D1006339

THE UNREMEMBERED

TOR BOOKS BY PETER ORULLIAN

The Unremembered

The Vault of Heaven, Volume 2 (forthcoming)

THE UNREMEMBERED

PETER ORULLIAN

A TOM DOHERTY ASSOCIATES BOOK  NEW YORK

This is a work of fiction. All of the characters, organizations, and events portrayed in this novel are either products of the author's imagination or are used fictitiously.

THE UNREMEMBERED

Copyright © 2011 by Peter Orullian

All rights reserved.

Edited by James Frenkel

A Tor Book
Published by Tom Doherty Associates, LLC
175 Fifth Avenue
New York, NY 10010

www.tor-forge.com

Tor® is a registered trademark of Tom Doherty Associates, LLC.

ISBN 978-0-7653-2571-6

First Edition: April 2011

Printed in the United States of America

0 9 8 7 6 5 4 3 2 1

For Cheyenne,
in the hope of more daddy stay-home days

• ACKNOWLEDGMENTS •

This artifact you're holding owes its existence to a multitude.

First, to Nat Sobel, the best kind of gentleman, who happens also to be a world-class agent. To Jim Frenkel, a great story guy, who also edited this tome and helped me through my first go at being published. And then there's Irene Gallo, who makes art happen; and the rest of the marketing, publicity, and editorial crew at Tor, all of whom have impressed me immensely. Finally, Tom Doherty. You, sir, are the very definition of "epic." Thank you for the opportunity. I'm humbled and grateful.

Here's to Mannheim Steamroller, and their song "Red Wine," in particular; I've had more early years writing fugues to this tune than I care to admit. Then to Terry Brooks, both in eighth grade and these last few years—another epic fellow. And oh my, to Stephen King, whose book *Night Shift* (my first King) I bought the year I graduated high school and realized I was indeed going to take hold of the flame (yes, that's a Queensrÿche reference). I should also thank a great list of writers—some of whom I've had the good fortune to meet—but that would make these acknowledgments overlong; so this time out, I'll mention Dan Simmons, whose work helps me strive to be a better writer. To all my writer compatriots in the Pacific Northwest: You're tops. Thanks to Dean Smith, who was there at the beginning and at the end—and points in between. And to Eph and Virginia, I'd be nothing without your example.

Of course—and not least of all—there's the family: Cathryn, for keeping us all sane and somehow happy; Alex, for his systematic chaos (yes, that's a Dream Theater reference); and Cheyenne, whose picture kept me company in the dark hours of early, early morning as I dragged myself to my writing chair and continued to hope.

SAECULA FOREST

'ALL MOUNTAINS

SOLEL STRETCHES

NALTUS
FAR

SOTOL WASTES

•NO'RHAL

ELYK DIVAD

•IR-CAUL

All the rest are walking earth, harsh dust, enslaving breath in imprisons

ZOL

LE WOOD

FALELL RANGE

LUHLM PASS

•A'VOTEL

WYNSTOUT
DOMINION

Y'TILAT MOR

REDTUV

NALTUS
REY

ALENS

KUREN

PATER FUL

FOR THERE ARE TWO ETERNAL TRUTHS THAT MAY NOT BE PUT ASUNDER,
THAT FORCE AND FORCE, OR MATTER AND ENERGY, OR BODY AND SPIRIT,
CAN BE NEITHER CREATED NOR DESTROYED, ONLY RENDERED CHANGED, MADE
NEW, AND NEXT THAT THESE ETERNAL ELEMENTS MAY CHOOSE FOR THEMSELVES.

O'DELL

AVEN WOOD

DYNLUL
MOOR

MASSON
DIMN

THE EAST OF
AESHAU VAAL
IN THE AGE OF
RUMOR

RIVEN PORT

VALLE

SOREN SEAS

CONTENTS

THE
UNREMEMBERED

The Whiting

An uncustomary quiet fell over the council as its last member entered the tabernacle. The One strode confidently toward the rest, who occupied their seats as though they'd convened some time ago. His steps echoed up colonnades of fluted granite columns that rose the height of thirty men and ended at the open sky. The depths of morning stretched above. Over ornate inlaid designs of marble his boot heels clapped, his dark mantle trailing him as if he were a bridegroom come to enter his final covenant. A mocking smile played on his lips, seen in snatches of shadow and sun as he strode between the pillars toward the council table.

Upon each pillar lay inscribed patterns of stars—bodies deep in the night firmament, many too deep to be seen from *this* world. They read like a book, a journal, an accounting of feats, travels . . . works. The One sneered, and muttered, "Arrogant, immortal biographers." With a narrowing of his gaze, he caused portions of the pillars to erode, the stone sloughing like sand in a time-glass and marring the designs with patches of emptiness. His smile widened, darkened. Then he continued on, returning his attention to the deliberation he knew awaited him.

Into the central chamber strode the last council member, still wearing his smile. He paused, gathering the measured looks of his eight brethren already seated at the great semicircular table. Above them, the sky shone a peerless blue, the winds absent from the day, everything a testimony to the creation they had sought to bring forth yet again. When he'd greeted each one of them with scrutinizing eyes, he folded his arms across his chest, making no move to claim his seat amongst them. Nor was there invitation to do so.

The moment stretched like one eternal breath.

Dossolum, the Voice of the Council, stood, his face drawn with both regret and resolve. "Maldaea, you were chosen among us, charged to ensure in the founding of this world the balance of hope and trial, growth and despair. Given into your stewardship was the power to refine the work of the council and create harmony." Dossolum stopped to regard the others. "You have corrupted the special sanctity of your office. And in your labors, the balance of Ars and Arsa, body and spirit, is lost."

"Am I too effective at the task you gave me?" Maldaea asked with casual sarcasm. "Or is the rest of the council too soft in its beneficence?"

The Voice of the Council looked up from beneath a stern brow, preparing his words carefully. "You glory in torment, Maldaea. You draw upon the Will to fashion and purpose life diseased from its inception. Your creations do *not* refine the races of this world. The intention of all that is given life at your hand is subjugation, imposition, dominion."

"The very qualities instilled in the breasts of your nobler . . . imperfect races." Maldaea sauntered several steps closer, threatening with his insolent informality.

"Imperfection is not always immoral or iniquitous," Dossolum countered.

Maldaea nodded appreciatively. "Then why the creation of this Bourne to banish and imprison all my work? I've not known a world where such a thing was necessary." The One took a square stance and leveled knowing eyes at Dossolum. "Or permissible."

"We are the Framers, Maldaea. We decide what is permissible." The Voice of the Council let his words ring in the vault of the open sky, echoing their dual meaning. "So we are convened to render a decision concerning your part in the foundation of this world and your seat among us."

A terrible, dark loathing drew Maldaea's features taut. "And what would you do, Dossolum?!" He turned savage eyes on the rest. "What would any of you do?! I am not one of your creations to be trifled with! Just as some stars burn brighter than others, so does the power to command the Will come to some of us in greater measure. Is that not the very reason that I alone was given the responsibility of setting avarice upon the land, forming prick and briar to smite the heels of men, siring life with a lust for war so that men might learn the value of peace?"

"Your talents are certain," Dossolum replied evenly. "It is your intention that makes you foolish . . . and dangerous. The wisdom and strength of the council is in its several members."

The Voice of the Council looked around the great table at those assembled. He nodded as he began again to speak. "In the formation of other worlds, each of us here has labored in the same office you occupy in *this* world. But never did the work of ruin become our delight. Even you, Maldaea, have peformed this dark labor before, and not allowed it to become your joy nor to overrun the balance you're meant to create." Dossolum paused, then softly asked, "What has changed in you?"

Hatred surged inside Maldaea. The arrogance and condescension were intolerable! "You are all fools! You convene to breathe life into a world as you have done for eons, but your own design has not grown or deepened. You've become complacent in your labors. Have you forgotten why we do this? These countless races, created on countless worlds, are not lifted up by the trials and hardships of their lives. They are not evolving to inhabit the divinity that you claim is their inheritance. They live and die and nothing more. Why is this tabernacle not filled with these children become your equals, to aid in the work? Perhaps something is amiss in *your* efforts."

"Enough!" Dossolum roared. The very sky shivered. "You desecrate these halls with your slander and lies! Do not twist the accusation back upon us. Your work is overgrown, it is grief for its own sake . . . nay, for your own glorification. That is the change in you."

Maldaea trembled with fury. "The time of the council is over! There must be one eminent among the rest. To lead. To ensure that souls are not lost to nothingness. Or else . . ." He looked up into the sky, forming his malediction. "Or else it were better that they never know life at all."

"There is no first among equals, Maldaea. The will of the council governs each of us."

"You hold no dominion over me!" Maldaea howled. He swept an indicting finger at the entire council. "And beware that you cross a line from which there is no return. Will you dare condemn me for doing only what each of us has done countless times before? Are you so elevated in your conceit that you ignore the jeopardy of taking open opposition against me? You are too far removed from the earth you are so fond of sowing."

"Maldaea"—Dossolum adopted a tone of finality—"once great and noble in the company of these, your friends, now condescension fills your breast and taints the renderings of your hands—"

"Silence!" Maldaea cried.

His call brought tremors to the Tabernacle of the Sky, the great pillars swaying against the blue, the floor quaking as if it might open and swallow them all. The air bristled and churned, the sound of Maldaea's command tearing at the fabric of reality and filling the tabernacle with an accompaniment like the rending of a thousand sails.

Yet Dossolum went on. "They are crimes of ambition, intolerable indulgences that have put at odds the work of this council and defiled the unique nature of your calling." Falling to a deep register and sure cadence, his voice calmed the surging stone, restored clarity to the visible world. "In consideration of all that has gone before, we have decided—"

"Enough!" Maldaea protested again. "You will not decide for me! The founding principle of the Charter is the right to choose! I defy you to place yourselves above the truths that guide the formation of life. *Eternal* truths that do not bend to the satisfaction of your own comfort or intention. You will either uphold these principles in every instance"—the words twisted his lips into a sneer—"or you will abandon them and give me place to *impose* order and claim what I have power to claim. Either these truths remain immutable, or, in denying them, you prove the validity of my work."

At his words, the earth shook again, the marble underfoot groaning, shifting, until fissures broke and spread across its glazen surface. His defiance, bright and fiery, ascended the fluted columns, jouncing over stone and rushing skyward where it blurred and discolored everything it touched. Chips of granite began to rain down, clattering on the floor. The smell of dust and a hint of charred rock rose all around.

Dossolum broke his formal tone, a fierce indignation infusing his words. "Quietus!" he roared. "Now and forever you will be known by this name! No place will you have among us! You are discharged utterly! You shall have always upon your tongue the taste of the death and hopelessness you take pleasure in visiting upon others."

As Dossolum spoke, chunks of granite spun and whipped back into the air, finding again their places upon the walls and pillars, fusing there to re-create an unblemished whole. The floor stretched and yawned, returning to its even, glistening plane. And wind rushed high against the heavens, as though claiming Quietus's bitter words and whipping them away forever.

"You will live evermore the simple law of consequence so manifestly absent from your rhetoric." Dossolum's words came with more rhythm and tone. "This is part of the Charter. You will answer for the choices that you willingly made."

Quietus trembled in his own malevolent anger. Without uttering a word, his hatred rippled outward from his quavering frame and sullied the visible world. Like a pall, the quiet stole the intonation of Dossolum's words and left the Tabernacle dim. It crept like a baneful prayer uttered from unhallowed lips, yet not a word did the One speak.

Then finally, in but a whisper, he answered. "If you persist in this action, I will set myself against you everlastingly. Long have I toiled, waxing strong in the knowledge and use of the Will as none of you ever has." Quietus raised his hands together in a cupping motion to signify the immensity of his gift. "With all that I am, I will also take those that sprang from my bowels and torment this world until each tabernacle is as this one is now." He gestured to the chamber without lifting his stern gaze. "Until every marriage of spirit and matter is corrupted, consigned to share the sepulchre you prepare for me."

Beneath such concentrated disdain, stone wept, tapestries moaned, books on the council table sighed with the resignation of the hopeless. The spirit evident in all things—the Forda that lived in all matter—protested the Quiet, cried out for respite. Even the sky withdrew, light and color fleeing, replaced by the endless stretches of space. Only indifferent starlight lit the Tabernacle, creating of the council vague forms like forgotten statues.

Somewhere in the shadows, Quietus smiled.

Dossolum stretched forth his own hands, but rather than cupping them up toward himself, he flattened them and turned them earthward. Staring through the shadowy light, he spoke his pronouncement upon Quietus: "You shall be Whited."

The darkness rippled, shadows and edges blurring as if seen through bent glass. A feeling of surprise passed quickly to a disregard that tore at the very existence of Ars and Arsa. An instant later, a deafening wail erupted from Quietus's throat. Waves of dark and bright coursed and careened off every surface. Like a living, maddened beast, the primal roar spared nothing, ripping indiscriminately at everything and everyone. In an instant, matter and energy were repurposed and sent racing at impossible speeds to wreak destruction and lay flat the variety of life given place in the land.

One by one, the other council members stood, each forming with their hands a personal sign to sustain Dossolum's action, and adding to him their strength in the Will. Their actions silenced Quietus's great cry before it could desolate the young world.

"This shall be the mark that shames you, announcing the pretense of working outwardly in the interest of others but hiding up your own wanton designs deep in your bosom." Dossolum's voice resounded. "From this moment, no more will Ars and Arsa be yours to spontaneously render; only with personal cost shall the power be known to you."

Amidst the tumult, Quietus began to slowly drain of color. His clothes bleached white, robbed of their vividness. Soon after, his hair streaked alabaster from scalp to tips. And as the wind howled, Quietus writhed, struggling to maintain control of his physical form. With a last show of strength, he pushed back the whiting, restoring color to his hair, greyness to his mantle. His lips curled back off his teeth, his eyes shut tight in concentration.

The Quiet surged again, fighting their collective strength, as Maldaea sought to impose his own will, to steal all hope and possibility from this young world. Abruptly, the One's efforts collapsed. The sound of words, many of them rising in musical phrases, rose above the din of wind and shearing stone, and pallor came again to Maldaea's—Quietus's—skin. Vapor shot from his pores, soon caught in the maelstrom and whipped away. He shuddered, howling imprecations at his brethren, reviling them all. Until finally there remained nothing of color in him save his eyes. He collapsed hard to his knees.

Dossolum spoke again, his voice like the rushing of water. "The vile creations wrought by your hand will be herded like beasts and driven into the deeps of the Bourne west and north: Bardyn, Fe'Rhal, Velle, all those given to you in their allegiance and lineage."

Quietus, his voice and body wracked, shot hoarse recriminations at Dossolum. "And what of your own creations? If you abandon this world, what care you for them?"

Dossolum's face showed a hint of sorrow as he looked skyward. "Some of these will go into the far reaches with your Quietgiven races."

"I see," Quietus managed, dark humor in his voice. "Handiwork whose promise you do not esteem, put away with those *I* brought forth. You are contemptible!" He again swept an outstretched arm in a violent arc to indicate the entire council. "What if any of these refuse to be compelled by you?"

Dossolum lowered his gaze to Quietus's own. "Then they will be destroyed. We will raise a veil to seal the rest inside the Bourne. And give those who remain in the eastlands at least the semblance of peace and hope."

"And what of me?" Quietus stood, his skin burning with the effort.

"You shall be bound and placed within the veil alongside the foulness you've created, there to spend time without end."

As he listened to the pronouncement, his terrible countenance shone with darkening hatred toward the council, the worse for the lingering color in his eyes—like a vestige of the Noble One he had once been.

"I am eternal, just as you are eternal. You can brand me, tear from me the glory of future worlds to frame. But you cannot take the authority or dominion that is mine." He showed an awful smile. "Be warned."

Straining against the whiting, he managed a final word before his irises and pupils turned forever white, a word, a name, both his sentence and ultimately his triumph: "Quietus."

For there are two eternal truths that may not be put asunder: that Forza and Forda, or matter and energy, or body and spirit, can be neither created nor destroyed, only rendered, changed, made new—yea, and all power within them lies, yea, even the First Ones were bound by these very laws in framing this world as in all the worlds that came before and all those that will come after; and next that these eternal elements may choose for themselves.

—Drawn from the apocryphal writings of
author Shenflear, during the Age of Discord

A grave I traveled past, and stopped to look upon the stone.
I read the tribute words aloud.
My voice seemed an intrusion in the silence
For a brave man gone to his earth fighting the Quiet.
And I despised myself for feeling reverent.
What then was his death about?
So I recalled a jest and spoke it to the stone
And laughed out loud, yawped a bit, and honored him with noise.
The grave's only power is this: that therein dies the laughter.
For this is life, and life is loud, or else the Quiet's you.

—"Reflections from an Ossuary,"
attributed to the poet Hargrove,
during the Age of Hope

• CHAPTER ONE •

The Right Draw

The taste of rain upon his lips and the quiet of the forest vales and hummocks usually eased whatever worries Tahn Junell brought with him on a hunt. But today the woods and skies held none of their customary peace. Storms had driven the animals from the hills. And it had been more than three weeks since he'd even fired his bow at game. The murk that descended closed him in, sealing the skies of the Great Fathers and leaving an unnatural stillness upon the land. Even the rain, which usually brought renewal, now felt like a weight being yoked to his shoulders, as though he ought to do something about the changes in the sky but was left only soaked and muddied by the downpour.

As the rain began to fall in earnest, Tahn sought the mouth of a natural draw deep within a stand of towering hemlocks. He'd had good success here in the past. He cut several low-hanging boughs and fashioned a lean-to on a thick bed of needles with a clear view of the ravine. Tucking himself up under his makeshift shelter, he took a drop of pinesap from a nearby bough and placed it on his tongue to cover the scent of his breath from his quarry. Then began his vigil.

The wind died as the storm came on full. Heavy sheets of rain deluged the land and diffused the grey, watery light, obscuring his vision. Tahn concentrated on seeing any movement up the draw.

Moments passed, and he lost himself some to the soothing sound of rain striking the ground and trees. Wet and cold, Tahn nevertheless took some small comfort in being still.

He had hunted every day for weeks now, but had been unable to produce any fare for the Fieldstone Inn. Hambley Opawn, the proprietor, was impatient for meat to replenish his storehouse, especially with an inn full of travelers awaiting the overdue arrival of the reader for the Northsun Festival.

It was odd that Northsun had come and gone without an appearance by Ogea the reader. In years past, his father, Balatin, and mother, Voncencia, (before they'd gone to their earth) had taken Tahn with his sister, Wendra, to watch the reader come into town. It was always the same. On a small mule, the reader rode stoically through every street in the Hollows. He never spoke to anyone, letting his slow progress announce his arrival. People would begin to follow several strides behind. Tahn had always noted the strange hush that fell over the crowd: Conversation fell off, carts and horses were stilled, even foot-steps sounded as though lightly taken. Ogea wound through the roads, allow-ing everyone time to hear of his coming, before heading for the Fieldstone, where Hambley would have put out a ladder against the face of the inn. The reader always dismounted, and, carrying a large leather book, climbed to the balcony on the east side of the Fieldstone. There he spent several moments looking over the men and women of the Hollows before beginning to tell the old stories again.

Every year Northsun brought people from distant parts to the Fieldstone, and for Tahn, providing Hambley with meat for his tables, it had always meant some extra coin.

But since the last full harvest, game had become scarce in the Hollows. Even a quarter-kill would fetch a hefty price from Hambley's purse. Tahn would of-fer a second quarter to his friend Sutter Te Polis's mother, for aid to his sister during childbirth; Wendra had expected her baby before the dark moon, which had come a day since.

And it would be Sutter's mother to help, because Wendra's circle of friends had diminished since the rape that caused her to become with child.

Rage burned in Tahn at the thought of it. He'd not been able to find the man responsible. Wendra's memory of her rapist had blurred to little more than sadness. The carrying of her first child should have been a happy time for her, but now served mostly as a reminder of its awful inception. It had darkened his sister's bright disposition by more than a shade. Tahn did his best to keep things normal in their home, but with Balatin gone, silences in the house brought morose thoughts more keenly. And not just thoughts of the rape itself. When he could admit it to himself, Wendra's pregnancy served as a reminder to him that his own childhood had somehow become lost to him. Anything before his tenth year had simply disappeared. It gave him the vague sense of being an adopted orphan. At times, it left him feeling like dried bread that might crumble at the touch.

The mournful and troubled thoughts of his and Wendra's home, Tahn now realized, were at least equally his own, especially with these incessant storms that darkened the skies and had apparently driven game from the Hollows.

A flash of light and savage thunder boomed all around, startling him. But it also focused him on his task.

When the last echoes of it had faded, Tahn breathed deeply and relaxed his grip upon his bow. Taking a leather strap from his belt, he tied back his long, dark hair. He then wiped his face with the lining of his cloak, pulled his hood forward, and settled in again. Moments later, from a copse of cedars at the bot-tom of the draw, a small herd of elk cleared the tree line. Their breath clouded the air as they snorted and chuffed. Cautiously, they regarded the ravine before starting to climb. Tahn slowly rose to his feet and nocked an arrow. Purposefully feeling every bit of tension in his bowstring, he made his pull and breathed easy as he aimed on the lead bull.

In a whisper, he said, "I draw with the strength of my arms, but release as the Will allows." He paused, seeking, as he always did, the inward confirmation of the rightness of his draw. In the same moment, he glanced at the scar on the back of his hand. Neither the old phrase or the hammer-shaped scar he bore ever betrayed their origins to him; those remained lost in that same childhood he could not remember. Yet somehow they also assured him that this bull was *not* the right kill. He shifted his aim, pulling down on a smaller male farther back in the herd.

As Tahn set to release, the rain erupted in a new explosion of light and sound. It whipped and leapt, and coalesced into a whirling spout. A shrill whistling filled the ravine, attended by the deep-toned creak of hemlocks swaying in the sudden wind. The spout rose up, seeming to rear a sentient head, gathering momentum and mass before driving its fury toward the lead bull. All the sky funneled down in watery aggression upon the animal. Tahn watched helplessly, his draw relaxing. The herd scattered into the trees. Darkness spun in the air above, gathering in the rain that hammered the elk. The creature struggled briefly against the onslaught, legs kicking, horns tearing at grass and throwing chunks of mud. Mewling desperately, it managed to stand. But the funnel of water seized it and thrust it earthward again.

Then it was still.

Almost immediately, the rain returned to a normal downfall, leaving only swirling dervishes of mist and a trail of blackness in the air.

It was the wrong kill.

Angered, Tahn traced the trail of darkness up the other side of the ravine to a figure standing in a small clearing between two large hemlocks. Its hands remained extended, filled with the same darkness. A cowl was drawn forward, leaving its features in shadow. But the being seemed to stare at Tahn, unmoving, sharing something silent between them. Then the figure knelt, never turning its head away from Tahn, and thrust its fists into the ground. A flash of brilliant darkness burst from the soil, causing steam to rise from the earth. Tahn thought he could see the shape of a smile in the depths of the cowl, a smile that spoke wordlessly.

It wanted me to see it kill the wrong bull, that it would take life that should be preserved. . . . It knows *me!*

Then the stranger stood again, his mantle shimmering with the faintest touches of crimson in an otherwise perfect blackness.

And pointed a pallid finger at Tahn.

Tahn's breath stopped in his chest. The ache of it threatened to drop him to the ground, his legs already shaking uncontrollably. What he'd just seen . . . the elements themselves controlled and brought down to kill . . . the wrong kill. He'd never seen a renderer, let alone . . .

Velle!

For all my Skies!

It was the only explanation he could find. Quietgiven from the Bourne, out of myth and story and secret lands so distant that they existed only in his imagination. Velle, the dark renderers of the Will, here in the Hollows! It was unheard of.

The reader!

Could this malefic creature have brought its dark craft to bear on the old man? It would explain his absence at Northsun. The thought brought fresh panic and the anticipation of deeper sadness.

Tahn remembered to breathe, and drew a cold stab of air that burned his throat and billowed out into the frigid air. He tried to breathe again, to calm himself. The figure across the draw only stared from the shadow of its cowl.

The motionless Velle and its dark intent were maddening, and Tahn felt again the pure, irrational dread a child feels when trapped in the dark.

He could think of only one thing to do.

His bow forgotten in his hand, Tahn ran.

He dashed into the cover of the trees, glancing back once to see the cloaked figure skirting the mouth of the draw, giving chase.

Tahn drove his trembling legs faster, and soon came to the forest path. He stopped, panting hard, his breath pushing short stabs of warm air into the cold. *Just like the elk.* He had to think quickly. The dark figure would track him easily and quickly down the path to the south road. Quelling the urge to hasten toward the Hollows, he ducked left into a dense stand of ash. Choosing mossy ground to quiet his steps, he doubled back toward the draw; the creature wouldn't expect him to come back toward it. Tahn knew these woods as well as his own home; he hoped his pursuer did not.

A moment later he heard a thrashing in brush to his left. The other had found the path. Tahn pulled his cloak over his face to mask his labored breathing, hunkered low, and listened.

A few wet steps on the path. Then a howl that shrieked into the treetops.

And silence.

Something about the quiet unnerved Tahn. Did the other know he'd doubled back? He didn't wait to find out. Staying low, he rushed back toward the draw where he'd seen the creature. He recalled its bony, pallid finger pointing toward him. But why destroy the elk? It was the wrong kill. And again Tahn thought that this creature had wanted him to realize that it knew the bull should not die . . . but that it did not care.

He flew into the draw, barely keeping his balance as he pounded down one muddy slope and up the other side. He finally shouldered his bow, using his hands to claw to the top.

Another howl. Closer.

The creature had found him out.

Tahn scrambled up, and stopped dead at the lip on the far side of the draw. He stood now where the figure had been. Underfoot lay a patch of ground as dry and untouched by rain as the Sotol Wastes. Rain beaded and ran across the spot as though it had been coated with wax. In the ground were two holes where the being's hands had thrust into the earth. Scorch marks flared from the holes. He knelt to touch the dry, black surface. Not wax. Glass. The soil had burned into a thin crust of dark glass.

"Great Fathers," he whispered. He'd never seen the work of a renderer. But here it was.

He knew little of such things, just what he'd learned from listening to Ogea's stories. Only the Velle and members of the Order of Sheason possessed the power to render. And rendering came at a price. The difference was that only the Sheason bore that price themselves, drawing on their own life-energy. Velle transferred the cost to something (or someone) else.

He ran his finger around the glass-encrusted holes.

But these were matters of myth, weren't they? No one Tahn knew had ever seen a Sheason, let alone a Velle. Velle were a Quietgiven race said to live only inside the Bourne. And the Sheason, though they lived in the nations of men, were spoken of almost as a cautionary tale, at best a secret. Somehow death seemed an equal threat from both.

A chill ran across Tahn's arms and down his back. *Velle! Here in the Hollows!*

He whirled, checking his back, just as the creature glided from the trees to stand across from him on the other side of the draw. It lifted its hands. Stepping over the scorched soil, Tahn plunged into the deep wood. The air behind him crackled and spat as if lightning sizzled after him. Trees splintered and cracked at his heels. He dove behind a great rock, just as a wave of heat pushed past where he'd been running.

Another howl rose into the murk.

Tahn got moving again, racing with a sure foot over terrain he knew well. Somewhere behind him, the Velle again gave chase.

He ran for an hour, never stopping to rest. Over chasms and through rivers and streams he fled in a wide turn until he'd doubled back again, angling for the south road. The woods had grown quiet, leaving him with no sense of how close the creature might be. He didn't wait. He lurched several hundred strides up the road to a stand of cedar where he'd tethered his horse, Jole.

His legs almost useless, it took him three attempts to mount. Finally, muscling his way into the saddle, he said simply, "Go." Jole flew toward the Hollows.

Rushing up the road, Tahn checked behind him often, trusting Jole to his course. His mind raced, wondering at what he'd seen. It seemed so deliberate, as though Tahn specifically had been tracked into the woods. The figure must surely have been following him to know where he would be hunting, because even Tahn had not known where he would end up. The images of the rain driving savagely upon the elk and the scorched earth belied the calming smells of loam and wet bark around him.

A Velle in the Hollows—something that had never happened, as far as he knew, in all its history. And it had tried to kill him.

He rode hard into the middle of town. A hundred strides to his left, great billowing plumes of smoke rose to mingle with the clouds above Master Rew Geddy's smithy. The smith kept a hot fire burning every hour of the day. The smell of his forge filled the air, even through the rain.

Looking ahead, Tahn spied the towering chimneys of the Fieldstone Inn through of the gloom. Reassured by the sight, he slowed Jole to a walk, then dismounted. He'd find his friend Hambley there. Hambley had a level head on his shoulders. After what Tahn had just seen, he needed the man's patient logic.

He took hold of Jole's reins and rushed up the muddy street toward the inn. It rose up like a square mountain, hemmed in by large, overhanging cedars. The stone structure looked palatial in the Hollows, where most homes were fashioned from the planks produced by the mill to the south on the Huber River. Gables protruded at even intervals along the top floor over the chamber windows. The roofing had been quarried from a red sandstone pit somewhere near the low steppes of the High Plains of Sedagin, or so Hambley said. He also claimed the Fieldstone to be the first edifice built in the Hollows after the High Season of the Great Fathers. But most folks in the Hollows felt sure he made that claim to attract customers. Still, the stones were smooth, washed and worn by countless cycles of the sun and winter's chill.

Tahn went through the stable yard to the rear outbuildings reserved for guest mounts. He stabled Jole, but left the saddle on in the event he needed to leave in a hurry.

He had just emerged from the stable when something hit him from behind, knocking the wind out of him and driving him off his feet and into the mud. He took a mouthful of sludge as he went down. Someone straddled him, pinning his arms to the ground. A strong hand pushed his head deeper into the mud, and his nostrils filled with muck. Panic seized his chest. Had the Velle gotten here so fast?

Then, vaguely, he could hear familiar laughter. Tahn twisted his head free and looked up to face his attacker. The grinning mug of Sutter Te Polis hovered above him.

"I'll bury you 'neath the Hollows!" Tahn cried, spitting out the mud, a smile of relief on his lips.

"I see. Well, my esteemed hunter friend, you seem to be the one half buried in the mud and," Sutter said as he picked up a bit of horse mulch, "the rich stuff." He smeared the dung over Tahn's face, barking laughter. Tahn began to writhe, struggling to get up, but Sutter simply rode him like a horse master taming a willful mount.

Tahn spat the foulness from his teeth and kicked up with his hips propelling Sutter over him and into a pool of rainwater. He jumped to his feet and untied his muddied cloak. Sutter splashed to his feet and whirled around to face Tahn. Hambley came to the kitchen side doorway to check on the commotion, retiring inside again after mumbling something about "that foolish Sutter boy."

"If I win, we leave the Hollows tonight, go find ourselves some maidens in the Outlands. I'll be done with harvesting roots and you'll be done with the woods," Sutter said, circling. "Maybe we'll settle for something a little less than maidens." He smiled knowingly. "How's that strike you, Woodchuck?"

Tahn spat again, the horse dung still pungent on his lips. Another time, he would have taunted Sutter that the Outlands had forbidden dullards from traveling abroad. Today, he didn't have time for their usual games.

Sutter whooped and feinted toward Tahn's belly. Tahn wasn't fooled by the old Sutter move. He dropped into the mud, swept his leg out in a wide circle, and upended Sutter. His friend splashed again into the large puddle. Before Sutter could right himself, Tahn jumped on him.

"Enough! Listen to me. I've just seen a Velle!"

Sutter stared up, confused. "What? Is this a new game?"

"No game!" Tahn blared. "I was down the south road and out east hunting. I laid up in a draw for a herd of elk." He stopped, still amazed at what he'd seen. "And a dark, hooded figure stepped out of the trees, raised its hands, and whipped the rain into a funnel to beat a bull elk to death."

"A dream," Sutter offered. "You fell asleep waiting on the herd."

"Then it looked at me," Tahn said, ignoring Sutter's remark. "I think . . . it knew me. And it chased me through the wood. I got away, but I heard the crack of lightning at my heels more than once." He looked at his friend, fear again seizing his gut. "It was trying to kill me."

Tahn relaxed his grip and stood up, letting Sutter free. He went to Jole for his waterskin, took a mouthful and washed out the foulness, spilling yet more water over his face and ears. "Has the reader come yet?"

"Not yet." Sutter took the waterskin and washed himself off before drinking deeply. He now looked a bit more like himself, his shoulder-length hair again the color of harvest just before it's taken in nearly matching his brown eyes. This, and an angular face make him look older than Tahn, whose own hair was again black, and whose blue eyes were bright in a lean face tanned from much sun. They both stood a little more than two strides tall, and had each gotten what they called "outdoor strong" from their respective occupations over nearly eighteen cycles.

"It's got to have something to do with the Velle." Tahn turned to his friend. "In the Hollows, Sutter . . . a Velle in the Hollows."

Tahn reached into one of the pouches on his saddle and took out a flake of salt. He dropped it onto his tongue as he tried to think of what to do. His heart still raced at the images in his head of the cowled creature smiling and a helpless animal beaten into a watery grave.

Sutter kept an uncustomary silence.

They stood together in the high doorway of the stable and looked up the road. Since the break in the rain, people had begun filling the streets. The clouds remained a complete canopy over the land, except to the east where small blue patches could be seen near the horizon over the Jedgwick Ridge.

"I thought the readers had some kind of special protection. . . ." Sutter cocked his head back and assumed an orator's pose, gazing into the distance— his humor had returned. "Riding from village to village, city to city, telling the old stories, stewards of the histories of the peoples of the land, even those in the Shadow of the Hand, and those . . . harbored deep within the Bourne." Sutter held his pose, glancing sideways at Tahn.

Today, the jokes wouldn't help his mood.

"I suspect you'll be a reader yourself someday, root-digger, you're so horribly poetic." Tahn tossed a salt flake at him, which Sutter caught and bit in two.

"And why not? There's certainly not much to listen to around here these days. Even the gossip is old." Sutter put the other half of the salt flake on his protruding tongue and coiled it back into this mouth with a flourish. Any moment he would return to his only topic of conversation: leaving the Hollows. Sutter wanted to leave digging roots behind, visit other cities, meet other races.

Tahn had just met one—today, as it happened, and Quietgiven no less. He had no appetite for more. He'd always been satisfied with the slow, easy way of life in the Hollows. Usually, just breathing Hollows air filled him with a sense of comfort. Now, his encounter in the woods had shattered his sense of safety and peace.

Panic again tightened his chest. "Let's get in to Hambley's fire. We need to tell him what I saw." He strode quickly, forcing Sutter to hurry to keep up.

They paused at the main door (Hambley didn't allow anyone but staff through the kitchen entrance) and scraped the mud from their boots on the last stone step before entering the inn. Already, Tahn could smell the fragrant scents of fresh bread and roasting duck, and the sour tang of ale hops. Muted conversation wafted from behind the door. Sutter pushed Tahn aside. "Let a man lead the way, Woodchuck."

Sutter shoved the heavy cedar door open so hard that it slammed against the inner wall, resounding with a loud crack. Talk lulled as guests turned to regard Sutter, who stood arms akimbo, chest out as he received their stares. Spying the root farmer, people went back to their conversations. Tahn shook his head and followed his friend inside, quietly drawing the door closed behind them.

The open area on the main floor of the Fieldstone extended several strides to the left, where a hallway serviced the kitchen, and twice that distance to the right where a hearth the height of a man blazed with fires fed by logs that were two strides long. Tables dominated the area, mostly filled today with Northsun travelers biding their time until the reader arrived.

People came from the farthest reaches of the Hollow Wood to hear the reader. Tahn thought the men from Liosh overly quiet and modest, while Evin's Creek residents seemed only able to bark. Mull Haven men wore double-breasted tunics, their women adorned in high-collar dresses; the latter always seemed to look up from a bowed head.

Hambley had set out makeshift cots in the rear hallways to accommodate the swelled crowds. Travelers, many of whom came three days' journey or more to be at the Fieldstone when the sun rose in its northernmost passage (signaling a complete cycle), hadn't abandoned hope that the reader might yet show. Though the sun hadn't been seen for days, Northsun was deep in the bosom of the people of the Hollows. Regardless of the rain, people knew when Northsun arrived. And despite the lateness of the reader, it appeared the tradition of his mule ride through town and ascent to the Fieldstone rooftop outweighed the inconvenience.

No one knew where the reader came from, but his bulging satchels thrilled the town. They were filled with stories passed down from ages past, hundreds of generations old, that became new again on the lips of Ogea the reader: Stories of the shaping of the Land, of the wars to save men from the Quiet and shadows from the Bourne. Tahn hoped he would be seeing Ogea soon, that the man didn't lie dead from a funnel of water rendered by the hand of the Velle he'd seen. Before today, he had wanted to ask the reader if he could tell them all something about the incessant inclemency and the desertion of the herds. The current age had no name and was now a season of storms. Today, Tahn wanted to ask just one question of the reader: What did it mean that a Velle had come so far south, and seemed to know him . . . personally? But he felt little hope that the reader would come this year.

The thought grieved him, and not simply for his own sake. He still remembered the first time he'd heard Ogea speak. The reader had never referred to his book, but held it to his chest with one arm while he gestured grandly with the other and projected a loud, resonant voice from his small, elderly frame.

The stories he painted with words had captured Tahn's heart. For hours Ogea spoke, sometimes singing passages of tales in a broken but energetic strain. When night came on full, torches were lit, lending the reader a formidable, eternal look as firelight caught his eyes and his flailing arm cast large shadows on the Fieldstone's upper floors. When he was done, no voices rose in appreciation, no cheers. A peaceful silence simply settled over the listeners as Ogea descended the ladder and quietly walked into the inn to sit beside the fire and sip a cup of warmed cinnamon tea.

Tahn hoped the reader lived to take his cup at the fireside again.

The lingering smells of nut-bread, berry wines, and sharp cheese drew him from his reverie. The tables were nearly full, so Sutter led them to the half circle of leather chairs closest to the fire—where Ogea always sat. Tahn hung his cloak from a peg beside the fire to dry and took a seat next to Sutter. The hearth passed through to the chamber and private dining room the Hollows townsmen used to hold their meetings; the fire heated both rooms. A door beside the hearth led into that adjacent chamber. Through the hearth, Tahn could see a pair of legs and dark boots.

His attention was shortly drawn away from the unknown person as Hambley came bustling toward them. The innkeep managed to carry a carafe of bitter and a plate of warm bread and cheese with one hand, and a meat cleaver with the other. Drawing near, Hambley put down the food and drink, keeping hold of his cleaver, and extended his long, thin hand to clasp Tahn's—it was always so with the man.

Tahn took Hambley's hand. The proprietor returned an iron grip. Tahn had once seen the Fieldstone owner bathing in the Huber, and had been able to count the ribs in the man's back. Still, his wiry frame had thrown men twice his weight out upon their tails when the ale had made them foolish. His place was clean, and Hambley never let a man or woman step inside without putting something hot down in front of them.

"We're almost out of meat," he said, pouring two glasses of Fieldstone bitter for Tahn and Sutter. "Did you have a successful hunt?"

Tahn shook his head. "We need to talk. Can you sit with us?"

Hambley seemed to sense the urgency. "I'll be back with some meat to join you." Important matters for Hambley required food.

Sutter piped in, "Yes, yes, that should do just fine, my good man. Have off with you now, and make a good job of it."

The innkeeper shook his head in bemusement and retreated down the far hallway toward the kitchen. Another great hearth burned there, one so large that Hambley boasted he could roast an entire bull in it. Tahn's mouth watered with the thought of food from Hambley's oven—he hadn't eaten all day.

But it wasn't the oven that made Tahn's mouth water. As he often supplied Hambley with his meat stores, he'd seen the secret of the Fieldstone's savory food. The inn owner fed his oven with only the most fragrant wood. And the cooks—Hambley's wife and sister—dropped wet sage, thrush cloves, pepper corn, and piñon bark into the fire, causing a sweet smoke to fill the oven and spice the foods they cooked there.

Hambley returned shortly, weaving through the crowd. As he sat, he put a plate of duck on the table beside the bread. "I have guests that are here twelve days since. The reader has not shown yet, and the older folks won't leave until he does."

"Have the townsmen sent anyone to search for him?" Tahn asked. He half expected Hambley to tell him someone else had spotted the Velle.

"No one will go out in the rain . . . except you, I guess. Northsun came and went and nary an eye has seen the reader. Ogea is old, but he is always here by Northsun. Even before I grew to my Change that old fellow was coming into the Hollows with plenty of time to dine on roast duck and gossip with the women folk. His absence puts me ill at ease," Hambley finished.

Tahn and Sutter shared a knowing look.

Then Tahn steeled himself for what he was about to say. It still felt like a nightmare from which he'd just awakened. Whispering low, he leaned close to the innkeep. "Hambley, today I saw a Velle in the Hollow Wood."

The proprietor's eyes darted to Sutter, where he surely expected to see a telling grin to reveal the sport they made of him, but the root-digger held an uncustomary gravity in his countenance. Hambley looked back at Tahn, who simply nodded, finding what he'd seen somehow more real as it lay reflected in the fear on the innkeeper's face. The three of them sat staring at one another.

After several moments, Hambley managed only, "You're mistaken."

"It doesn't mean the reader has been the Velle's victim." Sutter went right past Hambley's thin denial. "So, perhaps I'll go and find him myself."

Neither Tahn or Hambley responded, ignoring Sutter's bluster.

No one wanted to be taken seriously more than Sutter. Tahn suspected that was why his friend wanted to leave the Hollows. Turning soil to harvest the ground fruits would never be enough for him; it hadn't the respect or romance he sought. And while any other day his proclamation would be something to laugh at, today Tahn thought his friend might just be serious.

At the end of the first full moon cycle following Northsun both Tahn and Sutter would have their Standing—a rite of passage that, in the Hollows, was usually held in the townsmen's chamber in the Fieldstone. After that, their actions would be judged more severely. Consequences would be theirs to bear, unlike striplings who—for the most part—got away with everything. He wished his father, Balatin, could have been there to act as First Steward, but he'd died three winters past. Hambley would accept the honor in Balatin's place. But while Tahn looked forward to his own Standing, Sutter craved the Change more keenly if only for the way folks listened more thoughtfully to a man once he stood on the other side of his eighteenth year.

"Does Ogea come by way of the south road?" Tahn asked, breaking the silence and redirecting the conversation.

"Sometimes. I don't think he has a place to call home. Always traveling, always another village to visit." Hambley paused a moment. "Tahn, did your father ever speak of such things coming to the Hollows?"

"Balatin?"

Tahn had not spoken his father's name in a long time. The taste of it on his tongue was like grape-root, sweet but earthen. Men from far outside the Hollows had come to his father's burial. Some wore brightly colored cloaks bearing insignias Tahn had never seen. Others came quietly, saying nothing and sharing secretive looks with one another. Yet even before Balatin's funeral, Tahn had sensed that his father was more than he'd shared with either him or Wendra. But whatever it might have been, no one in the Hollows would talk about it—if they knew at all.

Sutter sat forward, his brow taut. "We'd know if this had happened before. What we need to decide is what to do now. Because if this is true . . . we may all be a few breaths closer to our last."

Tahn nodded, but could not shake the restlessness and panic in his chest that thrust his reason into chaos. His mind returned to the dark figure who commanded the elements and burned wet soil.

Unwittingly, he traced the hammer-shaped scar that marked him, which no one had ever really asked him about, and which Balatin had dismissed as a birthmark. Touching the scar, though, Tahn found words.

"We must spread the news. Now. People must be warned before—"

"Careful how you share such knowledge," a deep voice interrupted. "And keep your voice low to do it." Before Tahn even looked up, he saw beside him the dark boots that belonged to the man who'd been sitting in the chamber on the other side of the fire.

CHAPTER TWO

Strangers in the Hollows

Tahn sat, his plate of food forgotten in his lap. Raising his gaze to the face of the stranger, he saw sunken eyes ringed by dark circles. The man wore a closely trimmed beard with faint touches of dark red running through black. His hair was not as long as Tahn's own, but fell in long waves just past his shoulders. A black cloak hung from his shoulders, only the touch of firelight showing the deepest blue in its folds. At his neck, the man wore a short necklace drawn tight. The chain resembled a very thin, black rope woven from long thin strips of wood or leaves. From the chain hung a pendant in the hollow of the man's throat: three rings, each one inside the next, but all joined on one side. The pendant shone as dark as its chain. But the man's eyes communicated the most about him; a clear walnut color and edged by deep lines, they seemed to both worry and reassure in the same moment. He did not move, but stared down, appraising Tahn, as though he could see everything about him with a look.

"Were you invited into this particular conversation, stranger?" Sutter interjected. "It's all well and good for you to take a room at Hambley's fine inn here, but that doesn't give you the right to meddle in the personal lives of his friends."

The man looked directly at Sutter, showing him a flinty stare. Sutter retreated deeper into his seat. Then the stranger turned his hard gaze on Tahn. He leaned forward as he searched Tahn's face.

Hambley chimed in, "Master, he is a good lad. And we were discussing a family matter. There is no need for us to be at odds. Please have a seat." He gestured toward a fourth chair nearer the fire. The stranger appraised Tahn a moment more, still looming over him. Though he remained seated, he could tell the man would stand taller than him. The hilt of a dagger protruded from the opening of his cloak, but to Tahn the weapon seemed only an ornament. The newcomer's broad shoulders and stony visage inspired caution more strictly than anything else.

The man released Tahn from his gaze and took the chair Hambley offered. He drew it around, closing a circle with Tahn, Sutter, and Hambley.

"Would you care for a plate or a glass?" Hambley asked.

"No, I've my own, and much to say besides." He took a wooden case from the folds of his cloak and produced a small sprig. Thoughtfully, he placed it on his tongue. Tahn caught a whiff of something like peppermint.

"You are Tahn Junell," the man stated. He then waited as though he expected a response. Tahn finally nodded. "I am Vendanj." The man proffered his hand in greeting. Tahn clasped it in the customary salutation. Vendanj twisted their united hands, looking intently at the mark on the back of Tahn's hand. His grip tightened, hurting Tahn's fingers. Then he let go, returning his hand to his lap and his eyes to Tahn's own.

"Are you here for Northsun?" Tahn asked.

The man did not answer the question. "My concern turns toward the reader. It is not like Ogea to come late to retell the stories. The cycle of the sun has come and gone." Vendanj trailed off, his eyes appearing to see something Tahn could not. Something, he guessed, in a different place or time.

Sutter could no longer remain quiet. "The reader may need our help. Shouldn't we organize a party to search for him? He typically enters by the east road, I think. We could leave this very hour."

Hambley had finished his plate. "Lad, now that the rain has stopped, the bigger animals will be after meals of their own. It's best we wait on Ogea a while longer."

"But—"

"He is right," said Vendanj. "The land is mired in the wake of these storms. Foolish actions will only cause harm to the hasty." He spoke with a note of authority, as though not used to being contradicted. Sutter's jaw flexed as he bit back a remark.

"Are you going to finish that, Tahn, or shall I feed it to the dogs?" Hambley asked, pointing to Tahn's plate.

"I've no appetite for it now, Hambley. I'm sorry to leave it."

"Nonsense, you may leave anything you pay for." He grinned, and went to collect Sutter's plate as well. Sutter pulled his own plate back.

"I will finish mine, Master Opawn. My stomach is just fine." Sutter did not look at Vendanj when he said it, but his words were a challenge all the same.

Vendanj turned sharply, leaned close to Sutter, and captured him with his stare. "Listen, boy, I've no dislike for you. But you won't want to make an enemy of me so soon. There's mighty spirit in you, and I welcome it. Use it in the interest of something other than yourself, not in boyhood posturing. This is the season of accountability, and yours is nigh upon you. Wait and listen, reserve judgment until your actions are sure not to condemn you. I've no patience for foolishness."

Hambley shuffled off to the kitchen with a concerned look tightening his features.

The stranger's voice lingered on the air, accompanied by the smell of spent lantern oil. His chastisement had been severe, but he had spoken low, careful not to draw attention to himself.

Vendanj sat up in his deep, high-backed chair and ran a hand over his beard. "You and I have not rightly met. You know my name. What is yours?" He put his hand out again. Sutter took it with reticence.

"Sutter Te Polis," Tahn's friend said, his voice failing him as they clasped. Tahn guessed Sutter felt the same iron grip that he had.

This time the stranger did not turn his greeter's hand as he had Tahn's, but simply ran his long forefinger across the back of Sutter's knuckles. Then he let go. "What is it that makes your nails so black?"

Sutter mouthed something, his anger and fear slipping quickly into embarrassment. He fidgeted in his seat only a moment before placing his feet squarely on the ground and sitting still to offer his reply. "I farm the dirt. My nails are ripe with the loam of the Hollows. It's not an occupation of prestige, but still—"

"Don't apologize for it. When lent some mind, it is the vocation of a wise man." Vendanj looked closely at both Tahn and Sutter. "Knowing the right path is never as easy as when one physically puts his hands into soil. Causing life there, Sutter, isn't something to be ashamed of."

Sutter's mouth fell open in surprise. Tahn had seen the same reeling expression in his friend's face only once before, on the first day Wendra had responded to his advances and kissed him full on the mouth. The tension dissipated, and Vendanj raised a finger to Sutter to signal an end to the exchange.

This stranger reminded Tahn of his father: He was not petty, and his anger seemed appropriate, authorized somehow.

"Master—"

"You may want to become comfortable with my name," the man said.

Tahn nodded. "The boots you wear are not from the Hollows. The hide is too black and too thick." He paused, trying to assess how his question would be received. He couldn't read the man, whose face betrayed little of his thoughts. He came out with it. "What brings you here?"

Vendanj's lips curled into a slight but charming smile. "Spoken as only a man who watches the ground could." But still he did not answer, instead asking his own question. "What of your sister, Tahn? How is she since the death of your father?" The man crossed one booted leg over the other and sat back.

Vendanj knew much. And Tahn got the feeling he wouldn't do well to lie or ask what business it was of his. "She is well. She misses our father, and often writes songs about our lives together before he was taken from us. I think it's her way of dealing with his death." He looked up from the floor, harrumphed out a breath, and scrubbed at his face. "She has a lovely voice, but she rarely shares it."

Vendanj sat forward again, watching Tahn intently, seeming eager to ask a question. He fingered the charm around his neck for a moment. Finally, he did not speak, but sat back, still seeming to consider what Tahn had said.

Hambley returned and sat, wringing a wet rag.

Sutter cleared his throat. "So, are you here for Northsun or to ask about Tahn's sister?"

A sorrowful look touched Vendanj's eyes. "The observance of Northsun has mostly passed from the memory of the people." He smiled wanly. "In the larger cities like Myrr and Recityv, the Exigents have put an end to such things in public. Few dare to brave the League's wrath and be discovered keeping the day even in private."

"Exigents?" Sutter asked, looking at Tahn and Hambley for help.

"Yes. At least, that is how they started. They now call themselves the League of Civility." He frowned as he said it. "But in the beginning, they were known as the Exigency. In the Age of Hope, after the War of the First Promise, there was peace. In the midst of that peace, some men felt a need to record the histories passed down to them, to read and retell the stories of their forebears. Other men were compelled to stamp out this perpetuation of the past, believing it hindered men from fulfilling the promise of their own lives. These naysayers called themselves the Exigency, and soon the League of Exigents. Most scola believe the Exigents are responsible for ending the Age of Hope and for ushering in the Age of Discord; societies failed, losing connection with their past, becoming complacent. And those who defied the Exigents were put to death.

"Some generations later, after they were well established, the Exigents' mission became more measured, more often carried out in the halls of leadership. A thousand years later, Discord passed, and the Age of Civility began, so called because the League of Exigents renamed themselves after a new credo: to civilize mankind and root out arcane beliefs and practices . . . like the rendering of the Will." Again the stranger frowned. "There are League garrisons everywhere now, in almost every city. They are reason enough to visit the Hollows." Again he touched the pendant at his neck, an unconscious gesture that Tahn thought somehow comforted the man.

Sutter did not pursue the matter, and the four men lapsed into an awkward silence. The rumble of the hall continued unabated; a minstrel beginning to play his cithern, making expert melodies with his hands but bad accompaniment with his voice. After a few moments, Vendanj looked over the room behind Tahn and Sutter, studying the faces of those who had convened to eat and exchange words.

As though satisfied, he spoke, staring at Tahn. "I'm here for *you*."

A chill of warning shuddered through Tahn. The bustle of the Fieldstone faded in his ears. He saw and heard nothing, retreating inside himself where he could only repeat the old phrase for comfort: *I pull with the strength of my arms, but release as the Will allows.*

Then he thought of Wendra, Balatin gone to his earth . . . the Velle this morning.

Suddenly, he could see Vendanj again looking across at him, peering, Tahn thought, past his eyes into his mind. "I need you to come with me, Tahn, and leave the Hollows. Much depends on this. Soon, we will talk more about where we will go, and what must be done. But others must join us, and I have one errand for you first."

Tahn stared back, dumbfounded.

"I commissioned your smith. It should be nearly done. Simply use my name. Retrieve it for me on your way to the sodalist." Vendanj stood.

"Sodalist? You mean Braethen? Who told you he was a sodalist?" Tahn craned to look up at the man.

Vendanj gave him a hard stare. "I have heard it spoken."

"He's as much a sodalist as I am a reader," Sutter put in.

Vendanj seemed to consider. "Bring him anyway. Meet me back here as quickly as you can. Keep to the main roads, and don't venture beyond the town proper."

Vendanj drew his cowl forward and spared an even look at Sutter before crossing the floor to the double doors at the front of the hall. There, he paused for an instant as another figure appeared at his side. Tahn barely saw her. She moved with the simple grace of a plains deer, but also with the stealth of a mountain cat. Each motion seemed swift and sure. Tahn saw her light grey cloak for just a moment before she stepped through the door and disappeared, as quickly as vapor from a boiling pot. But in that moment, he thought her eyes had alighted upon him.

"Glad he's gone," Sutter exclaimed. "What a tangle of contradictions. I thought he was about to remove my head, and then he's complimenting me."

"Did you see her?" Tahn asked, staring at the door.

"The girl in the grey cloak, you mean?" Sutter laughed.

Tahn spun on his friend. "Yes. Have you ever seen her in the Hollows?"

"Barely saw her this time. She glided out as quick as a Far."

"Far," Tahn said, staring after her. "That's a reader's story." He tried to remember what his father had said about the Far. He recalled something about a great commission. They had been given the breath of life for but a short time in the world. Legend told that the Far lived a brief existence. It seemed a cruel matter to Tahn if it was true, but the Far themselves were little more than a myth in the Hollows. Even Ogea spoke about them so rarely that they hardly seemed real.

The one tale that the reader did share about them spoke of their city being consecrated by the First Ones at the founding of the world near the far end of all creation. It was said that is how their race got their name—being at the *far* end of everything.

Sutter broke Tahn's reverie. "Please, friend, don't tell me the Change is so quick upon you. Father will use it against me if you find yourself a wife and I'm still supping at his table." Sutter reached over and clapped Tahn on the back.

"I ask a question and you've got me married," Tahn said, a wry expression tugging his face into a smile. He turned again, though, toward the door the girl had just passed through.

"I see the look in your eye," Sutter retorted. "No. I've never seen her in the Hollows. But she left with Mr. Charming. What does that say about her character?" Sutter dug a knuckle into Tahn's back. "Did you happen to notice the color of her boots, too?"

Tahn swung around, catching Sutter's arm and slapping his friend's forehead.

"Take it outside, lads," Hambley said. "The travelers won't know you're just wrestling, and they'll want to join the bout. I'll end up with a lot of busted tables. Besides, don't you have things to do?"

Tahn released Sutter, ducking to avoid the parting blow his friend usually delivered to his left ear when they abandoned their sport. He strode quickly to the door, mostly in the hope of catching another glimpse of the woman at Vendanj's side. He stepped out into the dim light of midday. The murky weather had robbed shadows of their purchase, and left the Hollows feeling clammy and dank like the inner stones of a deep well no longer useful with water.

Sutter came up behind him. "Let's go, then. We must see the *sodalist*."

They shared dubious grins over that. Braethen was nice enough, but a bit fanatical about the idea of being a sodalist. He was an author's son who'd read too many books.

They got moving. Tahn still needed to speak of the attack in the woods. But somehow he felt that that would be part of the conversation with Vendanj later. It would have been lost on Sutter now anyway, who had begun to chatter in earnest about the possibility of leaving the Hollows. His friend had wanted to leave the Hollows for as long as Tahn could remember. The very thought of it had made him giddy. For Tahn, the prospect was somewhat less enticing. Mostly, he wanted to know where the man meant to take him. This was Tahn's home. The thought of the Velle in the woods still brought chill bumps to his skin. But he didn't know if he could leave the Hollows. Where did this stranger mean to take him?

A few streets over, Tahn and Sutter came to Master Rew Geddy's smithy. In girth, Geddy resembled nothing so much as a bull, but he was eighty years old if he was a day. He swung his hammer slowly, but powerfully. The crown of his head bore a dappling of age spots. A wiry fringe of hair horseshoed his ears and extended down the back of his neck into his coat. His only other hair seemed to grow from his nose. Geddy raised a hammer to the boys in mid-strike, finishing the motion with a resounding clang on a bit of orange-hot steel. Tahn and Sutter drew closer, seeking the warmth of Geddy's two large forges. The wind picked up a spark from one of the forge's flues and whipped it past Tahn's face. He ducked reflexively, causing a bark of laughter from Sutter.

"It's a wonder you ever succeed at bringing in any meat, boy," Sutter mocked, imitating the deep, resonant voice of Vendanj.

"You're my inspiration, Nails," Tahn replied, taunting Sutter for the dirt that lay perpetually under his fingernails. Geddy struck his anvil again. This time the flash sparked a blue-white color. Tahn realized that Geddy fashioned not a wheel casing or farm plow, but what looked like a . . .

"Sword," Geddy yelled, competing with the roar of his forge and the constant wind. He'd seen Tahn watching him work. "Have a look, lads."

The tip of the sword smoked in the frigid air and glowed red and orange from Geddy's fires. The smithy held it aloft. "Have you ever seen such a fine piece of steel?"

Tahn marveled at the blade, not because he recognized the quality of the metal, but because he'd never seen Geddy forge one before. To his knowledge, Geddy never had. Yet the man looked comfortable with the weapon in his hand. He dropped his hammer and hefted the sword from one hand to the other, an odd smile on his face. The steel's reddish glow gave his gnarled visage a garish look. The lines in his face seemed longer, the large black-filled pores of his face deeper. But his eyes did not look old as he studied the blade in his hands. Abruptly, the smithy seemed to remember Tahn and Sutter and held the blade out for their inspection, never offering to let them hold it.

"Don't know the owner. Must be here for Northsun." Geddy turned the blade to the flat edge and looked down its length, checking the straightness of the edge. "Came by a few days back and handed me a . . . by all my Skies I can still hardly believe it . . . a folded square of steel."

Geddy looked at them with crazed excitement, which turned to disappointment as he saw the blankness on Tahn and Sutter's faces. "Youth," he harrumphed. "This bit of metal, lads, has been turned over on itself several thousand times. No impurities. It is worth as much as . . . as the Fieldstone itself." He laughed from deep in his chest, the sound like rocks shifting upon themselves. "I've been at it. But it's a hard metal. Not, you might say, a Hollows metal."

Tahn shared a knowing look with Sutter. "You ever make a sword before, Geddy?"

"Just once," he answered. "Even told the gentleman that. He didn't care. Just handed me a small satchel containing the square of steel and a princely sum besides, in *silver*."

"Well it looks like a fine job to me," Sutter said.

"Thanks, lad."

Sutter reached to touch the sword. Geddy quickly pulled the weapon back. "Not yours to be putting your hands on. I just thought you might like to *see* it."

"Actually, its owner is a man named Vendanj," Tahn said. "He asked us to pick it up for him."

Geddy cast a wary eye on him.

Sutter gave an exasperated sigh. "Tall guy. Great sense of humor. The kind you want to upset so that he has to come get the sword himself."

Still Geddy didn't seem convinced.

"With a woman companion. Grey cloak," Tahn added. "She moves fast."

The smithy nodded. "Very well. I know I can trust you." Sutter faked a hurt look. Geddy put the tip of the blade into his water bucket, where it hissed and steamed. He then pulled the weapon out, tested its temperature with his thumb, and retrieved a rather ordinary sheath to stow the blade. "Tell him I had no time to polish or sharpen."

With some reluctance, Geddy handed the weapon to Tahn, who had to tug a bit to pry it from the smithy's fingers. "Thank you." As he and Sutter turned, Tahn thought he heard old Geddy mutter something about the sword and a strange light in the back of his barn.

• CHAPTER THREE •

A Late Reader

Braethen Posian sat in the warm light of his lamps and read. His father was Author Posian—A'Posian, as the tradition held—and the problem of it had been Braethen's access to books. He had little self-control when it came to them. Stories, histories, maps; didn't matter. And it led to the other hazard of his twenty-six years of life: He'd found the Sodality.

He'd discovered it at the tender age of eight, and loved everything about it: the purpose, the creed, the stories of sacrifice to meet and uphold higher truths. The Sodality covenanted themselves to the Sheason. Braethen had never actually met a renderer. But the Sheason's utter commitment to service—even at the cost of his own soul—left him holding that order in the highest regard, even though his father had spoken cautiously of the Sheason, warning that they walked between worlds, a path at the edge of what is and what may be, of what can be touched and what can be changed.

And so Braethen had spent the better part of his twenty-six years reading about and yearning to belong to the Sodality. So much so that he'd become a target for mockery—some of it good-natured enough, but a target nonetheless.

The real problem, though, was simply that the Hollows had no Sheason, and so no need of a sodalist.

Not yet, he thought. *But things could change.*

A knock came at the door.

He jumped up. He hoped to hear that the reader had arrived. He'd made a friend of Ogea. The old man always gave him an evening of discussion when he came to the Hollows, probably because Ogea and Braethen's father were such good friends. But the old man made time just for Braethen. He shared things with him that he didn't say from the rooftops. And Ogea was the only person who didn't tease Braethen about his obsession with the Sodality; in fact, the old man taught him more than he could ever glean on his own. He loved him for that.

With a book still in one hand and a quill clamped in his teeth, he pulled the door open to see Tahn and Sutter. "To what do I owe this pleasure? I know you two don't read."

They laughed and pushed past him into the room. "Can we come in?"

As Sutter passed by, he fingered the pin at Braethen's throat. It was the tarnished copper emblem of the Sodality: a sword on its side, a quill balanced on the blade at its center, the entire crest wreathed in a circlet of copper leaves. He had had it mongered by Geddy in exchange for a sign listing the prices of his various smith services.

Braethen shut the door on the wind and turned to his guests, waiting. He bore the two friends no animosity, even though they were among those who mocked him—though usually in fun. Because he was taller, and both fuller in chest and broader in shoulders than both Tahn and Sutter, he liked to believe if he really wanted to stop their mockery, he could.

"Who's there?" A'Posian called from a room at the back of the house.

"It's Tahn and Sutter," Braethen replied.

The author came into the room and removed his specs to shake the boys' hands. "What brings you here? I know you don't read."

They all laughed at the repeated joke, and the author clapped them on the back before going back to his writing desk. No one ever came to A'Posian's home without receiving his hand and some small witticism.

After he'd gone, Sutter and Tahn stood staring, a strange look in their eyes. So Braethen did the only sensible thing—he sat back down to his books. He proffered a plate of cheese and berries to the two, who waved it away.

Braethen marked his place in three of the books opened on the table before looking up at the two of them and asking again, "All right, out with it. What's going on?"

Sutter cocked his head to look at the books strewn across the table. "Why did you not follow in your father's path and take up the Authors' way?"

Braethen's smile faded, and his expression became thoughtful. "I thought I would. Father needed my help even when I was young, so I started copying books for him before you two could even walk." He was eight Northsuns older than Tahn and Sutter. "But I don't have Father's gift for words. I learned that about myself a long time ago. And somewhere in all those books, I found other interests."

"The Sodality," Tahn supplied.

"I was drawn to the purpose," Braethen said, and put his fingers to the brooch at his throat.

"Not a lot of call for it here," Sutter remarked, rolling his eyes.

"True enough," Braethen answered, unruffled. "I've no real acquaintance with the brotherhood, but I'm still learning, aren't I?" He smiled broadly.

"What are you reading?" Tahn asked.

Braethen's eyes glimmered at the question. "Histories mostly, with the occasional journal or map." He shifted on his chair. "I bought some of them from a merchant down out of Myrr." He began to gesture, his excitement growing with each passing word. "I suspect they were not gotten legally. I've read them all, several times, but there are inconsistencies and vast gaps. Entire ages summarized in a few pages." He ran a hand through his short, light brown hair. "Each time the reader comes, I have my questions ready." He paused. "This year I study even more because he has *not* come." Braethen looked toward the window, beyond which pine boughs swayed softly in the wind.

Sutter closed one of the books. "No offense, Braethen, but . . . why? Listening to the reader is enough, I say. What good can come of knowing the details of dead things? And after that, isn't the whole point of being a sodalist to protect a Sheason?"

Braethen replied, unabashed, "The Sodality defends in two ways: the arm and the word. I'm focusing on the word right now." Again he tapped the emblem at his throat.

This whole "focusing on the word" thing was a small evasion, and he hoped they'd be inclined to let him have it—though they didn't likely know any better. Besides, after all the joking done at his expense, Tahn had told him once that except for maybe Braethen's father he thought Braethen was the most ethical, dependable person in all the Hollows, precisely because he lived by the sodalist oath. That had been a good day.

Tahn broke the silence. "I think Sutter's trying to say that he's jealous, since digging roots is so awfully important."

"Yeah, that's it," Sutter agreed in a sarcastic tone.

"The past, all the ages of man, show us what will be," Braethen said, hefting one of the tomes before him. "They help us act today so that tomorrow doesn't come with all the mistakes that have gone before. This knowledge helps a sodalist serve a Sheason, the two working together in the common interest of others."

"You sound like a book," Sutter said.

Braethen ignored him, and turned with familiarity to a passage. "This is our purpose."

"Here he goes," Sutter muttered, "with the credo."

"'Change is inevitable and necessary, but the traditions of our fathers need to be preserved. Someone must watch. Someone must remember. And someone must defend . . .'" He trailed off, feeling again as he had the first time he'd read those words: humbled, yet eager to take the oath himself.

"You sound like the reader when you speak of such things," Tahn said.

Sutter waved a hand in front of Braethen's eyes. "Yeah, kind of spooky."

Braethen shook himself physically from his reverie. "The storms have never held so long. It bears another meaning, I think . . . rain, water . . . renewal . . . change. Maybe war."

A chill ran down Braethen's own back, and Sutter closed his mouth with an audible sound. Then the would-be sodalist looked up. The little room grew suddenly quite serious. "I'll tell you the truth. I'm more fond of Ogea than anyone, and I hope he is dead and that we simply haven't received word of it. Because . . . I don't like what I believe is the alternative."

"What, did you read something like that in your books?" Sutter wanted to know.

But before Braethen could answer, beyond the door the sound of slow hooves fell upon the street. At the lonely echo of a rider on the muddy roads of the Hollows, another chill rushed over him. They all went to the window to look out. The window began to cloud before his face and he unwittingly held his breath. Outside, the wind moaned over the eaves of the house and sighed through the trees.

The rider passed, so slowly that there could be no mistaking his identity: the reader. Ogea sat slumped in his saddle, his forehead resting upon the neck of his mule. In a moment, he vanished again down the road, lost beyond the trees surrounding Braethen's home.

"Let's go," Braethen said. He ran to the back of the house and told his father the reader had arrived. Then he donned his cloak and flew out the door, Tahn and Sutter close behind him.

It took but a short walk to catch up to the reader. Ogea's mount plodded along steady and slow.

As was tradition, the reader wound through the Hollows, saying nothing, his procession his only announcement. Townsfolk and Northsun travelers flocked to the street, as they always did, today drawing their coats and cloaks tightly around them as they followed behind. There was always a quiet reverence at Ogea's passage, but this time Braethen felt a sullen edge to the silence.

Dirt-stained and torn, the reader's cloak bore black-fringed holes as though left too close to a fire. Underfoot, the mud on the road, now being trod by a hundred boots or more, made soft sucking noises in the early dusk.

The wind continued to howl, and somewhere on the Huber River a water hawk protested the wretched skies that hindered its hunting, its call a faint but ominous shrill.

Finally, the procession drew toward the Fieldstone. A crowd stood in the street before the inn, ready to welcome the reader. The mass parted as Ogea's mule kept on straight, paying them no mind. Behind him, the crowd came together again. At the far corner of the inn, the reader stopped. He slid from his saddle, and steadied himself with his pommel. His satchels hung as they always had upon the flanks of his mule. Ogea reached inside, drawing out a scroll that bore a wax seal.

"My Skies. He's never read from the old parchment before," Braethen said reverently. "He usually carries a book with him to the roof."

In a broken gait, the reader hobbled toward the ladder that leaned against the Fieldstone. He clutched the scroll tightly to his chest with both arms. A strong gust of wind rushed in upon the crowd, and hands went up to hold hoods in place. Ogea's cowl was thrown back. A soft moan, so like the wind, escaped those closest to the reader—dried blood stained the reader's cheeks and chin.

The old man dropped to one knee just a pace from the ladder. But he stood on his own and slowly looked up the long ascent. Pausing for a breath, he tucked the scroll into his cloak and grasped the rungs.

And climbed.

The Fieldstone never appeared so tall to Braethen. Step by step, Ogea went up, gasping at every rung. The rasp in his lungs was audible above the white rushing sound of the wind. Two thirds of the way up, his foot slipped and caused him almost to lose his grip. One bony hand held tight, and he quickly hugged the ladder, pressing his cheek to a rung.

He started again. This time he climbed past the balcony with deliberate steps and slowly reached the roof, where he turned and beheld the people standing in the street below. Atop the inn, the wind whipped at his thin white hair and beard, his russet cloak flailing against the grey of the clouds blanketing the sky. After he regained his breath, he took the scroll from inside his cloak and thoughtfully ran his hands across its length. Holding the parchment in one hand, he surveyed the crowd again and began to speak.

"Northsun is past, another cycle come, and another measure of time to reckon our lives by. Hidden behind the clouds, the sun falls again into the west, and beneath these shrouds we huddle near our fires and share encouraging words." The reader sighed heavily. "The time for this is now past."

Ogea then stepped closer to the edge of the Fieldstone and raised his voice with more passion. "Before our fires, before the sun, the Great Fathers held their Council of Creation at the Tabernacle of the Sky. They called forth the light, the land, and filled both with life. Every living thing was intended to grow in stature and harmony with the elements around it.

"And this all was done for the good of everyone. But in their wisdom, the First Ones knew there must be counterbalance, a way for their creation to be tested and challenged. Else no learning or change could occur, and their council would bring to naught their intention: that we should become great ourselves. So, one of the fathers was given the charge to create all that would be ill to the land and its life. To one was given the task of creating sorrow and strife."

It was the old story, one Ogea told at every Northsun, but it enthralled the crowd to the last man, riveting them all as Braethen had never seen. Perhaps the endless storms had caused Hollows's folk to reflect more, of late, on their own mortality.

"For a time, the council served with great joy. Sound and song filled the land with vibrance, attending the creation of every living thing. But the One grew delighted in his charge to test men by affliction. He set upon the lands pricks and briars of every sort, creatures without conscience, to harrow the creations of light. Thousands of years did the council serve, the One becoming dark in his soul, consumed with his task.

"The Great Fathers knew the One must be bound, else men were lost. So, together they sealed him to the earth that he so wanted to destroy, creating for him a sepulchre in the farthest corner of the world to live an eternity in his rancor. And thus the High Season came to an end; the time of creation, of newness at the hands of the Noble Ones, passed from memory."

Ogea's hair flailed in the wind, his cloak pulled powerfully by the gales. The sash at his waist likewise twisted in the gusts that rushed over the Fieldstone roof. His pallor shone down upon the people, as though the warning in his tale had stolen his own vigor. Yet his voice rose into the wind. And into the face of it his eyes remained unblinking as he surveyed those who listened to his words.

"But by the time the One had been bound, balance had been undone. The land had gone awry of the Great Fathers' plan from the foundation, and they could not hope to salvage their vision. So they abandoned their work, sealing those given to the Quiet within the Bourne and leaving the unfinished world to mete out its own fate. And many scornful races there were who had, indeed, given their very souls to Quietus's hateful designs. So, into the land the First Ones introduced the Sheason, an order ordained to establishing peace and equanimity, set apart to guide the other races throughout the rest of Aeshau Vaal.

"But legions of the One pressed against the Shadow of the Hand where the veil between the Bourne and our world grew weakest. Quietgiven roiled with bitterness and chaos, unsure of their place since the Abandonment by the First Ones. But none more than the Draethmorte."

Gasps escaped the crowd at the mention of the Draethmorte. An unnatural chill rippled Braethen's flesh. He had heard Ogea utter the word only once.

"They were the first to be given breath at the hands of the One, in a time before his banishment, when the Gods yet held hope for this world. They knew well the power of the First Ones, for they learned at the feet of the council itself, serving in that first High Season, believing themselves chosen to set the world upon its path and guide it to its own glory.

"But like their creator, their arts grew cankered. And when the One was exiled, they, too, were sent into the Bourne, where their bitterness and hatred were likewise bound. There they served as the One's highest council, organizing his followers. These armies eventually penetrated the veil, passing the Pall Mountains. They marched south from the Hand into the lands of men after the Framers were gone."

From the roof the reader began to cough, the rasp in his chest sounding like the wet tearing of flesh. Blood oozed onto his lips, and when he spoke again the blood spattered in red-grey droplets down his tunic.

"The land has grown old since the Craven Season, ages passing, millennia now often forgotten. They have names, all of them, but it is enough to know that we have lived, survived, tended the land. Until this season that rests upon us now. The Sheason have dwindled, some lost to the weakness of flesh, unwilling to accept the cost to their own lives to bear the call. More often, they cannot find suitable initiates to learn their path. And in this Age of Rumor, there are those who have sought the execution of the Sheason."

Ogea looked up into the sky and shook his fist, a strangled protest tearing from his narrow chest into the neutral light of the clouds.

Braethen knew why the reader protested, and he shared Ogea's disdain. The League of Civility had passed the Civilization Order in most nations to execute Sheason for rendering the Will even when in the service of others. The League claimed what the Sheason did was superstitious and archaic, akin to the dark talents the old stories ascribed to creatures of the Bourne.

Ogea slowly lowered his gaze to the people. He held the scroll aloft. The wind riffled its edges, threatening to tear the seal. But Ogea took the red wax in his bony hands and snapped it in two. The sound, faint and brittle, sent yet another shiver down Braethen's back, and he muttered, softly so that others might not hear, "A seal once broken . . ."

Ogea unrolled the vellum but held it aside. Without referring to it, he began to speak again, a quiet humility in his voice.

"Good friends, I have read for the last time. Northsun has come again to the Land, and we are grateful for its light. We have hope, but it is naive if we sit idly and do nothing. There is a quiet darkness spreading. When its blight is complete enough, the power of the Will shall no longer be able to contain the Quiet. Forda I'Forza, body and spirit, earth and sky . . . will fail. The abandonment of the Great Fathers will be complete. . . . We will have proven that our growth did not matter; we will have shown that we hadn't enough desire and fortitude to be great ourselves."

Ogea fell to his knees. He held the parchment before his face and nodded to himself. Then he backed onto the ladder and began to descend. Only four rungs down, the reader slipped, his scroll falling from his hands and cast about by eddies of wind along the side of the Fieldstone. The old man dangled for a moment and then lost his grip on the rung. He plummeted, his fall seeming to last unnaturally long. Into the mud he splashed, letting out a thick mewling sound as he hit the ground. Braethen pushed his way through hundreds of townsfolk to reach Ogea's side. There, he turned his friend over and placed a hand on his chest to see if he still breathed.

Braethen suddenly felt eyes upon him. The crowd had crept closer, but they were all Hollows folk. Turning toward the back of the Fieldstone, he spied a tall, dark man, his face cast in sorrow and determination. Braethen's heart went cold when he saw the insignia at the man's neck: three rings, a Sheason.

• CHAPTER FOUR •

Dangers of the Road

The woman knelt at the side of the river, washing her face and hands and arms.

The highwayman watched from behind a thicket of scrub oak.

Leaf-shadow dappled the slow-moving water, the bulrushes, and the woman herself, who remained unaware that she was not alone. The low hum of the current cloaked his slow steps as his companions crouched in strategic positions downriver and across from her, in case she bolted.

She surely hadn't driven alone the team of horses and wagon that stood a hundred strides south. Somewhere close by, she had a man.

He would arrive too late.

Really, she should have known better. In the open places between the cities of men—with their garrisons and high outer walls—the world belonged to the man who would take the risk; the man who played his chances; the man who took the open road and sky above as his home and roof. For travelers in the places between, fair warning consisted of nothing more than a reflection in the water above you as you splashed a day's grit from the creases around your eyes and mouth . . . in the moment before you tried to scream.

The woman stood up fast, whirling, her lips parting to raise a cry of alarm.

The highwayman put his boot into her stomach to steal her breath before it could carry her distress to another. She went down on one knee, looking up with the surprised, pleading eyes he'd grown so tired of seeing.

Give me some real bit of anger instead!

His companions closed in cautiously—a caged and frightened animal will lash out.

"Now, before you start with any other ideas, let me tell you what is best for you," the highwayman said. "Because your options are few. For sport, my fellows here would like as not take you for a *ride,* then drop you in the river for the fish. These lads aren't delicate about anything, my good woman, so bear that in mind when you get your breath back and find your anger."

His companions smiled over his words, but the highwayman didn't have much use for them, either, and gave them a flat look.

The woman finally gasped a breath, her face pinched in pain and dread.

"For my part, I'd spare you that indignity, since I can't imagine the pleasure of a woman that is not freely given." The highwayman smiled genuinely, then caught a sneer on the woman's face. "But in exchange for my protection, you'll come along with us and keep your protests quiet. Otherwise, you are gambling that wherever we're going is worse than an early grave. And those are bad odds."

Deliberately, the woman stood, a steady defiance clear on her brow. "You think because my dress is worn I care less about virtue than my life? Is that what thieves on the open road believe?"

The highwayman laughed aloud, but low.

She went on, undaunted. "Any man with such a proposition can't be trusted to keep his word." She spat on him. "Kill me, then. Prove yourself the gentleman, save me from the itchy hands of your friends."

"Nah," one of his companions said. "If we aren't taking her with us, then let's do with her what a man can, and take what's on the wagon besides." The man pointed off toward the woman's camp.

The highwayman turned a questioning look on her. "Your play, my lady. What price for your virtue today?"

They stared at each other for several long moments. The years of toil and travel had given her salt, he had to admit that. The fact made him happier to have come upon her—the road had an indifferent beneficence if you spent enough time there.

Then he caught an imperceptible crack in her resolve. Just a glint in the eye, as her mind showed her the scene that could play out on this dappled bank in the early evening sun. He'd won. But not before her full lungs brought a scream of help that shattered the relative calm, scattering birds to the air and long echoes down the surface of the river.

A name. A name she cried out.

He knew she couldn't have been alone.

Before his men could wrestle her down, the heavy, thundering feet of a rescuer pounded the earth in their direction.

The highwayman nodded to the woman, and to himself, and took a position between his captive and the impending approach of this other. Resting a hand on his sword, he stood as still as a statue until the worried face of a man emerged from the trees on a dead run toward him. The man drew a pair of knives. Even from this distance, he could see that they weren't weapons. They were tools of some trade. Deadly perhaps, and likely the man was skilled in their use. But not a fighter. Not truly a threat.

He hoped he would not have to kill the man.

The woman dropped to the ground behind the highwayman, dodging his companions and screeching into the long shadows. She kicked and rolled until finally they pounced on her, smothering her thrashing arms under their bulk.

As the encroaching champion came near, the highwayman drew his sword, dropped to one knee, and placed the blade on the woman's neck. "That's far enough."

The other came to a skidding stop. "Leave her be! She's done nothing to you."

"Ah, but you can't really know that, can you?" the highwayman said, taking some sport of it.

"Aye, I can. She's not a combative soul, nor a *thief*." The man spoke his insult slowly.

"Hmmm. Well, let us get straight to it, then. I have invited this woman to join me. It is not a negotiable invitation. You'll want to attempt her rescue, and that's most noble. But mind you"—he fixed the man a stare—"resist that impulse. It will likely only get you both killed. I hope you'll trust me on that; it's not something you should gamble on."

Then a knowing, grateful expression touched the rescuer's taut features. "You're not going to kill her or you'd have done it already. And I don't see the signs of a man with forceful loins." He looked at the woman in a way that betrayed an intimacy the highwayman hadn't yet seen. "So then let's have a trade on it," the man resumed. "I'll take her place. Whatever need you have, let me fill it." Emotion crept into the rescuer's voice. "I won't argue or resist."

The man dropped his hands to his sides, a sign of good faith, waiting.

The highwayman relaxed his own grip on his sword and stood, marveling at the reason and proposed sacrifice. It was going to be easy to manipulate this man, since clearly he loved the woman.

But that could be dangerous, too. He'd have to play it just right.

"A noble request, but I'm afraid I must decline. You have my word, though, that I bear her no mortal threat." He signaled for his men to haul her to her feet.

"Don't do this," the man replied, both a plea and edge in his tone.

This is where it gets dangerous. Wonderful!

"Take care, man." The highwayman stepped forward.

The other's hands rose again, one knife swiveling about, tip back—a fighter's grip. *Maybe more than tools after all.*

Then he lunged, knives slicing through the air. The highwayman rolled left and came up, his sword just blocking another attack as he got to his feet. His men pulled the woman back as she thrashed against their clutch.

"There's still time. Let it go. If I kill you, you'll have no chance to track us in hope of revenge, or, better still, saving your beloved." He ducked as another knife slipped through the air near his face.

"She would rather die, here, now, than go with you one league!" The man danced from one foot to the other.

The highwayman sensed the truth in that. But he didn't have time for this. He had pressing matters. This husband or lover needed to more clearly see his choices. "Would she rather watch you die before accompanying us up the road?" As if on cue, another of the highwayman's men emerged with a bow at full draw on the rescuer.

At that the man paused, his knife handles creaking beneath his iron grip. His arms trembled with suspended action, even as he shared a long look with the woman they'd claimed from the river's edge. Tears began to stream down her face, silent, fearful, dignified tears. In response, her loved one's face pinched in a rictus of disbelief and horror.

"I will find you," he whispered. "I will never stop."

"There. That's sensible," the highwayman commented. He had his men tie the man up. Then, as the failed rescuer watched, they drew the woman through another line of trees, hoisted her into a saddle, and rode east.

CHAPTER FIVE

Quiet in the Hollows

I nside!" Hambley shouted, directing them to the kitchen door just twenty feet away. "Stay back, the rest of you! We can see to this. Take to your meals or homes, off now." No one moved. "Go!" The gathering slowly broke up, hushed talk shared between husbands and wives and friends.

Tahn, Sutter, and Braethen lifted Ogea and carried him into Hambley's kitchen, past the ovens, and down a back hall to one of the sleeping rooms. With care, they eased him onto the bed, and Hambley drew back the curtain to allow in the watery light. Braethen sat on the mattress and gently placed his hands on the man's neck and cheeks.

"What can you do for him, Braethen?" Hambley asked.

"Nothing." The answer came from the doorway.

Braethen looked up and saw again the Sheason, who stood now in the doorway. He'd often dreamed of the moment he'd meet a member of the order, imagined what he might say, how he might try to make an impression. All of those preparations fled him as he sat near a friend who might be taking his last breaths.

Hambley redirected his question. "Vendanj, can you help?"

"Shall we let Braethen answer?" Sutter said with an acerbic tone.

Vendanj ignored Sutter and moved to the other side of the bed, taking one of Ogea's hands in his own. "Hello, old man. I was here. I listened."

Though he'd only just met this Vendanj, the gentleness he heard now in the Sheason's voice did not sound like it often belonged to the man, who wore an iron visage. Ogea remained unconscious, his face still streaked with mud. Vendanj laid his free hand on the reader's forehead and spoke briefly in a tongue Braethen had never heard spoken. He couldn't be sure, but he thought he somehow *felt* the words the Sheason uttered. He regarded Vendanj with a look of disbelief. *The Conceiver's Tongue.*

Ogea's eyes opened slightly, and he looked up at the man holding his hand. "Vendanj." He coughed, swallowing hard against a spasm that threatened to steal his voice. "You should not have come. It is dangerous for you here."

"Quiet, friend." Vendanj spoke in mild reproach. "Use your voice only for what matters."

The reader nodded appreciatively. "Bar'dyn. Two days outside the Hollows on the east road. I escaped . . . used a trick Artixan once showed me. Tell him that for me." Ogea smiled, the expression turning sour on his face as the need to cough overcame him and he spat blood up onto Vendanj's cheek and lips. The Sheason made no move to wipe away the blood.

"I will tell him," Vendanj assured the reader.

"More. A Velle . . . with them. Careful, Vendanj." Ogea trailed off, his eyes conveying warning. His chest rose and fell in shallow pants, a soft wheezing sound rising from his throat with each breath. He then shifted his head on the goose-feather pillow and looked at Braethen.

"I don't think we'll be sharing that evenwine this year, my young friend. I'm sorry."

Braethen took Ogea's other hand and shook his head at the apology.

"Safeguard my scribblings," the reader said, smiling weakly. "They are important to the right eyes."

Another wracking cough seized Ogea, the ripping sounds coming from deeper within his body this time. A fresh stream of blood coursed down his left cheek from the corner of his mouth. He licked his lips to wet them, leaving a bloodred coating like the paint the womenfolk wore at Harvest.

"Is there more?" Vendanj asked.

"Yes. You must remind them of the New Promise, because a passage has been opened again into the Bourne."

The room stood quite for a long moment. The revelation chilled them all.

"Are you sure?" Vendanj asked finally, his voice strained.

"The veil has not yet failed, but from the Shadow of the Hand the firstborn of the One bellow deep into the Bourne to call their lost brothers. Some are able to pass through. They are here in the Hollows for the same reason you come. But how they got into the Hollows, I know not. Something must be—" He tried to cough, but his chest only heaved, too hollow to force the sound.

"Enough, friend. You have said all you will say." Vendanj gently clenched the old man's hand. Braethen still clasped the other.

"No, the—"

"Hush, my friend. Be still and remember. . . ."

The old man did not protest. He turned his head toward the ceiling, his eyes growing distant, a vague smile playing on his reddened lips.

Vendanj bowed, placing his forehead on the back of Ogea's hand and holding it there. Braethen regarded the two men reverently. Sutter and Hambley looked perplexed, but Braethen bowed his head. A calm settled over the room, broken only by the whispering sound of the reader drawing air. It came softly, slowing.

Sadness grew in Braethen's breast, his heart simultaneously filling with pride for a man who had earned the respect of others for the eloquence and boldness of his words without ever lifting a weapon. He reflected on the friendship the old man had offered him; a friend who had never judged his dream of being a sodalist, but instead traded tales about the order with him. His heart also pounded with the fear of losing his one supporter, as though the dream would pass if Ogea were no longer around to help him believe.

In those moments, Braethen also reflected on what it would mean to be a sodalist for real. And he knew suddenly a simple truth: Standing fast with a friend in his final moments, sharing whatever fear or pain or relief would come, was the measure of his devotion.

And so he held his friend's hand. And waited.

Sometime later, Ogea stopped breathing.

Vendanj looked up and brushed a gentle palm over the old man's open eyes, drawing down the lids. He gently placed the man's hand on the bed, then stood. His body formed a silhouette against the window behind him, nearly blackening the room.

He turned and spoke quietly. "The time has come for us to finish our talk, Tahn, but not here. Hambley, can we take dinner somewhere in private?"

Hambley still stared at Ogea. "He's really dead, isn't he? And he fell from my ladder."

"He was dead before he entered the Hollows," Vendanj assured Hambley. "There is no time to grieve for him now. We must speak in secret."

The innkeeper drew in a bracing breath. "We can use the townsmen's chamber."

"Well enough," Vendanj replied.

Hambley opened the door and disappeared to make his preparations. Vendanj went directly to Tahn and reached down to take the sword they'd retrieved from Geddy's smithy. He gave it a brief look, then motioned them into the hall. The large man brushed past Sutter and Tahn, his cloak stirring an indoor breeze as he went. They followed, but Braethen remained kneeling at the side of the bed, staring at the pallid face of the reader. After a moment, he reached out and gently touched Ogea's kind face. He whispered, "By Will and Sky, thank you for your belief in me."

Tahn strode down the hall and through a back door into the townsmen's chamber. The hearth, a fire blazing within, dominated the inner wall. Muted voices could be heard from the common room, where hushed talk conjectured on the condition of the reader. The windows admitted watery light from the skies without, leaving the private room in half shadow. Hambley drew a flame from the fire onto the end of a small dried reed, and returned to the wooden table in the center of the room. A brass fixture there held ten candles in a wide oval pattern. Hambley lit them all and extinguished the reed.

"I will fetch some bread and bitter." He bustled through the door and was gone.

Each of them stood behind one of the wide, high-backed chairs, as though sitting committed them to something they were uncertain they wanted to join. Vendanj sat and Sutter looked over at Tahn, who shrugged and sat down. Sutter and Braethen followed.

Vendanj glanced at Braethen, then began. "The things we must discuss are matters of import. Let's begin with Tahn. I think there is more to the story you started to tell here not an hour ago."

Behind them the sounds of the hall grew steadily more raucous, some men chewing hungrily, others arguing, many laughing nervously. But on this side of the fire, in the small circle around the rough table, quiet, intense conversation went on with a man whose face looked trustworthy, but who was also filled with the knowledge of an outlander. Would he have knowledge of the creature Tahn had seen in the trees controlling the very rain itself?

Tahn related his encounter with the creature in the woods, the darkness in the rain, and the dry ground with two scorched, fist-punched holes. When he'd finished, Vendanj regarded him a moment, but asked no questions. Then he spoke again.

"There are choices ahead. Only Braethen has made the Change, but Tahn has no father to counsel him, and you"—Vendanj pointed at Sutter—"I'd rather leave behind. But you know too much. If we leave you here, you're a danger to us, to yourself, and to your adoptive parents."

Tahn turned to his friend. Sutter was the son of Filmoere and Kaylla Te Polis, the best root farmers in all the Hollows. Tahn had been in their home a thousand times. Vendanj must be mistaken. *Adopted?* But his friend's sheepish look confirmed what Vendanj had said. Tahn raised his brows in question. Sutter only shrugged.

"Never mind the revelations," Vendanj went on. "As soon as preparations can be made, we must depart the Hollows." He fastened his steely gaze on Braethen. "Why do you wear the crest of the Sodality? Are you received into the order?"

Braethen had already started to shake his head. "Not officially. I've been studying—"

"Can you use a sword?" Vendanj interrupted.

"I've held a sword before—"

"Have you been in battle?" Vendanj's voice rose, impatient.

Braethen shook his head. "But I've been studying the Sodality for almost twenty years. I know what is required."

A dark question showed in Vendanj's face. "Do you? You knelt at the side of a dying man who spoke of the opening of the Bourne, of Velle and Quietgiven. What do you think, with all your wisdom, awaits us when we leave this place? Are you ready for that with your *studies*?"

Braethen looked abashed. The light Tahn had always seen in his eyes at the prospect of being a sodalist dimmed to nothing.

Vendanj wasn't finished. "Lives will depend on this. Ideal notions read in a book or shouted from a rooftop won't come to a single breath when the malice of the Quiet meets you in the darkness. Your mind will turn in upon itself and we will be forced to mother you while other lives fall."

Braethen shrank in his chair. Tahn had never seen him so seriously chided through all the ridicule he'd taken his long life for wanting to live the values of the Sodality. It was cruel. Tahn's own anger flared.

But words died in his throat as he watched Braethen not simply sit tall, but stand. Candlelight flickered, and shadows danced across the deep grain of the table. The smell of spent pine lingered from the fire, which popped and hissed as sap bubbled from the wood.

"Please, Sheason—"

"Hold, boy! Watch the mouth you use!" Vendanj himself stood up, his chair clattering back.

Terror rose in Braethen's face. "My apologies, but please consider . . ." He stopped, looking at the implacable gaze of the man. Slowly, he pulled a scroll from his coat. The parchment still bore the broken seal. Tahn looked at Vendanj's face, anticipating fiery anger. Instead, Vendanj said nothing, his face now placid.

Braethen placed the parchment upon the table, clearly unwilling to unroll it. He looked across at Vendanj, then down again at the scroll. It left silence in the room so profound that Tahn thought he could hear the candles burning.

"I know the stories," Braethen said. "My father is an author, and I *know* the stories. It is how I know . . . the path you follow. And Ogea was my friend. I want to come. If not to become a sodalist, then to honor the man who believed I could have."

In that instant, from the shadows emerged the girl Tahn had seen earlier. In the time of a thought, she stood at Vendanj's right shoulder. Her appearance startled them all, though Tahn was glad to see her again. Her eyes caught the candlelight, reflecting it like bright hazel-grey mirrors. Her skin shone smooth and without blemish over high cheeks and a delicately formed nose. She'd braided back her dark hair. A black leather strip high around her neck bore the insignia of two white blades.

Vendanj appraised Braethen's face. As he did so, the woman whispered into his ear. She stood taller than most women from the Hollows, almost Tahn's own height. As she spoke, Tahn observed the line of her jaw and watched her words silently draw full lips into round shapes. The sepia glow of the room bathed her skin. A hand on Tahn's shoulder made him jump. He twisted in his seat to receive Sutter's wide grin.

"Very well," Vendanj finally said. Tahn turned back, ignoring Sutter. "Only know this," Vendanj cautioned. "Your friend is my friend, and his dead body yet lies in this very inn. I will not stand to see his memory trifled with. It is not romantic to keep the stories, it is not a dream you grow to fulfill. It is labor and sacrifice . . . and dangerous. To be a sodalist isn't to know the word and use a sword. It's to use the sword to defend the word. Knowing doesn't qualify you by half. Not at all. Nevertheless, you may choose this for yourself. But mark me, more will be expected of you, Braethen, than to keep tales. More than you bargain for."

At that moment, the woman rounded the table and laid a blade in front of Braethen. Nothing more on the subject needed to be said. But Tahn caught a look of fear in the would-be sodalist's eyes.

In answer, Braethen returned the scroll to the folds of his coat and gripped the sword by its sheath. Vendanj nodded and turned toward Tahn, whose mouth hung agape.

Sheason!

Sutter, too, now stared. How did Braethen know?

This Vendanj was a renderer. Tahn felt the same awful portent he'd felt seeing the Velle in the woods. Raising the Will to his own design. It frightened Tahn to even bear him company.

Just then, Hambley entered with a large carafe of bitter and a wood platter of bread. The loaf steamed, bearing a glaze of goat butter. Behind him came his son, Mena, and kitchen help, carrying five large mugs. Hambley stopped short when he saw the girl. Adjusting quickly, he sent Mena back for another mug and proceeded to place a glass before each person seated at the table. The innkeep poured them all a full cup of dark, bitter ale, and filled the last when Mena returned. Hambley shooed his son away and took his seat, quaffing half his glass in one long pull.

"We will gather only what is necessary and go," Vendanj began. "Say nothing to your families. You only put them in danger by sharing any of this."

Tahn listened, his mind feeling fragmented. "Any of what?" he finally said. "If you mean the Bar'dyn, then we have to tell them. *That's* the danger they face. And not just our families, but all of the Hollows."

"He's right," Sutter added. "I don't know how you knew about my parents, Vendanj, but I won't leave my family if what Ogea said is true. I usually don't care for the old stories. But *something* got to the reader, and I'll be one who finds out what."

"You ignorant boy." The words were even, uninflected, and spoken by the girl beside Vendanj. "Have you no reason inside you? Have you not heard all that has been said?" Her words stayed Sutter's reply. "From beyond your wood we have come, witnessed the breaking of a seal, witnessed the passing of a reader, and heard the invocation of names spoken together only when the One sent his Quiet into the land, when the War of the First Promise raged against the Sky." Her voice carried cleanly as one who has not used tobaccom or bitter or been sick with the tremors. It rang with a certain wisdom that brought blood into Sutter's cheeks.

"What makes you believe that your life is entirely your own, that you can rush out and put yourself at risk?" A touch of derision crept into her voice. "Perhaps we should leave you here to dig roots."

Vendanj raised a hand, signaling an end to the exchange. "This is Mira Far. She will be accompanying us."

Tahn turned again in his seat, mouthing the word *Far* to Nails. Sutter stared, still embarrassed.

Braethen half stood. "Good to meet you, Mira." Mira dipped her head to acknowledge the introduction. "But accompanying us where?" he asked.

"I will not say the name of it yet," Vendanj replied. "For now, it is enough for you to know we must go."

Tahn looked back at the stranger. The vagueness of the man's reply gave him a sinking feeling in the pit of his stomach. What destination would need to be kept secret? The hidden answer unsettled him.

Hambley tore bread into large chunks and placed them within arms' reach of his guests. "Take bread together, friends. It is nigh time for supper, and eating together makes stronger ties besides." He lifted his glass and finished his bitter.

Each of the men ate, but Mira faded into the shadows near the outer wall, watching the street beyond through the window. In her cloak, she appeared little more than a shadow herself. But Tahn could still see the line of her jaw, held in a straight, almost regal posture. It reminded him of the mountain cats, the way their poised stillness belied readiness to strike. Rumors of the Far told of their gifts of stealth and swift movement. Still, the Far, if they'd ever existed at all, were said to be outlanders from the edge of the Soliel. Few believed the Soliel could support life anymore. Perhaps it was only her name, and not her lineage.

"Thank you, Hambley. You cause us to remember ourselves," Vendanj said. He then took from inside his cloak the small, flat wooden case Tahn had noted before and removed a green stem. Tahn thought he smelled again the scent of peppermint. The Sheason put the sprig in his mouth, neither chewing or swallowing.

Tahn finally had to ask the question. "Vendanj, why would it endanger our families to speak of this?" Both Braethen and Sutter grew still.

The man eyed him. "You ask a central question, Tahn. And we should come to the point in it." He motioned toward the door and, in a breath, Mira left the room. "The Bar'dyn are close. You heard this. But they have come because they seek to bring eternal Quiet upon the land, to cause it to dry and parch and yield no more its fruits."

Tahn listened closely, seeking the answer to his question, while images of dry earth and watered skies mingled behind his eyes.

"And it is more than this. By your own account the Bar'dyn bring with them a renderer, a Velle, out of the Bourne. We must leave, and go secretly. Or else the knowledge you share with your family of what you've heard and seen will itself attract the attention of those who seek to put an end to all things. Do you see?"

"No." Tahn's impatience grew. Balatin had not taught him to follow blindly. "I don't see!" He lowered his voice. "If it is Bar'dyn, if it is Velle, then we must stay and protect our homes, our families. How can you not understand that?"

Sutter nodded, putting his hand on Tahn's arm in a show of support. Braethen only watched for what Vendanj would say next. The Sheason did not raise his voice; he did not betray any emotion. Instead he looked steadfastly at Tahn and took a long breath.

"Your loyalties do you credit. But you are wrong because your first premise is wrong. Return to your question, 'Why does it endanger our families?' It is because those out of the Bourne have come here for *you*."

Tahn reeled at the suggestion, and shook his head. It was a mistake, or perhaps even a trick of the Sheason's to get Tahn to do as he wished. Why him? How did Vendanj know? The Quiet could have come into the Hollows for Ogea, or Vendanj for that matter.

As if reading his thoughts, Vendanj said, "You may deny it, or seek another answer to your question, but the truth remains. The sooner you embrace it, the sooner we can do what must be done."

Still struggling against it, Tahn felt some truth in what Vendanj said. And then something more occurred to him. If the Bar'dyn had come into the Hollows for him, then he was responsible for Ogea's death. Following that, another thought stole into his mind as cold as the winter ice in the eaves of a Hollows home.

"If we stay, we endanger all the Hollows, don't we," he said. It was not a question.

"It is more, Tahn," Vendanj explained. "They can sense you, taste your breath on the wind leagues distant. Leaving *may* preserve you, but it will *surely* preserve the town. They won't waste time warring on the Hollows if they know you are gone. But if you remain, they will set upon this place with a vengeance. Any friends you have here will die."

Dread tightened Tahn's throat. His stomach roiled as the things Vendanj said coalesced in his mind. His thoughts sped past his need to know why the Bar'dyn had come for him—something that would occur to him later. Desperately he looked into the strange man's placid face. "Ogea said they were coming from the east! Will and Sky, Wendra is alone!" Tahn jumped out of his seat and raced from the room, leaving the other men behind before they could speak a word.

Tahn rode for all he was worth and soon came to the rise where the firs thinned on the lee side of the hill. The road wound down to his and Wendra's home, a stand of aspen on the near side. Lantern light shone in the windows and fell from an open door in a small rectangle. *She waits on me,* he thought. But something deeper, something low in his belly put the lie to that.

An open door . . .

He began pulling his arrow, gripping Jole's sides tight with his legs. He descended into the shallow dale, the image of Ogea railing from atop the Fieldstone fixed in his mind. Bar'dyn, he'd said.

The road grew muddy. Jole did not slow, his hooves throwing sludge. A bolt of lightning arced through the sky. The peal of thunder shattered the silence and pushed through the small vale in waves, each one louder than the last. It echoed outward through the woods in diminishing tolls.

Vaguely, the whispering sound of rain on trees floated toward Tahn. The soft smells of earth and pollen hung on the air, charged with the coming of another storm. Cold perspiration beaded on his forehead and neck.

An open door . . .

Wendra would not leave the house open to the chill.

Passing the stable, Jole began to slow. As Tahn prepared to jump, another bolt of white fire erupted from the sky, this time striking the ground. It hit at the near end of the vale. The thunder immediately exploded around him. Simultaneously, a scream went up from inside his home. Jole reared, tugging at his reins and throwing Tahn to the ground before racing for the safety of the stable. Tahn lost his bow and began frantically searching the mud for his dropped weapon. The sizzle of falling rain rose, a lulling counterpoint to the screams that continued from inside. Something crashed to the floor of the cabin. Then a wail rose up, a strange howl filled with glee and hatred. It sounded at once deep in the throat, like the thunder, and high in the nose, like a child's mirth.

Tahn's heart drummed in his ears and neck and chest. His throat throbbed with it. Wendra was in there! He found his bow and the one arrow. Shaking the mud and water from the bowstring and quickly cleaning the arrow's fletching on his coat, he sprinted for the door. He nocked the arrow and leapt to the stoop.

The home had grown suddenly still and quiet.

Tahn burst in, holding his aim high and loose.

An undisturbed fire burned in the hearth, but everything else in his home lay strewn or broken. The table had been toppled on its side, earthen plates broken into shards across the floor. Food was splattered against one wall and puddled near a cooking pot in the far corner. Wendra's few books sat partially burned near the fire, their thrower's aim not quite sure.

Tahn saw it all in a glance as he swung his bow to the left where Wendra had tucked her bed up under the loft.

She lay atop her quilts, knees up and legs spread.

No, Will it not!

Then, within the shadows beneath the loft, Tahn saw it, a hulking mass standing at the foot of Wendra's bed. It hunched over, too tall to remain upright in the nook beneath the upper room. Its hands cradled something in a blanket of horsehair. The smell of sweat and blood and new birth commingled with the aroma of Wendra's cooking pot.

The creature slowly turned its massive head toward him. Wendra looked, too, her eyes weary but alive with fright. She weakly reached one arm toward him, mouthing something, but unable to speak.

In a low, guttural voice the creature spoke. "Quillescent all around." It rasped the words in thick, glottal tones, the way outlanders spoke when they hadn't yet mastered the common tongue.

"Bar'dyn," Tahn muttered. His disbelief fell away.

CHAPTER SIX

Payment in Oaths

The man with sun-darkened skin strode in the early morning light, a thin cloak wrapped around his shoulders. In the land of his home, he'd have had no need of the garment. But here in the frost-covered hills at dawn, the chill had its bite. And while, for his part, the man might have borne that without complaint, the child he cradled close to his chest beneath the folds of that cloak would not.

The babe slept as the man walked neither slow nor hurried. Purposefully.

He knew his destination, and would arrive soon enough. So he kept a careful eye and a measured pace. When he came to the place, he wanted the infant rested.

He also kept his own counsel as he climbed hills, descended valleys, and marched down long stretches of road beneath the overarching branches of sycamore, hemlock, and oak. The child slept all the while, unaware of what awaited it when sun would first touch the sky. The man had stopped to feed the babe several times a day; it made for slow going. But an end to that drew near. The man felt the pangs of relief and loss all at once. As he ever did.

He topped a rise and spied a small farm on a gradual slope a league distant. "Almost your time, little one," he whispered. "We will see how you are received today. I should not like to have to take you back. This is a one-way path for you."

The child woke, as if understanding it was being addressed. Quiet and thoughtful the way a babe can often be, it stared up into the man's sun-worn face.

"But we must have a discussion before we go our separate ways, little one," the man continued. "And I will pray they have sufficient means to make the offer you rightly deserve."

The child, still less than two weeks from its mother's womb, looked up. For the briefest of moments it appeared to understand the words. But the unfocused eyes soon turned in a new direction, and the man refocused his own concentration on the path ahead. He possessed the discipline not to allow the softness of the child's skin to recall to mind anything not useful in his errand. For his errand was his primary concern.

There was no equivocation in that.

Dew caught the radiance of dawn and shone back on the man a hundred points of bluish light. Long ago, in another life, he would have at least paused to consider the difference between his own life and that of the family he now approached.

He got moving again.

A small road blocked by a meager gate announced the farm he'd been angling toward. Up the path he went, the child tucked close to his chest, mostly covered by his plain, sun-ravaged cloak. Moments later he came to the back steps of the dwelling.

Always he rapped at a home's rear door (if he knocked at all), because women and men who earned their way by the sweat of their brow rarely used their front door. Life turned on the axis of a home's back entrance—closest to the kitchen and fire and stories. And while some did not recognize his subdued calling card (rear door and light knuckles), he felt it important that his errand be attended by the appropriate level of solemnity and discretion.

Life: traded at the back doors of the world.

There were bargains to be made.

And so today he rapped at this lintel, turning hard eyes on the yard as he cradled the child, who began to stir. No chickens scratched at the packed earth; no cattle lowed in the field nearby. He worried that these people would not have the resources to meet his demands. But then, there were many forms of payment, and that was one thing about which he felt good. For so many years . . .

The door drew back and a young wife dried her hands on a towel hanging from her belt before taking his hand in greeting and fingering the token of the hillfolk to identify herself. But as much as that, the look in her eye when she glanced down at the child in his arms led him to know that this woman would tend and love and teach and protect this child. To her credit, she kept any surprise or dread or gladness off her face. The man nodded to himself; her composure put her in good stead.

This may go well, after all.

The woman looked past him, eyeing the yard and everything else beyond, then stepped aside, indicating that he should enter.

So in they went, the man and the child.

He sat, resting his legs from his long journey, but still holding the babe close as he surveyed the modest home about him. Shortly, the woman's husband stepped in, showing a wary eye: a large man with large hands. Good.

They bore one another's company in silence for some time. There seemed no reason to speak, as the purpose of his visit manifested itself in the body of the infant he cradled. He measured the couple before him more by the appointment of their home than by anything they might have said.

Finally, the woman broke the silence. "Would you like some hot tea?"

The man with the sun-worn face shook his head at the hospitality. "No. But the child could use some milk. Have you any?"

In reply, the woman turned to a table behind her and took up a carafe. She crossed the room and waited for him to surrender the child. With interest he did so, and watched as the woman took the child in her arms, sat, and removed her towel. She twisted it at one corner and dipped it in the milk, then offered it to the babe in imitation of nursing. The child went right to it.

The man nodded his satisfaction.

Then her husband spoke. "We can offer you little for the child."

The traveler turned to gather the man's attention. "What is he worth to you?" The hill-man stared back, seeming to consider. But before he could speak, the traveler continued. "And be aware that payment is not always made in coin." The intimations were many, and the man let them all hang in the air in this early morning gathering in the modest home of some remote hillfolk.

"It will have a hard life here," the hill-man finally offered. "Many . . . most do not live to see their stripling years."

"So your payment is uncertainty?" The traveler looked back at the sure hand of the woman feeding the infant.

"The child won't go hungry," the hill-man replied. "I'll see to it. But beyond that, we've few promises here. And anything we give you will mean less to provision ourselves to care for it."

The visitor looked up with eyes that might have appeared faded from so long under a heavy sun. His own wages in this affair were hard-won. "Your assurances aren't grand, friend. There are others who have need of a child healthy as this one. A few days more on the road and I could return home with fuller pockets."

The hill-man did not hestitate. "Choose that if you will. I've little use for quick hands to make a prize of a child. I can offer the little one my home, and the knowledge of the hills besides. I've no delusions; this is all meager. And perhaps not the best place for the child, after all. We will have our own questions to answer on how it came to us and from whom. These will not be easy to avoid, and the truth brings its own risks to the walls of our home, if you take my meaning."

The man looked back at the hill-man. "I do at that. But I've my own balances to keep." He stood. "For payment I will have your oath. And heed me that I will call that marker if it is broken. The child's true parents, his origins, even me, we are all irrelevant now. No questions will you ask, or answer. And your covenant to the child will be as if your woman here bore him from your own seed."

The hill-man took three great strides and put out his hand. The two clasped, and the hill-man wrapped his finger around the visitor's thumb in the hillfolk token to seal his oath. The woman likewise nodded her assent. The traveler then went to the woman, whispering low, "He will grow to greatness, if treated hereafter better than was his start," and put a hand on the child's head in farewell.

He then strode from the room without another look at either of the hillfolk. Into the first light of dawn the sun-weathered man emerged, his darkened skin receiving the beams of the greater light as old friends. He set his feet back upon the road.

He had leagues to go.

CHAPTER SEVEN

The Birth of Flight

The Bar'dyn stepped from beneath the loft, its girth massive. The fire lit the creature's fibrous skin, which moved as if independent of the muscle and bone beneath. Ridges and rills marked its hide, creating a natural armor Tahn had only ever heard of in story—armor said to surpass the mail worn by men. It uncoiled its left arm from the blanket it held to its chest, letting its hand hang nearly to its knees. From a leather sheath strapped to its leg, the Bar'dyn drew a long knife. Around the hilt the beast curled its hand—three talonlike fingers with a thumb on each side, its palm as large as Tahn's face. Then it pointed the blade at him.

Tahn's legs began to quiver. Revulsion and fear pounded in his chest. This was a nightmare come to life.

"We go," it gurgled deep in its throat. Its cumbersome, halting speech belied the sharp intelligence in its eyes. When it spoke, only its lips moved. The skin on its face remained thick and still, draped loosely over protruding cheekbones that jutted like shelves beneath its eyes. Tahn glimpsed a mouthful of sharp, carious teeth.

As his eyes adjusted to the light within the house, he looked again at Wendra. Blood spots marked her white bed-dress, and her body seemed frozen in a position that prevented her from straightening her legs. That's when Tahn's heart stopped. He realized that what the Bar'dyn held to its barklike skin, cradled in a tightly woven blanket of mane and tail, was Wendra's child.

Pressure mounted in Tahn's belly: hate, helplessness, confusion, fear. All a madness like panicked wings in his mind. He'd had only one job: watch safe his sister through her birthing time. The horror of what he saw roiled inside him. It all came up in a rush. "No!"

His scream filled the small cabin, leaving it that much more silent when it echoed its last. But the babe made no sound. Nor did the Bar'dyn. On the stoop and roof, the patter of rain resumed, like the sound of a distant waterfall. Beyond it, Tahn thought he heard the gallop of hooves on the muddy road. *More Bar'dyn!*

He knew he must do something. In a shaky motion, he drew down his bow on the creature's head. The Bar'dyn's thick lips parted in the semblance of a smile, uneven teeth protruding at odd angles. It gave a rough, laughing snarl; its eyes and face twisted in hatred.

"I'll take you while I clutch the child. Velle will be pleased." It growled, and swiped its blade through the air in an impossibly wide, vicious arc. The sound of its awful laughter stole into Tahn's heart, and his arms began to fail, his aim floundering from side to side.

The Bar'dyn laughed again and stepped toward him. Tahn's mind raced, and fastened upon one thought. He focused on the mark on the back of his bow hand, visually tracing its lines and feeling it with his mind. With a moment of reassurance, his hands steadied, and he drew deeper into the pull, bringing his aim on the Bar'dyn's throat.

"Unhand the child," Tahn said, his voice trembling even as his mouth grew dry.

The Bar'dyn paused, looking down at the bundle in its arm. Again it showed its hideous teeth. The creature then lifted the child up, causing the blanket to slip to the floor. Its massive hand curled around the baby's torso. The infant still glistened from its passage out of Wendra's body, its skin red and purple in the sallow light of the fire.

"Child came dead, grub."

Sadness and anger welled again in Tahn, and his chest began to heave at the thought of Wendra giving birth in the company of this vile thing, having her baby taken at the moment of life into those wretched hands. *Was the child dead at birth, or did the Bar'dyn kill it?* Tahn looked again at Wendra, pallor in her face and sadness etching her features. He watched her close her eyes against the words.

The rain now pounded the roof. But the sound of heavy footfalls on the road was clear, close, and Tahn abandoned hope of escape. One Bar'dyn, let alone several, would likely tear him apart, but he intended to send this one to the Abyss, for Wendra, for her dead child.

He prepared to fire his bow, allowing time enough to speak old, familiar words: "I draw with the strength of my arms, but release as the Will allows."

But he could not shoot.

He struggled to disobey the feeling, but it stretched back into the part of his life he could no longer remember. He had always spoken the words, always. He did not release of his own accord. He saw in his mind the elk of his afternoon hunt. Neither should that life have been taken; yet the man in the black cloak had suffered it to die, had made certain Tahn saw him end a life that should not have ended.

Tahn relaxed his aim and the Bar'dyn howled in approval. "Bound to Will, and so will die!" Its words came like the cracking of timber in the confines of the small home. "But first to watch this one go," the Bar'dyn said, and turned toward Wendra.

"*No!*" Tahn screamed again, filling the cabin even as the sound of others came up the steps. Tahn was surrounded. They would all die!

Just then the Far woman shot through the fallen door, a sword in each hand. Close behind her came Vendanj, a look of determination on his face that frightened Tahn. The man came to the center of the room, placing himself between Tahn and the Bar'dyn. The Far—Mira—moved so quickly that Tahn could scarcely follow her. At the door, Sutter and Braethen filed in, each brandishing a short knife.

"Hold, foul!" Vendanj commanded, his voice a deep horn.

The Bar'dyn whirled, and Tahn thought he saw a worried look pass across its thick features. But it did not hesitate. It tossed the child onto the bed and lunged at Vendanj with a speed Tahn did not think it possessed. Vendanj prepared to take the blow, but before the Bar'dyn reached him, Mira stepped in, crouching low and driving her swords up in a sharp thrust. One blade bounced harmlessly off the Bar'dyn's thick skin; the other made a small cut in its chest. The beast came on, swinging its knife—as long as a man's sword—in quick back and forth motions. Mira had no problem avoiding the knife, but the Bar'dyn forged a path toward them, causing Vendanj to retreat. The creature from the Bourne was coming for Tahn. Helpless, he dropped his bow.

A whistling sound grew. He turned toward the sound and saw that Vendanj's hands had begun to rotate. The man raised them in a swift gesture and pounded one fist into the other. Mira dove out of the way, and a streak of light shot into the chest of the Bar'dyn, driving it back. The smell of burning flesh immediately filled the room, attended by a horrible shrieking. At the sound, far out into the wood, a chorus of shrieks could be heard above the din of the rain. Tahn and Sutter looked to the door, half expecting a band of Bar'dyn to crash in. None came.

Vendanj's blow threw the Bar'dyn back into the nook beneath the loft. The beast got to its knees quickly, and reached onto the bed between Wendra's legs, snatching the child's body. Mira rolled out of her dive and came up prepared to strike. But the Bar'dyn stood and, with a great howl, rammed the wall with its arm and shoulder. The wood gave and the beast tumbled out through the sundered wall into the rain. Vendanj rushed forward, Mira a step ahead. Tahn finally found his legs, and came up between them at the hole in the cabin wall. Together, they stared into the stormy night. The Bar'dyn, cupping Wendra's babe in one hand, moved incredibly fast, following a path to the closest tree line. Lightning flared once, illuminating the Bar'dyn's hulking form as it barreled away. When the flash vanished, so did the Bar'dyn, and only the sounds of rain and receding thunder could be heard.

Mira began to step through the hole, as though to give chase. Vendanj put a hand on her shoulder. "Patience."

Tahn turned from the ruined wall of his father's home and rushed to Wendra's side. Blood soaked the coverlet, and cuts on her wrists and hands bore testament to her failed attempt to ward off the Bar'dyn. Wendra's cheeks sagged; she looked pale and spent. She sat up against the headboard, a pillow propped behind her head, crying silent tears.

Sutter brought a bowl of water and some cloth. As Braethen cleansed her wounds and wrapped them, Tahn sat at her bedside wordlessly reproving himself. He tried more than once to look at Wendra, but could not meet her eyes. He had stood twenty feet away with a clear shot at the Bar'dyn and had done nothing, while the lives of his own sister and her child hung in the balance. He'd silently recalled the old words and known the draw was wrong. He'd followed that dictate over the defense of his sister. Why?

It was an old frustration, and a question to which he had never been able to find an answer.

It haunted him—had haunted him all his life, or what he could remember of his life.

Vendanj spoke softly to Mira. Tahn could not hear his words, but the Far listened close, then jumped through the same hole the Bar'dyn had used. Vendanj came to Tahn's side, looking down at his sister. "Anais Wendra," he began, using the old form of address rarely heard in the Hollows, "was your child born still?"

Sutter gasped at the question.

"Hasn't there been enough—" Tahn started to ask.

"Silence, Tahn, there are things I must know." Vendanj never looked away from Wendra.

She put a hand on Tahn's shaking fingers, and squeezed them warmly to reassure him. Tahn silently marveled at her strength. Her long, dark brown hair was still stuck to the side of her face from the exertion of labor, and her deep blue eyes were half shut in pain, yet she meant for him not to worry.

Her voice strained and hoarse, Wendra managed to say, "Yes, the child came still."

A dark look touched Vendanj's face, and he raised a hand, placing it over Tahn and Wendra's own. Finally he said, "You must leave the Hollows with us."

"She can't ride, Vendanj," Tahn argued. "After what she's just been through, how will she manage a horse? And I thought we were leaving the Hollows to *protect* our families. If she comes, she's in more danger."

Vendanj held up a hand to silence Tahn, then looked directly at Wendra. "Anais Wendra? Will you come?" She nodded. "Good. Sutter, gather the horses. Make them ready." Sutter stared, uncertain. "I've no time to wait, root-digger! Now go!" Sutter took halting steps backward toward the door, finally turning and darting into the rain. Outside, the horses whinnied loudly at another crack of thunder.

Vendanj went to the broken wall and stared out into the night, his face cast in shadow, though Tahn could still see the man's furrowed brow and clenched jaw. Without turning, Vendanj said calmly, "There is no time left to us."

The rain continued as Tahn aided his sister into a loose pair of his trousers and a heavy coat. He helped her pull on a pair of boots, but before she tried to stand, she reached beneath her bed and took a small wooden box from a hidden shelf. Wendra then tried to get up. She grimaced as she put weight on her legs and fell into Tahn. He shot a worried and angry glance at the tall man still watching the night, but Vendanj seemed not to notice. Why was he making Wendra come with them? A shrill cry erupted from somewhere in the woods.

Sutter hurried through the door. "The horses are tethered out front. But I don't think they'll be good to run far." He pulled back his cowl and brushed the water from his nose. Still, Vendanj did not turn. Tahn gave Sutter a fretful look, and nodded toward Vendanj.

"Her cloak is behind the door," Tahn said finally. Braethen took the garment from its peg and helped Tahn drape it around Wendra.

Vendanj pivoted sharply and surveyed the room. "Watch there for Mira," he said, pointing first to Braethen and Sutter and then toward the hole in the wall. They did as they were told.

Vendanj took two long strides toward Tahn and Wendra, gripped one of Wendra's hands, and eased her into a chair beside the overturned table. He knelt before her and looked intently into her face. He released her hand and then deliberately reclasped it, interlocking the bottom two fingers and folding her thumb into his palm. With his other hand he touched her brow. Almost inaudibly, he began to speak, never allowing Wendra to look away. A soft glow appeared in his face as he spoke, and Wendra's own face mirrored the luminosity. A look of wonder spread across Braethen's features, and Tahn suddenly remembered what Braethen had called the man back in the townsmen's council room: Sheason.

Even in the Hollows it was known that the Sheason were hunted. The League of Civility had branded them spies for the Quiet. The Sheason were expected either to keep their gifts hidden, or to openly disavow their use of the Will. If caught rendering, they were executed; otherwise they were tolerated. Tahn involuntarily took a step back. What if this man was the figure he'd seen in the trees early that morning? Few could summon the Will; it was a gift that had to be conferred, and that after years of training and careful study.

Vendanj reached for Wendra's other hand and helped her to her feet. Tahn's sister stood on her own, a combination of amazement and gratitude in her thin smile. "I—"

"You're welcome," Vendanj said. "Sutter, can you see Mira?"

"No."

Another shriek rang through the storm, this one deeper and more anguished.

"We can't wait," he said, moving toward the door. "Leave her horse tied to the stoop; we must be gone."

Sutter and Braethen came away from the wall and rejoined them.

"How can we run the horses, Vendanj?" Braethen asked.

"I'll see to the horses," the Sheason replied. "Now listen carefully. We go to Recityv. I did not speak it in town where someone may have overheard. But fix it in your minds. Much depends on us getting there."

Vendanj took a moment to look at each of them, then strode through the door into the night. Tahn looked at Sutter, whose jaw hung agape. *Recityv!* The thrill and fright of such a journey, such a large place, made his heart race. The revelation of where the Sheason meant to take them seemed to hit them all like another strike of lightning. In silence, many questioning looks were exchanged.

A moment later, they all followed Vendanj through the door. They clambered onto their horses in the pouring rain. Wendra came last.

Vendanj went from mount to mount, removing sprigs from his small wooden case and giving one to each horse as he went. Again, Tahn thought he caught a whiff of peppermint. The Sheason then jumped onto his horse. Tahn looked back at the lone mount still tied to the stoop post—Mira's.

In the darkness, a lusting, hate-filled cry arose.

"We no longer all need to return to town. Mira provisioned your horses before we left. And we have enough extra for Anais Wendra. Only Braethen need return." Vendanj sidled up beside him. "Ogea's satchels. Can you manage to retrieve them alone?"

The insult sliced through the downpour.

Braethen nodded.

"Meet us on the north road. Move fast. We'll be leaving the road soon."

Braethen didn't wait for further instruction, and was gone. As he raced away, Mira appeared as if from nowhere, jumped into her saddle, and kicked her horse into a dead run.

"Stay close." The Sheason kicked at his mount and disappeared into the rain after her. Lightning flashed in the sky. As thunder pealed and rolled across the Hollows, Tahn looked at Sutter.

"This is what you wanted, Nails." He kicked Jole to follow. The rest came after them in a dark blur of rain, wind, and fleeing hooves.

Soon the lights of the Hollows faded behind them.

CHAPTER EIGHT

Release of the Shrikes

Helaina Storalaith, regent of Recityv, ruling seat of Vohnce, threw open the doors to her High Office and stormed inside. Close behind came Roth Staned, Ascendant—the highest officer—of the League of Civility. Soon General Van Steward and Sheason Artixan followed. Four members of the High Council, which had just ended its session in acrimony, stood in the sunlit office.

The argument had followed her, unbidden, to her sanctuary.

"It is foolishness, my Lady," Ascendant Staned said. "Don't be baited into action by rumors. It sets us back as a people to fall victim to outdated beliefs and false traditions."

"Watch how you speak to the regent," Van Steward cautioned.

Roth cocked an eye at the general. "We are in open debate. Deference is set aside."

"Not while I am in the room," Van Steward said.

"The High Council has not ruled on this, Helaina," Staned reminded. "You cannot call a Convocation of Seats without a unanimous vote of the council."

Artixan lifted a finger. "That is not entirely correct. The regent alone holds the power to call a Convocation. She may seek the wisdom of the Council, but it is not a matter to be voted on, let alone requiring unanimity. You know this, Roth."

The leader of the League glared at the Sheason. "It is not an authority the regent can claim in these times. Once, yes. But that was long ago, when superstition ruled the wits of men and women. Calling a convocation of every ruling seat, nation, and kingdom cannot be the capricious act of a single individual. Right actions must come by the consent of even the most conscientious objector. If they are right, they will prove out. That is the civility we've grown to. Let us not devolve because of a few stories out of the west."

The regent finally turned. "You don't believe Quietgiven have descended into the land, Roth? Did you not hear the stories related to the High Council just now? What else explains them?"

"Dear regent." The Ascendant softened his tone, resuming a politic air. "The fears of the Quiet are deep in the race of men. We were all raised on the stories. But what we heard could be a hundred nightmares confused with Quiet. Will you displace so many kings and rulers without certainty? Suppose you call the Convocation after so many thousands of years, and you are wrong. What then?"

"I should rather think that prudence and solidarity would make an acceptable reason," the regent fired back. "Whatever the threat, a broad agreement throughout the eastlands would serve all interests."

"Except that of a man who would have that power unto himself," Van Steward offered.

Roth turned on the General. "Do you wish to say something to me directly?"

Van Steward stared back with the glare of a man who could no longer be threatened. "When at last I wish to do anything concerning you, it won't be to talk."

Roth Staned turned back to the regent, undeterred. "It is madness, Helaina. The other members of the council are deferring to you out of respect and duty. These are fine virtues, but not for use in governance. You above all should know this. I appeal to your wisdom. The other members of the council are well meaning, but they are not rulers, or even leaders. They are caught in the fear that grips a tiller or fisher, because these are the people they represent. But reason today resides in the places of learning and progress. Don't let all we've worked for pass away with a choice that smacks of superstition or shibboleth."

The regent did not immediately speak. She noted the thoughtful look of her most trusted advisor, Artixan, whose heavy brow told her all she needed to know of his opinion. Then she cast her gaze at the general, an iron-willed man the left side of whose face bore not one but three severe scars that ran down his forehead and cheek like white runnels. Van Steward was harder to read, since his place was to receive an order without question. But when the man dropped his chin ever so slightly in a half nod, she knew his mind, too.

Leaving only the Ascendant, Roth Staned.

He was an intelligent man, one she believed always represented the people's best interests, at least as he saw it. And for that she was grateful. But he had not been successful in turning the council to his view of the rumors. And so he had stormed after her when the council was dismissed. He challenged her now because she had countermanded his proposal to wait for incontrovertible evidence before committing Recityv to any formal action against the clear threat of Quietgiven.

He did this, she reflected ruefully, because when all was said and done, he wanted to possess the chair of the High Office, and couple his rule of the League with the regent's seat.

He might even admit as much, so unabashed was his ambition.

But why deny the rumors to do it?

Was civility threatened more by the possibility that these rumors were nothing but fancy and confusion, or by inaction should they prove true?

The regent, now in her elder years, could not puzzle it together.

But one thing she knew. If he'd not been her opponent before, he would become one if she did not align on his side of *this* debate.

The debate at an impasse, silence fell over the regent's High Office. She stepped to one of the great open windows and stared out over her city and away to the west, where thunderclouds rolled on the horizon. Even here, she caught the scent of ozone in the air, pushed ahead of the storm in gentle waves. In that instant, the promise of rain buoyed her.

It somehow made what she contemplated that much more real.

Quiet, again in the land. Could it be true?

Her spirit felt unsettled, and had for some time. Most days she attributed it to old age creeping up on her. Perhaps the truth was that she had been teetering on the verge of reinstituting something that had lain dormant for more generations than she could count. There were prophecies about what it would mean when a Convocation of Seats was recalled. Some said it would be the end of all things. Others spoke of new beginnings, dark beginnings, that would come as a shuddering whisper that rolled like contagion from rotted lips.

Would she be the one to do it—at her age?

Political maneuverings should belong to a younger regent, she thought, one who had the stamina to stand against Roth Staned for as long as was necessary. She grew so tired of his rhetoric that she often dreamed of exercising her authority to get rid of him.

But he had powerful allies, and the League's influence had grown and threatened to become a military power.

She had to keep him close, which made her decision in this matter so difficult. She could not afford to be wrong. Or perhaps more accurately, she could not afford to alienate the League Ascendant. Whatever she chose now could tear down all she'd lived to build, even if she proved to be right. And Sky help her if the rumors of Quietgiven were true, and the League became her enemy, too.

The regent made a slow turn, peering through the windows on all eight sides of the High Office. The horizon in every direction showed a singular view, and she'd grown to appreciate each of them. Indeed, she often went to them individually for the feeling inspired by the land distantly seen from each vantage. She was grateful that at her age, she could still appreciate each view with clear vision through hazel eyes; she was likewise grateful that her body did not yet force her to stoop. Her hair may have silvered with time, but age hadn't claimed the rest of her yet. Though, she was thinner than she'd ever been; perhaps it was all the worry of late.

Today, every view spoke the same answer to her: war.

Not today, and maybe not soon, but one way or another, reconvening the Convocation of Seats would lead to war.

And yet the cloud in her soul touched her with dark intimations of the blight that would come if she did nothing.

She feared it could be the very rending of the veil and the loosing of all the nightmare from the beginning of all things.

They were heavy thoughts . . . thoughts that at last brought her gaze to Roth Staned, unyielding and implacable at the center of her High Office. He did not blink, awaiting her command.

An oppressive silence had settled over the room. It bore the weight of choices that would take a heavy toll on the lives of countless men and women and children. Today, the people had no worry that the darker side of history could come back upon them: no fear of Quietgiven returning to the land, no concern that legends might actually be true. Most of the tales were no longer even recited in the streets of Recityv; the League had had a hand in that.

She had decided.

She finally returned Van Steward's nod. The general swept past Staned to the door and spoke a soft summons into the hall. Shortly a dozen young boys entered with caged shrikes.

"Roth—" she began.

But Ascendant Staned fixed them all with bitter, wrathful eyes and strode out, his heels tattooing the marbled floor in a quick, angry rhythm.

Helaina, the regent of Recityv, nodded once more, and the shrikes were set free from the windows of the High Office. The flutter of wings echoed from the hard marble walls as the birds escaped into the sky, angling in every direction from her eight windows.

"Send the riders and criers, as well," she said to Van Steward. "Every nation and king will be offered their seat again. Let us hope this is the last time."

Together, the three watched the birds fly until they could no longer be seen.

Will the rulers of men answer the call? she asked herself. The answer to that question threatened her heart with despair.

• CHAPTER NINE •

True Introductions

As Sutter rode after Vendanj and Mira on the north road, he tucked his chin against his chest. Gusts of wind drove rain like stinging nails into his face and hands. The Hollow Wood grew as dense as the firs just east of his home, and the night descended so black that at times he knew he was on the trail only when flashes of lightning revealed the landscape around them. Mostly he trusted that his horse wouldn't lose Vendanj and Mira. The thick smell of loam and sodden evergreens mingled on the path, and the cold rain cut into him, drenching his clothes and numbing his hands.

Occasionally, Sutter thought he could hear the strange high-low cry of the Bar'dyn echo deep in the wood just above the storm and the sound of their horses' labored breathing. But it never lasted, and he gripped his reins more tightly, hoping the mud would not cause his mount to slip and careen off the road into the trees hemming their way.

He was frightened, no doubt about that. But a thrill raced through him, as well: He was free of the roots, at least for a while!

What would Filmoere have thought of their leaving this way? The question bothered him. What if the Bar'dyn fell upon the Hollows, Hambley, the Field-stone? His family. A helpless feeling of cowardice gripped him. He didn't like leaving this way, he decided. He breathed deeply, and held the breath as long as he could. He'd found that a stomach filled with air chased fear away.

Twice they slowed to a walk, letting the horses rest. When they did, Mira stopped, allowing them to pass, and then turned her horse back down the road they'd traveled. Before they resumed their pace, she would reappear and shake her head subtly at Vendanj. Sutter understood that she was signaling: no Bar'dyn. He wished they could dismount, though. His thighs tingled on the edge of numbness, and he fought to stave off sleep.

It was well past dark hour when Vendanj called a halt. The rain had all but stopped, and far in the south, stars shone through two small breaks in the clouds. "We must rest," the Sheason said quietly. "There is an abandoned home a thousand strides from the road to the west. We will sleep there." Mira dropped silently from her saddle and disappeared into the trees to the left.

"We will walk our horses," Vendanj said. A flicker of starlight caught in his eyes, giving him a distant, menacing look. In the sky, moonlight illuminated the fringe of the clouds around the break in the south. The soft light near the horizon gave Sutter a wan feeling, as though he had been gone from the Hollows a long time, yet had such a ways to travel.

Still, he thrilled at the prospect of leaving, and was surprised that he felt drawn back toward the Hollows.

The feeling didn't last long.

Sutter helped Wendra dismount, and Tahn helped her navigate the trees. Braethen dismounted and pulled his horse along, coming astride Sutter.

"It's your Northsun, isn't it?" he asked. His profile in the dark still reminded Sutter of Ogea, and A'Posian—not a sodalist.

"It was," Sutter said. "I can't think how many days it's been since it actually passed. The skies have been grey forever. Terror on root farming."

"*Is* your Northsun, Sutter," Braethen asserted. "The next full moon brings the Change to you, regardless." He stepped around a large fallen hemlock. "Who will stand beside you as your steward?"

"My father. But I wonder if we will be back to the Hollows by full moon." Suter negotiated a path around the tree.

"I doubt it. It is Tahn's year, as well, is it not?" Braethen asked. Sutter saw him stroke his beard in a thoughtful manner.

"Both of us. We'd planned . . . never mind." He shuffled along; he could hardly hold a thought in his head for the adventure he'd just found himself on. He felt disconnected from the conversation.

Braethen put a hand on Sutter's shoulder and squeezed gently, saying nothing more. He then strode more quickly to catch up with Vendanj. Sutter concentrated on the ground and the rocks and fallen limbs from the storms that littered the forest floor. The smell of pinesap filled the air, trees having bled to heal themselves.

Sutter rushed to catch up to Tahn and Wendra.

"It's a good ache, don't you think?" Sutter said, and grinned despite himself.

"Oh, yeah, wonderful, Nails," Tahn rejoined.

"Truly, Tahn," Sutter replied. He understood things were serious. But wasn't that what the Change they were about to undergo was all about? Growing up? Things getting more serious? Taking life in hand once they were responsible. And no harm if adventure fell upon them in the process! "Did you mean to put meat in Hambley's storehouse forever? We are likely to be a story for the readers someday. Bar'dyn in the Hollows. It has never been spoken before, and they hunt the hunter." He poked Tahn in the neck and stifled a laugh at his own pun. "Besides, what did you have to remain in the Hollows for? Wendra's with us now."

His friend stopped, switching his reins to his other hand and urging Wendra to go on carefully with Braethen, who was just ahead of them.

The canopy of clouds overhead thinned, and the moonlight strengthened, shedding a lunar glow on patches of ground around them. When Sutter drew close again, Tahn asked, "Why didn't you tell me you were adopted?"

The question hung in the air between them, and for several moments Sutter did not respond. He had to think of how to say it. It had been a secret he had kept all his life. Sometimes it felt like a horrible burden, and he cursed those people who had left him behind. Other times he felt lucky to have found a home at all. And when he counted the people in his life, it got simple fast: his mother and father, a brother—his parents' biological son—and Tahn. In many ways he was closer to Tahn than to the others.

He'd often wanted to tell his friend. It was the only secret between them on his side of things. But something had always held him back. *Something?* Huh. He knew what held him back, but he would never share it. Some secrets would have to remain. . . .

"What do you say about yourself when your parents leave you because they have something else they'd rather do? It's not something I wanted people to know." He paused before continuing, "What difference does it make, anyway?"

"None to me, *Nails*," Tahn chided. "But all this time I could have been calling you 'orphan Nails,' or 'vagabond Nails,' or 'Nails the homely abandoned waif.'" In the light of the moon, Sutter saw his friend's smile.

He knew that that would be the end of it. Tahn would never bring it up again—except maybe to taunt him—unless Sutter wanted to talk. It just didn't matter. He slugged Tahn's arm in thanks.

Ahead, inside the tree line on the other side of the ravine lay a partially obscured cabin. Though the moon showed only a thin crescent, the light grew stronger as the clouds continued to recede. Tall ferns grew up around the place, helping to conceal it. More ferns and lichens covered the roof, and ivy vines crept along the walls and eaves. It appeared the forest had devoured the small cabin. The clearing sky brought a winter chill to the air and Sutter shivered as Mira emerged from the door. The Far simply looked at Vendanj and disappeared inside again. The rest of them tethered their horses to nearby trees and entered the house.

Condensation coated the walls of the small, empty rooms. Through tiny cracks in the floor and outer walls, the vegetation had found purchase, growing in straight lines. A rocking chair stood in one corner, coated in thick dust like fur. Near the south wall, a dinner table had been toppled. Mira busied herself at the cabin's hearth. The thought of a fire made Sutter more aware of the cold.

When Mira had finished her preparations for a fire, Vendanj knelt at the fireplace on one knee. He began rubbing his palms together. Braethen stood close, observing with obvious interest. A moment later, the Sheason opened his hands and touched them to the wood. Sutter's jaw dropped. He'd never seen the Will rendered in all his life!

The wood started to burn, but the fire burned dark. Black flames licked at the fuel, throwing heat Sutter could feel immediately on his cheeks. But the fire gave no light or smoke that Sutter could see. The cabin remained in deep shadow, though the chill in the air fled. Vendanj withdrew and stepped back out into the night; Mira was already gone.

"Darkfire," Braethen said, speaking into the black flames. "To hide us from the Bar'dyn."

Wendra sat on the floor close to the fireplace, and reached toward the flames.

"Not just Bar'dyn," Sutter added. In his enthusiasm, he retold Tahn's story of the Velle he had seen that morning so everyone would know.

"Hard to track, too." It was Mira. She stepped out of the corner near a lone window. Dim moonlight gleamed on the hilts of the two swords strapped to her back. She had removed the leather tie holding back her hair, allowing it to fall in wet strands around her face. She squatted next to Wendra and peered into the dark flames. "We can not stay here long. Velle can sense the Will. They will discover us even if the rain has washed our trail away." She stood. "You should all sleep now. When the horses can move, so do we."

Sutter watched Tahn exchange a strange look with the Far in the shadows of the cabin. He wasn't sure, but he'd swear his friend blushed. Then Mira left them again, joining Vendanj outside.

"She's quite the charmer, Woodchuck," Sutter joked. "I can see your attraction to her."

"She is right, though," Braethen said. "We'll probably leave before sunrise, and that gives us but a few hours to sleep." He lay near the fire, which seemed to burn hotter than Sutter ever remembered feeling a hearth fire burn. The walls of the small cabin began to dry, and the air grew warm and comfortable.

The Sheason appeared in the doorway. "Up, Braethen. Let us see how prepared you are in your defenses."

Braethen stood and followed the Sheason into the back room. Vendanj did not bother to close the door. For a long time, they listened while Vendanj slapped at Braethen, who didn't have the reflexes or training to stop him. Sutter couldn't tell for sure, but it sounded like some kind of defensive drill—Braethen trying to ward off blow after blow. All sat quiet as the session dragged on. Finally the slapping sounds stopped and they heard the Sheason say in a low, contemptuous tone, "You are pitiful."

A moment later Braethen slunk back into the room, his face obviously bruised even in the dimness. The sodalist-in-training did not meet their eyes. He merely crouched down, turned toward the wall, and sobbed himself to sleep.

Sutter shook his head. He took off his coat and crept close to Braethen, softly draping it over his shoulders for warmth and comfort. "I know I've always been the one to tease you about this sodalist thing, but if you want it, don't let that bastard knock it out of you."

Braethen might have nodded in the dimness. Sutter couldn't be sure. He left him to his silent sobs. Sutter knew the need of those at times.

Then he hunkered down next to the wall, the sword at his hip tangling in his feet. Tahn smiled. "And where did you get that?"

"Our fine friends outside. Braethen got one, too. What, you think mine should be longer?" Sutter grinned back.

"You ever even used one?" Tahn squatted down opposite him.

"Just the stuff your father taught us the summer before he went to his earth. I'm not going to win any fancy prize, but I know how to swing it. And I've got the callouses for it." Sutter held up his root-digger's palms. "Care to test me?"

Tahn shook his head, and gradually their smiles faded as they looked over at Braethen.

All were quiet for some time, when the silence of the cabin and the recent flight up the north road, and perhaps Braethen's unexpected beating and tears, got inside Sutter and his feeling of liberation. He got to thinking about his parents. Things had happened so suddenly.

Hardly knowing he was speaking, he shared a sad, reflective thought, just audible even in the silence. "I wish I could have said good-bye to my family." He looked up and found Tahn staring back. His friend's expression told him that he'd rarely heard Sutter spare a familial thought. And maybe he hadn't. He'd be first to mount to continue on their way—when it came to that—but just then he wondered if his own infant past (orphan, as he liked to call it) had mixed him up inside about family.

Mostly, he wondered if his father would be able to get the crop harvested without him. If he didn't, it could go badly for them this winter. They hadn't laid in as much as they had even last year. His departure might cost the man his farm. And suddenly Sutter's adventure, forced or not, meant something a little different, something more.

As Sutter sat against the wall, staring into his own thoughts about his parents, Tahn crawled near his sister.

Wendra had put aside a long dagger—probably a gift like the others had received—and curled up near the hearth, staring blankly at the dark flames. He could smell the coppery scent of blood on her blouse, and wondered if she could smell it, too, or if it was so close that she'd become inured to it. In his mind's eye he could still see the Bar'dyn fleeing across their field toward the trees, cupping the lifeless infant body in one hand. He was glad Wendra had not seen that.

"I'm so—" he began, but found that he hadn't any more words.

She lifted her hand and he took it. "Sleep, Tahn. There will be time to talk of it later." It wasn't forgiveness. Not yet. But neither did she shun him. He lay next to her, still gripping her hand, and found the smell of blood soon gone, his nose growing accustomed to it. In moments, sleep took him.

He awoke as he always did, while darkness still lay heavy on the land. The fire continued to burn hot in the hearth, and around him Sutter, Wendra, and Braethen slept soundly. Mira sat in the rocker near the window. One sword lay across her knees, her fingers curled loosely around its hilt. As he stirred, she turned her eyes and focused on him in the dark. Without moving her head from the chair's backrest, she closed her eyes again. Vendanj could not be seen in the back bedroom. Perhaps he'd gone to sleep.

Quietly, Tahn crept to the door, pulling the latch free.

"Where are you going?" Mira's lips were literally at his ear. Her voice came so soft, none would hear but him.

"Some things are private," he replied, intimating a natural need.

"Be quick," she replied.

Tahn stepped into the chill night air. The horses shifted uneasily as he passed them. He quietly stole several strides to the clearing above the ravine. There he stood, looking deep into the night sky. Stars winked like the sparkling bits of glass on Master Hambley's best tablecloths. His breath clouded the night, and droplets hung like frozen tears from low scrub and forest sage. He looked east and let his thoughts come naturally, as he had always done. Deep into the far reaches of the sky he let them wander, feeling as though his emotions and hopes struggled for form with the random groupings of stars. He traced the shapes of constellations, some from Ogea's stories, some from memories whose sources were now lost to him. The moon had risen high, its surface bright and clear. The pale outline of the darkened portion looked like a ghostly halo.

Tahn closed his eyes and let his thoughts run out even further, imagining the sun that caused the light of the moon; imagining its warmth and radiance, its calm, sure track across the sky. He imagined the change in color in the east from black to violet to sea blue and finally to the color of clear, shallow water. He saw in his mind sun flares that caught in his eyes when he looked directly into its great light. He pictured the eruption of color as sunlight came to the forest and touched its leaves and cones and limbs. And as he always did at such a moment, Tahn suddenly felt like part of the land, another leaf to be touched by the sun. His thoughts coalesced into the singular moment of sunrise and another hope risen up from the night, born again with quiet strength.

Tahn opened his eyes to the dark skies and the foliate pattern of stars. In the east, the first intimation of day arose as the black hinted of violet hues. A quiet relief filled him, and Tahn took a lungful of cold air. He turned to rejoin his companions and saw Vendanj standing in the trees twenty strides away, watching him. The Sheason said nothing. Tahn left him there, and started back when he ran into Mira.

The Far eyed him suspiciously. "You were not doing anything private."

"How would you know? Were you watching me?"

Unabashed, she said, "Yes."

Tahn studied her in a glance. He saw a latent energy in her hands and arms, as though they already had the thought to strike. When he met her gaze, he found himself wondering if she was really from Naltus Far. She had a strange hypnotic effect over him, which made him worry about what she might be, but her smooth skin and poise were hard to ignore or resist. In the shadows, she smiled just barely with the left corner of her mouth, revealing a dimple in her cheek.

Tahn found his own smile. "Are you going to watch everything I do?"

She canted her head subtly, the movement either inquisitiveness or suggestion.

Warmth rushed into his cheeks. He averted his eyes and went in to his friends.

The darkfire burned hot but had spent most of its fuel. Wendra had not slept. The images of the day refused to let her be. Made her cold. She curled ever closer to the fire to try and warm herself. There was no help for it.

Her child was gone.

The horror of facing the Bar'dyn alone when it had invaded her home, ravaged their belongings, and then seized her in the nook beneath the stair and loft, it could not be given words.

In a breath she felt as if she had been raped, all over again, at the end of her pregnancy—one to get her with child, the other to take that child away. Wendra couldn't help but feel as though she'd been used as a vessel and nothing more. The violation burned deep inside her.

But not so far as the precious life taken into the beast's hands and carried into the rainy night. However true that, if she could, she would undo the day of her first violation, she had grown to accept the child inside her; she had even felt the hope of it. She'd found herself thinking and humming most of the time about what it would be like to be a mother, and had looked forward to the day.

Most people scorned her, though some simply didn't know what to say to her and so kept their distance. But Wendra had begun to feel more like herself again, and settled back into her life with smiles and brightness in the small tasks she set herself about. That's what her father and mother would have done. If she'd learned anything from them, it was that life will come upon you with awful change; how you choose to live with that change is the measure of your worth and happiness.

Wendra had succeeded at that . . . until the Quiet fell upon her, and coaxed her child from her womb.

The horror of the recent violation caught in her throat as she lay staring into the darkfire. She could still feel the rough hands of the beast on her ankles, hear its guttural voice growling commands as if it knew something about childbirthing. Wendra could feel the passing of the baby into the world, knowing who received it, and that moment ached in her like no other.

She should have done something, but hadn't been able to.

And then there'd been Tahn.

Wendra had been delirious with fear and pain, but still she thought she saw her brother draw his bow on the Quietgiven but then relax his aim, never shooting. Confusion and anger roiled in her at the memory of it. Had Tahn been too frightened by the sight of the Bar'dyn? Had his friends come in so fast that he feared hitting them? It was a blur in her mind, but more than anything, she remembered the look in her brother's face. He looked as if he bore some shame, some unnamed, private shame.

Now it hung between them, and she didn't think she could simply let it go, even though she loved Tahn. Balatin had made it clear before he went to his final earth that when he was gone they must hold to each other above all else. But it would take time for this wound to heal. She knew, eventually, she would find it in herself to let this go. But not today. Her own body still thrummed with its physical loss.

The only other thought that entered her mind was why the Sheason had brought her along. Was it as simple as keeping her and Tahn together? Would she have been in danger if she remained in the Hollows? Though these questions offered some relief from more bitter thoughts, they likewise plagued her.

So she put her songbox on the floor before her eyes and hummed its melody. It reminded her of Balatin, and that was a comfort.

Soon she departed the familiar tune and wove melodies of her own as she often did, allowing them to escape her lips so softly that none might hear. These new airs came darker, mournful, and with a tinge of real anger. Something in them soothed Wendra's beleaguered mind enough that she fell into dreams, though they were haunted by the events of the day.

A shrill cry woke her from her doze. Blackness still cloaked the room. She sat up, her eyes staring wide into the emptiness around her. Braethen immediately stood and drew his sword. A loud thud struck the floor behind them. Wendra whirled to see Sutter had fallen from his sitting slumber. He smiled sheepishly. Mira was gone, her chair empty. Again the cry tore the silence of the predawn, this time louder and closer: "Bar'dyn!"

• CHAPTER TEN •

A Maere and Training

The door to the cabin slammed inward, falling from its hinges to the floor in a resounding crash. A figure filled the doorway, his cloak swaying behind him. "Come! Now!" Vendanj ordered, his voice low but intense. Tahn pulled Wendra out the door into the twilight. Mira had unlashed the horses and held them at the ready. Sleep still fogged Tahn's eyes, but he climbed atop Jole as the others clambered onto their mounts. Mira helped Wendra up.

"No talking, just ride. Follow me," Mira said as she returned their reins to each of them. In an instant she leapt onto her own horse and led them down the ravine that paralleled the road. Tahn tried to wait and come last, behind Sutter and Braethen. Vendanj came alongside him and grabbed Jole's tack.

"Stay close to Mira." There was no room for argument in the Sheason's voice. Tahn looked at Wendra. "I will watch her," Vendanj said, and pulled Jole forward.

The renderer and Wendra came after, leaving Sutter and Braethen at the rear. In the sky to their right, the sun strengthened beyond the horizon. They tore through scrub oak and trees overgrown as a result of generous rains. Tahn kept one arm before his eyes, protecting them from errant limbs, as they galloped into a shallow tributary to the Huber River. Mira veered right, following the stream toward the north road. The water splashed up around them as the horses picked up speed. The stream widened, strips of rock and sand emerging for them to travel on. They raced toward the sunrise as battle cries rose into the morning stillness around them. The din shook the very leaves of the trees, seeming to vibrate up from beneath them. A bridge appeared around a wide bend in the tributary, the horizon behind it now bright with the imminent arrival of the sun. From beneath the other side of the bridge, deep in the shadows of a stand of tall yews, a darker shadow appeared.

Maere!

Tahn knew it instinctively from the stories told at Northsun: a Quietgiven creature from deep within the Bourne, formed of shadow and broken promises.

The dim morning light pulsed and shifted through it, giving it the appearance of a shadow on the surface of a lake rippled by the wind. Mira pulled up short, and Tahn nearly piled into her.

Vendanj came around to the front to confer with Mira, but they had only just begun to speak when the Maere reared and bolted toward them with startling speed. It came smoothly, coursing over the river bottom without a bob or jounce. As it bore down upon them, Tahn felt a cold wind begin to blow, as though the Maere pushed intent and malice before it. Jole reared, and the other horses began to tug at their reins and dance at the sight of the Maere—all but Vendanj and Mira's mounts, which stood placidly. Mira jumped to the riverbed and drew her swords. Vendanj cupped one hand under his right forearm and held a fist out toward the Maere.

"Will and Sky," Braethen muttered. "Maere." A dark awe edged his words.

The thing traversed the distance with savage speed, and Tahn nocked an arrow, preparing to pull, when the sun lit the morning from the top of the towering yews, sending shards of coruscating light down upon the riverbed, erupting there in a thousand sparkling shimmers. As the streams of light fell upon the Maere, it vanished, gone like an exhalation of breath. Tahn looked through the space it had occupied, his arrow falling from his bow as he gaped in amazement. Precisely then, another howl lit the morning and four Bar'dyn crashed through the bulrushes behind them.

Their strange skin shifted loosely over the muscle and sinew beneath, but their deep-set eyes shone with brilliant hatred over the protruding shelves of their cheekbones. One pointed, and they all surged forward. Powerful legs propelled them in huge strides. Two Bar'dyn drew swords no less than five feet long. Over their shoulders, the other two hefted spears with dual prongs in preparation to throw them.

Mira leapt to her horse from her stance, both swords still in hand. *"Go!"* she screamed. The horses uniformly obeyed, and Tahn grabbed a fistful of Jole's mane to prevent himself from falling off as his horse bolted. The Bar'dyn stayed close as they fast approached a soft bank near the bridge. Tahn knew the horses would never make it up before the Bar'dyn pulled down Sutter and Braethen from behind.

They reached the bank and started to climb, the Bar'dyn mere strides behind. Tahn looked back to see Sutter and Braethen reach the steep bank and start up. Sutter's horse reared, and he almost fell. But his friend's hands were strong from working the earth. He held the reins tight, even as his feet slid from the stirrups. At that moment, a bright light exploded from Vendanj's hand and shot into the bank like green and blue shards of lightning. "Ride!" he yelled. Sutter got his feet back in his stirrups just as Braethen reached the top.

The Bar'dyn loosed a collective howl and began clawing their way up the riverbank.

A strange rustling began in the trees and brush around the creatures, like a fall wind through stalks and husks, whistling and groaning with an eerily human voice. Suddenly, roots leapt from the bank and limbs twisted toward the climbing Bar'dyn. Still knotted and gnarled, the branches, vines, and grasses laid hold of the beasts. Many tied around their feet, but others sought their wrists and legs. Still others shot into their mouths, stifling screams. One Bar'dyn hacked helplessly at the sinewy twists of vegetation, but for every one he severed, three more came on. The profusion of growth came alive and folded around the struggling Bar'dyn, muffling their cries. Animated with a hundred arms, the riverbank brought down the large creatures.

Mira slapped Jole's rump and Tahn held on as the stallion bolted for the road and headed north. The others came up behind, and Mira again found her place at the head, riding with one sword still drawn.

They rode north. A myriad of war drums pounded across the countryside, finally beginning to beat in unison. The strange high-low wail of the Bar'dyn rose on each third strike and the world seemed alive with a rhythmic, soaring chant. Tahn drove Jole on, and as the sun lifted free of the forests and rose strong into the eastern sky, he and his sister and friends followed the Sheason and Far girl up into the high plain meadows away from their home.

All morning they galloped, slowing to a walk at times and resting the horses before again pushing the pace. Shortly after reaching the road, Vendanj began swaying on his mount. In the stark light of day, his face looked more deeply lined, his skin drawn tight. His eyes were red and darkly ringed. Mira saw him, and looked as though she meant to jump to his horse and ride with him to keep him in his saddle. But the Sheason raised a hand and, by force of will, sat upright. He looked the way Wendra had when the tremors and fever had come upon her, but he kept on, his hands white upon the reins.

In the sunlight, along the road, a profusion of hyacinth showed in bright colors near pools of water. Scrub oak and low cedars dominated the rest of the terrain. The road had begun to dry, birds gathering at the muddy pools to drink and bathe until the horses' approach sent them fluttering into the air. They rode until midday, when Mira took them a good distance into the trees to take some rest.

But not right away.

After they dismounted, Mira had them all stand in a line with their new weapons in their hands, and taught them the fundamentals of steel. The Far loaned Tahn one of her blades to practice with. Some of it came back to Tahn and Sutter and even Wendra fairly quickly from some few sessions with Balatin years ago. Braethen struggled a bit more; he seemed to know better where to hold the weapon and how to position his arms—as though recalling pictures in one of his many history books—but the movements and feel came slower to him. After an hour of lunging, blocking, swiping, and stabbing the open air, the Far let them collapse and mop the sweat from their faces.

All except Tahn.

She pointed him to a field close by and supervised several dozen shots with his bow. That, at least, came easier. Balatin had been rigorous with Tahn in his practice of the weapon. Always it had seemed a means to an end—providing meat for coin or other food. But suddenly the care for judging the wind, elevation, and depth of pull all took on new meaning. Tahn didn't miss often. He wondered if his father had been preparing him for something more than shooting elk.

Again he recalled the dreams of the faceless man who likewise seemed often to be teaching Tahn to *draw with the strength of your arms. . . .*

It was that rote phrase he always needed to recite, and the image of himself drawing his bow in his dreams—questions and dreams about himself—that wouldn't let him alone even as he fled his home in the Hollows, chased by the Quiet.

That faceless man, leaving Tahn with a sense of more than mere hunting. . . .

But thinking about it never helped. It only upset him.

Mira dismissed Tahn after he'd shot and collected three rounds of his quiver. The Far seemed pleased, and Tahn didn't mind showing some prowess in front of her. He thought he saw a smile of appreciation at one point, but wasn't sure. His pulse quickened, regardless. Tahn walked back into the shade of some trees to check his fletching and tips, but mostly to rest.

Sutter found him. "Almost went to the earth back there, Tahn. Just another root-digger rejoining his worms." He clapped Tahn on the back, merriment writ large upon his face.

"Good thing you didn't, Nails, because I'm getting hungry. Go dig me something to eat."

"Just can't escape my past, can I?"

Sutter laughed aloud. It was nervous laughter, but it felt good to pause in the midst of all this and kid as they always had.

"I've only seen the High Meadows once in my life, Tahn. And I ate standing up for a week when I got home." Sutter pointed to the seat of his pants to indicate the lashing he'd received for straying so far from home.

Tahn felt little of the wonder Sutter showed at the sight of the North Plains. There were too many unanswered questions. The only thing certain was that the Bar'dyn sought them. Tahn wasn't sure anymore if the Quiet weren't really after Vendanj . . . except that for some reason he believed the Sheason. Traders in the Hollows often stopped by to barter for fur or dried meats. The talk usually turned to the League, and one would say that another Sheason had been put to death. Even small towns like Bollogh had seen the public execution of a renderer. And usually the traders spoke of the lynchings as good things. But Vendanj had healed Wendra, and it brought him no gain to do it. And more than that, when Vendanj chose an action, Tahn always somehow internally agreed, even when his reason cried against it.

"Why do you think we're going to Recityv?" Tahn asked Sutter. His friend had the uncanny ability to guess at such things.

"Recityv," Sutter repeated, clearly awestruck by the very thought. "Great Will and Sky, that's—"

"A long journey," Mira finished.

Tahn jumped in surprise. The Far was right behind them, kneeling at a small spring filling her waterskin, and they'd had no idea she was there. "Several weeks' journey, so pace yourselves." She lifted her waterskin and drank. Tahn heard mild reproach in her words, as if she were twice as old and much wiser, though she appeared slightly younger than they were.

"Don't wander too far when we stop to rest. And don't leave anything behind, do you understand? I wish you knew how to walk lightly." She surveyed the ground they'd passed over, and shook her head. "A child could track you. Watch your strides. Choose rocks to step upon when you can." She plugged her waterskin and turned back toward the horses. Tahn watched her go, each footstep placed quick and light, her cloak filled as a sail in a high wind.

"Forget it," Sutter said. "You and a Far? Never. She's too busy bustling about and swinging her swords. Besides, have you seen her smile? Even once?"

Yes, Tahn thought, *once.*

"Recityv," Sutter continued. "I don't think anyone in the Hollows has ever been there. We'll be legends."

"Legends," Tahn repeated, distracted. "They say Recityv is one of the largest cities east of the Divide. It's the home of the regent. And you heard Mira, it's weeks from here. Why is Vendanj taking us there?" He paused, considering. "Sutter, what of our Standing? Who will steward us if we are gone so long? You talk of legends, but until we Stand, we are still melura." Tahn stopped and looked toward the vast plain before them. Balatin had told him stories of places beyond the Hollows, but the tales had long since blended so that he could no longer tell truth from fable. Staring into the distance and thinking of the threat of Quietgiven and unanswered questions and the risk that he might never Stand, he finished, "It is of no consequence if we die. Our choices have no bearing. . . ."

"That's a cheery thought. Anyway, speak for yourself. I shall be missed." Sutter doubled his fists and placed them on his hips.

The familiar posture made Tahn laugh out loud. They turned back to the horses, jumping from rock to rock and chuckling as they went.

When they reached the horses, they found Vendanj sitting upon a large boulder and Braethen seated on folded legs before him. Wendra leaned against her horse, resting her head against its neck as she listened.

"Drawing on the Will is not given to all, Braethen. Haven't your readings taught you as much?" Vendanj took the waterskin from Mira and drank slowly.

"They have, Vendanj," Braethen said, his eyes bright with the opportunity to discuss such things with an actual Sheason. "But it is not written how the ability to direct its power is conferred on someone."

"Wisely so." Vendanj returned the water to the Far and closed his eyes a moment, resting. "It was never meant for a renderer to bestow the power of calling on the Will except by the prompting of his own surest feelings. The art and ceremony of conferring this gift is passed down by tradition. It was thought that if it should need to be written down, that man would have failed to fulfill the reason he was created at all, and so ought to perish." Vendanj spared looks for all those in his company. "I do not believe we have arrived at such a time, but there are those who believe we have."

"Who are these?" Wendra asked, still leaning against Ildico, her horse.

"They are many, Anais Wendra. Some of whom caused our flight from slumber this very morning." Vendanj stood, throwing a short shadow in the meridian of the day. His dark cloak fell to the ground in long folds.

Braethen stood likewise.

Vendanj appraised A'Posian's son, staring at him in the same manner he had stared at Tahn in the Fieldstone, as though reading the man like a book. An eerie silence settled among them, the wind gone with the clouds, replaced by a high sun that brought the first touches of warmth. The Sheason took a step toward Braethen and spoke. "You are a danger to me unless you understand Forda I'Forza as though they belonged to you as parents. And why, Braethen, did you not become an author? Why play at Sodality in the home of your father?"

Upbraided publicly, Braethen shrank, unable to answer.

"You fail again. What value are you to me if you don't speak and do so honestly? You must be a bitter disappointment to your father." Vendanj strode away.

Braethen's lips parted, but the words came late and sputtered in a whisper.

"He's a charmer," Sutter muttered.

Braethen slunk onto the practice field and began to weep. Tahn started after him, when Mira caught him.

"Leave him be. Self-healing is better this time." The Far gave Tahn a thoughtful look.

Tahn brushed past Mira and followed Vendanj toward the horses.

As he came up behind him, he watched the Sheason deliberately stride from horse to horse, softly feeding each a small sprig from the thin wooden case Tahn had seen before. "Strength to you, Solus," he said, feeding Mira's horse. "And to you, Suensin," he finished, proffering a sprig to his own mount. He stroked the horse's muscled neck and, without turning, said, "What is your question, Tahn?"

Tahn sputtered syllables, looking for his words. "Why do you assume I seek you with a question?"

"You've come only to talk then?"

Tahn approached cautiously, deliberately, coming to stand near Suensin's saddle. There was only one question, a single thing he wanted to know from the strange man who had come into the Hollows with so much knowledge and led them out just ahead of the Bar'dyn. But he needed to frame his question right.

"You agree to let Braethen come, then you tear him down. You compliment Sutter on his vocation, but question his character. And you tell me I must leave

my home to save it. Why the contradictions? Why should we follow you another stride?" Then Tahn came to his real question. "Tell me, why are we going
to Recityv? Does it have something to do with why the Quiet invaded the
Hollows . . . invaded my home?"

Vendanj continued to stroke his horse for a moment. He finally stopped.
Behind them, Mira had the rest of the group taking to their mounts. "Tahn,"
Vendanj said evenly, "you must trust me for now. You must all trust me. There
will be time to speak of these things. But your ignorance is still a protection to
you. Only watch. Take care in your choices. Your Standing is soon, and we've a
long road to Recityv. Stay close to Mira." He looked at Tahn with his focused
stare. "And don't ever let your feelings—even for those you love—get in the way
of the correct path, yours or another's. Such distractions are a weakness that
will undo us." Vendanj paused, his eyes momentarily distant. "Such is like an
interrupted song, whose melody, once lost, leaves you in an awful, deafening
silence . . . forever."

Done speaking, the Sheason looked away. He walked Suensin forward and
prepared to ride. Tahn turned in anger and took Jole's reins. He tried to hide
his frustration—Sutter saw right through him.

"What's gotten under your saddle?"

Tahn shot Sutter a cold look, and kicked Jole into a canter toward the road.
The others came after, Mira soon flanking him. He turned the same cold look
on the Far, but her stoic countenance robbed him of his ire. He thought he saw
the trace of another thin smile on her face before she rode ahead to check the
road.

• CHAPTER ELEVEN •

Harbingers

The North Plains rose and fell in long waves, as the road turned gradually
northeast. They rode for the better part of two days. Vendanj allowed
them a few hours sleep deep in the night, and each time they stopped Mira
lined them up to drill with their weapons.

At dusk the second day, they saw the lights of Bollogh far in the distance.

"By all my Skies, Tahn, look at that." Sutter's face shone with wonder.

Vendanj rode forward and spoke briefly with Mira. She nodded and again took them off the road, leading them several hundred strides into the trees. "We will rest here," the Sheason said, coming to the front of the party. "I will return before the dark hour. We will move when I see you again. Braethen, follow me."

Vendanj and Braethen rode in the direction of Bollogh, which drew comment from Sutter. "I think maybe I want to be a sodalist," he said.

Mira dismounted. "The Bar'dyn are close, so wear your boots to sleep and keep your weapons at hand."

"Yeah, this little sword of mine is going to help me if the Bar'dyn stroll into camp looking for a meal," Sutter said, his sarcasm given with a tired voice.

"Leave your horses saddled, but loosen the cinches," Mira said, performing that exact task, removing her cloak, and setting out to scout the outlying area.

"Will we have a fire?" Wendra asked.

"Not tonight," Mira answered. "Get your weapons. We will go through the movements again."

At twilight they practiced for close to an hour, many swords oft dropped as muscles tired. When the light grew too dim to be useful, Mira released them and headed off into the trees. Tahn followed the Far a short way beyond the horses and watched as she laid out dried leaves and small twigs in the flat areas that led toward their camp. All around the camp at fifty strides she did the same.

"You could help me, woodsman, it's not a difficult task," Mira said.

Tahn rushed forward, quickly picking up sticks and laying them down as he had watched her do. Together they worked, Tahn stealing glances at the Far from time to time. She reminded him not at all of a Hollows girl. Besides being nearly as tall as him, she had not grown broad in the hips as did most women in the Hollows. And while her looks were striking, she did not use her eyes and hands in coy suggestion the way melura girls typically did. When Mira had removed her cloak, she had let down her hair; a deep black, when the last rays of sun caught there, a vague tint of red, like fire, lay suddenly revealed. Tahn felt a stirring in his loins.

"You wear your desires too openly," Mira said, as she finished her precautions. "The art of esteem is subtlety."

Tahn likewise finished and stood up. They stared together into the west. "I didn't mean to offend you."

"I am not easy to offend . . . or interest." She let her mouth tug into that barest of smiles. Her face brightened even then; and while she didn't smile often, when she did, it was as if her smile had never left.

Tahn remembered himself then, the things in his heart besides the growing feelings for the Far. "Tell me why they want me."

"When Vendanj wants you to know, he will tell you. I understand your desire to know, but I would not betray the Sheason's confidence. Don't ask that of me."

In the distance, a dark bird flew into the light of the setting sun, bearing in their direction.

"He asks me to trust him, but he gives me no reason to do so. If my father were alive, he'd have had answers before agreeing to any of this." Tahn threw a stick he'd been holding.

Mira canted her head, looking more skyward. "Trust is only meaningful when you must proceed without certain knowledge."

Tahn thought about that, tried to refute it. Ultimately, he gave up, and turned to the other real questions in his heart. "Is it true that you live a short-ened life?" He stopped, wishing he'd framed his question better, and started again. "I mean, the stories tell that Far are blessed with quickness in the body, and that the price is an early death."

This time, both sides of her mouth found that slight smile. "That sounds like an author's pen. But yes, it's essentially true. My people share a very old cove-nant. Don't ask me what it is, because I must not say. But in trade for our ser-vice to that oath, we never pass the age of accountability. I believe you call it the Change. Our lives end naturally when we have seen the end of our eighteenth cycle of the seasons."

The bird they watched grew larger against the russet hues of dusk.

"Then you are going to . . ."

"I still have a few years left. But yes, that is the blessing of our covenant." Mira touched the insignia strapped high on her throat.

Tahn marveled. All his life he'd wanted to do little more than reach the Change so that he could be taken seriously, could have his choices *matter,* could find a girl . . . "Maybe it's the Hollows in me, but it doesn't sound like much of a bargain. I would think long life a better trade for your service."

"Such is a common view in mankind. And it is not that I don't value my life. But my spirit won't ever have to suffer a reckoning for the stain of misdeeds as one who experiences the Change will. The undying life after this world will be sweeter for that." In the soft shadows of the failing light, her face looked peaceful.

Tahn gathered the image of her in that moment to hold in his mind.

"Perhaps think of this, Tahn, when the Sheason tells you to watch after your choices. You will encounter the Change, and live past it. And I will tell you this: Our coming to you has much to do with you remaining as free of stain as you are able." She looked away from the approaching bird for a moment to get Tahn's attention.

He'd never spoken to a girl or woman like this, except for maybe Wendra. "How do I know what *stain* is, then?"

She showed him a third smile, a smile he thought (and hoped) held intimate suggestions. "Stain has much to do with what one holds as true."

Impetuously, Tahn kissed Mira. *No stain there,* he thought. And his heart pounded harder over that moment of time than any other he could recall, and was worth every bit of the embarassment and awkwardness that ensued, as he had no words to follow it with.

Mira, for her part, did not withdraw, but looked back at him with a mix of understanding and approval and amusement—but was not, he thought, dismissive.

The bird began to drop toward them. Tahn hefted a stone to chase it away, but Mira put a gentle hand over his to lower his arm. He thrilled at her touch, though he was a bit confused. She then raised her other arm, and the raven lit upon it, cawing into the twilight.

"Do you also have some husbandry gift I don't know about?" Tahn laughed a bit as the bird shifted around to look at him.

Mira shook her head. "It is a message from home."

"But there's nothing tied to its feet." Tahn looked more closely to be sure he hadn't missed it.

"The bird itself and the dark color of its feathers are the harbingers of this news." The look in Mira's eyes changed a third time that night, not the quick, appraising cast, nor the softer faraway look Tahn had just seen. This was the look of grief, and the difficult choices that often follow it.

"What does it mean?"

"My sister, the Far queen, has passed this life. It means I have a choice of my own to make. And you may have to finish this journey without me." She said it with new weight in her voice, as one mourning more than mere death. Mira cast the bird back into the sky and left Tahn alone to watch it wheel away north and east.

The city of Bollogh at night reminded Braethen of stories he'd read of the first years after war had ended. The Sheason led him past fires burning at street corners and down alleys crowded with carts where mothers huddled close to their children to keep them warm. The reek of waste was cloying. Braethen thought Vendanj meant either to conceal their movements by navigating these byways or else to put experience to the tales in Braethen's mind.

The Sheason spoke not a word until they came upon an ordinary door set in a far quarter of the city, situated in another remote byway. "Tether your horse and follow close."

Braethen did so, and stepped into the building. He could see nothing save a sliver of dim light beneath the door they'd just entered.

A moment later, the Sheason lit a lamp and went to the room's single window.

He opened the shutter and placed the lamp on the sill. He then seated himself and indicated a chair for Braethen to do the same.

In silence they remained sitting long enough for Braethen to recite the cycle of Promise poems—which he did silently—before a third man entered the room, closed the shutter, and took up the lamp. He went directly to Vendanj, and the two clasped hands, interlocking their last fingers in a cryptic token Braethen couldn't make out.

"This way," the stranger said.

They passed through a locked door, where the man used three different keys to open three different locks. Once in the farthest interior, where no windows stood, he turned, drew back his cloak, and Braethen finally saw the sodalist emblem at the man's throat.

"Braethen, this is Edias Faledriel, sodalist of Bollogh." Vendanj nodded to the man in acknowledgment.

"It's good to know you," Braethen said.

Edias tried to share the token with Braethen, but the would-be sodalist's hand and fingers made a bad job of it, fumbling unfamiliarly. Edias looked at Vendanj for explanation.

"In a moment," the Sheason said. "First, where is Palonas? I expected him to be with you."

Edias showed weary, lamenting eyes. "He was executed three days ago by order of the League of Civility. They've established a strong contingent here."

"For what—"

"It's worse," Edias cut in. "Palonas was the last."

Vendanj's eyes darkened. "Tell me!"

"Four there were at last harvest. But in the half cycle since, there has been much disease here. Karoon, Celenti, and Sahlieda were all found to have offered aid by the Will to the sick or dying. Their punishments came without trial." Edias walked to the wall of the inner room and lifted the lamp to it.

Braethen came close and read. A list of names too long to count had been carefully graven in a slab of marble mounted on the wall.

"Once a staging post for service and armies to march or defend the south," Edias said with sadness, "Bollogh has now lost every servant to the last. And here"—he moved the lamp to the right—"are the names of the sodalists who defended them."

Braethen followed the light and saw a few names recently carved. "And these?" he asked.

Edias's own anger and fear caught in his voice. "These are those sodalists bound to the Sheason whose names I've just given you. When they sought to memorialize them in public for their service and sacrifice, the League petitioned the ruling seat to try them as accomplices. Our lord is a weak man, and capitulated. These sodalists were executed for association with the Sheason to whom they were bound."

Braethen felt his legs go weak. He'd read of sodalists killed defending the lives of Sheason in the bitter tides of war. He'd read of long service and toil without recognition. But in the histories he'd somehow missed the writing of names on a wall of the dead whose only crime was memorializing another. Just now, he wasn't sure it *hadn't* been there, but if it had, his eyes were too enamored of the dream to have remembered it.

Vendanj stepped forward and retrieved the lamp from Edias. "Which is why we have come. Braethen wishes to be bound to me as a sodalist."

Braethen's knees buckled, nearly dropping him to the floor.

Vendanj looked at him sharply, and Braethen could only think of the disappointment he'd seen in his father's face when he'd told A'Posian that he would not follow the author's way, that instead he meant to meet destiny head on, meant to become a sodalist. But at this moment, he wasn't sure what he wanted to do.

His choice proved immaterial. Edias did not hestitate. He stepped close to Braethen and reached out to him, forcing Brathen's fingers into the handshake token of the Sodality. "Repeat after me: Change is inevitable and necessary, but the traditions of our fathers need to be preserved. Someone must watch. Someone must remember. Someone must defend. And some must die."

His study had been incomplete. Or was it another part of his dream that he'd selectively removed: *And some must die.*

Braethen stood on a threshold. He might be able to go back from here; he could retrace his steps to the Hollows. He certainly knew enough to be an author. His father would be so proud if he changed his mind. And this . . . this oath. The names on the wall. Killed only for memorializing . . .

Was following Ogea's encouragements of Braethen's dream worth this?

Braethen looked up at Edias, words caught in his throat. Vendanj stared at him, and for the first time Braethen could see neither contempt nor satisfaction in the Sheason's gaze. In the stillness, Braethen listened to the hiss of the lamp, his heart pounding. If he crossed this threshold, there was no turning back. Even so, he might fail, and then the long years of his hope would have been utterly wasted.

A loud crash erupted behind him. Braethen jerked his hand from its union with Edias and saw three men in deep russet cloaks storm into the room, swords raised: the League!

Braethen tried to move, but his legs were still little use to him, and he fell against the marble list of the dead and slid to the floor. Edias jumped past him, a short sword suddenly in his hands. The last sodalist of Bollogh stepped into the breach and stopped two hammer strokes meant for Vendanj that the Sheason had not expected and—for Braethen's coin—would not have survived. One blow Edias turned away, the other he took full in the chest.

Vendanj recoiled, his hands rising with darkfire, when Edias slayed both the leagueman closest to the Sheason before falling to the floor, blood gushing from his chest. The last leagueman raised a whistle to bring reinforcements, but never got it to his lips. His face melted first, followed by his head and shoulders, before he fell backward out of the inner room.

The smell of charred flesh and the bitter tang of blood rose quickly. The single lamp still burned near Braethen, who watched the smacking lips of the sodalist who'd tried to swear him in.

Then, looking up at the Sheason, he saw a look of disappointment that hit him powerfully, reminding him of an ache from the past that he mentally fought to push away.

He couldn't do this. His dream was a fancy that boys read to create games in the forest when the summer days were full upon the Hollows.

Then . . .

He remembered a crystal goblet.

A small, painful moment.

A moment when the disappointment he saw in his father's face had touched him, scarred him, in a way he had never forgotten. He loved A'Posian, and he loved the ideal of the Sodality. Those things had been in conflict in him for a long time. Would he now show disregard for the choice that caused him to turn his back on his father's path—the author's way?

Later, he would record this moment of his life, for the strength of will it seeded in him when brought to a moment of last things: Here, where Braethen knew the Sheason had believed the names of the dead and the severity of the call would scare him back to his books; here, where awful circumstance had raised on the Sheason's face a look of disappointment that Braethen would die to disprove.

With the image of that crystal goblet in his mind, Braethen crawled to Edias, took his bloody hand in the token, and repeated the words to the last: ". . . some must die."

A bloody smile came to Edias's lips before he gasped his final breath. Braethen stood, looked at Vendanj, and said, "We should go before others arrive." The look on the Sheason's face remained inscrutable, but that beat disdain or disappointment.

Wendra rubbed her stomach with her free hand in what had become a habit during the days she carried her child. Sutter wondered if she was even aware she was doing it. He thought perhaps the motion comforted her, and he decided he would never bring it to her attention.

But there remained a topic he'd tried to talk to her about many times. And he hoped maybe now she would finally speak openly with him about it.

"How are you?" he began.

Wendra's gaze remained distant. "Thank you for your concern, Sutter. I will be all right."

Sutter nodded. "I know you've not wanted to talk about it. But I can't seem to get away from it. You know how I feel about you—"

"You're not even through your Change yet," she said, smiling.

"Yes, yes. I'm melura, sure. But . . . I want to set things right, Wendra. The man who . . . the man who . . . He needs to be held responsible for what he did. And I want to be the one to put his name before the townsmen."

Abruptly, Sutter could see from the look on her face that he had unwittingly evoked in her a painful memory, and he wished he hadn't brought it up. She looked at him, seeming to understand his desire to help, but shook her head.

"You don't have to do anything. Just tell me his name. Tell me where I can find him." Sutter paused. Still she said nothing. But something in her eyes told him that however awful that rape was, something about Wendra's violation went beyond a moment of sexual violence. He asked one last time. "Wendra, I believe your father would have agreed with me. Would you tell him if he were alive?"

At that, she stopped shaking her head, a different look on her face. Then her eyes softened. "If you want to do something for me, make me laugh, Sutter. That's the strength I like best about you. Here, sing me this. Your voice is awful."

She got out the songbox she'd retrieved before they'd fled the Hollows and opened it to its tune. All the while, she continued to stroke her belly. As the night around them deepened and grew colder, they lay upon the ground, huddling close together for warmth, and Sutter made his usual bad effort at song. And she did laugh, the sound of it musical in the midst of so many other unmusical things.

Wendra's tragedy and her quiet resolve to stand by her brother were the only things Sutter didn't think he could find a joke for. And somehow that felt just fine.

CHAPTER TWELVE

Questions and Dreams

The Sheason returned with Braethen at dark hour. They rode north and east the rest of that night and all the next day. The vegetation on the plains grew variegated, with low cedar and sage that rose up to only the height of a small man; tall bushy pines bearing large cones; stands of aspen and great oak reaching heavenward—the Hollows were long behind them. In all directions, the vastness of the sky stretched down to the horizon where it met the earth, like two halves of one whole.

As untouchable as were the reaches of the sky, so was the earth underfoot tangible. The sky spoke of the possibility and the earth of reality. It reminded Tahn of the stories of Palamon, the first Sheason, wrestling Jo'ha'nel, first of Quietus's Draethmorte. Great ones and gods locked in conflict.

Palamon told of the strength in the arm of man, Jo'ha'nel the energy of what may be. Tahn's thoughts turned upon the necessity of both, how one could not exist without the other.

But he also wondered, beneath the lasting sky and above the abiding, patient feel of earth beneath him, if men could live if they had only one or the other.

As Vendanj led them off the road and they disappeared into the trees, the shriek of a night raptor pierced the quiet of the plain.

They came to an escarpment, a fifty-foot vertical wall that extended in both directions. Vendanj had already dismounted, and chose a shallow cave at the base of the cliff to rest in for the night. Braethen came last. Just after he had tethered his horse, Mira returned from a brief scout of the area and immediately began gathering wood for a fire. Tahn and Sutter hastily began to help. Soon, a bright, warm fire pushed back the cold and cast a softer light on the harried face of the Sheason.

Tahn expected Vendanj to speak. Surely something must be important if he allowed real fire to brighten their camp. But the Sheason said nothing, and Tahn liked it even less when the tall renderer kept his silence.

But he still wanted answers to his questions. Why did they go to Recityv? Why had he allowed Wendra to come along, when his leaving the Hollows was supposed to make their town and families safe? One question, in particular, though, he meant to ask again tonight—he needed to know. Drawing close to speak privately, Tahn asked, "Can you tell me now why the Quiet are coming for me?"

The Sheason did not reply, his eyes wide in the dark, searching Tahn's face yet again. Briefly, his gaze reminded Tahn of the way Balatin would look at him late in the evening when they all sat sipping juniper tea and eating roasted hazelnuts—a kind of knowing and not knowing. It was the only time that Tahn's persistent questions found favor with his father, though some questions he'd never asked: about the words he spoke when he fired his bow, or the dreams of a man he could not see.

Sitting so close, Tahn saw the thin, stern lines that framed Vendanj's mouth. Lines like Balatin's, though Balatin had earned them through a life of good humor. Tahn wondered what expression had produced them in Vendanj. He thought the weight of great worry all by itself could be the cause, such was the burden the man seemed to carry.

Finally, looking into the flames with a somewhat kinder expression, Vendanj said only, "Rest," and closed his eyes. The others soon spread their bedrolls near the fire and drifted toward sleep. All save Mira, who stood near a tree fifty strides away. Tahn only knew where she was because he had watched her take position. Now, the shadows claimed her.

Sleep came fast upon them all. The deep, slow cadence of breath taken in and let out marked their descent into slumber. Just when Tahn was giving over to it, low, hushed voices whispered in the background like a rumor. He kept his eyes closed, but listened as the voices spoke.

"You test the patience of the melura. They fear you more than you've won their confidence."

The Sheason said nothing to that.

"Do they convene?" Mira asked, slipping her blade back into its sheath.

"Yes."

"Who is invited?"

"All those given seat at the First Promise."

"Then why must it go before the High Council?"

"Because the land fails. Because reports of creatures out of the Bourne grow every day. History must first mark our efforts to reconcile ourselves."

"The Exigents sit at High Council. They will never endorse anything the Sheason put before the regent."

"It won't matter."

"And what of us? Why are children from the Hallows driven before the Quiet?"

The Sheason's voice shifted direction then, and spoke directly to Tahn. "Sleep, Tahn," the deep voice said. And with that, Tahn began to lose himself to his dreams. Falling downward toward sleep, he heard yet a little more, but would not remember. "We go ultimately to the Heights of Restoration, to know if these children from the Hallows have hope against the Quiet."

The sun burned hot in an azure sky. Tahn walked a dusty path over barren stretches covered only with sagebrush. Dust plumed beneath his feet where the sun had not baked the ground into a cracked hardpan surface. On the horizon, heat shimmered and rose off the plain. In some places, even the sage would not grow.

Tahn paused in mid-stride and raised his head to the intermittent breezes that drew the clean, enduring smell of the hardy foliage across the waste. Something new called for caution. He unshouldered his bow and silently nocked an arrow, pivoting on his toes to survey all around. He saw nothing, but a growing feeling of conflict rose in him.

The wind died, leaving him alone. The plain stretched out before him. It rolled to a mild descent several hundred strides up the path, and somehow he knew that was where he must go. Slowly he moved forward, crouching and holding his arrow at half pull.

A distant shrieking grew suddenly loud. Tahn dove to the ground as something whistled higher and passed through the air above him—an arrow. Staying low, he crawled forward into a denser growth of sage. Dust filled his nose and throat, and the sweat on his dirty brow ran into his eyes, stinging with salt and grit.

Turning in the direction of the attack, Tahn removed two arrows from his quiver and placed them in his mouth. He crouched and pulled his shot, holding the bow perfectly level. Then swiftly he stood, scanning the field for his attacker. Behind him a bowstring hummed and he jumped to the side, whirling. A second arrow shot through the air beside him. A low cloud of dust rose from his shifting feet. He saw a figure in the distance trying to nock another arrow.

"I pull with the strength of my arms, but release as the Will allows," he said in the heat. Instantly he let the arrow fly, nocking a second arrow behind it while his string still vibrated. Another figure bolted to the right toward a small hill. Tahn led the man, and spoke the words again, letting fly as his target raced for cover. Before he knew if his aim was true, footfalls were pounding the hardened ground behind him. Tahn brought his bow around in a sweeping arc and knocked a long spear from the hands of a tall, dark man. The assailant ran into him, lowering a shoulder into Tahn's gut. Tahn rolled backward, lifting his legs into the other's waist and using his own momentum to catapult the man into a large, sprawling cactus.

Tahn ran his hand down his bowstring to check for gouges, and quickly inventoried his quiver. Then he sprinted up the trail. The taste of dust in his mouth was familiar—the taste of soil that had forgotten the harvest. As he ran, dark clouds rushed into the parched sky, filling it with the threat of a storm. A cooler breeze touched his hot skin, but did nothing to ease the troubling thoughts twisting in his head. He thought he should know where this path led, but he could not remember it. Was it a place he wanted to return to? Far behind him, the chase had begun, and Tahn imagined his feet bare, touching the soil, no heavy boot leather weighing him down.

His pace quickened.

Without warning, rain fell from the roiling clouds, tinged red and orange from an occluded sun. Rolling thunder echoed deep in the sky. Tahn watched the trail to guide his feet in the mud that the rain would surely cause. But the ground repulsed the rain, soaking in not a whit. Each drop simply added to the one before it, rapidly creating a vast shallow pool. His boots caused a succession of splashes, and black flashes began to erupt from the ground, forming dark glass rings upon which the rain pattered in high-pitched pings.

As Tahn began to descend the path, he saw the frame of a small house, alone but for a solitary tree, stunted and clinging to life, at the bottom of a long gradual hill. Tahn pushed himself harder, the rain fell in heavier drops. As he ran, arrows flew by, harrowed by the wind. He lowered his shoulder against the strengthening wind and pushed on. Rain pelted his face and hands like small stones. The path became a small river, but the land still refused to drink.

On Tahn strode, drawing closer to the structure, which showed dark windows and looked altogether abandoned. Another arrow sped past, striking the house and protruding from the wall beside the door. Reflexively ducking, Tahn looked back, but could not see his attackers through the rain.

He reached the door and threw it wide, holding his bow before him like a sword and stepping inside. Beside a low bed sat a man, his face cradled in his hands, which appeared callused at every joint. From between his fingers he spoke. "Why have you come back, Tahn?"

Tahn knew the voice. As the man started to look up . . .

Tahn awoke.

Briefly, he looked deep into the night. High above, the stars shone like bits of ice. By the position of the constellations, dawn would be coming soon.

He thought of morning, of the sun's warm rays, and remembered Balatin mixing oats and honey over their fire. He wished he had someone to talk to who had the wisdom of many years.

Tahn got up and stepped away from the rest to think, drawn as he always was to consider night and day, near and far, the land and sky. The urgency always built in him, growing often in dreams until his mind overflowed and he awoke. Other times he lay awake, anticipating the feelings that came unbidden. But always he had to stand outside and allow his thoughts to turn outward. Closing his eyes, he imagined the eastern horizon, the farthest reaches of the land, and considered the dawn, considered the growing warmth and subtle change in color as light filled the day. As he did, the urgency left him, the anxious need to pause and simply listen to his own heartbeat, and reflect on the largest, steadiest rhythms, melted away.

Tahn opened his eyes, seeing the faint shades of violet and blue touching the night and signaling another day. Suddenly he heard behind him the sound of breathing.

He turned to find Mira also watching the dawn. She couldn't know what he was doing, but seemed to possess the wisdom not to clutter the moment with words. Somehow, always in this instant, Tahn felt like a witness, a lone observer to the coming of morning each new day.

As he watched on *this* day, the bluish hues of morning lit Mira's face, giving her clear, grey eyes the color of winter ice. And he was glad this morning that he was not alone.

Moments later, she went to her preparations. And just then, a phrase overheard last night swirled into Tahn's mind: *the Hallows.* Something about the words felt comfortable to Tahn, felt right. He would ask Braethen about it later.

CHAPTER THIRTEEN

Myrr

For two more days they rode north and east.

The storms they'd ridden through did not reappear in their same severity. The black clouds seemed to linger over the woods of the Hollows, leaving to the rest of the world bright cold skies and a high, grey haze. Or so it appeared as, just after dusk on the second day since leaving Bollogh, they emerged from the vast forest that had been Tahn's home.

They cleared a rise, where Vendanj stopped and stared into the shallow vale below. "Myrr," he said as Tahn and the rest came abreast of the Sheason.

It was like nothing Tahn had ever seen. Men in the Hollows told tales when the fire ebbed low and the night had gone to several cups of bitter, tales of grand cities, places where you never saw the same face twice. For Tahn, the stories were always little more than waking dreams, places he believed might exist, but which could never equal the teller's rendition.

"Bless my roots, who could travel its length in a day?" Sutter stared slack-jawed, realizing the fulfillment of a wish.

Vendanj turned back to them. "Everything from this point forward, every choice, will affect the end. See that none of you blackens the path with foolishness." He then leveled his eyes on Sutter. "There are paths whose courses are more important than those who travel them."

The Sheason let his words linger.

"Meet no one's gaze," the Far cautioned.

"You aren't to engage in conversation with anyone," Vendanj added. "And when you speak, never speak about yourselves or our destination. The people of Myrr have two sets of ears."

"How long will we stay here?" Braethen asked. "I'd like to meet with the—"

Vendanj cut him off. "You and I have business, sodalist."

Tahn and Sutter looked at each other, their mouths agape. The Sheason had never knowingly called Braethen "sodalist" before. Something had changed. After the slapping, the humiliation, the endless drills Braethen had struggled so hard with . . . Vendanj now acknowledged their friend by the title he'd sought all his life. For Tahn's part, hearing the sound of it in the Sheason's clear, resonant voice stirred something inside him. Looking at the author's son—a lifelong scholar—Tahn saw a new kind of resolve and confidence in the set of Braethen's jaw. Not arrogance or conceit. More like the true strength of his convictions.

To the others, he said, "We will take rooms, but our stay will be brief. Make rest your aim here, all of you. Tahn, you will remain with Mira at all times."

The Sheason then turned a kinder eye on Wendra. "Anais, I must ask you not to make your music in the company of others. They will misunderstand."

Wendra looked perplexed, but she did not contend with Vendanj.

Tahn opened his mouth to speak.

"Later for your questions, Tahn," the Sheason said. "Let us get food in our stomachs and rest for our eyes. Tomorrow is soon enough." Tahn shut his mouth.

A moment later, Vendanj nodded, pulled his reins about, and led them down the road to Myrr.

"That's telling him, Woodchuck," Sutter teased. He clapped Tahn on the back, and rode to catch Wendra.

For several hundred strides along the road into Myrr, small, ramshackle huts and market carts cluttered the highway. A few more permanent-looking structures were erected a stone's throw from the road. The roadside itself swarmed with merchants calling for customers to attend their wares. Children played wherever water pooled; young dogs barked and ran alongside their owners.

The smell of human waste was overpowering. It emanated from a large hole dug too close to the food vendors, who ladled stew into bowls, a copper a serving.

The closer to the city gates they came, the denser the crowd grew. Soon they were forced to ride a circuitous route through the milling masses. Rough torches set atop poles near the road gave light to the street, but left the faces all in shadow. Great gouts of laughter erupted from some of the larger buildings erected nearest the city walls. Tahn guessed these were taverns.

Thirty strides from the gates, the chaos ended. A low stone wall topped with rusted spikes mortared into the stone jutted straight out on either side of the entrance. A shallow ramp the height of a man's ankles rose from the earthen road, becoming a cobbled pavement. There were no outer guards. Braziers fixed to the low wall burned brightly, casting shadows upon the entrance. Iron barred gates, appearing to swing outward when opened, fronted heavy wooden gates.

"This is our welcome?" Sutter jested. "They must not have known we were coming."

"Quiet," Vendanj said brusquely. The Sheason dismounted and quickly crossed to the left side of the entrance. He rapped on the wood there in the same manner a man would knock at the home of a friend. A moment later, a small door cut into the larger inner gate drew back and a man appeared wearing a tight leather jerkin and a green cape.

The man started to protest until Vendanj gently placed one hand through the blackened iron and touched the sentry's wrist.

"What's he doing?" Sutter asked.

"Vagrants aren't allowed inside the gates at night," Mira explained, some ire in her voice. "The call for occupancy is always at last hour, before the heart of night. With such constant change in the citizenry, no census exists, only property holders or inn-residing travelers may stay. Property holders vote, merchants and travelers drink."

"Surely there are poor and homeless in such a vast city?" Braethen asked, incredulous.

Mira spared a look at the makeshift outer town they'd just passed. "Those poor who do survive within its walls are treacherous. Be wary of anyone you meet who has no place to call home. It surely means he sees you as a meal and a bath." She trailed off, watching as Vendanj concluded his instructions to the man at the gate. In a hushed voice, Mira added, "But these too must live."

The inner left gate pulled back just a few feet.

As Vendanj mounted, Tahn saw him cast his gaze one last time over the vagrant town that lived outside the great walls of Myrr. Looking out at the homeless masses, the Sheason spoke low to Mira, but Tahn overheard his words. "It's begun. The rumors of the Quiet are driving them from their homes."

Then the Sheason whispered something that Tahn alone heard: "These poor people." The utter empathy he heard in the man's voice startled him. But it also gave him a kind of hope he hadn't felt in a long time, perhaps because he sensed the single-mindness and vigor with which the Sheason would defend and advance his cause.

The party followed Vendanj through the narrow opening in the gate and immediately into a byway to the left, where they were enveloped in shadow.

One central corridor toward the city's center remained paved, but elsewhere the roads and alleys were earthen and strewn with straw to make the footing less treacherous on muddy streets. Pedestrians milled in the main thoroughfares, so Vendanj wove through narrow alleys close to the outer city wall. Clutter of barrels, broken handcarts, piled waste, and discarded articles of clothing lay near the base of exterior walls and alley doorways. Occasionally, they passed what looked like a beggar or what Mira described as "alley traders." But these human animals did not petition or accost passersby. Their eyes followed Tahn and the others as they crossed the narrow terrain these individuals called home, a hint of contempt playing upon their lips. Human waste fouled the air, and rats and carrion birds searched the straw for food, the latter as though they had forgotten their lofty capability of flight.

Distantly, the major causeways thrummed with activity. But here, on the city periphery, the streets were quiet, skulked by figures with forgotten scruples, plying secretive trades. Sutter clutched his knife as they passed appraising eyes.

Wendra looked long upon those who sat against the walls, and more than once Tahn heard Braethen mutter, "Is nothing to be done for them?" Tahn considered the question, but found himself wondering if these people, too, served a purpose. The thought surprised him and held him in its grip. But he had no answer.

Vendanj came to a larger cross street where squares of yellow were cast on the ground from windows all along the street. Far off, illuminated against the night stood a grand structure with several ascending planes and a half-dozen parapets. Other buildings rose magnificently, topped by flaming torches that winked like distant light-flies, but none shone so grand or tall.

Jole abruptly halted, and Tahn lurched. "Watch where you're going," Mira scolded. The others had stopped before a livery, and Mira had grasped Jole's harness to pull him about.

"Sorry, I've just never seen—"

"Watch what you say, Tahn," Mira said in a low voice. "Your observations reveal much about you to others."

A wide door drew back and a man with a thick, full beard ushered them in. No sooner had Braethen entered than the man slammed the door shut and threw the crossbar.

"Ah, Bean, good to see you," the man said.

His words issued from thick lips buried in a profusion of hair. Tahn had no idea to whom he could be talking.

"And you, Milear," Vendanj said, dismounting.

Sutter's head whipped about as if he'd been slapped, and he and Tahn mouthed the word simultaneously: *Bean?*

"Darling girl, what of you? Are you well?"

Mira slid from her saddle. "Much better seeing a familiar face, Milear."

The man wiped his hands on his leather apron and extended his arms to her. Mira embraced him, and he patted her on the back as he might a daughter.

Then he released her and pointed at Vendanj. "You, too, Bean, I've no mind to forsake you a squeeze." A sliver of a smile touched Vendanj's lips, and he took the shorter man's invitation. Milear patted Vendanj's back in the same manner.

Sutter's mouth fell agape. He and Tahn shared a look and with wide eyes again mouthed simultaneously to each other, *Bean.*

The rest of them dismounted as Milear released the renderer and stood back, appraising them all. "So this is what lives in the Hollows. Fine young people, Bean, I can see it in their jaws. Sturdy. Resolute."

"But say it softly, old friend. We are not yet known in the city," Vendanj said.

"Bean, you cannot come to Myrr but that you are known. Strangers, they will say, but they *will* say it. You cannot stay here long."

"A day is all," the Sheason answered.

The man looked up into the rafters of the livery, his eyes distant in what Tahn recognized as recollection. Then his eyes focused and he looked back to Vendanj. "Ayeah, I'm done now. No more will I speak on it." He brushed his hands again on his leather apron and set about stabling their horses. While he did, Mira checked her weapons and spoke in low tones with Vendanj.

Nearer the door, Braethen had retrieved a book from his saddlebag and sat on a bale reading from its pages. Wendra, too, sat, and rubbed her ankles.

Sutter approached Tahn. "How about you, old Bean, let's have a hug."

Tahn smiled. "I wouldn't have believed it if I hadn't seen it. But I don't think I'd mention it to him."

Sutter snickered. "Really, I was thinking of asking Vendanj for a hug. Anyway, we've got places to go, right? Did you see that palace? I've never seen anything like it. I thought the Fieldstone was big. Will and Sky, Tahn, this is a root-digger's dream."

"Maybe," Tahn said, "but you won't be going anywhere. You heard Vendanj, and even if you've got dirt in your ears, you saw the fellows in the alleys we came through. They'd roast you like a spring pig."

"Listen, Woodchuck, I didn't come all this way to sit in a room and talk." Sutter flicked Tahn's chest with his finger. "And neither did you."

"A man with his hands in the dirt is a grounded man," Tahn said, trotting out the old taunt. "All right."

A winning grin spread on Sutter's face. "You've got clay in your blood, Woodchuck. What stories we will have to tell."

A soft intake of breath, just audible from where they were, interrupted them; no one else heard the sound. Tahn looked toward the noise and saw the sodalist look up from his book, his brow deeply furrowed. Slowly, he shifted to look at Wendra, who was rubbing her calves. Tahn followed Braethen's eyes to his sister, then looked back at the sodalist, who shook his head so slightly that it might not have been a voluntary movement. Braethen closed his book and rubbed the binding thoughtfully with his palm.

Milear finished his task and came back to the center of the stable. "You folks gather round." He waved them toward him. Vendanj and Mira concluded their quiet conversation and came close to Milear. "You'll want to stay at the Granite Stone tonight. It's just two streets north of here. A friend of mine is the proprietor and he won't get overly curious about you. I'll send you with a horseshoe nail. He'll understand. People are wary these days, ever since the League established a permanent contingent here. Cursed fools, haven't the sense of a quarry mule. Ah, have done with that. Listen, the man's name is Ulee, his family is down out of Ir-Caul. A tighter lip there never was."

"Is there a rear entrance?" Mira asked.

"Every inn in Myrr has a rear entrance, but using it would be more suspicious than walking in the front door. The straw drift you would no doubt pass in the byways would try to sell the information, likely as not to the League, who are going to know you're here sooner or later anyway. Later is always better with the League."

"Are they making charges?" Braethen interrupted.

"Two just today. A man was seen neglecting to bow to the hat of Highborn Crolsus and was charged with sedition. The other had something to do with a tracker who came through Mal'Tara and was requesting an audience with Crolsus, talking about Bar'dyn legions as far south as Mal'Sent." Milear appraised Mira and Vendanj as he spoke. Tahn saw no visible change in either the Sheason or the Far, but Milear nodded. "Will and Sky," he said softly.

The stableman turned to Braethen. "And hide that blazon you wear, sodalist. It is not an emblem to the League's liking. Here." Milear took an iron nail from a pouch in his leather apron and handed it to Vendanj. "Now take your rest. We can talk tomorrow if you'd like."

"Thank you, Milear," Vendanj said. The Sheason handed the livery owner something wrapped in a green cloth and strode directly to the door.

"Solace be yours, my friends," Milear said, looking at Tahn and his companions. Mira put a hand on Milear's shoulder as she passed. The others quickly followed the renderer out of the livery into the street.

Vendanj strode without looking to either side as he led them north. The smell of wet straw commingled with a tinge of rot from the mud.

The Granite Stone stood five stories of magnificent granite. The face of the building was fluted at wide intervals, giving it an oddly striped look. A circular cascade of steps rose from the muddy, straw-covered street to a set of double doors. Passing wagon wheels and hooves had splashed mud three feet high upon the walls.

"Remove your hoods," Vendanj said. "Nothing will inspire someone to look more than concealing what you don't wish seen. Wear the expression of weary travelers."

That would be no problem for any of them.

The renderer pushed open the left-hand door and passed inside. Tahn took a deep breath and followed close behind Mira.

Stone partitions the height of a man's waist divided the room into at least twenty smaller sections. Two of the areas housed long tables suited for feasts. To the right, the conversation became quieter where men and women sat nearer the outer wall. Two hallways at the back of the great room were crowded with serving matrons and youths carrying plates of food. And on the far left, an area designated for contests was cleared, chalk lines drawn upon the floor and walls.

Vendanj did not pause, but found a table to the right that would seat them all. When everyone had taken a seat, a portly woman promptly appeared.

"Rooms or food?" she barked. She held one fleshy fist on her waist and a dirty rag in her other hand.

"Both," Vendanj said without looking at the woman. Tahn realized Vendanj had addressed the woman without the use of the honorific "Anais." "And we need to speak to Ulee."

"Ulee's busy and we're out of lamb." She began wiping the table in front of Vendanj, her ample bosom barely contained in the deep, square-cut bodice.

"He will see us," Vendanj said. His voice filled with violence at the hint of contradiction.

"Fine, I'll tell him," she whined. "Now what will you have?"

"Steer and root for all, and one bottle of evenwine."

The woman raised her chin in contempt and ambled away to the kitchen.

Tahn surveyed the room. Great carpets hung upon the walls, some with symmetrical designs rendered in cobalt blue and crimson. A small dais in the far right corner held stools; instruments leaned against the wall. Near them, two men and two women dressed in bright yellow and scarlet overdresses chattered and laughed, obviously the hall's entertainment.

At the table, little was said. Mira spoke occasionally to Vendanj, and Braethen had again taken to his book. Sutter's neck craned at nearly impossible angles to see all that the hall had to offer. Wendra's eyes had shut; she looked close to sleep.

A moment later, a man with deep auburn hair and wide shoulders wound his way from the kitchen toward them. He wore a loose white shirt with two thin blue stripes across the chest. His rolled-up sleeves revealed arms thick with hair. He had a day's growth of beard and deep-set eyes. He walked casually, nodding hellos as he came. Coming at last to them, he hunkered down beside Vendanj.

"Evening, friends. What can be done for you?"

"Hello. You are Ulee?" Vendanj asked.

"Since the narrow way into the land," he said, smiling.

As Vendanj started to speak, four men in deep russet cloaks bearing the sigil of the League of Civility appeared around the table. They carried spears and wore swords, as well.

"Gentlemen," Vendanj said, "what can I do for you?"

"You will come with us," the tallest replied. He wore a yellow cord draped over his left shoulder. "We have some questions for you."

As they spoke, the four scops in the corner donned large masks and began to play out a light, folliet skit.

"I've not yet eaten; can this wait until tomorrow? I'm not going anywhere."

The four leaguemen laughed. "You'll forgive us. We've heard your excuse far too many times." Then their captain's voice drew taut. "Now."

The entertainment rose into a grand song, all four scops linking arms and wailing into the high rafters of the common hall.

Tahn could see Mira and Braethen rising. Around them, the crowd had begun to sing with the scops, making it hard to hear. But it all felt like the precipice of madness and violence.

"Under what authority?" Vendanj challenged.

The man wearing the yellow cord brought a hard fist, wearing iron knuckles, against the Sheason's jaw. "Have you any more questions?"

Before Mira or Braethen could do anything, Vendanj held up his hand to stay them. He shook his head and gathered his composure. Tahn recognized the restraint the Sheason had just exercised. This was not the place for confrontation.

Vendanj then took Ulee's hand in farewell. "Thank you for your hospitality," he said, passing the horseshoe nail to the innkeeper.

He then turned to Mira, speaking under the sound of the crowd's adulation for its circus. "Do not leave them." He looked squarely at Tahn. "I will not be more than a day. If I am not back, leave at nightfall tomorrow, regardless." He gave Mira a strong, reassuring look. "You know I will be well. Do not leave them," he reiterated.

As a chorus of cheers and cups pounding on the tables applauded the performance, serving matrons rushed into the hall with bottles, where patrons were quick to want another drink. And Vendanj was ushered out under guard of the League.

Later in the night, when the others had fallen asleep in their rooms after hushed talk of Vendanj, Wendra crept back to the common room.

The drinkers and revelers were mostly gone. A few late suppers were being taken in corners by people whose occupations made late their time to eat. They remained attended by one serving woman, a hot but lower fire, and the scops who she'd come to see.

Wendra took a seat against one wall and listened. The songs these musicians played were unlike any she'd heard in the Hollows. When they were bright they were boisterous; when proud, courageous; and when sad, they were piteous and plaintive. Here, it seemed, the music became more than a performance by the singer, it grew into an accusation or challenge. There was boldness in it that she hadn't heard before. Even through the troubles and madness of this night and everything since fleeing the Hollows—and before, back as far as her rape—Wendra was entranced by this new sound and knew she must seize upon it in some way.

It made her think of where the simple, dark melodies she'd found when curled onto a cabin floor a few days ago might lead.

When the night at last found its end for the common room, the scops began to pack their instruments to leave. Wendra slid from her chair with questions she hoped they could answer.

"Thank you," she said. "You're very gifted. I enjoyed listening to you very much."

The woman, still packing, looked over her shoulder at Wendra as her male counterpart turned to receive his accolades.

"You're most welcome, my young woman. Was there a particular song you liked?" He smiled and bowed in thanks for her praise.

His companion shook her head without turning again.

Wendra decided her answers would come from this gentleman. "The songs of loss. There was something strong and comforting about them. I don't know. It seemed—"

"They didn't simply accept the pain, but demanded answers and retribution," he finished for her.

"Yes," Wendra said. "The music seemed to provide relief of a kind by not simply wallowing in grief and resentment."

"You are an astute listener. Are you by chance a musician yourself?" The man looked Wendra over from top to bottom.

She understood then his designs, her stomach roiling at the thought. Thankfully, the woman chimed in, finally turning to join the conversation. "If you are, don't waste any more breath on him," she said. "You'll want to talk to the composer, which would be me."

The woman hefted an instrument case over her shoulder and came to stand beside her companion. "He's quick to accept the credit, however he can get it." She gave him a look of amused disgust. "But he's never around to help create the music we earn that credit by. What's your name, my young lady?"

"Wendra. And yours?"

"I am Solaena. This is Chrastof. He's got packing to do. Why don't you and I sit so I can rest my feet, wet my lips, and I can give you the advice my father never gave me." She waved a hand at the serving woman, who showed attentive but weary eyes and went to get something from the kitchen.

Solaena and Wendra sat together, and shortly a tall glass of steaming tea was set before Solaena. She sipped, the warmth seeming to ease her features, and relaxed into her chair.

"You find some fascination with playing songs to a crowd like this," Solaena said. "Well, let me tell you. If you can find another way to earn a coin, do it. Most times we aren't paid, and patrons of a common room like this often think we're paid to do more than entertain them, if you understand me. Keep your music, my girl, but don't make it your life's path."

Wendra nodded appreciatively. But her questions were not professional. "How do you make them? The songs. How do you make them feel like anguish, not for its own sake but to justify revenge."

The scop smiled. "I see. Well, that's just writing from my own heart's desire. I guess so late in the night it's tolerable to admit that I don't believe in the same things I did when I was your age. And maybe because I don't, I write about them in my songs to remind me of a time when I did. What I mean is, the songs are a place where I can give voice to my inmost wishes, even if the world around me doesn't hearken to my words. Do you understand?"

"I believe so. But the world does hear you. The people in the room. Me."

A grateful smile touched Solaena's lips. "You're a dear heart, my girl. Thank you. And because of your gracious praise, I'll tell you the trick of it—as I think that's what you'd like to know." She leaned over her tea, and spoke in a sincere tone. "When you make your sad song, you mustn't be afraid to go to the bottom of your own pain. Any power in those tunes comes from the well of your own torment, and it's from there that the demand for relief will come. Anything else is simply a lament, and personally, I don't see a lot of point to that."

Wendra had an epiphany at the scop's words, there in the dark hours of night in an empty common room that reeked of bitter.

"And one more thing besides," Solaena added. "Those songs don't always need to be brayed out. We do it because these are noisy places." She looked around the room. "But what I'm sharing with you here can come with the same power and meaning in a lullaby. If you doubt it, listen to a mother singing the hope of her heart for a child born into a dangerous world."

Wendra stared back at the woman, loss and revelations warring in her soul. The late-night instruction on songs to be sung with sadness and authority would steal her sleep that night and for many nights to come, because the woman's words struck Wendra's deepest fear and regret. Her own recent melodies she now realized were, at least in part, lullabies for a child who would never hear them.

• CHAPTER FOURTEEN •

Subtleties

Tahn awoke to the smell of fried pig steak and root. A narrow shaft of light streamed through the window. Beside it, Braethen sat reading, looking like he'd been awake all night. Sutter already had his trousers on and a wild look in his eye.

"Any word on Vendanj?" Tahn asked.

Braethen looked up. "Not yet." Then he returned to his reading.

Tahn regarded the sodalist, still getting used to thinking of him that way for real. "What are you reading?"

"History," he mumbled without looking up this time.

"Are you coming to endfast or not?" Sutter asked, dressing.

The sodalist put down his book and pressed his eyes with thumb and forefinger. "I could use a break." He looked gaunt and pale from lack of sleep. "Mira said not to leave the inn."

"Wouldn't dream of it," Sutter said.

They left the room and found a serving matron in the hall near the kitchen. The common room stood vacant by comparison to the prior evening, though a few dozen men and women sat eating endfast. The serving matron led them to the kitchen where the sweet smell of honey frakes—a delicious potato cake—joined the bouquet of appetizing aromas. Tahn guessed Mira had arranged the location of this meal, where there were fewer eyes to notice them.

Pushing through the door, they found Wendra lending a hand in the kitchen.

"Come and eat." She dished out four plates and set them at a table to one side of the oven.

Sutter had seated himself and taken half a honey frake before Tahn even found a seat.

"Thank you, Wendra," Braethen said, and took a seat beside Sutter.

"You're welcome," she replied. "You are to eat and then wait in your room."

"We got the command," Sutter mumbled around his food. He nudged Tahn under the table, signaling him to hurry. If they finished their morning meal before Braethen, they might escape into the city without any further admonitions.

Tahn poured fresh grape mash from a carafe and drank deeply. He wasn't sure he wanted to venture any further into Myrr, even during the day. He remembered Balatin talking about the larger cities, and how he had moved to the Hollows to escape the constant intrigues and politics. Still, something stirred his heart at the prospect of seeing the sights, perhaps even the palace. Tahn began shoveling his food into his mouth. He wasn't a Sheason, or even a sodalist. He was a hunter of no repute—safely anonymous.

Shortly, Sutter stood. "I'm done. I guess I'll head back to the room," he said.

Tahn rose as well. "I'll join you. I need to fletch a few arrows."

Braethen looked at his plate, still half full, and appeared conflicted.

"We'll be fine, Braethen," Sutter assured. "You keep Wendra company while she finishes morning endfast, and we'll see you in the room."

Without waiting for a reply, Sutter turned toward the hall, where the stairs ascended into the Stone's upper levels.

"Delicious, Wendra. Thank you," Tahn said.

"A meal fit for the First Ones," Sutter called from down the hall.

Tahn hastened to catch his friend, who was already exiting the front door of the Granite Stone toward the streets of Myrr.

They'd just broken into the sunlight when a soft voice called, "I think you two are lost."

Tahn and Sutter turned simultaneously to see Mira standing beside a large cart to the right of the door.

"You're kidding. Really? Are you on guard here?" Sutter sounded more disappointed than incredulous.

"We were just—"

"Don't do yourself the disservice of a lie," the Far said. "This is not travel for its own sake. Remember our purpose. Remember what we've passed through to get this far. And don't try the kitchen entrance, either. I've got someone watching it for me."

Tahn pulled Sutter by the shirt. They walked back into the cooler environs of the Granite Stone, a bit dejected and more than a little embarrassed. For

Tahn's part, he'd have been as happy to stand with Mira on her watch. Her hair shone lustrous, seeming more a deep auburn than black in the full light of day.

As they reached the staircase, Braethen burst out of the kitchen, the crumbs of a honey frake still on his lips. His face made it clear. It had taken him another minute, but he'd realized why Tahn and Sutter had finished their endfast so quickly. Sutter shook his head. Tahn shrugged. Braethen smiled.

"Just as well," he said. "By the way, the inn has a natural hot-water spring in its basement. Ulee told me that generations ago this place served as a temple, built to honor the land for the blessing of its curative waters. They schedule it every fifteen minutes. I used it last night when I couldn't sleep. I put you two on the list, and your turn just began."

"I don't think—" Sutter began.

"You need to bathe," Braethen insisted. "You have fifteen minutes all to yourselves."

This time they both shrugged and followed the sodalist back to a hall just off the kitchen where a large granite door hung from great iron hinges. Pushed lightly, the heavy door easily swung inward. They followed him down a stair carved from the same stone. The sound of water grew and the feel of steam brushed Tahn's cheeks as they descended lower and lower. Lamps affixed to the walls dripped with condensation. At the bottom of the stair a natural cavern almost three times the size of their quarters opened up. Small benches had been set at the edge of a square fount rimmed with the same granite.

Sutter dropped to his knees and thrust his hands into the water. "Will and Sky, Tahn, it's like water boiled over the pit." He began tearing off his clothes. Before Tahn had removed his shirt, Sutter had jumped into the pool, splashing water all over himself.

Soon Tahn and Sutter were relaxing in the spring, their heads lolling back on the granite rim. They listened to the water drip from the ceiling and let the strain of their journey slip from their bodies.

As they rested there, the door at the top of the stair opened again.

Out of the shadow of the stairwell, a slender figure emerged: Mira . . . naked.

She held her clothes and weapons in one hand, having stripped them off as she descended the stair.

Tahn could do nothing but stare.

If he'd thought she was beautiful before, this defied every melura dream he'd ever had. Not even as alchera, after the change, did he think to see a woman like this. He became suddenly aware of his own nakedness, his physical reactions to the Far, and to his friend's wide-eyed, slack-jawed gape. Tahn wanted to cover Sutter's eyes, but realized how stupid it would appear.

Despite their gawking, Mira didn't appear the least bit inhibited or embarrassed. Nor was she clumsy or rushed, which made it that much more difficult for them to stop watching her. She placed her things out of the way of the water splashed onto the floor around the spring, and slipped into the warmth with them. She even traded looks with them, her expression one of confusion or wonder over Tahn and Sutter's sudden silence and attention.

Finally, she spoke. "I see neither of you are used to seeing a female bare."

Sutter said something unintelligible.

Tahn caught that slightest of smiles on the Far's lips. He looked through the steam rising off the water between them, and could think of just one thing to say. "Subtle."

It was the first time he'd ever heard her laugh. The sound of it could break a man's heart, or make him the best self he had to offer.

When her laugh had receded in the spring cavern, she said, somewhat matter-of-factly, "I value cleanliness, and at the Sheason's instruction, where you go, I go."

"I see," Tahn replied.

"In truth, the unclothed body is not as noteworthy in my country as it is in the kingdoms of men. Our customs aren't the same."

"Well, as long as that's the case, I do have a question, if you don't mind," Tahn said.

"I'll answer if I can," Mira said, slightly guarded.

"Was the Hollows ever called by another name?"

The Far gave him a wary look and brushed water from her face. "You overheard Vendanj and me talking near the fire."

"Guilty," Sutter sputtered. He sat forward, causing ripples in the water. "Tell us. It's our home."

Tahn nodded in agreement. "Vendanj hasn't exactly been free with his tongue, though he has felt free to thrust us from the Hollows into the path of Bar'dyn and Maere and a city full of secrets." He looked straight at Mira. "Can there be anything about the Hollows that we are not entitled to know?"

Mira eyed them both. Tahn thought he saw conflict in her face. "This is a reader's story—an old one not often told anymore—but still not a secret that must be kept."

"Tell us already, I'm getting to look like Merid Lavia's sunned fruits in here." Sutter held up his fingers, showing them his wrinkled skin.

"Very well," the Far said, resting her head back upon the granite. "You remember that toward the end of the High Season, the Great Fathers who sat at the Tabernacle of the Sky began to see the work of the One and grew concerned for the preservation of the land and its peoples."

Tahn and Sutter nodded.

"The Quiet were driven into the Bourne, and the veil was raised. But against the possibility that the veil should be breached, the First Ones consecrated an area in the land where the Quietgiven could not tread; where Velle could not render; where Quiet feet would find no rest; and where the lives of its people reflected their harmony with the Will. The very soil was sanctified, and its customs would in turn reflect understanding of the cycles—like your Northsun Festival.

"In such a place, it was believed that the future of the land could be safeguarded against the day that all believed would come, when the One would find a way through the veil and send his Quiet into the world."

Mira paused, cupping a handful of water and dripping it on her lips and tongue to moisten them.

The Hollows had been Tahn's home since he could remember, but the thought that it had been set apart by the First Ones amazed him.

Sutter seemed to have forgotten his concern for his shriveled fingers, examining them instead like newly found jewels. "In the soil . . ." he muttered.

"Before the Craven Season passed, the Hollows had lost its name. It is well that it was so, or it would have become a miserable refugee colony. Half the people of every nation perished in war and butchery. Most of those who survived quarreled and fought, until nations joined in the First Promise. Those who put their mark to that Promise did so in the safety of the Hallows. History records it differently, but that's where the First Promise was sealed after ratification at Recityv. With time the Hallows became a myth, leaving the ground there unremembered and uncontested in the ages that followed."

"And now?" Tahn asked.

"Now the creatures out of the Bourne walk freely into the Hallows to strip your sister's child from her." The Far's words reverberated in the warm stone room, echoing like an imprecation.

"Then the Will is no more," Tahn shot back.

"Nonsense. The Will is eternal." She stated it as fact, without passion.

"Then tell us how the Bar'dyn came trundling down a riverbed and nearly pinched our heads from our necks," Sutter said heatedly.

"Things are changing; no doubt this is why Vendanj came to you. And the Hollows is still she'holta, still blessed. No war has ever been fought upon Hollows earth, not even the Second War of Promise. The Hollows is known to those who serve the Artificer, yet they have never passed into its borders, until now. It has served its purpose since the establishment of the Bourne. And, my friends," the Far said, looking at Tahn and Sutter with narrowed eyes, "you ought to think on that when you find yourselves impatient with the Sheason. Regardless, these aren't times to be speaking of such things to strangers. You hold close the secret of the Hallows."

Without another word, Mira got out of the spring. Tahn regarded her with deeper desire and appreciation. "I'll get dressed and wait for you in the kitchen.

Take your time, my Hollows friends." She dressed unhurriedly in front of them, lashed her weapons on, then climbed the stair.

"We'll catch up." Sutter dipped his head beneath the steaming surface of the water.

They waited until Mira had shut the door at the top of the slick stair, then turned to each other with shocked expressions. They were simply too amazed to say anything. Neither was eager to stand, until the door at the top of the stair opened again.

The two listened closely and looked up. Had Mira forgotten something? A moment later, two elderly couples came slowly into view. As they descended, they pulled robes from their shoulders, revealing their considerably puckered and sagging flesh.

"Nudity was not meant for the aged," Sutter whispered.

"This spring must serve as one of those health bath houses for the elderly, among other things." Tahn stifled a laugh until he realized anew that he and Sutter were naked, too.

Tahn and Sutter jumped out of the water, grabbed their clothes, and looked for a place to hide. Nothing.

Except . . .

In the shadows on the far side of the spring, several stalactites formed something of a wall. The two melura from the Hollows dashed for the safety of the darkness and cover.

"What are we going to do? They can still see our feet." Sutter pranced a bit, dripping wet.

As their eyes began to adjust, they noticed something they hadn't seen before. Beyond the rock formation lay a second staircase. They smiled in the shadows and began to climb blindly until a crack of light showed them the way. Moments later they found a latch, pulled it free, and burst, still naked, into the alley beside the Granite Stone.

The door slammed behind them—no latch on the outside. The stunned look they shared gradually shifted to mischief. And that turned to embarrassment as two young girls began to giggle, seeing Tahn and Sutter's manhood hanging out in broad daylight.

But their embarrassment didn't last long. They'd gotten outside the Inn!

After Braethen let Mira know Tahn and Sutter were in the hot spring, he made an excuse for having to go back to the room. He was relieved when she descended the stair; he couldn't wait any longer to find out what had happened to the Sheason.

He removed his emblem. Clearly that would invite more speculation than would be helpful. Then he got himself out to the street and started to think. Ordinarily, he would have paused to recall tales that had described and depicted this place—there were many. But he needed to decide how best to help Vendanj.

And it occurred to him.

A book shop.

Ever had the place where authors congregated and sold their wares been the hub of information and advice. It was true on a smaller scale in the Hollows, but A'Posian had related to Braethen in both written and spoken ways the magic and majesty of the book shops in the cities of Aeshau Vaal. His father, in his younger days, had visited many, so he ought to know.

After asking just two passersby, he got directions, and made haste three streets over to Authors' Tell, situated on the corner of a fairly busy intersection. Braethen went straight in and immediately felt at home.

"Another young reader come to find a book, yes?" The stooped gentleman looked up at Braethen from his cane through thickish spectacles.

"Maybe. I'm Braethen, son of A'Posian out of the Hollows."

"Son of an author, how are you, my boy! Usually such lads will have nothing to do with the work of their fathers. I'm A'Thalia. Though I mostly scribble these days. Stories are work, and I figure I've earned time to dawdle." The old man began to pick up books and transfer them to a cart.

Out of habit, Braethen helped him. "I guess I'm looking for information."

"We have that, too." A'Thalia patted Braethen's hands. "Not that one, I'm going to take that one home. It's about a graellen and a lord who's lost his will to fight. Wonderful!"

Braethen thought carefully on how to ask about a possibly jailed Sheason. "I have a friend," he began. "He was accused of something and was taken, I think, by the League for questioning. I'm trying to find out if he's okay."

A'Thalia stopped in his tracks and gave Braethen a serious look. "Ah, boy, you're already lying. Or holding back some of the truth. Wait a minute. Jartamara, Molanerus, Rhye, scuttle on out here."

Braethen held his breath, expecting cloaked leaguemen to appear from the depths of the bookshop. He waited. And waited. Finally three more stooped gentlemen, all somehow retaining their hair in its silver antiquity, puttered slowly with their walking canes over to them.

After they'd introduced themselves, A'Thalia said, "All right, lad. Start again. And so you don't think the elder men are gullible, you're only getting this audience and second chance because I can tell you really do have an author for a pa, can tell by the way you handle the bindings on those books you loaded. Now, go on with it."

Braethen silently thanked his father. "I am a novice sodalist, recently bound to a Sheason. We came last night to Myrr, and almost immediately he was taken into custody by the League. He's done nothing wrong. I only want to find out if he's all right."

"I suspect it's all true up until that last bit," Rhye said.

"Yup," Jartamara agreed.

"You're right. If he's in danger, I need to help him. But how is that wrong?"

"I don't think any of us commented on morality here, boy," A'Thalia said. "And by the way, these fellows here happen to be authors, too. Though, mostly that garbage they use in teaching regiments. Except for Molanerus. He can spin a damn fine tale."

"How do I help him?" Braethen pressed.

"Well, it just so happens we've heard about your Sheason, Braethen son of A'Posian. News of accusations travel fast in the story trade. He's alive. Least-ways, that's what our reading fans tell us. And we have a few in the dungeons who need our wares to pass their lonely hours. So, we believe it."

"What's to be done with him?"

"That'll depend on him." A'Rhye loaded some tobaccom into a pipe. "Two stripes to the Sheason anymore. One will argue with his jailer, and like as not wind up swinging. Another will show his submissive side and be kept in jail for a piece of time. What's your Sheason like?"

Braethen panicked. "Is there appeal to the local ruling class?"

"Crolsus?" A'Thaila asked. "You're talking about a man who asks folks to curtsy to his hat when they pass it sitting on that pole in the square. That help you with your assessment?"

Braethen looked down at the four elderly men. They would help, but how? Then he hit upon an idea. "Can you tell me which cell he's in?"

"Aye," said A'Jartamara, "that too is something our readers in the pit would know. But I don't see how that's going to—"

"Architecture."

That was all he had to say. They understood immediately, and scuttled into the stacks to dig through the books.

And as they were looking, A'Thalia said, "Had a gentleman here a moon ago asking for books on the same subject. But not for Myrr. Recityv."

When Braethen heard those words, it was as if a warbird had flown warning overhead.

CHAPTER FIFTEEN

Crones

The highwayman led the woman and his men at an easy pace on the dark road. The stars shone bright enough to navigate by, and they were close enough to their initial destination that he didn't wish to set camp and waste another day. Besides, the night revealed yet another guise of the road, one he savored and held close.

After two days of travel, he finally turned off the road and followed a path so obscure that he'd never have recognized it at night had he not known of it before.

Many times had he come this way to visit the crone in her cottage set back deep in the whispering aspens.

The night air rattled the leaves, lending to their arrival the music of nature's applause. A dim glow could be seen behind heavy curtains at the window. A streamer of smoke rose in a silver wisp from the chimney above. She could not have been expecting them, but as they dismounted, the door to a shadowy room opened quietly.

The highwayman ordered his men to tend the horses and pitch camp as he took his captive by the arm and led her into the cottage. He closed the door and turned, his keen eyes already adjusted to the dimness. The woman sat in a rocker near the fire with knitting needles held in her knobby fingers, working bland yarn into what might become a shawl. The room seemed to press inward, confining them, the smell of old age, of one who rarely gets beyond her door, hanging on the musty air.

"Greetings," he said.

"And yourself, highwayman. What prize do you bring with you tonight?" The crone didn't turn, her eyes fixed on her knitting.

"I don't need much of you, and I apologize for the hour—"

"No you don't," she interrupted. "You're eager to have your answers. That's why you steer yourself through the shadows with this woman. But no matter. What will I have for your intrusion to make it worth my time? And don't play at lying with me. You're a good one at it, but I can see your deceptions, lest you forget why you come to me to begin with."

In the shadows of the crone's knitting room, the highwayman smiled to himself. He appreciated her directness and lack of moralizing. He suspected that she'd removed herself from the company of others precisely because she lacked the grace others tried to enforce in polite society. That, and her special talents, which he was sure others had not understood.

Special talents. The very reason for his visit.

"I have three bolts of fine cloth that are yours. And I've got a horse that you may have if you've a use for it." He waited to see if his offer would prove agreeable.

"You've some ale, too, no doubt," she said. "I'll have everything you carry."

"Done."

Her fingers stopped, and her milky eyes turned toward them. The woman recoiled into the highwayman from the crone's awful stare, and he put a bracing arm around her shoulders.

"Bring her closer." The crone's voice came softly, but cracked and thin, as if it had been abused somehow in her youth.

The highwayman had to use some earnest force to get the woman moving toward the crone's rocking chair. Finally, he whispered in her ear, "Consider the old woman a healer. She will do you no harm. Think carefully, what would it profit me to come all this way only to allow something to happen to you now?"

The woman let her feet be led, and they eased toward the crone's chair, their footfalls loud in the room. So close, in the glow of the firelight, he could see the hair on the crone's upper lip—vanity was clearly not her vice. The hag stared up at them both, her clouded eyes never seeming to quite look directly at either of them. Still, he knew a kind of *seeing* was taking place. Then she motioned for the woman to stand directly in front of her.

He let the woman go, and stood back as the crone put her knobby fingers on the woman's stomach and began to grope around her breasts and hips and loins and thighs, slowly returning to the woman's naval with an awkward caress.

"What are you doing?" the woman finally asked, and tried to step away.

The crone's bony hand shot out and grasped the woman's wrist, holding her tight and near.

"This highwayman took me from my husband by force!" the woman yelled. "Are you one of his conspirators? Are you so quick to profit from the lawless actions of this bandit? Where's your womanhood?"

The crone raised a dry cackle in the confines of her small room. Her milky eyes seemed almost youthful again with the light of the humor there. "Womanhood? Child, you are naive. You've seen too many skies to claim gender as a common bond with a stranger and expect it to be any kind of defense."

"And *you've* seen too many if you deal with a man who would seize a woman against her will." The captive stared at the crone with bright defiance and anger.

"Where was this husband of yours? Why did *he* not defend your will?" A slight smile drew at one corner of the hag's mouth.

The woman looked at the highwayman, who stared back evenly. "He chose to live in hope of my rescue."

"I see. Well, if you come to ill use, then you both will revisit the prudence of that choice, won't you?" Then the frown of the aged and bitter stole over the crone's face. "I don't have time for this. Come stand here or your captor will force you to do it. Either way, child."

Several moments passed, the highwayman relishing the battling emotions he could see in the woman's face. The contest of indignation and acquiescence. He remembered it well from his own life, and his mood darkened at the thought. Then finally the woman approached the crone, who again put her hands on the woman's stomach.

As the night waned, the old woman began to mutter to herself as she slowly moved her wizened hands in circles over his captive's navel. The scene struck him as ceremonial after a fashion, the two women locked in a strange union. But it also smacked of rape in a way he couldn't articulate. As the highwayman watched, despite his need of both women, revulsion touched his mind in long remembrances of other women in dark, small rooms. Other women who used and were used in unholy transactions that damned them equally. He recalled the tight, painful feeling of those rooms, and could almost feel in his throat the unanswered, sobbing prayers that he'd offered in them so long ago.

But those memories were interrupted when the crone stopped muttering and dropped her hands. His captive collapsed to her knees, spent. The hag took up the half-knitted shawl and wiped at her brow and hairy lip before turning her clouded eyes back to the highwayman. She stared a good long time, again not seeing but *seeing* him in a way that long ago might have disquieted him.

Tonight, he simply needed an answer.

"Get the bolts of cloth and the ale," the crone said.

"And the woman?" he asked.

The crone shook her head. "Her womb is ruined. She'll not bear children. Never has. Never will."

"Are you sure? She does not look too old. And she has fire in her." He didn't like to think that for all his effort he had come up empty-handed.

"Did you happen to notice any children when you snatched this one from her husband?" The crone's loose, wrinkled skin shrugged into an awful smile that showed gums bereft of teeth. "Something makes you hasty this time, highwayman. It's dirty work to seize the living. And it's worse when you get it wrong. Sometimes that can't be helped. But what makes you careless? There are signs that may be read to increase your odds of success, eh, besides just seeing children about. You know them, I think. Make your gambles, but do so wisely." Her smile faded, and she asked again, "What urgency causes you to forget such simple things?"

The highwayman looked deep into the milky eyes of the crone, his anger mounting. "Damnation!" he howled. He took a threatening step toward the hag and stopped. The desire to pull his knife across her throat was held just barely in check by the fact that she was not to blame. He then whirled on his captive, raising a fist. Someone must pay! His creditors would not be lenient with *him*.

He nearly struck the woman down before realizing that damaged goods fetch lesser prices.

The highwayman shot a gaze back at the crone. She was right. He'd been working too fast of late. He'd gotten sloppy. But there were still bargains to be struck. Oaths to be fulfilled. Though not things to be spoken of here.

"Get the bolts of cloth and the ale," the crone repeated and went back to her knitting.

The highwayman stepped into the darkness beyond the door, where the aspen leaves whispered in the soughing wind. The slow, chill breeze touched his skin, cooling his anger. Already he yearned once more to take his chances. Tomorrow he'd go back to the road, where he would try again.

• CHAPTER SIXTEEN •

A Need for Pretense

The sun shone bright upon the teeming roads of the city. A thick smell rose from the mixture of mud and wet straw. Small shops lined the byway, men and women hawking all manner of roots and elixirs. Others called to passersby to survey their fine coats or breeches, most fashioned of wool. A few carts displayed garish hats and scarves and belts. Most infrequent were the stores selling any kind of weapon. Rather, men selling dangerous wares stood in the recessed doorways of buildings that appeared otherwise abandoned. Knives or knuckle spikes lay on brown cloth near their feet, the proprietor standing back in a recess smoking from a pipe or a rolled bit of sweetleaf and watching the street cautiously.

"Which way?" Sutter asked.

"All gumption and no sense, Nails," Tahn said, and slapped his back. "Where else? The palace."

Sutter grinned. "You'll make a fine advisor when I become king."

Tahn laughed. "If you're ever king, root-digger, I'll wear the hat of bells and dance a heel-toe jig for your amusement." They started east toward the city center.

At each cross street they stopped and marveled at the throngs of people milling on the road. Tahn looked on in amazement as the palace slowly rose before them. Soon the straw gave way to cobblestones. Men and women walked more slowly here, their shoes low cut, and the women without stockings. Wagons were replaced by carriages drawn by a single horse.

"Look at that," Sutter said in a hushed, awed voice.

To their right walked two men in long amethyst cloaks, carrying spears. Each spear bore a short violet pennon emblazoned with a yellow hawk holding a set of scales in its talons.

"City guard," Sutter said with glee. "They've got to be." Sun glinted off their helmets and the studs in their armor. Not ten strides behind them came another pair of guards similarly dressed but bearing maces hung at their waist.

"Come on." Tahn pulled at Sutter's cloak. "Let's not look so conspicuous."

The two approached a crowd gathered tightly together. Their attention seemed focused toward a fountain.

"What's that?" Sutter asked.

Tahn led them through a maze of onlookers and soon saw the object of their attention. At the center of the large plaza, several men and women stood upon a broad, flat wagon declaiming to one another in strident, clipped speech. It struck Tahn as familiar, and he quickly knew why. These people were performing, just like the scops in the Stone the night before. Only these players wore no masks, and they did not seem to intend to provoke laughter. Several hundred passersby had gathered to watch; and the wagon platform sat high enough that the performers could be heard and seen by all.

"Come on, let's go." Sutter's face showed a twist of displeasure. "We can find something better in such a big city."

Tahn resisted. "Just a moment." He wanted to see more.

Sutter groaned. Tahn thought he saw more than simple impatience in his friend's face; Nails seemed to bear a real distate for these pageant troupers. Sutter fixed accusatory eyes on the wagon and watched. Tahn thought he heard Sutter mumble something bitter about "awful parents," before the players' voices drowned him out.

"They must be driven from the land," one player said.

A woman sang a phrase in a tongue Tahn did not know, her voice carrying easily above the crowd.

"Take hands, all, and this stand make," a second woman declared.

Sutter appeared disinterested, and began searching in the direction of the guards they had seen. But the crowd around them did not move. Many nodded knowingly, others shook their heads as if wanting to disbelieve, but unable to do so.

"The sky grows black," a young boy said. "Hurry, the sun flees this unhappy choice." The lad looked into the distance, his eyes seeing something Tahn's did not. Then the boy took hold of the hands of the players to each side of him; ten men and women and children formed a line upon the broad wagon and together looked over the heads of their audience at a distant event none could see. The boy was the shortest among them—at least two heads shorter than Tahn—with a shock of flaxen hair. But he looked wiry strong, at least in part to a face that didn't seem to know compromise.

Just then a commotion began at the edge of the crowd. Angry voices cried, "Disband, you! Enough of this!"

This brought Sutter's attention back to the stage. "Guards?" His friend shifted position, trying to see what was happening.

Tahn looked back the way they had come. The crowd had closed in tight behind them, and the warmth of close bodies suddenly caused panic to rise in his throat.

"This is sedition!" one of the voices cried bitterly. "Don't you know the law?"

Tahn stood on his toes and saw a small band of men and women parting the crowd and heading directly for the platform. Muttered talk erupted among those gathered to watch. The players released their hands and backed away from the edge of their wagon stage. The crowd grew larger, the sounds of strained voices rising from the edges of the gathering. People pressed forward, pinning Tahn and Sutter together.

The assembly parted to make way for the newcomers, who found the stage and turned to look back at those still watching.

"Have done with you, lest you find yourselves party to these here." The man speaking pointed an accusing finger in a broad arc over the assemblage. A few of those gathered grumbled low, emboldened by the anonymity of being so deep in the crowd. Despite the warning, the throng made no move to break up. The official pulled himself onto the stage and cast vicious glances at them all. He wore a long, rich, russet-colored cloak trimmed in white, with a round seal embroidered in white thread upon his breast. The insignia depicted four arms, each gripping the next at the wrist in a squared circle. Tahn hadn't seen the crest before, nor the rich, colorful cloaks, but he knew they belonged to the League. Near the leader, his comrades took defensive postures around the base of the wagon. Tahn thought it unnecessary; no one looked prepared to challenge them. The man's broad face radiated disdain. He whirled on the players.

"This rhea-fol is treason!" he yelled. "It is seditious to recount lies and fables that give false hope." His hand fell upon the hilt of his sword. "Who is responsible for this troop?"

The crowd hushed, those inclined to leave now riveted by this new scene being played out on the wagon. Sutter's hot, panting breath hit Tahn's neck.

Without a moment's hesitation, the boy who'd last spoken stepped forward, away from his companions. "I am. Whatever you have to do, do it to me." The lad's chest puffed out and his chin assumed a defiant attitude. He clenched his fists and stared openly at the man in league uniform.

A collective gasp issued from the crowd, like the awe expressed at Gollern-time in the Hollows when all gathered to watch the stars race across the sky in long, bright streaks. The league captain looked out of the corner of his eye at the throng, then focused his rage on the impudent boy.

"In your diapers you can scarcely know the harm you do, boy," he began. "I admire your loyalty to the troupe leader, but don't let it make you foolish. Loyalty is admirable only when well placed."

Tahn watched the man's lips curl as he spoke, leaving him with the impression that in a less public place, he might respond differently to the boy's defiance.

"How mighty you are," the boy replied, "to stop the performance of a simple rhea-fol, and our only means of bread and cups."

"Stay your tongue, boy," the man said, throwing his cloak over his shoulder to expose his blade. "The law holds no exceptions for age where sedition is charged. Find your mother's teat, and stop bringing shame upon whoever owns this company!"

The boy swallowed and began again in a soft, measured voice. "It is a story, sir. A story. True or not, it is no threat to you. It is played for them." The lad motioned with an upturned palm toward the growing crowd.

The man sniffed. "I'm done speaking with you, boy. What can you know of liberty, who have never put your life at risk in its defense?" He waved a dismissive hand. "Now, you will *all* be taken for the cowardice of he who lets a child stand in his place."

"No!" the boy yelled and rushed the man. In an instant, the leagueman's cloak whipped as though caught in a breeze, and the glint of steel rose in the air.

Tahn saw the moment unfold and began shaking his head, a sound erupting from his mouth unbidden: "Stop!"

The report of the command echoed off the stone of the courtyard beyond, filling the day with bright, hot contention. The boy skidded to a stop just a pace from the league captain, whose sword slowly dropped to his side as he searched the crowd. Men and women around Tahn and Sutter backed away.

"Will and Sky, Tahn, do you know how to travel," Sutter whispered, stepping from behind Tahn to stand beside him.

"Who calls?" the captain demanded.

Tahn studied the other's face as a wide path cleared between the wagon stage and him and Sutter. The league members standing around the wagon all drew their weapons. Tahn struggled with what to say; even the tales of the League in the Hollows were enough to teach him that you did not contradict one who wore its vestments. But as unsure as he was about what would happen next, he knew the lad should not be harmed.

"Leave the boy alone," Tahn said, his voice more defiant than he had thought possible.

"By what authority do you make such a demand?" the leagueman asked, squaring around toward Tahn.

Beside him Sutter's teeth ground. "By moral authority," Sutter said. Tahn looked at his friend, whose voice projected conviction that Tahn had never heard. "He is a child. Who do you represent that would strike down one not yet old enough to Stand?"

The captain smiled, his teeth menacing in a wide, clean-shaven jaw. "Your accent, more to the south I think, or perhaps the west." He put a hand on the lad's chest and pushed him back. Then he jumped to the ground and the crowd receded further still. "How far west, boys? Beyond the Aela River I think. Perhaps you make your home as far as Mal'Tara. It is no secret what manner of men come out of that place." He took deliberate steps toward them.

The leagueman's expression confused Tahn. It carried a mixture of confidence and belief in his calling, and a dark, seething hatred that belied that call. Tahn unconsciously shifted his stance, placing his right foot forward and slightly bending his knees.

"We are from—"

Tahn lifted his hand to stay Sutter's words.

When the captain came within three strides of him, Tahn looked closely at the crest on his breast, then to the ranks of leagueman that had fallen in behind him. He would say it once more. "He is a child, your honor, a melura. Impudent, perhaps, but not seditious."

"I've no immediate concern for the troupe now," the captain said, grinning. Again he threw his cloak over his shoulder, freeing his arm for movement. He spun his sword in his hand. "Do you know what accusation you have made, friend?" His words hissed like a sputtering candle.

"I know—"

"It is I, you Exigent hog!" The insult came from the stage. Over the leagueman's shoulder Tahn saw Mira atop the wagon. She held the boy by the hand. "He is my seed, and you and your league are a privy rag for his melura ass!"

The captain whirled to see Mira's fiery eyes inciting him. The league footmen rushed to the wagon. Mira took the boy and jumped from the far side, sprinting toward the alleys across the plaza. Though difficult to see, Tahn caught glimpses of the Far as she hoisted the boy up and slipped into the shadows with the speed of a prairie cat.

"Diversion," Sutter whispered.

Sutter pulled Tahn's cloak to get him moving, and together they turned back toward the Granite Stone. As they tried to find safety, Tahn's mind raced. *What did I just do?*

Preoccupied with Mira, the League gave delayed chase. Sutter broke into a run first, but Tahn soon overtook his friend, leading them into tight byways. Straw kicked up beneath their heels, and a few pedestrians shouted insults at them as they raced past. Tahn wove a circuitous route to the inn, bringing them to its doors an hour later.

They'd arrived safe. Mira had gotten back to the Granite Stone ahead of them with the boy. But Vendanj and Braethen were nowhere to be found. Tahn and Sutter took the boy and locked themselves in their room.

Vendanj lay in the guttering light of a single lamp, in the company of only his own dark ruminations. The blackened stone prison cell held a chill that seeped through even his heavy cloak. But the cold served as a good bedfellow. He needed to remember that it all came to this: choice. It was at the center of what he hoped to preserve. He smiled in his darkened room to think that the first thing civilized men create are prisons, because not all choose wisely.

And then he thought about the children out of the Hollows: the victim of rape newly delivered of a dead child, a farmer with Hollows dirt still beneath his nails, a boy pretending to be a sodalist, and Tahn . . . a hunter with no memory of his origins and a great task before him that Vendanj had begun to believe he could not complete.

Aeshau Vaal hung by a thread. The world stood at the brink and so few could see it, or would believe it. Governments, societies, families, even the Order of Sheason quarreled while the enemy sat behind the thinnest of walls that even now had started to fail.

A rough hopelessness got inside Vendanj for the first time in a long, long while. He could leave this jailor's pit when he chose. He had that power. But the repercussions of that could be dangerous, and he needed to measure them further before acting. Because right now, on balance, the result was bleak. He had not allowed himself to think on it until this very moment. Not in such depth.

He had required much of himself; that was fair and right. In the years since he'd been taken into the inner Order of Sheason—a rare second gift of knowledge and Will—he'd begun to require much of those around him, and he'd seen his own tolerance wane. His bitterness was that he saw this in himself, and approved.

His own conviction and faith were flinty things, and he could no longer bend them to appease the faithless. He only hoped that his inflexibility was the right tactic, was enough, because if not, then he was no longer the Sheason to carry this burden.

More than that, he didn't believe anything less would succeed.

There was so much to do; so far to go. Not only in distance and time, but in the inner lives of those called to surround him. Those inner frailties worried him most of all. Because if he shared what he knew, the others would break. Right now, they would break, these children from the Hollows. Even Mira would have hardships before long. And the exile out of the Scar that they must soon convince to join them . . . he was a rough stone that did not smooth by being rolled. That one could do the hard thing—if he followed Vendanj, if he chose it. But Vendanj had felt something more about the exile of late, that maybe he had a separate destiny. And his Sheason sight could not tell if it harmonized with the plans Vendanj had set in motion.

But he could not spare the whip. No matter how the hearts of those he tested cried. He must continue to push. His was a stony heart, a cold place that caged the hardest, most impassive soul. And that made him accustomed, familiar—not in body, but in spirit—with the dark, sweating stone of this prison cell.

And so he lay there, for a time, thinking, and hoping just a little for himself; for his companions; for the family of a man whose ignorance might usher in the Quiet after all.

When a scratching came, Vendanj sat up.

The sound came again, from the waste hole in the corner.

Vendanj went there, expecting to see a rat scrabbling for a crumb. Instead, the entire stone where prisoners put their asses to relieve themselves jumped. Then again. And finally moved up and over. Beneath it, out of the sewer, rose a filth-covered, stinking sodalist with a small lamp in one hand and a book to navigate by in the other.

The hope in his breast shone a little brighter.

A few hours after the commotion in the plaza, Tahn and Sutter sat in their room looking up into the iron gaze of the Sheason, who had just returned with Braethen.

"Mira told me," Vendanj said. "You were foolish to deceive her and the sodalist and take to the streets on your own." His voice hit them icily but low. "Why did you not listen to me?"

Tahn did not intend to answer. He could say nothing that would not sound preposterous to the Sheason, and he knew it.

But Sutter's teeth began to grind just before he opened his mouth to speak. "We have the right to decide where we will put our feet."

Vendanj fastened his steely gaze on Sutter and seemed to weigh his response. Finally he strode slowly toward Tahn's friend, taking a stance only a boot's length from him, their faces so close that Sutter surely felt Vendanj's breath. "And I may choose where my feet take me, root-digger," he said in a hushed tone that Tahn scarcely heard, even standing so close. "Be wary that our feet do not tangle. My charge is to you both, and I will not stumble in it."

Sutter stood still. Tahn had never seen his friend so scared. Always, a nervous smile crossed Sutter's face when danger or worry threatened him. This time, Sutter did not smile, and Tahn did not like the look of emptiness on his friend's face.

"A general call has been issued on you three and the boy," he said. "Discovery fees are promised." The Sheason locked the door, and moved to the window. "Milear will be here any moment with the horses. Can you all use a rope?"

They each nodded.

"Out the windows, and then north along the city's edge to the next gate. Those who've seen us would recognize their good fortune in turning us over at once. Keep your hoods up, and avoid looking directly at anyone. There will be many searching eyes."

"What is that smell?" Sutter asked.

Vendanj ignored the remark and looked out the window again. "Focus. He's here. Go."

Mira went first, followed by Braethen and the boy. Sutter went next and then Tahn and Wendra. Finally Vendanj came. On the ground, Milear camly held their horses. The liveryman did not speak, but took Vendanj by the hand and gave Mira a quick embrace. They mounted fast, and Milear waved them off.

Clouds hung low in the sky, casting deeper shadows in the narrow alleys they traveled. In the distance, thunder pealed, announcing a storm. The familiar smell of straw and mud rose from the street, now tinged with the ozone scent of the coming rain. Strawdrift watched them pass: Tahn thought their attentiveness had heightened in just a day's time.

Slowly they rode through the more brightly illuminated roads, where windows and street braziers glowed with fire. Then, through the dimness, Tahn could see the gate toward which they wound. Vendanj led them into another broad cross street, angling for an alley that passed toward the gate.

"Halt there, travelers!" A familiar voice called out of the shadows.

Vendanj did not slow, but Tahn turned toward the sound reflexively. In a shallow alcove on the far side of the street stood three figures. With careful ease the largest stepped from the darkness into the street. His vivid mahogany cloak looked like a night shadow in the sallow light, but the crest upon it shone unmistakably.

The Sheason continued on, the others following.

"I say, hold!"

Upon the frosted air, Tahn heard Vendanj utter the words, "Mira, gate."

In a blinding flash, Mira dismounted and dashed into the alley ahead of them. Tahn had never seen anyone move so fast.

"After her!" the captain called. Three more men emerged from another vantage point down the road and disappeared into the alleys.

Vendanj pulled Suensin to a halt, looked toward the leagueman, and then backward at Tahn. The play of dreary light in the Sheason's eyes made Tahn's neck and back prickle.

"Why might she have run, friend? Have you something to hide?"

Vendanj sat upright in his saddle. "It is best to be hidden from the eyes of the League."

The captain surveyed the party, stopping to take account of the boy.

"This fellow here is awfully small to be riding through the murk, don't you think?" He smiled, his clean, angular features sharp in the weak light of the street. "I believe I will offer him another place to rest this evening."

"We're of no interest to you," Vendanj said with diffidence. "We must be going."

"Be still!" the captain called. "There are questions to be answered. And I will have those answers." He walked close to Vendanj. "I believe you may be at the heart of it, too." He narrowed his eyes to try and peer through Vendanj's cowl. "You lead, they follow. You talk slowly in the face of questions. I will have a look at your face. I will know your affiliation."

A slight wind groaned in the eaves of a nearby building, and brazier fire sputtered and whipped. The rest was silence. Vendanj sat unspeaking for long moments.

Then the Sheason turned his head to the man in the russet cloak and inclined his head delicately toward him. "No!" he said, and the thrum of his voice roared like rushing water. He thrust a hand into the air, palm up and fingers curled skyward like talons. A stream of incomprehensible words followed his eyes toward the blackness above. Instantly a streak of red fire erupted from his fingertips and arced menacingly into the air. The fire swirled above all of them, leaping and falling back upon itself. It surged and licked above them like a living serpent, then shot earthward in sustained bolts. The street lit with ominous, reddish light, like the star fire seen deep in the night sky during dark moon. In the space of a breath, a wall of fire formed on each side of them, ending at the alley Vendanj had been heading toward. The horses pulled at their reins, shaking their heads and rearing.

"Ride!" Vendanj screamed over the fury of the blaze.

Tahn kicked Jole, who bolted past the Sheason. He could hear the rest following close behind him. In an instant, he entered the alley. Large, black, hulking shapes flew past Tahn in a blur. Jole carried him so fast through narrow paths betwixt boxes and barrels that Tahn thought they would surely slam into something.

The chill night air ripped at him, causing his eyes to water, roads and byways like a maze in his vision. Jole kept on, and the roar of hooves rose like earth-locked thunder in the confines of the narrow alleys.

Abruptly, they came to the gate. Solus stood placidly there already, his reins hanging to the ground. Mira could not be seen, though angry speech blared from the height of one of the parapets. The shriek of steel being drawn echoed down upon them as they all took rasping breaths. The horses, too, breathed heavily and shimmied about, their legs still blood-warm from their run.

"Now!" commanded a voice, unmistakably Mira's.

Vendanj came up behind them, reigning in Suensin. "Quickly!" he called.

Then the gates began to draw inward. Shouts echoed behind them, followed by a distant clatter of hooves and boots in the mud. The gate came open with aching slowness, and beyond the wall, the sound of heavy rain upon the trees could be heard, though the showers hadn't yet arrived at the city. Bolts of lightning fractured the night, booming just beyond the city wall. Mira appeared from the small gate house atop the parapet and looked at the ladder. Briskly she jumped, raising her cloak with her arms to each side. She landed, and fell immediately to a crouch, but more out of defensiveness than any apparent need to brake her landing. Immediately she went to the outer gate and threw the thick, iron crossbar aside.

As Mira pushed open the entry, Vendanj retook the lead and passed by her so closely that her cloak whipped in Suensin's passage.

"Go!" Mira yelled as rain began to deluge upon them.

Tahn heeled Jole and went directly after the Sheason, the others coming on fast. He looked over his shoulder and saw torches flaring against the rain, and a number of russet cloaks grown almost black from the sudden storm. Mira mounted and passed through the gate just ahead of the League. Into the downpour they raced, the sound of thunder filling Tahn's head from above and below. Myrr fell away like a dream image behind them and Tahn wondered if their numbers had been increased by one.

A child.

Why would Vendanj allow it?

• CHAPTER SEVENTEEN •

Beatings

The hard light of midday beat down on the man. But it could do no injury to skin that had already been darkened by long years in a desolate place of hot sun. He walked contented in the rolling hills, glad for the moment to be in a place of life and hope. There seemed precious little of that to be had.

His contentment was shattered by angry shouts from the cottage he'd come to call on. Raised voices, muted from within the dwelling, drifted on the still air. He hastened his steps, feeling an awful certainty of what he might find. The sun-worn man could discern three voices as he came to the stoop—two belonged to adults, the other to a lad.

As he stopped to listen, a loud crack shot from the cabin, sounding like a fist striking the face of another, followed by the thump of something falling to the cottage floor. A scream rose up, shrieking through the windows and cracks in the cottage walls—the wail of a woman. Then another crack . . . and silence.

The man's weathered face drew taut with grim lines. He ascended the stoop and pushed open the door.

Angry surprise registered on the face of a husband and father who stood panting at the room's center. On the floor to the right lay his woman, crying now, her head buried in her hands. On the left sat a boy of ten—the boy the weathered man had brought to this family long ago. The lad seemed to be struggling to suppress his anger and fear and helplessness. A heavy welt purpled one side of the boy's face, the skin there split. Blood dripped slowly down his cheek.

The lad shifted his gaze to the sun-worn visitor, and the two shared a long look. The man knew its message. The boy wanted to be rescued; this moment of anger and abuse was not the first. But any intervention would have to be permanent, because anything less would only invite more suffering after the visitor left the cottage.

The man sensed that the lad feared the time—perhaps when his father had had too much to drink—when the beating would be his last.

Indignation flooded the visitor as he shared that look with this father's son; a son he himself had given the man, had trusted to his care and safety.

He slowly turned his glare on the unworthy patriarch, who stared back with defiance.

"It is *my* family. I will do as *I* see fit," the abuser said. "You've no authority here. Get out!"

Instead, the visitor drew close, his limbs alive in anticipation of violence. He allowed his nearness to be his threat, staring, saying nothing. The abuser's breath reeked not of bitter, but of some recent meal; this cruelty had no reason. As the visitor looked deep into the abuser's eyes, he also looked inward at the long years of his own life abused in a forsaken place. Those years had given rise to another breed of malice and intolerance: one directed at low men like this, men who defiled the stewardship entrusted to them by denying their families the patience and kindness they deserved.

"Do you know how close you are to death?" the sun-worn man said. "I've no care for your life at this moment. Were it not for the family you've thrown down at your feet, I would end you here."

The abuser did not yield his own ire. "I don't owe you anything. I have fed and clothed and housed my own well enough these many years. Don't you show up and play the hero. I have my own way of keeping things right around here. And you gave up any part of it the day you left the brat." His eyes darted to the lad. "So you can take yourself back to your desert, and hope I don't share ill news of you with those who would see your visits here as a violation of your sentence."

The visitor shook his head in disgust and leaned in toward the man so that his nose nearly touched the other's. "You are a fool. If I am the criminal you suggest, what makes you believe I won't kill you to silence your gossip? And if I am not, then your threat is empty."

"You possess a double tongue," the abuser shouted back. "I will not be trapped—"

"It is this family that is trapped," the weathered man cut in. "Bound to you for sustenance and protection. But instead you feed them knuckles and fear, when they would have the better part of you to learn and grow by." The visitor's wrath seethed in his words. "You are more use to them dead than alive. For then at least their fear will be gone, and hope may enter their hearts."

The abuser sneered. "Hope?"

"The last victim of every prison," the visitor replied. In his mind he felt a thousand hot suns upon his cheeks and brow, tasted the dust and grit of his barren home, and recalled the countless children he'd carried into the care of others, bearing the simultaneous hope and fear that he was making the right choice of their guardianship.

With profound sadness and resentment—some of it at himself—he recalled that he had found others before today who had betrayed his trust, who had laid hands on the innocents he had entrusted to them.

If his banishment could be more bitter, it was in moments such as these when the only good of it was sullied by the neglect and abuse visited on the children he'd left to such men.

And it was in these moments that the soil of his heart grew stonier, when he sought—with all his training from so long ago (honed by decades of practice since)—not to protect, but to destroy.

Destroy a monster that would harm his own family.

With that thought, guilt pricked at the edges of his consciousness, but he would not let it stop him.

The weathered man gave the boy another long look. "Which is this man's strong arm?"

The lad's brow wrinkled. "His right," he answered.

The visitor then seized the abuser and ran him from the cottage. The other had no time to react or defend himself. With his precise, powerful grip, the weathered man steered the derelict father deep into the trees and out of sight. The abuser protested loudly, swearing oaths and calling for help. His cries echoed back into the grove and were lost around knotted trunks and deep ravines.

Then the weathered man let him loose, his indignation boiling over.

The abuser whirled, whipping a fist around at the visitor's head. The sun-worn man ducked and struck the man's chest, knocking the wind from him.

But the abuser did not give up so easily. He kicked at the man's groin. Again the weathered man avoided the blow and drove a crushing fist into the abuser's cheek—the same place the boy had been hit.

The other howled in pain and frustration, his eyes bright with rage.

But the man of so many suns had lost his patience. He barreled the man to the ground, and in one lithe motion drew out his sword and cut off the man's right arm.

As the abuser screamed in shock and pain, the visitor quickly cut off a swath of the man's shirt and used it to stanch the flow of blood spurting from the stump of his arm. He then tied it off and stood up. The abuser groaned and cried for some time; the weathered man watched with unfeeling eyes.

When he thought he could be heard again over the abuser's softer cries, the visitor took up the severed arm and held it between them. "You will either redeem yourself with the arm I've left you, or I will come again and find you. Don't fool yourself that you can take your vengeance on your family and run. There is no place far enough I cannot track you. And I have no other cause in life. If you ever trusted in anything, you can trust in that."

The man who wore the skin of many suns and winds and skies then tossed the arm into the high grass and returned to the small home. He paused at the steps again, considering what he would say to those inside. But that was a brief moment, since he now knew only one way to speak, even to a woman and child.

He strode in and found the boy comforting his mother, who had gotten herself to a chair. He knelt before her, holding her hands. The weathered man took one knee beside them, and sought their frightened eyes.

"He will never lay another hand on you. And if ever you fear he might, remind him of this day." He then fixed his gaze on the lad. "You're going to be all right, son. I am sorry for what has gone before. But even that will give you mettle when you are grown, if you use it well."

The sun-worn man put a hand on the boy's shoulder to reassure him. Then he stood, nodded to them both, and returned to the road that had brought him to this shattered home.

• CHAPTER EIGHTEEN •

Sedagin

They rode hard for three days through storms. The downpour discouraged talk; they either rode, ate, or slept. Little more. They were exhausted, but to Sutter, it was a good kind of weary.

The late-afternoon sun emerged, replacing the clouds that drifted south, carrying the storm away. Sutter closed his eyes and relished the feel of the warmth upon his cheeks. Birds bathed and drank from pools of water that had collected in the road. Ravens and crows squawked and flew away as they passed, returning to the puddles behind them.

It had been days since he had dug a root, at least voluntarily. And his nails looked great!

In the light of day, their run-in with the League seemed to him like a dream. A magnificent dream! The fire from Vendanj's hand, the clash of steel from the gate tower, and the drumming of rain and hooves and thunder all felt very far away as they walked their mounts over the sodden road and listened to the stirrings of the wild around them. A weary peace settled over them, all save Mira, who never seemed in need of rest. As they continued north under a bright sun, chatter ceased completely.

At the close of the day, the road forked, one path turning northeast, the other due west. Vendanj took neither route, instead leading them straight ahead into the dense trees, away from the traveled roads. He did not stop until the constellation of Kittel the ox had risen up from the watery grave legends confined her to each day. Mira left Tahn and Sutter to build the fire on their own, and returned quickly with three hares for supper. Not to be outdone, Sutter searched the soil and dug up several wild roots to roast over the flames. They ate quietly, sitting close to the fire as the chill of night pressed in upon them, the clear skies with all their stars feeling especially close and brittle in the cold.

When they were done, Mira stood and quietly took a position near a tree thirty strides from their bedrolls. Tahn watched the Far as she wrapped her thick, grey cloak tightly about her, and sat in the crook of a double trunk pinion tree. Ceasing to move, she became difficult to see.

Sutter's friend was smitten. Good for him.

Sutter had something else on his mind. "What of the boy?" he finally asked, his words jarring in the silence that had befallen them.

"Ask me," the lad said. "My name is Penit. I'm right here."

Wendra smiled and shook her head reprovingly at Sutter.

"All right, then. How did you come to be sitting on a horse fleeing the League and not staying with your friends back there in the city?"

"Truly a mystery," Tahn broke in. "Where might he have spent his night if the League had offered their hospitality?"

"Where indeed," Braethen said.

The boy cleared his throat. "I'm ten, not deaf."

Sutter turned to the boy. "I just mean, where's your family? Do you have parents? Aren't they going to be worried? We all started riding through the rain and no one stopped to think about that."

Tahn decided he agreed with Sutter. "Sutter's not making a joke of this," Tahn added. "A child has family, or should. If Penit has one, we shouldn't be interfering."

Penit nodded appreciatively. "I've got no one. Just the pageant wagons. And it's getting harder to play the stories. The troupe was only going to survive if we did well in Myrr. There's not enough money in the smaller villages anymore, and the larger cities all have the League. You were there," the boy said, looking at Sutter. "You saw what almost happened. Everyone in the troupe thought the rhea-fols important to portray, but it gets hard on an empty stomach. A scop must get paid. And besides, he asked me to join you." The boy gestured toward Vendanj. "I've got no one else, what do I care?"

Wendra frowned, but refashioned her expression into a smile of welcome for Penit. "It's nice to have you along."

Tahn and Sutter frowned as well. Each for his own reasons felt a fatherless child was an unhappy thing. For Sutter, especially, it brought up old, painful memories that this fatherless waif had come to them from a pageant wagon. Memories of his own true parents . . .

"I'd like to see you play the stories, Penit," Braethen chimed in.

Sutter groaned.

"I don't mind. So long as there's food enough for me," the lad said, and looked away as if to end the focus of attention on himself.

"Uh-huh," Sutter harrumphed.

Wendra broke the silence. "Do we put the boy in danger, Vendanj? Brave or not, this is no place for a child."

The Sheason put down the last of his meal, and looked across the fire at her. "It was his choice to join us," Vendanj said, appearing to feel as though his answer was all the explanation that was required. Then he added, "Penit, if you choose to stay with us, when we get to Recityv you and I will talk about what that means. You are welcome to remain with us beyond there if we are agreed on that."

Penit nodded. "Fine by me."

"So he joins us. But what are we doing?" Sutter challenged.

Vendanj gave the root-digger a narrow look. "You are constantly putting us in danger with your foolishness," Vendanj answered. "All is not as it was in the Hollows, Sutter. Watch closely."

Sutter's jaw flexed, but he controlled his anger and said in an even voice, "You helped us escape the Bar'dyn, and we're all grateful. And no one here is happier than I am to be out of the Hollows. But I'm worried that you expect to meet more trouble; if that's true, and you're not telling us, that puts us at greater risk."

Vendanj turned understanding eyes toward Sutter. "That is the first wise thing you've said, Sutter." Then the Sheason gathered their attention with his discerning gaze.

"You know our destination is Recityv. It is the seat of the regent." He received a number of blank stares, which seemed to await more. "Though she has no authority over your homeland of Reyal'Te, she rules the nation of Vohnce. And during the War of the First Promise it was in Recityv that most of the kingdoms of the eastlands formed an alliance to meet the threat of the Quiet. That convocation created the First Promise itself."

Vendanj frowned. "What is not told in your reader's tales is that many kingdoms did not join the War of the First Promise. And the Convocation of Seats lost generations of its youth to war. The First Promise did survive the Craven Season, and the Quiet was defeated. But in the countless years that came after, the Promise was lost. People forgot or, in the absence of any threat from the Quiet, no longer cared.

"Thankfully," Vendanj said, "the veil was sealed. The Shadow of the Hand lay dormant for a time; but its inhabitatants languished in their own scorn and discord . . . and waited.

"Ages later, the Hand was opened again, and hastily the defunct Convocation of Seats was recalled. Because the First Promise had been abandoned by the family of man, Dannan the Elder opened his shirt, drew his blade across his chest, and spilled his blood in the Great Hall of Promise at Recityv, uttering the words of the Second Promise, the New Oath. It is said that those seated at the table rushed to christen their swords with his blood and stand with Dannan till vanquish or void."

"And they vanquished, right?" Sutter interjected, his voice now bright with enthusiasm.

"Indeed they did." The Sheason touched one hand to his chest above his heart in an unconscious gesture as he appeared to reflect on the victory. "But that war cost dearly. Women who did not themselves fight bore children and raised them to join their fathers and brothers fighting in the farthest reaches of the North.

"The end came with a terrific battle. So powerfully did the Order of Sheason draw upon the Will that the earth itself was rent in twain. A hundred Sheason joined hands to force the land to swallow up the hordes of the Quiet in the Valley of Sorrow. Every last Sheason thus linked fell dead at the violent calling of the rent. But the Bar'dyn were destroyed, and the Quietgiven that survived withdrew to wait upon another day."

Vendanj paused as though assessing whether to share what came next.

"But balance had been upset, the stability of Forda I'Forza. The Hand had weakened enough to permit the darker creations from deep inside the Bourne into the world. And we have been living on this side of the veil ever since . . . waiting."

"And now the Bar'dyn have come as far as the Hollows," Sutter said.

"The Hand is open again," Braethen said in horrified awe.

"And whatever or whoever they seek is safer at Recityv." The Sheason looked at both Wendra and Tahn.

"Can any kingdom be safe?" Wendra asked, standing protectively behind Penit.

Vendanj nodded with appreciation of the sentiment. "The convocation has been dormant for generations. Even during the Mal Wars they did not reunite; a dozen disparate banners flew, and unrest between factions threatened the success of turning back the Quiet. But," he said, a hint of hope in his voice, "the regent has called again the Convocation of Seats."

A new question formed in Sutter's mind. "Is there to be a Third Promise? Is war upon us?"

The Sheason smiled gently, something he did more rarely than even the Far. "There is no need of another promise, Tahn. Only for men to keep those they've made." He paused, looking at each of them in turn, his searching eyes considering, weighing. "I know I ask much of you. And while you've exercised your own will to be here, it is not easy. There is more I would tell you, but the time is not right. I ask you to trust me. To accept that knowing certain things before it is prudent to reveal them would put us all at greater risk. Trust that I will not lead you down a false path." In a much gentler tone he said, "We will be safe, if we choose well. But neither will it be easy. Every day this journey will grow more difficult. You will despair, and some of you may even turn back."

For a long time, only the sound of the fire could be heard.

Sometime later, Vendanj spoke again. "I will trust you with this: Before we reach Recityv, we will visit the Scarred Lands. We will talk more of it later, to prepare. For now, if you have stories of this place, call them to mind and remember their warnings. It is a dire land that I would rather avoid, but cannot."

Sutter had heard of this place, known commonly as the Scar. But all he could remember was a vague sense of emptiness and despair. *Just what we all need right now!*

"How about a story, Penit?" Braethen finally said, clearly trying to steer conversation away from such dark topics. "I wasn't in the square to see you play a part. And you've promised us a fancy."

Penit smiled. "My pleasure. What would you like to see?"

"How about something about the Scarred Lands," Sutter jested, helping Braethen lighten the mood.

He then looked at the boy, and wondered if, in another life, he would have been Penit, if he would have been fatherless, playing for bread and cups. The dark thought threatened to ruin the good humor he was helping to invite.

"How about the Great Defense of Layosah," Penit said. "It's one of my favorites." He clapped his hands together twice. "Layosah it is," he announced, his voice falling to a deeper pitch than Sutter thought possible from the boy's small frame.

Wendra looked eager with anticipation of the tale. Vendanj sat back, his features thoughtful, as though still reflecting on the previous conversation. Braethen nodded appreciatively, and seemed to remember (too late) the story's essence, or else he might have tried to stop it.

Tahn looked again for Mira. Her shape was lost in the shadows beyond the firelight. He left the company of the fire to seek the Far. Searching the darkness for her familiar face, Tahn approached the tree where he'd last seen her.

From the stillness, he heard, "You give me away by coming on so directly."

Tahn stopped. "I did not mean . . . I will go back." He turned to go.

"Did you need something?"

Her voice was controlled, low. Tahn finally saw her through the charcoal hues of early evening. "No, nothing. You just always sit alone away from the fire. I thought you—"

"Thank you. I am comfortable. You may join me," she finished. Tahn wanted to say something more, but found no words that wouldn't sound clumsy. Instead, he looked up at Kittel and traced her outline among the spray of stars.

Behind him, Penit declaimed in a bold voice, "Do you not see the families driven from their homes? The Quiet is making refugees of the people, and they flood to every safe town or city, seeking safety. The food runs out and the people starve or riot. City arbors reek of the unbathed. Granaries are being ravaged. The streets are filled with every unsavory practice. Children forced into whore dens. All to survive while you send unprepared armies to die!"

Penit became a silhouette against the fire, gesturing and pacing, pointing and covering his heart with his hands.

Tahn, distracted by the lad's bold speech, turned back to face Mira. "I saw you grab the boy and spring from the wagon at the courtyard in Myrr. I've never seen anyone move so quickly."

A warm chuckle came from the shadow where Mira sat. "How many Far have you known, woodsman?"

"And now the largest legions out of the Bourne march into the east." Penit's voice echoed behind them. "And so I ascend these stairs of the great Halls of Solath Mahnus in the free city of Recityv, as one of King Baellor's Wombs of War whose grandmother's sons and mother's sons have gone to fight this enemy and fallen."

Tahn stepped closer so that he might discern Mira's face in the darkness. "One," he answered, indicating her. "But in the Hollows little is known of the Far. Even the readers do not often talk of your people. Braethen's books seem to have only passing references. We thought them legends and myths, and yet here you are."

Mira's grey eyes caught a reflection of the fire behind. "Here I am," she echoed.

"And I stand here," came Penit's strong, young voice. "On these chiseled steps with the child whose life I carried in my womb." Penit raised his hands high as though holding aloft a small child. "I stand here, denied an audience by King Sechen Baellor the Swift. Denied a hearing, though my family's blood has purchased this city's freedoms. I lift my child here and call upon you to form a council to represent *all* the people."

Tahn was suddenly grateful for the dark. Perhaps his awkwardness would not be so evident. "You said before, when the raven came, that you would have a choice to make. What choice?"

"It is not for us to talk about at this time," Mira answered. "Maybe never. But I am grateful for your concern."

He sat down with her, watching. "That was genuine. Not subtle."

"I know," she said.

. . .

Penit's voice came again, loud but tremulous, as if filled with the spirit of Layosah. "Or else I should rather dash my babe on this stone stair and snuff her life, than see her grow and bear another generation to go to war!"

It was clear that these weren't just sketches to the boy. Something of the valor and integrity in them surely must mean something to him personally.

"Well done, lad," Braethen said, his own voice soft, reverential. "Layosah's speech brought about the Convocation of Seats that ended the First War of Promise. She was a remarkable woman."

Wendra seemed not to hear. The wound for Wendra was too fresh, but the boy, Sutter knew, could not have known that. Still, Sutter's heart ached seeing Wendra in pain.

Vendanj looked away into the hills behind them, his brow a tangle of deep furrows over dark eyes.

For Sutter, the scene felt like the rub of salt on an old wound newly opened—the awful moment when he was orphaned. Despite being so far removed from the memory—by years and by distance (so far from the Hollows now)—it seared him still, his skin hot despite the chill on the air.

Of them all, that night, Sutter was last to fall asleep.

Tahn woke to the vague and distant sound of drums. He lay unmoving, the smell of frozen earth strong in his nose. At first he thought the sound was the beating of his own heart echoing in his ears, pulsing the way it did when he swam in the Huber River back home, diving under the water, the beating loud in his head. Then he recalled the reader's story of Nicholae's Drum—a pauper boy's toy that had, over the ages, become known as a mythic weapon.

But this rhythm pulsed out of time with his heart.

Tahn pushed himself up and looked around. Only Vendanj stirred. Tahn looked instantly to where Mira stood watch: the tree was empty. Vendanj rose and quietly woke the rest of them. Tahn stood and looked skyward. The lesser light hung near the high meridian; the dawn was still several hours away. Vendanj rolled his blanket. Tahn and the others took his silent direction and, beneath the silver shadows of the moon, they packed without speaking.

The drumming grew louder. Though they beat in unison, Tahn could now hear several drums, the sound repeating at long intervals from the road to the west which they had left. The incessant, monotonous beating unnerved him. If they returned to the road, the Bar'dyn would find them; the open country to the north led directly into a towering escarpment that ran east and west, in both directions farther than he could see. Tahn guessed the plateau above them led to the High Plains of Sedagin—a place of more legends about which he knew little.

Mira stepped into their midst, her face pale in the starlight. "Bar'dyn," she said to Vendanj. "An entire collough led by a tracker commanding an advance party. They are close." She paused, looking back the way she had come. "Closer than the drums."

"Sedagin, then," Vendanj said in a low voice.

"The Sedagin ceded too long ago," Mira countered. "The only thing longer than their blades is their memory. We may not be welcome."

Tahn saw Braethen nodding, though the sodalist kept silent.

The sound of movement interrupted them. Mira wheeled silently, drawing both blades in a deft cross-arm move. Before Tahn could turn, she had taken a position between the trees and the rest of the party. Vendanj came slowly past Tahn and stood beside Mira as four hulking figures stepped from the trees like shadows leaving the darkness. Beside them, a smaller, crippled-looking figure stood hunched, leaning on a short staff just a few strides away—the tracker.

A withered hand crept from the folds of its cloak, each bony finger wrapped tightly by translucent skin through which could be seen a lattice of blue veins. Then it pulled back its cowl, revealing a hairless head covered with the same strange skin. The tissue beneath ran in striated lines over gnarled bone. Its bulging eyes reminded Tahn of a dead animal bloated from several days' rot.

Tahn's breath hung on the air in a thin cloud. The sodalist stepped in front of Penit, but no one else moved, and for a moment, the small clearing might have been a court statue garden.

Into the quiet the hunched tracker croaked, "Did we wake you?" Tahn, peering through the darkness, saw the thick, tough skin of the Bar'dyn, their massive hands bearing a talonlike thumb on both sides of their palms. Most of them held large, double-sided axes. The last one in the line held a drum at its side and a mallet in its right hand. But neither the size nor their weapons frightened Tahn as much as the look of patient reason in their broad faces.

Again the crippled-looking thing spoke, its voice like the grinding of small stones. "Why do you flee?" it asked. It stepped forward, pointing its short staff at Vendanj. "Nola Will, Sheason, now and always." A sallow gleam opened in the thing's face where crooked teeth reflected the faint light.

Vendanj knelt down on one knee, and Tahn thought momentarily that the Sheason intended to yield. Vendanj turned his head slightly, whispering. Tahn only heard it because he stood directly behind Mira. "Don't let it strike that drum."

"Yes," Mira said softly. "But the rest will not be able to see to use their weapons when it begins." Her head nodded toward Tahn and the others behind her.

Vendanj shifted his hard gaze again to the tracker. "No," he said, his response calm, steady, peaceful. Then the Sheason swung one hand into the earth, his fingers tearing like iron tines at the cold, hard ground. He lifted a fistful of soil and tossed it into the air with a great sweep of his arm. The dirt erupted into shimmering dust, which hung on the air as particles of light illuminating the clearing. In that same instant, Mira crossed the distance to the Bar'dyn holding the drum and severed the leather strap used to carry it. The drum fell uselessly to the ground.

The tracker screeched with its wretched voice, "Velle'shea!" The Bar'dyn burst from their stances and charged them. Wendra grabbed Penit and retreated to the far side of the clearing. Braethen, drawing his sword, readied himself for their charge. Sutter lifted his own sword and crouched. Tahn briefly worried he would never again see his friend's gritty courage.

He raised his bow and drew an arrow quickly, internally speaking the old words *I draw with the strength of my arms* . . . and fired almost randomly at the large creatures. He let fly three shots. The first two glanced off the armorlike skin of the Bar'dyn. The third took one in the eye, stopping its charge.

The tracker threw a knife at Vendanj. The Sheason saw the attack coming and thrust up one hand. A sudden gust of wind felled the knife in mid-flight and blew the tracker off its feet.

The Bar'dyn nearest Mira swung its ax in a huge downward stroke. The Far sidestepped the blow and brought her swords up in quick counterstrikes to the beast's groin. When the Bar'dyn fell to its knees, Mira put her second blade through its teeth. The Given slumped forward. She turned immediately to the one who'd been carrying the drum, and narrowly dodged a waist-high stroke. The Bar'dyn swung past her, and Mira attacked its wrist with her blades so closely swung that they appeared to be a single sword. The Bar'dyn dropped his weapon, but countered with a blow from its taloned hand. Mira slumped into a back roll, regained her feet, and caught the beast's other wrist in a similar strike. The Bar'dyn howled and threw its massive body toward the Far, wanting to smother her beneath its immense girth. Again, she was too quick, leaping aside as the Bar'dyn crashed into the undergrowth. She jumped to the beast's back, rotating her swords in a blur, then plunged them into the creature's neck.

One of the Bar'dyn brought its huge ax up and swept it down toward Braethen. The sodalist retreated, one edge of the Given's weapon catching him on the arm. A spray of blood hit the Bar'dyn, maddening it further. Before it could draw back to strike again, Braethen pushed his sword forward with both hands in a straight thrust for the Bar'dyn's belly. The stroke pierced the skin, but the Bar'dyn uttered no cry. It grasped the sword by its blade and ripped it from Braethen's hands. The creature tossed the sodalist's blade aside and swung its ax around for a final blow.

Instantly, Sutter rushed in. He threw himself on the beast's arms, overburdening its attack. The Bar'dyn dropped its ax and clutched at Sutter, sinking massive hands into his flesh and throwing him down. The creature raised its foot over Sutter's head and was about to crush his skull. Before it could do so,

Braethen retrieved his blade and brought it down into the Bar'dyn's face, sending the beast reeling.

A second Bar'dyn charged Tahn. With no time to draw another arrow, Tahn took several steps back. The Bar'dyn bore down upon him, holding its ax in a wide grip. Tahn lifted his bow as though to strike the Bar'dyn, but knew the futility in it. When the Bar'dyn was just a stride from him, it erupted in flame. Red fire scorched its skin, and an awful-smelling smoke rose from the creature in black waves. The Bar'dyn opened its mouth to scream, but the flames licked at its tongue and teeth and muffled the cry in its throat.

Mira fell upon the Bar'dyn Sutter and Braethen had wounded, slaying it from behind before it knew what had happened. The last of the Given snapped the arrow that had pierced its eye, and looked with its other eye at the fire engulfing its companion. With that, the creature turned and lumbered off into the darkness.

The light in the air began to dissipate slightly as the dust settled. Rasping breath filled the air, but over the sound of labored breathing Tahn could hear the distant beat of drums.

Then, just beyond the clearing, someone struck the drum the Bar'dyn had been carrying. *The tracker!* And struck it again. The sound rose in a penetrating bass note that carried farther than any scream or cry might. In response, the chorus of drums farther south beat twice in quick succession.

"Your horses!" Vendanj commanded.

Tahn jumped on Jole and the others mounted their steeds. Mira rushed in from the dark as the last of the light dust disappeared. Sheathing her swords, she jumped in stride onto her horse, and turned an inquiring look at Vendanj. The Sheason did not hesitate. "North," he said. "To the Sedagin."

Mira nodded and kicked Solus into a gallop. Vendanj waved for the rest of them to follow, and took the rear position behind Braethen. Shapes rose up and slipped by in a blur: trees, large rock outcroppings. Tahn rode hard through the weave of foliage and knolls and sudden dips in the land.

The drums grew louder, each beat sounding to Tahn as though it was joined by still more mallets upon tightly drawn hide. The night air chilled his cheeks and hands, making them throb. He looked back at Wendra, who rode beside the boy, and found fierce determination on both their faces. Past them, he saw Sutter actually smiling thinly in the starlight. That was when he saw them. Just over Vendanj's shoulder several shapes were crashing through the trees. Saplings snapped under their feet, their footfalls like large stones rolling down a hill.

"Vendanj!" Tahn called, and pointed.

"Ride!" the Sheason shouted.

Tahn turned forward and saw Mira twenty horse-lengths ahead, jumping a ravine with Solus at a dead run.

Dear Sky, Tahn thought.

"Don't slow!" Mira called back. "Trust your mount!"

Tahn bent forward and spoke in his horse's ear; Jole raced ahead. "Come on, old friend. Dash!" Something quickened in Jole's legs and before Tahn could say more, the horse leapt into the air. The world felt suspended and silent. The chasm beneath them was deeper than Tahn expected, but they passed it quickly and Jole's hooves caught earth again, never slowing.

Penit's horse made the jump easily with its lighter burden, as did Wendra's. Behind them, torches flickered in the woods, and the sound of crashing branches came like a whir of droning crickets ten thousand strong.

Sutter came next, lashing his mount's rump before the leap. Up and over he came, yawping loudly as though initiating the Kottel Rhine back home. His gleeful cry was met with unearthly calls from the Bar'dyn just fifty strides behind Vendanj. Braethen came on, gathering his reins in both hands to steel himself for the jump. The sodalist's horse misjudged the slight pull on its reins and began to pull up as they approached the ravine. Dirt kicked up from the steed's hooves, and it whinnied loudly, spitting clouds of steam from its nostrils into the chill air.

"No!" Tahn screamed, pulling Jole around.

In an instant Mira was beside him. She grabbed Jole's reins and pulled Tahn close. "Vendanj said north. He knows the cost!"

She tried to yank Jole back into a run. But Jole faithfully obeyed Tahn, who used his legs to direct the animal toward the ravine.

Near the crevasse, Braethen's steed locked its front legs and slid toward the drop. The earth at the edge was loose, and the horse began to tumble into the ravine. The animal kicked furiously against its slide, and managed to steady itself. Vendanj came on, watching the struggle but preparing to make the jump. It seemed the Sheason intended to leave the sodalist to the closing Bar'dyn. Looking past them, Tahn saw small trees falling like a wooden wave in the Bar'dyn's passage toward them. The drums grew more frantic, beating out polyrhythmic cadences that began to confuse Tahn and confound his mind.

Tahn turned to Mira, beginning to frame a plea for assistance. Wendra, Penit, and Sutter reached them and slowed, following Tahn's concerned gaze back toward the crevasse.

Sutter saw it immediately. "Tahn, we can't leave him!"

Nails wheeled and headed back toward the ravine. Tahn tried to follow, but Mira held Jole's reins firmly. Then something locked deep inside him, a clear feeling that calmed his heart. He cupped his hands beside his mouth to throw his voice, and yelled, "No, Vendanj!"

Tahn's call rose powerfully, and the Sheason seemed to sense something in Tahn's voice. He immediately pulled Suensin to a stop. Vendanj turned to face the advancing Bar'dyn, who were but twenty strides from them now. At least a dozen of the figures rushed toward him without slowing.

"Help him!" Vendanj called. He clasped his hands and lifted his face to the sky. Sutter came to the ravine and jumped it again, yelping with delight as he had before. He jumped from his horse and extended his hand to the sodalist. Just strides away, the air began to rush in toward Vendanj, red and violet particles streaming toward him with increasing speed. Soon they were streaks of yellow and white, and it appeared as if the air itself were gathering inside him.

The Sheason unlaced his fingers and extended them toward the ground in front of him. Great shocks of lightning shot from his fingertips, lighting the ground in a blanket of popping, sizzling energy. The lightning brought the Bar'dyn to an abrupt stop, but not before it caught the first several in its field. The lightning leapt up their massive frames, coursing down their arms and racing around their bodies like a living thing. The smell of burning flesh filled the air, and great howls of anguish accompanied the searing sound of the earth-bound storm.

The sodalist took Sutter's hand, ripping his satchel from his steed's saddle just as the horse went over into the crevasse. Braethen's legs dangled in the air, and Tahn heard the horse land with a heavy crash at the bottom of the drop.

"Let go of the bag, Braethen!" Sutter cried. "I need your other hand to pull you out!"

"No!" the sodalist argued.

Sutter's grip slipped. He thrust his other arm over the precipice and grasped Braethen's wrist. "I can't hold you much longer!"

The sodalist looked down, then back at Sutter, but still did not release his satchel.

Vendanj jumped from Suensin and ran to the edge. He put his hand over Sutter's and in one motion, pulled the sodalist from the crevasse.

"Mount!" he yelled.

The Sheason jumped on his own steed, which sidled close to the edge of the drop, and, from a standstill, leapt the ravine.

Once Sutter and Braethen were saddled and ready to move, Sutter's face drew dark with concern. Their horse would never make the jump double-burdened. The Sheason came around, brought clenched fists to his chest, and began to fold his arms in and push with his chest, as a man does to pull a heavy handcart. The earth trembled and quaked, and the sides of the crevasse began to draw close to each other. In the space of just breaths, the chasm had narrowed enough that when Sutter kicked Bardoll, the horse jumped it with ease. Vendanj fell forward in his saddle. Mira left Tahn and raced to the Sheason. She pulled him from his horse and sat him in front of her atop Solus. She spoke directly to the Sheason's steed, which began to run north.

"Go!" she called to the rest. "Follow Suensin!"

They turned without question and pushed their mounts northward into the trees. Tahn didn't know how long they ran before the horses tired and finally stopped altogether. The sound of drums fell off behind them to a faint pulse that might easily have been their own ragged breath. Tahn climbed down off Jole and fell to the ground, exhausted.

He closed his eyes and turned to the east. It was more difficult than ever to think about the day, the light, but he remembered the calm hues of dawn and the reawakening of birds to the morn, and peace came over him, if only for a moment.

Mira stood guard at the south end of the small clearing where they'd stopped, but Vendanj lay unmoving at the feet of his horse, where he'd collapsed after the Far had helped him down from her saddle. Braethen sat close to the Sheason, his sword in hand. When Tahn's heart found its own ryhthm again, he sat up. The faintest touches of dawn had crept into the sky. Looking north, he could see where the High Plains rose dramatically in sheer cliffs to an immense bluff that stretched to the horizon in both directions.

Sedagin, another tale from the reader's books.

Suddenly, the crack of a drum shattered the silence, sounding as though it were right among them. Tahn rose on shaky legs, but did not believe he and the others could flee farther. They'd scarcely caught their breath. Vendanj did not rise.

"Mount!" Mira cried.

Sounds of the thrashing of undergrowth and trees snapping again filled the air. Before the rest could rise, six Bar'dyn emerged into the south end of the clearing. The sound of rough laughter coughed from one of the Bar'dyn.

"Run, run, run, you do," the Bar'dyn said. "Weak and slow. Foolish."

Mira raced to face them, silently drawing her swords and taking a low stance. Tahn marveled that she didn't look fatigued.

"One woman to fight for you," the same Bar'dyn said. "What of your Sheason?" Another laugh spat from its thick lips as it caught sight of Vendanj lying on the ground.

Braethen managed to get to his knees. He held his sword in front of him.

Sounding like a rock slide, a chorus of laughter erupted from the line of Bar'dyn. Then it abruptly stopped and their chieftain looked at Mira. "No one need die, Far."

"Never," she said. Tahn shuddered at the hatred in her voice.

"Velle'shea!" the Bar'dyn growled and its companions lifted their weapons.

As they did, a thrown sword shrieked through the clearing from the rear, burying itself in a tree a hand's length from one Bar'dyn head.

CHAPTER NINETEEN

Teheale

From all sides of the clearing, men appeared, each holding a blade like the one embedded in the tree near the Bar'dyn. The strangers took ready stances and rested their sword points lightly in the earth, each with hands relaxed confidently on the cross guard. At least twenty men could be seen, and Tahn sensed that others remained hidden in the trees, out of sight.

The Bar'dyn still looked implacable, but they eased their weapons back down, and retreated several steps.

"Not over, Sheason," the Bar'dyn said, looking at the still unconscious Vendanj. "We know where you are. Others will follow."

Then they vanished as quickly as they had come, their massive bodies forging new paths back through the thicket. The men around them made no move to advance, nor did they retreat. They wore heavy cloaks, some brown, some green, and each man carried only a large sword for a weapon. Beneath their cloaks, they wore thick, woolen shirts dyed a rich fir hue. They were tall men, and there wasn't one who had supped too indulgently at his dinner table.

Mira finally sheathed her swords. "Who speaks for you?" she asked.

"I do," said a man from the east. The fellow stepped out of the trees and into the clearing, then crossed to the sword embedded in the tree. He pulled it free and checked the blade, rubbing sap from the tip. He spun the blade once in his hand and sheathed it with expert skill. "I am Riven, First Blade to the Sedagin, and you are altogether too close to the High Plains."

Braethen reached beneath Vendanj's tunic and lifted the symbol of his necklace into the early light. "Safe Passage. For the First Promise," he said.

Riven's eyes widened at the sight of the pendant. The Sedagin First Blade looked quickly at Tahn and the others. Then he again set his watchful gaze on Braethen.

"Why are the Bar'dyn so far from the Shadow of the Hand, sodalist?" Riven asked.

"It is a fair question, but asked at an unwise time. These few you have scattered will return within the hour with a full collough," Braethen said. "And I fear there are more behind them. Our discussion, if had now, could be our last."

"We will take you into the High Plains. The Bar'dyn aren't likely to follow." Riven called three men to him. "Take the message ahead of us," he said to the first. "Make Sedagin aware of our guests, and find them beds." Riven turned to the second. "Take Henna, Elo, and Nittel and track the Bar'dyn. Learn their route and return to us. Go." The second man and three others disappeared into the trees to the south.

The third he commanded to build a litter to carry the Sheason. Tahn and Braethen assisted.

Riven pointed north and the remaining Sedagin disappeared into the trees, heading toward the High Plains. Retrieving a horse hidden north of the clearing, Riven took the lead. Less than a thousand horse-lengths farther, their path began to ascend the great bluff of the Sedagin. They followed a serpentine route that gave Tahn a clear view out over the meadows and plains beneath them. The land stretched on forever, divided by small rivers and showing itself in patches of cultivated earth and untouched wilderness. Distant smoke issued from a farmhouse, and the path of the road could be seen snaking west and northeast. Upward they rode, save Vendanj, who lay on the litter.

Tahn understood now that the Sheason's every use of the Will exacted a great price. And when he looked at Vendanj, it seemed the lines in his face were that much deeper.

When they reached the plateau, Tahn noted that the High Plains were perfectly described, as though the earth had risen straight up, rather than most mountains' gradual slopes and juts. Sutter grabbed Tahn and drew him to the edge, which dropped away a sheer five hundred strides.

"Look at it," Sutter exclaimed with awe. "Have you ever seen such a thing? If I look hard enough, I can convince myself that I'm seeing the Soren Sea."

A haze spread across the land far below. At the horizon one could imagine the vague, hazy blue to be the great sea, though Tahn knew better. But as they stood there, the wind began to howl up the face of the great cliff like an ocean gale.

"The winds that rise off the lowlands are strong, my friend," Riven said. "We call them the voice of the Sedagin."

Behind them, Braethen retrieved the wooden case from Vendanj's inner pocket and placed a sprig on the Sheason's tongue. A moment later, the Sheason sat up, thanked the sodalist, and took to his horse. They followed the path north through patches of needle trees and conifers, low scrub and quaking aspen. Most of the plains, though, were long, empty fields of knee-high grass. Gentle breezes blew across them, causing them to undulate like slow, green waves.

Toward midday they paused to drink at a small river that wended its way across a great open field. "It is clean," Riven exclaimed. "Fill your skins and drink deeply."

"It's like a separate world up here," Sutter said. He then lay on the river bank and put his lips into the cool, clear water.

It was too good an opportunity to pass up. Tahn pushed the root-digger's face under the current. Sutter kicked and pushed back against Tahn's hand, thrashing his face in the water. Penit laughed, Wendra and Braethen joining the boy as Tahn held his friend's head down.

"Any roots down there?" Tahn joked, then jumped back, ready for Sutter's counterattack.

Nails gasped as river mud shot from his nose and dripped from his chin.

"Woodchuck, you are going to see the soil side of my boot," Sutter challenged and jumped up, splashing in the shallow water of the river's edge.

Tahn laughed. "Is the world up here different in the river mud, too, Nails?"

Sutter smiled, mud running into his mouth and coating his teeth.

"You're going to see that up close yourself."

They began to circle in the grass, Penit cheering each of them when either feigned an attack.

"Actually, it is a part of our world, an old part," Braethen said.

Tahn stood, losing interest in the game. "An old part?" he asked. "What do you mean?"

Sutter seized the diversion, and tackled Tahn to the ground. Tahn let Nails pin him, distracted as the sodalist continued.

"This land was part of the rest of the plains around it, not rising into the high ground we see today.

"In the Age of Discord, the Sedagin longblades were the only ones who still kept the covenant of the First Promise. Holivagh i'Malichael presided over the Table of Blades. The table was known as the Right Arm of the Promise, and he took his banner into any kingdom or nation the Quietgiven marched upon.

"Holivagh never built a city of his own, though. He taught that the Promise was a constant call, and that his people must be always ready to defend it. Holivagh's people lived here, tended their fields and livestock here. But when the Table was called in to war, only a few were left behind to occupy and preserve their home."

Tahn and Sutter forgot to unravel themselves from their game. River mud dried on Sutter's face in the warmth of the sun. Penit and Wendra listened intently to Braethen. From the boy's expression, Tahn guessed the sodalist's story was one the boy had not heard.

"In the Age of Discord, the Shadow of the Hand lengthened. One of the powerful Velle called through the Hand the Maere; the Haelderod, known for its spread of contagion; and other creations not given names by the Great Fathers, creations never intended to descend into the land of men."

Braethen paused, looking into the clear sky, his face suddenly white and blotchy. "The scola say that out of the Bourne came beings older than these, some as old as the Great Fathers themselves."

Tahn's blood ran cold. Sutter fell off of him.

"It was against this movement that the Right Arm of the Promise was summoned," Braethen continued. "The Convocation of Seats was recalled at Recityv when the Tabernacle of the Sky fell to the Quiet. Representatives from nearly every nation, throne, principality, and sovereign city came to the convocation to ask for help.

"But those nobles and kings who came to Recityv would not commit entire armies to the cause, afraid to leave their homes undefended. Token regiments were offered to the regent as a pledge of good faith. The regent and the convocation met and debated for three days. Threats of secession from the alliance, accusation, threats of war among kingdoms, and personal maneuvers for advancement in the preeminence of the convocation marked the debate.

"The regent of Recityv, Corihehn, disbanded the convocation and issued the order to call upon Holivagh's Table.

"Corihehn sent word to Holivagh that the First Promise was given new life in a Second Promise, supported by the rulers of every principality represented at the Convocation of Seats. Holivagh was asked to send his legion into the fray against the storm of Quietgiven. The armies of the Second Promise would join them in due haste. The Second Promise was to build on the First by shutting up the Bourne forever, ending the shedding of blood by war and calling into the land civility and charity."

"Will and War," Tahn exclaimed in a whisper. "It was a lie."

"That it was," the sodalist affirmed. "Holivagh marched north the very hour he received the summons. He left only seven men behind to watch after the children and elderly and those women who did not bear a blade. The rest moved day and night into the breach at Darkling Plain. Forty thousand men and women armed with forty thousand swords, with as many Sheason as could be found, cut a path through the armies of the Velle toward the Shadow of the Hand. It is said that when they reached the mountain of the Hand, only two thousand remained. But this diminished army held the breach against the Bourne for eight days. Each day they expected reinforcements to arrive as Corihehn had guaranteed. The army of the Second Promise never came. And every bladesman who marched with Holivagh perished."

"But the war was won?" Sutter asked hopefully.

"When the Sheason realized that Corihehn had transgressed against the First Promise by sending its Right Arm to die, Del'Agio the Elder, the Randeur of the Sheason, sent his people into the courts of every known city. They threatened every regent, king, queen, and council with unnatural death if they did not pledge to honor the lie of Corihehn. It was known as the Castigation, both of the convocation and of the Order of the Sheason—since the Sheason were never supposed to invoke the Will as a weapon or means of compulsion upon mankind."

"Did they do it?" Penit stepped closer.

"They did, lad," Braethen said, smiling. "The Convocation of Seats reassembled. But one came *without* coercion, Dannan the Elder, King of Kamas, who had not been invited to the previous assembly due to rumors about the tyranny of his grandfather, Dannan the Stout Heart.

"In the Great Hall of Promise, the awful scandal of Corihehn's deception was recounted, earning him the title 'the Defamed.' Likewise, the demise of Holivagh's army was related. Hearing these things, Dannan stood and while reciting the words recorded on the writ avowing the Second Promise, he scored his own chest with his sword, sealing with his own blood the commitment of his throne. The realms would have gone to war on the threat of the Sheason. But it is said that with that single stroke, Dannan turned the hearts of men to their children, purpose replacing fear.

"A mighty army was raised, and its command was given to Holivagh's son, Sedagin, a boy just nine years of age. The Sheason went into battle alongside steel and wood, changing the Sheason order forever after—for no longer did they go only to heal—and the threat was put down, the Quiet destroyed or turned back into the Hand."

"Then what of these High Plains," Wendra asked. "How did they ascend into the sky?"

"When the war was over, Del'Agio the Younger gathered the Order of Sheason and journeyed into the fields and meadows of the High Plains. For one full cycle of the moon they linked hands and Willed the earth to move and rise. They built an earthen monument to the courage and honor of Holivagh and his Table. The High Plains are a testimony to the First Promise, and are said to show the distinction of its bearers above the frailties of those who sent them to die. In raising these plains, those Sheason gave the Sedagin a home easy to defend and as beautiful as anything I've ever seen.

"These plains are known as Teheale, which is thought to mean 'earned in blood' in the Language of the Covenant."

Tahn's heart thrummed in his chest, and he could see the excitement on Sutter's face. They all remained silent in reverence toward the sacrifice made thousands of years past.

Sutter broke the silence. "That is why they are called the Sedagin, isn't it? Because of the boy-king." He jumped up and wiped his face.

"Indeed." Riven nodded his approval. "And our lord bears that name still, in his honor."

CHAPTER TWENTY

Small Victories

Beyond a line of trees, the plain opened onto a cleared flat tract of closely cropped grass and neatly kept homes. Immediately to the left, hundreds of young boys stood in short lines before men who were demonstrating precise moves and attacks with the great swords the Sedagin carried. Their attention never drifted to Tahn and his companions. In turn, each boy executed the move and returned to the end of his line. The swords themselves were taller than their wielders, but the boys carried them and performed their drills without any apparent difficulty.

Farther to the right, a number of farms with penned sheep and cattle were being tended by men and women alike.

As they rode deeper into the plain, homes grew in number, wood-framed and modest in appearance. But it was the absence of street barkers that caught Tahn's attention. There were no handcarts filled with food or handmade trinkets; no beggars sat in the shadows of the buildings petitioning passersby. No loud, confusing din clouded the air, no smell of refuse rotting behind and between the homes and buildings.

"Not one house of bitter," Sutter suddenly said, riding beside Tahn.

A group of men standing beside a house was looking at them. Each wore a sword and exuded an air of calm confidence. As they continued down several lanes, they could see more of the Sedagin at their doors and windows and gathered in small groups outside, regarding the Sheason with a quiet respect.

They came to a stop at a particular house, and Tahn stepped off Jole at Riven's direction. His companions followed suit. No less than fifty Sedagin stood close by.

Sutter nudged him. "Did you notice that none of them looks like fat old Yulop?" He mimed a round belly in front of him.

The door of the house opened and a man emerged. His hair and eyes were the brown of brushed saddle leather. He, too, wore his long sword at his waist, but sported no cloak or cape. The other Sedagin bowed noticeably as he stepped outside, but Tahn could see nothing to distinguish him as their lord or king. The man made a quick survey of his guests, stopping to note their weapons. At a look, all the men dispersed, save a few who relaxed and began to talk quietly.

"Riven, my friend," the man said. "You always surprise me when you return from the lowlands." He offered a lopsided smile and stepped down from the short portico to the grass road.

Riven grinned and embraced the other. "I do at that, Sedagin, but this is different."

"Your advance has told me, but I suspect their report leaves the best of it unspoken."

Riven laughed. "You've a talent for understatement."

"Bring them in. Let us offer them rest and refreshment."

Riven motioned to a few of the men, who immediately came and took their guests' horses. "You are invited inside," Riven said. "Don't let the grass grow up under your boots."

Inside, a large room lay awash in sunlight from windows on every side. A sweet herbal tea steamed over the hearth to the left, giving the place a relaxed, homey feeling. Against the rear wall, sketches in charcoal of several men hung in a perfect line. Beneath each sketch, a sword stood buried in the wood floor. To each side of the door, bookcases reached to the ceiling.

"Please, be at ease," the Sedagin said.

"Thank you," Vendanj replied, and sat nearest the fire.

Riven brought chairs from another room, and they all sat as Sedagin watched patiently for them to be seated.

"It is a long time since a Sheason has been in the High Plains," the man said.

"Perhaps too long," Vendanj commented.

The other nodded. "I am Sedagin."

"I am Vendanj, bearer of the Will through Sheason."

"To come directly to it," Sedagin said, fixing his eyes on Vendanj, "the Quietgiven are come into the land again." He looked at each of them in turn. "And this time they chase *you*."

Vendanj followed the man's eyes, looking at his companions. "It is true," the Sheason confirmed. When the bladesman met Vendanj's gaze again, the Sheason spoke gravely. "We must reach Recityv. We thank you, as we do Riven and those in his charge, for assisting us this far. But we make no claim upon your honor, and we cannot stay long."

Sedagin shook his head as he lifted the teapot from the fire and began pouring several cups. "Any enemy of the Bar'dyn is an ally of ours. But what business has the Order of Sheason in Recityv, especially now that an entire collough of Bar'dyn is upon your trail?"

Vendanj took a cup from Sedagin, as did Mira and Tahn and the others. But he did not drink. He held his cup in his hands and stared long at Sedagin. Tahn knew what Vendanj would say, and how it would sound to this lord.

Finally, the Sheason spoke. "The Convocation of Seats has been recalled."

A grave look recast Sedgain's face; a very old wound shone in the man's eyes. Holding Vendanj's stare, he replied, "Why do you tell me this?" Tahn thought he heard some small challenge in the question.

Vendanj nodded. "Mark me. I did not intend to claim right of passage here. If a call to the Right Arm of the Promise is to be made, it will come from others than I."

"We will not answer," Sedagin said plainly. "We do not recognize anything that came, or will come, after the First Promise. You know why."

"Perhaps it is more than chance that brings us into your High Plain, Sedagin. It is not my place to ask anything. There are no declarations of war. There is no seal from the regent. But"—Vendanj gave the man a hard glare—"that time may come. And I would have you consider that the Quiet will reach every man's door if it comes into the east."

Sedagin looked at them each. "What business have you and your companions in Recityv that the Quiet track you?"

"These are not things I can discuss at this time," Vendanj answered.

A heavy silence followed. Then a warmer look returned to Sedagin's face. "We will talk more later. And I get ahead of myself. You must rest. Riven will find you beds, and food will be brought. Tonight a dinner will be held in your honor, Sheason, for the home your order bestowed upon us." The Sedagin lifted his own cup and drank a toast to the renderer.

"And in remembrance of your sacrifice for the First Promise," Vendanj replied.

"Just so," Sedagin said.

The sun danced on the treetops, filling the plain with golden hues and sepia shadows. To the west, over the roofs of homes smoke rose from several fires.

Men and women walked together in the same direction that Riven led Sutter and the others. At the edge of the community, the plain opened up onto a broad expanse of closely shorn grass. Large pits had been dug in the ground at intervals of nearly ten strides, each pit tiered and lined with stone. Great fires burned within them, and tables, covered with food and pitchers of drink, were set around the flames. Children chased one another about the tables, the sounds of their merriment lifting like the calls of morning birds.

Riven led them to a table near the fire where Sedagin sat holding a small girl on his lap.

"My daughter," he said as they approached. A woman came forward and took the girl from Sedagin. "And my love, Sonja," he finished, introducing her.

The woman bowed her head slightly. "You are welcome here," she said.

Sutter put a thumb in Tahn's back to get his Far-stricken friend to take note. Sonja was exquisitely beautiful.

"Let us begin," Sedagin announced. He went to the fire and raised a pole bearing the Sedagin banner. In turn, someone at each fire likewise raised the same standard. "Tonight, we celebrate the company of one who wears the symbol of the Sheason. And who in turn reminds us of our Oath."

The entire company fell silent. Even the children quieted. There was not a movement, not a cough or whisper. The eyes of all attended Sedagin. The leader of the Table of Blades waited patiently for something. In the moments that followed, Sutter realized why Sedagin waited. Presently, the sun dipped completely below the horizon, and blue shadows fell across them. Sutter could hear only the fires and felt the pride and reverence of these people in the profound silence.

Sedagin lifted his cup. "Drink now," he said. "And enjoy this moment of peace."

Every glass was lifted in the twilight, and all drank. Then Sutter and his companions were seated at Sedagin's table. Riven sat with them, and together they feasted on the grand meal set before them. Night came on, lighting the sky with brilliant stars. The fires glowed brightly and kept the chill at bay. All those present talked companionably and laughter rose from the plain with the sparks from the great flames.

"Woodchuck, I could get used to this," Sutter said.

Tahn nodded as he put several sweet berries in his mouth. "A man who sniffs the dirt is an easy man to please."

Sutter poked him gently in the side and resumed his meal with vigor.

When the food was nearly gone, several minstrels began to play and people began to dance. Taking his lead from those at other tables, Sutter quickly petitioned Wendra to accompany him, and the two began to imitate the steps of the many celebrants.

Penit jumped into the dance, taking Wendra and Sutter by the hand and capering in a circle.

A moment later, one of the Sedagin tapped Sutter on the shoulder. "I'd like a round with the lady," he said.

"Not this time," Sutter said.

The Sedagin raised a hand, and suddenly the music stopped. The Sedagin stepped close to Sutter, who dropped Wendra's hand.

"You are low born," the Sedagin man said with derision.

"I don't know what that means to you," Sutter replied, "but it sounds like an insult." The tone of Sutter's voice threatened action.

"So the lowlander can reason," the other mocked. "But you do not deny a bladesman a turn with a woman." The longblade spoke like a court counselor.

Sutter immediately looked back at the table, locking eyes with Tahn. The silent message was clear: *If you need help* . . . But he also saw the look in the face of the Sedgain lord—a ready contempt awaiting what came next. And that turned Sutter's anger more black.

He'd throttled stronger men for ridiculing his trade—always there were jokes about his dirty hands. But this. This somehow make him angrier. The interruption, the presumption of it.

"Hoping to find a friend to take your challenge for you?" the longblade taunted, following Sutter's gaze.

Sutter shut his eyes, his jaw working as he bit back a retort. Another word and he might explode. He knew the foolishness of it, standing here in the middle of a plain filled with Sedagin. But by the Bourne, he would not yield on this. Not simply to prove himself a man to Wendra, if this could mean that. Not because of the man's arrogance or any of that, after all.

But because he had to believe that a boy left by his parents to a life of root farming wasn't any less than a blessed, vaunted nation with a glorious history of promises and honor in war. Otherwise he could have, should have, stayed in the Hollows.

A hush fell over the the company, the plain now as quiet as it had been during Sedagin's toast. Only the sound of burning wood filled the air.

Sutter opened his eyes and shifted his gaze to the Sheason. Vendanj did not appear ready to offer assistance, but something changed in Sutter as he looked at the renderer, and remembered what Vendanj had said in Hambley's Fieldstone. His jaw relaxed, and his fists unclenched. A thin smile softened his features even more, and he looked back at the Sedagin before him.

"And what of the *lady's* choice?" Sutter asked in a low voice, his words nearly lost in the crackle of the fire.

"You're suggesting she would rather dance with you than with one who is highborn, given in blood to the Promise." The man chuckled.

Sutter choked back more anger, then shook his head. "So close to the sky, the sun has withered your wit," he said dryly. "I'm suggesting that *she* ought to have been asked, not me." Sutter stepped closer, his face only the width of his fist from the Sedagin's nose. "What is this First Promise that you invoke to give you station above another? Is it possible that it could have been meant for such a use? I have known the face of the Fathers more intimately in nurturing life from my soil than you have in all the grandeur of your sword and oath."

"You tread close to death, lowlander," the Sedagin said. The longblade's face tightened, and he took a wider stance as though preparing to fight.

"Then we will have ourselves a fight," Sutter said evenly. "And either your arrogance will come to an end, or my dirty hands will fall defending the will of another."

Sutter was a good fighter, but he was no match for the Sedagin's skill with a blade. Fear rippled through him; whatever happened, he would have to handle alone.

"Vendanj," Tahn said from the table, his voice sounding loud in the lengthening silence.

"Hold," the Sheason whispered.

The longblade reached for his sword.

"Or," Sutter said, his smile returning, "you could ask *Wendra* if she'd like to dance. Does your Promise allow for such civility?"

The man paused with his hand on the hilt of his blade. He looked across at Sedagin, who nodded. The man unhanded his weapon and turned to Wendra. "Anais, would you care to dance?"

Wendra's face shone as she looked at Sutter. Then she answered diplomatically, "Yes." The longblade took her hand, they made one turn, and the music started in again, as festive as before. Sutter was turning to leave when the longblade grabbed him by the wrist. Sutter wheeled about, surprised, but before he could think to strike, the man forced something into his hand. Sutter looked down, confused. When he glanced up again, the longblade nodded and returned to his dance with Wendra. Sutter ambled back to the table and sat, inspecting the present.

Tahn leaned close. Sutter held one of the wrist bracelets they'd seen the Sedagin wearing.

A wide leather band of the same deep fir hue, a thin cord meant to loop up and around his third finger.

"You're meant to wear it, Sutter," Riven said. "It is a gift."

Sutter put on the bracelet and flexed his hand into a fist. Riven and Sedagin appeared pleased, but neither spoke of it, returning to their food and conversation.

"I thought you were going to lose your nails," Tahn said as Sutter continued to study the wrist-band. "You're lucky it didn't come to a fight."

"Maybe," Sutter replied, finally picking up the last of his wine and finishing it. "We know their skill, but they've never fought a man from the Hollows before." He laughed and refilled his goblet.

Tahn shook his head, then jostled Sutter's arm, splashing wine on them both. "What happened?"

"The guy wanted Wendra to dance. Forced himself in," Sutter said, trying to sound incredulous.

"So you defended your love," Tahn teased.

"Of course," he said, smiling.

"And you're not worried Wendra will take a stronger liking to the longblade?"

Sutter laughed. "Nah, I'm sure his blade is the only thing about him that's long. Besides, I won the challenge, didn't I? I used his own virtue to defeat him."

Then, softer. "I wish my father could have seen it." He flexed his hand again, pulling the string tight over his fist. "I think he'd have been proud."

Tahn looked across the feast at Mira. At that moment, she reminded him of the purple logotes, a small stubborn wildflower that flourished where nothing else ever could—on the rocky, windy hills of Cali's North. Before he could stop himself, he'd rounded the table and asked her to dance.

"You think you can keep up?" she asked.

Tahn took her hand just as the music changed to a slow air played on a deep-pitched fiddle, sounding to Tahn like a lamentation. He put his arms around Mira and they swayed in time with the music.

"You're not very good at this, are you?" Mira looked down to where Tahn's feet had pinned her own to the grass.

"Just need more practice. I'd think you'd be used to that with me by now."

She smiled and they turned slowly under a canopy of stars.

"Your sister," Tahn asked. "Did she have children?"

Mira looked at him. "You're a bit of a clumsy dancer, but you're more perceptive than I thought."

"If she's a queen, and she's childless . . . will you be expected to bear the line an heir?"

"It is possible. Authority means something different to the Far than it does to others. It's not dominion. But in some ways, it's more important."

Her eyes held a distant look Tahn had rarely seen. This woman lived so completely in the present that to see her so distracted shocked him. A young boy and girl, no more than eight, danced by, a bit fast and not in time with the tune. "Do you want a family?"

The Far looked down at the children passing them. "It's not a question of what I want. I am Far. For us, even the most favorable conditions leave a mother but a very short time with her child. Our idea of family is different than yours."

Tahn caught her attention. "I didn't ask about the Far. I asked about you."

Mira stared back at him. They'd stopped dancing, and now, without speaking, were sharing a set of impossible questions. And except for when she sat vigil in the depths of the night over his sleeping friends, it was the only time he could remember seeing her motionless. He believed her heart stirred, mostly because his own told him it must.

A desire and ache for what one might wish but could never have.

For them both.

But Tahn would not let go of his hope for her that had begun in his heart, any more than he could give up his hope for a new sun each day, begun in the stillness of the dark hours of night.

. . .

Dust coated the path. In every direction earth rolled away, the crust parched and cracked, the sage dead, wind whistling over the plain. Tahn strode heavily across it, following a pair of footprints. The sun beat down upon him. It seemed not to move in the sky above. Beads of sweat rolled down his brow and into his eyes. He blinked against the sting, and wiped his face with his sleeve. Stumps of trees long dead, bleached white and forming jagged patterns, jutted up like gravestones amidst the dry grass.

The dreary plain continued, heat shimmering at the line of the horizon. Onward he trudged, his heart grieving for the loss of vitality. Occasionally, deep grooves scored the blackened, scorched soil, the sun hot on the sooty surface.

Farther up the path, stones cropped up in odd shapes, pocked and scabrous. Then more stones. And more. Tahn looked past them quickly, his mind refusing to see their shapes. Soon, he could no longer deny their stares, and he stopped to rub the eyes of one of the stones which rose from the ground like a human statue.

Past these he staggered, until he could see the sky growing bluer, green hills rising off the plain, and a tree rising against the horizon. Tahn fixed his gaze there and pushed himself toward it . . .

In the dark of early morn, Tahn slipped past a Sedagin sentry by going out his window. He crept to the stable and quietly mounted Jole. At an easy walk, he rode Jole to the edge of the High Plains, there to look out upon a crystalline dark. The constellation of Merade the Devout dipped on the eastern horizon, its head fallen below the edge of the plain. Tahn peered out over the vastness of the land that stretched out beneath him. It looked like a mural of shadows, veiled but beautiful. If not for the stars, Tahn would not have known where the earth ended and the sky began.

Sitting with his legs over the edge of the sheer drop, Tahn thought of Balatin and of the old questions that still plagued him: nightmares that felt like memories, faceless figures that seemed somehow familiar but unknowable, maddening words he was compelled to say each time he drew his bow—words that crippled his decisiveness. When did these things begin? It all made Tahn feel like he was slowly losing his mind.

In his worst moments, he simply didn't know who he was, slave to these things that had no rhyme or reason. A man with no history.

He kept thinking how all this strangeness had something to do with his father—the man he'd loved, and who'd loved him—since Balatin, Tahn had learned, had not always lived in the Hollows. But he'd learned nothing more than that about his father's early life.

Balatin had rarely spoken of things outside the Hollows. Tahn, for his part, was finding the variety and wonders of the land to be filled with possibility. He reflected on the way the Sedagin spoke of their own home, the High Plains, on the mirth and candor of Penit and his stories. Even Vendanj with his secretive tongue and hard face. These things led him somehow to his thoughts of dawn. But as he closed his eyes and considered the beginning of another day, more questions rose in his mind. Why did the Sedagin isolate themselves from the rest of the world? Why did they patrol their borders against intruders? What purpose existed in a troupe of players enacting the stories of the reader's books, bringing the tales on wagon-stages into each town they thought would listen and pay? And Vendanj, why did he speak in whispers with the Far? Why wouldn't he share their plans with those he compelled to accompany him? Why did the man's heart seem as hard and rough as stone? The questions tumbled over one another and brought darkness to Tahn's mind.

Then another thought occurred to him, and he opened his eyes to the wide reaches of the land below. These things were connected. He could not understand how, but all these strange things felt like part of something bigger, something that had, impossibly, the power to shape the lives of men.

"That is right."

The voice startled Tahn and he turned around to find its source.

No one.

He looked down the drop into darkness and saw nothing. The sky above remained empty.

He was alone.

Tahn refocused his attention on the color and warmth that would come into the land at the rise of the greater light. As soon as he did, the thought came over him that the lesser light should be allowed to rule, that the time of the reader's stories had gone by, their memory a testament to the failure of the Fathers, of men.

The voice came again. "You begin to see." It spoke as softly as a cottonwood seed borne upon a gentle breeze brushing his cheek. But it left a taint in Tahn's mind in its passing—he could feel it in the way that, in this dreamlike state, he couldn't focus on things that had always mattered to him. "You will see further with your mind, Quillescent, than you will ever see with the glare of your youth in your eyes."

Tahn panicked. The intrusion of the voice, its soft menace that spoke of barrows and widows and silent autumns, got inside him. He tried to stand. But his legs were numb, and he fell back down. The voice descended upon him from the air, rose into him from the earth, and echoed out from deep inside him—unspoken, but felt and understood. Like love or hatred. It began to bind him, close him in. At the edge of this great High Plain, looking into a fathomless distance, Tahn felt as confined as he had ever been. He struggled, trying to remember why he had come out away from the others. He kicked his legs and flailed at the night around him, disregarding the imminent drop beneath his dangling legs.

Someone grabbed him.

He screamed and forced his mind past the voice and its cryptic words to the single thought of daybreak. In that moment, he opened his eyes, and found himself sitting a few feet from the edge of the plain, staring into the openness, with light just touching the horizon. *A dream?* But somehow he knew better. He had fought a battle, a small one. But with whom? For what? His mind reeled in the wake of it, and he thrashed at the inexplicable implications.

The hands did not release him, though.

Mira.

She had dragged him back from the cliff edge. In the faint light of predawn, a look of concern showed in her eyes. They faced one another for several moments.

"Why do you rise before the sun? What prayer do you make that must be spoken at such a time? Every day?"

No one had ever asked Tahn about waking so early, about the purpose of his morning vigil. She had seen him spending those moments each day in reflection. She studied him closely.

Tahn had no reply. He'd never spoken of this to anyone, just as he had never spoken of his inner need to test the merit of every bow draw he made. Twice he had gone to Balatin to tell him, but had not found the words. Part of him believed they were secrets that must be kept, at least until he understood them himself.

Unable to lie to her, he said simply, "I don't know."

And together they walked back into the heart of Teheale: *earned in blood.*

• CHAPTER TWENTY-ONE •

Partings

Countless points of light shimmered as the sun reflected off the condensation across the plain. The horses stood saddled and ready. Vendanj gave Tahn a measured look as he approached the party gathered in front of Sedagin's home.

"We were going to leave you, Woodchuck," Sutter said. "But the Sedagin prefer guests who bathe."

Tahn mounted Jole. "And quiet guests, I think."

His friend laughed. "Well, you missed endfast, so stay downwind of me with that gamy breath of yours."

Penit giggled, and was silenced by a look from the Sheason.

"Have you forgotten what we are doing?" Vendanj asked. "The north face of the High Plains is a difficult descent under the best of conditions, and we will almost surely meet Quietgiven once we reach the lowlands again. We have many leagues to cross to reach the Scar; we must move fast, and still have strength to enter that place when we arrive. Turn your minds to these things."

With that, the Sheason rode toward Sedagin, who had appeared from a nearby stable on a sleek white stallion appointed with the customary fir-colored tack and saddle. Behind him came two more Sedagin, Riven and the man who'd challenged Sutter at the feast.

"Stay downwind of me, too," Wendra whispered. Her lips drew into a wry smile. Sutter stifled laughter, causing snorts and chortles.

"And me," Braethen added.

"And me," Penit joined in.

Mira said nothing, but the Far half-smiled, causing Tahn to do the same.

"Any idea why we're going to the Scar, Braethen?" Sutter asked. "It sounds like a lot of fun, for sure. But you know, details would be great."

Braethen stifled a laugh, and shook his head. "My knowledge of Scar history is sketchy. And what I do remember . . . no idea why we'd go there. Seems a bit out of the way, too, if we're going to Recityv."

Vendanj and the Sedagin returned just then. "I will escort you to the north face. The path from there is dangerous, but passable if you are careful," Sedagin said.

With that, they got underway. Just after midday on the third day of their ride, they came to the end of the High Plains. At its edge, Sedagin wheeled to face them. "It has been my privilege to offer you safe passage through our home-land." He nodded to Vendanj. "It is our custom to offer a gift to friends when they leave us. Sutter, will you come forward?"

Sutter looked up, putting his hand to his chest in question. Sedagin nodded, and Nails rode forward, casting a skeptical look back at Tahn.

Sedagin pulled his blade and flipped it into the air, catching it by the edge of its shaft. "Tylan made a present to you of our hand. Now I make a present to you of our arm." He extended the sword to Sutter. "Faced with the challenge to fight, you spoke the truth of the Promise so that the grounds of your action were clear. On the lips of a lowlander this sounded strange to us."

Sutter did not take the blade immediately.

Sedagin sidled closer. "Please take it," Sedagin said in a respectful tone. "It is as much a blessing to give as it is to receive. Do not deny us this."

Sedagin held the blade out so that Sutter would have to reach out to claim it. Hesitantly extending his arm, Sutter grasped the blade by its hilt. Tahn watched as Riven bowed at the gesture. Before letting go of the greatsword, Sedagin maneuvered it so that the point pierced the tip of his middle finger. He kept it there as Sutter continued to hold the blade, connecting the two men in that precarious position. Tahn knew the sword must be heavy, and Sutter's arm soon began to quiver slightly. Sedagin did not move his finger, but pressed more firmly to steady Sutter's hold. As he did, blood welled up over the tip of his finger and dripped to the plain below. For several moments Sedagin thus helped Sutter hold aloft the blade. Sutter's arm began to shake more violently, and he started to sweat. When Tahn thought Sutter would surely drop the blade, Sedagin pulled back his hand, and the sword swooped down harmlessly.

"Thank you, my friend," Sedagin said, and bowed his head slowly.

Sutter opened his mouth to speak, but found no words. At last, he bowed as well. Vendanj watched closely, seeming more pleased than Tahn ever remembered seeing him. Admiration shone in Mira's eyes as well.

Sedagin turned to Vendanj. "It must be done slowly. Even my own people take care on the Face."

"We will watch closely," Vendanj returned.

"If there are changes . . ." Sedagin trailed off.

"Thank you," Vendanj replied. Then he turned to the others. "Remember that we have been found by a Quietgiven tracker. The tracker is dangerous because he can feel the connection of Forda I'Forza in the land and in the air—*your* Forda I'Forza." He pointed at each of them. "It is how he tracks. And he can reason as you do, but *he* carries the craft of scrying. Now that he knows of us, we will not be free of him until he lies dead."

The Sheason visually surveyed each of them, then turned to start down the path.

"Did you see it?" Mira asked.

"Yes," the Sheason answered.

Tahn did not know what the Far meant until he came to the very edge and started his own descent. Enshrouded in a dense mist, the lowlands could not be seen. Somehow Tahn knew the mist was the work of Quietgiven.

The path wound more narrowly than the one they'd taken on the south side of the High Plain. Switching back on itself at sharp angles, the route became more circuitous, dropping hundreds of strides in a short distance. Before long, they dismounted and walked the horses down.

Tahn watched his feet, but found it difficult to look away from the roiling mists below. The mists bore the look of a storm cloud, dark grey and pregnant with thunder and sleet, except they moved silently as if with a patient, baneful intelligence.

Vendanj called a halt several strides above the fogs. Tahn looked out across the tops of the clouds, feeling as though he stood at the shore of a vast dark sea. He kicked a rock from the edge of the path. It tumbled downward, and Tahn jumped when a number of tendrils of mist rose like tongues and seemed to lick at the reception of the rock into its folds.

"Empty your minds," Vendanj said. "Think nothing of what you know about any one of us or where we are going. Find a single, pleasant image and fix upon it." He stopped and looked away at the menacing bank of dark clouds. "It is Je'holta. The caress of the Male'Siriptus. Be focused on whatever thought brings you comfort. Anything else will tear at the edges of your reason. Je'holta will inspire panic and madness by exaggerating your own fears. Mira, tie the horses one to another. Braethen, you will lead the animals. They are unaffected by the mists. Each of you will hold the hands of those next to you. The mists do not have the power to separate you."

Sutter shook his head and muttered, "Here we go, come Quiet or chorus."

Mira finished securing the horses, and Vendanj took Mira's hand, each of the others joining in turn. Together they walked into the darkness.

The mists folded around them, thin streamers reaching out to wrap them and draw them in. The sun became a pale disk in the sky, the damp and cold instantly chilling Tahn's skin. The mist touched his cheeks and fingers like icy velvet. Mira's hand firmly gripped Tahn's own, while Wendra's grasp tightened once they passed completely into the swirling grey and black fog. Vendanj led them slowly, peering into the depths around them.

Tahn could see Penit holding Wendra's other hand, but Sutter blurred to shadow and Braethen appeared as nothing more than a shape that might have been mists shifting and shaping themselves. The hoofbeats of the horses came as muted, dull clops, but the horses themselves were completely lost to sight.

Noises echoed in the depths of the dark cloud, faint sounds that Tahn felt more than heard—echoes like cries or laments, or death-side prayer offerings that traveled upon the mist. Desperation grew inside Tahn, manic and wild. He fought an almost irresistible need to turn and race up from the darkness, though he'd seen no evil. The mists would drive him mad if he stayed long in their velvet folds.

The shadows deepened as they further descended the north face. Soon, the sun disappeared completely. Charcoal-hued light encircled them, and Tahn somehow felt that they had become part of the mist itself.

The Sheason did not waver or slow, their progress cautious but steady. The Far, her eyes constantly searching and darting, seemed uncomfortable without a free hand to take up her sword.

Gradually, pressure built, constricting Tahn's chest and making it difficult to breathe. The mists plumed in successive shadows, pushing in upon them, as soft as cottonseed but as oppressive and suffocating as a dozen wet blankets. Tahn gasped, drawing into his mouth and nose gulps of the dark mist. From the blackness, he heard others coughing and fighting for breath. Suddenly, a wave of warmth coursed through him, entering from Mira's hand and passing to Wendra in an instant. His lungs expanded, and he breathed more easily. The Sheason had sent something through them, from hand to hand, and the coughing stopped.

Vendanj pressed forward.

Tahn had no idea how long they had been in the mists. His hands cramped from clutching the hands of Mira and Wendra. His eyes ached from the strain of trying to peer through the clouds that enveloped them. Finally, the path leveled out. They had returned to the lowlands.

In moments they were encircled by the mists on every side, and Tahn lost all orientation.

The languid calls from deep in the mists grew louder, more urgent. More than once Tahn thought he heard voices call his name. The words were shapeless and vague and sounded as though they were uttered from lips too pained to form them completely. Finally, the mists fell utterly quiet and calm.

Then distantly, a sound like tree roots pulling free from the ground rose in the fog. Deep, thunderous tones, like tall trees being felled, resounded all about them.

"What is it?" Sutter asked.

"Quiet," Vendanj ordered.

The sounds grew louder, accompanied by wretched cries in a cacophonous chorus. The din was somehow visible in the mists around them. It began to swirl in tight, angry eddies. Through the dim light, Tahn saw forms darting at the edges of his vision, moving in every direction and vanishing as quickly as they came.

"Do you see them?" Sutter called out, his voice desperate.

"Quickly!" Vendanj commanded.

The Sheason pulled them forward into a jog. Something that felt like saplings whipped at their feet, the mists swirling in a frenzy as they rushed blindly through the dense fog.

"Hold fast!" Vendanj called back. But his words scarcely reached Tahn over the sibilant rush of the wind and the dark song of rending earth and tortured cries.

Then came the beat of a drum, struck only once, but with a sound so deep and resonant that it seemed to Tahn as if he heard some god beating on the very land they rushed to escape. The air throbbed with the beat, which seemed to echo out and back from the north face. The pulse came at them from above and below, like a quake disrupting the very fabric of the world. The Sheason abruptly stopped. Again everything was preternaturally still. Tahn could see mist frozen in the air before his face, unmoving.

Then the mist began to take form.

The darkness swirled in front of him, coalescing into an image of . . . himself. The disembodied mask mouthed words. Its eyeless sockets looked nowhere, but also somehow saw inside Tahn. Then its features were gone, and the image hung before him like a canvas to be written upon. Tahn averted his eyes, turning to Wendra for reassurance.

Before he could find her eyes, a scream erupted in the mist. Penit's high, shrill voice pierced the cloud banks. The boy pulled his hands free and raced into the dark fog. Without hesitation, Wendra took off after him.

"No!" Vendanj commanded.

Wendra did not heed him.

"Find her!" the Sheason said to Mira.

The Far jumped into the roiling clouds and was gone.

A flurry of movement exploded in front of Tahn, as the misty face before him found its own voice. "Draw and release as you choose, dead man." The words came in a malevolent growl.

In his mind, Tahn suddenly saw sunrise after sunrise, but the greater light was moving backward, retracing its arc back into the east, time and time again. It was as though a thousand days were being taken back, and each time the sky became blacker, more blurred. He saw a desert wasteland, where children walked barefoot in the sand. He saw crags and dried roots, and himself standing at the mouth of a stone canyon, tearing at its walls with his bare fingers. Burning pages floated in the wind, becoming cinders and sparks that winked out against a violet sky. His voice was gone. He witnessed himself speaking, but the toneless words lived only in his mind. He saw broken swords lying like kindling, and bodies dissolving to ash under the lesser light. He saw a great white mountain thrumming and quaking. Then he saw the face of a man, the same face that twisted and writhed in the mists before him. And the face was his own. Tahn screamed.

"Don't betray yourselves!" Vendanj yelled.

But it was too late.

Tahn bolted from the line to escape the image. Blindly, he rushed through the mists, branches whipping at him, the black clouds hungrily licking at him as he raced aimlessly. He could hear someone in pursuit calling him, and he ran faster. Recklessly, holding his arms over his face, he thrashed through the foliage and undergrowth. He stumbled and went down hard, smashing his leg against a rock. But he did not stay down. He clambered back to his feet and rushed on, unsure which direction to go, only trying to escape the face and the voice that followed him incessantly no matter how fast he ran.

"You cannot outrun the consequence of another's choice." The menacing communication resonated in the mists around him, throaty and hushed. Tahn screamed again and redoubled his pace. The darkness descended upon him and still he ran, careening off trees and falling over boles. Forever he seemed to run, the images becoming stronger and more searing to his battered mind. His pursuer seemed to grow closer, to home in on the sound Tahn made in his flight through the wild.

Finally, the darkness began to break. The charcoal light softened to grey, and soon Tahn could see the faded disk of the sun through the mists. He lost his footing again, but scrambled on hands and knees toward the light, the pull of the mists strong in his mind and on his body. But he began to break free from the mists. A rushing scream of failure grew behind him, and suddenly with a cacophony of jarring thunder, he leapt from the mists into the full light of day. And collapsed.

Through the mists Tahn heard the voice of the Sheason call: "To Recityv!" Or did the cry sound only in his mind?

Gasping, Tahn touched his head and pulled away bloody fingers. The world turned and his eyes filled with blackness.

The mists rushed in, hindering Wendra's pursuit of Penit, the dark grey clouds swirling and thickening to obscure her sight. She crouched as she ran, and could just make out Penit's feet as he sprinted away from her. The boy dodged in and out of low alders and lunged through tight stands of bottlebrush. Images and forms moved maddeningly at the edges of her vision. Masses of dark fog leapt, encircling her arms, tendrils clawing at her. They lacked the substance to hold her, but their touch impeded her progress, filling her mind with thoughts of failure, of never catching Penit, of losing him as she had lost her own child.

"Penit, wait, it's me!"

The dinsome rush of wind and distant, anguished voices rose to swallow her pleas, making their cries indistinguishable from her own. The lad pushed on as though manic and rabid and terrified that stopping meant death. Then, from the left, two huge hulking shapes materialized out of the mists. Wendra ignored them for only a single moment before something told her that they were not insubstantial like the other shapes constantly rising and dissipating in the mists around her.

These were Bar'dyn.

The first dove at her, launching its huge body in a powerful arc to intercept her. Wendra found a reserve of strength and jumped forward to avoid the attack. The Bar'dyn crashed into the trees behind her and howled its fury. The second closed in from behind her, waving massive arms through the air in deadly arcs. It would be upon her soon; she could not hope to outrun it.

The mists thinned to a lighter shade of grey, and Wendra could see Penit clearly now.

"Run, Penit! Faster!" she cried.

The boy still did not acknowledge her, continuing to run at a breakneck pace through the mists. She was gaining on him, but the Bar'dyn was only two strides behind her. Its huge, powerful arms whistled through the fog as it tried to strike her down. Wendra heard a guttural grunt, and turned her head in time to see the Bar'dyn dive at her legs. She tried to push herself faster, but her muscles would not obey. One of the Bar'dyn's large hands clipped her ankle, the other her hip, sending her tumbling into the grass and brush. The Quietgiven's body landed with a heavy thud, but the beast quickly regained its feet and bore down upon her.

Wendra rolled over, pulling a small knife from her belt. She instantly knew the futility of her own defense, and saw a sudden rush of images stream through her mind: Balatin and the warm fires and brambleberry tea they used to share on winter nights; Tahn and the way he had cared for her, she in turn sitting at his side to soothe him during many nights of restless sleep; the child that had so recently been in her belly, and the Bar'dyn that had ripped it from her and carried its lifeless body into the night. With the cascade of memories, something happened deep inside her. It began in her bosom, a warmth like fire, reminding her of Balatin's anger the day he had driven the merchants away from the house when they came with bags of silver to trade for human flesh, but soft like tears of joy at seeing an infant learn to walk. The feeling shot through her and rose into her lungs and throat, needing someplace to go. As a thought occurred to her of where and how to release that feeling, the Bar'dyn arched its back and hissed, breaking her concentration. The Given's broad features pinched tightly, the mists seeming to recoil as though they, too, were wounded.

The beast fell, revealing Mira standing close behind. With a blade in each hand, she took a step back, setting her feet and extending one sword, holding the other in front of her breast in a defensive posture. The Bar'dyn jumped up and whirled around, issuing a guttural curse Wendra could not understand. The warmth in her chest abated, and she forgot the thoughts of a moment before as the Far lunged again, this time so quickly that the mists appeared to pass through her rather than around her. In a crosswise motion, she pulled down her blades upon the Bar'dyn's neck. The creature could not avoid the attack, but this time Mira's swords scarcely pierced the beast's thick skin. She backed up again as the Bar'dyn drew a pair of axes and started for her.

"Go!" Mira yelled. "Find the boy! We will look for you beyond the mist. But you know our goal, should we fail to find you."

The Bar'dyn seemed to take Mira's words for a lack of concentration and lunged forward, aiming with one ax at the crown of her head. Mira easily side-stepped the blow and brought her right sword down on the Bar'dyn's shoulder. The beast howled again. As if in response, the sound of many feet could be heard beating through the mists toward them.

Wendra did not want to leave the Far to fight alone, but she was little help with her knife. She stood, wincing from the pain of the gash in her ankle where the Bar'dyn had clipped her, and hobbled on as quickly as she could in the direction she had seen Penit go.

She heard the clash of steel muted by the mists behind her, and the sound of heavy feet grew louder, bearing down on the scene of the fight. Slowly, the sound of battle faded and the mists receded until the sun penetrated the darkness. Wendra caught sight of several broken stems and branches and followed them, hoping they led to Penit. Her entire leg began to throb, and she slowed against the onslaught of pain that washed over her in nauseating waves.

As she limped onward, the mists grew lighter still, until she could see several strides ahead of her. A few limping steps farther, Wendra spied Penit, crouched near the base of a large elm, shivering. She fell to her knees beside him. His hair and clothes were drenched with sweat, and he clung to the tree like a child holding his mother.

"It's all right, Penit. You are safe."

The boy did not respond, did not even look at Wendra. He trembled more violently, spittle falling from his lips. Wendra removed her cloak and wrapped it around him. Distantly, the sound of footsteps thrashing through the undergrowth cut through the thinner fog.

"We must go," Wendra urged, trying to help Penit to his feet.

The boy resisted, his small arms bulging with his effort to remain rooted to the spot.

"Please, Penit, trust me," Wendra pleaded. She knelt again, coming face-to-face with him. "I will protect you." As she spoke the words, she silently wondered how she would do such a thing, having not been able to protect even her own child. But in that moment, she vowed that she would do so, or die in the attempt.

The sound of voices came, accompanying the footsteps. Wendra looked over her shoulder and saw the mists enlivened and frantic, appearing to part in anticipation of the passage of one it did not care to touch.

Wendra looked back at Penit. "You must play the part of someone brave."

At that, Penit's eyes focused upon her. He seemed to suddenly be aware of who and where he was. He released the tree. His inner arms were marked with the pattern of the tree's bark. He blinked away the tears in his eyes and nodded.

Ignoring the wound in her leg, Wendra helped him up, and nearly fell as she placed her weight upon it. Penit put his arm around her waist, and together they started toward the lightest break in the mist. The dark fogs stilled, and in an unexpected moment, they stepped into the light of day, leaving the darkness behind.

• CHAPTER TWENTY-TWO •

Escaping the Darkness

The horses broke free from Braethen's grip, scattering into the mists. He tried to keep control of the one closest to him as it reared and whinnied and kicked its forelegs. Braethen stepped away, trying to flank the steed, but the horse went to ground and was gone before he could grasp the reins.

"Forget the mounts," Vendanj said. "They will find the light. Stay close."

Braethen ran to the Sheason's side, drawing his short sword and looking about them. "What happened?"

"The boy saw the face of Male'Siriptus," Vendanj said.

"I did not see it."

"The child sees with simpler, truer eyes, and his feelings are close to his skin. The mist laid hold of these things and used them."

"What now?" Braethen asked.

"We will hope that an entire collough does not await us at the edge of Je'holta."

The mists continued to form strange shapes, but Braethen paid them little attention, focusing on the words of A'Posian to keep his mind clear of fretful thoughts. He could hear the simple admonition as clearly as the day he'd first heard his father speak it: *Mind that your path is to be a creator. You may yet become an author. But creation of any kind serves the Will and those who bear it.*

Braethen still believed in those words, but his sword was unskilled and weak in the defense of Vendanj or Wendra or Tahn. The root-digger, of all people, had saved Braethen's life in their first encounter with the Bar'dyn.

The mists began to solidify in front of him, forming deep, wide holes where eyes might have been looking into him, and a slack jaw gaping in a frozen scream: his doubts given form.

"Hold now, sodalist!" Vendanj commanded, putting his hand on Braethen's shoulder.

Braethen recoiled, blinked, and the face was gone.

As if in answer, the mists began to list and heave, moving first one way, then another, but slowly, as though dancing to a silent, mournful dirge. Vendanj put a hand to Braethen's chest and cautioned him to step back. The mists began to part like a curtain, creating a clear, dark path out of the obscurity before them. He heard the approach of soft steps over the dank ground, and Braethen suddenly felt a terrible chill. A shape made its slow way toward them, draped in shadow, but with hatred clear in the simple inclination of its head.

Vendanj turned to Braethen. "Sodalist, are you completely sworn to the oath you accepted?" His eyes were stern, searching. "It is too late for guessing in this. Either you are in it marrow, blood, and sinew, or you are but a well-intentioned fool."

Braethen looked past Vendanj as the shadow came on, the mists undulating in a series of waves at its passage. How many nights had he sat at his table reading, rehearsing the words, the genealogies, the Covenant to the First Order? His elbows had worn thin the varnish at the table's edge, and the smell of candle wax had become his closest friend. In the small Hollows home he had dreamed of adding his arm to the Sodality, to defend all he knew against the changes men thought to write or cause in the land. Was he to go into the breach, or was he merely a reader of tales?

The image of himself seated as a child in the oversized chair of A'Posian, with a book wider than the span of his own arms in his lap, crystallized in his head. Then he immediately saw himself vowing an oath offered by a sodalist taking his dying breaths.

He was decided.

Gently he pushed Vendanj's arm down. "I am truly sworn, Sheason," Braethen said with conviction.

The renderer reached within his cloak and withdrew a sword. He handed the weapon to Braethen. "Then stand with me now."

Braethen took the blade, casting his other sword aside. Then the mists erupted in a din of snapping wood and rustling leaves and the roar of a thousand whispered voices from the dust of the earth.

The Quietgiven emerged completely, and pointed at Braethen and Vendanj. Just as it did, the world turned black in a heartbeat and Braethen could see nothing.

Struggling to see, the sodalist turned in circles. He began to feel weightless, having no idea which way was up or down. In his hand he still held the sword Vendanj had just given him, but he could see neither it nor his hand. He reached out, hoping to feel the Sheason, but felt nothing. Quickly, he crouched, sure he would find the ground beneath his feet . . . but it too was gone.

Braethen's mind reeled, and he wondered if he had been çast down that black tunnel in the mist. Or perhaps this was death, perhaps the stories of an eternal walk of life were a delusion created by the early storytellers to give men hope. He tried to speak; no sound came. He shouted; still nothing. He pressed his fingers to his lips to be sure he was opening his mouth. The only thing real, touchable, was his own flesh.

And the sword.

In his hand the solid feel of the hilt reassured him. Inside the blackness, he and the sword were all that remained. Its weight comforted him, and though he still could not see it, he lifted it before his face.

What is happening? Vendanj gave me the sword just as the darkness parted and the shape came upon us. Am I still in the mist? Did the creature destroy us? He squeezed the sword. *No. The sword would not exist in death.*

Then Braethen began to fall. He could not see the passing of clouds or rocks or birds, but his gut wrenched as though he were plummeting from the heights of the north face into the lowlands below. A feeling grew violently in him that he was rushing toward his own end, and must complete the riddle of his imprisonment in this stygian nightmare or be dashed against whatever came at the end of the darkness. His heart hammered in his chest. He gripped the hilt of the sword with both hands.

What am I meant to learn here? The question seemed to hasten his fall.

The Sheason asked if I was sworn to my oath. With that thought, an elusive awareness danced at the edge of his understanding. He reached for it, trying to bend his mind around the hope it represented. But it evaded him. His shoulders and legs began to cramp, and quickly the pain became exquisite in its intensity; he despaired of escaping it. Then he realized what the rushing was, the fall; it was him becoming one with the darkness. If he did not find the puzzle's answer, he would be swallowed by the endlessness of the blight around him, forever a part of it.

Then the awareness, the understanding, danced in again, closer now, and he reached out for it somehow, knowing there would not be a third opportunity. And the smallest, surest knowledge of it took hold in him.

"It is I!" he screamed, the sound bursting into the darkness like a horn blown from the heights of Jedgwick Ridge. "I am Forda. I am Forza!" He looked at the sword, which now glowed a brilliant white in the darkness. "We are here! Now!"

With his words, the world rushed in, the darkness retreating, and the ache and cramps were gone. He was back in the mist beside Vendanj; the creature stood before them in the same place, as though not a moment had passed.

The Sheason gave Braethen an approving look, and turned to meet the Quietgiven. Braethen lifted the sword before his eyes. Its blade no longer glowed as it had in the dark world he had just escaped, but he held it with a new purpose.

Before he could look up again, the being attacked. It lifted its tattered cloak like an evil bird preparing to take flight. A pulse of darkness rushed forward in a thick wave, cutting a path through the mists and knocking him and Vendanj off their feet.

A withering laugh escaped its cowl. "Mal i'mente, Therus." Braethen suddenly felt cold. Behind his eyes he saw the memories of his youth being rewritten and unwritten. As the changes continued, he recognized the creature: Maere. Unlike the stuff of cautionary tales, the hate and fright that beset him began to steal the memory of those events that made him who he was. He was being undone. In his mind he saw flashes of the past, many of his most cherished and formative memories being taken from him or reformed into painful scenes he would never want to revisit.

Braethen howled at the loss, and jumped to his feet. Unbidden, something rose in his throat. "I am I!" he screamed. The cry repelled the darkness and the shifting in his own mind.

He turned to see the Sheason regain his feet, a violet light growing in his hands. The Maere whipped its cloak back from its broad shoulders, its entire body seeming to rear as might a horse. But before it could do more, a series of bright pulses shot from Vendanj's hands into its chest. It yawped an unearthly scream.

Braethen did not hesitate. As the Maere screeched, he lunged forward and brought his sword around with all his strength. The blade tore into the beast and its clamoring intensified, shaking the very mist. One muscled arm flew with lightning speed at Braethen's head and sent him sprawling. He landed hard on the ground, his head ringing. But he did not let go of the sword. Hot blood ran from his ear down his neck. He tried to stand, but the world turned at dizzying speed, the force of it pulling him down. Braethen lost his balance and collapsed back to the soil.

Vendanj took advantage of the Maere's distraction with Braethen and reached into the folds of his cloak. He retrieved the small wooden case and withdrew one of the leaves Braethen had seen him eat. He held one between the second and third fingers of his left hand and placed the hand on his chest. His other hand he extended, palm down, and said something in low, quick words.

Instantly, the mists withdrew from around him, and a rush of light descended from the sky. Braethen looked up and saw a long, wide opening through the dark mists. The sun streamed down, returning natural, vibrant color. Radiance grew from below, even as the sunlight coursed down from above. The Maere began to thrash to and fro. Steam rose from its body and holes opened in its flesh as though it were completely insubstantial, a construct of their minds.

In a last desperate attack, the Maere charged Vendanj, whose eyes were shut as he focused his energy and words into the Will.

Braethen got to his feet, but fell forward onto his hands. He scrambled ahead, using one hand on the ground to keep his feet under him. The Maere closed in on the Sheason, but came hindered by the light, and losing substance with each step. Vendanj's eyes were still shut, and he stood, unaware. Braethen pressed on, gaining speed and resolve. He pushed away his dizziness, focused on the Maere and rose, bolting for the Sheason. The Maere raised its awful hands and darkness enveloped them, just two strides from Vendanj. Braethen howled, and the Sheason's eyes opened just as the Maere blew from its torn lips a rank breath across its darkened hands. The darkness leapt, flashing forward in jagged arcs toward Vendanj. Braethen arrived and with his last vestige of failing strength brought his sword up into the belly of the Maere. The sword thrummed as it met the Quietgiven. The beast doubled over, its dark magic dissipating as it crumpled, writhing, to the ground. The sun continued to stream down upon them, and in moments the Maere was nothing more than steaming ashes at their feet.

Braethen looked up again at the marvelous tunnel carved from the mist straight up into the light of day. The Sheason slumped to the ground, and Braethen sat down beside him, together in the light of the sun, surrounded by the darkness.

Tahn lay facedown on the ground, gasping for breath. Sutter collapsed on his hands and knees beside him, drawing his own ragged gulps of air. The smell of dirt and rocks warming in the sun helped reduce Tahn's panic. After a moment he turned over and propped himself up on his elbows. The mists remained just a few strides behind him, small plumes puffing outward, threatening to expand and engulf them again before being drawn back into the body of the great black fog. Distantly he thought he heard a shriek, but his heart still throbbed in his ears; he couldn't be sure.

In the distance, Jole and Bardoll were fretting and stamping.

"Will and Sky, what is that?" Sutter exclaimed, looking back at the mist.

"More than Vendanj told us," Tahn replied bitterly.

"Why did you run?"

The images flashed in Tahn's mind—the mind-cry of an infant falling off a broken stone monument, singed sheets of parchment rising on hot winds. He saw an image of himself tearing at stone with bloodied fingers. Tahn held up his hands and looked at them, but saw nothing save the old scar on the back of his hand. He tried to make sense of the images that flashed in his mind, but even now they were fading. The memories of countless suns folded into nothing; the gentle voice of Balatin teaching him on a summer porch with light flies winking in nearby piñons dissolved into a mirror of desert brush, waterless wastes, a barren tree, and finally to nothing. He was left with only the litany of flesh and Will he rehearsed every time he drew his bow, and that meant no more to him than before. He took fistfuls of dirt in his hands and recalled the cloaked figure near the ravine on his last hunt, a patch of earth turned to glass, and soil that resisted the nourishment of rain. He realized that he did not care to see another day come, and shuddered beneath the growing heat of the sun on his back.

Sutter gently grabbed his arm. "Tahn, what's wrong? What did you see? Why did you break the line?"

Tahn shook his head. "I don't know, but whatever the reason, it's gone now." He stared at the bank of dark fog. "It got inside me, Sutter. I don't know how, but I could feel it reading my memories like pages in one of Braethen's books. And then it was like something was writing the story forward." Tahn paused, trying to understand the feeling. "The story was the same," he finished.

"What story?" Sutter asked. "What do you mean the same?"

Tahn shut his eyes, trying to say it clearly. "I'm not sure. Maybe ours."

Sutter stared at him for several long moments. Finally, he said, "We have to go back in for the others."

Suddenly, Tahn remembered Wendra. "Great Fathers, what have I done?" He rose to his knees.

As if in response, the sound of pounding feet issued from the fog. Tahn sat up, hoping to see Wendra emerge from the grip of the dark cloud. Several feet inside the mist, the large shapes of several Bar'dyn appeared.

"Run!" Tahn yelled.

He scrambled to his feet and headed for Jole, Sutter at his heels. The stamping of heavy feet shook the earth behind them. Sutter quickly drew abreast of Tahn, matching his every step. Tahn looked back and saw the Bar'dyn emerge from the mist, their eyes fixed upon him and Sutter, massive legs carrying them with impossibly quick strides.

Tahn's chest burned. He'd not completely gotten his breath back before starting to run from these creatures that seemed not to tire. As he struggled up a low hill, something pierced Tahn's foot. Not watching his step, he'd planted a boot on a spine-root. Several needles shot through his boot and entered the soft flesh of his sole. He almost fell, but Sutter caught him, grabbing his waist with one arm and jerking him forward.

As they struggled toward the horses, something hit Sutter in the back. Nails pitched forward, breaking his fall with his hands. On his back, a small iron ball with several dozen spikes—like the head of a small mace—had struck just beneath his shoulder. Sutter got up. Blood spread in circles around the spikes. Tahn glanced back, and saw a Bar'dyn hurl a second ball. The beast threw the weapon with its bare hand, its fibrous skin too thick to be harmed by the spikes. The ball hurtled with tremendous speed. Tahn dove to his left, his foot jolting with pain as he hit the ground.

The Bar'dyn closed on them, their eyes set and determined, a bitter intelligence burning from within. Two took swords out without breaking stride, a third shifting a long ax into its other hand. The look in their large eyes somehow frightened Tahn more than the weapons they carried; there resided an old anger in them. Sutter stooped and helped Tahn up, reaching one arm around his head and arching his back against the intrusion of the ball lodged there. Leaning together, they hurried through the dry grass. Tahn could hear the labored breathing of the Bar'dyn, like horses going full-on. He fought to continue, expecting at any moment the steel of a blade or the huge, gnarled hands of the Bar'dyn to rip them roughly back. The horses were close, but each step grew heavier, more difficult. Tahn's legs threatened to give out. His hair fell in wet strands over his eyes and face; his friend's cheek and jaw dug into Tahn's own as they pushed forward, heads together. The mere heat of the sun fell like a weight upon him.

They reached the horses, and Jole nudged Tahn with his head. Sutter climbed onto Bardoll and looked back, riding around and putting himself between Tahn and the Bar'dyn. He lifted his sword as a challenge, but the Bar'dyn paid no heed and came on undaunted.

"Hurry, Tahn!" Sutter yelled. "They will take us from our saddles in another breath!" Sutter ducked, another ball sailing past his head.

The horses sensed the impending danger and began to sidestep, tugging at their reins. Tahn could not get his foot in the stirrup without stepping on the barbs that had broken off in his foot. He anticipated the agonizing pain of placing pressure on them to mount.

"Hold!" one of the Bar'dyn called. "You run only from lies!" Its voice rasped powerfully, the words glottal and hard to understand.

"I'll send you to eternal night!" Sutter cried in defiance. But even in his stupor, Tahn heard his friend's fear.

The Bar'dyn yelled deep in its throat. The proximity of the cry warned Tahn of their closeness. There was no time to move around Jole to mount from the other side, and he could not jump into his saddle with only one foot. Tahn gritted his teeth and thrust his boot into the stirrup. Intense pain filled his foot, shooting ripples into his entire body. Something snapped in the middle of his sole as though one of the spine-roots had broken inside his foot as it met bone.

Tahn screamed, and put his full weight upon his foot to hoist himself up. The force drove the spines deeper into his tender flesh. Seated, he let go the reins and put his arms around Jole's neck. He scarcely needed to tap Jole before his old friend ran like canyon wind. Sutter swiped down once with the flat of his blade and kicked Bardoll into a full run. Sutter raced away with Tahn, looking back warily for further spiked balls. Another ball hurtled past, missing badly over their heads. Each time he bounced in his saddle, Sutter's face twisted in agony at the sharp points driven into his back.

"Faster!" Tahn yelled. The Bar'dyn kept pace with them, one even gaining ground. Glancing back once, Tahn watched their gait, graceful despite their immense size, and the powerful muscles rippling beneath their thick, coarse skin. Their faces had eased into a terrible, placid expression, though their arms and shoulders pumped vigorously.

"We'll have you," one of them announced with an even voice, not a threat but a comment. "Then your lies and the lies of your Fathers will we show you." The Bar'dyn's face remained unchanged as it called after them, the eerie calm not unlike that belonging to the Sheason.

"They're gaining!" Sutter yelled over the fury of hooves and the pounding of Bar'dyn feet.

Tahn looked back. He could see that in moments they would be overtaken. *What can I do!* Suddenly a calm came over him, as though the world fell silent. Tahn felt still inside. Just then a cry shattered the air. The Bar'dyn all stopped and looked backward to the mist a thousand strides behind them. The creatures out of the Hand looked confused and without direction. The sureness in their aspects had fallen, though a cold hatred was still etched into their thick features. They looked at one another and then back at Tahn and Sutter, who now were well beyond their reach. One of the creatures pointed, and the Bar'dyn began to run again, this time south toward the north face.

Tahn and Sutter did not slow, and gradually the High Plains faded in the distance as they raced east toward Recityv.

• CHAPTER TWENTY-THREE •

The Help of Young and Old

As Wendra stepped into the light, she immediately saw six Bar'dyn and a figure draped in a long, oversized cloak that hinted at scarlet folds whenever it moved. The Quietgiven watched the mists farther to the north, and didn't see her or Penit duck behind a rock formation twenty strides from the mist's edge.

The exertion of freeing herself from the darkness had caused her hip and ankle to bleed freely, the blood pumping madly and coating her entire left leg.

Penit looked at her wound with horror. "Are you dying?"

"No," Wendra said, suppressing a nervous laugh. "But we must be quiet," she whispered. "They will not be kind if we are found."

Penit nodded and looked around, grabbing a rock and holding it with his arm cocked and prepared to throw. Wendra let him alone in his protective pose and tenderly touched her cuts. The wound burned hot, fever assuredly; it would get into the rest of her soon. A few drops of blood fell to the cool soil in the shade of the large rock. *Will the Bar'dyn smell the blood and track us down?* Wendra looked around and realized they were only paces from the north face. In their flight through the shadows of the mist, they had fled south and east. The dark cloud held steady, rising several hundred strides up the cliff. But on this side of it, the face of the sheer bluff shone red, orange, and white in jagged striations that looked like lightning. The summit of the north face was lost beyond sight, too far for help, but close by at its base she saw her answer.

A cave.

Wendra pulled the strapping from her left boot, tore a strip from her cloak, and tied it to her wound as tightly as she could bear. Then she tapped Penit and pointed to the hole at the base of the cliff. The boy understood immediately. He helped her up and, using the large rock as a shield, they stepped as lightly as they could toward the cave. Wendra watched closely for drops of blood on the ground, but soon lost her concern in the flashes of heat that stole over her.

Occasionally, strange sounds emanated from the mist, but Wendra did not stop. She fixed on the dark mouth at the cliff base and pushed all other thoughts out of her mind. She hoped the Far had fared well against the Bar'dyn. She hoped Tahn and the others were all right. But even her concern for her brother fell away under her determination to reach shelter for herself and Penit.

They reached the cave and guardedly entered, stopping to sit only when the shadows hid them completely. Penit eased Wendra to the cave floor. She felt the cool invitation of the ground there on her cheek and let everything else go to blackness.

When she awoke, she could not see the entrance to the cave. Worriedly, she looked around, searching for Penit, but all remained black. Finally her eyes adjusted, and she saw the flicker of several stars shining through what looked like a tilted arch—the cave entrance.

"Penit," she whispered.

"Right here," the boy replied. He reached out and touched her arm.

She jumped at his touch, causing a twinge in her leg. Her face slick with sweat, Wendra knew the fever had spread. The cuts were almost surely deeper than she had first thought. She sat up and leaned back against the cave wall.

"Any sign of the others?" she asked.

"No, but I found your horse," Penit answered, his voice proud.

"You left the cave?" Wendra asked with mild reproach.

"I crawled to the entrance and watched the Bar'dyn search the edge of the dark clouds, disappearing inside and coming out in different places. I didn't see them get anybody." Penit scuttled closer to her, his boots and bottom scraping the cavern floor. "Then the mist blew away in a great wind, scouring the ground. I waited a while, then I went out to look around for Vendanj to help you with your leg. I saw Ildico drinking at a small stream. I got him and brought him back. He's just outside, tied to a tree."

Wendra wanted to scold him for taking such a chance, but she didn't have the energy. Besides, he'd gotten them food and transportation, which might just save them.

"Thank you, Penit. That was very brave." Wendra, her eyes now more fully adjusted, saw a shadowy smile spread on the boy's face, though he said nothing. "Bring the saddlebags in. Let's have something to eat."

The boy rose and became a dark silhouette against the lighter darkness of the night beyond the mouth of the cave. Stars on the horizon winked in and out as he passed in front of them. He disappeared for a moment, then quickly returned, dropping the heavy bags to the ground.

"Can we start a fire?" he asked. "It's getting cold."

Wendra considered the risk, but heard the fear behind his request. "Gather some wood, but quietly. And don't stray too far from the mouth of the cave."

"Won't have to, there's plenty just outside."

Penit left again on his errand. Wendra retrieved a bag filled with dried meats and cheese, and another with Sedagin flatbread that she'd saved from the previous night's feast. Thoughts of the Sedagin left her dejected. They certainly would have come to their defense had they been close at hand. Instead, here she lay, far below them, holed up in the bedrock of their High Plain and bleeding out her life's blood. Suddenly, her thoughts turned to her lost child, and to the Bar'dyn who had come into her home and taken it from her, and who had pushed them up the road to Myrr, into the wilds and finally into the high home of the Sedagin. Then, upon leaving, they had passed through these mists. Anger brought bile to the back of her throat, and she tasted the hot acid of her stomach. Tears of frustration and loss shook her, but she let them fall without a sound, for fear of being heard by the boy and worrying him.

Penit returned with an armload of wood and laid it on the cave floor beside her. She took a flint and handed it to the boy, who readily built a fire. His face, streaked with dirt and tears, glowed in the orange glare of the flames with a thankful smile that warmed Wendra's heart. They ate in silence, building meals of the bread, meat, and cheese. Penit fetched the waterskin, and they both drank deeply before settling in and tending the fire.

Sometime later, Wendra decided to have a look outside, but her leg had grown stiff and numb and did not respond to her attempts to use it. She sat again and looked at Penit, who appeared lost in thought and somehow content here in the cave despite the events that had brought them here. She thought she could see all the terrible circumstances and nightmarish beings disappearing from his consciousness as he put himself in the present moment, fed and warm and tending a healthy fire. She envied him this, as she watched him live so contentedly even for a few moments without concern for tomorrow. Unwittingly, she smiled with the same expression that she'd seen on Balatin's face so often: wonder, love, admiration. She'd assumed her father lived a contented and happy life. It pained her now to realize that these moments were, for parents, but islands in a river current. But it made her glad as well that, though she hadn't known it, her life had offered him some respite from the hardships a parent knows.

"When do we go find the others?" Penit said, interrupting Wendra's reverie.

She looked at Penit with increasing amazement and wondered if life on the wagon beds had instilled such persistence and courage in him. "Tomorrow. My leg is stiff and I have the sweats. After I sleep, and it's light, we can search for them. They may well find us; Mira is an adept tracker."

"Good," Penit replied.

Wendra studied the boy's face, wondering if she dared jeopardize the feeling of safety he seemed to have. *Not tonight. Tomorrow. When the greater light is firmly over our heads, I will ask him what the mists showed him.* So she sat with him in the light of the fire. They steadily fed the flames and remarked softly about unimportant things, the way she and Balatin and Tahn had done in the years before. Sometime later in the evening, Wendra began to hum softly, her dulcet tones a perfect counterpoint to the crackle of the fire and the low hum of wood being consumed by flame. Penit watched her, grinning. Wendra returned the smile, spontaneously creating a soothing, lilting melody. Penit crawled closer and rested his head on her lap. Long before the fire had burned to coals, Wendra followed the boy into sleep.

She woke to the sound of wood being laid for a fire. Opening her eyes, Wendra saw Penit fussing over kindling and flint. Beyond the cave entrance, the day had already grown strong in the sky. Her attention returned to Penit, who began quietly singing to himself, though his efforts were not so practiced and squeaked in his adolsecent throat. Wendra sat up, several drops of sweat falling from her nose and forehead. The fever was worse. She had lost a great deal of blood. Even without standing she knew her leg would be of little use to her.

Propping herself up, she wiped her face and sat a moment as Penit finished relighting the fire. The boy had stripped a green switch and sharpened one end, threading several pieces of dried meat onto it for their endfast. He sat with his knees up close to his chest, heating the meat over the fire. Wendra smiled weakly through her fever at his innocence. What she must ask of him was too much. At what cost would it come for a boy who believed all the old stories enough to stand up to a league captain in his own defense to play the tales? But she knew she must ask. Merely propping herself up had exhausted all her energy; she couldn't even reach the entrance to the cave without help, and Penit could not carry her. He certainly couldn't help her reach Recityv.

"Penit, I need your help."

"Sure. What can I do?" He turned over the roasting meat and looked at her.

"I cannot stand." Wendra swallowed hard to keep her emotions from welling up. "I will need help if I am to make it to Recityv. I need you to find that help for me." She paused, looking into the boy's large blue eyes. "Can you do that for me?"

The boy did not hesitate. "I will." Then he surprised Wendra. "It was hard for you to ask me that, wasn't it?" He put his meat down on the saddlebag. "I am young, and I have been without parents for as long as I can remember. And," he said, hesitating, "I don't want to meet the Bar'dyn again." He smiled nervously. "But I can do it. I can follow the stream. Deleira always said water leads to people. He was the troupe leader."

"You must be careful. Even if the Bar'dyn are gone, a child . . . a young man alone is not safe in the world of men."

Penit smirked knowingly. "I've seen my share of scalawags. They're always close to the wagon pot or spinning a tale to see your pocket stitching." His smile faded and he looked distantly into the fire. "I will be careful. I don't want to see any more of the darkness in the clouds."

He offered no explanation, and Wendra chose to hold her questions for another time. "You'll be all right, Penit." Her voice broke with emotion. She wiped her brow and eyes with the hem of her cloak.

"You, too," the boy said.

Penit gathered a great stack of wood for her, and refilled the waterskin. He took four strips of meat and a slice of cheese and put the rest in the saddlebag. When he finished, he knelt beside her.

"You're sick because of me, because you came after me and got hurt. I won't fail. I will come back."

Wendra put her arms around him and kissed his cheek. "Go safely, Penit."

Then he rose and walked to the mouth of the cave, where he stopped and looked back. "I lied before. I did care about the pageant wagon, the troupe. And I miss them." He stopped, reflecting. "But I had to get away. I saw what happens after a life on the boards."

He left off there, and jogged from the cave. She heard him mount Ildico and pass briefly across the mouth of the cave, heading east. "And come back to me again, son," she said to herself and lay her head back down on the cool loam of the cavern floor.

Wendra drifted in and out of consciousness. Too weak to even lift herself up, she lay on the ground inside her cave and watched the last dances of fire-shadow on the uneven surface of the rocky ceiling. Fever sweat drenched her back, and her lips were dry and cracked from panting and dehydration. The food Penit had left was beyond her reach, but the thought of it nauseated her anyway, so she gave up on eating.

As the fire died, the cave grew quiet and cold. Dim light shone from the entrance as the day came fast to a close. Chills shook her violently, alternating with hot waves of fever. She managed to pull her blanket up over her shoulders and listen to the sound of her own heart in her ears.

Perhaps the Sheason or the Far would find her before Penit could return with help. But she had been here more than a day. If they hadn't come to her yet, they had likely turned east toward Recityv.

When Penit tore from her grasp in the mists, she had reacted without thinking, chasing him, hoping to catch him before whatever darkness groaned in the clouds could destroy him. Her thoughts grew darker still. She would probably have failed if Mira had not come after her. The Bar'dyn had put its sharp, powerful nails into her and she had crawled into this large tomb to die.

Wendra pushed back the morbid thoughts. There was still hope. Hope that she would live . . . a hope her own child had lost at the hands of the same brutal beasts. Her throat tightened with weak anger at the thought of what they had cost her: her home, her child, and now possibly her life. Wendra started to cough from the thick emotion. The convulsions from the coughing tore at the wound in her hip that was trying to heal.

Lying on her back, the coughing worsened, each fit reopening her wound. She summoned all her strength and rolled onto her side to try and calm the spasms. Her coughs now stirred the fire ash into small clouds that settled and clung to her sweat-slickened face. The smell of spent alder and soot nauseated her, but the wracking convulsions stopped, and she breathed easier. Lying still, Wendra felt an uncomfortable lump protruding into her side. She reached into the folds of her cloak and removed the box she had brought with her from beneath her bed back home.

Carefully, she placed the songbox beside her head. A wan smile touched her lips at the memories the box's cedar smell evoked, and the gulf that seemed to separate her from her life when the box had been so important. Then her thoughts turned bitter, and she considered how much better this token might serve as wood for her fire than to remind her of what was no more. Salty tears stung her eyes and ran over her nose and cheeks. She liked the feel of them and did not wipe them away, tasting them as they ran onto her lips.

The songbox reminded her of home, the Hollows. The thought of it raised the question to her mind again: Why had the Sheason brought her? Was she supposed to support Tahn? Would she have been in danger if she'd remained behind? Something told her there was more to it than simply keeping siblings together. But no matter how she concentrated or reasoned, she could find no good answer. And now she was alone; left to try to make it to Rectiyv with only the help of a boy.

Wendra fingered open the box's clasp and lifted its lid. Softly, its melody began, small gears turning the roll inside, which plucked a tune through the tiny tone prongs. The delicate song was too soft to ring as high as the cave's ceiling, but it fell on the fire pit, the cavern floor around her, and her own tired ears like a memory, and she closed her eyes. The gentle notes called out their tune like a wounded bird, and Wendra felt herself falling into a fevered sleep.

Suddenly, Wendra had the feeling that she was not alone. Opening her eyes, she saw seated across from her a kindly looking man in a brilliant white robe. Between them, the fire had been rekindled. Distantly, like wind causing chimes to jangle, she could hear the melody of her box.

A fever vision?

Maybe. But despite not feeling any immediate fear, she sensed that her life had just irrevocably changed.

• CHAPTER TWENTY-FOUR •

The Rushing of Je'holta

Braethen lay on the ground staring up through the great hole in the mist. His chest still heaved from exertion. He clutched in his left hand the sword Vendanj had given him. The Sheason remained still, his eyes shut, one hand to his chest, the other extended. Not far from either of them, the ashy heap that had been the Maere still smoked in the bright shaft of light that broke through the gloom. Sometime later, the Sheason opened his eyes.

The sound of hurried footsteps could be heard in the mist, vague sounds that were retreating from him. The cries and moans deep within the fog bank slowly faded, leaving the sodalist and the Sheason in a pervasive silence. The hole torn in the mist began slowly to close, but for several moments the two sat in the sunlight, catching their breath.

"Do we wait, or do we continue on?" Braethen asked.

"The Maere likely means Bar'dyn are close by," Vendanj said. "I believe I heard their heavy strides chasing the others when the line broke. The Quiet-given will feel the death of the Maere, gather quickly, and come for us. We will wait for Mira to return, then we will try to find Tahn and the rest."

"What of the sounds in the mists?"

"Always a threat, sodalist, but they are no longer alive in the flesh. The mist gives them shape to the eye: their influence is in the mind. Their voices belong to souls lost while serving the One. They cry from beyond death, their hollow voices audible within Je'holta, like corrupted remembrance."

"You said the Bar'dyn were here in the mist," Braethen said. "Are they not affected by it?"

"Not as you or I. The Bar'dyn and other lost races that serve the Artificer no longer feel hope. Abandonment is what they know, and so the taint of Male'Siriptus has no hold over them. It is said that all the Bourne is Je'holta. For them," the Sheason said mournfully, "it is like home."

The Sheason's words drew Braethen's thoughts back to the black world that had enveloped him as he'd taken the sword he now held. In stark contrast, the brightness of the sun above him made his eyes water, but he did not turn away. He decided it was some kind of test.

"When you gave me the sword," he asked Vendanj, "darkness swallowed me . . ."

Vendanj looked first at him, then at the encroaching wall of mist. Cautious footsteps could be heard approaching. The Sheason put a finger to his lips to silence the sodalist, stood, and turned in the direction of the sound. From the bank of darkness, Mira slowly emerged, her swords drawn, her face flushed.

"The girl?" he asked.

"Bar'dyn found her and the boy deep in the mist. She fled while I fought them back."

Vendanj nodded. "Are you all right?" he asked.

"Out of patience with the beasts out of the Hand," she said sternly.

The mists followed her as she approached, and quickly Je'holta filled in the large hole above, occluding the sun. She stopped near Braethen and appraised him carefully, her gaze alternating between him and the sword in his hand. Under her scrutiny, Braethen got to his feet and replaced the sword in its sheath. Around them, plumes of mist rose and fell, their touch feeling as a willow bud might in early spring.

"We will go north to the edge of the mist," Vendanj said. "Perhaps the others have reached safety beyond its grip." The Sheason extended a hand. "The power of Male'Siriptus still exists around us. If even one of the Velle came with Je'holta, we are far from safe."

Braethen took the renderer's hand, and put his own out to Mira. The Far sheathed one sword, and took the sodalist's hand in a firm grip. Together they walked on through the mist.

It took time, but eventually they emerged from the low, dark cloud, into the light of day beyond. Braethen raised his arms and turned to face the sun.

"I'll find the horses," Mira said. "The Je'holta cloud will not go quietly."

"I know," Vendanj replied. "It will rage soon."

Mira left at a run, covering ground at great speed, scanning the terrain she passed. In a moment she disappeared from sight. Braethen had not seen her move thus. He gaped openly at her rapid departure.

"We must find shelter," Vendanj said. "The rushing of Je'holta is painful to the point of death. It will howl and blow like a storm dropping off the slopes of the Pall. The despair and loss of those that inhabit Male'Siriptus race over the body in torrents and tear at the mind like daggers. Come."

Vendanj hastened up a low hill. A dense copse stood halfway down the lee slope, the rain and weather having hollowed a space beneath the gnarled root system on the downhill side. Braethen and the Sheason ducked under the cover.

They sat silently in the protection of the hollow, looking out on the day and watching cloud shadows move across the land. Then a wind rose up, mild at first, nothing more than the breeze that precedes a summer shower. But soon it became a gale, carrying leaves and dust in streams down the hill below them. The trees swayed, low oak and sage rippling in the fierceness. Above them, the sky darkened, and the wind screamed in horrible gusts. Braethen squinted at the mists that rushed past them at incredible speed. Branches were torn from their trunks and smaller plants uprooted entirely. Small sticks wheeled into the sky like feathers, and the dark cloud rushed out. The gale raged for several minutes, the tree roots around them groaning and straining against the onslaught of wind. The noise was deafening, like standing beneath a waterfall during spring thaw. Braethen grasped a root nearby to anchor himself, and hoped the Far had found cover. The Sheason sat with his cowl drawn up, a shadow in the rooted hollow, patiently waiting out the rushing of the winds.

The angry cloud expanded outward, dissipating to nothing. Soon, the howling died and the wind grew still. Light filtered through, replacing the darkness, and revealed the terrain around them, ravaged in the passing of Je'holta.

"Will and Sky," Braethen muttered.

"Let's go," Vendanj said, and stepped out from under the trees.

They hiked back to the top of the hill, and watched as Mira appeared over the rise to the west, leading four horses. Moments later, the Far arrived with their mounts, and Penit's besides. Her hair had blown free of its band and fell in long, silken strands about her face and neck. Braethen had not seen Mira like this; the difference surprised him.

"We may find them traveling east toward Recityv," Mira said. "But the rushing winds have erased any trail we might have followed for leagues in any direction. The boy is either on foot, or with Wendra. They should be easy to find."

The Far did not mention Tahn and Sutter.

They mounted and rode east, Mira taking the lead, constantly scanning the ground and horizon. All the rest of that day they rode, stopping finally when the light became too dim to see any further.

Mira secured the horses, then started a fire. Braethen helped her gather wood before sitting near the blaze and placing his sword in his lap to look it over. The blade bore the mark of a craftsman's care, but had not yet seen its polish and finish. The metal was unyielding though. It glowed in the night, but so imperceptibly that Braethen half doubted any glow at all. Yet, when he looked closely, he could see the metal held a faint white cast, as though lit somehow from within.

Vendanj took a seat near the fire and removed his small wooden case from his cloak. Opening it, he took two leaves from a stem and placed them in his mouth, then, without once looking at Braethen, settled in, clearly exhausted, to savor the fire's warmth.

Mira left for some time, returning without a sound. She seated herself on the trunk of a fallen tree. "There is no sign of them. But there is also no sign of Quiet-given, either," she reported. "We are beyond the land affected by the rushing. Perhaps they moved farther north before turning east." Mira shifted her attention to Braethen. "We need to continue your training."

"And you asked me of the darkness, sodalist," said Vendanj. "I have not forgotten. But that must be left for another time." The Sheason drew back his cowl and looked at Braethen. "There are things from your books that you must know the truth behind if you are to fulfill your oath as sodalist. I know your heart now, but your inexperience and lack of understanding are more dangerous to us than the boy, Penit."

"Why?"

"Because you are aware of the histories and the truths they offer us, but you haven't comprehended them. To hold that sword, to lift your arm with others as your emblem suggests, you must have an understanding of the power of the Will, its meaning and purpose."

Braethen listened intently.

"The Will is the power of creation, sodalist," Vendanj declared. "You've read this countless times. It is what moves us, the wellspring of all life. The Will is without beginning or end. It is the power that resides in all matter, and the matter that resides in all power. It gives purpose to each age, those past and all those that will ever be." The Sheason lifted the symbol fastened to his necklace, three rings, one inside the next, all joined at one point. "Each age is a part of the one before it, its consequences spreading, resonating, outward like ripples on a pond. But you may also read the emblem in its opposite, focusing inward." Vendanj ran his finger across the circles toward the point where they were joined. "An inner resonance reducing forever to a single, perfect point." He traced the woven figure of the rings thoughtfully. "The Will is both these things. Indeed, its meaning is forever dual."

"And Forda I'Forza?" Braethen asked.

"Yes," Vendanj answered. "Called also Ars and Arsa in the Language of the Covenant. Its true meaning is 'energy and matter.' All things are a marriage of the two, or one that becomes the other through transformation or growth or offering. Matter and energy have always been and will always be. They can be neither created nor destroyed. They list and heave under pressure from each other, becoming new, sometimes refining each other into beauty and balance, sometimes becoming discordant and unstable in a struggle to reach harmony. The Will is the union of these separate and everlasting elements."

The Sheason spoke with deep reverence. Braethen thought that it must be because he invoked the power of the Will, taking it inside himself to cause change in the way of things, the cost of its use evident in the sunken cheeks of his face.

"To be confirmed a Sheason," Vendanj went on, "is to accept the responsibility of wielding the power of the Will. The authority cannot be claimed; it must be conferred by those who already possess it to a pupil worthy to bear such a mantle."

Mira tossed two pieces of wood into the fire. "It is a noble call, sodalist, but not all those who receive it live to know its worth." She stared at him across the fire, her grey eyes bright and knowing.

"She is right," Vendanj said. "But you must understand this first." He touched an open palm to his chest. "We ourselves are Forda I'Forza. Our physical bodies are one half; thought and feeling the other half. For some this second part is known as the spirit or soul. In the covenant language, it is called us'ledia. But it is all Forda."

He lowered his eyes and took a handful of dirt from the earth between his feet. "The Will was not intended to be drawn upon and used to influence this age, or any age since the High Season when the Noble Ones walked among us and used the Will to give form and variety to the land. It was their first hope that there be balance sufficient in this world that men would strive together to know the Will without trying to manipulate it.

"But while the Great Fathers yet held council at the Tabernacle of the Sky, the One put at odds all they had hoped to achieve. The peace begun in that blessed age started to fail."

Vendanj looked away, the words distasteful in his mouth. Flaring eyes returned to Braethen.

"It was the Sheason who kept the dream of the Fathers alive. The Sheason were those who served the First Ones with untiring arms and perfect conviction. No power did they wield, only the desire to serve, to assist, to sustain. Sheason means 'servant' in the covenant tongue." He took a deep breath and let the dirt slip from his palm as though it were sand in a time-glass. Then he gathered Braethen's attention with a hard stare. "The world all but surrendered itself, becoming wicked and craven, and the age that followed the departure of the Fathers was given its name for it. It was a dark season, when the veil was thin and the emissaries of the One wrought havoc and destruction over most of the kingdoms south of the Pall.

"When all seemed lost, a Sheason known as Palamon rose in battle against Jo'ha'nel—the first dark messiah out of the Bourne—and defeated the beast. Palamon was a simple servant who had studied the writings left behind when the scola—the first disciples and scholars of the Framers—fled their colleges after the Fathers departed. He learned how to vender the Will, to use its power to direct change and organize matter. But he could do so only because he had been deemed a servant by the First Ones, and so was conferred the ability to render."

Vendanj paused, lending weight to what he said next. "That ability came with a price."

Several long moments later, he continued. "Since matter and energy can be neither created nor destroyed, to draw upon the Will in order to change things as they are requires an expenditure of Forda I'Forza. The Sheason were ordained to serve the land and its people; they were entrusted with this authority by the Fathers, and Palamon would not abrogate that trust. So he drew the power of the Will from himself, costing so much of his own Forda I'Forza that he could never fully recover. All those who have come after him have honored this covenant of personal sacrifice."

Braethen stared with wide eyes in amazement. "Then each time you draw upon the Will, you die a little?"

Vendanj said nothing, but Mira's eyes answered Braethen plainly. The Far rose and glared across the fire at Braethen. "Mark well what has been added to your understanding this night, sodalist. It is dangerous knowledge. It inspires your compassion and admiration, I can see, but joining yourself to this cause has put a price on your head." She stopped, the sound of her words replaced by the yowl of coyotes in the prairies to the west and the crackle of pine boughs in the fire between them.

Braethen's hand tightened instinctively upon his blade.

Mira noticed his whitened knuckles. "Well enough, sodalist. Tomorrow then. We will show you better use of that steel."

Mira left the fire, disappearing in an instant beyond the circle of its glow. Braethen knew he would not see her again until morning. He still had so many questions. Some of the gaps in the accounts he'd studied had been filled, but what of himself? What of the Sodality? And he desperately wanted to know what had happened in the mist when he'd taken hold of the sword.

He turned to Vendanj. "What of me? What of—"

"Not tonight, sodalist," Vendanj interrupted. "Sleep. We will talk of these things again. But now we need our rest. We have a longer route to Recityv than the others, stops to make."

"The Scar," Braethen said.

"And before that, Widow's Village." The Sheason's voice became thoughtful, soft. "We have names to record. . . ."

The Sheason lay down and soon his breathing slowed. But Braethen's mind would not be quieted. For hours into the night, he sat pondering the words Vendanj had spoken. What was Widow's Village? What names did he speak of? But mostly, Braethen worried that every time he used the sword lying in his lap, the darkness would return.

• CHAPTER TWENTY-FIVE •

The Tenendra

The land and sky turned bronze as the sun began to fall toward night. Shadows lengthened and the hazy light of end of day rose over the full-bellied roll of the land north of the High Plains. The trees became dark shapes, and the whir of cricket song came as the heavens exposed themselves again.

But Tahn and Sutter did not fully stop until Sutter fell from his saddle.

They'd ridden for many hours, pausing only when the horses' legs had flagged beneath them. They'd allowed their mounts a brief rest to drink and graze a bit. Then they'd continued toward the east. Tahn had ridden with his injured foot free of the stirrup. The pain of the spines in his sole sharpened with Jole's every stride, but bothered him less with his foot unrestrained. And unable to concentrate, Tahn followed Sutter's lead.

Until his friend tumbled.

Tahn jumped from Jole's back, taking care to lessen the impact on his damaged foot. He got to Sutter's side. His friend lay on his stomach, his nose in the dirt, the spiked ball bloody and still protruding from his back. But the bleeding had been relatively light. Sutter's fall had not resulted from loss of blood.

"I feel weak." Sutter's words came soft. Too soft, even after having fallen.

Something on the spikes?

Tahn looked around, panic seizing him.

They were alone. There was no help.

"Let's sleep here," Sutter said. Something in his voice struck Tahn's mind like a warning. *Don't let him slip into sleep. Keep him talking.*

"How about you stand your lazy ass up? I could use some help. My foot's killing me." Tahn jostled his friend.

Sutter managed to look up with a tired smile. "Ah, Woodchuck, stuff that swollen foot of yours into your mouth so I can't hear you complain."

Tahn needed to get Sutter back on his horse. But he'd never do it still hobbled by these spines in his foot. He carefully removed his boot and stocking. The coppery smell of blood rose from the wool sock, sodden with sweat and blood. In the dim twilight, his wounds did not appear too serious. Tahn slowly probed the sole of his foot. He winced when his fingers brushed the entry marks.

"How about some help with this little prize in my back?" Sutter spoke from behind Tahn, his words slurring a bit.

"I think it suits you fine. I say we leave it for a while and see if it grows on you."

Sutter laughed, and immediately groaned. "Don't make me laugh. It hurts too much."

"Never thought I'd hear those words from you." Tahn stood on his one good foot.

"Only when you're telling the joke, Woodchuck. Now about my back."

Tahn drew his knife and doubled his cloak in his hand to pull the ball out with a quick yank and toss it aside. It fell to the ground with a thud. Sutter bit back a curse before Tahn tucked a cloth in Nails's shirt and patted his shoulder. "Good as new. You'll be stooped over the dirt again in no time."

Sutter returned a wry half smile and stood, the pain dispelling some of whatever had gotten into his blood. Tahn sat and took a drink from his waterskin, then washed his foot.

"Ah, Dust and Wind!" Tahn exclaimed.

"What you whining about now?"

"I can't even see the spines. They're too deep inside." Tahn continued to probe, grimacing as he touched each buried needle.

"I can get them out," Sutter said. "But your cries will be heard all the way back to Hambley's if I do it." His lips tugged into a lopsided grin.

Tahn mocked him. "It's all those marvelous years plucking twigs from the ground that qualifies you to do surgery on my foot. Is that it? Because if that's what you're thinking, forget it. I would rather burn the foot off. It would be less painful."

"Your will is your own, Woodchuck." Sutter made a show of two good feet by stomping down hard on the ground. "My father taught me how to use a short knife to remove the slivers that a professional root-digger such as myself is bound to get working the soil. And those spines are a great deal larger than some of the barbs and thorns I've coaxed from my hands."

"Have you any of that balsam root to dull the pain?" Tahn asked.

"I think there's a bit left if your womanly foot is too delicate to stand for man's work."

Tahn smiled defeat through gritted teeth. "Find the balsam root."

As Sutter looked through the saddlebags, Tahn had his first moment of quiet and calm since they entered the mists of Je'holta.

By the Bourne, what have I done?

He looked west, the way they'd come, as though he might see Wendra even now in her own flight from the Quiet. Only the hues of sunset there. He thought of her, of the simple life they'd led in the Hollows, of the awful moment of her childbirth . . . of abandoning her defense then, of leaving her in the dark mists a few hours ago . . . He hoped she was all right.

He chastised himself for allowing the mists to get inside his mind, to send him fleeing recklessly away from his friends and causing himself and Sutter to be separated from the others. He wanted to go back and find them, to make sure Wendra was safe. He owed his sister that much.

But he needed to get Sutter and himself to a healer. Even now he could see his friend's hands trembling as he searched for the balsam root. Still, the guilt of abandoning her again plagued him. What would Balatin have said? Tahn examined his throbbing foot, delicately fingering the wounds. Sharp pains shot up his leg. Balatin would tell him he was no good to anyone unless he was *whole*.

He needed help.

With unexpected suddenness he missed the Far. He had grown used to her certainty, to seeing her at the edge of camp looking out into the night. He had become accustomed to her unsmiling way, and the sureness with which she moved and spoke and knew what to do.

If nothing else, Wendra would be safe with Mira and Vendanj to protect her, though unlike the thought of the Far, recalling the Sheason did not comfort him. Tahn sensed that Vendanj had sought him out because Tahn might prove useful or important, not out of regard for his safety.

Then like a crack of thunder, the images he'd seen in the mists flashed violently in his mind. Tahn pushed them back, refocusing on his sister. He should have made her stay in the Hollows. Whatever danger the Sheason placed him in, Wendra should not share it. But even as he had these thoughts, Tahn knew them to be false. Despite the danger, it had felt right for her to come. He just wanted to find his way back to her as soon as possible. Because after all, perhaps being near her had less to do with keeping her safe and more to do with the mutual comfort they could give each other. As they always had. And moreso now than ever: She with the recent loss of her baby, and Tahn with his growing dread of where this journey was leading him.

And the sacrifices it may require.

Tahn then considered Penit, the boy his sister had grown so fond of so fast. The boy's presence troubled him. Why would the Sheason permit a child to accompany them? The dangers were very real, and this orphan belonged on the boards of a wagon-bed, performing. Now he accompanied a renderer. The Sheason surely had a use for him. The thought of Vendanj's manipulation burned in Tahn until Sutter returned, hefting two roots in his hand.

"Here," Sutter said, and threw a root at Tahn.

The root hit him in the stomach. "Such compassion." The words came out more bitterly than he'd intended—thoughts of the Sheason still lingered in his mind.

Tahn stripped the shoots from the main root, then broke the root in two. He ate the first half, grimacing at the bitter taste.

"You're a picture of loveliness," Sutter said, pulling a short knife from his own boot.

"And you're a credit to dirt everywhere, Nails—" Tahn gagged on the root. He forced himself to swallow.

"Eat the other half," Sutter admonished. "It's a thin root. You'll want it all if the pain is as bad as you're making it out to be."

Tahn frowned and put the second half in his mouth.

"Chew it," Sutter said. "It works faster that way." Sutter took his own root and gobbled it up.

Tahn bit into the balsam and quickly chewed it into small pieces before swallowing. "How long until you can start?"

"The balsam won't dull the pain of getting them out, just the throb once we're done." Sutter was slurring his words again.

"Come here," Tahn said. "Let me check your back."

Sutter turned. "Why?"

Tahn slapped Sutter's wound, eliciting a yowl. "What in all your days was that about?" Nails complained.

"Something was on those spikes, Sutter. I don't know what it was, but you're slurring your words and your hands are trembling. The sting keeps you sharp. Now, get these spines out, and try not to enjoy causing me pain. Then let's find some help for us both."

A look of disbelief on his friend's face quickly changed to worry. Sutter sat, lifting Tahn's foot to the last light of day. The smile left Nails's face as he carefully put the blade against one thumb and started on the punctures near the toes. He folded back a flap of skin, and pressed the knife into the wound. Terrible pain shot up Tahn's leg. He muffled a cry, and in a second, Sutter lifted the first spine for Tahn to see.

"Not bad for a root-digger, wouldn't you say?" Sutter commented, though his face held no hint of humor.

Tahn gritted his teeth against the next operation. One by one Sutter removed the other spines, and as he did he began to speak in a faraway voice. This, Tahn thought, was not the poison on the spiked ball, but remembrance.

"This was my father's knife when he was a boy," Sutter said, holding up the bloodied blade along with another spine dug from Tahn's foot. "He gave it to me when I saw my tenth Northsun. Told me a good knife and a bit of root knowledge was all a man needed."

"He's a good man," Tahn offered.

"I know." Sutter nodded, returning to his task. "And he was always good to me. Never said a bad word about the parents that left me. Never asked more or less of me than he did of Garon." Sutter was quiet a moment, as if thinking of his stepbrother. "He needs me on that farm," he said, mostly to himself.

Tahn heard guilt beneath the words.

"We'll go home eventually," Tahn offered.

Sutter looked up and caught Tahn's eyes, a question passing unspoken between them: Neither of them knew if they'd ever get home again. He worked another spine out of Tahn's foot. Then he stopped, and stared at the knife. "It wasn't for shame of him or my mother that I never said anything about being adopted, Tahn. I want you to know that. Never of them. It was . . . it was the parents who left me to begin with. That's what I didn't want . . . I love my father, my mother. I wanted to come with you, yes, but I love them . . . I do. They were never anything but kind to me."

"You're a good son to them, Sutter."

"Am I?" Tahn's friend squeezed back sudden tears. "They don't deserve the hardship of that farm without my help." Then softer. "Maybe the Sheason is right. Maybe putting my hands in the loam should have been noble enough."

Sutter's words were painfully clear. No poison, Tahn thought, could have dulled them.

"Your secret is new to me," Tahn said, "but it's not the reason you left the Hollows. Remember what Vendanj said. Staying there would have put them in danger." Sutter looked up. Tahn nodded. "They know you love them."

In the dying light, Sutter looked at Tahn a long moment, then nodded. His grimy face showed the vaguest hint of a smile.

"Now, can we get on with it?" Tahn concluded, pulling them out of the past. Sutter's smile came on full.

The last two spines felt as though they slid from bone-deep inside Tahn's foot. The pain in the flesh of his sole was excruciating. When Sutter finished, Tahn's body fell limp. His foot throbbed while his friend gently wrapped it with several lengths of cloth torn from the hem of his shirt. Sutter then helped him into his saddle, and the two friends turned east and rode hard enough that the jouncing of their mounts kept their pain fresh.

The terrain undulated in long, rolling hills and vales. As darkness descended more fully, the pain in Tahn's foot grew. When they came upon a road stretching north and south, Sutter reined in his horse. As Tahn looked both directions, Sutter handed him another balsam root.

"Eat and be well, Woodchuck." This time his friend's words slurred badly.

"Your face is pain enough to need this bitter medicine."

"You're feeling better, I can tell. Any thoughts?" Sutter pointed up and down the road.

"Yeah," Tahn replied. "But your face would still be ugly." Tahn looked both directions again and turned Jole north. After another hour, they crested a low rise and found a town nestled in a narrow vale. Firelight flickered in windows like light-flies, and people ambled along the streets. A few rode in overland carriages—the type built strong for long journeys that might encounter highwaymen.

At the far end of the town, several large tents glowed like the hollow gourds fitted with candles at the commencement of Passat each Midwinter in the Hollows. But these were grand tents, decorated with stripes that flowed from their pinnacles to the ground. Tahn could see six tents in all, and from a distance could hear the thrum of voices and activity. People were entering and exiting like bees coming and going from a hive. And in the air hung the scent of animals sharing close quarters.

"A tenendra?" Sutter asked.

"Looks like it," Tahn said. "I've never seen one in the Hollows."

"My father says they're low entertainment, unworthy of our coin." But Sutter's eyes were alight with curiosity. "I don't suppose it would hurt to test the wisdom of our elders." He turned a devious grin to Tahn, his smile lopsided, as though the left side of his face was growing numb.

Tahn looked back at the brightly lit town below. He wanted to see the tenendra. The stories of the feats and wonders they exhibited were known almost as widely as those of the reader. And the bright tents looked warm and welcoming, the kind of thing he and Sutter had talked about finding ever since he could remember.

But more importantly, they needed a healer.

"We will go," he concluded. "But we find a healer first. And remember there's no one to stand behind us if we get into trouble."

"You couldn't even stand behind *me,* gimpy," Sutter said. "Come on, before we miss all the fun." Then, in a worried tone, he added, "Tahn, I need help. I can't feel my hands." Sutter looked unsteady in his saddle. They were running out of time. Whatever had gotten inside Sutter had gone deeper, and would continue to work at him until . . .

Sutter clucked at Bardoll and Tahn hurried to catch up. Together they descended into the vale as night closed in completely.

Tahn guardedly watched the faces of people he and Sutter passed as they rode into the town proper. To his surprise, no one seemed to take note of them. Men and women crossed in front of their horses without care. More than once, he and Sutter slowed or wound their way around pedestrians who stopped to share a greeting or an insult with one another. At the prospect of dipping into this new town and its culture, Sutter gave Tahn a look of delighted, unrestrained glee as comic as the scop masks they'd seen in Myrr. But his friend's eyelids seemed to droop, giving him the look of one deep in his cup of bitter.

They needed to hurry.

The variety of fashions gave Tahn the impression that the town hosted travelers from near and far. Every third building either let rooms or announced itself as a full-service inn to this town called Squim. Brightly painted signs nailed to building facades listed what could be purchased within and at what price. More than a few led their menus with blandishments like "Fairest Anais east of the Sedagin," and more plainly, "Bed Company."

And if there were a lot of inns, there were scads of taverns. Loud laughter and the sounds of challenge poured from open doors, and the jangling strains of poorly tuned cithern and badly carved pipes and flutes floated on the air. Each of the taverns had one or two large men sitting near doors propped open for ventilation. Dull expressions hung on their faces, and their massive arms rested in their laps. Hambley had never needed such men to control his clientele, but Tahn felt sure that was precisely these fellows' purpose.

Most of the buildings were wood, built with little care for appearance. Rough, ill-fitted planks showed slices of the light within. Narrow alleys ran alongside many of the shops and passed through to secondary streets. Shadowy forms huddled in the darkness of those alleys, the wink of lit tobaccom stems and pipes flaring orange as they smoked there.

They passed a long building with multiple entrances, each lined with signs two strides high. The signs were large slabs of slate carefully quarried to remain intact. Upon the black surface, long lists of sundry items were scrawled in white chalk. As Tahn and Sutter passed, a short man with thinning hair and wearing an apron bustled out and used a cloth to erase a number of items on two of the slates. Men and women in various states of agitation entered the store. Tahn watched some who carried wrapped parcels, whose heads twitched and who looked around nervously as they passed through the doors. A few women went in looking distressed and mournful, their gait halting as they neared the entry. One woman strode briskly up to the door, her face heavily painted and her bosom threatening to free itself from its tight, constraining bodice. She carried a man's belt over her shoulder like a hunter returning with game from a hunt. The buckle glinted in the light from the shop's windows, casting shards of blue and violet and red on the ground behind her. She disappeared inside without a backward glance.

"What's that?" Sutter asked.

"I would guess it's some kind of trade shop."

Without realizing it, they'd stopped in the street to observe the traffic in and out of the many doors to the long store. Dirty men with knotted beards carried soiled bundles into the place. At one point, Tahn was saddened to see a young boy and girl sneak into the first door on bare feet, holding something together in their small hands. Whatever this place was, Tahn wanted no part of it.

Farther into town, narrow streets were filled with horses hitched to posts and overland wagons unloading large barrels and chests. People gathered together in storefronts and windows, their shadows falling in long jagged shapes across the road.

The byways were dry from the recent sun. From their shadows, emboldened beggars reached up toward the street's edge to harangue passersby, their cant so much like liturgy that Tahn wondered at their potential as readers. The repetition of their pitches soon combined into a deafening white roar that compelled Tahn to cover his ears.

That's when Tahn saw it: HEALER, the sign read.

Tahn and Sutter moved as fast as their injuries allowed, hitching their horses with double knots in this questionable place, and going right in. A diminutive man with stubby fingers and thick spectacles sat in a chair against the back wall. Seeing them, he said simply, "You pay first," and pointed.

A metal box with a thin slot in its top stood bolted to the floor in the corner.

"Three handcoins. I'll need to see them first." The little man waddled over and looked up at them.

"How do we know you can help us?" Sutter slurred.

"Sounds like you just need to sleep off some bitter, except your eyes look funny. Come now, my fee."

Tahn found the payment and showed the healer, who snatched up the money and rushed to put it into his box. His face lit in delight at the clanging sound of the coins as they rattled. He then turned back toward them. "Okay, what ails you?"

Tahn looked at Sutter, who had begun to weave now that he'd come to a full stop. "Get him a chair."

The healer scooted a seat up behind Sutter, who sat heavily.

Tahn considered what to say. He didn't think he had time to dissemble. He didn't know what was at work in his friend's body, and caution might kill him.

Tahn knelt to be close enough to speak low and still be heard. "We were attacked by Bar'dyn. One hit my friend in the back with a spiked ball. I pulled the ball free, but in the last several hours his speech is slurring, his eyes are heavy, and his balance is off. I think he's been poisoned."

The short fellow buried his face in his stubby fingers. "The first fee of the night and this is it? What did I do to deserve you?" He stabbed a finger into Tahn's chest and immediately went back to his lockbox. He produced a key from inside his shirt, opened the box, and drew out Tahn's money. Stumping back, he lifted Tahn's palm with one hand and slammed the coins into it. "I can't help you!"

Tahn stared, slack-jawed. "Can't? My friend is sick. What do I do?"

The diminutive fellow went back to his chair to resume his vigil. "He's got Quiet poison in him. You need a healer from the Bourne. Good luck."

Tahn's ire began to stir. "But I don't know where to find one. Can't you do something?" He stood, feeling for the first time the kind of righteous anger he remembered of his father. Things had grown serious, and now so was he.

The small man seemed to hear it, too. He puffed air from his wide nostrils. "The tenendra. They have a tent of low ones at the far end. They say there's a creature from the Bourne caged inside. Good luck."

With some difficulty, Tahn got Sutter to his feet, and the two stumbled back into the street. The peaks of the several tents to the north glowed like beacons and lured Squim residents to come and pay the admission fee. Tahn and Sutter followed the crowds, which all seemed to stream in the same direction. The closer they got to the the brightly lit tents, the stronger many sweet smells wafted on the air: honey, molasses, and flower-nectar creams. But so, too, did the acrid smell of people long without a bath, massed together for whatever entertainment the tenendra brought to this shady town.

"There," Sutter said, getting Tahn's attention.

They rounded the last large building near the end of town and stopped at the massive tent that seemed to swell before them. It rose to at least the height of Hambley's Fieldstone. Ropes the thickness of Tahn's arm anchored to great iron stakes, holding the tent in place. Great swaths of color ran in wide stripes to the peak—red, green, yellow, blue, violet. Straw had been laid all about, but in the heat, there was no mud to cover, so chaff rose under the hundreds of feet that trampled it, filling the air with the smell of a dry field.

Along the perimeter of the tents, carts filled with honey-glazed fruit, sugar wines, and rolled flat-cakes filled with berries and dusted with powdered sugars were surrounded by men, women, and children all clamoring for a taste. Torches blazed all around the tents, casting rope shadows and the occasional figure of a man upon the outer canvas, while the light from within bobbed and shifted with the movement of talking heads and arms raised in applause. Excitement carried Tahn along with the flow of the crowd. Roars of approval erupted from the tent at frequent intervals, often followed by gales of laughter. Outside, those still standing in line for their food looked anxious to gain admittance to the tents and join those inside before whatever entertainment within came to an end.

The tide of the throng took them around the first tent. Two more tents rose against the darkness like enormous, pregnant light-flies. One of these glowed a peerless aqua blue color; the other was covered with sketches of faces in exaggerated expressions of pleasure, pain, joviality, sadness, anger, and contentment. Booths were erected close to each tent, others in the thoroughfare that ran between them. The intoxicating smells of food and drink wafted over the crowd like an invisible cloud.

Several booths were manned by men and women who hollered the merits of one game or another. Tahn passed one woman wearing an eye patch who barked about the ease of tossing a small dart through a hole in a plank of wood set fifteen feet from the front counter of her stand.

Farther on to the right stood three more tents like the first, all in a row. But on the left, out of the way, sat a long, square, dimly illuminated tent. Tahn thought he detected a more acrid smell from that direction.

No one stood in line there.

This had to be the tent of the low ones, with a creature from the Bourne.

CHAPTER TWENTY-SIX

A Songbox

Don't be alarmed, Anais," the gentleman said.

His long white hair was drawn back in a ponytail. Clear blue eyes shone beneath thick white brows, and the clean scents of sandalwood and oak leaves seemed to emanate from him. He sat with his elbows on his knees and his fingers laced, smiling paternally at her across the fire.

"Who are you?" Wendra asked, looking around for Penit. Perhaps this was the help the boy had brought back with him.

"Your friend," the man said. "What else would you have me be?"

Wendra shook her head and tried to push herself up. She collapsed quickly from the effort.

"Do not exert yourself," the old man said. "I will do you no harm, and you must conserve your strength." He took a piece of wood from the nearby pile and stirred the coals with it before tossing it into the flames. "It is a joyous sound, is it not?"

Wendra looked at him, confused. "What sound?"

"The fire." He closed his eyes. "If you close your eyes it sounds like the wind filling a sail, the rush of water over a falls. Yet it is both gentler than these and stronger." He smiled with his eyes shut. "The life of the wood is consumed, re-born into flame and warmth. The force that gives the tree its form, still deep within the wood long after it ceases to grow, is offered up in a bright flame that warms our meals and soothes our flesh."

Wendra licked her cracked lips, but said nothing.

"It is an old song, older than the races, and one they've forgotten." He opened his eyes. "Its power is still harnessed, but the sacrifice of the touchable becoming untouchable is no longer appreciated. The song is no longer sung." He did not speak reproachfully, and the same kindly smile remained on his lips. "This is the way of things," he concluded, and rested his gentle eyes on Wendra.

"What has this to do with me?" she asked. "How does this help me? Heal my wound?" Her voice trembled as panic closed in upon her. The man was not re-ally there, and he could not assist her. She was having fever visions, death dreams. She remembered her dying father holding entire conversations with the empty chair that sat beside his bed. Tears welled in her eyes. Distantly, the tune of her box continued to chime.

"Only you can decide what it has to do with you, Wendra, how it will help you." He looked down at his hands, then held them up without unlacing his fingers. "What is their song?"

"I don't understand."

The man unlaced his hands. "I may use them to fashion a home, to cup the face of a loved one, I may even use them to take up instruments of war." He turned his hands over each time he listed an example. "I may even put them before the light and create forms of things which are not." He joined his hands in odd ways and cast shadows of animals and people on the cavern wall behind him. Slowly, the images there became more distinct, moving independently and taking on color and sound. Suddenly, Wendra was watching Balatin play a cithern on the steps of their home while she and Tahn danced. Her father, laughing, showed them how to perform the next step in the jig while his fingers plucked the strings and the yard rang with a lively tune. Tapping one foot, Balatin finally stood and joined them in their dance, while continuing to play. A freshet of tears escaped Wendra's eyes, and instantly she remembered the tune her father played, the same tune as her box.

She laughed out loud, and the images disappeared, replaced by the old, white-haired gentleman sitting deathwatch with her at her fire.

His smile never wavered. "Do you understand now?"

Wendra shook her head, then stopped. "Yes. Maybe. These are my comforts as my body fails, as the form inside of me rises and departs, leaving these memories behind."

The old man's smile broadened. "Dear Wendra, death is a song worth singing, but not yet for you." He again rested his elbows on his knees and settled in as though preparing to tell a story. "With my hands I can create many things, many good things. But my art, the things I touch and shape, are only my best interpretation of what I see and feel inside." He touched his chest. "They can be glorious, as Shenflear's words or Polea's paintings. They may ascend into the sky with magnificence, as Loneot's great buildings that arc and rise in sweeping bridges and spires on the banks of the Helesto. But"—the man leaned forward, excitement clear in his features—"can you imagine what thoughts, what images existed in the hearts and minds of such men and women, but were not so perfectly reflected in the efforts of their hands?"

Wendra began to feel cold inside. The fire burned on, but held no warmth for her. Its flames, even the old man's kindly face, blurred and wavered before coming into sharp focus again. Beyond it all, her wood box played on, slower now as it wound down, and she tried to fix her attention upon the melody, to grasp something she knew was real, something she could understand.

The old man sat up and flung back his great white cloak. In the firelight, his white hair and beard looked regal. He again fixed his stare upon her, never losing his warm smile. "You, Wendra. The instrument you must play is *you*. It is the first tool, the first instrument. It is a uniquely wondrous symmetry of Forda I'Forza. And there will be those who will teach you. But you shall have to get up off this floor." He patted his leg. "So, how will you do that, Anais? Tell me, what song will serve your need?"

"I've no strength to rise," Wendra said. "I've sent a boy into the world to bring me help, and I worry that he is harmed."

"The Quiet do not seek you or the boy. Trust me, you are safe here."

"My brother . . . they came to our home . . . my child . . ."

"Indeed," the old man said. "And these are strains of a song that should be sung with reverence and hope, because they create in you what only you can voice. Learn from them, Wendra. I have stood in places for days at a time to hear and know the voices they sing with. Even this place, this dark cave, knows a song. It is inside you now, in the rocks and fire and ash, and the lad Penit and what you see in him that is forever lost to you. It is a lament, Wendra, that you may sing of this place, this moment . . . but there is joy in that, too. What reprise of joy in sympathetic understanding might that give to another, who cannot for themselves express such things. Not unlike your box." He motioned toward her music box. "What is captured there that causes you to return to that simple melody? Things forever lost to you in flesh, but alive to you in spirit. Like the wood relinquishing its form to exist as something brighter. We create as we can, but the end must be to fashion something finer of ourselves."

For the first time, the old man's eyes grew distant. "But the songs are changing, and there are few who can sing the songs that have given us courage and hope. And greater still, Anais, is the call of the Descant. And so you must arise." He smiled kindly. "I ask you again, what song is it?"

In a moment, the old man was gone, leaving Wendra in the darkened cave on a bed drenched with the sweat of her fever. The smell of ash rose in cloying waves. And more clearly, more intimately, she could hear her box plucking its tune in the darkness. The soft click of the gears hummed just beneath the melody. In the shadows, Wendra parted her lips to hum in time with the song of her box, and her chills began to fade.

As Wendra sang, she found her voice gaining strength rather than tiring. The natural reverberation in the cave carried her soft intonations farther than she projected them. But her humming soon strengthened, and as she remembered Balatin singing to the melody, she began to intersperse words. Every few minutes, when her box wound down, she rewound the cylinder and sang again to its accompaniment.

Penit had not returned and Wendra began to fret over him, but she could do nothing if she remained ill, so she continued to sing, listening to her own voice echo and re-echo off the rock walls. In the welling sound that filled the cave, she found unique comfort ... and more. Wendra's fever broke before the mouth of the cave darkened on her second day there. She nibbled lightly at some of Sedagin's bread and sipped cool water. But even while she ate, she hummed around her food, beginning to make subtle changes in the melodies, singing counterpoint to the original tune. The creation of new rhythms and harmonies to the music excited her and she found strength to build a fire to keep her warm as she continued to sing changes on Balatin's simple tune.

The sun had not yet risen before feeling in her hip and lower leg returned. She had continued to compose her own lyrics and harmonies to the weave and flow of the music begun in her box, and the swell of sound caused her heart to quicken. The vaulted cavern resonated with a score that wrapped Wendra in its healing embrace.

When dawn touched the cavern entrance with the light of day, Wendra realized she had been singing all the night through. Yet her arms were light, her eyes alert, and, without thinking, she stood and felt only the faintest trace of pain in her wound. She lifted her voice in exultation, then ceased her song, listening with gladness as her final notes echoed into the recesses of the cave and outward to the coming day.

Carefully, she walked to the entrance and squinted into the light, allowing her eyes to focus. Early morning haze hung upon the land, leaves and grass glimmering with dewdrop emeralds. The sweet smell of vegetation washed over her, and she took it in gratefully after the old earth and ashes of her fireside bed. Looking out, she could see no sign of Penit, or of the others. They had surely started for Recityv. She hoped Tahn had made it out of the fog. Her brother was prudent, but apt to get into trouble when paired with Sutter—though she genuinely liked Sutter. She had little choice but to try and make it to Recityv herself. But how long should she wait for Penit to return? He'd promised he would. Still, he was so young.

Wendra returned to her fire and took a quick meal. She packed her box and blanket into the saddlebag Penit had left her, snuffed out the fire, and returned to the mouth of the cave to wait for him. She sat on a large rock in the sun and closed her eyes, enjoying the warmth and light that penetrated even her eyelids. She forgot for the moment where she was and why she was there, and found again on her lips a few notes of the melody she'd sung all the previous night. Then suddenly, the image of the old man with a white beard and cloak surfaced in her mind, startling her. *Fever visions!* But it had seemed so real. A smile touched her lips as she thought of the old gentleman's fatherly smile. It spoke of certainty and understanding, and Wendra longed for such reassurance.

With growing clarity, Wendra realized what had just happened. She had healed herself by doing nothing more than what came most naturally to her. Music had always been a central part of her life. Balatin had played cithern and often sang with her. It had never been more than entertainment, distraction, perhaps reverie. What had happened in the cave was something spoken of only in rumor, a story repeated more in legend than history. Always it was interpreted as metaphor or symbol, the power of song to affect the way of things.

Wendra lifted her pant leg so she could examine her wound. The cut had closed over and was now only slightly discolored, the blood completely gone. One might have thought the damage to be years old. She touched the scar lightly, feeling a dull pain from the flesh inside. "Will and Sky," she muttered. "How can this be?"

She pulled her hair back and fastened it with a short strip of hide. The sun burned hot upon the face of the cliff, causing her to sweat. Half the day she waited for Penit's return, scouting around nearby, singing softly to completely mend herself. After eating a bit more of her food, she found a trail leading east along the north face. Her rations would not last, and she began to more fully regret sending the child out to seek help.

Hoisting the saddlebag over her shoulder, she set out, following the trail of hoofprints and hoping Penit would use the same path to return . . . if he was able to return.

The trail took Wendra east until dusk, when it veered southeast alongside a small river. She made camp, lit a fire, and ate a small supper, her concern growing for the boy. The sun dipped below the horizon, and gentle shades of brown and red streaked the sky, leaving sepia shadows on the land. Wendra filled her waterskin from the river and washed her face. Kneeling at the river's edge she listened, truly hearing for the first time the musical cadence of the current, the babble and chuckle of the water over stones, the rush of it around stems and branches growing or dangling in its flow. Wendra thought she could also hear the deeper, quieter pull of the current from the bottom of the river, where cold, blue water moved more slowly, more powerfully. The several voices of the river commingled in her ears in a lulling melody, its soothing power draining the fatigue of the day away from her tired muscles.

She returned to her fire and sat patiently as day gave way to night. Softly she began to hum, creating her own tune in dual harmony with the fire and the river, her concentration so complete on her song that she did not hear the approach of feet. Before she knew what was happening, three figures stood immediately opposite her, smiling devilishly in the glow of her fire.

"What fortune," the man in the center said. "This place is like a garden; we leave it and it grows new fruit."

The two other men laughed, their eyes appraising Wendra the way she'd seen herders do with new breeding stock.

The man who spoke had rough, handsome features, two days' growth of beard, and thick brows. His eyes shone with an intelligence the others lacked, and his clothes were simple but better cared for.

Suddenly, she knew these men for what they were: highwaymen.

Wendra discerned from the man's first comment that their intentions were not charitable, but Balatin had taught her never to show fear. Half the battle is what they don't know, her father had been fond of saying. She composed herself, allowing a bit of an edge to her voice, and inclined her chin smugly, preparing to ask the only thing she cared to discuss with these men.

"I seek a child, a boy, about ten years old," she said. "He would have been traveling this way a day since." She leveled her eyes at each man in turn. Their stares were filled only with greed and wantonness.

The man on the left spoke up in a voice bruised by too much tobaccom. "You ought to be worried—"

"Silence," the first interrupted. He looked at Wendra, his eyes appraising her in a different way than the other two. A softer look spread on his handsome face. "Indeed, lady, we have seen the child." He ceased talking as though he had more information and intended Wendra to know he was holding something back.

It shall be like that, then, hare and wood-cat. One pursued, but both a part of the game.

Wendra steadied her eyes in an unflinching stare upon the obvious leader of the small band and gave a knowing smile. "You've seen him, have you? Well, perhaps you also know where I might find him." She reclined a bit to show her lack of concern.

Straightaway, a wide grin spread on the highwayman's lips. "I think we might, lady, but how could we ask you to travel these dangerous roads alone?" He paced past his men to one side of the camp.

"Do I look as if I am in need of assistance?" Wendra asked. "Unless of course, my new friend, you mean me some harm." She lowered her gaze to the man's sword, holding her smile as surely as she'd seen the old man do in her visions. Inside, panic gripped her, but she knew she mustn't show it. "I seem to be quite well in this suspicious land you describe. Not a jot of trouble, not a curious word, until now."

The highwayman bowed persuasively. "Well said, lady, well said. Allow me to introduce myself, and then you and I will no longer be strangers. Jastail J'Vache." He held his bow, but inclined his head to watch for Wendra's approval.

A great game you play. We trade places as the hare. Wendra nodded. "A man of breeding," she said, her words laced thinly with sarcasm. "How fortunate for me to have met you, if, as you say, the world about is so corrupt."

"My lady," Jastail said. "You've not yet given me your name." He stood, his devilish smile pronounced upon his rugged face.

"I am Lani Spiren," Wendra said. "Make yourselves warm at my fire." Wendra knew they would have stayed regardless. Whatever their intentions, her game with Jastail would at least allow her to retain some freedom, for a while anyway. And if they did know where Penit was, then she would have to convince them to either tell her where or take her to him. She rubbed her stomach out of habit, a reassuring gesture during her pregnancy.

Jastail eyed her closely. He then motioned his companions to a fallen log. The men appeared disgruntled, but finally acquiesced. One of them produced a bottle of wine, and the two began to whisper in harsh, sibilant exchanges. Jastail sat with a flourish near Wendra and turned to look at her directly.

"Be true, lady. Why would you travel alone in open country?" He looked away thoughtfully, relaxing as though he shared a fire with an old friend.

"I have told you," Wendra answered, not needing to pretend. "I am searching for a small boy." She turned to him. "But you have not told me where I might find him, or how it is you came to see him."

Jastail smiled, and Wendra watched the rogue's profile dance in the firelight. He was preparing yet another prevarication, and she meant to catch him in it. "For my own truth, I see many people, young and old, and remembering a solitary one is a daunting task, even for me."

Wendra persisted. "You are falsely modest, Jastail. I don't believe that you forget much of what you see or do. A man traveling with such men"—Wendra looked over at Jastail's brutish traveling companions and wrinkled her nose—"is clearly upon an errand. Or would you like me to believe that you *choose* to keep this company?"

Jastail laughed aloud, and his two comrades reached for their weapons in a start. When Jastail stopped, they resumed their muffled whispers and sidelong stares. "A sharp eye and reason besides, Lani," Jastail said. "But would you also expect me to share with you all my secrets so soon?" He grinned suggestively, the smirk embodying the roguish wit and wisdom Wendra knew must serve him well. "And would you have me believe that I know all I must of you?" Jastail continued. He held up his hands to forestall Wendra from repeating her objectives.

"Yes, yes, I know you seek a boy child. Perhaps yours, perhaps a blood relation, but how carefully you dance around your solitary state in this endeavor. Something, lady, is missing in your story, and I forgive you for not coming straight out with it. Just as you must forgive me for guarding my secrets from a stranger. However"—he leaned in and spoke in a low, conspiratorial voice—"my friends there are not as inclined as I to extend courtesies. They listen to me most of the time, but the errand you mention is in their arms and legs, and as with most men who follow another, they don't trouble with questions of civility or morality. They understand what they can touch, what they can take, what they can buy, and the work that brings them money to do it."

He put a hand gently on Wendra's leg. "I may even grow to be fond of you, Lani, but paid men mutiny when their salaries are threatened. And gifted as I am, I can neither remain awake all the time, nor predict their intentions when they part with my own."

While her mind raced to understand Jastail's veiled threats, Wendra forced herself to wear a smile. This man, she decided, was far more dangerous than the rogues she'd heard about. His eloquent language always traveled two steps away from its truest meaning. But she kept smiling.

"You undersell your persuasiveness," Wendra began. "You convinced me to invite you to my fire, and your concern for me"—Wendra raised her voice so that the others would surely hear her—"gives me confidence that these two will abide your wishes when it comes to me." She put her opposite hand over Jastail's own. "You are right that I keep secrets from you. A lady is allowed such discretion, is she not?"

Jastail's eyes narrowed. "I believe you're right, Lani. How clumsy of me to forget. You must never allow me to interrogate you further about such things. My concern for you, however, is quite genuine. Whatever brought you here alone, and what the boy flees from or runs toward, is beyond our control." He placed his other hand over Wendra's. "But I must insist on conveying you safely to your destination."

Wendra spared a glance at the men across the fire. They had ceased talking, dazed expressions on their faces, their eyes fixed upon her and Jastail's clasped hands. She could not be sure that they would lead her to Penit, or that they had even seen the boy. But playing Jastail's game might afford her an opportunity to escape, while attempting to dismiss them would only force Jastail to do whatever he meant to do more quickly, and perhaps more painfully.

The dark memory of her rape threatened to surface, but she pushed it back.

He had started by saying that this place bears fruit, perhaps his only mistake, suggesting that they had discovered someone, maybe Penit, here, just as they had discovered her. She was their prisoner, and looking into Jastail's lying eyes, she believed that he knew she understood it. These things didn't matter; it only mattered that she locate Penit. Her desire to find him grew in her with each passing moment. She would not have two children taken from her, even though one she had not borne.

Wendra searched Jastail's angular face, trying to imagine what Balatin might do. Finally, her forced smile became natural, widening, and she put her second hand over Jastail's, trumping him and coming out on top. "And together we will find the boy," she concluded.

One side of Jastail's weathered face tugged into a bright, fetching grin. This one, Wendra thought, had more the look of real humor. "And we've better than a gambler's chance at that, lady," he said, noting the final position of their hands before withdrawing his own and beginning preparations for supper.

But something in the way he used the word *gambler* left disquiet in Wendra's heart.

• CHAPTER TWENTY-SEVEN •

The Wall of Remembrance

The regent took private counsel in the darkness before the dawn. With her were her most trusted advisors, the Sheason Artixan and General Van Steward. Somewhere out of sight, shadowing them, were a half dozen of her Emerit Guard; they would never be seen, but were always as close as a word.

She had been unable to sleep. The implications of calling the Convocation of Seats plagued her, so she had taken to the street that encircled Solath Mahnus to walk the Wall of Remembrance. The Wall rose to the height of three men. It had been fashioned of granite quarried in the mountains south of Recityv, and carved in relief on its face was the history of the city; perhaps the history of the world. Or at least of those events that should not be forgotten.

Many of the stories depicted on the wall's surface had begun in the halls of Solath Mahnus, which rose in palatial expanse behind it. Solath Mahnus was her home, just as it was home to all the courts of Recityv. In the darkness it sat, a hulking presence, at the center of the city. From the street where Helaina now walked, she could see all the way up to the pinnacle of her High Office at the top of Solath Mahnus, outlined now against a spray of stars.

Once again the regent recalled sending the birds of war; some few seats had already answered her call for the convocation to begin.

But unrest ruled even closer to home. Her own High Council stood in disarray. And she bargained from a weakened position that would undermine her voice when the convocation finally commenced.

"The League has begun to politick with those still loyal to you," Artixan said. The Sheason kept his voice low in the stillness. "Some will remain faithful regardless. But others have weaknesses the Ascendant will exploit. And though they'll loathe themselves for doing it, they'll vote against you, Helaina, when Roth asks it of them."

Van Steward nodded. "Staned's lieutenants have been lurking around our garrisons. They are making their own appraisals of our capacity."

"Are you concerned about a coup?" The regent continued to walk, noting the histories in the wall to their left.

"No, my Lady. We will hold. But anyone gathering information on the size and readiness of your army should be seen as more than a political adversary . . ." Van Steward let the rest go unsaid.

"The inns of Recityv begin to fill with the retinues of those answering your call to the convocation. And those they serve are directing *them* to appraisals as well."

"Of what?" Helaina asked.

"Of you," Artixan replied. "Many of them know you by reputation, some only by name. But all will want to come to their own seat at Solath Mahnus knowing your own council is uncompromised, that you possess the strength to draw them together. There will be alliances, Helaina, even before the convocation begins. Indeed, though no one has brought the hammer down in the great hall, the convocation has *already* begun."

The regent said nothing. She had guessed as much. But hearing it from Artixan made it real and dire. There was no Layosah in this age of men to inspire the minds of rulers, to force their collaboration against a common threat. Instead there was skepticism and maneuvering.

She stopped again on the stone-cobbled road that encircled Solath Mahnus, and looked up at the Wall of Remembrance, where the Wars of the First and Second Promise played out forever upon the stone. She could see Layosah even now, depicted in the granite with her child raised up in risk of imminent death. The sculptor had given the figure an attitude of resolve the regent could see even in the darkness.

The Wall of Remembrance served its purpose well for Helaina in the dark hours before dawn. She considered a mother sacrificing a son against the threat of nations . . . of the Quiet.

No measure must be left untaken.

"Your recommendations?" she asked. "What do you advise?"

"Dispatch Roth," Van Steward said without hesitation.

The regent looked around at her general, at his uncustomary joke. The three chuckled lightly in the darkness.

The general spoke again. "Truly, Helaina, put the call out to bolster the army. As peacekeepers we're content. But we have not taken to the field in open war for a long time. If that is coming, we should train a contingent twice the size of what we have. It will also give you more weight against the League's shadowy aims."

"Are there men in Recityv to answer such a call?" she asked.

"No. But I would invite the whole nation of Vohnce to our ranks. And if even then we fall short, I would recruit beyond our borders." The general spoke with earnest passion. "There are men who would take a post with us who have no allegiance elsewhere. I can find such men."

The regent heard secrets in her general's words, and was considering pursuing them when Artixan placed a gentle hand on her arm to draw her attention.

"You would expect me to ask you to rescind the order set against the Sheason, which even now imprisons one of my own. But it is not the time. The League needs to believe it remains in control where justice is concerned. Their propaganda convinces the people that they are their advocates. While you fortify the halls of Solath Mahnus with alliances, you should not give your people cause to question you."

"It is an unholy law, Artixan. You know how I feel." Helaina's anger rose.

"I know. And the time may come. But that time has not yet arrived." The Sheason himself looked at the Wall of Remembrance, his gaze growing distant.

The three then took another stroll around the wall, walking for a time in silence before Artixan spoke again. "It is your own council where you must begin, Helaina. Roth is right that many of its members are not rulers, and certainly not leaders. Their appointments were made in a time of peace, and most will either completely defer to your judgment, offering you no real counsel, or they'll vote with the League, who will offer them false security for their support."

"Are you suggesting that I remove members of the High Council?" she asked.

"Replace," Artixan corrected. "Many of them will be relieved to go, I promise you. And you will have the advantage of qualifying their replacements before they take their position. You need to employ the shrewdness that won you the regent's mantle to begin with. We need that now, more than ever."

That was all it took.

In the many years of her rule, she'd been firm and fair, but her statecraft had not often been needed. As if new breath entered her bosom, she felt renewed. She would be the iron fist of Recityv again, by Will or war. The carvings on the wall around her home and courts helped give life to these old stirrings.

And with this decision, the path before her became clear.

"General, begin your recruitment. I will draw up the Note of Enmity before the day is done. But don't wait for the note to begin; get started the moment you return to your offices." She turned to her closest friend, and possibly most powerful ally. "Artixan, find those who have come already to Recityv to answer the call of convocation. I will see each privately to either discover their allegiance or create a new alliance. I will take those audiences in the High Office, where the glory of Recityv may be seen from the windows to inspire their honesty . . . and choice."

She thought a moment, considering her next words. "As for my own High Council, it is made of old friendships, and I must speak with them, too. So we will do that in their homes, where they are comfortable. But we will do more than replace those who no longer have the capacity or desire to serve. We will find our next generation's stalwarts. I daresay our incumbents can help point us toward them. They know well the guilds and orders they represent."

Helaina paused, not from doubt, but from gratitude for her own renewed purpose. She had but needed to remember. With the image in her mind of the shrikes taking wing to carry the message of the Convocation of Seats, her resolve hardened further.

"And we will fill again the council chairs that we have thought unnecessary for far too long. The Maesteri will be recalled; I will make this request myself. My own council will be whole and strong when the convocation begins. Send the riders and criers to proclaim it: Recityv's High Council will be made whole."

The regent then considered one last seat at her table. "And announce that we will once again seat the Child's Voice. Let word go forth that we will run the Lesher Roon. And the winner of the race, as in times past, will speak for the children and give us balance."

Artixan smiled in the darkness. "Roth will take exception to it as another false tradition better left in the past. He won't care to listen to the opinions of a child."

The regent spared a last look at the Wall of Remembrance, where she saw the granite image of the Lesher Roon being run by countless children. "Come, we have much to do."

CHAPTER TWENTY-EIGHT

Widows Village

Braethen's muscles ached. For two days they had pushed on. It was not the ride that made him sore, but the incessant training. Each night Mira worked with him, though he practiced with his old sword, not ready to take up the Sheason's gift again so soon. And neither Vendanj nor Mira spoke of the blade; their silence unnerved him.

Late in the third day, under gathering clouds, the hills rose up to the north and east. Through a dispersion of oaks they entered a village of humble dwellings thatched together of tares and plant husks and rough wood huddled against the ground.

Meager to the last home, something was missing, but Braethen could not put a name to it. The closer they drew to the dwellings, the bleaker everything seemed. The threat of rain came with peals of thunder not too far distant. He welcomed the promise of rebirth that the rains might bring to this place. But he sensed that the rains held no such promise here, likely only to cause muddy feet and the musk of wet thatch.

The sparse village looked abandoned. Perhaps the residents had retreated indoors with the coming of night or the storm. Yet the windows held no lamp or candle, seeming cold and unfriendly in the grey twilight. A gentle breeze pushed by the coming storm tugged at their cloaks. The wind unsettled the horses, as though carrying a harbinger of bad business; they rolled their eyes and tugged at their reins. The sizzle of rain falling upon the hills began to drone like a distant hive. Braethen hoped they could find lodging before the storms came on full.

They passed through the center of the village, coming to a longer building near the end of the few homes. A woven rug had been hung from the cross brace to serve as a door. Vendanj lashed Suensin to a post and rapped on the lintel as rain cascaded into the streets behind them. Braethen heard nothing stir, and no light or fire could be seen through the windows. Vendanj waited as Mira and Braethen tethered their mounts.

He rapped again, more softly this time, the sound of it meek and hollow, nearly lost in the hammer of rain upon the thatch of the small building.

Several moments later, a woman drew back the rug and stared coldly at them. She wore a featureless smock the color of clouds at night. Around her shoulders she had wrapped a shawl of the same shade. Its weave was so coarse that Braethen wondered if it held any warmth and was not abrasive to the touch. But it was her face and eyes that caused pity to swell in Braethen from first sight. Her ashen skin lacked the flush of womanhood or even the natural color of flesh. And in the pale skin, the woman's aspect conveyed no emotion. The plain, unexpressive cast of her face could be described only as haunted.

She looked at each of them with indifferent eyes. Under her gaze, a sudden feeling of guilt washed over him, guilt for his ability to feel emotion, to know fury and joy. Her eyes lingered on him for a moment, then she stood back and held the rug aside as she motioned for them to enter.

The room within seemed smaller than it appeared to be from the outside. Braethen took it to serve as the town tavern or common room; a table with a few bottles set to one side served as a little bar or kitchen. The hearth opposite the bar sat cold and silent, the hollow sound of rain echoing down its flue. One lone table stood at the room's center, three chairs at each side and one on each end. A gourd in the middle of the table held an unlit candle. In the rear wall Braethen noticed a second doorway, also hung with a shabby rug. The floors were clean. And despite the house's abandoned feel, he could see no cobwebs or dust anywhere. A feeling of habitation resided there, but not of life.

Penaebra, he thought, an old word that described the untabernacled spirit, a soul with no body. This place felt like a body, a husk, left behind when its pan-aebra had gone.

Vendanj took a seat at the low table, and Mira sat beside him. Braethen stepped fully into the room, allowing the woman to let back the rug. She gave him another appraising look, then shuffled past him toward the others. The rain began to fall more strenuously, pounding the world outside. The hollow sound of drops hitting the window filled the empty room. Middle-aged, the woman slouched like the elderly as she took a seat opposite Vendanj.

Braethen sat at the end of the table, feeling uninvited to the triumvirate gathered at the table's middle. He wrapped his cloak tightly about him to stave off the growing cold, and focused his eyes toward the others, where grey shadows absorbed them.

"You should not have come here." Her voice never changed or rose, but fell out in soft, diffident rhythms.

"I would not have," Vendanj said, "but it is important. Only a list of names. That is all."

Braethen listened, noting in Vendanj's exchanges a deference he had not heard before. The tall, imposing Sheason sat and looked across at the frail woman and spoke with a hint of kindness beneath his unwavering words.

"Important," the woman echoed. "How interesting is that word. And names . . ."

Vendanj did not reply, merely waiting as the woman seemed to consider.

"North is Scarred land, Sheason. As inhospitable as its inhabitants," she began. "Foolishness." She scoffed, but still her voice remained even and unin-flected. "The Far perhaps, but this one." She pointed at Braethen. "He is a strip-ling, cowering in the windbreak of the tall ones. Shallow roots. The Scar is no place for him."

"You are right," Vendanj agreed. "But there is no choice in this. He will learn as he can."

The woman nodded, then turned to Braethen. "Do you know this place, so-dalist?"

Her question caught him off guard. He returned her stare, discomfited by her waxen cheeks and flat eyes. "Anais, I am in a dreary place. And forgive me, but one I hope soon to leave."

The woman coughed a bitter laugh, but the sound came without mirth. "Your father taught you honesty; I'll wager he was an author. Well enough, sodalist, but I am going to tell you a fuller truth. And your stripling soul will be cankered by the knowledge, but so be it." She paused to light the candle between them. The sudden flare of light into the room made Braethen squint. The woman turned more fully toward him, her nose, chin, and brow throwing the right side of her face into shadow. "My name was Ne'Pheola. I walked freely the Halls of Self-Sacrifice at Estem Salo, where the Sheason make their home. For twelve years I lived there, not as a renderer, but as a companion to one. We were wedded, and our life was happy. But that name has no meaning for me now, not in this place, not after his death."

No emotion cracked her voice as she spoke of her loss. The strange calm of her words continued.

"Yes, sodalist, it is a dreary place. It is Widows Village, where the use of names is no longer meaningful. Those here are the severed halves of such unions as mine, men and women left to live after their companions have been taken. They come here to live out the balance of that life, but it is a desolate heritage we have, sodalist, long and forgotten."

Braethen did not understand. The death of a spouse was tragic, but didn't the widowed eventually find some peace?

Ne'Pheola's eyes lit in understanding. "You don't believe I deserve my sorrow."

Braethen did not get a chance to speak.

"That emblem on your breast is a dangerous one, sodalist. It represents what was well begun a thousand generations ago, but is now mocked and ridiculed and denigrated. Beware of yourself. Standing where you will be called to stand with that oath threatens the fabric of your life almost as much as the Sheason's insignia dooms him.

"We here are *baenal*." She looked to see if he understood the word. Braethen shook his head. "Eternally left behind," she explained. "The Inveterae and Given have swarmed into the land many times. But their last coming wrought one mighty work on our side of the Veil, sodalist." She paused, her silence lending weight to what would follow. "The Undying Vow."

Braethen stopped breathing. He knew of it, of course, had read about it. But references to it in the books he'd read did not give a lot of information, and even then had been found only in the oldest texts his father owned, as though the writers of the histories were reluctant to disclose too much.

"Of course you've heard of it," she said. "But you most assuredly know nothing of it, and that is as it should be." Her eyes narrowed. "Except that now you have placed yourself alongside those who walk into the breach, and the burden is yours to share.

"When the war was all but lost, the Sheason convened at Estem Salo to consider what could be done if the Quiet took all the Land beneath the Hand and Pall and Rim. G'Sare, the greatest among them, returned to the archives, hidden deep in the vaults of the Sheason. In the ancient texts he found an answer: to bind husband and wife together for all time, to eternally sanction their union and ensure their happiness beyond the dust. In this way, even if the Sheason could not defeat Quietus in life, after death, they would defeat what he stood for, by knowing happiness forever with those they loved. What G'Sare did not know was that Quietus had written many of the texts hidden by the order. And the Velle which the Whited One sent into the land wielded a dark power as they drew upon the Will, a power to sunder the Undying Vow and bring not just physical death to the Sheason, but the death of their eternal bond to those they loved.

"Each man and woman of the order that fell, fell alone . . . forever. Those left behind would likewise go to dust, their union broken, and their spirit, their penaebra, left without the promise of reunion with their spouse. In this way, the One made our defeat complete. Valiant Sheason, confident in their struggle because of the vow, were struck down by the unhallowed, and their companions instantly knew the vow was null. We are these, sodalist. This is Widows Village . . . and ours is a desolate heritage."

"But this war was a thousand lifetimes ago," Braethen said.

"No, sodalist," Ne'Pheola said, "the war continues. It is more careful now, more subtle. And growing, stripling, growing as sure as the Scar. My love was killed by the Exigents under the Civilization Order sanctioned by a council of men with greed in their fingers and wine in their gullets. Something of the Bourne rests in the vaunted halls of civility. And so your emblem puts you in danger, because standing next to Inner Resonance, your own life isn't worth a pinch of salt."

The candle danced slowly in the quiet of the room. Inner Resonance, a rare term for the Sheason. Few knew or used it. Vendanj, appearing lost in thoughts of his own, did not look at Braethen. But Mira looked carefully at him, her eyes seeming to test the conflict the woman's words might have caused in him. The scrutiny angered him; did she think he would now become a liability?

He mustered a harsh look, forgetting the patience and benevolence A'Posian had taught him, but remembering one of the great truths written by his father's own hand: "And this is the great gift of life, is it not?" he said bitterly. "That I may choose to go where others have found sorrow?"

He stood and stalked out into the storm.

The rain descended in great drops, hammering the ground like stones. Braethen pulled his hood up and strode through the downpour. There was no place for him to go, but he needed some time alone. He slogged south, the way they had come, watching his feet kick through the gathering puddles. Then the splatter of the rain changed as hailstones replaced the drops, beating the sodden ground more heavily, tapping an endlessly complex rhythm against the earth. The hail fell on his shoulders, and quickly stung him through the thickness of his cloak.

In moments, the world filled with a dizzying white roar, hail striking the ground so hard that it jounced up at odd angles and skittered against other hailstones like glass balls that children rolled in their games. The hail fell in sheets, shortening his vision, the hovels of Widows Village nothing more than low, hulking shadows through the gloom. Braethen looked desperately about for a place to take cover. The tree's bare branches rattled in the hailstorm assault, offering no cover. He almost turned to dash back to the room, the Sheason, and the Far when a voice rose through the storm.

"Here," said a voice, "quickly." The invitation came muffled by the beating of hail upon the earth.

Braethen peered around him, shielding his eyes as he searched for the owner of the voice. He could see nothing, and the hail bit at the flesh of his hand.

"Quickly," the voice repeated, "to your right."

Braethen still could see no one, but he hastily followed the directions, finding himself in front of a dwelling a short distance away. Drifts of hail already collected against the outer walls, and rolled from the thatched roof in thick clumps. The shutters had been latched tightly against the storm. A rug similar to Ne'Pheola's, serving as a door, hung from the lintel of this even smaller hovel. A hand drew back the rug, offering entrance into a darkened room. Braethen hesitated. In the darkness he could not see a face. Hail continued to pelt down in painful waves, covering the ground in a blanket of white. Unable to stand the thrashing, Braethen dashed inside, away from the onslaught.

Without even the neutral light that had seeped through the glass windows at Ne'Pheola's, the room was utterly dark. The sound of feet was the only evidence of the presence of Braethen's rescuer. Slowly, his eyes adjusted; dark shapes showed themselves against the lighter shadows. Behind a table stood a figure wearing a coarse wrap much like the one Ne'Pheola wore. She stood patiently looking at him through the darkness.

"Thank you," Braethen said. "I'd nowhere else to go." He wiped his face with his cloak and looked around. A small bed, cupboard, and desk furnished the modest home. In one corner stood a trunk half covered with a piece of some delicate fabric. Atop it a slender vase held a number of green stems. It appeared to be an attempt to brighten the spartan room, but the stems, bearing no flowers or buds, seemed more dismal for their thinness.

"How often I've said the same thing," the voice came again. This time Braethen heard the soft inflection of a young woman, different from the even tones of Ne'Pheola. He guessed this voice had not been in Widows Village as long, her remark almost witty, satiric, but bleakly underscored by the sizzle of hail upon the roof and streets outside.

"Do you have a candle?" Braethen asked, growing tired of the dark.

"Yes," she answered, "but the dark might be preferable to you."

"The dark has never been preferable to me," Braethen said. "Would you light it?"

The woman went to the hearth behind her and struck flint to a bed of straw. When it flared alight, she added several small sticks before taking one lighted piece of straw and touching it to a candle wick. The room brightened, but seemed emptier in the light.

"That is better," Braethen said, and looked back toward the woman. Terrible burn scars had ruined one side of her face, the disfigurement running from her forehead across one eye to her cheek. Scar tissue had grown completely over her left eye; she refused to look at him with the other.

She could not have been much older than Wendra. She wore a shapeless grey dress. Her hair and skin were as drab as her clothing. Over her ear she had tucked a green stem like the one in the vase. It was all the color she bore, apart from the blue of her one good eye. Around her delicate shoulders, she had wrapped a shawl. Her hands trembled, as if unfamiliar with visitors, which Braethen imagined were few here.

"You may leave if you wish," she said, still not looking at him.

"But I may stay, too?"

Her gaze finally found him. "Yes." Braethen thought he saw a thin smile touch her lips.

"Well then, I am Braethen. What may I call you?"

"Names have no—"

"But I am not from here," he said. "And where I come from, our custom is to know a person's name."

The woman's gaze grew distant. "I was once called Ja'Nene."

"Then I shall use that name," Braethen said cheerfully. "And it suits you well. You should make a habit of using it."

"You do not understand," Ja'Nene said.

Braethen looked about and lowered his hood. He spoke loudly, hoping to fill the room with sound, and paced as he spoke, hoping to fill it with movement. Ja'Nene stood still and did not speak. "I've not seen such a storm in ten years," Braethen said. "In the Hollows, we wait for the hail to stop, then rush into the streets to gather it into balls and throw at one another. Usually only the young ones play the game. But can there be anything funnier than someone getting hit in the ass with a hail-ball?" Braethen chuckled.

Ja'Nene may have smiled weakly, or it may have been a trick of the light.

He went on. "Wait, there *is* something funnier. We have a grand inn at home, and the roof *is* not quite even on one side. In the winter, melting snow falls at the foot of the kitchen door. When the skies clear or the night comes, the water there freezes. Our good man, Hambley, can never seem to remember this, and I've waited in the morning cold for him to arise early and come out his kitchen door to fetch eggs from his coop. The funniest sound is a man slipping on the ice and *falling* on his ass."

Braethen laughed more genuinely, seeing Hambley in his mind's eye pinwheeling to stay on his feet before landing hard on the seat of his trousers. This time, Ja'Nene clearly smiled, the smile turning to laughter, and the look and sound of it stole his breath. It was beautiful and weary and sad, like the first touch of yellow in the leaves at the arrival of autumn.

Their laughter faded to smiles.

"It has been a long time since I laughed. It feels strange now." She motioned to her scarred face.

"What happened?" Braethen asked.

"The Exigents came for my husband. When I tried to stop them, they threw an oil lamp at me." She faltered, a tear escaping her good eye before she resumed. "It struck my face and shattered, spilling burning oil. I ran into the street to find a water trough to douse the flame. By then, the damage was done. And when I returned to our home, Molinu was dead. I felt it even then; I knew we would never be together again. The Undying Vow was torn asunder. And so I came here, as all of us eventually do."

"Do none of you have families you could go to?" Braethen asked.

Another weary smile pulled at the ruined half of her mouth and cheek. "It's hard to explain, but when that union is severed, you need the company of those who know the feeling. And yet . . ." She paused, her gaze distant. "With time, the sisterhood and empathy die from the burden of grief. For me"—she looked up at Braethen—"well, a woman wants to feel womanly. The night they killed Molinu, they stole that from me, too."

Braethen got up and came around the table and took her hand in his own. "I think what a woman is has very little to do with how she looks, Ja'Nene. On this topic, I will suffer no argument."

She looked up at him, another tear falling from her useful eye. "Would you kiss me?"

Braethen stared back at her. Ja'Nene did not look away. Deep gravity etched her gentle, ruined features, touched with a pleading hopefulness.

"Is that proper?" was all Braethen could think to say.

"Then you will not," she said.

"Wait—"

"Questions are the last effort to avoid action or honesty. Is it because I am ugly?"

Braethen felt as though he'd been slapped. It brought him back to himself. "I have come a great distance in a very short time," he began. "And I have seen things I had only read about in books, some things I did not believe to be more than tales created by gifted authors." He knelt to look at her eye to eye. "And today I came into this sad and dreary place and found a village of people who have removed themselves from the company of others. People who believe their lives are over or of so little worth that they choose to live apart from those who might care for them. It isn't proper—"

She shot him a scathing look. Braethen bit back his words, and painfully watched as her anger turned first to sadness and then quickly to apathy. He much preferred her scorn. The diffident look left upon her face served as an indictment Braethen could not bear. She sat at the table silently and ignored him, the shadow of her head cast large upon the table.

Braethen desperately looked around the room, searching to find something to talk about, something to say, to investigate, praise, comment upon. He lit upon the thin, green blades of tall grass, the stems sitting in the vase. They, too, cast long shadows upon the wall, like ethereal fingers trying to claim purchase upon the physical world. The image struck him.

Finally, in an emotionless monotone, Ja'Nene began to speak. "Forgive me. I forgot myself. They say I will eventually come to understand, to accept what I am now." The haunted sound of her words was more disturbing than Ne'Pheola's. Perhaps because of her youth.

"What you are now?"

"It was rash of me. But please understand." She turned her one good eye on him. "I don't ask because I am love-starved, though that is certainly true. Nor because I seek a memory to warm me on bitter nights." A tear fell gently down her cheek from her eye. "I sense a gentleness in you. A kind of caring. I have always been fast to know such things about men. And I"—she swallowed, tears coming more freely—"I just wanted to remember . . . the closeness."

Braethen looked from Ja'Nene to the long blades of grass and back again, understanding dawning in him.

"Why do you pick the grass?" he asked. And answering his own question, said, "It is because it is not so desolate. Because you hold out hope against the life left to you. Because whatever joy you knew has not been bled from you, even if it is only seen in a blade of grass."

Something awakened in him at the revelation of what he had just said, an admiration for this woman dressed in grey and living in such a vacant, dreary place. He put his hand on her scarred cheek. She jerked away at first, but after a moment inclined her cheek toward his hand, a warm tear falling on his knuckles.

"Despair overtakes my heart now, as for all of us it eventually does. One day I will wake and will not walk to the hills to pluck a few blades of grass. I fear that day. I can feel it coming. . . ."

Braethen looked at her, and in that moment did not see her ruined face, but the girl she had been. And thinking of her, he leaned in and kissed her tenderly on the lips.

When he drew slowly away, he saw wonder and gratitude in her eyes. He smiled kindly and nodded to her. Then gazing around the room, Braethen memorized the look and smell of desolation. Fixing on the blade of grass, he turned back to speak directly to her. "It will not always be this way. A blade of grass might sire a forest."

He stood and crossed to the rug-door. When he looked back, he saw Ja'Nene, sitting in the shadows of her small fire and candle, staring after him. He remembered the darkness he had felt when he took the sword, and his cry when he lifted that sword to defend the Sheason's life. It stirred in him the one thing more he could leave her with.

"You are beautiful. And I will not forget your name . . . Ja'Nene."

The sodalist stepped back into the hail and strode toward the others with more purpose in his step than he remembered ever knowing.

• CHAPTER TWENTY-NINE •

Reputations

The sun-weathered man arrived at the small town of Solencia. Today he traveled with one of his wards for whom he had been unable to find a home. He would need help in transporting and protecting the provisions he had come for—the road back to the Scar could be treacherous. And these excursions away were good opportunities for his wards to learn more of the ways of men, and a means to test their desire and readiness to strike out on their own.

Solencia squatted against a hill, little more than a collection of merchant shops and a smithy, which did most of their trade with overland travelers. A few homes dotted the road into and out of the place, and some few tents and wagons had been set up along the highway, where travelers—who could not or would not afford a room—took a day of rest while they gathered supplies.

It was a town of little talk. Prices weren't negotiated and passersby didn't stop to trade greetings. Even the one tavern hunkered small and quiet at one end of the main road—a place to get a drink, nothing more. While outside, the sound of wagon wheels or horse hooves seemed the louder for the lack of human voices.

All of which suited the man and his ward, who were used to the absence of human sound.

They stopped in front of the general store and went in. The traveler handed a list of items to the shopkeep and dropped exact payment on the counter without a word. They waited patiently while the order was filled, then began to shoulder the provisions out to their small wagon for the trip back.

On their last haul, voices finally interrupted the solitude of Solencia.

"So it is our outcast come to take our food and water back to his desert home. And he brings with him one of his bastards this time."

The man turned toward the sound. Three men stood in the road several strides away, challenge in their stances. They held weapons in their hands. The traveler took a quick survey of the scene, noting the men's positions, full complements of weapons, the ground itself, onlookers, everything.

This was not the first time someone had called him out, hoping to make a reputation.

"Go home," the weathered man said. "We have no quarrel with you. We will take our supplies and be gone in a moment's time. There is no need of a contest between us."

His challengers laughed, and the leader said, "It is not enough that you take our goods, but the word is you also take our arms. I think you have much to answer for. And we will not wait upon the councils of justice to put things right."

The man placed his sack of oats in the wagon bed and spoke softly to his ward. "Be calm. I will talk with them. If it comes to conflict, remember your training. You are young but practiced. Have confidence."

Despite his words, the sun-worn man did not want to see the youth—barely in his thirteenth year—tested on the road of Solencia. He approached his challengers, his weapons still sheathed.

He glared at each one, being sure they saw the look in his eye—something he knew a wise fighter could use to gauge what would follow. "You are not the first to call me out so that you might earn your reputations by putting me down. But if you persist, I promise you, you will not be the last."

The lead man looked back evenly, deploying his men to encircle the traveler.

"Your reputation is known, both for prowess and betrayal. And now for crimes against the innocent. For all these reasons we will not heed your threats."

"Don't be a fool," the man replied. "We need not shed blood this night. But I will not ask again. We are packed and ready to leave."

The traveler could see immediately that his words had fallen on deaf ears. He cursed the circumstances that made another man's ambition of him. There were always those who sought to claim they had slain the outcast. But this many years into his isolation, it had less to do with the *reasons* for his isolation, and more to do with the notoriety killing him might win a man.

And down those years, the skill and refinement of his combat gifts had sent more men to their earth than he could count. Nor did he lament a single one.

"Prepare yourself," the challenger said into the cool night air.

With that, the weathered man's blood cooled and he set himself.

The attack came fast, but predictable. A knife shot out from the lead challenger's left hand, meant to put the outcast off balance while his sword arm brought down a hammer stroke that could end the contest before it began.

The man dodged the knife and in a fluid motion stepped to the side, unsheathing his own sword as easily as he drew a breath. He removed the challenger's arm in token of the offense with which they'd charged him, then put his sword through his heart. A scream shot out across Solencia.

But it did not issue from the throat of his attacker. The man pivoted around in time to see the two accomplices fall upon his ward, who blocked one stroke, but took one in the belly from the other man.

He rushed to the boy's aid, howling defiance to distract them as he went. But they seemed not to hear, as they each raised their blades against his ward. The lad ducked and rolled, grimacing with the pain of his wound. The boy brought his blade up to deflect another strike and thrust, sticking one of his attackers. His sword hung in the flesh of the man, and as he fought to pull it back, the other smiled wickedly and used both hands in his final swing.

"No!" the outcast cried, now a mere stride away.

But he was too late, and the blade of the second man tore out the boy's throat. The lad's eyes showed awful surprise at his own death, followed fast by a look like a longing for home that the weathered man would never forget.

Then the boy fell back, his head striking the edge of the wagon bed before he landed on the hard earth.

In fury, the outcast laid into the killer. With a single raging stroke, he took the man's head from his body. He followed the momentum of his sword, doing a complete turn, and brought it around on the other man, ripping his throat out as his cohort had the outcast's young companion's.

The challengers fell almost simultaneously, their heavy bodies thudding against the road and bleeding out. The man dropped to his knees. He had a few precious seconds to hold the lad and look some comfort into his eyes before the light there went out forever.

It was once again quiet, and terribly still, as he sat alone on the road of Solencia, holding a child he had been entrusted to protect. He mourned his ward, dead because prideful men had sought the outcast's death to bolster their own esteem.

It struck him yet again, as it had so often before, that no matter where he went, he never escaped his condemnation, which would spread with the death of this lad. The poor boy, dead so young. His heart ached at the sight of him, while growing yet harder and more rancorous.

Something fundamental had to change.

The land of men could not endure with such pettiness, such selfishness as had banished him into the desert to begin with, and now threatened him and those he safeguarded . . . even when merely buying a bag of oats.

He had his own set of sins, he knew. But they were long in the past, and more than atoned for, to his mind.

No, something fundamental had to change.

The weathered man picked up the lad's still body and gently placed him in the wagon, covering him with one of the blankets he'd just purchased. He should not have brought his ward. The dangers of traveling with the outcast were more than ordinary. He knew it too well. Alone, he could have killed all three contenders. Instead, the hopeful life of this stripling lad had been snuffed out before his bright contributions to the world could be made. The man hung his head over the boy's body. His every breath became a painful, conscious act of grief.

The dark irony in it all came when he realized that even this purest of human emotions added to the rest of the stains on his life and made his heart stonier.

Then he ascended the few steps to the store again. He stepped up to the counter and looked across at the shopkeep, to whom this time he would have to speak his order. The thought in his mind was heresy. But he had reached a final outpost in the land of his heart, and he might be the only one, given such a vantage, to consider such impossibilities.

For what he contemplated might well be impossible.

But the act alone would ease his troubled mind.

"Parchment," the weathered man said.

CHAPTER THIRTY

Emblems

Wendra slept restlessly in the presence of Jastail and his comrades. She had been unwilling to sing at her fire after their conversation ended, and so was left without the calming benefit it might have brought her. But it was less her own circumstances than those of Penit and Tahn that caused her to struggle with sleep. Though one was much younger than the other, neither had grown past the age of melura, and both were fatherless and now lost to her. She tried to focus on memories of Balatin, and on the vision of the elderly gentleman in the white robe who had visited her the night before in her fever. But she could hold none of them in her mind. The soft whir of crickets and the stream nearby did nothing to improve her mood. She lay silently until dawn, hoping her unspoken pact with Jastail would not prove foolish.

The two other men left after endfast and returned with three horses evidently tethered close by. Jastail helped her onto his own horse and they followed the stream northeast all day. Toward nightfall, it turned southeast through a series of steep hills, where rills out of several small canyons joined the stream, enlargening it. They soon came through a pass, and unexpectedly, in the valley below, the stream merged with a large river that flowed south from the other side of one low mountain. The river stretched nearly a hundred strides wide.

Several hours into the night, as they followed the river, they came in sight of a huge wooden dock. Jastail moved them into the cover of nearby trees where, for a time, they waited and watched. Resting on pilings that rose like dark columns from the water, thick, uneven cross timbers formed the landing on the riverbank. Wendra looked out over the flow, noting for the first time its beauty, a thousand ripples shining with moonlight, and the low musical hum of the vast passage of water.

Jastail gestured, and the first man rode to the dock's end and lit a torch fastened to the last piling. The torchlight bounced harshly on the water, unable to completely dispel the darkness from the black timber of the dock. The first rider returned, and together from the cloak of the trees, they again watched the river and dock, now with the torch burning its lone flame from the end of the pier.

Distantly, a sound like geese honking floated across the water. Jastail looked north. Soon a large riverboat, multiple torches flaming from its runners, rounded a bend in the river. The sound of laughter came more clearly now, still sounding something like geese, and the boat angled toward the torch on the dock. The parting of water around its hull whispered with the clamor of voices. Wendra looked on in amazement at the sheer size of the watercraft. Several buildings rose from the deck, with second and third stories. At the rear, a team of oxen had been yoked to a thick crossbar fastened to a revolving post. As the animals walked a never-ending circle, the slow-spinning post turned a set of large wooden gears that powered the rear paddle wheel.

Men appeared on deck with ropes in hand, some guiding the vessel to a deft stop beside the dock. The sailors, six men in all, then brandished long knives. One extinguished the torch. Jastail seemed to take this as a signal. He spurred his horse from the cover of the trees and led them all to the pier's end.

The clop of hooves on the wooden planks drowned out the sound of the river, but not the jollity streaming from the brightly lit middle deck of the boat. The incessant chatter reminded Wendra of Northsun Festival back home: animated laughter, punctuated shouts, and an occasional remonstration.

Jastail brought them to a stop before the men who'd lashed the riverboat to the dock. He lifted his hand in greeting, but folded one finger down.

"Name it," said the deckhand who had doused the torch.

"Defiera," Jastail said, and the men relaxed the angle of their daggers.

"What is wanted?" the other asked.

"Passage downriver to Pelan," Jastail said. "We've business there." His head turned slightly, and Wendra had the impression Jastail was indicating her.

The sailor, his face lost behind a protuberant nose, shifted and peered around Jastail at Wendra. He nodded appreciatively, then sized up the two men who kept them company.

"And these?" the sailor added.

"Hirelings," Jastail replied. "Honest enough if they're paid. Sullen enough on an empty gullet."

At that the sailor laughed, joined by a number of the other deckhands.

"Three horses, three men, one woman"—the sailor leered at Wendra—"a handcoin, no less, and a stem for each man here so that their lips are occupied when asked about the business our new fares have in a place such as Pelan. Putting in there is hazard enough. You'll not want the captain poking into your merchandise."

Raucous laughter fell hard upon the wooden dock.

Jastail did not join them, but reached inside his cloak and pulled out a handful of coins. The sailor came forward and greedily reached for them. Jastail pulled back his fistful of money. "I've ridden your vessel before, Sireh, and find that I tend to . . . lose things. I will pay you for boarding, but the rest I will give when we are safely upon the dock near Pelan. If I am complete at that time, twice your price will you have. If I am not, then all the money will I give to but one of you without a word to the others. You may then share the money as you see fit."

The sailor glowered at Jastail, who dropped a single silver coin. The man snatched it from the air with a quick hand and walked away muttering under his breath.

"Why do you spar with them?" Wendra asked. "They outnumber you, and you've no place to hide on the boat."

"Ah, lady, it is good that we paired together in this enterprise," Jastail said as the other sailors stood aside to let them pass. "Unwise is the buyer who pays his fee in advance. And with rivermen there are precautions to be taken. I have made this deal for your safety. These men are without consideration of what belongs to another man, let alone the proper treatment of a woman. They may well take us to Pelan, and hold their tongues about our particular transactions. But it is the time between then and now that I have purchased, the safety and assurance of our property and well-being. They will think three times before stealing what is ours, because I would then give all the tongue-money to one man among them. The distrust and danger created when each believes the other is holding money that belongs to him will insure us against pilfering while we travel. Rivermen are as greedy as the river is cold. The one I would pay would never share it with the others. The result would be that each of them becomes a target for the daggers of the others while he sleeps. They are as predictable as the rise of the sun."

They boarded the great ship and passed into a building used for stabling horses. There they dismounted, unsaddled their horses, and walked through a door into the glare of the middle deck.

Wendra followed Jastail around odd tables that held sunken pits bottomed with slate. Between those standing around the tables, she caught glimpses of grids drawn across the slate with different numbers marked in soapstone in each square. Men and women moved colored markers in a flurry of hands until a man in a bright yellow shirt cast several triangular rods into the recessed area of the table. He then quickly counted the numbers scrawled on the stained surfaces of the rods.

Jastail pulled Wendra along. The two hirelings they'd been traveling with quickly found room at tables and tossed coin onto the slate to enter the games. On the left, a handful of large men stood stoically overlooking the whole of the room. They wore swords menacingly on their backs, the handles protruding in bold advertisement of their function. A black and white patch had been sewn to the left breast of their tunics. Next to them, a very small man, perhaps only three and a half feet tall, stood on a raised platform serving bitter and wine. He waddled in a strained gait, having to throw his left shoulder up to lift his right leg, and his right shoulder up to move the left. His pants were held in place with strange belts looped over his shoulders and fastened to both the front and back of his trousers. He looked terribly uncomfortable, but he smiled constantly, apparently happy in his work.

They wound past the long counters near the entrance and found men seated at short square tables, a man in the same yellow shirt standing as in mediation next to those who were seated. Intense eyes met over a series of square wooden placards that appeared blank. Each man took turns overturning a placard. Disgusted looks rose in their faces until one took up a placard whose underside was graven with the image of a bird. The mediator handed him a fistful of coins.

At still another of the small tables, two men sat engaged in simpler contests. Wendra watched as one of the gamekeepers placed a wooden block in the center of the table, asking the players to put their hands in their laps. The mediator then stood back and waited an indeterminate amount of time before quickly saying, "Take." The contestants then both anxiously grabbed for the block. The man who took it won the prize.

As they meandered past various games, a general hilarity swirled around them. Wendra noticed that many of those gambling were dressed in unrefined wool, a few even in pelts; these men and women bet more meager amounts than those better dressed, but they drank more deeply, loosing bawdy laughter from wet lips. Beside them were players adorned in silk and twilled cotton, linens of extravagant color and design. Their wagers often flashed of gold, sometimes several coins high. And their cups were just as full as the rest.

The participants seemed to share a familiarity. It was common, Wendra saw, for a man here to put his hand on a woman's breast, or she to cup another man's loins. Even men and women who appeared to be here together seemed to feel free to lay hands on others. The gestures fetched bouts of laughter and calls for more bitter. Sweet-leaf tobaccom stems flared and puffed like small cloud makers, filling the room with a pungent haze. The revelry never abated, but fed upon itself as the boat moved down the river.

Jastail took hold of Wendra's hand to guide her more surely through the throng. Toward the back of the great room, a few round tables sat partitioned off from the rest by a low wall. One of the swordsmen stood at the passageway into the area. Upon seeing Jastail, he stood aside and let them pass. Only a few men sat at the tables, most of the seats empty. Jastail led Wendra to the last table, where just one man sat with a stack of thin wooden placards like the ones

Wendra had seen moments before. He wore a smartly tailored russet tunic with golden piping and a double column of silvery buttons down the front. A ring on each forefinger bore a weighty, elegant gem. And his beard had been frosted to match his buttons. The fellow did not rise, did not take note, but sat shuffling the placards over and over. Jastail's tall shadow fell across the table; the man surely knew they were there. But he refused to immediately acknowledge them. Jastail waited, holding Wendra by the wrist.

The seated man took a tobaccom pipe from the lining of his jacket and tamped fresh weed into its bowl. He pulled a straw from a wooden canister beside the table lamp and lit one end in the lamp's flame. With deliberation, he applied the flame to his bowl and puffed his pipe to life. With his head wreathed in the sweet smell of perfumed tobaccom, he looked up with smiling eyes and greeted Jastail.

"Hello, my friend," he cooed. "Come again to test your luck, have you?"

Jastail flashed his standard smile. "You are a temptation to me, Gynedo. How can I resist the game?"

"And you play well for such a young man," Gynedo said. "But young men should not be so willing to pay the price of the game, I think. Old men as I haven't the . . . concern for reputation or consequence that young men should. How say you to that?" One brow rose in expectation of a response.

Jastail motioned to the chair opposite Gynedo.

"Please," the older man said, puffing at his pipe.

Jastail sat, pulling Wendra to the tableside where he could see her, and let go of her wrist. "In any other time, Gynedo, I would say you are right. But these days we live in are filled with rumors. This is not a time for a man to lay stores by in the hope of surviving the winter. I—"

The old man pointed his crooked finger at Jastail, arresting his answer mid-word.

"You're a philosopher, my young man," Gynedo said, his eyes narrowing, "but leave the rhymes and riddles for those you intend to betray. Tell me why you come to game here." The old man tapped the table with his finger, seeming to indicate not the boat, or even the room, but the very table at which he sat.

Jastail's smile failed him. Wendra liked the look of his face plain, absent the attempt to distract or deceive. He appeared to earnestly consider the question, his eyes thoughtful and directed despite the confusion of noise from the outer room. "Because it thrills me," he said finally. "It is a base logic. Fah, no logic at all. I play because no other trade makes me feel alive, no other contest or wager speeds my heart." His voice grew quieter, but somehow cut through the din. "I come, Gynedo, because I am a young man, younger than you, and I have learned already the intoxication of where you are willing to go. I can no longer do less."

Gynedo sat appraising Jastail, considering his answer. Finally, he nodded.

"A pity for you, I think, Jastail. Your trade in human flesh has dulled your senses." The old man looked at Wendra.

Jastail said nothing

"But it *is* a thrill." And the old man's eyes lit with excitement and energy. "None greater that I know, no paltry thing as what the herds come to partake." He motioned in disgust at the outer room. "They with their pittance upon the slate, their heads dulled with watered bitter, their wanton hands betraying their animal nature. I need my wall." He gave a wan smile. "But yes, it is a thrill, one that I will enjoy until my flesh is gone to dust. But you, friend, you may live to tire of even this game, and then what is left to you?"

"I will never tire of it," Jastail said in a convincing voice.

"No?" Gynedo remarked, his voice rising with incredulity. "Well, I will hope you are right, because I have seen what is next, and it were better that you should perish now than live to know such stakes."

Jastail had no reply.

"Then let us make our accountings," the old man said and stood up, leading Jastail into a small anteroom.

"Stay here," the highwayman said to Wendra. She sat, glad to finally rest her feet.

But she watched through the open doorway as the old man, Jastail, a woman she could not see well, and a few others took turns holding up various items, pointing and touching them as they seemed to describe what they were. Wendra couldn't hear what was said, but solemn faces and appreciative nods followed the presentation of each item. Assessing value, she imagined. It seemed clear that the various articles they discussed would be what the players would wager in their game. For the moment, the highwayman was embroiled in something that didn't involve her. It gave Wendra a much needed respite, and she relaxed ever so slightly, realizing how weary she was.

What Gynedo called *the accounting* took an hour, and Wendra had nearly nodded off when the group came out of the anteroom.

Gynedo sat, as did Jastail. The two men stared at one another for some time before Gynedo divided the placards and pushed one pile toward Jastail. "Pick them up, my young friend, and let us see where the chances take us this night."

Jastail picked up the thin wooden placards and fanned them out, studying each with great interest. Wendra could see a number of designs on the placards, but could not understand what they meant or what game they might indicate. As the two began to play, the other players who'd taken part in the accounting gathered around them. Three were men, all elderly like Gynedo, and all puffing pipes as though in imitation of the man. One was the woman, younger and wearing a beautiful satin dress. Her hair had been tied up above her head, exposing the delicate, white flesh of a neck that had never been exposed to the workaday sun. Gold earrings dangled delicately against her skin, and on each thumb she wore a gold ring with a large white stone. But she did not watch the men: she turned her attention immediately to Wendra, looking closely at her hair, her lips, her bosom, and her legs.

"Set three ways," she said, speaking to Gynedo and Jastail, but looking still at Wendra as if with some prescient knowledge.

The men stopped their analysis of the thin woods in their hands and looked at the new player. Gynedo sat deliberating, smoking his pipe, savoring the sweet blend of the weed and the power he had to make others wait. He looked at Jastail, who nodded his agreement.

"Just so, Ariana," the old man said. "Take a chair and three will play." He looked up at the other men. "But no more."

Wendra thought she could feel peering eyes, and looked over her shoulder to find a number of gamers and gamblers watching the development of the contest. She hoped Gynedo or Jastail would send them away, but the men were busy reshuffling the placards to divide them into three piles. None of this was getting her any closer to Penit, or to Tahn, and her frustration mounted. A stirring of song came darkly to her mind and fought for release, but she held herself still and thought of Balatin and his words concerning patience: *Fortune serves he who is long-suffering.* She turned her attention to the game, trying to understand how it was played.

After several minutes of consideration, Gynedo put a placard down on the table in front of him. Both Jastail and Ariana looked surprised at the play. The placard held the image, rendered in red, of a serpent with great wings.

"To you, then, Jastail," the old man said, taking pleasure in his pipe and smiling around its stem.

Jastail spared a look at Ariana, touched one placard, then quickly removed the leftmost one in his hand and set it before him. It was Gynedo's turn to show surprise, but only in the raising of one brow. The old man nodded, then shook his head, still smiling around his pipe.

Ariana's face showed nothing, and she did not hesitate in making her play, immediately putting down a placard bearing the same symbol as Jastail's.

"One round," Gynedo said. "What have you to carry you to the next?"

Jastail removed an earring from his belt that bore the likeness of a tall woman.

"Most impressive," the old man said. "It was you that did it, then." He nodded appreciatively.

Ariana turned baleful eyes on him. Jastail did not favor her with a return look. The woman's composure failed for only a moment, though, before she removed a glove from a small silken bag tied to her wrist. Woven of metal shavings, the warrior's glove shimmered in the light.

"He went to battle for you, dear Ariana," Gynedo said. "How better suited to play the game is a woman, don't you agree, Jastail?"

Wendra's captor looked at Ariana, whose obvious hatred now burned through cold, inscrutable eyes.

"We shall see," Jastail finished.

The old man laid a small drawing on the table, rendered in an unpracticed hand, like that of a child's. A hush fell over all who saw the wager. "That gets me to round two. Does anyone disagree?" No one spoke. "I will accept that as my invitation to continue."

Another round of placards was laid down, and again each of the players produced an item that seemed to shock those gathered to watch. Wendra didn't immediately understand the significance of the objects being used to buy the players an opportunity to present another placard, but her mind danced close to understanding that they represented people in some way, and that the literal value of the item was secondary to what it signified.

Around they went, laying six cards on the table. Each time was followed by some token that appeared to be the personal effect of someone the wagerer had known.

Then Wendra understood, looking at the pile of items on the table: a mourner's kerchief, a child's diary, an author's quill, a worn doll, a stringless fiddle, and more. Things she'd seen them presenting and discussing in the back room before the game began. These were tokens of loss, of emotional pain, of death, the voices of which were the sounds of silence and sorrow, of life's sacrifice and bereavement. And somehow these gamblers were the cause or custodians of these moments of grief and regret, gamblers whose souls were so hardened to the effects of money and wine that all that remained worth betting—that could stir their desire to wager—was the despair and tragedy represented in the offerings heaped on the table before them.

Only human suffering seemed able to move them, and perhaps thereby convince them of their own lives.

Wendra's heart ached with the knowledge.

"Young friends, you've played well," Gynedo said with a hint of condescension. "But your placards don't make a strong bid against your last play." He leaned back and drew deeply on his pipe. "There is only small shame in getting up from the table. But to do so, I require you to take back your wagers."

The few men who had first gathered to watch gasped. Gynedo seemed to be demeaning their efforts to play the game and devaluing their wagers. Wendra guessed that in doing so, the players lost more than the game, they lost reputation. Gynedo was mocking them.

Then Jastail smiled, as wicked a smile as Wendra had yet seen upon his lips. "Not I, old friend. I will turn my last placard."

Ariana studied the placards on the table, appearing to weigh her chances. She looked at Jastail and Wendra, then nodded that she, too, would play to the last.

"Your will to do," Gynedo said. "Then what shall be the prize that gets you your last turn?" He took his pipe from his mouth and watched Jastail with curious eyes.

Jastail looked at the old man, his cunning gaze holding back something, a secret that he seemed to enjoy not immediately sharing. Ariana leveled her icy glare on him, an angry beauty in her that Wendra admired. The entire area again fell silent, players pausing to hear the last turn even if they could not see the play.

As he leaned forward, Jastail's chair creaked loudly in the suddenly quiet room. He seemed to want a close look at Gynedo's face as he put in his last wager.

He slowly reached for Wendra, taking her again by the wrist and drawing her toward the table. "And with this, I buy my last turn."

• CHAPTER THIRTY-ONE •

Names of the Dead

Vendanj sat across from Ne'Pheola in the darkest, smallest hours of the night. By the light of a solitary candle, they worked. Through the rug door, the cold encroached, leaving his writing hand slightly more pained after the cramp of putting the stylus to such long use.

But he would have none other write these names.

It took time, because he would not add a name to the parchment until he'd asked Ne'Pheola to relate the story of both the one that was gone and the one left behind. He would know of the severed union, and to do so, both halves must be understood. These marriages, which had borne a promise binding two people together beyond this life, had also been torn asunder by the the power of the Whited One. For Vendanj, perhaps the most nefarious of Quietus's evils was that even in his victories, he would not leave those fallen a happiness beyond death.

And so one by one, in the soft tones of mourners, Vendanj and Ne'Pheola told the stories of the fallen, and the barren life of the other half that remained behind. The long hours stretched, but Ne'Pheola went on, and Vendanj recorded the names thoughtfully.

For much of the night those names were drawn from wars with the Quiet. But after a time, the names on the page reflected the will of men to execute Sheason for the use of their gift, even when done in service.

Ne'Pheola drew a tepid cup of water to wet her dry throat and to steady the emotion that crept there as the names now were friends, even her own. "I still do not understand, Vendanj. What power is there in this law that should make the execution of a Sheason everlastingly final for him and his wife?"

Vendanj paused, laying down the stylus at last and putting his fingers near the candle's flame to urge some warmth into them. "I do not yet know," he answered. "I used to believe that part of it was that, as servants, we have bound ourselves to honor those we serve. That we should not act contrary to the laws they use to govern themselves and define what is right and good."

"But you—"

Vendanj held up a hand. "I know. That is why I say I *used* to believe this. It is at best only half an answer. I have not been able to discern the reason." Then he said lower, "I am sorry."

The widow stretched a cold hand across to him, and they locked fingers beside the candle. They remained unspeaking for some time.

"If the law was rescinded," Ne'Pheola asked, "would it remake the bonds that have been severed?"

Vendanj looked into her eyes. They were etched deeply with lines of grief and sorrow felt over many years. She had once been beautiful, once the flower of Estem Salo. He wanted to give her hope, wanted to see the radiance again, as he had long ago. Her warmth had once done much to make serving as Sheason a more joyful and estimable calling. But he would not give her false hope, for such was the torment of the damned.

"I don't know, Anais. I do not believe so. Some things cannot be remade. A nail can be removed from a piece of wood, but the hole it created remains. I cannot see if repealing the law would also give the wood its wholeness again." Vendanj saw despair etch itself deeper into the lines of her face, and he couldn't leave her with that. "But I will hope with you," he said. "And I am on my errand to do everything in my power to put an end to the Quiet that threatens all our futures."

Then briefly, he saw it. The flower of Estem Salo. And in that small hope, he was doubly paid for any loss he might suffer farther down the road.

"You have much to give, Anais. Why don't you return to the Halls of the Servants? There is yet wisdom and strength in you that could train a new generation—"

It was Ne'Pheola's turn to raise a hand, cutting Vendanj off. "They are kind words, Sheason, but I do not think my heart could bear it. And more than this, these here"—she tapped the parchment on the table—"have need of whatever strength I have left. Some days are a struggle to convince them that they should want to see another sky."

Vendanj did not press. This he understood well enough. Yet he also understood that this list might bear fruit when he carried it into the Scar, where yet others bore the sentence of endless, lifeless days.

And so after a long moment, sharing without words the separate griefs and burdens they each bore, Vendanj again took up his stylus and they resumed recording the names of Sheason widows. With each name the magnitude and toll of their service mounted, the document growing. The weight of it thickened the air.

The list they created whispered of the abyss, and he wished that there'd never been need to create it.

Wished especially, as the last name he put to it would be his own.

Mira leaned against the outer wall of Ne'Pheola's home in the dark of predawn. She surveyed the street, the land beyond the last homes, the sky. Now she understood why Tahn took to the dark for his moments of solace. The peace of a sleeping world before lying tongues and dire threats came into the day was something to be savored.

In those few moments Mira forgot the Quiet, forgot even the changes coming for her and the Far. Mira stood in the still serenity with no need to do other than breathe and listen.

"You don't sleep, do you?" Ne'Pheola shuffled into the street to stand beside her. Her voice, though soft, seemed loud in the silence.

"Return to your bed. I will watch here," Mira said.

"I've been up at this hour for more years than you've drawn breath, Mira Far. That's not going to change now." The old woman leaned against the wall with Mira, and stared out upon the unwaking world.

Together they shared the calm for some time before the widow spoke again, her words so soft this time that Mira had to strain to hear her.

"Do you know where your road ends, my girl?"

Mira understood that she meant the journey they all had undertaken. "If it ends prematurely, no."

Ne'Pheola might have smiled in the darkness. "You will go into the belly of the Quiet if you would see this thing done. And for my part, I hope that's where you go. It's selfish of me, but I believe I've earned a wedge of selfishness for my own burdens."

"I think we're all going to come to the belly of the Quiet before we are through." Mira did not say it lightly. She'd thought on this.

"We might at that," the widow said, nodding. "We might at that. But here's the question: Is it your intention and heart to stand at the Sheason's side to see it done?" Mira started to answer when Ne'Pheola held up her hand. "I don't need an answer, girl. I only want you to have considered the question. Vendanj will make an enemy of himself to most before this is done."

"Enemy," Mira repeated. It wasn't a word she'd ever attributed to the Shea-son. He was a hard man at times, driven and uncompromising. But those qualities were the reason she'd joined him some four years ago.

Ne'Pheola looked up, surveying the stars above Widows Village. "The world is changing. The things a Sheason stands for, his service and sacrifice, are con-sidered by many to be at best irrelevant, at worst criminal. The Quiet stirs, and this, Mira Far, is not simply another war. The very instruments we have always had to protect ourselves—the Song of Suffering, the Tract of Desolation, the Will itself—are under attack from within our own borders."

Mira followed the widow's gaze skyward. "You speak of the League."

"Not only of the league, my girl." Ne'Pheola sighed. "If you intend to stand beside Vendanj to the end, you will stand not only against the secrets held deep inside the Bourne. You, child, will stand against nations and kings. Yes, the League, as well. But before it is over . . . the very Order of Sheason."

Mira stared intently at the old woman, waiting for her to explain.

Ne'Pheola remained silent for a time, taking in those stars as if she'd never seen them before. Then she looked at Mira again. "I have seen and felt this even just this last evening as I sat with the man. A terrific burden he has placed on his shoulders. You must decide if you are truly yoked with him to carry it. Yes, you've brought hope out of the Hollows." The widow paused, a grave look pass-ing over her eyes. "But hope often fails. Vendanj knows this. He seeks to sur-round himself with those hardened enough to come against these threats and who will not falter. And that, my girl, will mean looking into the faces of those you've esteemed as friends and being willing to do what is necessary."

Ne'Pheola stopped. She rubbed her eyes slowly, then looked heavenward again. "Before it is done, your friend there will likely become a fugitive, and yet his heart will remain fixed upon the goal. A goal that would see the world safe again. Safe from the Quiet. These things, Mira Far, are not trivial. And one who makes them his purpose must know on whom he can rely. This is why he can be cruel; there is no middle ground. His foot is upon a path from which he will not stray. And it is why this old woman will carry a thought of hope for her lost family when you leave here."

Mira pondered all Ne'Pheloa had said. At times she and the Sheason had disagreed, and while he trusted many things to Mira, if he set himself on some-thing, there was no further debate. In fact, that quality had made them com-patible.

But Ne'Pheola's words fell like prophecy on the stillness of Widows Village. Standing against Sheason, looking into the faces she'd esteemed as friends and doing what was *necessary*—these were dark portents to Mira's heart. It amounted to a war against all of creation on both sides of the veil. There could be no victory for them in such a cause. How the widow could feel hope against such hopelessness escaped Mira.

But that was not the question.

Had Mira considered where this ended?

The answer came when Ne'Pheola spoke again into the stillness. "And what of your own family, Mira Far? You are come to the age to bear your own heritage a child, are you not?"

Mira remained undecided on the choice her king would put to her when next they spoke. And the thought of it brought fresh sadness about the death of her sister. But regardless of what Mira decided about bearing an heir, the larger choice seemed clear. The Far would need no heir if the purpose she set out to aid the Sheason with fell to ruin. On the other hand, perhaps the Far and their commission would have a larger part to play in Vendanj's plans than she could now see; and if so, they would indeed need an heir.

She desired to go into the belly of the nightmare on either side of the veil to stand beside the Sheason and the children out of the Hollows. But Mira knew that part of her motivation was selfish, even as Ne'Pheola had just self-ascribed; only for Mira, her selfishness had more to do with escaping family than preserving it.

Mira wondered, though, about Ne'Pheola's other words. She wondered which friends she might be called on to lift her sword against.

• CHAPTER THIRTY-TWO •

Inveterae

Cheers continued to erupt to the right, noise and laughter and applause rising from the great luminous tents. But Tahn ignored them, shuffling Sutter away from the throng. The feeling changed as they walked toward a distant part of the field. Tahn's skin began to tingle with goose bumps—a warning and expectation. *What is in there?* But he did not falter, and the two friends made their way to the low, darkened tent hoping to find help from the Bourne.

"Some taste in entertainment you have," Sutter slurred, and nearly fell.

His weight hung on Tahn, making it difficult to walk. But Tahn managed to get them to the flap of the tent, where he stopped dead, staring at the most captivating woman he had ever seen.

She stood leaning against the stand at the tent's entrance. A sign nailed to the front of the stand read: STAY TWO STRIDES FROM THE CAGES.

Her long curly hair was drawn back in a tail. Tight-fitting leather trousers, cut extremely low across her hips, clung to her calves and thighs. Her blouse plumed in the sleeves, but stretched across her bosom and ended above her ribs, showing a lean stomach. She could only have been a few years older than Tahn and Sutter, but the experience he saw in her face made her look more exotic yet. Her brow rose with impatience over large, brown eyes and a delicate nose.

"Find what you're looking for?" The woman used the tip of a knife to clean her nails, sparing an occasional glance at them.

Regaining his composure, Tahn wasn't sure how to ask. If she knew his desperation, the lucre in this woman's eye might be beyond his ability to pay. She was tenendra-folk, after all. He could see her already sizing them up. Before he could concoct a lie, she uttered a warning.

"I suggest you speak true words when you open your lips, boy, or your friend here is likely to gather some scars." With her dagger she delicately caressed Sutter's lips, which now hung loose, wet with spittle.

Tahn pulled Sutter back out of reach and shot an angry glance at the tenendra girl.

"I will wait on your reply for a moment or two, and then you'll either turn around and leave or you'll be food for whatever carrion eaters occupy this tent." She pointed with her dagger toward the flap to their right, then spun the blade in her hand in a quick circle, and sheathed it against one trim thigh.

Tahn thought quickly. He decided on the truth, and something more. This girl looked both beautiful and dangerous, but she would not stand between him and any chance of healing Sutter. At any cost, he was going in, even if that meant violence. His shock was not that he considered such hostility (maybe even anticipated it), but that such measures didn't this time make him anxious. He was not long out of the Hollows, but something inside him had begun to shift.

"My friend is sick. The healer in town said you held a creature here that might be able to help him. I need to go in." Tahn nodded toward the tent.

A wicked smile crossed her lips. "I hear the hope of free admission in your voice. Are you appealing to my sympathies for your friend's ailment? Because I tell you, you are not the first young boys to try and connive a private show at no cost. Either your friend is feigning his sickness, in which case I'll make you pay double. Or you tell the truth, he's truly sick, and you'll pay triple. Ha! There are sights you are not accustomed to in these cages, boys, things from your dreams and nightmares." She looked at Sutter. "So, which is it?" She tapped the dagger at her thigh.

Tahn stared back. "How much?"

"I will take you in, and three coppers each."

Tahn raised the price. "Four. We may need to get close." He nodded toward the sign on the front of her stand.

The woman's eyes darted to the sign and back to Tahn, measuring him closely. Then her face lit up with savage amusement, a dangerous humor that lent her features an exotic sensuality. Tahn's face flushed at the sight of her. Competing needs made his head swim: Sutter's sickness and the intoxication of this tightly clad tenendra girl. *Perhaps,* he thought, *this is what it means to go beyond the Change.*

Through smiling lips she said, "Well enough, boys, but that will cost you three and six, you understand? Three handcoins, six coppers." She gave Sutter a careful look. "I believe I know what you need, and to have the beast's cooperation I'll have to threaten it. It's a dangerous business." She pulled her dagger from its sheath and pointed it at each of them separately. "And you take the risk knowing I will not help you if you come to harm. The beast is not human, and mad as the Kaemen Sire when he marched upon the Sky." The girl twirled her dagger again between her fingers. "Pay now, and you shall have your chance with the low ones. But mind you, no tricks. Real coin. I can smell alchemic ore a league away. And I can throw my stick half that distance at the thief who flees with my wage." She waved her knife.

Tahn stood. "One and eight, now. The rest once we're done."

The girl slowly laid the point of her dagger on Tahn's chin, just barely pricking him. The wicked smile widened, arousing Tahn even over the threat of her blade. "Another time I might put you into your earth for such a veiled insult to my honor. A dead man's purse is no longer his." She leered at him, a wanton look that made him ache in a surprisingly pleasant way. "But I am feeling generous tonight. We are made," she said, sealing the deal. She sheathed her dagger and straightaway put out her hand.

Tahn took the toll from his pouch and paid her.

"You may call me Alisandra, lover," the girl said, hiding the coins in a pocket of her trousers that Tahn had not seen. "It is not my true name, but it will help you find me if you have further . . . desires." She again looked him up and down, still smiling her infuriatingly seductive smile.

She then strode toward the long tent, her tight leather pants showing a firmness Tahn could not ignore.

"That girl is all greed and muscle," Sutter whispered as soon as she began to lead them away.

Tahn continued to look after her, noting the hint of sinew beneath the smooth skin of her back—lithe as a mountain cat, and just as dangerous. He rubbed his chin and hurried to follow her, when Sutter collapsed for the last time.

Alisandra reached the tent and pulled back the flap. "In you go, boys," she said, wearing a half smile.

Tahn hoisted Sutter over his shoulder and ducked inside. The humid smell of caged life hung in the air with the thick, rich scent of straw and unclean skin. Alisandra came in after them, passing to lead them forward.

Inside, small torches lined the far right-hand wall, the light scarcely more than a candle might emit. Straw had been thrown down to walk upon. The fetid smell of mildewed canvas permeated the tent. To the left sat darkened cages fashioned of close iron bars, separated by canvas flaps. The smell of animal waste and flesh left too long to inaction commingled with the smell of the canvas to make Tahn's stomach heave. Above each cage dim lanterns burned, fastened well out of reach of whatever might occupy each stall.

The first cage stood empty. Tahn walked ahead without speaking. Rustling sounds, as things shifted in the straw, inspired his anxiety. He swallowed and slowly passed the first flap to view the second cage. There, two young girls, naked, huddled together in the straw at the back of their cage. The flickering light played delicately upon their skin, but seemed somehow intrusive. He did not immediately see why they might be caged. Then they moved, as one. The girls were joined at the hip, sharing a middle leg and part of the same stomach. Dirty, ratted hair hung over soft, supplicating faces. They looked away and cowered in a corner, gathering up straw to hide their nakedness. Tahn noted a bowl of wormy fruit and another of filthy water in the opposite corner. The sight disturbed him. But more than that, it left him feeling despair and sadness for them. Somewhere, these two girls had parents who had surely loved them. Yet here they were, an attraction meant to disturb or cause the ugly wonder of ridicule in the onlooker.

Or maybe, Tahn thought, *the parents of these poor girls had been glad to be rid of them. Perhaps even at a price.*

He moved on quickly to the next cage, Sutter grunting on Tahn's shoulder with each step.

The lantern above the third stall had burned out, casting the cage into deep shadow. Tahn peered into the darkness, but could see nothing. Then a hoarse cry shrieked from within and a form rushed forward to the bars of the cage. Tahn recoiled, tripping and sending both him and Sutter sprawling. They landed heavily in the straw.

Tahn turned over and looked back at the cage. Vaguely human, the creature's flesh had been replaced by scar tissue as though it had been rescued from the belly of a fire. Its features appeared to run like liquid. It made noises with its tongue through one side of its mouth, but Tahn could discern no words. Its shortened limbs bore no hands or feet, and in the faded light, it appeared hairless. Without fingers it could not grasp the cage bars, but it beat at them with its stubs, its one good eye fixing Tahn with an imploring stare. *Kill me or free me,* it seemed to be saying. The thing lost its balance and fell back into the straw, making no effort to get up, but just whimpering with its lipless mouth.

Again, despair bloomed in Tahn's chest. And pity. *What kind of person profits by the misfortune of another?* Indignation began to replace his disillusionment. He looked up into Alisandra's face, and saw an inscrutable look. Did she find him pathetic, or was there a touch of guilt buried inside her?

It didn't matter. He grabbed Sutter's arms and dragged him forward, following the tenendra girl onward, staying close to the outer tent wall. Then, she stopped at the last cage. Tahn let Sutter's arms drop. His friend was now unconscious.

The sheer size of whatever lay captive beside them drew Tahn's attention. The bars restraining it were double the diameter of the others, casting vague shadow-stripes on it. Sitting in the pen, something very like a Bar'dyn patiently watched them. It was broad in the face, but the bones beneath the eyes did not protrude as he had seen in the Bar'dyn. And its skin, though thick, did not appear as fibrous. Immense legs did remind him of the Given they'd fled, as did the bulging muscles in its neck. The sheer size of it frightened him. Its dense musculature was enough, Tahn knew, to pull him apart. Its fingers rested as passive and hard-looking as stones, and its eyes, fixed upon him, did not move.

He stared back, increasingly sure that this was not Bar'dyn. Though in one way it did seem entirely the same: the reason and intelligence reflected in its eyes, belying its monstrous frame. To his own astonishment, Tahn stepped closer.

He found pity swelling in him, just as it had for the girls a few cages away and for the burned boy. Tahn guessed that the proprietors had meant for this last cage to inspire the most fear and awe, culminating the experience of the wonders of the low ones. But something more gnawed at him, and he struggled to understand it. He dropped his eyes to his own hand, looking again at the mark there, tracing its familiar pattern with his eyes. They were prisoners. All these strange misshapen creatures were captives, and suddenly Tahn wanted to know why. To give others pleasure, to draw money for the tenendra. Forgotten were the delightful smells outside the tent and the rank smell all around him; forgotten were his travails since the Hollows. He looked up in desperation again to the massive creature jailed before him.

He was startled to see the creature standing at the edge of the cage, just a hand-length away—well within reaching distance. The beast had moved close soundlessly while Tahn had looked away. His senses swam and clouded as he stared face-to-face with the being, its eyes still placid. It could take him and kill him with one hand, but Tahn did not budge. Calmly, he studied the intelligence in its eyes.

Then, softly, but in a deep, proud voice, it very clearly said, "Lul'Masi." It never looked away, and Tahn blinked in ignorance. Was that its name? The word came so quietly, he wasn't sure he heard it correctly. Before he could ask a question, Alisandra pulled him back.

"All right, back up, back up." She waved her hands at the beast, who slowly stepped backward to the far side of its cage. "Here's how it's going to go. You," she said, pointing at the creature, "are going to stay where you're at while I open this door and let our young friends here inside. They want to ask your help. And you're going to give it or the beatings on this little family of yours are going to start back up again." She pointed toward the other cages.

The beast's eyes never left Tahn while she spoke.

Alisandra lifted a lantern from one of the poles behind her, and shined its light deeper into the cage, her face more stern. "Do you understand me?"

The creature nodded.

"You may have come here to dig your own earth," Alisandra said to Tahn. "This beast may tear your arms from your body. You are either brave or foolish."

He looked down at Sutter, whose breathing rasped over open lips. His friend was still alive, but for how long? "You took our money with quick hands. Use them to fetch your key and let us in."

The girl turned reproachful eyes on him. "Don't grow brave with *me*. I may feed you to it for half our agreed price, just to silence your tongue." She replaced the lamp, and retrieved a set of keys from a flap in her boot.

"Mark me, lover. Nothing can be done for you once you are inside the cage. The beast will decide whether my threat is worth its obedience. The strongest five men in the company cannot harness it alone; it takes them all." She looked in at the massive creature. "I share no blood with either of you, so take your chance, and either I will increase my fortune, or one less low one will need feeding when the supper bells chime."

"Open it," Tahn said.

She stepped forward and inserted the key in the lock. A small click sounded as a tumbler fell back, and the lock opened. Alisandra kept her eyes on the beast at the back of the cage as she slowly opened the door.

It finally dawned on Tahn that he had paid to take himself and his friend into the company of a creature out of the Bourne. The madness of it struck him. But a glance at his friend bolstered his resolve. He took Sutter's arms and dragged him through the hay and into the cage of the Lul'Masi.

Alisandra closed the door behind them.

As Tahn turned his attention to the beast standing back in the shadows, sudden helplessness filled him. A chill raced down his back as he considered the possible consequences.

A chuff of breath came from the great shape in the shadow, and Tahn laid Sutter down and began to creep toward it. Drawing nearer, he marveled again at its immense size. Its sides heaved as it stared at him in the dimness. *What if it is Quietgiven?* The thought exploded in his mind. The creature resembled the Bar'dyn in so many ways.

Something kept him moving, though, and slowly he crept to within a stride of the creature. Its thick skin rippled with muscle. One hand could easily have fully encircled Tahn's neck. This close, he noticed fine, dark hair growing on its legs and arms. He stared up into its broad face.

The beast stared back, and bent toward him. The ground vibrated with the shifting weight, and Tahn's legs locked in fear. His heart thumped in his ears and chest. This was mad. The creature's arm measured at least the size of Tahn's leg. He began to feel claustrophobic and started to pant. Waves of hot and cold ran over him, threatening to tumble him to the floor. He turned to look at Sutter, trying to recapture his resolve, and heard his friend moan and his eyes tighten at his unnecessary poisoned dreams. A moment later, Sutter cried out in witless pain.

Tahn whipped around and stood face-to-face with the beast. Its glassy eyes were like large black pools, so close that Tahn could see himself in them. Tahn thought he saw a pain-fed apathy in the creature's visage. The presence of the beast was dizzying, its silence more menacing than any shriek or cry it might have uttered. Intelligent eyes peered through Tahn, assessing him as the Shea- son had done.

For several moments the thing stared at him, unmoving, unspeaking. Then it said in its deep voice, "We are Lul'Masi. I am Col'Wrent."

The creature said it as if it should mean something to Tahn, but whatever it was didn't register.

The beast looked back, seeming to consider behind its intelligent eyes. Then its features tightened. "I am Inveterae."

Warmth rushed into Tahn's body, like the thaw of winter all in an instant. He knew this word from the reader's stories. This creature had surely escaped the Bourne. But it was not Quietgiven; it was of the Inveterae, one of the *unredeemed*.

CHAPTER THIRTY-THREE

The Stakes Are Raised

At the revelation of Jastail's last wager, Gynedo's face fell, making him look every year of his age. Murmurs erupted throughout the gambling deck. Wendra felt claustrophobic, and struggled to breathe as the smoke and stares seemed to rush in upon her. Darkness stirred within her, but before it found form, her knees buckled and she fell to the floor. No one moved to assist her. Over the lip of the table she could see Ariana, who alone appeared unsurprised.

"And now you, Ariana," Jastail said softly.

The beautiful young woman looked a moment longer at Wendra. With steady hands she turned over her placards. She did not speak, but sat with quiet dignity waiting for the game to finish.

Gynedo found his composure, his face twisting into a semblance of the amiable smile he'd worn before. He took a long drag at his tobaccom before speaking. "More than a fair price," the old man said. Then he bent forward and peered into Jastail's eyes. "You were too young to learn such a game, friend. You have gone past me. Earth and Dust, I hold no value for your life."

Jastail did not avert his eyes or blink at the strong condemnation. "Will you try to match this wager, Gynedo?" Jastail asked with a mocking reverence.

The old man sat back, looking over the placards, the wagers, and all the faces surrounding them. "No."

A collective gasp was heard in the room, mutters slowly filling the silence. Jastail sat back in his chair. He and the old man's eyes locked, each searching the other. Wendra looked up again, noting the disdain in Ariana's face, but also familiarity in the way she looked at Jastail. The thought of what had just happened left her breathless and tasting bile in the back of her throat. She had been the last raise, the last wager. And something told her it wasn't merely her life; that vague thought churned like panic in her throat.

"Great Fathers, what is this man?" she mumbled. The roar of the gaming room rose to its previous volume, clouding her mind further. She longed for the Hollows and Balatin and a forgetfulness of this riverboat and its vile occupants.

As Wendra sat dumbfounded on the floor, the crowd went back to their gambling. Two gentlemen clapped Jastail on the back before taking their seats again at their own game behind the low wall. Gynedo stared at the heap of to-kens, shaking his head. Soft words fell from his lips like prayers to broken stones, but Wendra could not make them out. Ariana glowered at Jastail, but whether from hatred or jealousy Wendra didn't know. Her captor remained at the table, a defeated look on his face though his final wager had earned him the game. He laid his hands splay-fingered upon the tokens and swept them into a bag before extending a hand to help Wendra up.

Wendra slapped his arm away roughly and pulled herself up using the wall at her back. Blood rushed to her head, and she steadied herself, waiting for the pressure to ease. The din of wage-makers calling odds and gamblers squealing delight or shouting misfortune rose in a dizzying cacophony. Laughter and angry barks punctuated the chorus of voices. No one looked twice at her now, involved in the play of their own chances.

"Come, it's time we go," Jastail said. The command was salt in an open wound. Wendra's attempt to play this man's game, to salvage control over her circumstances, had failed in one raise of the stakes. She thought to jump at him and tear at his eyes, but his companions stepped behind the wall as her balance finally returned.

"Hold, Jastail," the stately woman said. Her words bit, but retained an air of dignity.

Jastail half turned and smiled wanly. "Not tonight, Ariana. I haven't the patience for it."

The woman pushed back her chair and exited the rear gambling area without another look at any of them.

"Bring her," Jastail ordered his men, and started to leave.

"Too far," Gynedo blurted.

Jastail paused, though he would not look back at the old man, who went on, his words weak against the noise in the room, but clear in their intent.

"I've seen it, but only once. Take care, Jastail. You and I, we know the lie of the wager. It is meat for our wine, and tobaccom for our pipe, but always these things sate the user. What you play at now . . . it will never satisfy—"

"Enough!" Jastail blared.

The old man's face sketched itself in stern lines. "Don't forget yourself, boy." Gynedo sat tall in his seat. "And mark you this: Will you come again to my table? Will the chances of the riverboat be enough to entice you?" The old man re-clined again into his chair. "I judge that the game has more of you than you of it. You are too enamored of the stakes to maintain control. You're reckless." He took his pipe to his lips. "Do your trade and leave me in peace."

Jastail left, briskly striding through the game room and out onto the deck. His companions urged Wendra to follow, and reluctantly she made her way past the revelers into the night air.

She found Jastail leaning upon a rail, watching the lesser light ripple upon the water. Without turning, he dismissed his men, leaving Wendra at his back, unguarded.

"You're thinking to attack me," Jastail intoned calmly. "Take your chance."

Wendra stood, her fingers clenching and unclenching as she thought of shoving him over the railing into the river. She'd lost sight of her goal in complying with this highwayman: Penit. She knew Jastail had used the promise of taking her to the boy to manipulate her. The thought darkened her mood further. What use had he for her now, if she was only to be a prize for a game of stakes? And if she failed to find Penit, how meaningless was her struggle in the cave against the fever of her wound? A dark pressure filled her lungs, burning her from within, but also warming her against the night, against this place, this man. She took a step toward Jastail and raised her arms.

"Do you suppose you can do it?" he asked. His words stopped her. "I mean to say that you do not appear to be one acquainted with death." He spoke evenly, as he might to a friend, but still he did not turn toward her.

"But there you're wrong," Wendra answered. "I've seen it." An image flashed in her mind, and she rubbed her empty belly. She lowered her hands, the dark pressure in her lungs subsiding. "I've had it coaxed from my body and torn away from me before I might give it a name."

At that, Jastail turned. His eyes looked strange as he searched Wendra's face. His lips parted as if he meant to pursue her comment, a wary concern folding the lines of his mouth and eyes. He looked at Wendra's stomach, seeming to understand a part of her story. But he left unspoken whatever questions he had. After a few moments, the same smile as he'd given Ariana played upon his features.

"Acquainted, perhaps," Jastail conceded. "But not the cause."

Wendra came to the railing beside him and looked out at the expanse of river. Moonlight rippled on its surface, a silent dance accompanied by the music of small waves lapping at the prow and the din of gamblers inside the game room.

"No, not the cause . . . unless the boy dies," she threatened. "I will find him. Either you will help me, or you will not. But you will not prevent it."

"Anais—"

"Anais?" Wendra interjected. "I don't want to hear that word from your lips. You may be smart at the table, and more than a match of wits for those two dogs you keep with you, but I am not blind to your lies and empty promises. You've made a mistake in bringing me into the company of others as greedy as yourself."

Bitter laughter escaped Jastail's tired face. It fell flat upon the deck and river.

"There is fire in your belly," he said. "The dust won't take you easily. But there's no help for you on this riverboat." He considered a moment, a more wry smile returning to his weathered features. "In truth, I am your only friend here. You may have need of my protection against other, less friendly passengers."

"And what if I should cast myself into the river and swim to shore?"

"In this water?" Jastail asked, his smile lingering. "Not likely. Your legs would seize and drag you down before you stroked half the distance."

"And if I should kill you while you sleep?"

Jastail regarded her. "Then you will never find the boy." He took up his vigil upon the river, his amusement gone.

Wendra could not divine the truth. Did he know where Penit was? Or was he playing her false until the last?

The chill off the water bit at her skin while she kept her captor company beneath the lesser light and the river carried them south. On another night, the sweep of stars in the sky above the wide river basin and the reflection of their light in the water would have caused her to sing. But Jastail muzzled her, not with hands or cloth, but with vague promises and deadly wagers. And in her lungs, her breath for song scarred like smoke and threatened to give voice to a dissonant rasp like a cough from winter winds.

They watched the river together in silence for some time, and the tranquil rush of water along the side of the boat nearly caused her to forget the strange relationship she shared with him. She might have been standing with Tahn at the edge of the Huber in the Hollows. The thought of her brother suddenly sharpened the pain of their separation. It had been long since they'd been separated, starting—in some ways—with the death of her child and Tahn's inaction against the Bar'dyn that had coaxed her child from her womb. That moment, the flight from the Hollows, and not knowing now if Tahn was still alive— because she still loved him—made her need to rescue Penit that much stronger.

And as she stared into the cold depths, she heard new sounds, not the water sluicing down the side of the riverboat.

Wendra heard water splashing.

And the zip of arrows penetrating the river's surface.

Angry voices suddenly barked commands, fear tingeing their orders. *The Bar'dyn,* Wendra thought suddenly, realizing what must be happening. Could they have tracked her once she got aboard the boat?

"Bring her!" Jastail yelled, calling his men to action.

As they rushed down the side of the boat, deckhands stood along the railing firing arrows at the Bar'dyn swimming toward them. Wendra looked toward the shore, where dozens of Bar'dyn rushed south to get ahead of them. Hundreds of strides downriver, the Bar'dyn splashed into the water and began swimming toward the middle to intercept them. The large creatures moved swiftly in the river, their long, powerful arms and legs pulling them with ease against the swift current. Arrows continued to strike the water, some bouncing off of thick Bar'dyn skin. Two men manned the front ballista, firing spears toward the Quietgiven with little accuracy.

Jastail led her toward the stern. The riverboat yawed as the wheelman turned away from the Bar'dyn, hoping to put some distance between the watercraft and the Given. The oars and paddle wheel worked wildly, slapping the water and pulling with the current to increase their running speed. Celebrants lined the gambling room windows, their moon faces peering into the dark with concern. Wendra ran past them, and at the rear of the boat watched as Bar'dyn swam to catch the swiftly moving craft.

They came to the building that housed the horses, and Jastail threw the door wide. His men came from behind and darted into the stable, saddling the mounts in a hurry as Jastail watched the railing for any sign of boarding Bar'dyn. Moments later, the two hirelings emerged with four horses, having appropriated one for Wendra.

"The other side!" Jastail barked.

The men led the mounts to the side of the riverboat opposite the attack. The hull sliced across the current, angling toward the east side of the river. Wendra could see no torchlight marking a dock. The clash of metal chimed in the night air, drawing their attention forward, where strangled cries rose and echoed out across the water. Men and women streamed from the large gambling rooms, filling the deck with chaos and more desperate cries. The large sword-bearing guards of the gambling room were first, jumping to meet several Bar'dyn who were rounding the corner. Given eyes found Wendra, and the creatures broke into a run toward her. Jastail lifted Wendra onto her steed, jumped onto his own, and slapped her horse's rear. Together they vaulted the railing. Their mounts crashed heavily into the freezing waters. Jastail's men came directly behind, splashing into the river at their back.

The instant cold forced a cry from Wendra's throat. But her horse began working alongside Jastail's mount toward the opposite bank.

Already, Wendra's legs were growing numb from the cold. The horses chuffed and swam, struggling to make the far shore. Behind them on the riverboat, the Bar'dyn howled, meeting the swords of the boat guards and dispatching them quickly. Then the riverboat begin to burn. Some people jumped into the river ahead of the swinging blades; others fell beneath the onslaught. Some jumped to escape the flames, which danced on the river water beside the reflection of the lesser light.

Then into the water came the Bar'dyn, pulling with ferocious strokes. She glanced ahead; could they reach the east bank ahead of the Quietgiven? The Bar'dyn gained on them, snatching the slowest of Jastail's henchmen from behind and pulling him from his horse. His scream ended in a gurgling sound.

The boat had gotten them close to the bank, but Wendra did not think the horses could outswim the Bar'dyn. Downriver, dozens of Quietgiven had seen their escape and now swam swiftly for the shore.

The riverboat became an inferno of swirling flames on the water, men and women trying to swim away from the heat, their arms succumbing to the freezing cold water and slowing their flight for land. More than a few slipped soundlessly into the depths.

Hearing another splash just behind them, Wendra turned in time to see a Bar'dyn crush the second of Jastail's men before sending him adrift, blood flowing from a wound to his neck.

Then Jastail's horse lurched from the water, jumping onto the bank. The Bar'dyn uttered indiscernible words and kicked harder toward Wendra. But before they could close the distance, her own horse gained the land and pulled her from the river. In a heartbeat, she followed Jastail north along the riverbank into the trees, the feeling in her legs all but gone.

The wind cut at Wendra as her horse raced to stay with Jastail's fleet-footed mount. Tree limbs and tangled roots whipped past as they forged their own path through the dense wood that clung to the riverbank. Twice, her horse nearly went down, the swim having exhausted its legs. But the steed righted itself and fought to stay close to Jastail.

The forest rose like a series of dark columns frosted with the glow of the moon, but its beauty hid itself from Wendra, who clung desperately to her reins. They splashed through an estuary and up into a dense stand of firs. Jastail slowed at the top of a short rise and cocked his head toward the river to listen. Wendra looked in the same direction and saw a shape moving among the trees.

"Run!" she screamed, and kicked her mount hard in the sides.

The horse bolted forward past Jastail just as a Bar'dyn dove from a thicket of saplings. Jastail scarcely had time to draw his sword and turn. The Bar'dyn's bulky body sailed through the air with a strange grace, hitting Jastail's horse full in the side. The horse, the Bar'dyn, and Jastail all went down in a knot of arms, legs, and drawn weapons. Immediately, the horse stood and bolted into the trees. Jastail rolled aside, one large Bar'dyn hand clasping his ankle. A wet tearing growl escaped the Bar'dyn's throat as it yanked Jastail back. Wendra could see blood on her captor's pant leg where the beast's razor-taloned hand held him firm.

The gambler struggled against the Bar'dyn's strength, but to no avail. Jastail's left hand scrabbled for purchase on root or rock to pull himself away, the other clinging to his sword. Finding it useless, he stopped fighting the Bar'dyn, twisting his sword in a quick spin and clutching it with both hands like a plunging weapon. As the Bar'dyn pulled him in, Jastail used the creature's force and drove the blade into the beast's shoulder.

The Bar'dyn let go and stood erect, howling in pain. The sound vibrated in the trees and hummed in the forest floor. Jastail's sword rose like an ornament from its body, the creature touching it tentatively as it mewled in its throat. With a painful jerk, the Bar'dyn pulled the blade from its fibrous skin, a soft, wet sound accompanying the sword's removal. One of its arms hung slack, but the other lifted Jastail's weapon to its eyes and surveyed the blood streaming in runnels down the blade's flat edge. It grunted and tossed the sword aside, fixing its baleful eyes on Jastail, who crawled backward, kicking with one good leg.

Wendra realized she could flee. Jastail would die, or he would find a way to defeat the Bar'dyn, but either way she could be several thousand strides north of here when the battle ended. She looked north and considered kicking her horse into a run.

The Bar'dyn took large steps toward Jastail, who seemed unable to climb to his feet. In a moment, it would pounce upon him and Jastail would be dead. To Wendra's right, water suddenly splashed at the river's edge: more beasts out of the Bourne. In the space of seconds the fury of many Quietgiven would descend upon them. The forest trees and low growth and Jastail and the Bar'dyn all swam before her eyes, her lungs burning with hot breath that longed to pass over her teeth in violent song. She shook her head, dismissing the strange irrelevance of the inclination and thought. *What would Balatin do?* Still, her legs would not move—they were still numb from the river cold—she could not stand to defend Jastail.

Dear Will and Sky, I prepare to help my captor. I should like to see him suffer at the Bar'dyn's hand. This very night he played me like a token.

The Bar'dyn took another menacing step, now seeming to deliberately threaten Jastail, knowing the man was beyond self-defense. Jastail butted up against a tree, turning on his side to crawl around its base. Then the Bar'dyn grew still, a serenity entering its face as if it contemplated the death that would follow in the next moment. Heavy feet pounded the forest floor, growing louder from the direction of the river. Time fled—Wendra knew she must intervene now or not at all.

In the tense moment of calm, Wendra slapped her horse with the reins and plunged forward to place herself between the Bar'dyn and Jastail. The Bar'dyn looked up at her in surprise, its death mask gone and hatred twisting its features.

"Sa'hon Ghetalloh," the Bar'dyn shrieked, compacting the very air around Wendra. It turned at the sound of its brothers racing to its side. "Your blood will nourish the dust, Womb, then no more will you people the land with their plan."

The coarse, ripping sound of its voice caused her horse to rear, kicking with its front legs. One hoof caught the Bar'dyn in its wounded shoulder, forcing it to double over in pain. A second hoof landed on its head, driving it back into the saplings.

Wendra yelled to Jastail, "Get up!"

The gambler struggled to his feet, leaning against the tree. Wendra pulled her mount backward by his reins and Jastail struggled onto the saddle. As the highwayman put his arms around her waist, three Bar'dyn emerged from the trees behind the saplings where the first Quietgiven had recovered its balance. Wendra kicked hard, spurring her horse into a dead run. Through the trees Wendra pushed, gathering speed. Behind them, the Bar'dyn pursued, their feet pounding the ground. But slowly they outdistanced them, and before the lesser light fell west of the river valley, Wendra was alone again with her captor, who slumped against her back.

Wendra did not stop to tend Jastail's wound, nor to warm herself or eat. She followed the riverbank, keeping it just within sight through the trees, but stayed far enough away to avoid being seen by anyone traveling by boat. She had done as Balatin would have, and she wondered now if she should attempt to push Jastail from her saddle and regain her freedom. But the man still claimed to know where Penit was, and the promise of finding the boy held her in its grasp.

The cool smell of evergreen softened the heat of their flight, and at dawn Wendra stopped and helped Jastail down to rest. Her horse needed rest, as well. She hoped the Bar'dyn would need to regroup and sleep, or her intervention would have been for nothing.

Birdsong filled the strengthening daylight, and Wendra pulled up Jastail's pants leg to check his wound. The gambler muttered incoherently, flinching at her touch. His leg where the Bar'dyn had held him was purple and black, lined with several deep cuts from its sharp nails. Wendra cautiously wound her way to the river and wetted a length of cloth from her cloak. Crouching at the water's edge, she looked both north and south along the smooth surface that reflected a clear morning sky. No boats or Bar'dyn interrupted the perfect glass image of the water. She closed her eyes and muttered hopeful words about the others reaching Recityv safely.

Silent, she paused there, listening to the lapping of water at her feet and watching swallows fly close to the surface gathering food. The steady burn in her lungs subsided, relieving her need to rasp out an angry song. The soft melody of her songbox played in her mind, and she allowed herself to briefly forget Jastail and all that had happened since descending from the plains of Sedagin. Into her repose rose the face of Penit promising to return. The image scathed her, chided her for poor judgment and selfishness. Though she did not fully understand how, she'd been able to heal herself, but had done it too late, after the boy had gone to find help. She realized she had not attempted to sing the song for Jastail, to try to heal his wound. But even should it work for someone beside herself, she did not intend to ease his suffering. He would live; that was enough. Wendra wrung the cloth out and returned to find Jastail more coherent.

"Why did you save me?" he said as she knelt close to him and softly wiped his wound.

"I believe you tell the truth when you speak of the boy," she explained evenly.

"And if I don't, you have made a very bad wager."

She lifted her face from dressing his bruised and cut leg and prepared to press her point with a murderous look. But his words hit home. The anger abated and her face fell slack. "The second time my life will be the stakes," she replied. "But this time, I choose it."

Jastail frowned at her words. "Why is this child's life worth risking your own? You could have left me to the Bar'dyn and been free. Or you could leave me now; I am too weak to stop you. But you tend my leg. . . . Have you not considered how the child came so far from you, who brought him, or why?"

Wendra returned her attention to Jastail's leg. She finished cleaning off the blood, and wrapped the cloth around the bruised and damaged flesh, tying it loosely to avoid paining him.

"If you know of him, it is likely it was you who took him, just as you took me," Wendra reasoned. "For what purpose I don't know, but I've seen how you treat others, and I've no delusion that you will repay this kindness."

Jastail's hard, angular face betrayed no softness. In his aspect Wendra saw the same look as she'd seen at the game table the night before, the look of abandon and considered revenge wrought on anyone he knew. He would become whole, and become again the deceiver and user that knew no bounds to winning any game.

"Come," he said, "we've lost much time."

Jastail stood, favoring his hurt leg. Wendra stood beside him and allowed the man to lean on her as they walked to the horse and mounted.

"And let us talk of why the Quietgiven are so deep in the south and so intent on finding us," Jastail said, cocking a quizzical brow.

Wendra clucked mildly, allowing the horse to walk at an easy pace. They made their way slowly until sun covered the river valley. Shafts of the greater light, filled with dust motes, fell through high boughs of fir and towering hemlock.

"Tell me why Bar'dyn swim a cold river after a girl," Jastail said as they wound east through the canyon.

"They did not knock *me* from my horse," Wendra said, smiling. "I think they sought a highwayman, perhaps someone who has stolen something that belongs to them."

He laughed. "Yes, yes, they are swept up in their need to reclaim a few coins, which mean nothing to them in the Bourne." He paused before continuing in a mirthless voice. "Or perhaps what I have is less of metal and more of man."

"The Quietgiven want nothing of man but his death," Wendra returned blackly.

"Perhaps," Jastail began, "but the one may serve the other." He laughed again. "It is rare fortune that I won *two* bounties at Gynedo's table last evening. Though the second is one whose value I'm likely to have to discover on my own, yea?"

Wendra considered. "You find me the boy, and you'll be glad of it, I assure you."

"Clever," Jastail said, squeezing Wendra's waist affectionately. "Making a partner of me. You've seen how well my companions fare, lady. Be careful how you make your alliances. I expect that a time shall soon come when we have fewer secrets from each other. But the time in between is fuller for the ignorance." The highwayman smiled.

The small earthen highway snaked through the canyons until the mountains fell to wider rolling hills. A fork in the road turned a smaller path south along the back of the mountains that fronted the river valley. Jastail directed Wendra to take the south fork. Within an hour their horse could go no farther.

That night Jastail made a fire from wood that Wendra gathered. Her chill ran deep, having lingered in her flesh ever since the river. The bones in her legs felt brittle and shaky. A lazy sun westered against the mountains to their right, casting them in shadows while touching the few clouds with bright russet and crimson hues.

Jastail had led them off the road to avoid contact with travelers, though Wendra was sure he knew she had no intention of seeking escape. *An odd man,* she thought, *but one who makes every decision with careful deliberation.* He warmed his hands at the fire, the mellow glow softening the angular shape of his face, which might never have spent a night's sleep beneath a roof.

Despite the clear sky, the air did not grow overly cold, and slowly the chill ebbed from her body. Jastail warmed some dried meat and bread on a rock beside the fire, giving half to Wendra and settling back against a low boulder to eat his supper in silence. The highwayman stared into the flames, his eyes distant and flickering with the light of the fire.

As night closed in, prairie wolves howled and small birds chittered, reminding

Wendra of the quiet peace of the Hollows. She and Tahn had spent many nights like this, stirring coals and reminiscing about their father. She remembered how she had loved to visit the Fieldstone, sip honey wine aged in a cold earth cellar, and listen to travelers' tales rendered in florid speech. Balatin had often accompanied her there. Together they would walk home beneath the lesser light and her father would explain to her which parts of the tellers' tales were truth and which parts exaggeration for the sake of his audience. In time it became a game, and soon she could discern the truth behind the lie nearly as well as her father. She did not remember Tahn always accompanying them, but when he did, he seemed less interested in the tale and more interested in why the teller told it. On those walks home, he'd stroll quietly and occasionally interject something about loneliness, which Wendra never understood, instead always recalling the merriment that surrounded Hambley's guests.

Looking across the fire at Jastail, she considered that the lines of laughter in his face were the work of sarcasm, mockery, and deceit. His handsome features used a smile or laugh less because of amusement and more to paint the picture he wanted another to see. The sallow, tired mask he wore at the close of such a rough day was as close to anything Wendra might consider natural. In her mind she heard the words of the old man on the riverboat: *Too far.* And yet when Jastail laughed, it looked and felt genuine. The thought caused Wendra to shiver even as she basked in the heat of the fire. That Jastail may find delight in the labors she'd witnessed him undertaking chilled her as the river never could.

"Are we close to the boy?" Wendra asked, hoping to end the bleak thoughts carrying her away.

"Indeed we are," Jastail replied. "Tomorrow we will come to the place where I believe he may still be." He tossed a dry piece of cedar on the fire. "I cannot guarantee it, but the odds are likely that he is there. And I will have kept my part of our bargain by helping you find him."

Wendra eyed him suspiciously. "And what is your price?"

The same wry smile creased his face. "Isn't it possible that I have done this for charity's sake?"

At that, Wendra lips curled into a grin. "Honestly," she said, "I would bet against it."

"That's not a wager worth taking," Jastail answered. "We will come into Galadell midday. You should sleep."

"I thought we were going to Pelan?"

"That is only what I wanted the deckhands to believe," Jastail said, smiling.

The name of the town—Galadell—was unfamiliar to her, but it was Jastail's unwillingness to say what he stood to gain that unsettled her. She had not expected him to reveal it to her, but she'd hoped to encourage him to lie, and have the chance to look behind it for some indication of the truth. Part of her knew the truth, though. Jastail had not asked for money in exchange for information about the whereabouts of the boy, and he had not sought intimate pleasures from her. His desires must be more fundamental, or more extravagant. The riddle of it only led her back to the certainty that there existed no bargain between them. His promises were possibly lies, but he'd not made a habit of lying to her, either. What was she not seeing?

Jastail covered himself in his blanket and closed his eyes. The last rays of light escaped the sky and gave birth to a thousand stars. Wendra persisted in trying to discover Jastail's intentions. Then suddenly, something came to her.

"What were the tokens?" she said, her voice tremulous but louder than she'd intended.

Jastail opened his eyes and looked up into the night. "You should sleep," he repeated. But he did not close his eyes again.

"You made me a final trump in a game of chance," she said, emotion tightening her throat, the sound of the words somehow more painful than the thought itself. "I don't know the game, but I saw their eyes when you drew me to the table. By Will and Sky, I want to know what you made of me!" Something stirred in Wendra's chest. In an instant, the peaceful dell and fire and sky twisted in her vision and no longer reminded her of the Hollows, but of the fragmented skies and dry, charcoal stretches said to exist within the Bourne.

Jastail peered upward, ignoring her indignation, as though threats held no barbs for him, loud language and the wail of the innocent as meaningless as wind in dry grass to his weathered ears. "You do not want to know, lady; on this you should trust the liar."

"Liar?" Wendra asked, confused. "What game is this? Stop your tricks! I've no sympathy for you. I have been brought low, and I scarcely care for my own safety anymore. Tell me the truth!" Her voice rose in querulous pitch, falling in strident rhythms and beginning to rasp in her throat. At her words the campfire pitched like a dervish stirred by the wind. The change was slight, but she could not be sure Jastail did not see it. She noted it distantly, burying the observation beneath her ire as soon as it was made, and accepting it as wind upon the plain.

Still Jastail remained unmoved. As he continued his gaze upon the firmament, his face remained slack and still, like the stuffed grain sacks she and Tahn used in the summer to erect scarecrows to frighten foragers from their gardens.

"Then I will tell you," Jastail said. "But mind you this, the land east of the mountains of Lesule Valley belong to an unrestrained few. Alliances are all that matter, and I am known at Galadell. Without me, tomorrow will become the worst Sky you ever see."

The gambler did not know Wendra's recent skies, but she said nothing.

The highwayman continued to stare into the heavens, half of his face lit by the fire. Cricket song whirred in the night around them, as Wendra waited.

"I care nothing for money," he began. "Coin is the currency of the ignorant, those imprisoned in the trappings of custom and convinced that it elevates them. The earth provides food, the animals clothes, the timber and mountains wood and stone to build homes and cities. With flint we warm ourselves, and the birds teach us music. All this is given to us freely, the world is plentiful, and each age inherits something of the marvels of the age before it." Jastail's voice quieted. "But the deeds of men, the measure of their lives, these are things that cannot be obtained from the land.

"They cannot be bought and paid for, or if they are, they are not natural choices or honest actions." Jastail slowly turned his head toward Wendra. "The great game is to know the offering in these deeds, these sacrifices people make; to weigh their price, and barter them; to hold them in token is a dear thing." Wendra remembered the many items upon the gambling table, and feeling that they represented actions, choices of sacrifice.

"Dearer still," Jastail went on, "is the one who can *direct* the choice, up the wager, hold the action suspended in one's hand. It is no less than holding life, for what is life but choice?"

He held up the metal glove won from Ariana. "Our fair lady at the table spoke but a wish to a doting warrior, and sent him to his death, knowing it beforehand." Jastail's smile flared. "Do you see, his was the choice, but by her influence he chose a path of ultimate sacrifice. The glove became an emblem of his life, his will offered to another."

Anxiously, Wendra rubbed her belly, now flatter absent her child. Only vaguely did she note Jastail's observant eyes as she tried to soothe herself when her mind raced again to understand what else lay upon the table of the gambling boat. Her thoughts, though, went quickly past those tokens to Jastail's final play—pulling her toward the table's edge. And then a dark revelation came.

Will and Sky, he does know where Penit is! That was his wager. It was not simply my life. It was my choice, my chance, to find Penit!

Wendra rose from the fireside and raced into the darkness with her mouth open, gulping lungs full of crisp night air to cool the fire that burned within her.

CHAPTER THIRTY-FOUR

The Scar

The quiet roar filled his mind like silence, like listening while submerged beneath a swift-flowing river. Braethen's heart raced as it had when first he'd accepted Vendanj's sword.

For reassurance, he fingered the hilt. He needed to know he was not really in that place again, that unnatural blackness. The sensation of being both in and of the dark filled him. He fought the duality, trying desperately to see something through the thick pall of black.

The night will not lift! I am inexorably caught in it. But I am not born of this desolate place!

He took the sword in hand, weeping at the sky. But somehow the fevered action left him disconsolate. Was it the sword that defined him, led him, defeated the dark?

His skin ran hot and cold as he denied the violence inherent in the blade but reveled in the peace it seemed to offer. He felt like a child in the womb, blind and helpless and safe. In that moment he started to fall. He could not see the sky turn, or the ground rise up and roll as he slid toward nightmare. He clung to the sword, but released himself to the descent.

"Open your eyes, sodalist!" The command boomed through the obscurity.

Braethen did not understand, and relaxed further into his tumble. He would be glad of some rest in the peace of that obscurity.

A hand caught him. And a wave of disappointment began to wash over him.

"Your eyes!" the voice said again from down a long black tunnel.

But still he did not fully understand. Images cascaded through his mind, all blurring, tumbling, fading, claimed by the dark as quickly as they rose, until he could see nothing save a blade of grass.

He blinked his eyes open, and looked into the hard eyes of the Sheason awash in white light. Vendanj gave him a hard stare and heaved him from his bedroll. Mira looked on, standing still in the fall of rain and lit dimly a few paces away in the same radiant light. The realization hit him as he traced the source of the illumination back to his hand, where the sword burned brightly against the night.

Vendanj continued to stare at him, his sharp features catching the light of the blade, his brow drawn tight. Braethen thought he could feel the force of the Sheason's thoughts spreading like the weight of a graveside requiem. The turnings of the Sheason's mind were palpable, living things. Whatever their true message, they fell so heavily on Braethen that they threatened to overwhelm his own sense of purpose.

"Will you still take this mantle?" It was a question without an answer, because the decision had already been made. The real intent was to say that Braethen may fail.

Vendanj shared a final pained look with the sodalist, then walked away. The weight of the Sheason's thoughts departed with him, and Braethen gasped in relief. He didn't believe Vendanj had meant to let them get away from him; Braethen had never felt that weight before in all his moments spent near the Sheason. It felt like a yoke, harnessed tight to a beast of burden. In his mind flashed the skeleton of an ox, white bones bleached in the sun, the tatters of its yoke still fettering the skull and hitched to a wagon laden with an immense white stone sculpted at long vertical angles. The flash seared his mind like a portent of things to come. Braethen shook his head and dashed to catch the others.

"It was given too soon," Mira said evenly.

"It doesn't matter now," Vendanj replied, his voice soft. "Two journeys, sodalist. May they converge for you."

Vendanj rode ahead, leaving Braethen holding the dimming blade. As the light receded on Mira's skeptical features, he thought he heard the words "For us all." But the sound of them seemed carried away by the night as they again found themselves in relative darkness.

Mira strode to where the Sheason stood, and the two spoke as they looked east under a starry, cloudless sky.

Watching them, Braethen's face flushed with anger. He was being left out while being asked to put everything at risk. He wanted to justify the Sheason's initial confidence in him when he gave Braethen the sword, but now he felt like the boy who first sat at his father's table and thumbed books he could neither read nor understand.

With as steady a voice as he could muster, he asked, "What is it that must remain a secret from me?"

Neither the Far nor Sheason acknowledged his question.

Again he asked.

This time they stopped. Without turning, Vendanj replied, "You gave light to the sword, sodalist. Any Velle within a week's ride will now know of us. We have only to anticipate wherefrom the Quietgiven will come, and choose our path appropriately."

Mira's level gaze caught him. No contempt showed there, but no consolation either.

"Do not concern yourself, sodalist," Vendanj added. "There is only one way for us, and the Quietgiven aren't likely to follow too closely."

Braethen sat again. In the east, dawn hinted at its arrival, night holding sway everywhere else. They'd been traveling for two days since Widows Village, and thankfully the dreariness had been left behind. Overhead, the patterns in the stars turned slowly. They called to mind stories given to the shapes there: Adon'Imesh the Unyielding, six stars describing the sword in his hand, which was said to have brought an end to the Craven Season behind the might of Adon's arm and legions of men pledged to put down the Quiet; and the open book of Cervis'Leo, the first author known to have penned fancies and parables to show men to themselves without the use of real names or history. Braethen remembered one journal entry recorded in spidery script that related how Cervis screamed the original creation of a tale as he was burned at the stake by a gathering that an age later would be known as the Exigency.

Shapes and stories fixed in the night sky; a sword and a book. Braethen thought of the irony, his own life ruled now by the stuff of legends, myths. Near his left hand rested the sword given him by the Sheason, near his right, one of Ogea's books. There was room enough in the sky for both, but would he be big enough to reconcile the two disparate elements that warred in him? Braethen put tentative fingers to each—both reassured him, both appalled him.

"By Will may I find a way," he whispered.

Soon light shone strong enough to see by; and no sooner had it done so than Mira returned.

"Take up your sword," the Far said.

Braethen looked a question at her.

"Don't force me to ask you twice, sodalist," Mira said, a slight edge in her tone.

Reluctantly, Braethen took the sword in hand, holding it awkwardly. Mira led him to a flat clearing. As he followed the Far, he cast furtive glances back at the fire.

"You seem to fear the sword," she said, still facing away from him.

"*This* sword," Braethen corrected.

"And why this one in particular?" she asked. "Is it different from other swords you have wielded in battle?"

"I have been in battle but once," he answered, aware of the Far's deliberate choice of words. He had longed to raise his hand and claim the sword sewn in the crest on his garment, but he feared that he lacked the nobility he had attached to the emblem. He'd sworn to it, but the darkness he'd experienced when taking the sword in hand still haunted him.

"Nonsense," Mira countered. "You have been in battle many times, it is only the instrument of the sword that you have used but once." She drew one of the blades she wore on her back and ran a finger down its edge. "Is it physical conflict that you fear?"

Braethen considered the question. Many times he had raised his hands in his own defense or in the defense of another. It was not an activity he relished, but neither did it cause him fear.

"No," he answered. "I cannot explain it. I've little experience with weapons, and the wars have not touched the Hollows in my lifetime." He looked at the edge of the sword he held, the dark surface catching the light of early morn. "But this blade is . . . unique. It is more than metal."

"Oh?" Mira said. She turned to face him. "And why is that?"

Why such games? You and the Sheason hold answers you are unwilling to share with others. His face felt hot in the cool air of dawn. "Because," he began, then did not finish.

"I see," Mira replied, a mix of condescension and disappointment in her voice.

"No, you do not!" Braethen yelled. His explosive outburst surprised him as much as it did the Far. But he could not stop what came next. "I took the oath. I believed in the stories, that the Sodality honored what was best about the Sheason, standing beside them to record and remember, to place themselves in the way of whatever risk. It is part of the oath to take up weapons of war if it is needed, to brandish steel and leather and bone and mind to safeguard the keepers of the Will."

Mira shifted her stance, her gaze fixed on him.

His breath came fast and shallow, the silver rays of daybreak streaking the clouds of angry exhalations that billowed from his lips. "But I did not know the cost. I was naive. I idealized the tales of heroism, the banner, and even wars so old that they are unremembered in the minds of men. And now that I have taken hold of steel and lifted it in conflict, however right or necessary, I have found myself in darkness." His breath faltered, catching in his chest, and he went on in a softer voice. "Will and Sky . . . deep, eternal darkness. No sound could I make, no thought could I hold, as if I was swallowed in the belly of a great beast out of the Bourne. I was gone to nothing, and in keeping what I swore to, had nearly lost all that I am."

Braethen cast a scathing glance at Mira. "Is it so with all who first draw a weapon of war? Or perhaps it is me, and I am a small, foolish scholar who belongs in the Hollows instead of carrying the scrolls of a dead reader into the east." He raised the sword. "Or is it this weapon? And should I crack its shaft across the nearest stone because of the well it cast me into when I took it up?"

Mira stared back at him, her face stony. Vaguely, Braethen was aware that the Sheason stood nearby, listening, watching. The Far shared a look with

Vendanj, then stepped closer to Braethen, her steady gaze at once strangely re-assuring and frightening.

"Listen closely, sodalist, and remember these words." She placed a hand on his shoulder. "The darkness is all these things. Taking up a weapon to end life is a black business. Better it would be if all those who lifted the sword fell into the place you found yourself. There is more than a little comfort in knowing that the potential in your arm and weapon causes you disquiet. If it were other-wise, I should have left you in the Hollows." The Far looked at Braethen's hands, which shook as he held the sword Vendanj had given him.

"But it is much to do with the sword you carry. It is not mere steel. Much of what it is will occur to you in its use, and more will the Sheason teach you. But I will show you how to hold the weapon, how to keep another from tearing it from your grip, and how to use only what energy is necessary to meet an attack. In time you will hold it steady, and see its edge and end without looking at it."

Braethen tried to stop his trembling fingers. But as he considered her words, his shaking would not be stilled. "I do not want to grow familiar with such a thing," he finally said.

"I spoke nothing of familiarity, sodalist," Mira answered. "You should never make yourself a cousin to death. But now more responsibility is yours, so more is expected of you. To help you meet that expectation, I will teach you things you must know. Now lift your blade and we will begin."

Braethen stole a glance over his shoulder. Vendanj still watched, his eyes sober in the light of sunrise. *What will he show me about this thing?* Braethen wondered as he began lifting the sword in his quivering hands.

For an hour, he repeated movements and grips, his and the Far's swords glinting almost playfully in the rays of another day.

But when they'd finished, Braethen still felt dejected for having unwittingly called the sword's power in his sleep.

The Sheason appeared next to him and pulled his wooden case from be-neath his cloak. "Don't waste your energy with guilt and regret for what is done, sodalist." Vendanj took a leaf from the case and held it toward him.

Braethen looked at it with reluctance.

Vendanj raised it higher in offering. "Take it."

Trying to peer within the Sheason's hood, Braethen leaned forward and ac-cepted the leaf.

"What is it?" He turned the thin, dark green leaf over in his palm, studying it closely.

"It was harvested from the Cloudwood two summers ago."

"But it is fresh," Braethen said, unbelieving.

"It is a resilient tree, sodalist." Braethen thought he saw a look of deep sad-ness within Vendanj's cowl. "Do you know it?"

"It is written of in the histories. Some pages call it the Eternal Grove, saying its roots have woven the land itself. Others say it is the wood to harvest for our gallows, where the last trial will be held and punishment swift." Braethen looked up from the small leaf. "But these accounts were compiled from diaries and the oral tradition of reader's tales stretching over ages we cannot even name. Some of them were written in the hand of my father himself."

Vendanj nodded. "The oldest stories come with interpretation. It is the price we pay to preserve them. Put the leaf upon your tongue. I will tell you of its origin." Vendanj exhaled and looked skyward. Braethen caught a clearer look of the Sheason's pale cheeks and brow. The man was aggrieved, yet indignation flamed in his eyes.

"The name is right," he began. "It is the Eternal Grove. Its leaf and stem and branch were among the first in creation, drawn from the purest and most enduring elements. Its height is magnificent. Poets have had to test the limits of their craft to describe its grandeur. Its strength is unmatched even by iron and steel, and it takes a hundred years for its trunk to increase by just one growth ring.

"The Cloudwood stands at the end of the Saeculorum Mountains, at the edge of creation, its roots growing into the abyss, claiming form and substance from the mists there, creating earth where none existed, forcing the land to expand."

"Would it not have overcome all the world then?" Braethen asked.

Vendanj smiled dryly. "The weave of the root is slow. It adds, and in time some of our world passes away. The process occurs too gradually for us to mark, but as the earth is made new, so, too, is it eroded and washed to silt in distant places, in the west near Mal'Sent and on a hundred other shores across the oceans."

Braethen put the leaf on his tongue, letting it rest there. He did not know what to expect, and for several moments nothing happened. It was simply a leaf after all. Then sweet nectar flooded his mouth. The leaf dissolved and Braethen swallowed hungrily. In an instant his aches subsided and whatever self-doubt remained in him faded to nothing. A quietude and calm came over him, and he felt as though he'd rested for a week.

A curious smile crossed Vendanj's face as the sensations made their way into Braethen's body. The sodalist imagined that he must look like a child tasting his first molasses stick.

As the taste lingered on his tongue, Braethen marveled at the effects of one small leaf. "Why do you share this with me now?"

"Do you think me selfish, sodalist?"

"That is not what I meant. I—"

Vendanj held up a hand and led Braethen to the small rise he'd been standing on moments before. Cresting the rise, Braethen found himself staring out over a blackened plain.

"The Scarred Lands," Vendanj said.

This was why the Sheason had shared the life-giving leaf. Looking out upon it, Braethen felt hopeless.

Vendanj rode ahead, descending into the vast plain. Braethen followed him onto the dark soil, which reminded him of soot.

A smell like dead candlewick assailed him, and all around an empty stillness surrounded them, more desolate than the despair of Widows Village. The land was nearly devoid of all life. Only the hardiest sage grew, and that sparsely. Fissures yawned like sores in the arid expanse of sand and hard-baked stone.

Small wind dervishes licked at the earth, tugging at brown grass that bristled with their passage. The sun pounded down as though drawn to the land, which cracked like a vast dry seabed.

"What caused this?" Braethen asked, hearing the consternation in his own voice.

Vendanj waved Braethen to his side. "The War of the First Promise lasted close to four hundred years. It was not constant battle. Years of peace would pass with little threat from the Bourne. But then the Quiet would surge again. And so generation after generation watched their fathers go to war. The activities in schoolrooms focused on combat strategy, whatever knowledge could be had of the Quiet, and the production of clothing and arms. For nearly twenty generations, literacy belonged only to those children whose mothers sang the teaching songs and read to their young. Women created the implements of war and bore the men that would wield them. Before the war was over, they were known as the Wombs of War. On the fields, the fruits of those wombs lay unrecorded, unremembered as the procession of war marched on."

Braethen lifted his face to the sun, wanting to both honor the dead and clear his mind of the images the Sheason's words created.

Vendanj took a drink from his waterskin and continued.

"Despite all the people could do, the Quiet came, driving families from their homes. Refugees flooded every safe town and city. Food shortages caused riots. As people strove to survive, the streets filled with every kind of unsavory practice: prostitution, slavery, gambling. City arbors began to reek of the unbathed, granaries were ravaged, livestock purloined to feed hungry mouths.

"It went on like that for nearly the entire span of the First Promise. So it was that at the end of the fourth century of war, when the largest legions out of the Bourne were reported to be marching on the world, one of the Wombs of War ascended the palace stair at Recityv with a newborn babe."

Braethen mouthed her name: Anais Layosah. They had seen Penit play this rhea'fol not a week ago.

"For three days Anais Layosah called for the formation of a council of nations to answer this threat. King Baellor heard her, dispatching birds and riders to the other remaining independent nations. And by sunset on that fourth day, a proclamation was read calling for appointments to a convocation."

Braethen's heart quickened at the tale of Layosah holding her child aloft and decrying a king and the noble elite to which he pandered. He had read a different ending to that tale, though, one of pity for the infant.

"Appointments were made from every quarter of society. Dethroned kings, leaders of cities under attack, all took a seat. These rulers committed every last man and weapon to the amassing of an army to march against those cutting a swath into the nations of the south, a force numbering two hundred thousand. But it became clear that steel alone could not put down the Quiet or drive them back to the Bourne. Scouts reported the presence of renderers and other creatures of nightmare from beyond the veil. When King Baellor heard that dire news, he went to Maral Praig, randeur of the Order of Sheason, asking him to violate the oath of the order and commit his followers to the use of force, to war. Baellor convinced Praig, and the army that marched west from Recityv to the blare of brass horns grew by four hundred Sheason."

Vendanj pointed to the land around them. "Into this place they came, sodalist. It was here they met the Quiet, here that the War of the First Promise was decided. Baellor's army was outnumbered four to one. Wave upon wave of the Quiet descended into the plain. Baellor knew he could not fight a war on many fronts, so he commanded his line to form a great circle, leaving no flank.

"At first, only flesh and steel clashed on the plain. But soon, Velle lifted their hands to the sky and called terrible fire and wind and lightning to smite Baellor's army. They drew the great power of life from the world they sought to own, from the earth upon which their enemies stood. Their drain upon the land was massive, stripping it of life and vitality, color and scent, the very marrow of the world, leaving the land an utter waste."

Vendanj looked about him.

"But the Sheason refused to draw upon the land or others to exercise the Will, so they exhausted their own Forda at an alarming rate. Journals record Sheason giving unto the last, expending their spirit until nothing remained to give.

"The battle raged on for eight days. The Quiet sought a way through Baellor's line. The army of the First Promise fought a final battle in that great ring. There could be no escape, and Baellor's circle of defense shrank through attrition.

"It was then that Maral Praig, First Servant, gathered his fellows together at the center of the great round. While the remnants of Baellor's army held the line, the Sheason stood together, each one joining hands with the Sheason next to him. In an attitude of prayer, the Sheason bowed their heads, and Praig uttered a soul-rending cry that filled the entirety of what would become the Scar. A light flared with the magnitude of a thousand suns, and with it, every man with the stewardship to direct the Will, Sheason and Velle alike, fell.

"In three days, those Quiet that were still alive retreated. And across the dry, dusty land lay the stain of blood like an artist's spillage. Ten thousand men still stood when the Quiet vanished into the north. Here"—Vendanj swept his arm across the horizon—"the stench of the dying filled the air, and the heap of Sheason forms in their long, dark robes lay like a benediction on the Battle of the Scar."

Vendanj cast his gaze from left to right, finally looking back at Braethen. "It is an ugly wound, sodalist, but one that reminds us of the cost of freedom from the Quiet."

Braethen gazed across the barren landscape. Beneath the smells of dry sage and grass lingered a smell like dirt from a burial cave. But there was something more. Ever since they had come into the Scar, the quality of light, of movement, seemed strained. A lethargy permeated the place, like the broken spirit of a man. And as the sun rose over the vast inhospitable waste, it grew hot and oppressive.

When Braethen sensed that the Sheason had finished his recounting, he asked, "All this time, and still so little grows here?"

Vendanj took a deep breath of the dry air. "Some have tried to cultivate crops in the Scar. They've given up. The Forda is gone, drawn into the bodies of Quietgiven to replenish their life's breath ages ago. It is a mark upon the land, a reminder, a remnant of violent thoughts and deeds. This place will yield none of the promise inherent in the world beyond it."

"A promise forgotten by most of those who trod upon it," Mira said, loud enough to be heard but not so loud as to become part of the conversation.

Braethen took Vendanj's silence as agreement with the Far's comment.

"If it cannot be healed or changed," Braethen asked, "then why do we ride directly into it?"

Vendanj regarded him, and first asked a question. "Your books, sodalist, they did not prepare you for this, did they?"

Braethen looked again into the bleak land around him. "No," he finally answered, "they did not prepare me to see the scale on which life might be snuffed out by the actions of those who render the Will." He gave a furtive glance at the Sheason. "The dark soil is stronger testimony than that written on the pages of my books."

Vendanj seemed satisfied by this answer. But Braethen's mind churned with the horror that what he saw around him could be the fate of the world beyond the Scar.

Then the Sheason finally answered Braethen's question. "We seek out the man Grant, who lives in the Scar."

Someone lives *here?* Braethen shuddered at the thought.

"You mean for this man to join us." Braethen wasn't asking.

"What if he says no?" Mira said.

"He mustn't decline," Vendanj replied. "This place he lives in has no doubt gotten inside him, so it will not be easy. But he must be convinced. He was the first to challenge the Exigents and the Sheason and the Recityv council. I deeply fear what will happen if he refuses us."

• CHAPTER THIRTY-FIVE •

The Wages of a Kiss

A thousand tales of caution and distrust and hatred resounded in Tahn's mind. Inveterae were creatures of the Bourne. Some stories spoke of them as synonymous with Quietgiven. Others related a malevolence and stain so terrible that the gods had deemed them unfit to live among men. The very word—*Inveterae*—that described these races sent into the Bourne ages ago with the Quiet meant literally *unredeemed.*

Yet something in the Inveterae's unperturbed stillness belied all Tahn had heard. As Balatin had always taught him when greeting someone strange in peace and friendship, Tahn put his hand out with his palm up and thumb out. "I am Tahn Junell," Tahn replied in a whisper. "And I need your help."

The Lul'Masi did not respond. The two stared at one another in the dim light of the cage. Then the creature spoke, but low so that only Tahn could hear. "No man has ever helped my kind; the Lul'Masi have no friends in the land of men."

Tahn spared a look at Sutter lying in the straw. Returning his attention to Col'Wrent, he raised his hand higher. "Then let me be the first."

A strange look passed across the Lul'Masi's thick features. And with some hesitation, it raised its massive arm and locked hands with Tahn, whose fingers were lost in the massive palm. When they joined hands, the Lul'Masi's face softened. "Quillescent," it said. The word disconcerted Tahn a little, but he had no time to ask about it.

Sutter could be dying. He suddenly had a new bargain to strike.

He leaned closer, the sharp smell of the creature strong in his nose. "The te-nendra girl threatened you to force your help. I will make you a different prom-ise. Help my friend and I will free you from your cage."

The Lul'Masi's grip on Tahn's hand tightened uncomfortably—reflexively, Tahn thought. The creature closed its eyes for a moment, the way Tahn did when he thought of the sunrise. The Lul'Masi breathed deeply, its belly ex-panding, the air it drew producing a deep rumble in its chest as it exhaled.

Finally, the Lul'Masi nodded, its face as unreadable as the moment before. But Tahn thought he saw gratitude pass across its eyes. "What is wrong with your friend?"

"He was struck with a spiked ball thrown by a Bar'dyn. He lost his balance, his speech, and now he's unconscious. I think he's been poisoned. The healer in town said you may know what to do."

Panic filled Tahn's chest again as Col'Wrent did nothing more than stare at him for several long moments. Perhaps there was nothing he could do, and Sutter would die in the straw of the low one's cage.

"Bring him to me."

Tahn dragged Sutter to the back of the cage, the straw heaped around him.

Col'Wrent knelt over Sutter like a mass of boulders. "Your friend will not die. The poison in him is meant to slow, not kill. But without a cure, he could sleep for days." Col'Wrent put a massive finger in its mouth and drew out a thick stream of saliva and mucus. It gently pried Sutter's mouth open and wiped the viscous fluid on his tongue.

Then together they waited several long minutes in the hiss of the lantern and stink of the tent. Sutter lay unmoving for some time. At length, his eyes opened. He began to writhe in the straw and spit foulness from his lips. "What the Sky did you put in my mouth?"

"You don't want to know." Tahn put his hand on Col'Wrent's shoulder in appreciation, feeling the strong, rough skin of the Lul'Masi.

Suddenly Sutter realized where he was, and looked up into the massive face of his healer. He scrambled back against the side of the cage, trying to free his sword but fumbling with the weapon.

"Easy, Sutter. There's no need of that." Tahn pointed at Sutter's blade. "You were poisoned by the Bourne, and you've been healed by the Bourne. Maybe a thank-you is in order."

Sutter stared, incredulous. "Thank you?"

"Good enough," Tahn said.

From behind them, Alisandra called, "Looks like you're finished. I'll take my second half now."

With his back shielding their exchange, Tahn spoke in low tones. "The girl is quick and wary; she won't allow you to approach the door. I will go out and get the key from her—"

"No," Col'Wrent said in a deep whisper. "Her mistrust will guard against your task. Tent folk thrive because they are greedy and assume all others are like themselves. You won't succeed without feeling her blade."

"Then how?" Tahn asked.

"What's going on?" Alisandra asked, impatience edging her tone.

"Yeah, what *is* going on?" Sutter echoed.

"Not now, Sutter. Be quiet for once."

Alisandra called again. "Your friend looks fine. Get out here."

"What bribe bought your entrance to my prison?" Col'Wrent asked with a hint of distaste.

"Three and six," Tahn replied.

"You were wise enough to hold back full payment?"

"Yes. Half before, half after."

The Lul'Masi looked over Tahn's shoulder. Its patient eyes surveyed the cage door, then returned to Tahn. "Tell her how low and stupid I am. Tell her you believe you've already trained me to perform simple tricks, like a dog. That you got me to lift my hand, and that you are going to have me hold out the balance of her payment in my servile palm for her to take. The tent folk are wary, but infected with greed and pride beyond their caution. I will play my part, until her hand is close enough to grasp."

There was no murder in Col'Wrent's eyes, but Tahn had not yet seen any real emotion in them, either. Caging the Lul'Masi was wrong, but he didn't want Alisandra slain.

"I can't help you if you intend to kill her," Tahn said.

Col'Wrent's brow tightened. The Lul'Masi hovered over him. Tahn craned his neck back to look up at the towering creature. Slowly, Col'Wrent extended both arms toward the roof of the tent, then lowered them while bringing them slowly together. When its hands touched, they were at Tahn's chest. The Lul'Masi interlocked its thumbs and pressed its palms against him. Tahn peered up in confusion. Col'Wrent removed its hands, and spoke earnestly. "I vow, from the sky to one, to do as you ask."

Tahn took out his money pouch and dropped the coins in Col'Wrent's large hand. He then immediately whirled, fixing a self-congratulatory grin on his face, and strode confidently to the door.

"He is indeed low," Tahn said to Alisandra as he came close to her. "But hardly the monster you described. He has the mind of a child."

"But the body of a Slope Nyne," Alisandra put in.

"I've never seen such a thing," Tahn answered. He leaned casually against the inner bars of the cage. "A dog bites when it is threatened or beaten into a corner," he explained. "But let the dog smell you, show no fear, and it welcomes you into its home. Will even perform tricks for you."

"Tricks?" Alisandra said suspiciously.

"Nothing as fancy as the feats in your larger tents, but I have given the beast the rest of your money, and some extra besides, and asked him to bring it to you."

Alisandra took up a dagger.

"There is no need of that," Tahn said. "The creature wants to serve. A kind word and second meal bowl will earn you his trust. Think of the money to be made by bringing people to this cage and letting them inside to pet its hoary skin. You could train it to do small tricks; your mastery over it will make you rich." Tahn leaned in conspiratorially.

Alisandra's eyes danced with the prospect. She appraised the Lul'Masi, greed written large upon her face. Then her lust for lucre gave way to the guarded look she usually wore. "What gain is in it for you? Why tell me such things? Do you intend to petition for partnership in the tenendra?"

Sutter laughed, causing Alisandra to frown. "No partnership," Tahn said. "A kiss."

The request startled the girl for a moment, and she drew her head back in obvious suspicion, a grin teasing at one corner of her mouth.

"I don't care for the beast, and I don't seek my fortune," Tahn said confidentially. "My friend is healed, I have what I want . . . mostly."

"Mostly?" Alisandra's beautiful, dangerous smile returned.

"I'll have a kiss from you without price, and then I'll carry the memory of winning your favor without lightening my purse. It will warm me when my fires grow cold."

Sutter laughed from behind him, but this time Alisandra regarded Tahn with appreciation.

"Well, boy," Alisandra said, "you may have your kiss, and that will put paid to all future claims you might make." She inclined toward him, stopping short. "And you will take this information with you when you leave Squim. Should another come to understand the gentle nature of the beast, I will find you and show you your earth."

Tahn shook his head and puckered clownishly. Alisandra put her soft lips to his own, and Tahn's pucker melted beneath the heat of her mouth. She moved her lips across his for several moments, taking, he thought, some pleasure in the kiss. The touch and taste of her lips, the danger and mystery of her, the striking beauty, all of it raced through Tahn. It was part of the ruse, and part of his own fledgling desires—together they made it a kiss he would never forget. Alisandra gave a soft, submissive sound before pulling away. Tahn's mouth hung open as she called the beast toward her.

The Lul'Masi walked sheepishly, cowering, but advancing at her call.

Tahn could see Alisandra had bought his story; a wild light shone in her eyes like that of a child waiting to be given gifts. Hesitantly, Col'Wrent approached until he was within arm's reach. He turned his head, looking away as he proffered his palm filled with coins as though he were afraid. His fingers trembled as the girl reached to take the money. In her confidence, she made no haste, gathering the coins with arrogance.

In an instant, the Lul'Masi took Alisandra by the wrist, its grip stopping the flow of blood into her hand. It yanked the girl toward itself and wrapped its mighty arms around her. It squeezed until her face reddened to the hue of summer apples. She lost all her breath before she could utter a cry and moments later she slipped to the floor.

Tahn dove to his knees to check her breathing. She was alive, merely unconscious.

"We should hurry," Sutter slurred, still woozy. "The town will not be safe once they find out what we've done."

Tahn stood, dwarfed beneath the Lul'Masi. "Thank you."

"The debt is mine," Col'Wrent answered. "Now go. Your friend is right. I will free the others."

Tahn and Sutter raced to the end of the tent. Sutter ducked outside, but Tahn looked back to see the Lul'Masi take the key from Alisandra's hand and begin to open the other cages. The Inveterae looked up and caught Tahn's eye. A look of gratitude passed between them, and it made Tahn wonder about the nature of the Inveterae.

Then Sutter pulled Tahn through the tent flap and they ran back past the tenendra toward town.

They rode most of the night north out of Squim. They didn't speak, pushing to put leagues between themselves and the tenendra. In the waning hours of night, Tahn turned his attention east and thought about the coming of dawn, about another day of life. He imagined the rays of sunrise striking a more peaceful world, one where Wendra hummed over morning pig steak. The thought of his sister ended his ritual predawn reverie. Skies, he missed her. There seemed a hole inside him. He couldn't remember a time without her in his life. Not where he couldn't go to her if he needed to. Or if she needed him.

And again he recalled the moment when he hesitated in releasing his draw on the Bar'dyn hovering over his sister's birth bed. *I'm so sorry, Wendra. Forgive me. Are you okay? Your child . . . it's not your fault.*

Those maddening words—*I draw with the strength of my arms*—Tahn's frustration returned. Long ago, he'd learned to live with the ritual saying. It flashed in his mind so quickly that it posed no encumbrance to his skill with his bow. But the origin of those words, and now the trouble it had caused Wendra, plagued him anew. Would he ever understand what made him say them?

No, there had been no good reason to let his sister's child be carried into the night by one of the Quiet. He would not forgive or explain that away.

All he could do was let the wind and rhythm of Jole's hooves lull him toward less troubling thoughts, and hope he would find her in Recityv with the others.

Some time later, full day lit the sky.

Sutter reined in. "We've got to get off this road." His words were no longer slurred, and his friend looked more like himself.

Tahn pulled up beside him and wheeled around. There was no sign that anyone was following them, but he nodded. With Quiet on their trail as well, and tent folk they'd be best off avoiding, getting off the road made sense. Having forgotten his tender foot, he winced as he jumped to the ground.

"Watch those delicate toes," Sutter jested as he dismounted. "I have it on good authority that they intend to dance a turn with a quick-footed Far. You'd better stay on the mend."

Tahn grinned through his pain. "Perhaps I ought to fix you with the bit and bridle and ride you a distance. I could do with the rest and quiet, and so could the horses."

Favoring his left foot, he ducked into the dense trees on the east side of the road, and pushed himself and the horses as quickly as he could. Blue shadows clung to the ground in the early light of dawn, the smell of dew thick over fallen leaves and low rocks.

When the road had been left far behind and the trees thinned, Sutter pulled abreast of Tahn. "Explain something to me. How does a melura, who rubs the reproductive scents of animals across his boots and shoulders to attract game while hunting, fetch the smiles of so many women?" Sutter grinned wickedly.

"Those gamey smells have gotten me a few friends, too." Tahn smiled back.

"I hope you're not talking about me," Sutter said. "I'd just like to know why *you* got to kiss Alisandra."

"These women you talk of are all deft with a blade. Isn't that somehow unwise?" Tahn furrowed his brow in mockery of reason.

"You looked plenty *wise* receiving Alisandra's lips. And don't play coy with me about the Far. You may as well have branded your intentions on your forehead."

"And what about you, root-digger," Tahn put back. "You've declared *your* intentions for my sister. Do you esteem her less than a tenendra girl?"

"How did we end up talking about me?" Sutter asked. "You're the one flapping your lips all over the place. And while we're at it, for one who wanted to live out his life isolated in the Hollows, you've taken a keen interest in poking your nose into the private affairs of others."

"You mean like taking a square stance against a ranking member of the Sedagin?"

"Just defending your sister's honor," Sutter said, bowing as he walked.

They laughed together and wound their way through leaf-shadow.

Tahn found a comfortable rhythm. "You know what we forgot?"

"Yeah, directions," Sutter replied.

"The ravine runs east there," Tahn pointed, "but turns north before reaching that range." He indicated a mountain ridge visible through the trees. "I think we should leave the road alone. You can dig—"

Sutter put his hand on Tahn's arm, his smile fading. He turned to face Tahn. "Thank you."

"What?"

"Don't get me wrong. It's no treat to taste the snot of a brute from the Bourne. Thing gave me the crawls." He paused. "But you went into that cage and could have been that thing's next meal. You didn't know any better than the girl who sold you admission what it might have done."

Tahn tried to dismiss it. "It was nothing. You'd have done the same—"

"Yeah, I would have," Sutter cut in. "But . . . it's just that I think often about the people who put something at risk for me. There's precious few who ever have."

Tahn understood that Sutter was thinking about the man and woman who raised him as their son, and about his actual birth parents who had given him away before he was old enough to know them. In hindsight, Tahn thought maybe a lot of who his friend had become had to do with trying to reconcile himself with—or maybe leave behind—the decisions those people had made. He thought maybe his friend felt dispensible, and needed to get past that. And suddenly some of the jokes they'd shared all their lives echoed back a touch darker.

"Well," Tahn said, "my guess is you'll get to return the favor. So hold on to your good intentions."

Tahn tried to continue east, but Sutter held him back. "It's more than that. I don't know why the Sheason and Far came for you. I don't think you know, either. But whatever it is, I think it's a lot more important than we've given them credit for. I mean, they didn't come to the Hollows for a root-digger. You take my meaning?"

Tahn stared. He understood. Maybe Sutter was right. But he looked back with defiance. "I won't be caught on the wrong side of the choice to help a friend, Sutter. Not ever again. Anything the Sheason means for me to do will have to be in harmony with that. Or else he's got the wrong melura. Doesn't that seem right to you?"

Sutter thought, then slowly nodded. "It does. But then, this whole business is backward, Tahn. Seems like you could do what feels right, and be wrong. Just remember that."

Tahn nodded. "Or perhaps we are decoys in a larger, more complicated plan." The dark, cloaked figure spinning rain down upon a bull elk flashed in his mind. "But so you know, I'm not at all sure this is about me. For all we know, it *could* be about you." He jabbed a playful finger into Sutter's chest.

They laughed again, the moment behind them, and headed down the ravine, angling northeast.

They traveled the rest of the day, mostly walking. Near dusk, they descended a low ridge. The distant hum of a river rose into the forest, a soothing, familiar strain. The ravine descended to a river running south. They led their mounts to drink. An orange sun reflected its double in the glossy surface, river flies and other insects darting to and fro over the calm water. The ripples of fish surfacing to feed briefly interrupted the languid smoothness. Near the shore, the river tapered gradually, the water clear enough to see the sands in the shallows.

Tahn looked out over the river with relief; this, at least, was good fortune—rivers meant food and water, and always rejoined a road if you followed them far enough.

"See," he said. "Just stick with me." He swelled his chest with a lungful of air and inclined his chin toward the rising moon in a heroic pose.

Sutter caught him off guard while he was striking his pose, shoving him into the river before Tahn could catch his balance. The chill of the water bit at his skin, but not unpleasantly.

Tahn got his feet under him and turned on his friend. "Bad foot or none, Nails, you're going to gulp your share of river water in a moment."

"You should take the opportunity to bathe," Sutter said, laughing. "I'll cut you some peppermint leaves to perfume your delicate skin."

Tahn rushed him.

"Now, Woodchuck, you really ought to accept your wetness like a man." Sutter barked laughter, allowing Tahn to grab him around the waist and hold him up. "This won't help either," Sutter sputtered through laughing lips. "I'm not baring my shoulders for you."

Laughing, Tahn pulled Sutter back into deeper water, both of them submerging for a moment. Tahn let go, welcoming the soothing cold on his foot and slowly floating to the surface. He heard Sutter splashing toward him, no doubt preparing to take up their bout. Just as he was about to surface, a hand grasped the nape of his neck and thrust his head deeper under water.

As he went down again, he smiled at the impetuous, tireless antics of his friend. The same prank had been shared between them endlessly on the banks of the Huber. He waited a moment, determining whether to counter, or simply to wait for Sutter to let him up and continue the contest. The hand did not relent, but grew tighter, pinching savagely around the base of Tahn's skull and thrusting him deeper.

A dark certainty filled him. This hand did not belong to his friend.

• CHAPTER THIRTY-SIX •

Dust on the Boards

The day after the fire on the riverboat, Jastail and Wendra rode slowly north. Two hours after meridian, Jastail turned off the road toward the east. Flat land stretched into the distance, broken occasionally by undulating hills. Wendra noticed the roll of wagon tracks in the soil, though they trod no established road. Jastail took them into unmarked territory for yet another hour before they crested a knoll, where Wendra looked down upon a makeshift town with no real roads. A sudden feeling of despair stole over her as Jastail walked their mount slowly into Galadell.

Not a single man or woman failed to take note of them as they came. A few nodded to Jastail, but did not verbally greet him. He nodded in return, an air of authority in the angle of his head. Something bothered Wendra about the place. It felt impermanent, as though it could be abandoned at a moment's notice. She sensed no sort of commitment, or community, or tradition here.

Then it hit her.

The silence.

Merchants did not bark their wares, men did not argue prices, women did not wag their tongues at their husbands, and the few children she saw swept or carried or lifted in the performance of some chore. This accumulation of life did not have the vibrance of towns she'd recently visited: the rapid exchange of insults in jest, or tales of the road, or arguments about overpricing; the raucous play of children under the feet of their parents. None of it lived here. The town itself did not feel like a town so much as a huddling of disparate folks all engaged in some dark, illicit business.

Jastail led Wendra to a ramshackle establishment near the center of town. Beside the door hung a weathered sign nailed to the wall announcing the

OVERLAND BED AND CUP. Jastail looked both ways along the street before entering into the dimness beyond the door. Wendra shot a glance over her shoulder at the passersby, catching one of them in a long, appraising gaze; the man continued to unabashedly stare at her. Quickly, she followed Jastail inside.

The room stood weakly lit by a few sparsely placed candles inside glass lanterns, and by a bit of daylight that crept through cracks in the poor carpentry along the outer walls. The smell of stale bitter hung in the air, and that of boiled roots and a meat odor unfamiliar to Wendra. The tables sat empty save for two nearest the back where a set of wine barrels had been fastened to the wall. Drips fell at long intervals from spigots into cups placed on the floor to catch them. A man in a long leather apron sat beside the barrels with a short-brimmed hat drawn low on his brow. His chair stood tilted back against the wall and his chest rose and fell in the slow, steady rhythm of sleep.

Jastail moved soundlessly across the floor and made as though to take up one of the cups catching the spillage. With immediate swiftness, the chair legs came down and the man's hand latched onto Jastail's before he could lift the glass.

"You're slowing down with age, Himney," Jastail said.

The other laughed. "Of course I am," Himney replied. "But the land has yet to produce a thief swift enough to take bitter from me without me knowing and stopping him."

Jastail put the cup back under the drip, and pulled Himney to his feet. They clasped each other by the wrist and shook in two deliberate up and down motions.

"And I don't suppose there will ever be a thief who can cut your profits."

"Not till I go to my earth." Himney let go of Jastail's hand and nudged the cup the highwayman had attempted to take so that it could receive the drops in its exact center.

Jastail dug into his cloak and pulled out a coin, walking it along his knuckles with deft skill. The coin danced as though flipped, passing back and forth from one finger to the next. When he had apparently satisfied himself, Jastail tossed the coin up. Before it could finish rising, Himney snatched it out of the air. The little man licked the coin, running his tongue over its surface and along its edge, then rolling his eyes up as he concentrated and wagged his tongue just behind his teeth. Seemingly satisfied, he hid the coin so fast that Wendra wasn't sure where it went. He then picked up two fresh cups from a shelf between the wine barrels and filled them for Jastail and Wendra.

"Still the best nose in open land," Jastail said with bemusement.

"Can't run risks with the dreck that scuttles through these parts, my friend." He led them to a table away from the few patrons and put their cups on one side, positioning himself on the other with a clear view of his wine barrels.

Once seated, he eyed Wendra with a long, hard look, making her feel as though she were a coin held between the little man's sweaty lips. "You've been busy lately, friend. The open country is treating you well."

Jastail took a long drink from his glass. He wiped his mouth and leveled his gaze at Himney. "Must be my honest face."

The two chuckled over the jest.

When their chuckles had faded to smiles, Jastail said, "Tell me the most recent news. Things have not been"—he looked at Wendra—"easy. Tell me all you've heard, Himney, and leave the garnish for the next man. I've no patience for tales, and no money for lies or rumors."

The other man raised his hands before him and waved them to shush Jastail. "I understand. Earth and dust, but you do go on. Drink your bitter and let me do some talking." Himney leaned forward in his seat and rested his elbows on the table, one eyebrow cocked upward quizzically in preparation to speak. His tongue lashed out in a quick motion, licking the sweat from his lips. He then drew a breath, paused dramatically, and began in a cautious voice.

"Dust is up, dust is up," he said. "Men come into Galadell two and three a day, north out of Ringstone, south from Chol'Den'Fas, even from the east they come from as far as the coast of Kuren. But you," Himney said, pointing at Jastail, "you go to the west. What do you know that the others don't?" He pondered for a moment, then went on. "Some say that the order is aware. Others are not convinced. But less than a handful know what business they trade in, Jastail. Not like you."

"Know the seasons, do they? When we come to the lowland?" The highwayman waved a hand in a tight circular motion to indicate Galadell.

"We haven't seen any sign of a three-ring here. But rumors are loose on the tongues of my clients. Some say the dust belongs to the Quiet." Himney nodded dismissively. "Nothing new there. But most of the newcomers have no sense of what they do, only itchy palms for coin."

Wendra noted the way this man Himney looked when he used the word *dust*. Something about it unnerved her. It sounded somehow like something dark that she wasn't sure she wanted to learn.

"A different breed entirely," Jastail mocked, looking directly at Himney's waist belt, from which hung several leather purses.

"Men and women such as these, taking to the highways on the merits of rumor and the lucre of gold shining in their eyes. They're dangerous. They come in here to drink when the dust has settled, their stomachs tender to the trade."

"And what of that?" Jastail asked. "How does it go?"

"Little change, my friend, except . . ." Himney bent forward toward them and talked so low that many of his words were nothing more than the movement of lips. "There is talk that a full collough is down out of the Hand as far south as Reyal'Te." Himney swallowed. "And rumors that the Velle lead them." He stopped, thinking about what he had just said.

"There are those who have seen it with their own eyes?" Jastail asked.

"One," Himney said. "The others relate only what they have heard. But as for myself, I take the talk as truth. The skies are not as friendly as they were ten, nay five years since."

"Your barrels empty sooner with less copper in your purse," Jastail said without humor.

"No!" Himney barked, immediately quieting himself. "I mean that the night holds longer upon the land, and the cycles seem confused of their purpose, winter coming early, spring coming late, summer falling upon the earth like the heat of the smithy's forge. It feels like an ending in every turn."

"Dreadfully poetic for a bitter salesman in a leaky tavern nestled in the lows of Galadell," Jastail said, the mockery still dark.

"Fah. You ask for the recent news. This is it. We do our business in the spaces in between, you and I," Himney said, pointing a finger at Jastail. "But private though it is, most of us never go into the north, nor near the west. Never near the Hand. But now the Hand reaches south and east, escaping the detection of nations and kings as if it had some direct purpose. It's all changing, Jastail, a shift in the way of things, and I don't mean just for the cities and regents and nobles, who, you might like to know, have called for a running of the Lesher Roon."

A grim look tugged at the lines in Jastail's weathered face. Wendra could not place the look. Her captor's usual cynicism remained, but now it appeared broken, tentative. She thought about the Bar'dyn swimming toward the riverboat and their confrontation near the banks of the Lesule River. Perhaps Jastail understood more of the truth in the rumors than he let on. And he already thought that Wendra was keeping something back from him. Sooner or later he would force the issue: why Bar'dyn seemed to chase a girl with nothing of apparent value; why such a girl fled unprotected, and sought to rescue a boy.

Jastail turned his narrow eyes toward her, scrutinizing every pore of her face. Still looking at her, he asked, "Has the dust gone up today?"

"Not yet," Himney said. "You'll know when. The tables fill with men who take a cup before heading to the boards."

Wendra looked at Jastail and the serious tavern keeper, and finally had to ask. "What is the dust?"

Himney's gaze shot to her, and he retracted his head the way a turtle does when it feels threatened. Jastail's brows lowered, a simmering look roiling in his stare. Wendra met the look squarely. He may not honor it, but he owed her the debt of his life. No longer would she remain silent. Whatever his intentions concerning her, he had proven at the gambler's table how he viewed her. He continued to speak of Penit, drawing her farther along, tempering her instinct to flee. Abandoning that tactic would not serve him, whether Penit was alive or dead, so Wendra would not stay still anymore. Nor could she. Some new feeling inside her grew stronger each hour, insisting on release.

"Shut her up," Himney said emphatically. "She has no business uttering such foolishness."

"Calm yourself, Himney," Jastail replied, darting a threatening glance at the shopkeep. He returned his attention to Wendra. "Lady, this, too, is something that you'll understand when you meet the boy. I must ask you—"

"Ask me nothing!" Wendra cried, rising from her chair. "You will not treat me this way any longer! I played your game, highwayman, from the north face to the river, accompanying you so that I might help Penit. I sat in ridicule and blasphemy as a token for your gambling." She glowered with menace. "And I saved you from the Bar'dyn because I believed you knew where Penit was. Now take me to him! If he is in this place, then now! If not here, then let us go. But you haven't any idea what game of chance you play by holding me and putting my life at risk!"

Jastail regarded her passively. His perpetual look of apathy, so deeply rooted in him, did not change. But something else surfaced in his aspect, though Wendra could put no name to it. And as she noted it, something began to surface inside *her*. It began with her fury, but took a new form as she began to hear it in song inside her mind. Merely thinking of it made her skin tingle in expectation; it emboldened her. She stepped closer to Jastail in clear defiance.

The gambler stared back, unconcerned. "You may be right, lady," he began. "But haven't you learned that chance is all that matters to me? If what you say is more than a desperate threat, then I will have less inclination to be civil than before. And in either case"—he sat forward in his chair, so that his face was directly beneath Wendra's—"you could be dead long before any risk presents itself." He smiled calmly. The look of it was the most natural thing Wendra had ever seen on his rough face. "Hold your tongue and you'll have your answers soon enough."

Wendra's song stirred inside her, and she shuddered under its intensity. She grasped the table's edge to stop herself from collapsing and eased herself back into her chair. "Do you have a wet cloth?" she asked Himney.

Himney looked to Jastail, who nodded. The barkeep stood and scurried to the back of the room, where he found a table rag and dipped it in a bucket that sat against the far wall. Wringing the cloth out as he came, he extended it toward her. Though it smelled of a thousand wiped spills, Wendra took it graciously and leaned back, placing it over her face. Slowly, she blocked out the continuing conversation, focusing on the thrumming in her head, a pulse that

THE UNREMEMBERED • 281

emanated from every part of her and reminded her of the sound she'd heard when a musician's bow was drawn slowly across the strings of a bass fiddle. The low register sang in her flesh like a mournful requiem.

An hour later the tables filled, just as Himney had predicted. The tavern remained quiet, with low chatter or none at all as people took one cup, drank it quickly, and left the way they had come. When the tables emptied, Jastail stood and shook Wendra from her self-induced trance. She started at the intrusion, but got to her feet with the expectation of finding Penit. Jastail put a coin on the table and gave Himney a watchful stare. Then out he went, not looking to be sure Wendra followed.

Into the street they strode. Men and women were running past them toward a square where all the town seemed to be gathering. Wendra could feel an excitement in the air, nothing spoken, but nonetheless singing in her nerves as if everyone in town knew the same secret. The crowd did not jostle for position, but found places from which to see and then waited. She noticed that many of them held in their hands colored sticks, marked with numbers. An ominous feeling crept over her, like the darkest prophecy ever spoken by Ogea from the rooftop of Hambley's inn.

Jastail led her to a place near a raised wood platform. "The boards," he said, indicating the single most finely crafted structure in the ramshackle town. Long slats of oak lay fitted neatly together to form the raised platform six feet off the ground. On either side, stairs ascended to the platform, which stretched thirty feet long. A short table and chair stood near the left edge, a locked ledger and quill set upon it.

Moments later the crowd parted and several individuals came in a line toward the platform led by a tall man, thick in the waist and shoulders and well muscled. Wendra could not see who they were, but the procession stopped at the foot of the stair. The tall man bent to do something before escorting a bound woman to the desk. A second man, clasping a key fixed to a chain he wore around his neck, rushed up the stairs to the right and took a seat at the table. Quickly, he put the key to a lock that sealed the book, and opened it. Dipping the quill in a reservoir of ink, he inclined his ear as the big man said something softly to him. Then the big man ushered the bound woman to the center of the platform and turned her toward the crowd.

Looking on, Wendra now knew what "dust is up" meant. The woman's feet had been powdered with chalk, and with each step dust rose in a faint blue-white cloud.

The big man raised his hand and gestured with several fingers, whereupon Wendra watched as members of the crowd lifted their colored sticks with the painted numbers on them. No one spoke, allowing Wendra to hear the mild breeze occasionally whistle through cracks in the poorly built structures around them. The woman stared at her feet, her bedraggled hair hanging limp from her scalp and obscuring her features. She wore a shapeless smock to her knees, drawn in at her waist with a length of rope. The man pointed to one of the many sticks, then raised his hand again, performing a complicated series of hand gestures. More sticks went up, but not as many as the first time. Again the pattern was repeated, each time fewer sticks rising into the air, until but one stick rose above the crowd. The bullish man pulled the woman to the stairs at the right, where she met the woman who had purchased her.

The officious little man at the table wrote in his ledger, dipping his quill feverishly to record the transaction. Then the large fellow descended the stair, and again bent out of sight before rising and escorting a young girl to the boards. Information went into the book under the small man's quill, and powdered feet trod the boards to the center, where frightened eyes looked out on the bidders.

Wendra's gorge rose. *This is madness! People cannot be bought and sold!* But Jastail stood beside her, a living rebuttal to the notion that even Wendra was free. And something more lingered beyond her awareness, something awful, something that her mind shielded her from, would not let her see. Wendra desperately tried to recall a melody or lyric to give her comfort, but at the sight of the young girl her throat swelled shut. Jastail put a hand on Wendra's arm to steady her. She did not shrug it away.

Again the large man lifted his hand and declared some unknown price. All sticks went up. The man smiled, showing a mouthful of bad teeth. He'd grossly underestimated her value. This time his hand fingered a simple gesticulation. Half the sticks remained still this time. The cycle repeated, and the girl on the boards watched in dawning horror at the event unfolding around her. The rounds of bidding extended further this time, but still only the wind talked, ruffling the girl's downy hair and kissing her chalked feet with delicate plumes of dust over the neatly planed lengths of wood.

As the bidding wound down to two, one of the bidders waved his stick. At that, the auctioneer removed the young girl's dress so that her potential buyers could view her naked body.

Wendra fell against Jastail. The realization of this horror stole her strength, but also stirred a song deep inside her. The tingling began to crawl into every part of her, leaving the disorientation of a body at war with itself—weak but angry, unable to act but desperate to do something, to release the anger and bitterness mounting inside her.

More came to the boards, chalked feet, vacant eyes. Mostly women and girls, occasionally a frail man, but never the old.

And then a young boy was put upon the boards.

CHAPTER THIRTY-SEVEN

Wards of the Scar

The place was aptly named, Braethen thought. The Scar felt like a wound opened up to the sky. The earth rolled in dry stretches, desperately needing the nourishment of rain, but unable to make use of the moisture. The sodalist could see low spots where rainwater pooled, leaving behind alkali flats. Juts in the land showed coarse streaks of limestone; other spots had turned red from long exposure to the sun, their surface rough like the dry tongue of a mongrel dog. An unsteady breeze blew in fits and starts at long intervals. When it had passed, the Scar returned to the heaviness of the unforgiving sun.

That sun lay on their left near the horizon, its weak light casting violet shadows. It struck Braethen as the loneliest moment he could remember. Only the sage remained behind, clinging to life in the arid, eviscerated land.

"The Scar runs deep," Vendanj said, drawing Suensin to a stop.

"Will it ever be alive again?" Braethen asked.

"A question better for a seer," Vendanj answered. "But as long as the Quiet remains, I don't believe that it will ever flourish with life again."

The light of dusk lingered in the sky. Braethen started a fire and Mira joined them as they opened their food bags. She looked away at the darkness to the north. "A voice will carry far across this stretch."

She did not need to interpret the warning for Braethen. The sodalist nodded and continued at his bread.

"They could cast him into prison when we arrive at Recityv." Mira looked to the east.

Vendanj regarded Braethen with appraising eyes. "He'll be questioned. And the league will take undue interest in him if he arrives with us. But that can't be helped."

"You speak of this Grant. Who is he?" Braethen asked.

"Perhaps you ought to work with your blade some more," Mira suggested. "Before the light is gone."

"A fine delay, but I won't let this one sleep," Braethen warned with a smile, and went to practice with his sword.

But the answer would find him before he returned to the fire.

Braethen strode well away from their camp. In the twilight beyond the fire-light, the faintest white glimmer in the steel shone against the night. It might have been little more than starlight reflected in the blade. He touched the workmanship softly, running his finger up the fuller to the tip and testing the point gingerly with his finger.

Then slowly, he began to practice the strikes Mira had taught him, moving with careful deliberation to position his legs and center his balance. Braethen paused to wipe his brow, dropping his blade to his side. In that instant, he caught sight of a shadow streaking through the darkness. Before he could look up, some-one dealt him a crushing blow to the chest, and he fell gasping to his knees.

Immediately, a boot struck him in the face and he went over on his side, his sword peeling from his grip and landing on the dead soil a stride from his hand. Quickly, he rolled, expecting the jolt of another boot in his ribs. The sound of scut-tling feet rose in the air, and several more shadows darted in his blackened vision.

In a panic, he swept his arm out toward his sword. His hand slewed across it in the darkness, the blade cutting easily into the meat of his palm. He fought the immediate urge to pull his hand in as he looked over his shoulder and caught a glimpse of a human shape lunging forward. Again he rolled away, the stamp of boots loud just behind him. A wave of nausea swept through him, blood rushing to his head, his chest still tight from the first blow. He could not draw breath, could not call to Mira or Vendanj for help.

He scrambled on his hands and knees toward a line of the faintest white—his sword! Quick steps followed, but Braethen retrieved his weapon and twisted onto his back, lifting the blade toward the figure closing fast upon him.

The shadow stopped, a ready, catlike posture in the evening light. Braethen could not see its eyes. His chest heaved with the desire to pull air into his lungs, but his bosom yet felt constrained. He could not call for help. The figure drew a sword, and in that moment, Braethen slammed his blade down three times upon a nearby rock. The clank of steel on stone rose sharply in the still, dry air like a vespers call.

The figure before him raised its head toward new foes who were fast ap-proaching and stepped back lightly, shifting its blade toward the sound. Brae-then watched as three forms coalesced from the darkness to stand in a staggered line facing the approaching help—like shadows born out of the ground, spirits of Quiet put down in the Battle of the Scar ages ago.

Blood ran down Braethen's arm from the cut in his hand, making his grip slippery. Movement to his right: Mira and Vendanj running.

Braethen hunched low and turned to see Vendanj shooting red fire into the sky from his hands. Hellish light lit the faces of their attackers. There stood four striplings—not wraiths, not creatures out of the Bourne. None of these lads could have seen more than twenty Northsuns. Their eyes dilated in the sudden glare, awe and fascination clear upon their faces. Immediately they lowered their weapons.

"We thought you were Given, Sheason, forgive us," a voice said out of the night. "The use of steel here is always accompanied by darker intentions."

"Is Grant with you?" Vendanj said, coming close.

"No."

Braethen slowly dropped his sword as understanding came over him. Only a renderer of the order would use the Will here. Velle would have nothing from which to draw power; the ground had already been sapped of its Forda.

He rose from his knees as he recovered his breath. He'd come close to his own ground. But he thought they'd found their reason for coming into the Scar.

"How far?" Vendanj asked.

"Another day," the boy said. "I can take you there. It is not easy to find."

"I think I know the way," Vendanj answered. "But before you leave, sit near the fire and let us talk."

The four striplings cautiously walked past the Far.

Mira watched as the striplings sat down near the fire and began talking softly with Vendanj. "You don't have a lifetime to learn your art, sodalist. When your body is at rest, you must practice in your mind. There will not always be someone at hand to assist you. You should go to the fire and let Vendanj dress your wound."

He looked down at the sword in his hand and turned it over and back, catching dim glints from the far-off flame. Then he sheathed the weapon and walked wearily to the fire. Braethen shook his head and sat a few strides from the boys who'd just tried to kill him.

"I am Meche," the man who had struck Braethen said. "Please accept my apologies. Grant sends us to the borders for much of each lesser cycle. We set markers, watch for intruders, and learn the folds in the Scar. Shall we go ahead and announce you?" he asked. "If we do not, it is likely that others will respond to you as we did."

"I will not let that happen a second time," Vendanj said in an uninflected tone that Braethen nonetheless thought held some disgust.

Meche turned to Braethen. "Are you all right?" he said.

Braethen raised his sliced palm.

"A practicing swordsman in the Scar is not a man to be questioned, only taken down." Meche showed no hint of remorse.

But the logic eluded Braethen. "And why is that?" he asked, a more acerbic tinge to his voice than he'd intended.

Meche looked at the sodalist with level eyes. "Because only one type of man comes into the Scar. And he is one who would try to bolster his reputation by killing its warder."

"This Grant," Braethen surmised.

"Braethen," Vendanj said, trying to end the conversation.

"And we are his wards, sodalist. We watch here, live here much of the time, and when it's necessary we defend the only good thing in the Scar." Meche ran a hand through his hair.

"Which is Grant," Braethen said again, a bit incredulous this time.

Meche nodded. "And the primrose at his hand."

Vendanj noted Meche's words with dark concern.

But Braethen had had just too many mysteries. "Wonderful, a primrose. But how did this man become warder of the Scar, and why would he possibly stay in such a scorned place?"

Meche looked at Vendanj. "We'll see you soon." Then he stood and nodded to Vendanj before departing into the darkness southward with a subtle placement of two fingers beside his mouth in a cryptic salute. The others followed him, each in turn performing the same gesture.

"Get some rest, sodalist," Vendanj said, and closed his eyes as he leaned his head back to rest on the rock against which he sat.

Braethen watched as the Sheason began to pull deep breaths; Vendanj had fallen asleep with a swiftness he'd never seen. It left the sodalist alone with questions. Mostly, why were they seeking a man so reclusive that he lived at the center of the most tortured place outside the Bourne?

• CHAPTER THIRTY-EIGHT •

The Tracker

Tahn struggled to free himself, pushing his hands into the soft river bottom, trying to rise up. It was no use. Whatever had him was much too powerful. His lungs started to burn, and he thrashed from side to side, twisting his neck and bucking his feet. The water around his head clouded red, the fingers digging into his skin. Tahn thought fast. He collapsed his arms, hoping to surprise his attacker and win some advantage. His face quickly met the bottom, his nose filling with wet sand.

His chest spasmed, trying to force a breath. Tahn stifled the need, but knew he would soon suck water in and start to drown.

Around his face, the water clouded, obscuring his vision. He reached back desperately, hoping to clasp his assailant's arm and force a withdrawal, perhaps pull him into the water, as well. He could gain no purchase on anything. The water roiled. Murky light, filtered through the river, bent and shadowed in his eyes. As he twisted, his back struck the being's legs, and he began trying to kick the man off his feet.

The legs did not give, rooted like iron in the river bottom.

The urge to draw breath became too much, and Tahn heaved a huge rush of cold water through his nose and mouth. The feel of it down his throat came like a dagger, and he immediately began to cough. Panic swelled within him, and he thrashed more violently, trying not to breathe a second time.

Gathering his feet under him, Tahn pushed up with all his strength, and broke the surface. He gasped a breath, and saw a water-blurred image of Sutter rushing to his horse twenty strides away. He heard a sound—half snarl, half chortle—just before the creature gripping his neck thrust him back into the river to drown.

He clawed at the hand around his neck, beating relentlessly at the fingers and wrist. The being's grip held him fast. Tahn's lungs began to burn again, and in his eyes he could see red dots flashing. His resistance ebbed, his arms tiring, growing heavy.

Then vaguely, the sound of rapid, harsh splashes echoed under the water like dull thuds. They seemed to grow nearer, deeper, louder.

Just when he thought he must surely take more water into his spasming lungs, the hand pulled away from his neck as if forced, the fingernails tearing away thick strips of his skin.

Tahn shot to the surface, gulping air in a loud, hoarse rush. He retched and fell back down, coughing and choking, the feeling of water in his gullet still convincing him he would drown.

Casting his gaze around, Tahn saw a darkly clad figure regaining its balance, and Sutter thrown aside in the shallow water. He realized the splashes he'd heard were Sutter's running steps as his friend had thrown himself at Tahn's attacker and by sheer force ripped its hold away. The figure lashed at Sutter, who stumbled out of the way and fell back into the river. Wasting no time on Nails, the creature wheeled about, fixing its eyes on Tahn. Instantly, he recognized the tracker from their encounter north of Myrr. Its pale skin glistened with water beneath a drenched cloak that clung to its emaciated frame.

"Patience, child," the creature admonished. "I've no intention of killing you. Just breaking your spirit before taking you back."

Tahn scrambled backward through the water like a river crab, trying to regain his feet and reach his bow. He stole a look over his shoulder at the horses, which had retreated some distance away and milled nervously near the trees.

The tracker came on, its feet gliding through the water but never breaking the surface.

A snarling smile spread on its face as it fast closed the distance between them. The grin drew rough, unnatural lines in the tight, thin skin, which threatened to split over the tracker's sharp, angular features. It came on, hunched, bent as though stooped forever to the ground to track the passage of its quarry. Its fingers coursed across the river's surface, likewise making no mark.

Tahn tried to stand, but his wet cloak caught beneath his foot and tripped him back into the shallow water. He flipped over to meet the attacker face on. The tracker rushed him.

Tahn heard the keening of a blade drawn from its sheath; the fast arc of that blade pierced the dusk.

As Tahn watched, Sutter's greatsword lodged itself in the right shoulder of the tracker, causing a terrible grimace of anger and hatred before a great howl roared from its throat, echoing down the river like a loon's call. The Given swung around to deal with Sutter, giving Tahn time to gain his feet and sprint to Jole. Pain shot through his foot with each running stride, but he forced himself to ignore it and move faster.

Reaching his horse, he pulled his bow and wheeled about, nocking an arrow as he rounded.

His back rashed with chills to see the tracker almost upon him. Sutter knelt at the riverside, blood on his hands, staring helplessly toward Tahn. The Given rushed toward him, cold finality in every step. Tahn lifted quickly, the words racing through his mind: *I draw with the strength of my arms, but release as the Will allows.* Then one arrow, a second, and a third whistled from his string, biting the tracker in the chest one after the other.

A primal scream split the air, waves welling in the river, leaves quaking on their branches.

The tracker slowed, but still came on. Tahn backpedaled, fumbling for more arrows as he retreated. The sound of heavy footfalls came across the riverbank. Knowing eyes rolled in the tracker's head and it shuffled to meet Sutter's charge. Sutter skidded to a stop, using his momentum to swing his sword with reckless abandon. The sound of steel biting the air menaced even Tahn, but the tracker evaded the blow and shot one long arm at Sutter, taking his neck in its powerful grasp. He dropped his blade, using both hands to try and loosen the tracker's grip. His face reddened, and veins in his neck and forehead welled with blood. The Given lifted Sutter from the ground. A terrible stream of clucks and choked words fell from his lips.

Sutter's legs flailed, trying to kick the Given, but he only feebly hit the thin body within the wet folds of the dark cloak. His mouth gaped open, trying to draw air; Tahn feared the tracker would, at any moment, simply crush Sutter's neck. Blood welled onto his lips and began dripping from his nose.

At last, Tahn fingered some arrows. Already speaking his cant as he nocked them, Tahn let three more arrows fly into the tracker's humped back. The creature immediately reared, releasing Sutter, who fell to the ground clutching his throat.

The wizened visage turned on Tahn, bloodied lips rasping curses Tahn did not understand: *"Je'malta yed solet, Stille. Sine ti stondis roche."* It crumpled to the ground at Tahn's feet, one withered hand creeping forward toward his boot. Then it ceased to move altogether.

Giving the tracker a wide berth, Tahn rushed to Sutter's side. His friend sat huddled, wheezing, his hands working ineffectually at his throat. Lifting his wet cloak, Tahn wiped Sutter's face and helped him lie back on the ground.

"Slowly, breathe slowly," he instructed.

Sutter shook his head, gulping air. His neck was already purpling from the attack, dark blood suffusing the skin. Tahn began taking exaggerated breaths in a slow, steady rhythm to help Sutter regulate himself. After several moments, they both calmed, lying wet and bloodied in the shade of a river tree just strides from the dead tracker.

When the pounding of their hearts subsided beneath the sound of the river, Tahn looked at his friend, whose eyes seemed lost in the nearness of his own death. "Would it be too much to ask you to find that balsam root now? I'm kind of sore."

Sutter rolled his head over to look at his friend. "Foot still bothering you, is it?" Neither laughed. "That creature wasn't interested in me, Tahn."

"Not until you picked up that sword of yours." Tahn spoke in a grateful tone.

Sutter shook his head. "Even after I knocked it off you, it just turned back." His eyes darkened momentarily. "What does the Bourne want with you?"

Patience, child, I've no intention of killing you. Just breaking your spirit before taking you back.

Suddenly, Tahn realized what peril his friends had placed themselves in, but he still had no answer for Sutter's question. They were all Sheason secrets. But the tracker's words took root in his heart like a weed nourished on doubt and fear and nightmare.

"I don't know," he finally answered. "Maybe we'll find out at Recityv."

Sutter studied Tahn's face for several moments, his eyes moving over every feature as if he'd never seen Tahn before. Then he propped himself up, grimacing with the effort. "We'd better get moving. Where there's one, there may be more. I can't promise to save you more than once a day."

While his friend looked for more balsam, Tahn filled the waterskins and gathered the horses. Sutter quickly mashed his harvested roots into a paste, which he and Tahn spread liberally over their abrasions and cuts, wrapping them with strips of cloth. They grinned at the similarity they bore to each other with their necks thickly swaddled. Sutter applied poultices to cuts across both of his forearms. Tahn took some of the paste under his tongue, sucking the bittersweet juice to ease the throbbing in his foot.

Before setting out, they dragged the tracker to the river and cast it facedown in the shallows. Tahn fell to his knees beside the body, the panicked feeling of not being able to breathe still aching in his chest. He dropped his bow and looked toward Sutter, who stood over the Given, a grimace twisting his lips.

In sudden anger, Sutter raised his sword and brought it down on the lifeless form with a mindless scream. Bloodied water erupted from the blow as the body bobbed from the attack, sending ripples outward. Then Sutter fell to his knees as well. Water splashed up on his pale face; a mixture of shock and fear tensed his features.

"It's dead," he proclaimed in a loud voice. "It's dead." The second time he whispered.

Sutter was in shock. Tahn didn't think there was a root his friend could dig for that. This whole business was mad.

Then Sutter pushed the shape from the shallows into the deeper water, where the current began to pull it downriver. Tahn watched as the tracker floated away into the scarlet-tinged water of sunset. Soon, the lump might have been nothing more than a fallen log pulled from the shore during a heavy rain. After another moment, the body was gone, swept south and away.

"I didn't hear it coming," Tahn said.

Sutter continued to watch the river where the figure had disappeared. He shook his head. "It didn't make a sound. Even in the river its steps were silent." His hands and arms shook, trembling from cold and fright and weariness, the blade in his hands dangling in the water. "We were lucky. I've never come so close to my earth."

Tahn followed his gaze. "Part lucky, part brave."

Sutter shook his head again. "Instinct. Survival."

"That, too," Tahn admitted. "But we got the best of it the way we always beat Maxon Drell or Fig Sholeer: One fighter can't concentrate on two men."

"Yeah, but you were under a long time. I thought you drowned for sure."

"Me?" Tahn said with mock confidence. "I was just letting you test that sword of yours."

Sutter turned back to Tahn, and the two shared nervous laughter in the waning light of day.

When quiet returned, Sutter looked Tahn in the eye. "You know what I thought about?"

Tahn didn't understand the question.

"When I thought it might kill us. When I thought this was truly the end." A pained look drew Sutter's eyes and mouth taut. "I thought of that root farm. I thought of Father and Mother, and that they must think they failed somehow in making me feel loved. And when I thought it, part of me wanted to kill that thing so I could go back and tell them the truth." He stopped, swallowing back emotion. "But part of me wondered if dying today . . ."

Tahn looked out at the river, letting the admission pass without comment or judgment.

But his friend had struck a chord. "You know what *I* thought about?"

Sutter wiped moist eyes and shook his head.

"I thought about my parents' funerals. The sound of the earth covering them over one shovel at a time. I also thought of Wendra, and how I wasn't there to protect her when she was raped." Tahn shook his head in gentle self-reproof. "But then I saw her happiness at the coming of her child. She's all the family I have left, and it was good to hear her sing again." Emotion thickened in his own throat. "Then I thought about the loss of her baby."

And Tahn finally shared a secret of his own, the very old compulsion to utter those words before he could release a single arrow. He shared how it had kept him from his own sister's defense in her time of greatest need. And when he was done, he hung his head and wept. Because now she was lost to him in a world preyed upon by Quiet, and she was too far away, Skies knew where, for him to make it right. His own fears and needs had taken him away from her when she needed him most, again.

Tahn looked up at his friend, who sat wet and bleeding beside him, a gift sword laid across his knees, less than a day removed from Bourne poison in his blood, and caring for little more than the feelings of two people who had taught him to farm the dirt.

And that *little more*, other than the bluster of his adventuresome spirit, was Tahn.

Maybe they each had a bit more family than they'd counted.

It was not a secret, but it didn't need to be said, either.

Under a crimson and violet sky, they led their horses north, taking a course just inside the river tree line, each carrying his weapon in hand. A few hours later, they returned to the river and found a shallow cave in the high bank from which the water had receded. They made camp there, eating a cold meal to avoid the smell of fire on the wind, too weary even to jest. Alternating their watch, they finally slept.

Images from his flight from the mist spun in his dreams like bits of flotsam in a river eddy. Under it all was the vague dream of scorched earth feeling both bruised by an endless, savage sun and touched by the unwholesome taint of the

Bourne. And a faceless man teaching him how to aim . . . When Tahn awoke from his troubled slumber, the stars still held their places in the heavens.

Despite his exhaustion, Tahn remained awake and stared into the firmament in the moments before the land began to awake from its hibernation.

A dull ache reminded him of his foot and the friend who had gone to sleep just a few strides away. They might have been on a hunting trip, going as far east as the Ruleigh Hills or even the Aela River, ignoring the admonitions of Balatin and Filmoere. They might have spoken of the girls who had recently made the Change, even of Wendra, and laughed about their inability to grow full beards. Tahn might chastise Sutter endlessly about his dirty fingernails, knowing how he longed to do something he deemed important. And Sutter would surely have chided him about being a loner, spending all his time in the trees, and smelling a bit too much like the game he hunted. They would have spent hours in the ponds near Gehard's Ridge, each trying to hold the other underwater. When night came, the smell of duck roasting over a fire of mesquite or cedar would have soothed their tired bodies and enlivened their senses. And just before sleep claimed them, they would have spoken honestly of their fears and hopes, and the future would have followed them into their dreams beneath the calls of loons upon the ponds and bright stars winking through the boughs.

Tahn's foot twinged, reminding him that on this night, he and Sutter were far from the ponds and the Hollows. And the future was upon them, carrying them forward. Quietgiven had come south into the land and nipped at their heels. The tales of the reader, the books of the sodalist, were no longer entertaining stories. Sheason and Far and Sedagin were real, as real as the League, as real as the Bar'dyn. *Never mind all that! Concentrate on this moment! On what comes next.* The self-reproach somehow brought the old forgotten scent of parched wood to him.

Tahn pushed away his reverie and propped himself up on his elbows. He looked east and wondered if the greater light would ever cease its cycle, and why each day he felt compelled to pause and consider the dawn. Maybe it was more than mere solace. Strangely, it occurred to him that the pure and singular moment of sunrise was his truest friend. No guile, no pretense, new life, new light, and all the possibilities that came when first the sun met the sky.

The smell of ozone came to him as dew rose from the ground. The comforting reassurance of the fragrance eased into him, and Tahn closed his eyes to envision the dawn. The moment stretched out as he watched in his mind's eye the path of the greater light. Suddenly, the image flooded with red. The sun shone a bloody hue, and the mountains, clouds, treetops, everything in his mind turned scarlet. Then the world ignited, the air burning and the rocks melting into rivers of blood. The sun shimmered crimson and sable, flickering like a man blinking blood from his eyes. Tahn began to choke, the horror in his mind making it hard to breathe. He could not open his eyes, could not free himself from the images in his head.

Strangled pleas gurgled from his throat, as he thought that he might die here, now. And with the thought of his own mortality came the desperate desire to see Wendra. She was now his only family, and the pit of his stomach seemed to fall with the troubling thought that he would never see her again. Then hands were on his shoulders, shaking him. Words cascaded down to him as though spoken from very far away.

"Tahn, wake up!"

But he was awake. He tried to say so, only his swollen tongue would not obey.

Hands slapped his face, but the vision held. His heart thumped in his ears and behind his eyes, the rhythm slowing, growing louder, like the single, great beat they'd heard in the mist. Then stillness. The scarlet sun faded, and Tahn could no longer summon the name of his sister.

"Will and Sky!" he screamed. But the sound of it echoed small and only in his head.

A hand struck his back, batting him. Soon after, water splashed his face. But the sensations were distant and soft the way a bird's wing sounds across a lake, or the cry of a loon comes muffled by the cloak of night. Like sounds over the ponds at Gehard's Ridge . . . and Tahn remembered with a rush of regret and stark understanding that he and Sutter were alone, fleeing the Bar'dyn. That he'd stepped into the spine-root. He began to feel very heavy, as though the energy to move or think escaped him.

"No!" he howled.

"Tahn! Breathe!" he heard, and thought he knew the voice, but could not place it.

He gasped a breath as if he was that loon on a Gehard pond, surfacing from a long dive, and a painful rush of air seared his lungs. He panted as a jumble of fiery colors streaked through his mind. In their wake a solitary disk of light hung in a blue sky. He opened his eyes and stared into Sutter's worried face.

"What happened? Are you all right?"

Tahn stared at his friend without answering. When his breathing returned to normal, he again felt the throbbing in his foot.

"That must have been some dream you were having," Sutter said. "I hope there was a girl in it, at least."

Tahn looked over his friend's shoulder at the break of dawn on the horizon. He hoped there were answers in Recityv. He hoped they *reached* Recityv. He hadn't yet passed from melura to adulthood, and he had never felt further from it.

They started north again in the early light of day. Mist rose from the river, edging into the trees around them. The damp chilled them both and slowed their progress. Everywhere he looked, Tahn encountered moss growing from rocks and bark, in places hanging like drapes from branches and smothering the brush at his feet. Gradually, the sun burned the mist from the air. Tahn and Sutter kept a companionable silence, the memory of their recent assault making them both cautious.

They followed the river north for two days, finding a few abandoned homes built along the shallow coves in the bank, but otherwise not encountering even a hint of man until the afternoon of the third day, when something curious fell from the sky and settled on Tahn's cheek. He wiped at it, and drew back a finger smeared with ash. Thinking nothing of it, they rode onward. But soon flakes of black and grey were falling with some regularity.

Sutter held out a hand to catch a wafting speck. When it fell into his palm, he proffered his hand to Tahn in question. It could mean only one thing: forest fire.

"Perhaps we're near Recityv," Sutter offered.

"I doubt it," Tahn answered.

Sutter nodded. "Then let's stay near the river. My neck is too sore to fight today." He smiled weakly.

Ignoring him, Tahn cautiously maneuvered Jole in the direction of the smell.

"Of course," Sutter said with a shrug, falling in behind him.

Soon the smell of fire filled the air, but what burned was something more than wood, more even than the premature burning of trees still green with life. The forest itself felt pregnant with the terrible consequence of things forever destroyed, the way a few years earlier the last of the singing trees had been harvested from their grove in the Hollows, leaving the land there naked and silent. Tahn remembered the auction conducted beside the sighting stones to fetch a high price for the famed wood—money to pay a debtor whose name no one in the Hollows seemed to know. Tahn had visited the grove later, as a woodsman, and sat upon the dusty ground where bare roots no longer fed a sheaf of leaves above. The specter of the last felled singing tree clung there like a revenant. In this distant wood, thick with the smell of burnt ash, the same feeling hung thick and smothering as a death pall.

Judging the direction, Tahn turned west from the river, and climbed the wooded hill that rose from the river valley. Ascending higher, the ground grew increasingly carpeted with soot and ash, the rain of spent embers coming like a strange, quiet storm. Tahn checked his fletching, and urged his mount upward through a tight bank of spruce.

Immediately on the other side, blackened trees stripped of foliage spired like bony fingers. Some still smoldered, smoke lifting lazily to the sky. The ground was charred with intricate patterns of burnt needles like tight embroidery. But the number of burnt trees did not explain the fall of ash that piled now at their feet, the flakes continuing to descend softly around them.

Tahn dismounted and tethered Jole to a nearby tree. Sutter slid to the ground and came in step, holding his sword with both hands. Pulling his bow to half draw, Tahn crept forward. As he skulked around the scorched remains, his skin began to tingle. The very air felt charged. Scarcely thirty strides from the first burnt tree, they emerged into a small semicircular clearing. Sutter's eyes widened as Tahn whispered denial.

Ahead, the face of a short granite cliff hung in graceful, molten waves, as though a banner sagging where it had lost its mooring. Steam issued from pockets of the liquefied rock, sending tendrils of smoke up against the blackened face of the escarpment.

"Earth and dust," Sutter muttered. "What makes rock run like honey from a hive?"

Unconsciously relaxing his draw, Tahn quickly surveyed the ground, searching for something specific. To their right, a circle of earth glinted dully in the light filtered through the ash-laden sky. Tahn's heart fluttered in his chest. He took four long strides and bent to brush ash from the glazen surface. At the center of the black glass ring, two holes burrowed into the earth, holes the size of a man's hand. Surveying the rest of the clearing, Tahn noticed several more dark rings, some larger than others, some at the center of depressions in the level clearing around them.

Brushing ash from his hands, Tahn stood, again pulling his bow to half draw, and continued forward. Dark ripples in the cliff hung like stone curtains, and appeared to seal a doorway into the granite where an obvious footpath ended at a puddle of cooling rock.

"That'll do." The strange voice rang out over the clearing and startled Tahn, causing him to fumble his arrow from its rest.

• CHAPTER THIRTY-NINE •

Heresy

Alone candle lit the home of the weathered man. He sat at his table in its glow, the silence and emptiness of his home wrapping about him. His hands still bore the dirt of his ward's grave—the lad buried in the soil of the barren land, adding yet another layer of remove from the world beyond.

In his dirty hands he held a charm the boy had always carried with him, the remnant of the child he had been—a token left to him by a mother he had never known. The lad had never worn it, but still had never been without it. Maybe it harkened to some hope he had of reunion, or perhaps was a reminder of the neglect that had brought him to the weathered man to begin with.

Whatever the reason, the boy had never shared it, nor had the man asked.

But now he turned it over and over in fingers soiled with the boy's final earth, and thought about choices and death. He thought about his many wards. And he thought about the land of his soul, as barren now, he imagined, as the soil beyond his door.

He held little use for the family of man. Little hope. The few who bore their burdens well and strove to raise up a child in this age of rumor earned his esteem. But they would surely be beaten under when the tide of bad choices came back upon them all.

He'd known it when they sent him here.

He knew it better now.

He couldn't stand against it without thinking boldly, even if what he considered was only an exercise to ease his battered mind and spirit.

The man looked about, taking in the modest appointments of his isolated home. It held no touch of warmth. He only *existed* here, forever on the edge of either abandoning the honor of his sentence or of death. The walls kept out the sun, and there were some few beds for his other wards. Besides this, and the basic necessities, it was shelter, nothing more.

It seemed barrenness had gotten into everything in and around him. And maybe there was a blessing even there. Perhaps it dulled the reality he sensed had consumed the lands of men; and if dulled to *him*, how awful might the reality be?

And yet, however hard and pitiless he now was, he nevertheless felt a seed of hope. Perhaps his purchase of some parchment had been a small act to cultivate that seed. He guarded against undue optimism; blessings and surprises came when expectations remained low. Still, a seed of hope . . .

His weathered face turned up in a bitter smile as he considered that his cultivation of hope would be named by others as an act of heresy. The world had been stood on its head. He saw that more clearly, he decided, because of the dire circumstances his life had come to. And it might take such to set down what he dared now to write.

The patter of small feet interrupted his thoughts. He looked up to see his youngest ward standing at the mouth of the hall, staring at him. She was just four years old. She'd been born with a disfigurement of the lips, so that she could never quite smile, or quite close her mouth. Always you could see some of her upper teeth, crooked as they were.

He had not been able to find a home for this child.

Nor, as he thought about it now, would it have been wise to do so. The life she'd have known in the company of cruel children and adults who traded darkly on such disfigurements would have been drear; he thought of tenendra camps where oddities were caged, and he thought of panderers with base clientele.

How unfortunate. For the sunny spirit of the girl often proved the only cheer the man knew in a day. In the absence of the looks and cruel jokes and misunderstanding here in his isolated home, she had all the confidence she deserved. He waved her over, and she ran and leapt into his lap, hugging him close.

"Where did you go this time?" she asked, always eager to hear stories of any kind.

"Just supplies, dear one." He would not tell her yet of the death of the boy she considered a brother.

She smiled, a smile he knew would be reviled in the cities of men, or laughed at and mocked. Yet to him there existed no sweeter expression, none he would rather receive as payment for any joke or laugh or play. He smiled back.

"Did you get any molasses sticks?" Her voice slurred around the words of the confection, her lips unable to make the sound. She looked up expectantly.

He took two from his breast pocket and handed her one. "Make it last," he said.

She nodded. "Did you meet any interesting people?" In addition to the stories, the girl always wished to know of others, as in all her life she had only ever known the other wards—she longed to travel and meet new people.

The man returned her nod. "Some interesting people indeed. But not, I think, anyone you'd have cared to meet. You're much nicer than they."

"You always say that," she replied. "Maybe sometime someone will come to visit us, and then we'll know who is the nicest."

The man smiled. "Yes, maybe."

The girl looked at the tabletop. "What are you doing?"

Finally, he set aside the charm and put his own molasses stick in his lips. "I've got some things to write down," he said, and ran his hands over the parchment laid flat on the table before him.

In the sallow light of his single candle, the parchment looked brown, like his skin. He was no author, reader, or scrivener. His profession and skill came first of the body. But he had a keen appreciation of ethics, his rigor in their observance among his most prized qualities. And to be honest, he lived by wit as much as skill. He knew how to write this. Whether it would come to anything, he knew not. But, he did know the act alone would comfort him.

And just now, that more than anything was all he hoped for.

"Can I help?" the girl asked. "I know all my letters."

The weathered man looked into the girl's eyes and wondered if it wouldn't be most appropriate, after all, to have a babe help him write such a thing as he was set to write. After all, it was for her and all those like her that he meant to do it.

"I will write, and you will ensure I make the letters well."

She put her molasses stick in her mouth and leaned forward to begin.

He took up his pen and dipped it into a phial of black ink. He paused a moment and looked into his candle. He wondered if, once he had finished writing the parchment, he could find a way to give it power and purpose.

He knew but one way. And access to that means remained a myth and mystery to most. Going into the deeps where it lay guarded by vows given in a time before memory was a fool's errand.

But pausing with his ready pen, a dried-up creature in a dried-up place watching after the world's orphans, an outcast with the audacity to even consider writing what he now planned, he thought himself the perfect fool. For only fools went where courage and reason would not. And that, he admitted to himself, was where he would need to go if tonight's scribblings were more than simply his need to purge his anger and frustration and sadness.

With one rough hand, the sun-worn man stroked the honey-colored hair of his youngest ward. With the other, he put ink to parchment and began to write.

He penned deep into the night, thinking of a better world for the wards that came into his care, a better world for this girl with her beautiful, ruined smile. On and on the weathered man wrote, pouring out the quiet thunder of his heart.

• CHAPTER FORTY •

Reunion

The lad came alongside the muscled auctioneer, his head straight, his feet heavily chalked. He strode the boards, his feet producing large dust clouds with each step. He took his place at center stage as though he was accustomed to the bidding, the judgment, accustomed to treading the boards. This time the man's hand did not even fully rise to indicate a price before sticks flew high against the late afternoon sun. Many simply did not lower their sticks.

Wendra looked on through hazy eyes, sweat stinging them and blurring her vision. Penit stood bravely for several moments before she recognized him.

When she realized the prize at auction, a flood of strength ripped through her. This was what she had not allowed herself to consider, to know. The auctioneer's hand gestured convulsively, acknowledging the raised bids, his eyes wide with the number of sticks unyielding in their determination to purchase the young boy they did not know. All bidding, all wanting, all but Jastail. He had not yet bid on a single person. But Wendra cared nothing for that, or for the highwayman. The song leapt in her beyond any pain or anger she had known, the feeling alive and anxious to be birthed into the air. Dark, disturbing snatches of melody occurred to her spontaneously, haunting and fierce, seeking a voice to give them violent life in the auction yard, *on* the auction yard.

Wendra struggled with the painful emotions, lurching from Jastail's grasp, her eyes fixed on Penit—the child who went to bring her help, now tied and priced and subject to this humiliating doom. The thought of it overcame her, and Wendra turned to the sky and howled with a fury she had never known. Her aimless wail rose in strident, ululating tones, shattering the silence and knocking her to the ground as soon as it had begun. Her scream ascended harmlessly, echoing above the larcenous crowd.

Jastail helped her to her feet. His eyes carried a hint of fear, but not, Wendra thought, for his life. But she was too angry to worry about him. The blinding white rage began to build again within her. She looked at Penit, who stared at her from the boards, a grateful smile on his lips. He raised his bound wrists to wave to her, and was roughly cuffed by the auctioneer.

"Be still, lady," Jastail said. "You've no need of any of this. I intend to purchase the boy."

Wendra looked with a strange mix of revulsion and gratitude at the highwayman, who slowly lifted his stick and did not drop it again until only his remained high against the pitiless sky.

Wendra awoke before she opened her eyes. She lay quiet, aware that she did not occupy her own bed. She always washed the linen and bedclothes with soap cured in spruce buckets, and she always beat the dust from them with spruce switches. She liked morning to arrive with the clean scent of spruce. The heavy blankets on her now smelled of rough wool and men.

The back of her throat throbbed, as though a bruise were forming there. But Wendra refused to discover where she was just yet and continued to regulate her breath in the slow cycles of sleep. A slight movement made her conscious of another hand in her own, and reality crashed in upon her in happy, bitter waves.

She opened her eyes and saw Penit at her bedside. The boy slept in a chair with his head against the bedpost, his small hand curled around her fingers. He appeared peaceful, wearing a vague smile on his dirty cheeks. Wendra squeezed his hand; hot tears ran from the corners of her eyes. Soon, Penit awoke, and the smile grew on his lips.

"You're all right," he said with bright enthusiasm.

"And you," Wendra said. "I thought I'd lost you forever. What happened?"

Penit's smile faded as quickly as it came. "I followed the river once I came to it," he said, avoiding her eyes. "Sooner or later, you always come to people if you follow the water. I made good time, too. No dawdling, no sidetracks. Kept to my script, you know. I kept thinking of you alone in that cave with the fever. No one ever depended on me that way," he said, trailing off.

Wendra put her other hand on top of Penit's, pressing it between her own. "You did all you could," she said softly. "Do not be ashamed. Tell me what brought you here."

The door to the small room opened and Jastail walked in. "You're awake, good. You look weak, but we must leave. Be about it." He went to a dresser opposite her and pulled it back from the wall. He pried the back panel off and began loading a satchel with items hidden within. He smiled at her with one side of his mouth, and went back to his work.

Penit stood from his chair and squared his shoulders toward Jastail. He kept Wendra's hand, but raised his chin. "You must let us go."

Jastail did not look up. "Boy, for the trouble this is turning out to be, I'd almost agree with you. I admire your asking it. Now, see that you help the lady, and save your comments on me until we're clear of this place. I don't want to have to gag you."

Penit fumed, shaking with pent-up anger. Wendra raised herself on one elbow. "What now, Jastail?" she asked. "You bought Penit's freedom. It's time for us to part company."

Jastail looked up. "You can't buy what you already own." He cinched the satchel shut. "You are an insightful woman, but your ill-founded belief in people cripples your judgment."

A hint of regret edged his words, but Wendra could not tell if it was for her or for hopeful people in general. He rose and shouldered the parcel. "Don't dawdle. Get to your feet and come to the rear door. Mind my warning; you are not among friends here. There's not a soul in this place that cares more for you than the price you'll fetch. And they'd have use of you before the chalk is put to your feet.

"I must buy a horse. I'll be at the door in a meal's time. There's bread and root for you at the table, and clean water. Eat and be ready."

He closed the door and left them alone again.

"He is the one that brought me here," Penit said. "I'd followed the river half a day when he rode upon me with four others. I tried to explain about you, I told him you were sick and needed help. He asked me for directions. I told him I would lead him to you. But he said I looked ill, and that he would send me with his friends to a safe place, and bring you back himself. He would not listen to me. So I finally gave him directions to the cave." Again Penit trailed off. "And now he has us both."

"What do you mean?" Wendra asked. She sat up to the edge of the bed and pulled Penit around to face her.

"You saw it," Penit said. "He intended to sell me. All of us were being sold. That's what he meant when he said he couldn't buy what he owned."

"He does not own you," Wendra protested. "Or me. We will leave here together, right now."

Penit backed away, shaking his head. "No, Wendra. I do not like him, but the others know we are not traders. That's what the others call them. They will capture us as soon as we are alone among them. The others . . . they do horrible things . . . and it would have been worse if it weren't for Dwayne."

"Who's Dwayne?"

"I met him when they put me in the pen; that's where they keep everyone that will go to the boards with chalk on their feet. They put me and him together and made us fetch things, running all the time. Dwayne helped the younger ones."

Wendra took a short breath. She didn't want to think about how young the children he spoke of might be.

"He also helped the older people, kind of showing them how to deal with the traders in order to get better food, or at least more food. He made it all kind of a game. And it kept me from getting too scared."

Wendra drew Penit close and hugged him to her breast. "I am glad to hear it. If we could, we'd take him with us. As it is, we'll let Jastail take us away from here. But I won't let him sell either of us." She swallowed against the fear and rage that threatened to overwhelm her. "We will purchase our freedom from him one way or another."

With Penit's help, Wendra stood up. Before they went out into the outer room to sit and eat, she shared with Penit the false name—Lani—she'd been using. The boy nodded and winked as they went out. At the table, Penit scarcely chewed his food, devouring mouthfuls and washing it back with long gulps of water. Wendra sliced a root with a knife beside the bread. As she ate she considered how to escape. She rose, leaving Penit to finish his meal. She then hid the knife inside her boot, and searched the other rooms of the small ramshackle house. She found nothing of any use. The austere utility of the shack suggested it was always used for the same purpose: housing people he intended to sell.

She went back into the bedroom and quickly rummaged through the dresser, finding a few items of clothing, laundered and folded, though threadbare for all that. She pulled the dresser from the wall and used the knife to pry back the panel she'd seen Jastail get behind.

A hollowed compartment sat empty save for a small piece of parchment bearing a handwritten note:

> *Meet me at the wayhouse two days from the final auction. Bring every man you can trust for five handcoins. We'll set the balance right, and you may have yourself a route of your own for the trouble. Watch that you're not followed. And should you feel ambitious, know I've taken precautions against your greed.*

Wendra tucked the note inside her bodice, and checked to be sure she hadn't missed anything. Satisfied, she replaced the panel and rejoined Penit at the table. She didn't know the nature of the meeting, but if it involved her, then preventing the arrival of the number of "men available for five handcoins" improved her odds.

Something Jastail will surely understand. She smiled.

She took up a crust of bread and was eating it when she heard the sound of steps approaching the outer door.

Jastail entered; he surveyed the room in a quick sweep. "You may have been tempted to steal the knife," he said dryly. "Perfectly understandable. I'll give you the opportunity of putting it back."

Wendra considered playing coy, but decided not to test the rogue. If she were to use the weapon at all, it needed to be once they were well outside town. She produced the knife from her boot and laid it next to the bread crumbs on the table.

"Good," Jastail said. "Quickly, and hold your tongues."

Penit went grudgingly and Wendra followed.

They got onto their mounts, and Jastail led them casually down a vacant alley toward the east, never turning onto the main street. The sun lay low in the west, sending their shadows in long, dancing rhythms on the ground before them. Penit fought to ride alongside Wendra even through the narrowest lanes. His face shone with the conflicting emotions of hatred when he looked toward Jastail and relief when he saw Wendra.

Would we make it if we made a break for it now?

She dismissed the thought. They might be able to break away, but it would have to be once they reached the open road, and even then it would need to be planned. If Jastail caught the boy, Wendra could not leave him again.

They passed a cluster of tents and rode into a field dotted with cook fires.

Shallow rain ditches had been dug to catch the rainwater as it rolled from oiled canvases stretched over wooden frames. The smells of roasting grouse and prairie hens rose on the dusk air. Wendra's stomach growled at the savory smell.

"What is this then?"

As a group of men stepped into their path, Jastail called them to a halt.

"I've business elsewhere," Jastail said, looking past the men at the open land along the horizon.

"So pressing that you would leave at suppertime," the man retorted. "And taking your stock with you." The others laughed, their eyes passing from Wendra to Penit and back. "How far the great trader Jastail has fallen that he buys his own wares. Damaged goods, my friend." The man shifted his head to the side to affect a sidelong glance of reproof.

"Business elsewhere," Jastail repeated.

"Is that so?" the leader of the group replied. "Well, perhaps. But I don't like what this means to those of us you leave behind." The man raised his hand to his mouth and bit at a fingernail before continuing. "What information do you have that causes you to forfeit the price of a boy on the block? It isn't like you." His eyes narrowed. "And it isn't fair to those prepared to pay good money for him, either. And what of this one?" He walked past Jastail and laid his hand on Wendra's thigh. She kicked him in the chest, and would have put her boot in his face if the stirrup had not inhibited her blow. The man stumbled backward.

When he regained his balance, he rushed toward her, one arm brandishing a deeply curved knife. Orange sun glinted on the beveled edge as Wendra tried to shy away from the charge. Instantly, Jastail was off his horse and between them. He ducked beneath the man's arm and drove a leg into his ankles. The other went over on his face. His jaw slammed into the hard-packed earth. The report rose in the mellow evening like the striking of river stones together.

Wendra had seen men cower when their leader was put down, but these men rushed in on Jastail the instant he swept the first man off his feet. Two smaller fellows tried to flank him as the largest among them came directly on, a moronic grin showing but five existing teeth. Two more drew short blades and skirted the edge of the fray like dancers anxious for a turn with a courtesan.

Jastail lunged for the largest man, feigning an exaggerated roundhouse toward the man's face, and drove his knee into the fellow's groin. The lout doubled over with an airy *whoosh*. One blade swept near Jastail's face, but before the man could recover to strike again, Jastail drew his own sword and struck a deft jab to the man's sword arm. The wounded brute dropped his weapon and turned tail.

The other swordsman rushed at Jastail's back. Wendra saw the blindside attack and bit her lip against warning Jastail. The instant seemed very long, but finally she yelled his name. Her captor did not look back. He fell into a forward roll and narrowly missed a jab at his spine. He came up and whipped his sword around in a deadly, level arc, catching the man in the neck as his momentum carried him toward Jastail.

The fight had drawn the attention of nearby traders. Troubled shouts rose, and the faint clink of blades and armor accompanied bellowed questions sounding from the tents. Wendra realized she needed Jastail to win. Whatever the highwayman had planned for her and Penit, he was their only chance of escaping Galadell. If they were captured, these ruffians would show no mercy toward her or Penit.

Wendra turned her mount on one of the men trying to flank Jastail and spurred the horse. In a burst, the mount leapt, trampling the man before he could cut Jastail. A frenzied whinny erupted to her left. Penit had followed her lead, knocking the other thug to the side with his horse's broad chest.

As running steps and calls of concern flooded the street, the last man slowly backed away. Jastail jumped into his saddle and rode toward the shadows. Wendra and Penit raced at his heels. She'd saved her captor's life once again, but she expected no gratitude from the man leading them past the last tents of Galadell.

When the tents disappeared behind them, Jastail immediately took them off the trail and into untraveled patches of trees. He sped through gullies and over hills, sometimes turning left, sometimes right, as though he were not wholly unacquainted with the terrain. But he forged through low intertwined limbs, and twice forded rivers deep enough to require the horses to swim.

Wendra suspected Jastail of trying to take them far enough from possible rescue to discourage hope. But more than once she saw him stop on a rise or bluff and look away to the west through the gathering darkness. The highwayman feared pursuit. Perhaps he'd violated the code she'd seen pass unspoken among the traders while the bidding had gone along—cutting your own kind with a sword might defy their ethical mores (if they had any). But Wendra reminded herself that the highwayman had always seemed to be a cult of one. Every association she'd seen him acknowledge had been used to further his own ends. Among those who appeared to know him the best, he acted with the most deceit, putting the most at risk. The thought of it made her eager to test her chances with the boy in these wild hills.

The final traces of light left the sky to a faint moon.

"Can we stop now?" Wendra asked. "The boy is tired."

"Keep your voice down," Jastail said in a rough whisper. He looked up. "The starfire is bright enough. We will keep moving."

"What are you afraid of?"

He drew his horse to a quick halt and shot an unnerving glance at her. "I'm afraid of you dying before you prove useful to me," he said. He threw one leg over his horse and slipped to the ground. "Rest then, but keep quiet. The night sky is a better friend to the pursuer than the pursued." He left them and began scouring the ground.

Penit came close, leaning toward her. "We could run now," he said so faintly she could barely discern his words.

"No," she replied. "Running a horse in the dark is foolish when you don't know the way and have no road for your horse to follow."

"What if they come for us?" Penit's shoulders slumped. His tireless enthusiasm appeared at last defeated.

"Then we'll fight them," she answered, giving his arm a reassuring squeeze. "But it isn't the traders that concern me."

"What then?"

"If he stood to gain from your sale at the auction," Wendra said, "then why forfeit his bounty? He fought his own thieving friends to keep silent rather than answer the question." She stopped, looking back over her shoulder toward the horizon and a dozen hills they'd already passed. "Perhaps we should have left his fight to him and not interfered."

Penit laid his own hand on Wendra's forearm. "I know I'm just a boy, but I'm not helpless. I learned a lot on the wagons. And I won't let anything happen to you again."

Wendra smiled at the naive promise of the child. It sounded like something Tahn might have said. "I believe you," she answered. "For now, be ready. We shouldn't forget that we're here because of the Bar'dyn and other Given. If they come again, Jastail's friends will be the least of our worries."

Penit nodded. They dismounted and sat together on a fallen tree while Jastail worked at something behind them. Wendra put her arm around Penit and felt his small body's warmth. He nestled closer to her in what looked like a very uncomfortable position. But he did not stir. For the briefest moment, Wendra thought to sing the song from her songbox the way Balatin had sung and played for her. She imagined that this was the kind of moment she might have shared with her own child. The mixture of love and regret caught in her throat. She inclined toward the boy and kissed the crown of his head.

Looking back toward the horses, she saw Jastail watching her. In the darkness, she could not see his eyes, but he clearly took note of the tenderness she showed Penit.

He got up and walked close so that she might see him gesture toward their horses instead of having to speak. He had fastened several fallen limbs to his saddle horn with a length of hemp. He meant to drag the branches to cover their trail, but he'd have to be careful that it did not make their passage more evident. The highwayman pointed ahead. "To the next ravine and then north," he whispered. "Slowly."

They rode another three leagues before stopping.

Jastail said nothing, tethering the horses and throwing his blanket near the base of a tree. Wendra and Penit slept close together but far from Jastail.

A rough boot at her calf awoke her the next morning. "Pack and eat," the highwayman said. "Stretch your legs and arms before you mount."

Jastail had already seen to his blanket, and had allowed a small fire over which a pot of black tea heated. Wendra saw a handful of juniper berries laid on a clean rock near the pot to spice the tea once it brewed. He sat reading from a book, making notations with a thin piece of graphite.

Penit insisted on packing both his and Wendra's blankets and fetching food from their packs. She allowed him the task and sat opposite Jastail on a low rock, watching him.

Jastail lifted his eyes. "Did you assume a ruffian like me did not read?" he said with a hint of sarcasm.

"No," Wendra replied. "I just did not expect to see you reading poetry."

Jastail partially closed the book, his brows rising in interest. "And how did you know it was poetry, dear lady? Have you been rummaging through my things without my knowledge?" His voice held a hint of humor.

"No. Your eyes move unevenly to each line. History and fancy run the width of the page."

"How astute. And why do you wonder at my choice of literature? No wait, let me guess. Is it because the dreams of a laureate would be lost on one like me, who trades in living commerce and kidnaps women and children? Because if it so, lady, then you make an ardent case. And I may be at a loss."

Wendra wanted to scowl, but she did not let the desire reflect in her aspect. Her silence seemed to disconcert Jastail more than her words might have. His charming demeanor fell like an ill-fitted mask at a folliet.

"I was not born near the blocks, dear woman." This time the appellation came bitterly from his lips. "And not every scop looks heavenward when he contrives his rhyme."

"You want me to believe in the noble savage," Wendra said tersely.

"Not at all." He rubbed the binding of the book the way Balatin used to touch Wendra's hair before he kissed her good night.

"What you think of me is none of my concern. And the differences between nobility and savagery aren't as clear to me as they are to another. I've sat at fires where a man who doesn't read is distrusted and shunned. In other lands my knowledge would not even earn me the shoveler's spot in the court wastery."

Jastail's eyes flared. "But that is precisely why I read these works, precisely why I don't care what you might think of me."

"I see," Wendra observed in an even tone. "Your education has confused your morality. You are like water left atable overnight, neither cold to refresh nor hot to brace. A hallmark of mediocrity."

Jastail smiled sourly. "Perhaps," he said. "But it is that very place you name, that very . . , temperature, that gives meaning to more than a few of these bardic phrases." He tapped the book. "These men did not scribble about with dirty quills because they hoped to profit by it. They bared their torment at being caught *in between*."

"You feel tormented?" Wendra interrupted. "You think you appreciate such reflection?"

Jastail sat with his mouth slightly agape, his words apparently lost to him. With a pleasant grin, he closed his lips and opened the book with ready familiarity to a page that Wendra could see was often read. She expected him to recite a verse to her, something to prove his point, answer her accusation. The highwayman read in silence, a curious twist upon his lips that tugged his mouth into a slight frown. In that moment, Wendra thought she saw a glimpse of the unsure child this highwayman had once been. Then he closed the book again, setting it aside near his bedroll.

"Shall I talk to you of being caught in between?" Wendra said. She sent Penit back to the horses to retrieve the waterskins. "What of being taken into the company of thieves by one who barters you upon the table like a loose coin, or of watching a child marched upon the block before a crowd to be auctioned like a hog or goat at breeding season? Do these things strike you as being in between?" Her voice continued to rise as she lashed at him with vicious accusations. "Tell me how as a child you offered your hand to your elders to find an ally, elders who used you to cheat another, a friend, as you did the boy." Wendra stood, her hands clenched into fists.

Jastail shot a menacing glance at her. "My answer to that might surprise you. But you forget yourself, woman. We are not in a place you should dare to be bold." His glare did not falter, but his voice softened subtly. "And none of what you speak tells of being in between." He rose and kicked dirt into the fire. His broad mouth and bright eyes again shifted to the inscrutable expression he'd worn at the card table where he'd wagered Wendra's life. The look sent a shiver up her back. The heat of their exchange still burned in her, but the utter indifference of the man robbed her of focusing the anger into action.

Without a word, he mounted and led them north. He would not give her a clear opportunity to escape. Sooner or later she would have to make a gamble of her own.

CHAPTER FORTY-ONE

Memory of an Emotional Scar

As a boy Braethen had once taken down a crystal goblet Author Posian kept high on the shelf in his study. It was the only fine thing the man owned, something he'd gotten as a young apprentice himself.

Early in his own readings, Author Posian had traveled south with his own mentor, Author Selae, to the court at Kali Firth during the high festival of Summer Eve. There, A'Selae read the work of his winter's pen. People came from every corner of Reyal'Te, many from neighboring nations, and some from dominions and principalities far distant, to the celebration. The artists of cloth, parchment, and song gathered there each year to entertain and edify and remind the celebrants of the harshness of the most recent winter and celebrate the warmth of summer sun. Musicians played every hour of the day, and tables assembled in the great square were kept filled with early harvest vegetables, roast goose, smoked fish, and chilled wine.

Posian remembered the tables of nuts and fruit candied with syrup and molasses, and the sweet punch ladled out to children whose cheeks showed the red-orange stain of several glasses. The air filled with the sweet smells of food and the haze of sunset; men and women danced and clapped as fiddles played lively tunes and tambourines marked time. Women strolled and skipped, their blouses falling off their shoulders and their hair let down from the pinch-combs he usually saw them wear.

At night, large torches lit the square nearly as bright as day, and the food was continually replenished, but the gaiety abated as people gathered to witness the shapes and fancies of authors and dramatists and sculptors.

Sometimes a burst of laughter would swell from one small crowd here or there. But on one night, Posian listened near a group of people whose eyes glistened wetly in the torchlight. That Summer Eve, Author Selae had drawn a large group to him at the steps of a tall building. Standing within the stone entrance, Posian's mentor used the natural echo to add resonance to his voice as he read aloud from his pages. Late in the evening, Posian had gotten the signal from Author Selae that he needed something to drink, and had rushed to the tables at the Center Square to draw him a cup.

In his haste to return, Posian dodged around a coach and ran into a tall woman wearing a white satin dress. The mug of red wine splashed and spattered across the perfectly white gown. Posian looked up to apologize, and was immediately forced to his knees by two guards wearing heavy chain mail and holding spears. The woman looked at her gown, a stern frown on her lips. Suddenly, at her side, a third man appeared, this one dressed in raiment as fine as the lady's. He wore at his side a sword in a sheath encrusted with colored jewels. His cloak, trimmed gold and red and bearing the mark of sheaf and scythe, hung loosely from his shoulders. At the sight of the stain, a scowl narrowed his eyes, and he began to direct the soldiers to take Posian away.

Just then the woman raised her eyes from the ruin of her dress and saw Posian kneeling in front of her. The boy had never seen her, but knew from the descriptions uttered by all that he had just spilled Author Selae's wine on the queen's dress. She was an exceedingly beautiful woman, and it worried Posian, because the stories he'd read in the books always equated beauty with vanity and an intolerance for imperfection. He was sure the king prepared to have him cast into prison, or at least taken from the festival; either would earn him disfavor with Author Selae. The queen and king were not known to come to the festival, not due to arrogance it was thought, but because they believed their presence might distract the revelers. Their appearance any other time would have been fortuitous for Author Selae. But this was disastrous.

In an instant, the queen raised her hand to stop the guards. She gave them a commanding stare and then turned her eyes back to Posian.

"What have you to say for yourself, son?" Her voice did not shrill, and she did not bark her question. Posian immediately felt hope that he could extricate himself from this situation.

"I was sent to fetch a cup to moisten A'Selae's lips while he reads his winter's pen, and in my haste I did not pay attention to my path."

The queen's eyes did not waver as she considered his words. She touched her sodden dress and rubbed the moisture between her fingers. "Author Selae, where is he from?" she asked.

"North from the Hollows," Posian replied.

"Are you scolito to Author Selae from the Hollows? And do you pursue your study diligently?" she asked.

"Yes, for two years now," he replied.

The queen dismissed the guards with a slight elevation of her chin and motioned for Posian to stand.

Humbly, he rose to his feet but found that he could not meet the queen's gaze.

"Then you shall be pardoned for this infraction upon one condition," she said.

Posian could think of nothing he could do to redeem his error. He licked his lips and stared into the spreading wine stain on the beautiful satin of the queen's dress.

"You will create for me a parable," she said. "Something new. It must be something you've never heard, written, or thought before." She raised her brows to determine if Posian understood the terms.

"I am a novice, your Majesty," he protested lightly. "I do not write well, and I am not gifted with fancy."

The queen held up her hand, wet with wine. "I'll not have bargaining," she said with the authority of her office. "I am convinced you can entertain me, remind me . . . teach me. It is a royal request, scolito. Will you deny your queen?"

Posian stood dumbfounded. The guards looked on through their heavy beards, and the king stood beside his wife, a plaintive look on his face.

He wanted to do as the queen asked, but nothing came to mind. He tried to remember the things Author Selae had taught him, but all he could think of was the darkness of a prison and weak light cast through iron bars, or straw for cleaning oneself and bedding down at night, and the squeak of rats rummaging for food. He looked again at her soft shoulders, milky white even in the firelight, and of her words: *teach me.*

Slowly, Posian began to speak, the words sputtering out in half-formed thoughts.

"There was a bird. And the bird was still in its shell. All the other birds had hatched and left the nest before this bird could be born. The Northsun festival came and went and still the bird did not hatch. Maybe because the mother bird had left the nest after laying her eggs. Yes, the bird was alone from the start. But he didn't know it really, because he was still in his shell and he didn't know anything different."

Chortles from the guards were silenced with a look from the queen. But Posian's parable began to crystallize within him, and he spoke more confidently.

"Then one day the bird hatched and looked around at the emptiness of the nest, and felt alone. He knew he had to get out of the nest because he was hungry, but his legs and wings were still too weak. So he began to squawk and twitter, using all his energy to attract attention.

"A hummingbird flew close, hovering above the nest, and asked in his singsong voice what the new bird was doing in the nest still. The hatchling didn't understand the hummingbird at first, but after a while, he began to imitate the hummingbird, and pretty soon they began to talk, the hummingbird humming old tunes to the young bird.

"But the hummingbird became hungry. He invited the hatchling to join him, but the hatchling still could not fly. So the hummingbird had to leave the nest alone. And before the hatchling could ask for any food, the fast hummingbird was gone."

The queen granted him a thin smile, and Posian felt encouraged. He drew a deep breath and rushed on. He thought he now knew how to finish the parable just right.

"Then a red finch flew close and began chirping at the hatchling. Again the young bird couldn't understand the song. He began to imitate the chirping noises, and soon they spoke to each other. The hatchling was so pleased to have a new friend and know a new tune that he forgot to ask for something to eat and soon the finch darted away."

Posian looked at the soldiers and felt a streak of pride to find their attention on him. Their gruff beards seemed less ominous to him under the sparkle of interest in their eyes. The spears in their hands leaned at unconcerned angles as they waited upon the rest of his tale.

"For three days birds flew close, each one calling a different tune, and the hatchling learned them all, though none of his visitors ever returned with food or offered to remain close by and keep him company. The hatchling grew weaker, not just because he was hungry but also because he was lonely. He now knew many great songs, but there was no one to share them with.

"He realized he must learn to fly, and he beat his wings to test their strength. They felt fine, but they seemed small to him for carrying him on the wind as he'd seen the other birds do. Pretty soon, he couldn't wait any more, and he jumped to the edge of the nest, ready to try his wings. He called out several songs and leapt into the air. He beat his wings furiously, but he could not stay up, and he fell to the ground."

One guard gave a surprised sound, tilting his helmet back to free his ears.

"The fall hurt, but not too badly; the ground was close. So the hatchling started off to find food and friends. In no time he had regained his strength on worms and plant seeds. But his wings still did not work, and he hadn't found any other birds to talk to.

"Then he spotted a quail and several baby quails, and realized they kind of looked like him. They were not flying, either, and he got excited that he wouldn't be alone anymore. With all his might he ran to the covey of birds. But his legs were not yet coordinated and he lost control and skidded toward the mother bird. Before he could stop, he fell into her downy plumage and knocked her off her feet."

Posian saw that now even the king was listening to his story. The king took the queen's hand in his own and watched Posian with a father's gentle eyes. The queen's other hand, wet with wine, was forgotten to her, her face filled with expectation.

Posian took a breath and let the story take its final shape in his mind.

"The mother quail got up and looked at all her babies and their sure feet. Another child to protect would be difficult. The hatchling understood the concern in the mother quail's eyes and feared being left alone again, especially because he was still weak, had no friends, and was all alone. He didn't know what he could say to convince her that she should let him stay with her and her children. Then it occurred to him. He knew the songs of all the other birds, wonderful melodies that might be lost to birds on the ground that could not fly.

"So quickly the hatchling began to chirp the tunes of the other birds that he had learned. Their melody seemed to please the mother quail. She began to speak to the hatchling, and it was only an instant before he could understand her song, too. He told her that he would keep the songs of the others, the large birds and the predators, the beautiful mountain finch and the fragile hummingbird, and that those songs would live forever. He told her that he would sing her song, too, and that her kindness in protecting him would live as long as the songs of all the birds of the air."

Posian finished and watched the queen closely, hoping he had satisfied his end of the bargain. The queen did not look angry, but her face held no hint of acceptance. Then a tear ran from the corner of her eye, a single drop that hung delicately for a moment from her chin before dropping into the wine stain Posian had splattered on her dress.

She then turned her head and said something to an attendant behind her. Posian glanced at the guards; their beards framed smiles. He realized that an audience had gathered around them, but he'd focused so narrowly on the queen's eyes that he hadn't noticed.

"Your name?" the queen asked kindly.

Posian turned back toward her. "Your Majesty?"

"What is your name, my boy?"

"Posian," he answered, feeling uncertain what she thought of his tale.

A courtier came forward and, smiling, handed the queen a crystal goblet. Another courtier then poured brandy from an elegant bottle. When the glass was full, the courtiers withdrew and the queen looked down at Poisan. She smiled warmly, and causing a gasp from the onlookers, knelt before him.

"Posian, as a reminder to me of this night I will not wash my dress." She handed him the crystal glass, the smell of brandy sweet and sharp in his nose. "Your parable did all I asked and more. I will sleep well tonight knowing you have learned those songs." She winked. "Now go to Master Selae, but go a touch more slowly."

Awestruck, Posian put his second hand around the goblet and received a kiss from the queen upon his cheek. She did not, as he thought she would, return to her carriage so that revelers would not see her stained dress. And when her lady-in-waiting came forward to protest, the queen dismissed her with a simple smile. She then walked freely among the people, wearing the wine proudly. Posian watched her for several moments in a daze, then hastened to

Author Selae's side. He believed his mentor would pardon his lateness once he heard his story.

And so he did.

When Braethen began as scolito to his father, Author Posian, he saw the crystal goblet displayed on the top shelf in his study. His father dusted it once a week, and looked reflectively at it in the early light of Endweek morn. Then he sat at his desk and read and wrote.

One evening, Author Posian was away to offer some solace to Relan e'Foraw, whose wife had died in childbirth. The story of the queen and the goblet fascinated Braethen, and he'd drawn a chair close to the shelf and reached to take the glass in hand. Stretching for the goblet, Braethen fell against the shelf and knocked the glass from its perch. Off balance, he grasped at it as it fell, not quite catching the goblet before it dropped out of reach. A horrible shattering sound rose in the quiet of A'Posian's study. Braethen regained his balance only to find shards of the crystal gleaming in the light of the oil lamp atop A'Posian's desk. He knew in an instant that the goblet could not be mended, and his heart sank.

He'd destroyed his father's single most precious possession, the symbol of the life he'd taken as an author.

Their front door opened and closed. Braethen jumped to the floor and knelt, preparing to gather the pieces together and hide them. But before he even began, he knew it was useless. He waited there for his father to come.

Shortly, the old man entered the room, his eyes tracking down at his son and the broken goblet. Braethen's chest heaved with guilt and sorrow. He wanted to express it, but words would not come, and he only looked at his father, whose hollow cheeks to this day still defined infinite sadness in Braethen's mind. He expected the wrath of the old man, or perhaps a torrent of tears. Neither came. Author Posian had simply looked woefully at Braethen and the ruined token of the queen's esteem and closed the door, leaving him there with his clumsy mistake and its awful consequence.

Braethen woke from sleep with the nightmare memory alive in his thoughts. He had finally placed the feeling of this wretched place. That awful moment of his childhood was the feeling of every moment in the Scar. It was the weight of disappointment, sorrow, and irreparable damage to something precious. Just as Braethen had felt in his father's study that night.

He had broken something he couldn't mend. He would have lived better afterward if his father had struck him, at least reproved him. Instead, Braethen had lived with that awful look of disappointment and loss on his father's face. He wondered now if it was at least part of the reason he hadn't followed his father in the author's way: a fear of disappointing him.

His father had come to him not long after, and they'd made peace over Brae-then's mistake. A'Posian had just needed some time to himself after finding the broken goblet. But those few hours had felt like a lifetime. Nothing, Braethen thought, would ever feel worse than utterly disappointing someone you love.

But this feeling of the Scar, forever . . .

And that someone *lived* here—this Grant—left Braethen's heart cold; what kind of man could endure such a place every day? What unfathomable penance could keep any man so deep in the Scar? The sodalist wanted to journey on to meet this man Grant as badly as he wanted to flee the Scar and never return.

In the heat, Braethen shivered.

• CHAPTER FORTY-TWO •

Qum'rahm'se

B ehind Tahn, Sutter's feet shuffled, and his friend emerged beside him, his sword raised menacingly toward the destroyed cliff face. Tahn nocked his arrow again and aimlessly pointed ahead.

"And what damage would you do that hasn't already been done?" the voice asked with sad sarcasm. "I, for one, am relieved to see the fright so evident in your trembling weapons."

Tahn traced the source of the voice up the melted cliff face, and saw a hollow-chested man sitting beside a rock. The fellow had seen maybe fifty Northsuns and wore both an unkempt greying beard and spectacles perched on a rather protuberant nose. A feather stood tucked over his ear and several more fixed into his vest, which buttoned over his right breast. Beside him lay a staff. Not far behind him, plumes of smoke issued continually, flakes of ash rising into the air in a steady stream. Instinctively, Tahn lifted his aim toward the man.

They waited for the man to speak again. Instead, he sat where he was, saying nothing. He moved not at all, except every few moments, he lifted a small book secured to his waist by a rope and heaved a sigh over it.

Sutter whispered, "Let's get out of here. He may be more dangerous than he appears."

Tahn nodded, but stepped over the black crust of glass at his feet. "Tell us what happened."

The fellow's head cocked, then made a long survey of the world around him.

"I should think that it was evident. And quit pointing that thing at me. Can't you see the kind of day I've had?"

Tahn lowered his bow and looked about, noticing for the first time several melted columns of rock evenly spaced on both sides of the clearing. He guessed they might have been statues before the fire that had consumed the cliff face and trees.

Knowing the answer, Tahn nevertheless asked the stranger, "Then who is responsible for this?"

Hefting a small stone, the man threw it at them weakly. "Go away. Two quivering boys don't need these answers. They'd only send you sniveling back to your mother's teat."

Sutter laughed in spite of himself. "I like him," he whispered.

Tahn ignored his friend. "Perhaps not as quivering as you," he said, having an idea about the man. "How is that everything is burned, even the rock, and yet you sit unscathed?"

He seemed to have unnerved the stranger. The fellow glared back at him, then began to pick his way carefully down the cliff. As soon as he got to level ground, he strode across the charred earth of the clearing toward them, crusts of glass cracking beneath his boots. Anger grew in his eyes. They were the astute eyes of a scholar, an observer. He struck Tahn as someone on whom little was lost. Nearer, Tahn saw not one but two small books fastened by silken bands to his waist. In his belt he carried a vial and several more quills.

Striding with his thick staff toward them, he stopped directly in front of Tahn and stared up into his eyes with open scorn. "You needn't speak your third assumption, stripling," the man said, his voice a mix of self-loathing and detestation. "I will own my ignominy, but be sure it has nothing to do with your feeble attempts at deduction. Fah, language is too precious to be abused in the mouths of those who think themselves clever."

"I didn't—"

"Of course you did," the man returned bluntly. "So, hear it now. I am Edholm Restultan, a scrivener of Qum'rahm'se Library." The man looked back over his shoulder. "Or what was once Qum'rahm'se. It has come to this. And in the hour of its destruction, while sitting watch atop the cliff, I raised no defense against those that brought fire to incinerate a hundred generations of study." He brought baleful eyes back around to Tahn. "However impudent, boy, you are nevertheless right. I survived the attack by keeping quiet whilst my colleagues . . . my friends . . . cried mightily for deliverance. It is the weakness of men that they think first to preserve themselves. And as you will both be men someday, you will no doubt also someday understand my shame."

Hanging his head, the man fell silent. Tahn had no response. The scrivener began silently to weep.

In a whisper, he said, "I am undone as surely as if I'd stepped into the blaze."

"Quietgiven," Tahn said solemnly.

Edholm nodded. "Past innumerable wards they came, past the guard—though a small detachment to be sure—and past the vault doors, granite twice as thick as a man is tall. Unnatural fire spread from the hands of hooded beasts. The sheer heat seared the surrounding trees. But their object was the library, the books. . . ."

Tahn looked past the scrivener to the cliff face. "The entrance was there?" he asked.

The man nodded.

"What interest would the Quiet have in books?" Sutter said, resheathing his blade.

"Not just books," Edholm explained. "Qum'rahm'se has stood for milliennia with one purpose." The scrivener looked back at the charred earth and rock, seeming to judge if even now it were appropriate to speak its function. "I'll have your names first," he finished.

"Flin," Tahn blurted, "and Crowther." He nodded to Sutter. "Just hunters."

"I see," the scrivener said, unbelieving. "Well if not your names, at least something to call you. Have you been hunters long?" the man asked.

Neither Tahn or Sutter answered.

"You understand my question, since seasoned hunters know that their quarry flees from fire." A tone of condescension drifted on the man's words.

Tahn put away his arrow. "True enough. But fire does not melt stone."

"And common hunters do not deduce Quietgiven so easily," Edholm put back. "But neither do your trembling limbs speak of allegiance to the Bourne." The scrivener gave them another solemn look, gathering their attention. "Look upon it, striplings, the ruin of Qum'rahm'se. The vault and library dedicated to discerning and deciphering the Language of the Covenant."

Tahn nearly dropped his bow. Sutter gave Edholm an appalled stare.

"That's right. Our commission since even before the time of the Convocation of Seats has been to gather the most remote, arcane documents we could unearth, and piece together what remains of the covenant tongue. Scholars from every nation and realm committed their lives to this place, this work.

"Each generation, the library has grown, expanding deeper into the safety of the mountain, filling new shelves with theory, commentary, minor breakthroughs, bits of translation.

"It was thought that one day the language would be needed to turn back the minions of the Quiet. Or that knowledge of its use might call forth the promises the First Ones set in store for us." The scrivener paused, grief tightening his face. "The darkness out of the Bourne surely seeks the same power. Their depraved goals would be within reach, their power unquenchable, were they to have the language as a weapon."

Edholm sighed. "We did not have it for them. We had not yet revived the covenant tongue. But what we have learned over time might have been enough for the Quiet to hasten the end of peace and light upon the land." A bit of ash fell between them. "How many lifetimes are now reduced to ash," the scrivener said mournfully, "their labors so much char to litter this mountain."

Something occurred to Tahn. "Wait. If you weren't inside the library when the attack came, how do you know it has been burned? Perhaps all is not lost. Perhaps the Quiet's fire only sealed them out from the books they hoped to steal."

The scrivener pointed to the top of the cliff at the vent of steam and ash issuing into the sky. Tahn suddenly knew why his first whiff of fire had not been of burning pine alone. Edholm spoke darkly, mocking Tahn's hopefulness. "Perhaps the pages burn by the flames cast from Velle hands, the heat igniting the gentle tinder of bindings and parchment even through the stone. Or perhaps to deny them their prize, those scholars trapped inside the library set the books alight to keep them from Quiet hands." Edholm whispered, "How it must have pained them to do it."

Tahn watched the ash spew into the mountain air and waft lazily south on a gentle breeze. The empty feeling of defeat stole into his chest. Edholm finally explained.

"The dust of those who fell defending the library is now appropriately mixed with the dust of the pages they died to preserve," the scrivener said, as if in eulogy. "The fire burned them utterly, consuming even their bones. They put themselves in harm's way to try and save the library. You tread upon them even now." The scrivener looked at their feet.

"When all lay dead, the Quiet prepared to tear the mountain down and have at the books. It was then that the ash began to rain down upon them. They knew what it meant. They knew those inside the library had burned its contents rather than lose them to the Quiet. In their anger, the Quietgiven shot their fire into the mountain, burning the very rock, and sealing those scholars inside forever. I could not even die with them." Edholm kicked softly at the coat of dust and ash that layered the clearing.

Tahn could hear the man's disgrace plainly in his words. "You could not have made a difference in the battle to save the library."

The scrivener shot a fierce look at Tahn. "You are a fool! The difference is my willingness. I wear these emblems and tools," he said, lifting the books tied to his belt, "not for convenience or comfort. I wear them because I have committed myself to the preservation of our dearest words. That I stood by, whether my death might have been the cost, is the surest comment on my virtue . . . and it is my condemnation!"

Edholm turned his back to Tahn and Sutter. "I can only imagine the suffering of those trapped within the library as the flames and smoke filled the chambers."

The scrivener was quiet a few moments, then finally told the story.

"Early this morning, before the greater light shone free of the eastern ridge, three Velle came into the clearing just as you did. They wore their cowls up, and I supposed that they were couriers from Recityv as have come more frequently during this last cycle. I was there." Edholm indicated the cliff. "I stood watch. They spread out, facing the cliff. The first to greet them, Bene, was struck down by the fire in an instant. His screams brought the guard and others to the clearing, where they made their defense.

"They were all burned.

"But before the futile battle was done, the ash began to fall. Those inside had begun destroying the library to keep it from the enemy. When the Velle saw this, they screamed their fury. Flashes of white fire and lightning erupted from their hands, growing larger and sending flares out in jagged bolts. They unleashed it all at the mountain itself, the fire and lightning scattering across the ground, the statuary, the trees, the cliff, scrabbling at every nook and seam. Soon, the acrid smell of singed thatch and crumbling stone filled the air. Mortar and stone bubbled and ran, the lightning feeding the fire, and the fire the lightning. All of it expanding outward, igniting more trees, soil, stone."

Edholm faced the cliff, his head shaking as a man trying to disbelieve. "It sealed the door closed in moments, before leaping upward and covering most of the wall. The rock began to flow, and I thought I heard . . ." The scrivener fell silent.

"What?" Tahn prodded gently.

"I thought I heard the cries of men and women being consumed by the awful white fire deep inside the vaults of Qum'rahm'se. Like their voices streamed up through the very earth on which I stood, the sound of it vibrating through my soles and into my bosom. It was a horrible thing to feel their cries . . . a horrible thing. In all my years, I've not copied a word that describes, nor translated a passage that conveys such utter hopelessness. It is an awful thing to learn: All ink, all vellum, all graphite and parchment are imperfect receptacles for the thing we call life. And poorer still to record the sorrow of death."

The scrivener became silent again, standing with his back to them as he stared at the low escarpment. Sutter looked at Tahn and shrugged.

"I lay upon the ground to hide." Edholm took a quill from his vest, and continued in a whisper. "And I could feel the shape of these instruments pressed into my belly as I hid myself. They are something of a shame to me now.

"I will be remembered as part of the old trust that failed to safeguard the only documents worthy of preservation. It was a trust begun when the First Promise was not yet necessary, a trust carried forward through the ages until now, protected by anonymity—few know of the library—and by the wards of the order, and by a vault of living rock." His lips snarled as he formed the words. "Now the library is gone, and there is no trust."

Tahn had no words of comfort for the man. He understood too well the guilt of not rising to the defense of someone or something you care for.

As if sensing his sympathy, Edholm said, "This is none of your concern. My apologies." Abruptly, the scrivener asked, "Where are you going?"

Reluctantly, Tahn admitted, "Recityv."

The man brightened. "Aha! Come with me!"

The scrivener rushed to the cliff face as though he meant to walk through a flow of steaming stone. He stopped, and plunged his staff into the rock. The thick flow yielded little, but the man had put a small dent in the face of it. Again he struck, grunting with the effort. "Don't stand there idle," he chided. "Come, put your arms to it!"

Tahn found a pair of blackened tree limbs nearby, and handed one to Sutter. They shared a quizzical look, Sutter smiling and crossing his eyes at the mystery of the task. Then they began to pick at the stone.

Shortly, the scrivener had pierced through. The sudden smell of burnt flesh filled the air. As though unaware, Edholm turned a sweating face to Tahn. "I'm through!" he said excitedly. "Help me bear down on the staff!"

Tahn lent his weight to it, and together they widened a small hole in the rock. Smoke and steam rose from the opening, but the scrivener did not slow.

"Place a rock beside my staff. We'll use it for leverage," Edholm ordered Sutter.

Nails did as he was told, and held a large rock in place while Tahn and the scrivener continued to work at the stone. The wider the hole became, the more furiously the frail scrivener worked.

Sometime later, drenched in sweat, they all stopped. But they had created an opening large enough for a man to crawl through.

Growing hope lit the scrivener's face. He mopped his brow, and in a rush started through the hole. "Follow me, lads."

Inside, the smell of burnt flesh became nauseating. Tahn covered his mouth and nose and surveyed the hallway. He expected the library to lay in total darkness. Instead, he found a dim light shining from the very stone itself in a small radius around him and Sutter. The light followed them, the walls themselves lighting in response to their movement. For several strides down the first hall, the rock around them cascaded in gentle, melted swoops.

A few strides ahead, a charred, hunched figure lay curled into a ball on the hallway floor. Tahn advanced slowly toward the body, the radius of light continuing to track his movement. The soot and smoke caused the light to shine darkly, like midwinter dusk through heavy clouds. But it was enough to see the gruesome death mask of the burnt man lying on the floor. The figure's hands stood frozen in the attempt to ward off the fire that had claimed him.

The scrivener did not wait for them, but scurried ahead. Tahn, running to catch up, continued to cover his mouth to avoid breathing in the dust and ash kicked up by Edholm's shoes. The floor lay littered with larger bits of parchment, charred and crumbling in the gentle wind of their rushing steps.

And more curled and huddled bodies.

Tahn rushed past, trying to avoid looking at the lifeless, blackened forms.

The hallway branched, and the scrivener turned right. Tahn stayed close and saw him duck into a room. Following the man, Tahn found himself looking into a large sunken chamber, great drifts of ash and scorched parchment lining the walls as if bookshelves had once occupied the perimeter.

The smoke became overpowering, forcing Tahn and Sutter to cough even through the cloaks they held over their noses and mouths.

Edholm dashed past them and farther down the hall, seeming now to move with purpose to someplace specific. Tahn wondered if the scrivener hoped to find survivors deep within the sacred library. Passing several more rooms, Edholm took quick glances inside. Each time he saw a fallen scrivener, small whimpers escaped his lips.

They swept on, trampling the ashes of books and scrolls and sheaves smoldering on the floor.

At the end of the hall, Edholm turned right and descended a stair. At the bottom, the air cleared a bit, and Tahn wiped his brow, the heat still intense.

The scrivener raced ahead, no longer looking into ruined offices, chambers, reading rooms. They descended several more sets of stairs, and turned down countless corridors, rushing through the labyrinthine maze behind their knowing guide. It gave Tahn the impression that the scrivener had concealed something of the library's worth or function. Quickly, Edholm outdistanced them so that they could no longer see where he ran to, but only follow his receding steps.

Moments later, a tortured scream echoed from deep inside the mountain.

Tahn and Sutter sprinted toward the sound, their running steps echoing off the walls.

Again came the soul-shattering cry.

Down another short stair, a long hall stretched deep into the library to a single room at the end of a passageway that branched no more. From within shone a pale glow—the stone shining dimly to the one life within the room. Tahn and Sutter slowed to a jog at the arched passageway that led inside. A stone lectern stood in the middle of the room, a slanted vacant altar where a book might have lain open from which to read. Its placement gave Tahn the impression that a tome of particular importance had rested there.

"No," the scrivener muttered. "All my Skies, no."

Edholm stumbled about the podium, as if he might discover something other than its bleak emptiness and the filmy layer of soot that covered it. He turned in circles, regarding the vacant walls; shelves carved directly into the stone, bearing smoldering piles of waste similar to what they'd seen throughout the library; the remains of desks half burned upon the floor like empty, leveled ramparts in this repository of learning; and along the back wall, gossamer threads of what once might have been a large tapestry now hanging like sooty webs. Then the scrivener fell to his knees in the banks of ash and withered sheets and thrust his hands deep into the remains. He crushed fistfuls of the ruined pages in his palms and raised them to his eyes as he mouthed words Tahn could not hear. Black motes of dust hung in the air about the scrivener, given light from the stone floor beneath Edholm's knees.

The scrivener quaked, his senses appearing to have beheld too much. Wrathfully, he cast away handfuls of the ashes, the reality of the fire's destruction descending upon him.

Tahn watched the man grieve and said nothing. The moment seemed to belong to the scrivener alone. Edholm bowed his head in an attitude of prayer, and the floor around him brightened through the soot that coated it. In a voice of quiet resignation, he muttered, "We are undone."

Thinking to give the scrivener more peace, and seek out any possible survivors, Tahn touched Sutter's arm and nodded for his friend to follow him out of the room.

After a single step, Edholm spoke. "Even if some still draw breath," the scrivener said, his voice hollow, "they would rather perish than learn this news."

Tahn turned back toward the man. "What news?"

With reddened eyes, the scrivener looked at Tahn as though he'd never seen him before. Then his countenance changed, the flinty edge returned, and the acute intelligence came again to the man's face.

"No more games, melura," he seethed. "A hunter you may be, but this is not what brought you to Qum'rahm'se. You are the first witness to this." He lifted his hands filled with parchment ash. "Now I must require something of you."

Edholm violently cleared the floor about his knees of the debris. "Come close," he said in a broken voice. Tahn and Sutter obeyed. Without looking up, the scrivener lifted one of the books tied to his waist and tore three clean sheets from the back. Setting them on the stone, he handed them each a quill from his belt. "Do you know how to write?"

They nodded.

"Good. You will write what you have seen, my friends," he said emphatically. "Leave nothing out. Describe the destruction, the smell, the ash, the burnt rock. Write of me, my shame. But mostly, write of the empty vaults you have passed through, the fate of the books, the pages, the destruction of the library at Qum'rahm'se. And put your name to it at the bottom."

"But why—" Sutter began.

"Do not cross me in this, boy." The scrivener spoke sharply. "I won't be a coward twice."

Sutter raised his hands in surrender to ease Edholm's fierceness.

Edholm removed a vial from his belt and opened it, placing it before them. Without further instruction, he dipped his own quill and began to scribble madly upon the parchment.

With the stink of so much soot and burnt timber about them, and a layer of ash as deep as Tahn's ankle—spreading to knee-high mounds at the walls—Tahn did as he was asked. From his own loss of his father, he understood the sometimes inexplicable needs of a mourner. This scrivener, in his shame and loss, needed something to do, to accomplish, and Tahn would not deny him. In the vacancy left by the fire, their three scribbling quills sounded loud in the chamber.

As he wrote, Tahn nodded to Sutter, who shrugged again and stuck his tongue out playfully, concentrating as a child might over a mundane task.

Nails finished first, his page half written upon.

Tahn filled his sheet, noting the smell of singed flesh and charred wood and iron as he related the devastation around him.

Together, Tahn and Sutter waited for Edholm to stop writing. The man used three pages to make his account, his fingers moving lithely, tracing words in quick, elegant strokes. Tahn watched letters and symbols fill the parchment, lines being written in alternating directions—left to right and then right to left—all in a language foreign to him.

The scrivener then put his quill aside on a layer of ash, blew the last strokes dry, and rolled his parchment tightly. He bound it with several strands of what Tahn thought must be hair. He then produced three ordinary-looking sticks from an inner pocket of his tunic. Taking the first in hand, he opened one end, revealing a hollow compartment within. Into it he stuffed his rolled parchment.

He sealed it again, the seam undetectable. Reaching for Tahn's and then Sutter's parchments, he read each with amazing speed, seeming to take it all in at a glance. Then he rewrote their epistles on new pieces of parchment, having them sign their names again to words they could not read. Afterward, he likewise placed their parchments in the remaining sticks. Having sealed them all, he stood and surveyed the room, a profound look of melancholy drawing his face. Then he gave both Tahn and Sutter a grave look. "Now come," he said curtly.

Through the maze of halls and stairs and small inner courtyards they re-traced their way to the entrance, but not before searching each room of the library. The hope that had lit the scrivener's face never touched it a second time. More figures lay curled into charred human balls, the fire having consumed everything in the vast library. The soft glow of the rock bore them company, shining dully through warped mortar and stone. At the entrance, the scrivener peeked through the hole they'd created to assure himself that all was well in the clearing.

"They succeeded, Tahn," the scrivener said. Tahn immediately realized that he and Sutter had signed their real names to their parchments. Edholm did not draw attention to the uncovered deceit. "The Velle came to this place and by destruction stole countless ages of accumulated thought and wisdom."

Having spoken it like an epitaph, Edholm went through the hole, and out of Qum'rahm'se a final time.

Tahn and Sutter ducked back out into the light.

Standing together, the two of them shared wary looks before the scrivener handed the sticks to Tahn. "Never allow these out of your hands. These are sealed words. The encryptions are a simple matter, understandable only to those pre-pared to know their truths. But the parts that a foe might decipher could be nearly as dangerous to them, to *us,* as the full truth.

"They are safe against water," the scrivener explained, "but take care not to break them. You'll present these at Recityv. Not to some low officer or pundit. Take the sticks to Dolun'pel, head of my brotherhood, and watch as he removes their seals. Attest to their contents. If you cannot find him, give them into the hands of someone you trust, someone with authority to act on what they find therein. Do you understand?"

"Why don't *you* take them?" Sutter asked.

"I won't need them," he replied. "If I make it as far as Recityv, my presence and testimony will be proof enough that Qum'rahm'se has fallen." He poked Tahn's chest. "*You,* however, are just striplings, and I'm guessing by your garb you are unknown at Recityv. These will be needed should I never make it there, and our chances are doubled if we both go separately.

"Those in authority must know what has befallen our work here. It is im-perative." Edholm's eyes grew distant once more. "They must know the loss and decide what must be done."

Focusing again, he said, "Make haste, lads. Don't dawdle. This season may end sooner than you might imagine, and if it does, it will come with desecra-tions we can only imagine. Don't be a party to it by failing in this simple com-mission. The Quiet are still very close, so I will head west for a time, traveling obvious roads, burning bright fires, and singing loudly at every step to draw undue attention, before proceeding to Recityv. You follow the river north. Make no fire, stay beneath the shadow of the leaf. If you can see the river blue, you are too close to it. In a few days, you'll come to an old overgrown road. Any other time, I'd tell you to follow it west to the main road north." The scrivener shook his head. "But not this time. Follow the road east back to the river. There you'll see a grand old bridge arcing toward high cliffs. That's the way for you. It's an old road, a forgotten way. But the Given won't look for you that way, either. Take care and you'll be all right."

Tahn could feel the scrivener holding something back. "Where are you sending us?"

Edholm motioned them close and whispered so softly they almost couldn't hear him. "It is a very old city, very old." He looked them each in the eye. "Take care and you'll be all right," he said again.

As an afterthought, the scrivener reached for one of the books at his belt. He tore out several written-upon sheets, and rolled them as he had done the others before stuffing them inside yet another stick, this one larger. "Take this with you, as well. Those to whom you present the sticks will be glad of its reception."

Edholm fell silent, his aspect weary. "I am but a scrivener, boys. I have loved my days recasting what has been, laboring over it with bone and muscle, carrying forward in time the simple and dear words that authors in the tradition have given us." He lifted a quill and spun it slowly between his fingers. "There are other methods of producing the words, but none that imbue the text with all the depth of soul and intention set out in the first seasons of man."

Shaking himself from his reverie, the scrivener looked a last time at Tahn and Sutter. "It is an imperfect plan, but likelier to succeed than three untested men leaving together to outfoot the Quiet."

Edholm was right, and even if he had been wrong, it would have done no good to try and convince him otherwise. Tahn sensed that the scrivener had written upon his scroll things that Tahn and Sutter had not put to their own: a last testament to his life because he didn't believe he'd ever reach Recityv.

"Should Will and Sky smile at once, we may meet in cleaner air, and I may take your hands to show my thanks."

The scrivener extended one hand, which Tahn took willingly. With his other hand, Edholm traced a circle around his and Tahn's thumbs. Without another word, the scrivener set out through the still smoking trees and spared no backward glance.

"Whew," Sutter exclaimed. "I don't know what to make of that little fellow."

Tahn stuffed the sticks into an inner pocket of his cloak. "Really . . . I thought he was your brother."

Bandying a series of similar retorts, they retrieved the horses and marked a northward course. They soon reached the river and resumed their journey under the cover of the tree line not far from the river's edge. Until evening they traveled, speaking low, Tahn occasionally clutching the sticks inside his cloak to assure himself that they hadn't worked themselves loose.

In the twilight, ignoring the scrivener's admonition, they agreed to a small fire and warmed their meat and cheese together over bits of stale bread.

Smacking his lips with delight over the makeshift supper, Sutter asked, "If the cycle turns and there is no one around to witness for us at our Standing, do we still pass into manhood, the fullness of alchera?"

"You won't," Tahn jibed. "I think 'manhood' is rather picky about who is allowed in."

"I see. And you feel confident that 'manhood' has a place reserved for a hayseed whose only manly activity is shooting helpless animals." Sutter chortled through his food.

"I think I'm in line right ahead of the clodhopper whose closest friend is a worm." Tahn threw the last bit of his fusty meal at Nails. Then he thought more seriously. "I don't know. I'd always thought Balatin would Stand for me. And when he went to his earth, I chose Hambley." He adjusted a log on the fire. "I don't think we'll be home in time for that to happen. I guess one way or another we'll get older. . . ."

Sutter brushed his hands together and drew up his blanket. "Not me, Woodchuck. I think I fancy that if we never Stand, we never age. Imagine an endless lifetime of trackers, scriveners . . . and women." He winked at Tahn and rolled over to sleep, leaving the first watch to Tahn.

In moments, long, slow breaths rose from Sutter as he went to his dreams. Tahn leaned back against a fallen tree and looked up through the darkness toward the lesser light, his thoughts turning to Mira: A woman who looked his age, but who seemed to have lived a lifetime of experience; her reserve; the latent skill and energy in her arms as they rested near her sword. Something did seem ageless, timeless, about her.

Removing his neck wrap, he rubbed at his wounds. Despite the foulness so recently pursuing him, Tahn lost himself in reverie of an imagined life with the Far. The responsibility of the sticks, the ache in his foot, the guilt of his inaction over Wendra's child, all receded if for but a moment as he thought about possibilities.

They rode a full day, speaking little, each caught up in his own thoughts. Evening meal and night watches were more of the same. On the morning of the second day after leaving Qum'rahm'se, they broke through to a road choked with foliage, high grass growing in the middle, nearly obscuring the wheel ruts. Tahn angled east toward the river, stems brushing his legs and the bellies of their mounts. In the breeze, the air filled with seeds blown from river cottonwoods shedding their plumes. The soft fall of the light, downy seeds seemed to assuage the urgency that had been growing in him to safeguard the messages entrusted to him by the scrivener.

The ripple of leaves rustling together in the wind like the rush of whispers reminded Tahn of the Hollows, and he relaxed in his saddle. Slowly, the sound of running water grew. The dappled light gave way to an open sky above them as Tahn and Sutter suddenly found themselves at the edge of a bridge arching up to span the river.

Neatly cobbled stones mortared together with clay and sand made up an elegant overpass. The bridge was bordered by balustrades and supported by stout pilings of seamlessly fitted larger stones. The architect had invested great care in fluting the masonry posts that rose at even intervals to the flat stone ledges on both sides of the bridge. Beveled edges marked the ledges themselves. The stone, darkened from long years of river moisture and sun, stood stately in the morning light.

Grasses grew over the foot of the bridge, some taking root in the cracks where wind and water had eroded the mortar.

Across the river, the bridge dropped to the base of a sheer cliff, a chasm there opening like a rift in a risen plain. Suddenly, Tahn wondered if the chasm had been built to service the bridge or the bridge to service the chasm.

Sutter, giving Tahn his cavalier smile, started across the bridge. The clop of hooves on stone seemed loud, causing Tahn to swing his head about like a thief wishing not to be heard. Reluctantly, he followed his friend.

The great arching bridge ended at a stone gate. Sutter pushed on it with his left hand. The huge block did not move.

"Your assistance?" Sutter requested in a sarcastic tone.

Tahn rode to the gate and together they pushed. The gate gave, slowly. A moment later they had opened it far enough to pass beyond.

Sutter hesitated a moment.

"Scared," Tahn mocked.

Sutter's smile broadened. "You'll remember that I was the one who pegged Anais Polera in the ass when she turned to flee our root attack." With that, Sutter went in.

CHAPTER FORTY-THREE

More Scars

Mira had been to the Scar once before. She understood its secrets and silences. Not as well as the Sheason, whom she believed could hear in the dust the voices of those fallen ages ago in a final act of defiance against the Quiet. And not like the man Grant, who lived here. But the way of it haunted her the way the Soliel Stretches did when she walked their vast tracts alone, save that here, the reminders were far more bitter.

Mira knew this time her visit to the Scar would bring more painful memories. She knew it because of the recent arrival of a raven bearing a message from Naltus. She knew it also because the Children of the Soliel all shared one common childhood misfortune. As she considered that misfortune, she remembered when she realized how hard it was to have more than one mother.

"I don't understand," Mira said. "I thought you said you were my mother."

She stood in the warmth of her home, going over basic movements she'd been taught. Only arms and feet so far; she was only four. They'd get to start practicing with weapons the next turn of a cycle. As she repeated the forms again and again, taking correction from her mother, they spoke. This was her favorite time, because her mother, Genel, always taught Mira things while she was practicing the basic movements. Her friends didn't seem to have the same kind of relationship with their mothers.

"Mira, you need to listen closely. I am your mother because I am taking care of you right now. But I did not give you life. The woman who brought you into the world was called Mela. She fulfilled her call in your first year." Genel cautioned that her foot was too far back for proper balance.

Mira corrected her stance. "What does it mean to fulfill her call?"

"When a Far reaches the age of accountability, she is called home, into the next life. This is the honor given us for our stewardship. We will never have to taste the fear or pain of reckoning for stains of word or deed. It is a great blessing."

"It's a blessing to go to the earth so young?" It confused her. Mira naturally thought that doing well meant the reward of pleasant things, not something like dying.

Her mother interrupted Mira's next movement, and took her face in her hands. "Yes. You must understand. We protect a very important knowledge. To do so means we must be willing to do anything necessary to keep it safe. And that will sometimes mean doing something that seems wrong to you. But understand," she said, commanding Mira's attention, "that in the service of our oath, nothing is wrong. And so when our life is done, we go unblemished."

Mira looked back, understanding dawning in her young mind. "But accountability is when you have eighteen cycles. Does everybody die then?"

"If they are Far, they do," Genel said. "Though we are given the full turn of our eighteenth year."

"How old are you?"

"I have seen eighteen turns of the sun, Mira. I will go into my next life in but a few months."

Mira began to cry. "I don't want you to go. Please. Can you stay? I will be very good. I won't beat up on any of the boys anymore."

Her mother smiled. "As long as you don't really hurt them." Then she wore her serious face, her teaching face. "Mira, this is who we are. You will have many mothers in your life. And they will all love you and take care of you. And then one day, you will take care of a young Far. And then you can tell her it's okay to beat up on the boys."

Mira didn't smile. "I don't want to. I just want you to stay. I don't want any more mothers. One is enough. Just until I'm old enough to be by myself."

Her mother held her close and hugged her. And rocked her. "One day, you may even have a child of your own, Mira. It is such a blessing when that happens. Especially for you, because you belong to an important family for our people. And then you'll be happy to know that when your time comes, there will be able and willing Far to take care of that child, just as I am doing for you."

Mira shook her head. "But then the only way she'll ever know me is because someone else told her my name. And we'll never be able to sing the Soliel songs or Run the Light as you and I do, because I will be gone before she is old enough to do those things."

The woman who called herself her mother tried to hug her again. But Mira didn't want her hugs right now. She didn't want to love Genel anymore, because she was going to die and give her to another mother. And she couldn't understand why this was a blessing. So she ran. Ran out the door and into the city and moved as fast and long as her small body would allow her.

Why do I have to be a Far? she thought. Just train and learn and fight and . . . die. What if I just want to be a mother and keep being one?

. . .

As the memory receded, Mira stood from her vigil and sprinted into the Scar night, running with every whit of speed with which she, as a Far, was endowed. The rushing night air cooled her skin, but could not calm the troubled thoughts in her mind.

There was life and love and duty. For a Far these were supposed to mean the same thing. But somewhere in her youngest childhood had been sown the thought that perhaps they needn't be. And while the broken hopes of that four-year-old girl had never healed—could never heal, because she was after all, Far, and always would be—she had made peace with her own brief, childless life.

Until her sister died.

Mira didn't know how long she'd been running when she arrived back at camp. The heat of the day had receded, leaving the night air pleasant—not cold enough for a fire. The sodalist lay asleep, fitfully dreaming. The Sheason sat awake in the dark, looking northeast toward where they hoped to find the exile they sought.

"You should rest," she said, and sat on the ground opposite him. "This may be one of the few places the Quiet will hesitate to follow. I'll keep watch."

Vendanj said nothing for some time. When his eyes finally left the dark horizon to find her own, he said, "Does running help you forget?"

Mira had shared the Sheason's company for too long to be surprised at his ability to divine the inner concerns of those around him. Still, she was guarded. "And what do you believe I run to forget?"

"Your sister. The mantle she's passed you by her death. The struggle with childhood—yours, and your people's." His eyes seemed sad as he said it, though she had the impression the sadness was not for her alone. "This place," he went on, "it causes us to remember. And for you and I, my friend, remembrance is not cheerful. But neither let it cause you despair. Coming through this place, bearing our memories . . . it is a good test for what may come."

Mira stared back, saying nothing.

"It is hard, though, isn't it?" Vendanj said. "Especially when feelings stir inside you for the boy."

It would be pointless to deny it, nor did she feel inclined to do so. "It has no bearing on what I must do, or why I came," she said.

Vendanj showed a wan smile. "I know, Mira. But be careful that in spending so much time with me, that you do not become too much *like* me. Your future may be short, but it is worth living. Don't let anything, even a Sheason, influence your decisions."

She looked back at him for a long moment, then offered her crooked smile. "You say that now . . ."

In the dark of the Scar, they shared between them a rare laugh, low and even and mild. She had the thought that it might likewise be rare that laughter was heard by *anyone* in this place. Afterward, they sat in companionable silence for some time, each seeming to carry lighter thoughts, even if just barely.

Finally, she said again, "Get some rest. I'll keep watch."

As Vendanj nodded, she saw his brow furrow and his face change, as one who anticipates troubled dreams.

Vendanj never slept well in the Scar. More than the land's loss of Forda, or the memory of war that lingered ages later across its barren surface, the problem was that the Scar had a way of reminding its travelers of their own emotional wounds. Sheason were no exception.

Looking up at the hard, dim flicker of stars, Vendanj knew that what plagued his sleep wasn't a vestige of the Quiet's power. It was the emptiness and hopelessness that was rooted in this place. It came near the feeling of the Bourne, where Vendanj had traveled more than once—a place he would not visit again, if he didn't have need.

Because the memory of a moment long past pricked like a canker in his soul, and each visit to the Bourne tore the wound wider still.

As it did here in the Scar.

Vendanj ran. The streets of Con Laven Flu still showed signs of the Quiet attack. Black scorchmarks on the sides of buildings, some homes razed to the ground. He thought he saw smoke in a distant part of the city, though that could have been a cook fire.

But all he could think about was Illenia, his wife, and their unborn child.

He tore through the streets at a maddening pace, cursing himself for being overlong in his journey to Recityv on Sheason matters. He'd helped bring a dissent against the new law forbidding Sheason to render. The league had sponsored the law for all of Vohnce and he'd fought it at the seat of the regent. But their baby wasn't due for some time, so he'd felt safe in leaving for a few days. And Illenia was also Sheason; she could serve equally well without him.

He turned into their street. No!

The mortar stood in rubble. He raced to their doorway and stepped past the half-broken door. Fragments of wood and fallen stone lay all around. He picked up long crossbeams and peered beneath piles of broken rock. She was not here.

But his panic did not abate.

He jumped into the street, thinking to try the homes of people she knew, when Amalial called, "Vendanj!"

He followed the voice, and saw the woman. "Where's Illenia?"

"She was taken to the league's hospice, yesterday, when the attacks came."

Vendanj heard the last in fading tones as he sprinted toward the far end of the quarter where the league's healing ward stood. His lungs burned and his head pounded with dark suggestions that threatened his sanity. Please be all right, Sweet One. I will be there soon.

At the door he slammed through and shouted her name. A scholarly looking gentleman in a dark brown tunic bearing the league's emblem came right up.

"Calm yourself, my friend. We have sick people here. Tell me the name of your friend or family and we'll see what we can do." The fellow smiled paternally.

Vendanj hated the obtrusiveness and grabbed the man by the arms. "My wife's name is Illenia. I'm told she was brought here. Please, I must see her. Is she here?"

The man then spied the three-ring sigil Vendanj wore, and his countenance visibly changed. He asked to be unhanded and then called to a standing guard, who came forward with his palm on the hilt of his blade. Vendanj let the healer go and implored them to tell him where his wife lay.

"Please, she is with child. I need to see her!" Panic seized him afresh. He thought he would scream soon and keep screaming.

Shortly, three more guards came to reinforce the first. They did not snarl or curse, but simply barred him from two shadowed hallways that led to several doors and private rooms. The healer then took Vendanj gently by the hand and patted his knuckles.

"You are probably a fine man. And I understand your worry. These fellows will accompany us, and we'll take you to see your wife. They are a necessary precaution in these troubled times. That seems most reasonable, doesn't it?" He smiled his patronizing smile again.

Vendanj nodded.

The four sentries went first, directed by the healer down the left hall and through the third door. Vendanj came after, still fettered to the healer, who held his hand in a tight embrace. He thought the gentleman may have thought this a supportive gesture, but Vendanj was going to need his hands free soon, and the grip of this other began to irritate him.

But it all faded when he entered and saw Illenia lying in a bed of white linens. Her face had been heavily bruised and her arms were completely bandaged. Still, the noise of their entry brought her eyes open, and when she saw him a pained smile rose on her purpled lips. "You came," she said. "You came."

Vendanj tore free and rushed to her side. "Dear Sky, Illenia, what happened?" He wanted to caress her face to comfort her, but the bruising advised against it. Instead, he put his hand on her stomach, as he had grown accustomed to doing, and stroked slowly.

She could speak only in the barest of voices, and then just a few words at a time, but she managed, "Quiet came. They had Velle with them." She swallowed. "The guard failed. Didn't know what to do. League"—her eyes darted to the men behind him—"ran. The people started to fall, Vendanj. Fall." A tear coursed across a yellowed bruise at her temple.

He could see how the memory upset her. "Don't talk. You're going to be all right."

"Had to do something. I went to the gate. Called the Will." Her voice cracked, and she squinted against some pain.

"I think this is not helping her," the healer said. "She needs rest. This whole affair has been most . . . unbelievable. We need to assess. And she's taken serious—"

Vendanj silenced him with a stare. The guards moved closer to him. Their presence angered him all the more. He didn't need them; Illenia didn't need them anymore, either. Vendanj could care for her now.

"Wasn't enough," Illenia said. "Too many. I'm sorry, Ven. I'm sorry. I wouldn't have gone. The baby. But no one could stop them. . . ." She ceased to talk, crying openly now, her tears silent and hot and painful, he knew, in more ways than one.

"Leave us," Vendanj said. "Thank you for everything you've done. But we don't need your assistance any longer. I will care for my wife now. If we owe you anything, I will pay when I'm done. Please allow us some privacy." He looked at them each, being sure they understood that he meant all of them.

None moved.

And then the healer came forward. "Sheason. These are troubled times. I am a man committed to healing the sick. And I will continue to watch over your wife. I hope you'll have confidence in me, as I've taken her to my care while you've been away." The indictment in his voice was gentle but clear. "But there are two things that are certain, and not easy for you to hear, which is why my colleagues are present." He indicated the league guard.

Vendanj stood, knowing what the man would say, and preparing himself for whatever course he must take. The leaguemen drew their weapons. Behind him, he heard Illenia whisper, "No." But he couldn't see her eyes to know whom she addressed. Didn't matter. For Vendanj there was only one acceptable course: He would heal his wife, ensure the safety of his unborn child, and they would find a new home beyond the Nation of Vohnce, far from the sight of the League.

The healer looked up passively. "Your wife, sick as she is, did nevertheless violate the law. When she is well, there must be a trial on it. And despite your grief, Sheason, you must entrust her care to me. You will not be allowed to call upon whatever arcane rituals you practice. And I will tell you true, I believe they hold more danger for her besides. The best thing for you is to go home and get some rest. It would seem you've been on the move for quite some time."

Vendanj stared into the man's bespectacled eyes. "There is no man or army that is going to stand between me and my family, leagueman. I am grateful for *your ministrations thus far. But that is over. What I do with and for my wife now has nothing to do with you."*

Then it all unraveled so quickly.

"No," Illenia cried again.

This time, Vendanj heard the message in her voice. And so, apparently, did the league healer. Something was wrong with the baby. As he bustled past Vendanj, he called, "Get him out of here!" In an instant, the four guards grabbed Vendanj by the arms and legs and began to force him from the room.

An anguished cry rose from his wife's bruised lips. "Please, no. Vendanj. Vendanj." She could not cry loudly, but he heard her husky call and fought for all he was worth to free himself, or at least his hands so he could call the Will and escape the dirty grips of these leaguemen. But he couldn't muster enough strength to outman four guardsmen.

Vendanj thrashed, kicking and yelling for assistance, for someone to take pity on him. He could save his wife and baby, if he could get free. "Help me! No. Illenia! Illenia!"

As he was dragged from the room, he caught one last look at his wife. Her bruised, tear-streaked face; her eyes shut tight against pain and grief; one bandaged arm raised toward him.

He fought and fought until his strength failed him. Screamed until his voice sounded like stalks brushing each other in the wind. And then he was struck on the head and all fell to blackness.

Illenia died.

Their child died.

As Vendanj looked up into the bitter skies over the Scar, he thought again, as he had countless times, that if he'd had the experience he had now, if he'd have been willing to call the Will in those few moments . . . he could have healed his wife, and saved their child.

They were a fool's thoughts.

In that time he'd strictly followed the path of the order—never rendering the Will to harm another man in anger or frustration or fear. It was a path most Sheason still followed. Not Vendanj; not anymore, and not since the day his observance of the principle had cost him so much.

Vendanj shook his head. No good could come of reliving the past. The choices today and tomorrow were all that mattered anymore. He had learned that at a dear price. Others did not see it so clearly. But where matters of import lay, with the threat of the Quiet, and the choices ahead for himself and some few others whose lives were now bound for good or ill to the outcome of Restoration and all that would follow . . . in these matters, Vendanj would make them see. Not simply because of the scars of *his* past, but because someone must, else the value of a man's wounds would be as nothing.

And for Vendanj, it would never be so.

CHAPTER FORTY-FOUR

Stonemount

The chasm reminded Tahn of a box canyon near Jedgwick Ridge in the Hollows. Except this passage felt constructed. Ahead, it stretched into the rock until its walls seemed to meet. Some birds had managed to build nests high up the sheer facings, using small imperfections to gain purchase. The walls rose up more than a hundred strides. Beyond them, the sky appeared as a river seen from high above. The sensation of peering up and seeming to look down caused Tahn to swoon in his saddle.

He steadied himself and noticed figures carved into the stone on either side of the canyon, one showing a man, the other a woman, both with tightly shut lips. It struck Tahn as very odd, and was more than a little unnerving.

"Come on," Sutter scolded. "We're wasting time." His friend pushed his horse into a gallop down the chasm.

Tahn stared after Nails, who raced into the riven stone. Something gnawed at him, and he clutched again at the sticks concealed within his cloak, assuring himself they were still there. Then he followed.

The chasm ran deeper than Tahn had thought possible. On each side of them the walls continued to grow up to impossible heights, though the chasm itself never varied in width. He no longer felt queasy looking up, the ribbon of sky receding to a thin blue line as the walls rose out of sight.

Soft loam accepted the hard iron of Jole's tread, muting the sounds of their passage. Suddenly, Tahn remembered the chiseled figures with tight-shut lips and had a thought. He stopped and turned. Sutter stopped beside him.

Tahn raised his hands to the sides of his mouth to project his voice, and called, "Hello."

The word rose on the hard, sheer faces of the narrow chasm. A long, deep echo jounced against its surface, then another, the second hardly diminished from the first. Soon, a chorus of voices repeated the word, rising in a voluminous rush like the running of water over a falls. The syllables echoed, and the word itself became lost, replaced by a sound like that of a throng. The din found a strange forcefulness of its own, interrupting thought and forcing confusion into Tahn's mind.

When the sound finally echoed away, Sutter leaned close and whispered, "A fine discovery, Woodchuck, but even *I* don't want to try that a second time."

They rode for some time before the narrow canyon came to an end. The shadows of evening were falling fast, casting the gorge into darkness. Only careful attention kept them from riding into the walls.

When the rock at last gave way, it was as though the mountain before them had been hollowed out. In the belly of a great depression lay a city, stretching a league wide. In a great circle, sheer cliffs rose around the vast basin, in some places higher than others, the whole thing looking like a vast crater. From where he stood, Tahn could see no other entrance, no chasms like the one they'd just traversed.

The westering sun caused a sharp line of light and shadow to fall across the city, leaving its western half in darkness. But nowhere could he see the flicker of a lamp.

The city seemed to be abandoned.

Tahn expected to smell cooking fires, livestock. He thought to hear men's voices as they retired to a mug of bitter or their women. Nothing. No dog barked, no recalcitrant child protested his bedtime. An unsettling quiet held over the city. Outer buildings were covered in creeping vines that had gained purchase on their timbers. Deeper into the town, smooth white walls rose in lonely majesty as though seeking the light that fled the sky. But even these showed cracks and fissures. This city's protection—the great cliffs—had also become its tomb.

"Look at this place," Sutter said in wonder. "It must be a thousand years old, two thousand. I've never heard Ogea mention such a place in his stories."

Maybe some places are left to the dead.

"Come on!"

The soft loam in the chasm ended, letting them into a shallow gully that dipped to a natural spring before rising again to the plain of the city proper. They watered the horses and tied them out of sight in a grove of ash before climbing to take a look at the city itself.

At the edge of a copse of aspen began a cemetery. It extended several hundred strides to a low stone gate, and ran along the perimeter of the crater like an outer circle of defense. *Or warning,* Tahn thought.

They stepped over markers set squarely on the ground and walked around stone tombs erected like small bathhouses. The line of shadow falling across the city seemed to move faster as the day came to a close. In only moments, Tahn watched that line of darkness move up the eastern cliff. The sense that the sun had opted to climb from this monstrous hole in the ground would not let Tahn alone. He and Sutter found themselves picking their way more slowly across the graves. Untended grass bristled around their feet, the peculiar smell of uneven earth and leaning stones accompanying the fragrances of night-blooming flowers that seemed to grow only where bodies were gathered in death.

The stridulant sound of crickets began to whir, arrythmically at first, but soon in a common pulse.

Then above it, Tahn heard a scratching.

He froze in the deepening shadow of a stone mausoleum, raising his finger to his lips to warn Sutter not to speak.

Sutter furrowed his brow and prepared to ask something. Tahn put a hand to Nails's mouth before his silence could be broken.

The scratching came again, like bare winter tree limbs blown by the wind, scrabbling against one another or scraping the side of a barn. No wind blew. And the sound came as though with human intention. Tahn nocked an arrow and Sutter slowly drew his sword. Ducking low, Tahn peered around the corner of the stone monument. Through the dark night he squinted, searching for the source of the sound.

It came again, stealing his breath. Tahn blinked sweat from his eyes, his mind fevered with images of charred earth and running rock. Through the night he saw movement. Hunched over a grave, a shadowy figure examined the writing on a marker. It gently touched the ground there, its long, thin fingers moving easily into the earth as it seemed to ponder.

A mourner?

It raised an arm against the night and then plunged it deep into the earth. The ground moved only slightly as the shape cast its arm back and forth as though searching, feeling, digging toward something. It stopped, perhaps having found the object of its desire, and pulled its arm out. The figure's cowl slid directly over the hole in the grave, and it lowered its head so close to the ground that it might have inhaled the dust of it.

There it remained still for a moment.

The form huddled but twenty strides from them, and Tahn feared that even a breath would reveal them.

Suddenly, the black figure raised both arms to the sky. Its long, thin fingers curled into knotted fists that shook in defiance as it tilted back its head and screamed in an airy hiss. Tahn's skin immediately rose in chill bumps, and his muscles weakened. His fingers and toes began to tingle and his temples pound with the beat of his own heart. He wanted to retreat back from sight, but his legs failed him. Should he move, he would surely stumble and alert the figure to his presence.

Tahn held still and waited. The tension grew interminable, and he knew that at any moment the creature would whirl around and put its knotted fist into his chest as easily as it had into the hardened earth.

Finally, the thing stood, rushing from the grave to the north. In a moment, it vanished behind a forest of grave markers. Tahn collapsed against the cool stone of the mausoleum, and pressed his face against it. Sutter whispered a question that Tahn did not hear for the rushing of blood in his own ears.

Reflexively, he traced the familiar pattern of the scar on his left hand. The shape calmed him, and slowly his breathing came under control. He remained silent for several minutes, shaking off Sutter's questioning gaze. By the time he felt it safe to speak, the light had completely drained from the sky, showing a bright tapestry of stars on a sable backdrop that ended in a wide circle where the cliffs rose against the night.

"Something," he said. "I don't know what, digging in the earth of graves." He didn't explain that the being hadn't needed to remove the dirt to pass its arm freely through solid earth.

"You should have let me see it," Sutter said, ire just under his concern.

"If you'd moved, it would have come."

"Let it," Sutter boasted. "We took down that tracker on our own."

Tahn touched the poultice still wrapped about his neck. But rather than explain that he feared this creature more than he had the tracker, he simply nodded. "Next time." He peered around the corner of the low stone gravehouse and searched carefully for any movement. Nothing. Holding an arrow half drawn, Tahn led them through the cemetery to the low retaining wall separating the earth of the dead from the abandoned city.

The first buildings they encountered were houses, most of them single-story structures. Near the walls rested a few produce baskets and water barrels, blown by winds and chewed in the mouths of rats and whatever life now occupied the dead city.

Under the cover of darkness, Tahn skulked slowly, Sutter at his side. Each gaping window, opened door, and alleyway brought him to a stop, where he expected a face or arm to sweep out of the shadows. Sutter huffed air out his nose in exasperation, but Tahn did not rush. Farther on, the buildings rose two, three, four stories, blocking more starlight and blurring the edges of the buildings in deep shadow.

"There is no point to this," Tahn whispered. "Let's bed down for the night, and leave at first light."

"As long as we find one of these grand old houses to sleep in," Sutter said. "I'll be the lord of the manor."

Tahn shook his head. "Let's get the horses."

After retrieving their mounts, they returned to the same street. Tahn pointed to a towering building on their left. Dim light showed a series of windows empty of glass or shutters. Nor did it have a door, the wood apparently gone to termites or rot.

Tahn crept inside, trying not to let his heels fall and make too much noise. Sutter stepped more noisily, but paused to produce a candle from his pack and light it. The room looked like a cavern: ceilings the height of two men, rough chunks of stone fallen from the walls, the lonely smell of dust blanketing everything. Bits of glass lay strewn near the windows. A few paintings dressed the walls, appearing to have become sepia-colored from endless days. And a handful of broken tables and chairs littered the floor in jumbled masses, broken and marred.

After hobbling the horses in an adjacent room, Tahn headed for an inner wall. There, he swept the rubble aside with his boot and sat with his back against the firm rock. Sutter sat beside him, laying his sword across his legs and exhaling tiredly.

"Is this the adventure you wanted?" Tahn whispered.

Sutter emitted a single, low chuckle. "You forget, Woodchuck, I didn't see your grave robber."

Tahn pulled his cloak tighter about him as the chill of night set in. "I'll see if he can tell me how I might bury you without arousing suspicion."

"Wouldn't do you a bit of good, Woodchuck," Sutter said, dousing the candle and closing his eyes. "I have the skills to dig myself up from the roots. Probably find myself a meal along the way."

Nails fell asleep fast, leaving Tahn with the darkness. How much more comfortable he would have been knowing Mira watched nearby. He fingered the outlines of the sticks stuffed in his cloak and wondered if the others had reached Recityv yet, wondered if they had escaped the dark clouds at the north face.

His mind turned and raced with the images and events of his life just since Northsun. He huddled against the wall, staring through the empty, darkened window at the abandoned streets. So many unfamiliar things swam in his mind and in his eyes, he soon had no power to discern if he were awake or asleep, dreaming.

His feet dragged over the harsh terrain, carving shallow furrows in the dusty trail. The height of the sun put it near the meridian. Its heat fell like the yoke of a peddler's wagon on his shoulders. No wind stirred. There was only the painfully patient smell of aging sage and earth left baking under a cruel sun. The horizon wavered with heat, blurring the dips and rises in the land.

Tahn stumbled, catching himself with his hands on the hot ground. He allowed himself to kneel and rest, raising weary, half-shut eyes to the glare of light from a pale blue sky. The firmament appeared washed and bleached and absent of clouds. Images began to turn in his vision: Pages fluttering in the wind; a woman with a child still wet from birth; seats covered with soft cushions hand-sewn with plush red fabric arranged in a series of shallow arcs facing a podium. Suddenly he felt very cold. Tahn fixed hateful eyes on the greater light.

"All your glory and still I shiver here." He breathed and saw the plume of breath that winter air might show.

"Ah, you do understand," a familiar voice said softly.

Tahn whipped around at the intrusion.

Behind him an elegant-looking man stood posed as though for a portrait. Heavy white robes hung in several layers from his shoulders, fastened at his throat with a silver pin, a ring with a small disk somehow fixed at its center. His hair hung in silken white strands, his hands nearly the same color.

"Understand what?" Tahn asked.

"You said you shiver here," the man continued. "Why are you cold, Tahn, with the perspiration of heat upon your brow? Do you choose to be cold? Do you choose to be here?" The man cast vengeful eyes in a wide scan of the world around them.

Tahn followed his stare, then brought his eyes back to the smooth skin of the stranger. "I don't know," Tahn replied.

"How pitiful," the man mocked. "Dutiful and ignorant. You are dangerous, Quillescent, but only to yourself." His eyes flared with indignation. "I am done with these games, melura! Done with the feeble antics of vain men stuffed on the power I made possible for them. Nobility? Hah. It is at an end, melura, do you understand? You may live in ignorance of what they do, a blind servant to do another's bidding, but the shadow of your ignorance freezes your blood even now. I hold the keys, melura. Your threat to me becomes more diluted every hour, every day, and with every age."

Tahn struggled to understand what the man said. But his mind slipped and failed. His skin continued to grow cold, chills raising goose bumps as the sun rose toward its zenith. Conflicting smells of warm rocks and cold fingers combined in his nose. He fell upon the ground and tried to crawl from the man's presence.

"Upon your belly will you go then, melura?" he chided. "Or shall I save you?" The man waved a hand and a small spark ignited in a dead tangle of sage roots. "The tinder will be spent in a moment. How shall you nourish the flame, boy?"

Tahn watched the flame gutter. Desperation seized him. He felt sure he would die if he could not build a fire against the cold that emanated from the man. Tahn stretched one hand toward the flame, the constriction of his muscles from the wintry air making him unable to even fully extend his arm.

"Will and Sky!" he screamed.

The man laughed harshly. "Again, child, I don't think your cry has reached as high as you'd like."

Tahn distantly heard the mocking laughter as his mind raced to the need of fueling the flame. He clutched at the rough ground, trying to pull himself forward. His fingers clawed through the dusty earth, scarcely moving him closer to the dying flame. Then a thought lit in his mind. He reached within his cloak and drew out the sticks given him by Edholm. Without hesitation, he tossed them into the small flame.

Behind him the man wailed in a triumphant laugh that shot roughly from his throat. The sound of it shimmered in the air like bright, fiery ridicule.

Tahn did not care. He watched the sticks, forgetting their hidden notes, and hoping they would catch. The bitter cold wracked his body. With brittle hands he clawed at the ground, inching closer to the fire. His limbs were turning numb, and he flapped them uselessly.

"How important they must have been," the man said through dark laughter.

Tahn tried to shout his defense. His tongue clucked, thick and numb from the cold.

The man hunkered down before him, his breath steaming in the air, though somehow the sun still shone in all its strength. "It should leave a lasting impression with you, Quillescent." He pointed to the scrivener's sticks burning coldly just beyond Tahn's grasp. "Consider it when all the secrets begin to unravel in your mind, and give you a taste of the dust you willingly race toward." The man then picked up one of the flaming pieces of wood, the fire burning him not at all. "You are no more than this stick, no more than the contents hidden up within it. . . . Just as easily cast upon the flame . . . just as easy to burn . . ."

The laughter returned as the man stood. Tahn could no longer hold up his head, collapsing, chin first, into the earth. He managed to turn over and peer up, wanting to defy the man if only in a look.

The man was gone.

Instead, Tahn looked at the sun, which still seemed to beat down upon him with punishing heat though he could not feel it. The contradictions swam in his head: the ease with which he'd sacrificed the sticks entrusted to him; the familiar landscape known to him only in his dreams; and the almost recognizable shape of a cowled face he never fully saw.

The dream ended, and Tahn awoke in the darkness beside his friend and felt for the four wood sticks tucked into his cloak. They were there. He tried to regulate his breathing, slowly pushing away the images as he focused on the emptiness around him.

"Will and Sky," he muttered, and knew he would get no sleep that night.

Tahn left Sutter sleeping and ambled through the first story of the building in search of a window facing east. Around the corner, a stair rose through

shadows into the upper levels. Gossamer threads hung between the posts supporting the dust-covered stair rail. Tahn warily climbed through successive
stories, the stairs ending after six flights and letting him out onto the roof.

Under a veil of starlight, Tahn could see the beauty of the hidden city. Its
surface rose and fell across rooftops and streets silhouetted against the outer cliff.

Tahn faced east and started to recite the names of these stars. He knew them
all like friends, friends met of necessity each morning. He couldn't remember a
time when he did not rise to see them. It was a quiet, peaceful time. Voices did
not rush to fill the silence; his thoughts could run outward without interpretation, without resistance.

Tahn remembered sitting on the front stoop with Balatin and Wendra and
trying to describe how far the sky went, the speculation soon becoming so preposterous and cumbersome that they all laughed and turned their attention to
the light-flies and songs. But there were moments, Tahn thought, when that
farthest point could almost be understood, almost glimpsed. He braced himself against a gentle breeze sweeping in from the tops of the cliffs and thought
involuntarily of dawn.

The thought surprised him, and he briefly suppressed it, longing to entertain the stillness of his reflection and the cold, silent stars. The subtle glimmer
suddenly offered a moment of hope. He peered again into the heavens and opened
his mouth to speak, but in an instant his words were lost to him. He shut his
eyes, and imagined again the image of the sun, elegantly slow as it rose into the
eastern sky, the gradual strengthening of the light an unassuming, wakeful
promise.

For a moment, in his mind, the two images dwelt together, night and day,
and Tahn thought he heard the echo of laughter from his dream.

In a panic, he flashed open his eyes and saw the stengthening light at the
eastern rim of the cliff. A wave of relief stole over him. He nodded a greeting
toward the dawn and descended the stair the way he'd come.

As Tahn reentered the room, Nails woke. "Find anything good to eat?" he
said, with a sour morning smile.

"I thought you'd dig us some roots from the graveyard," Tahn answered.
"Aren't the plants there especially tasty because of their human fertilizer?"

Sutter smiled. "No, that's around the outbuilding, Woodchuck. Graveroots
aren't crisp, they're . . . fleshy."

Tahn laughed in spite of himself. "Let's get out of here."

In the watery light of predawn, they stepped into the street. The sound of
their mounts' hooves clopped loud against the hard stone and morning silences.

"Hello, gentlemen," a voice greeted them as they cleared the door.

Sutter pulled his sword in a clumsy movement, his eyes trying to fix on the
owner of the voice.

Tahn nocked an arrow and made a full draw, bending at the waist and swinging his bow in a full circle. He could see no one.

"Those are not necessary," the voice said. "If I'd wanted to kill you, you'd be dead." A man stepped from between two of the buildings. "May I ask what brings you to Stonemount?"

Tahn considered his answer as he spied the jewel-encrusted sheath of a long curved blade hanging from the man's hip. The fellow wore brushed leather breeches and tunic, with an embroidered belt done in scarlet colors of varying hue. Gold rickrack graced the collar and cuffs of his loose white shirt. On his head he wore a tricorne hat likewise garnished with gold thread, sitting at an angle on his head. His cloak—really more of a cape—was bright red, and gave Tahn the impression that the man cared more for fashion than warmth.

"Come now," the man insisted, "cease your careful scrutiny of my sword and answer my question." He spoke with a merry expression on his face, as though the things he said were of no consequence at all, things charming and lightly conversational.

"I know you crossed the Lesule on the Ophal're'Donn Bridge; I heard your shout in the Canyon of Choruses. You're not men of the valley, or you'd never have set foot upon it. And I don't take you for trophy hunters, because you brought no cart." All the while the man's face remained jolly, unconcerned.

Tahn listened intently. He relaxed his draw and dropped his aim to the ground. He started to speak when Sutter chimed in. "We're adventurers!"

"On our way to Recityv. We're just passing through," Tahn amended.

"But a grand place to pass through," Sutter added honestly.

The stranger seemed to like Sutter's response better. "Grand, indeed," he echoed.

"Abandoned by its residents by the looks of it. And some years ago if I'm not mistaken." Sutter removed a waterskin from his horse and took a draught from it, then offered the stranger a pull.

"No, my young friend. But thank you all the same."

Sutter corked the skin and refastened it to his saddle.

Tahn put away his arrow and took tentative steps forward. "May I ask what business brings *you* here?"

"I am an archivist and historian, good fellow," the stranger replied with enthusiasm. "Where else should I be?"

"In a school or library?" Sutter retorted, appropriating the grin the man wore so ceaselessly.

The other's waxen smile dipped, but only for a moment. "Fah, not so. This is my school. This is the place to find what matters." The stranger turned a wry look on them both.

"Not for us," Tahn corrected. "We're on our way *through*."

"Well, into the city we'll go, then," the stranger said. "I to record and discover, you to find your way through. And while we go, we will talk of what matters: fallen cities, long journeys, eating, drinking, aches of the body and the mind, life and breath, and new friendships . . . wonderful unions."

Tahn thought he heard some second meaning to "wonderful unions," and put another arm's distance between himself and the stranger. "We don't have much time to waste," Tahn interrupted.

The man's friendly smile finally waned. "You do if you want to leave Stonemount, my new friend."

Sutter drew his sword again.

"Hold there," the man exclaimed in a calm but commanding voice. "All I'm saying is that you cannot exit the way you have come. The wards in the Canyon of Choruses will prevent egress." He indicated the deep chasm through which Tahn and Sutter had entered Stonemount. "There is but one other passage beyond these walls. And energetic as you are, you are not likely to find it alone." His smile returned. "Come with me and all your better deeds I'll add to my histories. Then away you'll go to continue your adventure."

Sutter slowly sheathed his sword. Tahn leveled his eyes at the man, realizing that he had not yet offered his name. But neither had he asked for theirs. Tahn let it lie there for the moment as they silently agreed to the man's offer.

The city itself rose like a grand mausoleum built up over centuries for an entire people to sleep their last.

The light strengthened on the eastern rim of the cliffs that encircled the city, bathing the walls and immense towers in bluish hues. In the dawn of another day, the city felt safe, protected.

"A marvel of engineering," the stranger was saying. "Everything you see was sculpted, erected, and fashioned by the hands of the Stonemounts. An industrious people, gifted as few in the raising of stone to art." The man scanned the city with appreciative eyes. "It is a shame they are no more."

"And why is that?" Tahn asked.

"Because," he said, immediately, "it is rare to see a place so committed to the aesthetic of the entire city. Tell me, where do you come from?"

Sutter shot a guarded look at Tahn, forcing his friend to pause as he considered a response.

"Keep your secret," the man said before Tahn could come up with a lie. "But answer me this, in your homeland is every house, shop, and stable of equal beauty despite its size? There is no revelation in answering that, is there?"

"No," Tahn replied. "Each is as decent as its owner can afford."

"The equality of selfishness," the man retorted.

"No one goes without," Tahn argued. "The land is bountiful and hard work earns each his place."

"Then you were content with your life there," the man pressed, his gait unflagging as he strode through the city.

"Yes," Tahn said, anger rising in him. "I have a good life there."

"I see, and that is why you left that place to seek adventure." Tahn caught a glimpse of the man's cheek and saw a wry smile drawing up his lips. Before Tahn could counter, the man went on.

"Don't be angry. Your home, I'm sure, is very nice. But look there." He pointed behind them to the first distant outbuilding near the barrows. "Even these are raised with careful splendor, wouldn't you agree?"

The man was right. No sign existed of an underclass here. Smaller buildings at the edge of the city had been given the same care in design as the towering structures that rose near the city's center.

Tahn raised his eyes now and saw the sun striking the immense gables and beautiful archways that joined the high buildings hundreds of strides up. In the distance they looked like flags unfurled from parapets into these man-made canyons of stone. Despite the wear of time and cracks creeping into the walls, the symmetry mesmerized him.

"Makes you wonder why they left," the man said, following Tahn's gaze.

"They left?" Sutter remarked, incredulous.

"It is the fodder for scholars, and theories abound. I, of course, have my own." He paused dramatically. "I believe they found a harmony between death and life, like the circle of stone that surrounds the city. They found a way *past* death, past *life*."

Tahn raised his brows at Sutter, as everyone did when Liefel "Smooth Hands"—the great mooch and braggart—told his incredible stories at North-sun Festival. Sutter smiled back as he ambled beside him.

"I intend to find it," the man said so quietly that Tahn was not sure he heard him correctly. The words sounded like a secret uttered in the shadow of a dying tree.

As they walked, they fell into a comfortable silence. The heights of the surrounding buildings reminded Tahn of the narrow canyon they'd entered at the river. Deep into the rivers of sky, bridges bisected slivers of blue, arcing like limbs from tree to tree. High up, wind whistled thinly around the corners of the edifices. Occasionally, a bird took flight from the landing of a portico set high off the street. It might have struck Tahn as a lonely sound, mournful perhaps, the burring of wind across a grave marker like those encircling Stonemount. But this wind coursed through a monolithic city that was itself one immense testimony to life gone by. Regardless of the city's vacancy, Tahn felt oddly at home.

Around a corner, they suddenly were in an expansive square ringed with water fountains now home to accumulated drifts of wind-borne dust and dried leaves. From each fountain ran a tributary channel downward to a great fountain at the square center. All the empty pools were recessed into the ground, so that the water might have lapped near a person's toes as he stood to appreciate the mists it produced.

Tahn walked close to one fountain. A large bowl stood poised atop the back of a large, granite-sculpted man, the musculature of the figure still evident in the skillfully textured work of the sculptor. Around the perimeter of the great square stood several such statues, each facing the fountain at the center, their eyes peering along the channels that fed the central fountain. Tahn followed a channel, forgetting the stranger as he passed him by.

The channel emptied into a deeper basin. On one side, a set of stairs descended into the fountain.

"Grace and utility," the stranger said. His face appeared in conflict, admiration contending with envy. The struggle twisted his smile in a horrible line. "This is where they were sanctified. Where they completed their journey."

The man's words disquieted Tahn, despite the beauty being described. He didn't care about this lost city-nation anymore. He and Sutter had concerns of their own. They had to get to Recityv. Wendra would be worried sick, if she was not in need of help herself. Tahn subtly placed a hand on the sticks hidden within his cloak. There were other reasons to hurry, as well.

Tahn refocused on the man. "How do we find our way out of this place?"

The man did not look away from the fountains. "What, so quick to leave so remarkable a place?" A wry grin spread on his lips as he finally turned to marvel at the immensity of the palaces and towering stone edifices that faced the great square. "What adventurers you are proving to be, young friends."

"Will you help us, or not?"

Unsmiling, the man pointed to the northeast. "Between those two towers."

Several towers rose to the north, spires reaching skyward. Tahn could see away to the cliffs, a morning haze in the air washing the crisp edges that touched the sky. But he didn't immediately see.

The stranger pointed once more.

Then Tahn spotted the towers. Each rose with prim majesty from an edifice several blocks away, a stone staircase on the outer wall of both towers spiraling toward the top. A narrow bridge passed between them near the pinnacle. Just under the footpath, Tahn thought he could see a dark, vertical line in the distant cliff wall obscured by the haze.

"Must be a gap like the Canyon of Choruses, huh?" Sutter remarked.

"Indeed," the man said. "But it is a great deal more difficult to find than it appears. The streets in that direction are not square, and the cemetery there is less . . . habitable."

Something in the way the man used the word *habitable* was unsettling.

"We'll just follow the rim around until we come to a break in the cliff," Tahn stated matter-of-factly. "We should be able to reach it well before dark."

"And so your eyes would deceive you." The stranger stared at both Tahn and Sutter. "The envy of the outside world forced the Stonemount people to protect themselves. In the west there is the Canyon of Choruses. In the north"—he looked again to the dark line between the towers—"the canyon is bordered by wild growth. People here learned to navigate the wilds, but foreigners often found their final earth early by trying to pass through them without a guide." He turned a mirthful eye on Tahn.

"Don't tell us: you know the way through these wilds."

• CHAPTER FORTY-FIVE •

Ta'Opin

Jastail and Penit rode side-by-side ahead of Wendra. The highwayman had astutely discovered that if he kept control of Penit, he controlled her. At times he spoke in avuncular tones to the boy, at other times as though they might be brothers, giving advice and smiling over the lad's imperfect knowledge. Penit seemed just young enough to forget their circumstances and lose himself in conversation with an adult. Wendra stewed in her anger over Jastail's easy manipulation of the youngster. Once, he even patted Penit's shoulder, the boy laughing at some comment. Wendra's heart was gladdened to witness Penit's resilience, but the dirty hands of the trader on Penit forced her to close her eyes and hum the discordant strains chiming in her head.

Colors swirled in her vision. She could feel blood coursing through the veins at her temples. She could hear the blood coming in rushes like the reprise of a song, ebbing and flowing with regret and violence as each beat of her heart pushed it along. When she opened her eyes again, Penit and Jastail were looking back over their shoulders at her, curious looks on their faces. She hadn't thought she'd been loud enough to be heard. She ignored their looks and fought for balance as the fading harmonies of rhythmic sound, like strings being plucked by calloused fingers, brought tears to her eyes. They were not the peaceful tunes of her childhood, or her box, and she couldn't remember their melody, only the rough feel of them on her tongue and the image of broken glass on cellar floors.

After that, Jastail did not speak as often to Penit, nor did he put his hands on him. But he continued to keep the boy close, even when they stopped to rest and eat.

Near meridian of the second day, they came to a road that stretched north and south.

"We'll use the road," Jastail said. "But keep your wits about you. The road is filled with travelers whose business it is to deceive. Don't let them know anything about you, or you're likely to wind up dead." He looked at Penit when he spoke, but clearly meant his words for Wendra, too. He turned north and kicked his horse into an easy canter.

They passed a few homes. Wendra badly wanted to make a break for safety among those strangers. But each time, the people they saw remained silent and distant, their eyes following them from behind window glass or over the backs of standing cattle. Others turned their own backs to them in counterfeit gestures of labor, while searching from the corners of their eyes as Jastail and Penit passed by.

Farther on, at a fork in the road, Jastail called them to a stop, surveying each direction. Finally, he led them fifty strides from the intersection and asked Penit to build a fire. The boy eagerly took to the task.

"Not concerned about your fellow tradesmen pursuing us anymore?" Wendra asked as Jastail took a seat on a flat rock.

The highwayman smiled. "They'll wait their chance upon me. For now, they will return to their trading." He carved a slice of cheese. "When we meet again, they'll remember what their efforts earned them, and I will be wealthy enough to have them whipped for harboring ill thoughts of me."

Wendra looked for Penit, who bent gathering sticks near a copse of alder a stone's throw away. "There's no mystery in you," Wendra said, seething. "I have saved your life more than once and for it I must watch the boy learn to trust a salter's hand. You don't live to build wealth; the shine of a copper has long since lost its luster for you."

"Ah, but remember that each time you helped me you also helped yourself." Jastail took another slice of cheese and looked away with a studious gaze. "The irony is striking, don't you think, that by helping me you preserve your life, which also helps me? It is true charity, thank you."

Wendra clenched her teeth and a flush of heat raced through her body. "Keep your thanks to yourself. Do you think I will not find a way to escape—"

"And shatter poor Penit's illusions," Jastail interrupted, a wry look upon his face.

"You are a fool to be so confident."

Still smiling, he said glibly, "And you are a lovely woman far from home whose views of the world and its people are not useful beyond the limits of the most rural town. And maybe not even there." Jastail scrubbed at his beard and motioned toward the trees and sky. "A different season turns now, and the covenants of the early fathers no longer apply to us, if they ever did. Dear lady, you may be right about my waning desire for coin, and any man is grateful to the hand of his rescuer, but it ends there." His tone became serious. "A day ago you asked about the book I read. Well, let me tell you, line and verse it opens a spyglass to the farthest reaches of what man is. And where the lens blurs on too distant an object . . . there, there is where I long to be. To know what I am capable of . . ."

Jastail looked into the distance, recalling the words from the poem.

> *The bird that uses wings only to gather insects,*
> *No matter how finely plumed,*
> *Is a meaningless creature.*
> *The horse that uses hardy legs*
> *To but pull a plow through the soil,*
> *Is a meal waiting to be prepared.*
> *What then of man, so noble in reason, fine in particulars, crafty with wit,*
> *Who rests his body and rises again at dawn to weed a furrow,*
> *Draw a mug, or argue over the shifting of a line upon a map?*
> *How lesser is he, to have been endowed with such capability*
> *And yet negotiate each breath to the breeding of yet another man,*
> *Who will but eat and drink and argue until his own rest is come.*

Jastail's smile returned. "So now you have it . . . the all of me."

"Bitter words for a poet."

"The truth always sounds bitter to an unfamiliar ear." Jastail put his cheese away and pointed at Penit. "It is forgivable in the boy, but you'd do better to understand the poem."

Wendra regarded Penit for a long moment. "I understand it well enough," she asserted, still watching Penit. "They are a coward's words, written with his own grave at the back of his mind. Some men come to nothing because they aspire to nothing."

"And this is how you value an author?" Jastail said, interest arching his brows.

"No," she said sharply. "It is pity for one who thinks so little of his own contribution that he must do as the starling and soil his home for those that come after him." She directed a searching look at Jastail. "Is this really all of you? Are you like the maker of your poem? Perhaps that is why you drag the boy and me toward some hidden destination. You are the starling soiling the nest by killing or corrupting a woman and child."

Jastail did not reply, but stared at Wendra. She returned his gaze with equal measures of hate and empathy. She did not know if she believed what she had said, but it eased her mind and satisfied her sense of justice to insult him using something he cared about, as Jastail had done to her in using Penit as leverage.

"No words from the apprentice wordsmith," Wendra finally said. "Your wisest choice in a week's time."

Jastail stood and positioned himself between Wendra and Penit, who was now coming back with an armload of dry firewood. "You have a sharp tongue and clever mind, but on the highroads away from the walls of your cozy home, there is an immutable truth. Everything may be bought and sold, and what is not can be taken if you are willing to risk." The corners of his mouth dropped to the utter look of apathy she hated so much. "For all your clever words, you will do what I say because the risk for you"—he nodded subtly back toward Penit—"is too great. And when our verse is written, dear Anais, you will be a notation writ in small script, and that will be a good deal more than the grave marker will say."

Wendra opened her mouth to respond, but just then Penit returned. She closed her mouth with a sour smile to cover the comment she'd intended to make. Jastail grinned a mouthful of smiling teeth, and took some of the load from Penit's arms.

Staggered clouds floated high in an otherwise clear sky turned russet with dusk. Wendra saw to her horse, taking her music box from her satchel and gripping it tightly. She would not play it, for fear Jastail would have something to say about it, but holding it was enough. She heard the tune in her mind and watched the fire-colored sky give way to violet hues as Penit helped Jastail feed the fire. Soon, the crackle of burning wood echoing behind them accompanied their voices like ghosts in the dark beyond the horses.

She wondered if the others would find her, or she them. And if so, would it be in time to escape what Jastail had planned for her and Penit? He used people the way his poets used their words, each stroke carefully placed, each word just the right choice to carry off the intended meaning. Her head ached with the constant effort of sorting things out, tracing her steps since the High Plains and wondering how she came here.

The sound of metal clanking drew her from the dark thoughts. To the east, toward the road, she could see two lanterns swaying with the gentle motion of a large wagon. By turns, the lanterns struck the sides of the cart, causing a dull, tinny *whop* in the night. The slow clopping of hooves came next, and then the sound of song, evenly measured and hummed low in the chest of a large man.

Before she could think, Jastail was beside her. "On the highroads it is unwritten grace to share a man's fire and offer him a cup of tea. He'll have seen our fire, and he's made no secret of his presence on the road. When he comes, remember all that I have said. He may be yet a rougher man than I, and you may be glad of my company. Or he may be more your suit." Jastail sniffed. "But even if I am taken down, you may be sure I won't go down alone. And you know where my first strike will go."

Wendra marveled still at the indifferent timbre in Jastail's voice. "Would you sooner we die than let us go free?"

"I would sooner you keep your manner as cordial as when we first met in the shadow of the north face," Jastail said. She could not see his eyes, but he had already affected the charm that had first allayed her fears of him. He wore a different face as easily as a player wore a mask.

The wagon creaked to a stop at the crossroads. "Hail there," a voice called.

"And you, traveler," Jastail said in a raised voice. "Come off the road and share our fire."

Penit left the fire and jumped through the high brush toward the wagon as it turned from the well-worn ruts. As the stranger came, Wendra regarded Jastail's handsome profile silhouetted against the firelight behind him. She thought how strange—and deviously useful—a face he had, to show apathy in one moment and to be striking in its strength and affected good-nature the next.

The horses' muzzles emerged from the darkness into the dim glow of the flame, their backs already striped by the glare of the wagon lanterns. Their tack and harnesses jangled and yawed until the driver pulled them to a stop and tied the reins down to the hitch. A tall man with a deep chest hopped spryly to the ground. His buckle gleamed in the flicker of the firelight, but his face remained obscured until he came close. Nearer, Wendra realized the man was Tilatian— one of the dark-skinned peoples out of the east. Some of Ogea's stories hinted that the Tilatians were Inveterae, once confined to the Bourne; though Ogea thought that particular bit of wisdom to be nothing more than a myth.

And though Wendra had never seen a Tilatian, the real shock came when she realized the man had shaved every last bit of hair from his head and face and wore no tunic; he was not simply Tilatian, and not a man at all, but Ta'Opin—a race within a race, as Ogea would have said. If Tilatians were uncommon, the Ta'Opin were rare, perhaps mythical. The Ta'Opin were rumored to live six generations, and to end their days with a strange madness, such that most took their own lives before the dementia beset them.

The shock of seeing one of the Ta'Opin made Wendra forget Jastail, who strode confidently past her and put out his hand.

"Off of the road when greater light has failed, share our tea." Jastail said it with a strange rhythm. It carried the sound of a routine greeting.

"And a tale when our tobaccom is lit," the other replied as if by rote.

They clasped hands, and Wendra wondered if she could communicate her predicament to the man without alerting Jastail. As the two approached the fire, Penit flitting about their legs like a light-fly, Wendra put her box away and joined them.

Jastail produced two tin cups and poured steaming tea into each. He handed one to the traveler. "What name do you carry across the highroads?" Jastail said, settling himself again on his rock.

"Seanbea," he answered, and sipped his tea. "Thank you for the tidings. Not every fire near the road is the welcome it used to be."

"Truer words were never spoken," Jastail said, nodding. He pointed his cup of tea at Penit. "This is Penit, a fine young man I'm escorting to Recityv to run in the Lesher Roon." He raised his other hand with his open palm up. "I am Jastail. And this is Lani," he said as Wendra came into the circle near the fire.

The Ta'Opin stood and bowed slightly at the waist. The deferential gesture took Wendra by surprise. It struck her as strange but pleasing to see a wagoneer so far from the trappings of society perform such a simple but genuine acknowledgment. Perhaps he would be just the one to help her and Penit get free of Jastail. She nodded in return and sat on a fallen log next to the boy. She nudged him subtly with her elbow.

"I meant to tell you," Penit whispered. "Jastail told me about it today. The Lesher Roon is a race with a great prize. And we need to go to Recityv anyway, right?"

Had the boy become so completely blind to the highwayman's manipulation?

Jastail cleared his throat with the obvious intention of ending their exchange. "Have a seat," he invited the Ta'Opin. Seanbea sat directly on the ground close to the fire and drank his tea. "You drive your horses late," Jastail said over his own cup.

"And would have gone on another hour or two if you'd not welcomed me to warm my hands," Seanbea replied.

"What makes a man brave the roads at night, and without protection?" Jastail said, refreshing his own cup of tea.

"I go myself to Recityv. And my haul is awaited." Seanbea put his cup out to be refilled, and spoke as Jastail filled it to the brim. "But it is hardly a bounty for the highwayman: music instruments and census records, collected for Descant Cathedral."

Descant! Wendra remembered the name from her fevers. She looked away at the wagon; its load had been tied down with thick cords. What accompanying instruments might he be freighting?

The Ta'Opin went on. "The instruments are old, serviceable maybe, but only to the hand that remembers how to play them. Your man around town wouldn't have any idea how to go about it with any of these. As for the rest, moldy parchments and rotted books, little to interest a thief."

"Still, to ride alone is risky," Jastail commented as he settled himself comfortably with his mug.

"Right you are," the wagoneer agreed. "But an escort would draw attention to my parcels, and really, it isn't the kind of haul that needs extra riders. Besides, the legends of my people make average men wary, and dull men faint of heart." He snickered. "And it is my good luck that a smart man rarely takes to the road to earn his fortune."

Wendra gave Jastail a vindicated look.

Returning her expression, Jastail spoke, his pleasant demeanor undisturbed. "To your good luck," Jastail said, raising his cup in a toast. "Luck to have found us, and not the kinds of men you describe." Wendra despised the way the highwayman relished the irony that the Ta'Opin could not appreciate.

Jastail then proffered his cup toward both Penit and Wendra. The boy giggled a bit, and Wendra forced herself to hold the semblance of a smile on her face. Seanbea followed Jastail's lead, and hummed a few happy notes as he took another drink of his tea. A comfortable silence settled over them for a few moments. Finally, Wendra could restrain her curiosity no longer.

"Tell me of Descant Cathedral." She tried to speak evenly to disguise her interest, but she could scarcely contain her desire to hear more of this place of which the white-haired man had spoken during her days in the cave; a place she was amazed to learn was real.

Wendra immediately sensed Jastail's anger; it emanated from him like a palpable wave. But he couldn't know what her inquiry meant, so she ignored him.

"Ah, Descant, it is a grand place . . . or was," Seanbea said. "There was a time when it was the pearl of Recityv, the very reason for it, if you can believe it. The city itself lived for the music they wrote and performed there. It became the heartbeat of Recityv, of all of Vohnce. Children like young Penit here were entrusted to the Maesteri, who would teach the prodigies who lived among them to study and learn the art and passion of song."

The Ta'Opin stood. "Its spires rise above vaulted ceilings." He pointed into the sky as though he could see them even now. "Brass cupolas that once blazed like fire in the sun, now colored by rain, dress the cathedral like green crowns." He stared a moment, then dropped his gaze, as if looking at the street-level memory of the cathedral in his mind. "Its stone walls are dark now, and many of its colored-glass windows are boarded against vandals. It lies in the old district of Recityv, where rent is cheap and boarding houses stand next to brothels for convenience. The stench of goat pens can be smelled from the steps to its iron doors. These days it is more of a museum than a place of study."

Wendra could see the affinity the Ta'Opin had for the cathedral. He wore it plainly even when he described the ruin it seemed to have come to. "You've been there, then?"

"Been there, lady?" Seanbea said with good-natured incredulity. "I sang there, more than once." He sat again, draining his tea in a gulp.

Penit's face glowed with the thoughts Seanbea's words must have created in his mind. "I've done the skits in many cities," Penit said. "But never in Recityv."

The wagoneer looked across the fire at Penit. "You're a player?"

"For a while," Penit answered. "But only on the pageant wagons, never in the theater houses."

"All the same," Seanbea said, beaming. "What a chance meeting is this: A child of the stage, a brother to give me haven at his fire, and a woman—"

"Indeed," Jastail cut in. "But we have traveled long today and I think—"

"We should travel together," Wendra suggested over Jastail's attempt to put an end to their camaraderie. "We are faster on the horses than your wagon, so we can keep your pace, and it would be a blessing to hear you sing, Seanbea."

"I don't see why not," the Ta'Opin answered.

"No." Jastail spoke harshly. The edge in his voice silenced them all. She turned on him and found him glaring at her. The searing stare lasted a long moment. When Jastail realized he'd momentarily dropped his facade, the anger melted from his face. "My apologies," he said. "We *are* going to Recityv, but we must stop at a friend's. That will take us a day off the trail. I don't suppose you can spare the time, my friend. Though I, too, would have liked to hear you sing."

The Ta'Opin held an affable expression on his face, but Wendra thought she saw concern in the set of his jaw. He took a lingering look at Penit and then at Wendra before looking back at Jastail. "I cannot, you are right."

"A shame," Jastail said, his control reestablished. He offered his cup to Wendra, and she fought the urge to push it back into his face.

"I've no stomach for it," she hissed through clenched teeth.

I could snatch the boy and dash to Seanbea's wagon. Surely he would defend us against Jastail. He is a good man.

The thoughts pushed her to her feet, and she carefully eyed Penit, who looked wistfully at the two men, his elbows propped on his knees and his head held in his hands. She took half a step toward the boy, but then Jastail rose to his feet and cut in front of her. He took a quick seat next to Penit and wrapped an arm around him.

"We think Penit's going to win that race," Jastail said. He turned to the boy, his fingers riffling Penit's hair. "Isn't that right?"

Penit smiled, slightly embarrassed, then put his own arm around Jastail's waist.

"He's your boy, then?" Seanbea said, careful eyes studying them.

Wendra knew Jastail would register the curious way the Ta'Opin eyed them as he asked. And she suddenly feared for Seanbea.

I'd hoped he could rescue us, and now I may have to rescue him.

"Not my son," Jastail said.

A pained expression tore the smile from Penit's lips.

"Closer than that," Jastail added quickly. "We're like brothers, right?"

Penit nodded, but Wendra thought the boy looked as though he was still reeling from the powerful shift in emotions that swept through him.

The Ta'Opin looked at Wendra. "Then you—"

"Will you sing with me?" she broke in.

Seanbea's confusion seemed plain. He slowly shrugged his massive shoulders. Wendra could not bear the feigned closeness Jastail used to inspire respect in Penit and turned away from them when she went and sat near the Ta'Opin to sing.

"What shall it be?" she asked.

" 'The River Runs Long'?" the Ta'Opin suggested in a distracted tone.

She could see that behind his eyes he still worked at the problem of the relationships among the three. Jastail may have claimed closeness to Penit, but by virtue of what? And Wendra had not explained her affinity for Penit. She could tell it had raised questions in the Ta'Opin's mind, and where Wendra had thought he might be able to rescue them from Jastail, she now simply hoped Seanbea would safely ride his wagon away.

"I don't know it," Wendra said, "but sing it through once, and I'll join you."

Seanbea eyed her, then looked back over his wagonload once before putting his cup aside and clearing his throat. She heard a deep hum in his chest, like water on a whetstone to prepare it for use. Then suddenly, the concern that had tensed his jaw relaxed and the Ta'Opin began to sing. The melody settled low around them, as though hugging the earth and rising only as far as their ankles. It came softly, and soothed out in legato strains that flowed effortlessly from his throat. Wendra heard the refinement in his voice, the sweet richness and clear call of each phrase. He sang slowly, allowing each note a life of its own. After but a moment, Seanbea shut his eyes and followed the song where it led him.

Across the fire, Wendra glanced briefly to see Penit paying rapt attention, a smile of wonderment lifting his cheeks and arching his eyebrows. Jastail listened, too, but the deep resonance seemed to capture something different in him, leaving the highwayman to stare at things he alone seemed to see. The blank look of indifference she'd learned to hate in him hung heavy in his lids, drawing the lines at his mouth taut in an expression that bordered on sadness.

The melody slowly rose, coaxed by brighter tones from Seanbea's voice. The tune quickened and in her mind Wendra could see the river for which the tune was named. She could almost feel its current, visit its shores, and see the world reflected in its smooth surface. The melody did not inspire dance, but filled Wendra with a kind of hope. Not for herself exactly, but in general, the way spring brought hope after a cruel winter.

Seanbea moved into an elegant passage of music, calls from one voice in the song's story and responses from a second voice. The first rose like simple questions, a child's questions about the river and where it led, to be answered by the second voice in a deep register, the voice of experience, of a parent, teaching the child the beauties and dangers and destination of the water's path.

Abruptly, Wendra's mind flooded with the image of a Bar'dyn standing over her, coaxing her unborn baby from her womb. The thick smell of copper filled her nose as she saw again the wide, unsmiling face of the Quietgiven standing at the foot of her birthing bed and seeing her exposed womanhood. She reeled with the memory of her home and the distorted look of everything through tortured eyes. She listened to her own unanswered cries for Tahn to come to her defense.

Seanbea's song went on, growing lightsome in the sharing between a parent and child of such a simple wonder as a river, discovery recurring in each question and answer, simple truths revealed to the child's mind. But every note in the Ta'opin's song made Wendra's remembrance more vivid. The beauty of the melody ached inside her, reminding her of the child she lost to the rain and night, but also showing the hope inherent in birth.

Then her own mouth opened as though separate from her, and Wendra began to sing. Seanbea's song repeated with new questions, new answers, and deeper metaphors for the river. As he went on, Wendra wove her own harmonies of aching beauty to his lines. She sang without anticipating what she would sing next. Distantly, she was aware of Seanbea turning to look at her. But she sang past him, giving voice to the single cruelest moment of her life. Her lament rose up in a long echo like a loon's call at dusk.

The image changed then, and in the Ta'Opin's song-fashioned world the skies emptied rain into the river, somehow further darkening Wendra's countermelody. She lifted her song higher, but softer, a delicate huskiness edging the timbre of her voice. She'd never sung like this before, but it seemed right.

The Ta'Opin's melody sank to a whisper, falling to his deepest register, holding long notes with open lips to keep the river running while Wendra wove her dark tale above it. The rush and rasp in her throat sputtered and dipped like an injured bird, falling toward the river mud of Seanbea's vision. And when she thought her song was ended, when she thought giving voice to the pain of losing her child might close her throat, a crescendo of song filled her chest, and reached a height of pitch and pain she'd never imagined. Seanbea followed, in perfect time. Wendra's chest vibrated with the powerful basso of his voice. But she ascended higher, a clear, piercing note rising and turning in melodic groups until the moment of her loss became as real as this moment by the fire.

She sustained the note, the sound of it pounding in her head, making her aware of every beat of her heart, while she felt the explosive power of Seanbea's pulsing rhythm beneath. Then she stopped; Seanbea likewise ceased his song, anticipating the moment as though they'd rehearsed the duet. The brutal memory departed instantly. And she sat next to the Ta'Opin, listening to the echo of their final notes into the alder and out upon the hard roads that had brought them both here.

When the sound was gone, and all that could be heard was the fire, she looked at Seanbea and saw anguish in his face like that of a father agonizing over a lost son. Had he seen what she saw?

She glanced quickly at Penit, relieved that the awe in his face remained. But she did not meet Jastail's gaze. Quietly, she stood on weak legs and left the circle of fire.

• CHAPTER FORTY-SIX •

Hidden Jewels

The regent slid through the shadows in a seamy section of Recityv. Fires burned openly in the alleys, and animals lapped at spilled bitter and nosed through refuse on the ground. Here, a woman on the street past dark hour had but two intentions, and Helaina had come alone; walking without purpose would solicit invitations.

She held her shawl up over her face to guard against being recognized. She'd risked her visit to Descant Cathedral because so much had been put in motion, and there remained at least one more thing to do.

The cathedral had once rivaled Solath Mahnus as the jewel of Recityv. Its marble gables and towering vaults had risen at the same time as the palace and courts. Now it lay surrounded by a rough working class that took no delight in, or even noticed, its splendor. And the coarser among them tended to vandalize or deface the cathedral such that heavy boards had been secured against the lower windows, and its base showed the stain of men who stood against it to urinate.

All this in her own time, when the league proclaimed that civility had rescued them from the superstition and myths of the past. Free of such *burdens,* apparently men's civility amounted to pissing wherever they pleased.

Even on the symbols of things they once held dear.

The regent ascended the Descant steps and quietly knocked. A moment later, the door cracked open wide enough for a pair of eyes to see, and surprise lit the doorman's eyes when Helaina lowered her shawl to reveal her face. He immediately stood back and motioned her inside.

The door shut smartly behind her. "I wish to see Belamae."

Helaina's use of the Maesteri's true name startled the doorman. He would not have heard it often used. But the musician-composer and she were friends since their childhood, and she could think of him in no other terms.

"Of course, my Lady." The man bustled ahead, retreating into the dim halls of the cathedral. The regent followed.

She registered the distant sound of song, like a hum emanating from the marble pillars themselves. Among the things she must discuss with her old friend, this song was the most important.

The doorman led her beneath great vaulted celings until they came to an unremarkable door. The man knocked and bowed as he stepped back. Shortly the door opened, and her old friend with his blazing white hair offered his wide smile in greeting before wrapping Helaina in a firm embrace.

"You don't come to see me often enough," Belamae said.

"Nor you me," Helaina countered. "But mine is the greater sin; your cathedral is a more pleasant place to spend an afternoon."

"Yet you have come after dark hour, choosing secrecy for your visit. I think I may not like what you have come to discuss." Belamae nodded in satisfaction to the doorman and sent the man away.

Together, Helaina and Belamae went into his brightly lit office and took chairs beside each other before a cold hearth. She relaxed back into the leather, made for comfort and not ceremony—a fine treat. And for a brief time, she closed her eyes, concentrating on the distant hum, before coming to her purpose; she needed a soothed heart. The requests that she carried with her were heavy, indeed.

Moments later, Belamae said, "You've come about the Song of Suffering."

The regent sighed, then nodded. "There are rumors, Belamae, and if they are true, there is likely only one cause. I know you will not lie to me, and I need to know the truth."

The Maesteri patted her knee, then stood and went to his music stand. There he fingered several sheets of parchment. He gathered them into a pile and sat once more. "I read it every day." He handed the sheets to Helaina.

She took them in hand. "What is it?"

"The music that accompanies the words of the Tract of Desolation." He sat back into his chair. "I do not sing the notes. That is left for the Lieholan in the Chamber of Anthems. But I review it in my mind. It gives me some comfort to do it."

"The tract is safe?" It was not truly a question.

"I would have come to you if it was not," Belamae said.

Helaina grew thoughtful. "How long have you been its steward, my friend? Since long before I became regent, I think."

Belamae laughed warmly. "I hadn't even had my own Change. And I sang the Song for twenty years before I began to teach."

"Responsibilities fall too much these days to the young." The regent looked into the flameless hearth.

"If I recall, you were rather young when you were called to be regent," Belamae said. When she looked up again at him, he was smiling. "Daughter of the wealthiest merchant family in Recityv, a year, maybe two, beyond your own Change, when the commerce guilds asked you to represent them on the High Council. What was it, a year later when you took the regent's seat? We were both young once," the Maesteri said, wistfully, "both making far-reaching decisions at a tender age."

Helaina nodded, thinking that she was here now, at a not-so-tender age, with more far-reaching decisions to share. "I have called for a running of the Lesher Roon."

"That is what I hear," Belamae replied. "You're filling your table in preparation for the convocation. It is wise to do so. Is that why you have come? You'd like me to sit again on your council?"

"That is only part of it, but yes."

"The others do not accord the opinions of the Maesteri much consideration, but I will return to my seat there if you wish it." Belamae patted her knee again. "So now I must tell you the truth about these rumors. There is word of Quiet in the land again, yes? That is at the heart of it."

Helaina nodded.

"Then I will tell you that I believe it is true." The Maesteri uttered a weary sigh, and scrubbed his woolly brows. "The Leiholan are tired. There are few of them left, Helaina. The gift to create with song does not come as often to the family of man as it once did. I have less than a dozen who can sing the Song of Suffering, and they are mostly young and inexperienced. You know the song is long—the entire Tract of Desolation sung without pause takes seven hours, and it must be sung constantly. One Leiholan rests a full day after performing it."

"Belamae," Helaina said, staring at him straight, "do they falter?"

Her old friend looked back. "Some days, yes."

Empathy swelled in her for the keeper of the tract, even as utter dread gripped her. "Then the veil weakens, and the Quiet slips through."

Belamae said nothing.

Helaina handed back the parchments. She did not blame her old friend. The gift of Leiholan was rare to begin with. And not all who possessed the ability to create with song could even learn the Song of Suffering. Fewer still could endure singing of the horror described in the Tract of Desolation. The act of singing it took a heavy toll on the Forda of the one who sang. In some ways, it was remarkable that there were even a handful who could do so.

And now, this last bulwark against the Quiet, hidden among the rags and filth of Recityv, had begun to fail. The Song kept the veil in place. Without it, the veil would fall.

"It is time," Helaina finally said, breaking the ominous stillness that had settled around them.

The Maesteri met her confident gaze.

"Time for what, Helaina?"

She cleared her throat and spoke as the iron hand. "I have recalled the Convocation of Seats. Suitors with dangerous ambition flood our gates, looking for position and alliances. This will take time. And the League has its own agenda. I have instructed General Van Steward to begin recruiting to build his army. But now . . ." She paused, taking her own fear in hand. "Now the veil, our best defense against the Quiet, is at risk, and I am convinced the Quiet does come into the eastlands. I will leave no request unmade, however dangerous. Do you still deal with the Ta'Opin?"

Maesteri Belamae nodded in grave understanding. "Yes."

"Then send word that I wish an audience." She took a deep breath. "It is time that we seek the Mor Nation Refrains. Their warsong is written of in the Tract itself, is it not?"

"It is," Belamae affirmed. "Helaina, once we start down that path, we cannot turn back from this. Are you sure?"

The regent fell quiet, listening again to the distant hum of the Song of Suffering. In truth, she'd started down this path long before she'd arrived at the cathedral. She reached out and placed a hand over his. "How soon can we speak with the Ta'Opin?"

"You know that the refrains are just a part of the need. You still have the problem of finding Leiholan to give voice to those hymns." He glanced down at the parchments of music—the Song of Suffering—in his other hand. "It isn't known if the Ta'Opin have kept the Leiholan tradition alive. I've had but one Ta'Opin student in many years that has come to me."

Then Belamae offered a gentle smile. "But I have not been neglectful of my stewardship . . . or the changes of late in the Song of Suffering. Even now, I have voices on the roads of men seeking records that might help us find those endowed with the talent." He squeezed Helaina's hand. "And there is at least one bright hope out there, my Lady. I have seen her."

CHAPTER FORTY-SEVEN

The Wilds

The day cleared steadily as the greater light rose high toward the meridian. Tahn and Sutter walked their horses through Stonemount toward the northern rim. In the full light of day, the empty city left Tahn feeling hollow. Somehow, in the brightness of the sun, the place felt even more alone. The iron-shod hooves of their mounts clopped on the stone street, echoing loudly against the walls. Spaces between the stones showed dead grass, riffled by an occasional gust of wind. That is what it had come to—the glorious city that Tahn imagined as a vibrant center of thought and skill and family still stood tall, but at its edges unruly grass grew and died. All the craftsmanship had become a mere shell left behind when the lives that inhabited it were gone, and each street felt rather like a bone left after a body had decayed.

They crossed a wide bridge near a riverhead. The weathered emplacements were as solid, Tahn thought, as the day they'd first been set. Along the crystal clear waters, broad granite stairs descended into the river. The stranger paused at the bridge railing and looked out across the river's course.

"A place to take comfort from the heat," the mysterious man said. "Can you practically see the children wading in the water there? Splashing one another and running to hide behind a mother's legs?"

The image hit Tahn forcibly. He could think of no better use for the long stone terraces. Along the stair, a number of decanters lay overturned, some broken, many still whole. He imagined that water was fetched here for use in the homes of Stonemount. The simple task of bringing in water to prepare supper reminded him of the Hollows. Though his hometown was far less grand in design and size, its needs, some of them anyway, were every bit the same. Yet the people of Stonemount had left this paradisiacal home. He found himself wondering what their strange companion might discover about their demise. Or what he knew that he wasn't telling them.

The water could not be resisted. Tahn dismounted, jogged ahead, and rounded the last bridge post, hopping down the three wide stairs to the water's edge. He could see the bottom clearly. The scent of the clean, fresh spring caused his mouth to water. He cupped his hand into the stream and drew several mouthfuls. When he finished, Tahn pulled the cap off his waterskin and dipped the opening into the flow. Waiting for the skin to fill, he watched the mirrored reflection of the sky above in the surface: the tops of the tallest buildings west of him, the sky, the bridge, Sutter, and . . . where was the stranger? Tahn looked more closely, a cold chill running up his arms and down his back. He could see nothing more in the glassy surface.

His waterskin was full, but he kept it submerged and casually looked up. He saw the man striding from the bridge without looking at Tahn, his movements swift and effortless. It might be foolishness, but he'd thought the man had been standing beside Sutter. He didn't know what, but there was something dreadfully wrong with this stranger. He turned his attention back to his waterskin, drawing it up and corking it again.

As casually as he could, Tahn stood and climbed the steps to the end of the bridge, where Sutter joined him.

"What's wrong?" Sutter said immediately.

Tahn shook his head, looking away at the stranger, whose back was still to them.

"Later," Tahn whispered and swallowed. "But let's just keep an eye on our new friend, huh? There's something about him."

"You think that's news?" Sutter said and threw a light tap to Tahn's chest with his knuckles. "I don't trust anything I can't dig whole from the ground."

"Come," the man called back without sparing them a glance. "We've a way yet to go, and the roads get tricky from here on. But never fear, once we reach the wilds, I'm a sure foot to get you to the north canyon."

Tahn slung his waterskin over his head and nudged Sutter. He fell in behind the man again, but allowed several extra strides between them this time.

Late sun was touching the last outbuildings when they suddenly came upon a narrow strip of unoccupied ground, beyond which lay a profusion of trees and brush.

"The wilds, lads," the man said in self-congratulation. "I told you I would get you here."

"It's late," Tahn said. "We can sleep in one of the houses close by. There is no need to rush into the wilds tonight."

"Nonsense," the man replied. "You can be clear of them while light still clings to the eastern rim. Besides, a Stonemount bed is a hard thing to sleep on. You'd do better with a plot of earth." He grinned broadly. "Never mind me," he said. "I've overstated their danger. I'm not entirely sure the Stonemounts even called them the wilds. Come, come, I'll show you the way."

The man started again, a decided clip to his step. Sutter shrugged and fell in after him. Tahn felt for the sticks in his cloak. The sooner they arrived at Recityv, the better. Twenty strides on, the trees rose up around them.

The thick hardwoods of the wilds were coated with damp, mossy lichen, and the air rolled with the smell of rot after the rain. Root systems snaked along the ground, as though unable to find purchase deep in the soil. It made for uneven footing and labored walking. Branches did not naturally grow skyward, seeking the sun, but reached in strange directions, seeming to turn at random, many growing back toward the ground, where they took root or continued to grow laterally. Tahn wondered if, in time, the whole of the forest would be an impenetrable wall of wood.

Soon, the light diminished, obscured by the densely interwoven branches overhead. The trees bore small, budlike leaves, hardly enough to provide shade, but the profusion of limbs, having grown together in tangled knots, more than compensated for the lack of foliage.

Tahn listened for the natural sounds he'd become accustomed to when hunting in the Hollows. Instead, he heard a low sound deep in the woods, like a mallet striking a hollowed-out timber. Infrequently, he heard the stridulation of a cricket, but the chirp never lasted, cutting off for several moments before repeating the same halting cadence. As they passed deeper into the wilds, a musky fog began to rise from the loam.

"Never mind the fogs," the man assured. "The heat and cold battle in the topsoil; it will settle soon."

"You said this was the Stonemounts' defense against attack?" Sutter asked, picking his way over a confluence of roots.

"Effective, don't you think?"

"Seems to me it offers an enemy cover while he comes closer to battle," Sutter said.

"There's more to the wilds than trees, adventurer." The man stopped and turned in a full circle, nodding as he surveyed the trees overhead. "The wilds have a way of turning a man around, making him forget himself. Many graves lay within the wilds, but none are marked, because none were planned. There are glyphs in the city that say the square came first, and others that say the wilds came first. Whichever is true, this dark grove has stood here for a long time. I suspect it reminded the Stonemounts to be humble as much as it warded off malefic trespassers." The man smiled at his own insight. "How glorious a people. How enlightened. Beside the measure of their ingenuity and monument in stone, they allowed this grove to grow untamed, its natural state a marker to measure the height of their advancement."

Sutter gave the man a curious stare.

"Or perhaps they are just trees," the man said unconvincingly. "Perhaps I'm too long in my documents and studies here to have remained objective." He turned a bright eye on Tahn. "You see, this is precisely why I hoped to escort you to the north canyon. A good student of the past must test his conclusions against the sensibilities of living, breathing . . . adventurers. Does that not seem right?"

Tahn nodded and surveyed the woods around them. The light fell in weak, diffused patterns. The tight weave of successive branches above them left him with the impression that this was as light as it ever got in the wilds, and that night would be deeper and darker than he imagined.

The man whipped his cloak around as he spun and continued deeper into the wilds. His route wound like a snake, and Tahn, even with his keen woods skills, soon felt completely lost. The land dipped and heaved, the roots growing more closely together and leaving little ground between. All about them was wood: roots underfoot, dark bark upon the trees, and a low ceiling of branches. A cavern of it. In every direction, Tahn could see nothing but the deep dark of endless trunks, grown black in the shadowy confines of the wilds. The smell of rotting wood hung thick in the air.

Then, in an instant, the light vanished. The dim half light fell nearly to utter darkness, the sun gone behind the western rim. Distantly, the strange sound of wood striking wood echoed in deep tones that Tahn felt more than heard. And, strangely, the cricket song ended, leaving a deathly quiet in the grove that undid even Sutter's natural smile.

"I suppose we aren't going to make it to the north canyon," Sutter said with sarcasm out of the dark.

"It isn't far," the man replied, "but travel at night in the wilds is . . . ill advised. Don't fret. I'm a cautious one, and I'll see you through."

"I'll build a fire," Tahn said. The abrupt darkness had brought with it an attendant chill.

"If you must," the man answered. Tahn thought he heard a quarrel beneath the man's assent, though it may have been that the damp feel of the wilds and the gloom that enfolded them had put Tahn himself in an objectionable mood.

Carefully, he shuffled his feet, seeking an open section of ground clear of roots. Sutter gathered a few fallen limbs and shortly they had light again, and warmth. Tahn sat on a humped root and pulled out some bread for himself and Sutter. The firelight glistened darkly on the nearby bark. Sparks from the fire drifted up on the heat, and winked out against the tight weave of low branches. Their guide sat close by, watching the fire and looking alternately at Tahn and Sutter. He produced nothing to eat.

"Do you trust me sufficiently now, after coming so far through the wilds," he began, "to share with me your true vocations?" He cocked an eyebrow at Tahn.

Sutter put down his own crust of bread. He fixed the man with a hard stare until the stranger turned his eyes to meet it. "I dig roots," Sutter said with fierceness. "Or did," he added. "But now that I spend my time listening to tiresome stories, I long for the roots again."

Tahn tried to quiet Sutter with a look, but his friend would not meet his gaze. The man looked back at Tahn, undisturbed. "And you?"

"I'm tired," Tahn said.

"Nonsense," the man rebuffed. "Going into the wilds is easy enough. I've no particular care for your true labors, but they're surely more interesting than your pretense of being adventurers. Life itself is adventure enough, wouldn't you agree?"

Tahn studied the easy smile on the man's face. The stranger likely suffered from a lack of companionship, and was intrusive only because of it. His jeweled scabbard, long cloak, and tricorne hat were the affectations of a man not sure of himself. He spoke with an elegant confidence, like the polished way a trader spoke. But he hadn't anything to gain from helping Tahn or Sutter, and Tahn could sympathize with the feelings of lonelieness.

"I would," Tahn answered. "I hunt game and watch after the forest near my home."

"And where is home?" the man asked.

Tahn did share a look with Sutter then, his friend shaking his head in a nearly imperceptible motion to warn him off. "Reyal'Te," Tahn said.

The man nodded to the small reservation. "At the edge of the Mal. You're a long way from home. Maybe there is a bit of adventurer in the pair of you, after all."

Their guide sat comfortably, looking rested after a day's walk, and vital without a speck of food. The night air grew colder still. Tahn and Sutter circled closer to the fire, warming their arms and chests and cheeks while goose bumps from the cold rippled on their backs. Their guide seemed equally content in the dipping temperature.

Something had been bothering Tahn about their route through the wilds, and it occurred to him as he rubbed his hands near the flame. "How do you mark your passage through these woods? You can't have learned the way after one trip."

"Oh, I've been here a very long time, my fellow," the man said. "The irony in studying the past is that we too often boil an entire generation into the notes on a single page. If history is properly studied, I do believe it may take as long to learn it as it did for others to live it. And if I am to discover what became of them, what led them to vacate this beautiful city, I must learn all the things a citizen takes for granted: the multiple meanings of words that are used to insult, edify, and produce laughter; the unwritten standards of behavior that show respect or intolerance; if the attitudes of their populace were harmonious with their poets or if the poets spoke individually, rebelliously."

"I don't see the purpose of it," Sutter chimed in. "I mean no disrespect," he added cautiously. "But they left, one way or another, and the world went on without them."

Their guide's face fell slack, the convivial look gone. He shifted his eyes to Sutter without turning his head. "You have answered your own question, root-digger. How does it escape you? Today we stood in the vaunted square of the most glorious city ever erected. From its central fountain to the edge of the graves around it, you walked the streets of a city that showed no despair in the architecture of its least citizen. The whole of it is a lasting tribute to unity, equality. This people literally traded on the understanding they accumulated by such common fellowship. And then they disappeared without a trace of contention or a single indication of where they went."

The man stared at Sutter with wide eyes, clearly feeling as though his point should be obvious. Sutter shook his head. "Maybe they were invaded. If they were overwhelmed and taken captive, they could all have been led away some-where. That would explain the city being deserted but showing no signs of war."

Their strange guide continued to stare quietly for some time. It was his turn to shake his head.

"Boy." It was spoken with utter evenness, an insult more searing than a curse. "Look at you, far from Reyal'Te, searching for something, I assume, keeping your little secrets because you don't trust me, but ashamed of the life and work that held you there. And now you wear a sword and walk the high-roads seeking more. Doing whatever you will, crossing the Ophal're'Donn Bridge and sauntering down the Canyon of Choruses as though you'd earned the right. And yet you fail to see the miracle of Stonemount, that those who lived here overcame the kind of arrogance that makes you feel deserving of more than you have, overcame the combative nature such arrogance creates. In so doing, the Stonemount people outgrew their own city of rock and mortar, and when they left for something better, nobler, the world did indeed go on." The man paused, the crackle of wood seeming suddenly very loud in the si-lence. "I want to know what they knew, go where they have gone. I am tired . . ." He stopped, a genial smile returning to his lips. "I apologize, I get very passion-ate about my studies."

Sutter's face paled. His hand found his sword's handle, but he looked inca-pable of effectively using the weapon.

In a soft voice, their guide said a few words more. "All the rest are walking earth, upright dust, consuming breath in ignorance." The words were familiar to Tahn, but he could not place them. He finished his bread, and later fell asleep watching the guttering fire, his hand on the sticks hidden within his cloak.

He couldn't see the man's face. He never could. But Tahn could feel the figure behind him, prepared to correct an errant move or loss of concentration.

The horizon rose pale blue at the break of day. Tahn stood upon a precipice of rock, looking out over an ancient canyon carved by a slow-moving river deep in its valley. The red stone and bleached sands appeared tranquil in the gentle light of predawn. The form shifted his weight to his other foot, the crunch of pebbles beneath his sole accentuating the quiet that had settled over the canyon. The air remained still over the outcropping he stood upon, and Tahn held his breath as he aimed his bow over the vastness of the canyon below.

"Breathe naturally," the man said. "A rigid chest makes weak arms, causes anxiety. You must shoot your arrow without fear in order to hit where you aim. Every arrow, every breath is one less to your last. And each arrow is important, and must fly with the fullest intention of your heart."

"But there is nothing here to shoot," Tahn said. "The canyon is wide, and there is no game to hunt."

Tahn felt the man's head incline toward him, coming close to his ear. "We come at dawn to this place because when you release you must learn to focus on yourself, not the quarry." His voice came softly, but firmly. When he spoke in such a way, he expected Tahn to listen and remember. "You create the energy of the weapon by making your pull. You can feel the force of it suspended in the string and the give of the haft. None is yet offered to the arrow. This is the moment of balance between Forda and Forza, the bow and the energy you give it. In this moment you stand armed with the potential to take life or save it. Your intentions are everything, Tahn."

"How will I know when to shoot, and when not to shoot?"

The man let a slow breath out through his nostrils. "You will ask this question each time you draw. It is not something that can be answered once and for all. But the ability to make that choice is a power of its own. There are those that do not possess that power, but who will seek to own your portion of it."

Tahn was confused.

The man went on. "Your life is a precious gift that you must safeguard against a particular enemy. They are known by many names, and often simply called the Ancients. They are forgotten in the land now, passed away beyond the memories of even the oldest reader. They may come to you as tempters, even messengers. But they are charlatans whose pride doomed them to a stagnant life deep inside the Bourne. With a thousand lifetimes they made their way out of their prison and began to walk among men, conniving like thieves to steal what their ambition robbed them of: a chance to feel the melding of Forda I'Forza together in their own breast."

"And I must shoot them," Tahn said naively.

"No, boy, listen to my words." The man stretched an arm past Tahn's face, pointing at the emptiness of the sky above the great canyon. "You must learn and remember the power of the draw itself, not the arrow. It is potential power, just as a boulder perched upon a hill. And it would be your only weapon against them."

The man stopped, seeming to give Tahn time to comprehend what he'd said. But Tahn hadn't grasped the man's meaning before he went on.

"To test the honesty of an Ancient, put forth your hand in greeting. The Ancient will want to greet you, and in so doing forget himself. You will not feel the palm of his hand in your own. From this you will know of his appetite for your destruction."

The man ceased speaking, and Tahn knew it was time for him to shoot his arrow. He looked into the gathering light of dawn and sought a target: a blackened tree a thousand strides distant on the far side of the gulf, then a mountain peak at the edge of the horizon, then a cloud gliding low across the hills to his left. He could hit none of these things, and his fingers began to ache from the constant tension of his draw. He took a deep breath, immediately exhaling as the man had instructed. But his young arms could no longer sustain the long pull, and began to quiver. The pain of maintaining the draw burned in his shoulders and ached in his knuckles. Was this the lesson, learning the power that existed in the weapon? Learning that a man must yield to it eventually? That the dual components of Forda I'Forza existed in men at the same time?

He let go the string, and realized as it relieved the tension in the haft that he held no arrow. The string hummed, but nothing sailed against the light of dawn. A mocking laughter descended out of the heavens, rolling on waves of mist and brushing his face like the kiss of a mourner, all heartache and loss. Tahn whirled to see the man, but behind him all was emptiness. The hum of his bowstring rose like the tolling of a great bell, the vibration tingling his fingers, turning his hand numb. He lost feeling in his arm and dropped the weapon. Beneath him the soil turned white, spreading outward to rob everything of color. In a frenzy, he thrust his fists against the rock of the outcropping and screamed to hear anything but the awful hum. Hearing nothing, he stopped. Quickly, he took two large rocks and smote them together. No crack. There was nothing in his head but the ringing buzz of his bow's last release, and nothing in his eyes but colorless earth.

Tahn looked up and screamed into the sky.

He started, and came awake in the wilds, a scream dying to echoes in the trees around him. Sutter still slept, undisturbed, while their guide sat poking at the fire with a slender stick, his eyes on Tahn as he probed the embers. The flame burned low, casting deep shadows over their companion's eyes but hinting with reddish hues at the dark pupils.

Casually, Tahn passed a hand over the concealed pocket in his cloak. . . . The sticks were gone. In the same moment, he saw their guide reach down and take them into his hand as though prepared to feed the fire.

Will and Sky, no!

The man did not take his eyes away, appearing to judge the sticks' value by Tahn's expression. In the flickering light, Tahn could not be sure if the man smiled. He tried to mask his fear, but could feel his eyes widening in alarm.

What had the man said in his dream?

The thoughts blurred in his mind as he focused on the sticks concealing the *messages Edholm had entrusted to them. Their guide raised the sticks near his eyes and considered them. Then he tossed them into the pit, where the fire had burned down to nothing more than a bed of coals. The heat seared them, and they exploded in flame. Tahn lurched from his bed and thrust his hand into the coals after the sticks. The smell of his own burning flesh rose on the smoke, and the stranger's odd mocking laugh surrounded him. Try as he might, Tahn could not take the sticks in hand. They danced out of his reach, forcing him to stretch farther into the flame. Then the fire's tongue bit him sharply and Tahn bellowed his pain and frustration into the wooded ceiling of the wilds.*

Tahn sat up with a weak yawp following him out of his dream.

"Keep it down, Woodchuck," said Sutter. "I'm trying to get some sleep."

Tahn rolled over and looked at the man who had led them from Stonemount toward the northern rim. He sat placidly, staring at the fire, which burned low, just as it had in Tahn's dream. Attempting to be subtle, Tahn gathered in his cloak so he could sit up. He swiftly checked for the sticks. They were still safe in his inner pocket. The man turned a disarming smile on Tahn, nothing like the clever manipulator of Tahn's dream.

Tahn, getting to his knees, took several small pieces of wood and cast them into the fire. The man gave him a quizzical look, but said nothing. As the fire brightened, the memory of an unfinished thought nagged Tahn. He'd been trying to recall something as his nightmare had played out.

"You sleep restlessly. You've got things on your mind," the stranger said.

"We all have things on our minds," Tahn replied.

"So I've noticed." The man settled a thoughtful gaze on Tahn. "Some of the old texts say that sleep is our preparation for death: a day of life and light followed by a quiet, restful end to it in a night's slumber. Rehearsal, you might say. A pattern we follow often enough to accept when our time is gone and we must return to the earth that makes us. No riddle then why men tussle with it. But it is a noble fight, I say. I would not so easily give in to my barrow."

The man's face looked pained as he spoke. Tahn stared aimlessly into the night, thinking of a scholar, here in a forgotten city, alone. He reviewed all they had seen: the great fountains at the city's great central square; buildings grand and modest fashioned with equal care; a wide ring of untilled land, spotted with groves and dotted with grave makers for those from Stonemount who went to earth before the exodus that abandoned the city forever.

Something flashed in Tahn's mind, something he'd seen as they'd first passed through the Canyon of Choruses, a figure, little more than a shadow itself, hunched over a grave. The nagging thought took form as he recalled the man's words from his dream: *Put forth your hand in greeting.*

Without turning his back to their guide, Tahn stood and shuffled to where Sutter lay. He nudged his friend's shoulder with his foot.

"Don't tell me you're kicking me just as I was about to fall asleep," Sutter protested in a thick, surly voice.

"Get up," Tahn said softly. Something in Tahn's tone must have struck Sutter, who stood up fast and shrugged off his blanket.

"Are you ready to go?" the man said, rising gracefully. "I sense you're quick to be shut of these wilds and on your way to wherever fortune next takes you."

Tahn cautiously picked up his bow and caught Sutter's gaze before looking down at the sword at his friend's hip. Sutter understood and rested a hand on the handle in readiness. If their companion noted their apprehension, he did not show it. His gaunt cheeks held shadows in the flickering firelight, but his eyes remained easy. The jewel-encrusted sheath caught the light in colorful prisms, and he pushed back his tricorne hat on his head as Tahn stepped around the fire toward him.

"We've come all this way together, borne you company, and haven't made a proper introduction."

"How do you mean?" the man asked.

"We do not know your name," Tahn replied, "though you've been good enough to ask after ours."

"I believe you're right. How foolish of me." He fixed them with an earnest, apologetic smile. "The prospect of companionship has made me rude. Forgive me. I am Sevilla Daul."

"Clumsy of me not to have asked," Tahn offered. "Accept my apology." And Tahn extended his hand to Sevilla.

CHAPTER FORTY-EIGHT

A Primrose

Braethen opened his waterskin and drained the last few mouthfuls of warm water, hardly enough to wash the dust and grit from between his teeth. He upended the skin and three drops fell into the dirt. While he watched, the earth absorbed the water, leaving no trace. He put a hand where the few drops had fallen; the ground was burning to the touch.

Then he raised his head, shading his eyes and looking both east and west.

There still was no sign of the man they sought. There was only the Scar, and the Scar never changed. He'd thought that even this place would be beautiful in the first light of morning. But it was only like the fallow fields west of the Hollows where scarecrows hung limp and forgotten on posts, their stuffing a memory and their clothes faded by the sun.

They'd been moving since before sunrise, Vendanj contining to lead them north and east. All day they walked in the oppressive heat. Late in the day, Braethen swooned. He caught himself with several shuffling steps. Beads of sweat ran down his neck. He clutched his shirt and mopped them away. Their water was gone, and the horses, too, stumbled more frequently each hour.

Ahead, the trail disappeared where the earth slid away down a hill. Mira's head popped up from the gully, and the Far came running toward them, one hand raised for them to stop.

Vendanj pulled up, and one of the horses immediately lay down, chuffing from its nostrils with the exertion. In a moment, the other two mounts had done the same. The thought of sitting daunted Braethen, and he remained standing as Mira sprinted toward them. Simply watching her tired him further.

Her hair and shirt hung wet with perspiration. Her face, too, ran with sweat, but she did not wipe it away.

It took her but a moment to catch her breath. "A thousand strides. Down the hill and over a second shallow rise."

"Did you see him?" Vendanj asked.

"No. And I did not look to see if it was occupied. There are strange tracks crossing the path at the base of the hill, where those in the house could not see. Less than a day old." She looked back the way she had come. "Quietgiven could have come this far into the Scar unnoticed. If they know why we have come, then they may lie in wait for us."

"We've no choice." Vendanj looked at their mounts. "We'll go the rest of the way without the horses. If the house is still occupied, whoever lives there will have water and we can return and refresh the animals. If it is abandoned, then they will have filled a noble purpose." The Sheason turned to Braethen. "Keep a ready hand at your sword, sodalist. You'll be all right."

Braethen licked dry lips.

Vendanj began walking. "Circle wide," he said to Mira, his gait quickening. "Come at the house from behind. Do not be seen. If it is not him, we will want your presence to be a surprise."

The Far left without a word, running east. Braethen watched her go, admiring the ease with which she moved, the grace and speed, like a wager-horse running the loam. She moved as though unaffected by the heat. Seconds later she disappeared over the edge of the hill. Braethen steeled himself, and worked to keep up with Vendanj. A new determination seemed to burn in the Sheason, and with each passing step, Braethen felt it grow inside himself.

Vendanj and Braethen came to the crest of the hill that dropped to a gulch below. A dry riverbed twisted away to the north and south. After a brief survey in each direction, Vendanj started down toward the small house, standing like a lone way station in very a long route. It appeared somehow like both a part of the landscape and an intrusion on the emptiness of the Scar.

Fifty strides from the structure a natural circular depression in the land surrounded it. Large red masonry bricks stood at each corner; they looked like the baked clay of the Scar. Wood planks ran in vertical rows, bleached and coarse from exposure. The roof had been covered with thin pieces of sandstone, and several ladders stood against the roof's edge, giving Braethen the impression that it was used as a lookout.

He followed Vendanj a few steps closer. A slight wheeze of wind around the chimney trailed in the air like an unseen streamer, and stirred dead grass here and there.

Vendanj put a hand across Braethen's chest to stop him.

The Sheason waited, listening, then dropped his hand and pointed toward an empty weapon rack standing against the house.

"It may be hard to respect this man," Vendanj spoke low. "But hold your tongue. His bitterness is earned."

As they stepped full out of the shallow gully, it occurred to Braethen where they must be: the depressed ring where Maral Praig and his Sheason had stood in a circle to call their last power from the Will in the Battle of the Round. The sodalist's heart jumped at the thought of being at the center of where it took place. He wondered if the Sheason who died here were buried nearby. Looking at the house before him, it struck him how like a grave marker it seemed now, as if each stone represented the life of one who fell in the final call of the Round. Whoever this Grant was, he either admired those who died here or held them in contempt, to make his home in the midst of their death.

They went to the house and stopped. Vendanj listened. "Hello," he called, keeping a short distance from the door.

No reply came.

"Grant," the Sheason said, his voice softer.

Still silence.

Shutters fastened from inside stood closed over the windows.

"Take your weapon in hand," Vendanj said.

Braethen drew his blade, as quietly as he could. The Sheason went forward and rapped at the door.

"If you are there, Grant, we have urgent things to discuss with you." The Sheason's voice seemed a loud intrusion in the silence of the Scar.

Braethen eyed the corners of the house and wondered where Mira was. His belly churned with expectation. He might need to use his sword; the thought thrilled and troubled him. A flash of the darkness he'd experienced when he'd first held it raced in his mind.

"Do not judge us because you are sentenced here," Vendanj continued.

Nothing stirred inside the home. A gust of wind kicked dust into their eyes. Vendanj waited for a lull in the warm breeze, then tried the door. The handle gave easily and the door swung inward. Vendanj stepped back, bending slightly at the waist.

Before Braethen knew what was happening, Vendanj disappeared inside. A moment of indecision swept through him. Standing alone with his sword, he reflected how different it was for him to call on a home, any home, without a book in his hand. But the moment passed in an instant, and the sodalist jumped through the opening, both hands tight upon his blade.

Everything went black, and panic struck him. *I am back in the darkness!* He gripped tight his sword, trying to remember the words he'd spoken the first time, words that had allayed his fear. He could not remember, and his heart pounded. Then the blackness receded a shade. *I am a fool!* It was not the same emptiness as before; the interior of the home simply lay cloaked in darkness. The stark change in light had left Braethen temporarily blind. He swung his head back and forth, trying to fix his sight on something. Shapes and shadows seemed to dance around him. He jerked his blade toward them in rigid strokes.

"Easy, sodalist," Vendanj's voice called out of the blackness. "We are alone. Grant is not here."

As Braethen's eyes acclimated to the dark, Mira came through the door, her swords in her hands, but lowered to her sides. She looked directly at Braethen, then at his sword. "Your hands are too rigid to use that weapon," she said with reproach. She moved past him into the back rooms of the house. Braethen sheathed his blade with an embarrassed smile. Vendanj paid him no attention, studying a small pile of documents left on the table.

Inside the home, furnishings sat mute, and a cooler, settled air eased the heat in Braethen's cheeks. Shielded from the sun outside, the trappings of the home nevertheless appeared sun-worn: A wash basin atop a table; a book cabinet largely empty, save for three books lying flat in a pile on the uppermost shelf; a rough table attended by four rough chairs; and open cupboards with a few dishes. No art adorned the walls, only bow-pegs and a narrow weapons rack near the door. A graying rug, its pattern faded to almost nothing, covered much of the floor. Then Braethen saw something fixed to the wall near the hall to the back rooms. His eyes had fully adjusted, and he could make out an elaborate sigil scrawled at the top of what looked like an edict.

When he drew close, his jaw dropped at what he read:

> *This writ shall serve as witness that Emerit Denolan SeFeery has willfully committed treason against the stewardship entrusted to him and against the right order of progress as held by the High Court of Judicature and the League of Civility. It is hereby declared that Denolan SeFeery is unfit for citizenship in the free city of Recityv.*
>
> *In the interest of justice he is thus permanently exiled into the emptiness known as the Scar. With the exception of the First Seat at the regent's Table, he alone will know the trust this sentence represents.*
>
> *Any known to abet Denolan SeFeery will be considered a traitor and judged accordingly.*
>
> *From this day forward, Denolan SeFeery will no longer be referred to with the emerit honors of his former office. Should he ever return to the free walls of Recityv, he shall be punished by immediate execution.*

A dozen names marked the bottom of the page. The parchment itself drooped with sepia tiredness. Only the seal at the top indicated the official nature of the document.

"Emerit," Braethen repeated with awe. He recalled that an Emerit was a warrior with fealty sworn to someone of high station, one whose physical prowess might only be surpassed by his keen intellect. It was a title accorded to only the greatest fighters by the highest mantle of government.

As he spoke the word, Mira returned from the rear hallway. Hearing it seemed to touch a personal wound in her.

Braethen hardly noticed. "Was this Denolan SeFeery the same man? Was he also Grant? And if so, why this other name?"

The Sheason ignored him. "Someone left in a hurry. The ink here is not yet set."

"There is no one in the house," Mira confirmed. "The beds are made, a change of clothes in each room. Oil lamps, and recently burned by the smell of it. A journal on each night table." She came into the room to stand next to Vendanj. "No one left the house while I watched. And I've seen no footprints." She sheathed her swords and began inspecting the common area.

The Sheason gingerly touched the top sheaf of parchment spread on the table. "He's rewriting the Charter," he said in a whisper.

The sound of it chilled Braethen's blood. He'd only heard the Charter spoken of once, and then it was when A'Posian had been deep into a bottle of Winemaker Solom's brandy. The things he'd said came out in incoherent phrases that sounded like dream talk. But Braethen gleaned that the Charter preceded the Tract of Desolation in age and exceeded it in consequence, and that it came from the hands of the First Ones themselves.

It was believed the Charter had been wrought in the Language of the Covenant, setting forth founding principles and privileges governed by universal law, granting and sustaining life itself in the world. Many accepted the reality of the Tract of Desolation as an instrument fortifying the veil and holding the Bourne at bay. But most scholars, if they mentioned the Charter at all, referred to it as folklore, a romantic notion that no longer seemed reasonable, certainly not an actual document. More like a set of ancient beliefs, but some so powerful that they existed in the fabric of life, even if generations who lived by its tenets no longer had direct knowledge of it.

Braethen had come to think the Charter now lived in the stories retold by readers and authors to share beliefs and give meaning to what men do, what they die for.

But the way Vendanj said it, Braethen found himself believing it was something more than he had thought. For whatever the Charter may have been, that Grant had begun writing it anew was surely a harbinger of change.

Did this man Grant have the power to create such a document? Or was his an act of heresy?

"There is nothing for us here," Vendanj finally said. "There is light left to travel by. And we must either find water or make haste to the edge of the Scar. Come."

Mira swept to the door before Vendanj could leave. She crouched and laid a nimble hand on the sword at her hip. She darted out, Vendanj a step behind. Braethen took a last look around. Something tugged at him about the home. Perhaps the edict on the wall, or the stark simplicity of the furnishings, or the pages left on the rough table that were being written in this far place—somehow, he thought, an act of belief that did not belong in the abandoned environs of the Scar. What man wrote such a thing?

Braethen strode to the door, and his knees locked up when he nearly walked into Vendanj's back.

"Visitors," a voice said from somewhere ahead.

Braethen stepped to the Sheason's side. A man stood silhouetted against the sun. Braethen raised a hand over his eyes, but the light was too low against the western horizon to be blocked out. The man's shadow fell in a long line toward them. Braethen instinctively began to draw his sword. Vendanj put a hand on his wrist. "Hold," he said in his softest voice.

"Indeed, sodalist," the man said. "A three-ring man and a fleetfoot as traveling companions, and you are first to draw. Brazen or foolish, I don't know, but you wear your sword like new shoes."

Vendanj stared ahead directly into the sun. "We have news."

"Of course," the man answered, a hint of condescension in his voice. "What else could convince someone to come so far from home? And your news, Shea-son, you believe it somehow involves me." The man took a few steps closer. Braethen could see the dark brown of his weathered, sun-worn skin, and the deep lines at the corners of his eyes.

"I do."

"And of names," he said. "Will you give me yours, or will there be lies and secrecy?"

"This is Mira of Naltus. And this is Braethen of the Hollows." Vendanj lifted a hand toward the man in greeting. "And you know my name."

Braethen watched the stranger frown, but the man with the sun at his back did not move.

"I am dead to you," the other finally said. "Why come now?"

"Because a new age may call men to forget their past," Vendanj replied. "Will you become what they accused you of being?"

A dark look passed across the man's countenance. Braethen felt the same chill he had felt inside the home. It was more the sameness of those feelings than anything else that left no doubt that they had found Grant. The man's eyes might have inspired fear in a Bar'dyn. The expression in his face pierced Brae-then and made him suddenly aware of his own ingratitude and naivete. He never wanted to see that look again.

Vendanj left his hand up to be received in welcome, but Grant made no effort to take it. Braethen felt a certain respect in addition to the wariness he already had for this resident of the Scar, who gave no deference to even a Sheason.

"Leave me be." His words sounded as both command and plea, and, Brae-then thought, resignation.

"I cannot." Vendanj began slowly walking toward Grant. "I will not. You know better even than I that sometimes a man must speak. And you must hear what I have to say, just as Helaina needed to hear your words long ago."

Mira moved with the Sheason, more slowly than Braethen ever remembered her moving. Her hand rested on her sword in an unthreatening way, but he knew she could have it out in less time than Braethen could think to draw his own blade.

"Leave your trained dog behind," Grant said without anger or resentment.

Braethen cringed at the insult to Mira. She stopped, an even expression on her face. She was close enough, Braethen thought, to take Grant down if he moved against the Sheason.

The sun now loomed large and low in the sky, a great russet orb. As Braethen watched, Vendanj stopped before the deeply tanned, leathery face of the other, and studied it as though he were suddenly unsure this man was indeed

Grant. Several days' growth of beard peppered the man's jaw; the Sheason scrutinized his brow and nose and shoulders. Finally, Grant took Vendanj by the hand, the grip unfamiliar to Braethen. The Sheason looked down at their united hands.

"I'm glad to see you, Denolan."

Grant's head drew back in a start. "I've not heard that name in a long time. You are fortunate we stand so far from the ears of court pages. Using it might earn you a night in the cuffs." A long pause stretched between them. In a saddened whisper, he finally said, "Don't use the name. It is not who I am anymore. I am only Grant."

"Your new name should be a proud one," Vendanj replied. "You were right to speak against the injustice of the council."

Grant let go of Vendanj's hand. "Surely you don't bear clemency. So what brings you here?"

The Sheason looked intently into the other's face. "No lies or secrecy," he began. "But let us talk later, after we have retrieved our horses."

Grant smiled at some inward joke, but it looked unnatural on his face, unnatural in the Scar. Braethen thought that these two were now indistinguishable, reflections of one another, and mirth simply didn't belong to either.

Grant raised a hand. Four young men and two young women rose from the depression that surrounded the home. They ran to where Grant stood. Each of them, skin as deeply tanned as Grant's, wore a sword and carried a bow. All had long hair tied back with strips of cloth. Mira showed no surprise, but Braethen wondered if she knew these six had been so close. The Far observed them closely as they came. Before they moved again, she would know each one's physical limitations and weaknesses, simply by watching them run, their stance, the movement of their eyes, and the way they held their weapons. They weren't much younger than Mira, and they wore the same stern look he saw on Grant's face. The Far seemed to appreciate them in a way Braethen had not seen her admire anyone before.

"See to their horses," Grant ordered. He pointed in the direction from which Braethen and Vendanj had come. "Take water and salve."

The six left at a run, and Grant turned toward the house. "There are questions in your eyes, Sheason. Let's answer them and send you on your way. You don't belong here." The man brushed past Braethen without acknowledging him.

Inside his home, Grant lit a table lamp and started a fire against the coming of night. From a hidden basin beneath the rug he drew a jug and poured them each a cup of cool water. He waited while every cup was drained, then refilled them. He left the jug with Braethen and took a seat beside the fire.

Even with the warming color of firelight, Braethen still felt the chill on the back of his neck. He continued to glance sidelong at the aging parchment tacked to the wall.

"You bring a novice sodalist out of the Hollows," Grant said. "Does he realize what danger he must be in, simply traveling with a Sheason?"

"You might ask me," Braethen said before Vendanj could answer.

"First to draw *and* to speak," Grant said. "Well then, let us hear it."

Braethen felt Mira and Vendanj's eyes fall on him. Another awkward smile twisted Grant's lips. Braethen looked at the wall again, where the edict had been placed. "I don't know your story," Braethen said. "It is not in any of the books I have read, and no reader has ever come to the Hollows and shared it." He looked at Grant, whose gaze now held the same black severity he'd seen before. Braethen quickly looked toward the fire to avoid the stare. "You are condemned in the Court of Judicature, but apparently not by the Order of Sheason. You feel free to insult a woman, but are glad to revive a horse. And you stock your home for defense, attracting striplings to yourself like a rogue captain, but there is no war here because there is no life here."

"A stripling calls another child a stripling," Grant said, a chuckle escaping him.

Braethen resumed. "I know there is danger. But it is danger of losing the life I have. It appears to be no less than what you have done in your own past." He looked at the exile order on the wall.

Grant's laughter caught in his throat. "Astute words for a boy just out of his books. Before the three-ringed man and his fleetfoot ask me what they must, let me answer you." He pointed a finger at Braethen. "I chose to be here. That parchment on the wall reminds me of that. It is an ugly place, and not for any of the reasons you think. But because *I* am here, those striplings you mention are not sold into the grip of Quietgiven. And while these youths are here, I show them how to keep from having their own choices taken from them." Grant sat back, his face relaxing again. "And it must come by physical defense; all is coming to that. Or perhaps you knew this, since you wear a sword of your own and were prepared to draw it against me."

None of them spoke, and the fire hissed in the silence.

Against the quiet hum of burning wood, Vendanj asked, "Then why redraw the Charter?"

Grant gave Vendanj a bleak, unsmiling look. "Perhaps only to define what we have become, what lies ahead for us when the Hand is opened and the scourge of the Bourne spreads to the farthest reaches."

"For such a condition no Charter needs to be written," Vendanj countered.

"Since you are here only once I will tell you." He stood and went to the table where the parchments lay open. "It is my primrose in this desert. You can't imagine what it is like to write these words, and not believe they are possible.

But not writing them is like admitting the League of Exigents is right. And if that were so, then I could not remain here." His eyes seemed to look far away. He muttered, "And the cradle would be more merciful as a casket than as a promise of life."

"What evidence have you that the Bourne will ever spill through the Hand?" Vendanj asked, eyeing the documents beneath Grant's fingers.

"You," the man said.

Again no one spoke, the only sound the popping of sap in the flames. Mira stood as still as a statue. Outside, the sound of hooves approached. Grant went to the door and gave a few instructions. Three of the six ran back into the dusk; the other three came inside and stood back near the hall entrance.

Vendanj gave the newcomers a look. "Can they be trusted?"

"As you would trust me," Grant answered.

The Sheason appeared dubious, but turned to Grant. "The regent has called for the filling of every seat at the council table . . . and for a Convocation of Seats."

Grant frowned, unimpressed. "There's never been a regent who didn't want to fulfill that prophecy. But the words of seers don't like to be forced to fruition before it is time."

"Perhaps," Vendanj agreed. "But it is not only Vohnce that answers the call."

"And the nations of the sea, those across the Aela, the northern kingdoms past Ir-Caul?" Grant asked. "Do they care about the Second Promise any more than the First? Do they even remember? Those are old alliances, seasons without memory behind us. It is political posturing of the same brand that brought me here. Your Court of Judicature will fatten themselves and squabble over appointments to military stewardships and land resources, and those are the ones that even attend. The rest defend their own farthest boarders if they can, and have no use for convocations."

"You may be right. But it is not all the same. . . . A cry has begun to end the Song of Suffering sung from the Tract of Desolation."

That statement silenced the room.

This secret the Sheason had kept was one Braethen wished he had never heard. This song, sung from the lips of a select few, remained one of the few gifts of the First Ones, a protection against the Quiet. The singing of that song kept the Veil in place, and the dark races and creations of the One sealed away from the light of men . . . or, at least, was supposed to. From his books, Braethen had gathered that the Tract only became efficacious when rendered in vocal melody . . . the Song of Suffering.

Finally, Grant asked, "Who raises this cry?"

"It passes on the lips of people in the street," Vendanj said. "But even there it sounds like the League."

"Ah," Grant grunted.

"There are Quietgiven deep in the land," Mira added. "As near as the southern perimeter of the Scar. They came at our heels not four days ago."

"Nearer, fleetfoot, than that." Grant sat himself back by his fire. He watched the flame a moment. "You were not hard to anticipate, Far. You've likely seen the plodding tracks of Bar'dyn in hardpan dirt. They are near, but they won't engage us. They either fear us . . . or they use us as bait." Grant shifted his attention to Braethen. "How long before they come through that door, sodalist? Is that the kind of danger you speak about, the life you esteem highly enough to hold your sword beside a three-ring man?"

"Enough!" Vendanj said in a raised voice.

But Grant didn't stop. "And you, Far, what covenants do you break by coming into the lands of men? You are either more like me in exile than you'll admit, or the mysteries of your people are about to be laid bare for a tribe of Velle too fast for even you."

"Enough!" Vendanj yelled again. His voice boomed in the house, crashing down from the crossbeams and echoing off the floor. "These are not the words of the man who kept a straight back beneath the weight of irons and named his accusers. Beware that your sentence does not make you foolish."

"Speak softly to dead men, Sheason," Grant returned. "There's no threat that moves us." His gaze did not flinch from Vendanj.

The Sheason returned the stony stare. "We went to the Hollows to find Tahn."

At that, Grant's eyes lit with interest.

"Through Myrr and over the High Plains we came," Vendanj related. "But on the north face we were separated. He is lost to us, hopefully moving toward Recityv."

Grant clenched his jaw. The man from the Scar looked past them all at the three standing in the shadow of the back hall. Whispers passed among them.

"I belong here, Sheason," he said. "The world beyond the Scar is not mine anymore."

Vendanj sat stiffly in his seat and shook his head. His eyes flashed with disgust. From where Braethen stood, the force of his anger was palpable. "Then answer me this one question," the Sheason said.

Grant looked him in the eye.

"Why have you hardly aged a day since you were exiled?"

CHAPTER FORTY-NINE

The Untabernacled

The man showed a toothy grin and reached to take Tahn's hand in greeting. Tahn held his arm rigid, gritting his teeth beneath his lips. His jaw dropped when Sevilla's hand passed through his own without so much as a bump.

Tahn stared in disbelief at his fingers. Everything around him began to happen very quickly. Sevilla snarled at himself in disgust, seeming to have forgotten his true nature. In an instant, his body began to change. The fine garments fell to loose rags, worn with holes. The hat and scabbard that showed such refinement became a filthy sash and a spate of unkempt, knotted hair that hung like the dark strands of an old mop. Behind him, Tahn heard Sutter draw his sword, the scrape of metal being bared somehow reassuring.

Sevilla looked up at Tahn, a strange mixture of bitterness and regret in his eyes. "So long in that dark country, little hunter, digger of roots," he said. "There still, though through the vaults of Stonemount I may wander." Anger surged in his visage, pure hatred contorting his face. "I want my own temple!"

Sevilla leapt forward with startling speed, his hands rising toward Tahn's throat. Sutter called a warning, and Tahn dropped backward into a roll. Sevilla raced through the air where Tahn had stood. As Sevilla turned, a shriek tore through the wilds. Sutter jumped between them as Tahn struggled to gain his feet.

"Little man with a steel toy," the thing barked in savage mockery. "If I could I'd take your strike to know the glory of the sting." Sevilla launched himself again, moving with surprising speed. Sutter started to swing, but had only cocked his blade when Sevilla shot an arm into his chest, the creature's gnarled fist plunging deep within Sutter's flesh. Nails dropped his sword, his body tensing.

Tahn watched his friend writhe on Sevilla's arm and knew with sudden, dark knowledge that the creature could touch man when it meant to cause him harm. Cords stood out in sharp relief on his friend's neck as he twisted and fought to free himself. But it appeared as though the being had hold of his friend's heart. Around them the air began to whip and swirl, stirring sparks from the fire in dervishes and tugging at their cloaks. Sutter sputtered calls for assistance, his movements starting to slow.

Tahn nocked an arrow and made his draw before he realized his weapon would not harm the insubstantial creature. There was nothing he could do. How could he destroy something he could not touch? His mind filled with the sudden image of himself standing upon the precipice prepared to fire into emptiness. His heart told him it was the answer, but he did not understand.

Relaxing his draw, Tahn charged at Sutter and Sevilla, diving into his friend and wrapping his arms about his waist. His momentum tore Sutter from the creature's grasp, and Nails uttered a weak, throaty cry as Tahn severed his connection to the beast. His friend fell to the ground beneath him like a loose bag of grain. Quickly, Tahn turned over and sat up, again drawing his bow and pulling his aim down on the dark creature. He must shoot, but he had no faith in the arrow.

The being lurched forward, menace contorting its withered features. Words hissed from Sevilla's lips, but Tahn could not discern their meaning. It did not rush, but came on slowly, as though preparing for some arcane ritual. Tahn thought he could still see the prim hat and decorative scabbard, the fine cloak and trimmed hem of his garment, all still somehow in the ratty remains of the figure before him.

Tahn slowly stood and uncertainly faced Sevilla. He then cast his arrow to the ground between them and drew back his string again. Sevilla paused, concern narrowing in his contorted features. Distantly Tahn heard Sutter howling in pain, but the sound of it was lost behind another sound, like the hum of a potter's wheel heard turning. His entire body began to quake uncontrollably, as though vibrating with the same strident hum he heard in his head. If he'd had an arrow prepared, it would have fallen from its string.

The air continued to howl about them as Sevilla took another guarded step forward. Tahn drew his string farther, his heart pounding in every joint of his body. He looked at the shape of the hammer on his left hand to gain steadiness, and whispered the oldest words he knew: "I draw with the strength of my arms, but release as the Will allows." The familiar phrase was both a prayer and an imprecation. Despite the terrible tremors wracking his flesh, his strength and thought and emotion coalesced as he had never before experienced.

The small camp became a maelstrom of embers, leaves, twigs, and dust. Eddies of the mixture swirled in the crevices of trees and large roots. Tahn's hair whipped about his head, flailing at his eyes, but he kept his arms up, trying to hold steady on the figure of Sevilla. He saw the ledge from his dream, the impossible targets of a cloud, a mountain, a horizon, and closed his eyes against them. He felt close to the precipice, and was ready to release, wanted to release and give way to the feeling that welled inside him.

Then abruptly the wind ceased, the fire immediately falling to a slender flame. Tahn opened his eyes. Sevilla took a step back before turning and starting to walk away.

Tahn watched, unable to stop his own shaking or release his draw. His muscles ached but would not obey. At the edge of the light, Sevilla half turned and looked back. His clothes still hung in mottled rags, but his face had again become the amiable, sure man they'd first seen. He appeared ready to say something, his lips working silently. Then he was gone among the trees. Tahn collapsed, still gripping his bow and staring into the low ceiling of tightly woven limbs.

Then everything went dark.

Sutter writhed on the root-choked floor of the wilds.

His soul ached.

The moment Sevilla had put his unearthly hand into his chest, he'd taken hold of something inside him. It hurt differently than a cut or broken bone. This hurt was not of flesh, but somehow of spirit. He felt as though this creature had laid hold of his soul. And its icy touch had taught him an awful, immutable truth: His Forda could be separated from his body.

For a terrible moment, he thought this disembodied spirit wished to possess him and force Sutter's soul into the empty existence in which *it* had lived. But as soon as the thought came, it dissipated like breath on glass. And then he realized he knew what Sevilla (or whatever its true name was) sought. It hunted for the Stonemounts to try and find its spirit a tabernacle of its own. Did it also then hope that if it could somehow inhabit the *bones* of a Stonemount man, it might take on a mortal life?

Even through his pain, Sutter's mind flashed on the notion that true life, true *wholeness*, came not when spirit merely inhabited flesh, but that there was something more to it. And so Sevilla, lacking that, was . . . damned!

The creature wailed at the thought, somehow, through its unearthly connection with Sutter, hearing and knowing his mind.

Then the struggle began in earnest.

With the intention of taking possession of Sutter's body, this penaebra meant to rip Sutter's soul from his body and cast it to the wilds. Sutter could feel himself shifting inside his body, his spirit wrestling to remain whole within its bodily tabernacle.

His vision swam, one moment looking into the creature's terrible rictus, the next awash in blue where images of the countless dead walked, watched, or wailed. Somehow, with the eyes of his inner self he could view the unseen world filled with the untabernacled—spirits with no body. It haunted him with its severe serenity, even as he struggled to get free of Sevilla's hold.

Only vaguely was he aware of Tahn—movement somewhere nearby.

And his soul began to slip.

An awful comfort stole over him, a dreadful security in leaving the uncertainty of future choices. He looked about him, embracing the final reality that existed all around. He caught the violet and black and cerulean world in snatches through the creature's mortal embrace.

And at the furthest reaches of his mind, a wry thought halted his surrender: *I am being plucked from my own body like a root from dry ground.* And on its heels came another thought: *I am more than a single shoot. And I mean to honor the sacrifice of the hands that gave my own a chance in the soil.*

So he fought back against the snatching of his life from his body.

But the burn and tear of spirit from flesh became too exquisite to bear, and soon real death seemed to beckon.

Then Sevilla's hand was ripped free of its grasp upon his heart. Dark thoughts and dreams receded in a blinding rush, and he crumpled to the forest floor with his friend, who had forced the creature's release.

He knew in his agony that a part of him had been lost, stolen.

And something else gained.

Drops of rainwater struck Tahn's cheek. He woke and more rain fell into his open, troubled eyes. The knit of intertwined branches obscured his view of the sky, and caused the rain to gather in the leaves before falling. The fire had burned out, hissing as rain plopped into the cooling embers. He wiped his face, spreading the moisture to try to refresh himself. He lay unmoving and listened to the sizzle of the storm as it struck the upper leaves of the wilds. He'd never been to the port of Su'Winde, but Hambley had been there once in his youth, and described the sound of waves crashing against the shore as nearly the same as a good storm whipping against the bark and limbs of Hollows pine. This was that sound.

Tahn wanted to lie and let the rain fall on him and lose himself in the sound that seemed to hide him. But Sutter let out a weak moan, and Tahn forced himself to sit up. He could discern Nails only as a familiar dark shape in the recess of night-shadow beneath the canopy of trees overhead. Tahn tried to stand, but his legs cramped under him. So he rolled over and dragged himself to Sutter.

His friend lay clutching his chest. No wound marred his clothing; no blood stained his hands.

"Are you all right?" The words sounded foolish as soon as they came out.

Sutter drew breath to speak, but coughed in the attempt and winced in pain, grabbing his chest with both arms. He rolled onto his side and curled into a ball until the convulsions passed. Weakly he whispered, "Cold."

"I'll get your blanket," Tahn said and tried again to stand. His legs refused, and he sat hard next to Sutter.

"Inside," his friend added, touching his chest.

Tahn looked back to where Sevilla had disappeared into the trees. *What if he returns? What if I had tried to release an empty bow?* He scanned the trees around them and satisfied himself that they were alone. They couldn't stay here. Maybe the strange creature whose hand he could not feel would not come back. But maybe there were more of whatever he was.

"We have to get out of here," Tahn said.

Sutter nodded, his eyes still shut tight. He peeled his lips back and spoke through gritted teeth. "I can't ride."

The rain began to fall in earnest, growing louder in the flat leaves and running to the ground like miniature waterfalls. The fire coals hissed and steamed more loudly, sending waves of smoke into the air. Tahn folded his knees under him and again sat up. He looked around for long branches to build a litter, and spotted a deadfall not far from the horses. He tried a third time to stand, but his legs held him for only a moment before tumbling him forward into the gnarled surface roots of the trees. One knee cracked hard against a large, knotted root. His head pulsed with the rapid beating of his heart, blurring his vision. Each breath seemed to rush into his blood and push his heart faster. He shook his head and dragged himself through the mud and mulch to the dead wood. Lying on his side, he pulled two long limbs and one shorter piece from the tangle.

Working against the growing pain, he retrieved a length of rope from Jole's saddle. He lashed the wood together in a slender triangle, and rigged a sling between the poles before laying his blanket across it.

He then gathered their horses' reins, hoping to secure the litter and find the north passage.

The wilds lit as lightning flared in the sky above. A mere second later, a powerful clap of thunder boomed around them. The air seemed to explode with the smell of ozone, rushing as though propelled by the boom. Sutter's horse bucked and tried to tear free. Tahn held on, the reins pulling him up like a puppet whose leg-strings have been cut. The horse reared again, this time tearing the leather from Tahn's hand, slicing his palm. In an instant, the horse sprinted into the darkness of the wilds and was gone. Jole rolled wide eyes and stamped about, but did not jerk his reins from Tahn's hand.

When he got Jole back to Sutter, he attempted to hitch the litter to Jole's saddle horn. But when Tahn stood, his head swam, and he fell to the ground. He beat at his legs, but could feel nothing, the numbness spreading into his fingers and back. *What's happening? I don't have time for this.* He buried his face in the mud and screamed his frustration, tasting the richness of the soil and the decay of last year's leaves, ground mites, and worms. The earth muffled his cry.

Tahn crawled back to Sutter to roll him onto the litter. As he pulled at his friend's shoulder, Nails opened his eyes, a pained but clear look in them. "Leave me."

"What?" Tahn asked, his head ablaze with pain.

"You can't make it hauling me like this. And I can't take the ride over the roots." Sutter grimaced, trying to smile. "How do you like that, Woodchuck, undone by the very things I tried to flee."

Tahn ignored him. He pulled Sutter's shoulder over and laid his friend on his back. Tahn then worked himself onto his knees and heaved Sutter into the litter. He retrieved the blanket and covered him. His friend was wet, but the wool would keep him warm. Tahn looked back at Jole. How would he hitch the litter and mount his horse?

Another burst of light flickered, the thunder seeming to come before the light faded. The noise eclipsed the patter of rain and the sound of his own heart in his ears. Rainwater ran into his eyes and plastered his hair to his cheeks and neck. In his mind he tried to recall the words of the man from his dream, and touched the familiar shape on the back of his hand. All he could think of was a funnel of water driving a bull elk to a muddy, watery death . . . and the moment he did not avenge Wendra in her birthbed.

His friend began to lose coherence, babbling, "The spirit is not whole, Tahn. It's not whole. It can be divided. Given out. Taken. Small portions separated from the whole . . ."

Tahn paused to listen to his friend. A strange truth resonated in Sutter's demented ramblings. Then Sutter passed out. At least the pain had left his face. Tahn rasped breaths, his throat pulsing now like his head, aching and burning. He wondered if Sutter might dream of waking to a still dawn, cloudless and warm.

Tahn dropped to his belly and inched his way to Jole. Clenching one end of a rope between his teeth, he cut another length and tied the other end of it to the apex of the litter. Then he took hold of the stirrup and hoisted himself up. On his feet, he could not tell that he stood, save that his eyes told him so. He hooked his arm under his knee and lifted his foot toward the stirrup. He jabbed his boot in and took hold of the horn. His hands went numb and he could not feel the jut of the saddle against his chest. With one great effort he thrust himself up over the saddle, and shimmied around until his leg fell onto Jole's other flank. He managed to get his other boot tucked into its stirrup, pulled the rope from his teeth, and wrapped it around the horn. With clumsy fingers, he tied it, then took a deep, searing breath.

On the ground, water now traveled in small streams, pooling in low hollows. Tahn was glad Sutter had fallen unconscious; he would not feel the jouncing of the litter across the roots.

Last, Tahn cut yet another piece of rope and fastened it around his own waist. He then tied the ends to the saddle horn, as well.

Clucking to Jole, he let down the reins. He would trust his old friend to take them ahead and out of the wilds. It was all he could focus to do. Trees passed, one the same as the last. His eyes burned as if they, too, had fever, and moments later he could no longer feel his arms or chest. He slumped forward and tried to keep his balance, whispering encouragement to Jole until the numbness entered his face and took his ability to speak.

On they went. Tahn remained awake, but felt like little more than a field suit in his saddle. The rain did not let up, and the thunder shook the forest floor as though the lightning shot up from the ground. Flood pools accumulated in low areas, and Jole trod through them, casting his head about, seeking direction in the absence of a path. The wind soughed in the trees, stirring wet leaves and dropping rain in sheets over them. Tahn hoped Sutter would not be thrown off the stretcher because neither of them would ever know.

After what seemed like an endless number of hours, like stepping from behind a curtain, Jole emerged from the trees. Less than four strides from them the northern rim rose up into the blackness. Jole paused for direction, and got none. Tahn made a thick sound deep in his throat to urge him on, and Jole turned right, following the rock wall. Shortly, the wall opened on the left into a narrow canyon like the Canyon of Choruses. Rainwater ran in a shallow river from the mouth of the narrow aperture into the wilds. Tahn moaned again, and Jole turned into the canyon and took them away from Stonemount.

The sound of the rushing water reverberated endlessly up the high stone walls along the narrow road. The shadows were impenetrable in the canyon, leaving the rushing of water to guide them. The roar of the rain and current blotted out thought, and only the constant ache in Tahn's head remained. Each pulse of his heart reminded him that he was alive, and soon the fevered ache became a grateful prayer to him.

But would Sutter live?

The night stretched on, and Tahn wondered how long Jole could keep going.

Finally, the canyon ended. Tahn moaned again, and Jole understood to stop. The storm had abated a bit, the heaviness of the drops lighter and their fall less pounding. Tahn turned his head as high as he could and looked east. He imagined the sun burning away the clouds, touching the treetops with orange light and steam rising from the soil as the rain evaporated in the early morning sun. He imagined the smell of green things and the stirring of bird wings. The familiar image might have warmed him in a time before the Bar'dyn came to the Hollows. Sitting on Jole's back without feeling in his body, he now hoped to live only because Sutter would need his help.

Tahn found himself glad for the cloud cover. Somehow today he had no need of the sun. Whatever beginning it intended for him, for the land around them, could lay cloaked as far as he was concerned behind the veil of dreary light that passed through the thickness of the storm. He wanted the sun to come, but not with the same earnestness as in days past. He simply cared less.

He needed to get Sutter to shelter, but if his own arms did not regain feeling, he would need someone's help. Atop Jole's back, he fell asleep thinking of Wendra, and was glad he could not feel the wind that began to riffle his sodden hair.

"Ho, there, do you need help?" a voice said. "It is night soon. Do you intend to sleep in a ditch?"

• CHAPTER FIFTY •

Fever Dreams

Tahn opened his eyes. Jole stood close by, the walk gone out of his legs; his head bowed the way Tahn knew it did when his old friend was tired. Evidently, Tahn had finally fallen from his saddle, the rope he'd fastened around the saddle horn slipping its mooring and leaving him to tumble to the ground. Above, the sky remained dark with rain clouds, but Tahn noticed the leaves of trees sprouting delicately on thick branches. Wherever this was, Jole had worked long to bring them here.

A set of legs strode into his field of vision. Tahn tried to raise his head, but the numbness remained complete, leaving only his eyes useful. The boots were hard leather, lashed with black cords that had been tipped with silver links to prevent fraying. Rolling his eyes, Tahn looked up into a rotund face.

"Do I look like an angel, my friend?" the man said, his voice gentle but crisp. "Because you have the look of death in your cheeks. I daresay you're not capable of assisting in your own rescue. No man sleeps in the mud when he has power to avoid it."

Tahn rasped something out.

"And coherent, too," the man replied. "Never mind, you'll be wanting to know about your friend. He's in bad shape, but no worse than you. I'm going to assume you'll be glad of some help. Now you may grunt some protest, but I'll live with your hatred better than the thought of you dying here, picked clean by highwaymen and catching shivers deep to the bone."

The man hunkered down beside him, and Tahn followed him with his eyes. The gentleman's rich, russet cloak parted as he squatted, and Tahn saw the emblem of the League clearly over the man's left breast, and likewise fashioned in the pin that closed the man's cloak at the hollow of his neck. The stranger put a hand to Tahn's brow. A worried expression touched his eyes. "I've no interest in alarming you, my friend. But I've pulled up children from the river who feel more alive than you." He smiled, seeming to think better of verbal diagnosis. "Grunt if you understand."

Tahn heard none of it. He could only stare at the insignia on the pin that closed the man's top garment. Did he know that Tahn had challenged the League at Myrr over the boy Penit? Would word have gotten to him this quickly? Could he know Vendanj had taken him out of the Hollows just ahead of the Quietgiven? Anything the Quietgiven sought so relentlessly was something the League would want destroyed. But the stranger's face did not convey concealment, nor did he appear to recognize Tahn. The suspicion he'd seen in the eyes of Exigents before was not mirrored in this man's gaze. But the thought lessened his concern only slightly. He lay powerless against the man's any whim. He might discover the sticks in Tahn's cloak, misuse them in any manner, turn them over to a higher league authority.

"I am Gehone." He withdrew his hand but stayed there, his elbows on his knees. "When you're dry, warm, and able to speak, I'll be interested to hear how you came to travel north on a road that goes through the mountains." One eye cocked. "This will give you time to construct a lie, so craft it carefully." He smiled wryly. "And think while you're doing it that either you'll pass this world attempting to deceive, or you'll live and make a mockery of the fellow who saved you from your final earth." The smile turned to a chuckle and the big man lifted Tahn as though he was a scarecrow. He put Tahn in the back of a wagon and tethered Jole to the rear axle. With his left ear pressed to the wagon boards, Tahn listened to the creak and roll of the wheels, wondering how he had ended up paralyzed and in the hands of the League.

Gehone drove them for some time, eventually passing into a town. He steered from the light of the main streets to a darkened rear alley. Bats flitted in the air, swooping near the wagon and away again. Gehone pulled to a stop, and shortly scooped Tahn up and took him inside, directly to a bed. Tahn watched him depart and promptly return with Sutter, whom he laid in a second bed on the opposite wall. With fatherly disinterest, the man from the League stripped Tahn and Sutter bare and covered them over with thick wool blankets.

From a pouch at his belt, Gehone produced a small jar. With one thick finger he took at a generous portion of a green salve. "Hold this under your tongue," he said, and deposited the goop in Tahn's mouth. He then took another fingerful and gently applied it to Tahn's lips. He did the same to Sutter, opening Nails's mouth for him and setting the paste beneath his tongue.

Gehone wasted no time, but stood and left the room, taking the lantern with him. Tahn waited in the dark, expecting someone to crash through the door and point accusing fingers at him and Sutter. Instead, he heard only the thin rasp of his friend's breathing. Peppermint and parsley cooled his tongue, and a mellow feeling crept over him, inviting him to sleep once more. Before he succumbed to weariness, he looked around for his cloak and saw it hanging on a peg beside the door. He couldn't see if the sticks were still there, but he hadn't seen Gehone rummage through his things. Hoping his movement would return by morning, Tahn distantly wondered if he would wake before the sun as he always had, or if this time he would simply continue to sleep, lost in the darkness behind his eyes as the numbness climbed inside him and stopped his heart.

"What they've told you are lies." The disembodied voice came to him like whispers echoing from the sweating stone of sealed caves. "Flee us, and flee yourselves."

"Lies?" Tahn asked. "What lies?"

"Every record you possess bleeds from the pens of historians and authors who forget or ignore the abomination of the Whiting." The voice rasped with anger, rising to a growl. "It is you who are imprisoned, bound by manacles you cannot see. And still you walk in chains, even to the ledge—which is where they always go—to discard the life you treasure." Howls of laughter followed, brittle, pained sounds like falling crystal.

"I don't understand," Tahn said, and started to run. Blindly, he forced himself to lift his legs. He held his hands out in front of him and moved faster through the darkness.

"Is this the Will you claim? Running toward nothing? From nothing?" The voice fell low again. "And this because you are *nothing. Nothing to the Will. Nothing that belongs to, returns to, the Quiet." The last word came so softly that Tahn thought he did not hear it.*

"No!" Tahn screamed. He dropped his arms to his sides and pumped his legs, forgetting the possibility of running into anything, sprinting faster into the absence of light.

"How many more suns, Quillescent? How many until the pages burn, the song is ended, and the throats of Leiholan shriek because the covenant is broken, and all promises of men are silly, unkept things, just like the betrayal of the One by the Many? Sleep, Quillescent. Like the sleep of the Bourne. This is where you belong. We are you."

Tahn tried to scream; no sound came.

The darkness seeped inside him and closed his throat. He ran harder, feeling the sweat run down his face and neck. In the distance, brilliant pools of darkness gave life to crisp shadows that glimmered darkly as he ran onward: words floating in the air, parchment spiraling on gusts of hot air from burning rocks and rents in the earth that vented heat in gouts and spumes. Birds fell to the ground as the air itself seemed to catch fire. Broad, dark shapes scrabbled from cracks in the mountains beneath a lowering grey sky. Armies were trampled under by terrible waves of hoary, powerful creatures, the metal in their blades snapping like brittle winter twigs. And tall men, Sheason, knelt, producing feeble light that dissipated in the air like so much dust from an uncultivated field.

Suddenly, all these things were past him, and Tahn ran directly through the image of a sullen creature seated in a low cage in a carnival tent. The image surprised him. It did not feel like part of the others. He looked back over his shoulder to be sure of what he'd seen.

"Leave that be!" the voice commanded. But Tahn saw nothing. The darkness now wrapped around everything, yet glimmered as though alive. Tahn ran up a mountainside toward a pinpoint of light, his body drenched in sweat, his nose running freely. His feet stabbed at paving stones he could not see, becoming raw, but he pushed on, flailing toward a goal that seemed to come no closer despite his pursuit. A chorus followed him, dismal sounds like the unheeded petitions of a street fellow and the sob of a mother over a fresh grave. He could hear the resigned voices of men, creatures, standing in the shadows of a cell. And the din of it all ran out flat across stony ground, flint and ash too hard and dire to embrace these lost souls in the sleep of death. Tahn tried to hum the melodies of story songs to replace the sounds of the dreadful chorus. His own voice failed, swallowed by the dark. Ahead, the pinpoint of light flickered, growing even more distant as his legs tired. He could run no more. With a great leap, Tahn dove toward the single point of light, wherefrom a single voice seemed to emanate, directing him as much as the ray of light could.

Tahn gasped and opened his eyes to a darkened room. In the small bedchamber, shadows seemed to move. The smell of drying wool and pine floorboards reassured him that *this* darkness was real. Across from him, the window showed night beyond, but not so deep with shadow as his room. It was sometime before dawn. Tahn managed to envision the break of rays over the lips of a desert plain and consider it appropriate enough before falling to dreamless sleep.

The sound of boots on the floor roused him sometime later. Tentatively, he opened his eyes, half-expecting to see Jole, rainy sky, and treetops, or perhaps the stiflingly low knit of wilds branches overhead. Instead, he found the rough carpentry of a small room bathed in sunlight.

"It's about time, Woodchuck." The voice was feeble, but only one person called Tahn that.

He tried to raise his head, and was relieved that he could do so, even if just a little.

"Don't strain yourself. Heroes always push themselves too hard," Sutter said from across the room. "But don't go thinking this means I owe you. Hero or not, I'm still a naked man who chafed all night beneath itchy wool blankets."

Tahn licked his lips and attempted to speak. His voice cracked. He swallowed, beginning again more slowly. "Did you say *man*?" Tahn laughed weakly. "You sound better, Nails."

His friend chuckled in return. "I feel like one of your arrow tips is lodged inside my chest. Just talking is sending little spikes of pain into my neck. But I think I like the pain. Means I'm alive and away from Stonemount." Tahn heard Sutter shift in his bed. "By the Sky, what happened to you? Some large fellow walked in this morning and spread some disgusting goop on my lips. I meant to know the reason, but he put a hand over my mouth and said you needed to sleep."

Tahn let his head drop back onto the pillow. "It's all hazy. After Sevilla left, I started going numb. Before my arms went, I built a litter and hitched it to Jole. Eventually we found the rim and canyon. Somewhere along the way I passed out. I woke up when Gehone found us and brought us here."

"Where is here?" Sutter interjected.

"I don't know."

They fell silent. Beyond the door, the occasional sound of boots over wood reminded them that they were not alone.

"You said you went numb? Did Sevilla poison you?"

Tahn considered the question. Perhaps he did at that. He might have had the opportunity while Tahn was sleeping. But somehow it didn't ring true. He shook his head, still happy to have some movement back. "Maybe," he concluded. "But whatever happened, you should know we are now guests in the home of a member of the League."

Tahn heard a quick intake of air. "Does he know about us? We've got to go, Tahn, come." The rigging under Sutter's bed creaked as his friend tried to rise. Tahn listened to the pained effort, Sutter taking shallow breaths and holding them long before grunting them out and continuing to try to hoist himself from his bed. Finally, Tahn heard Sutter flop down as he gave up. "All this way," Sutter said, "and it ends like this."

"Nonsense," Tahn said. His lips still worked slowly. "It's all a blur, but Gehone seems decent. And if he'd known, we might have spent last night in a less comfortable bed."

"You're delirious. Do you hear what you're saying?" Sutter's voice became simultaneously vehement and quiet, as he attempted not to be overheard. "Vendanj told us to beware of the League. I'm grateful for a warm bed, but how many stories do you remember in which the accused are nursed to health so that they may walk the gallows?"

Tahn raised his head again. "And what of your mistrust for the Sheason? Suddenly you believe Vendanj? When did he ever tell us enough of any story that we could decide what to believe? Did you ever consider that he is the reason the Bar'dyn came into the Hollows? They may have been chasing Vendanj and Mira—" The words caught in Tahn's throat at her name. The image of her clear grey eyes rose in his mind with terrific force. Suddenly, he recalled seeing her seated in a rocker beside a window in an abandoned cabin deep in the Hollows. Even in that dark he had seen her eyes.

"Is that what you think?" Sutter replied. "Have you forgotten the Bar'dyn came to your house, came to Wendra . . ."

Sutter trailed off, and quiet returned to the room. As they held a companionable silence, light ebbed and returned as clouds passed over the sun. Then down the outer hall, someone began to approach the door.

Tahn spoke quickly. "You're right. We will leave here as soon as we are able. Don't let Gehone know you've regained your strength."

"What strength?" Sutter laughed, sending him into a coughing spasm. But the absurdity of their condition kept him laughing through the wracking convulsions.

Tahn smiled. He and Sutter had always been able to make peace easily.

The door opened and Gehone entered, carrying a tray with two small bowls and two narrow mugs. Steam rose from them all. He put the tray down on a dresser and crossed to Sutter, propping him up with his pillow until his coughing subsided.

"You're a winsome lad," Gehone said, retrieving the tray. "But I'd save the humor until your lungs can withstand the pressure." He put a bowl and cup at the stand beside Sutter's bed. "Don't waste a drop," he admonished. "The blend of herbs will give you strength and the broth will heal whatever ails you."

Gehone came to Tahn and sat at his side. "Any movement in these arms of yours?" Tahn shook his head. "Ah, but your neck has returned. Good." Gehone lifted Tahn easily and propped his back against the headboard. He lifted the bowl and spooned out some broth. "Are you ready to tell me what business you had in Stonemount? And don't deny you've been there. Your boots are caked with soil that belongs to that place." Gehone put a spoonful of the broth in Tahn's mouth. The savory potage soured on Tahn's tongue.

"Adventure," Sutter said around a mouthful of the hot broth. Gehone turned a questioning look on Sutter. Under the leagueman's gaze, Sutter pulled back a bit. "Accident, really," he added.

Gehone turned again toward Tahn. "That the truth of it, lad?"

Tahn simply nodded.

"Indeed." The man spooned another bite into Tahn's mouth. "Well you're lucky to be out of it alive, then. Lore holds that Stonemount has belonged to the walkers since the hour its residents abandoned it. If it is so, you two must certainly have gone unnoticed there." Gehone watched Tahn closely.

"What are walkers?" Sutter asked, his voice tense.

Without shifting his careful gaze from Tahn, Gehone explained. "Walkers were the first creatures deprived by the Whiting of the One; they were left with no physical form to house their Forda. They are known as untabernacled; they've no bone or muscle, and so they seek to take it from other men. They are the revenants of Stonemount because the bones of the dead there are believed to be able to give life to vagabond spirits. Silly, superstitious stuff, but creatures out of the Craven Season are creatures of appetite. They would not have allowed you to leave, if they exist at all." A careful smile crossed Gehone's lips.

"Perhaps we defeated these walkers," Sutter said. "Perhaps that is why we came to you weak and in need of help."

Gehone put down the bowl and shifted to face Sutter. When the man's back was turned, Tahn shook his head, trying to shut Sutter up.

Gehone spoke with fatherly patience. "Not likely, my young friend. Unless you boys are more than you seem." Gehone ran a hand through his beard and shot a look at the leather piece on Sutter's hand given him by the Sedagin. "But let me be honest. I've seen you both without your breeches, and if you're not melura, you're just my side of the Change. If you really came by way of Stonemount, then I'll wonder what brought you through. Melura or no, there is something different about you lads, and I'm hoping it isn't your penchant to lie. Because tomorrow my commander pays his usual visit to gather my reports and bring me orders. He'll want to know about you, and he'll be a good deal more insistent." Gehone turned around again and began to feed Tahn, who ate quietly, the leagueman occasionally mopping his chin.

When Tahn's feeding was complete, Gehone gathered the dishes and prepared to leave. He stopped with the door halfway shut. "My colleagues direct the course of the fraternity, and that course is my course. But a serpent's tail is where the head was several turns ago. So far from the leadership, I cannot be sure what changes may be coming. And for it all, I think the progress..."

Gehone departed without finishing.

Tahn and Sutter sat looking at the door as the sounds of the leagueman's boots retreated down the hall.

Sutter got out of bed twice that day, quietly pacing the room to test his strength. Nails winced with pain at every stride, but he could stand, and the sight of it eased Tahn's own discomfort. The first time, Tahn had him check for the sticks in his cloak; they were still there. By evening, Tahn found himself capable of moving a few of his fingers and toes. He'd never been so happy to feel the stirrings of such inconsequential things. Gehone came again at dinner, this time bringing thin slices of meat and quartered tallah roots covered in meat drippings. With it he served a mild bitter. "Good for your circulation," he said, and held the cup to Tahn's lips.

The leagueman didn't again mention their travels or the impending arrival of his superior the next day. Instead, he limited himself to idle banter, allowing Tahn and Sutter to enjoy the meal, and taking his leave without a further word when he was done. After supper, Tahn found he could ball his fists and raise his arms. As the night descended, Gehone left a lantern burning for them, the flame just barely taking the chill off the air and lending warmer tones to the surfaces of their beds and skin.

Looking at the scar on his hand, Tahn spoke. "He never once went through our things."

"What?" Sutter asked with a preoccupied voice.

"As far as I know, Gehone has not once tried to know us by going through our belongings." Tahn looked up at Sutter.

"Maybe he didn't need to," Sutter answered. "I get the feeling he has a good idea about us already."

"You think he knows, and is protecting us?" Tahn looked nervously toward the door.

"No. I don't think he suspects we've come from the Hollows or Sheason or Far. But he senses we're running from some danger. And he knows we came out of Stonemount. He has to be wondering what made us sick. Maybe he knows it was a walker, because he knew how to help us."

"Green goop," Tahn muttered.

"Yeah . . . And if that thing was a walker like he said, then he'll be wondering how we got rid of it. My Sky, Tahn, that thing was Quietgiven. How *did* we get rid of it?"

Tahn sat quietly, thinking of an empty bow and an aimless pull over a vast canyon. Weakly, he clenched his fists and lashed out with both arms, striking the headboard to either side. *What do these images mean?*

Sutter waited for his anger to dissipate. Through the hiss of the lantern he said, "I've been thinking about the Bar'dyn, Tahn, when we were first separated from the others. They said things, something about lies. Do you remember?"

"No," Tahn answered immediately. "They are abominations out of the Bourne. The lies belong to them."

"I was just thinking," Sutter continued, "Gehone does not speak like a member of the League, and offers to help us, while Vendanj is closemouthed, even when his silence seems to put us in danger. Things seem twisted, backward. I can't figure it. I'd like to get back to my roots just now."

Tahn laughed in spite of himself.

"I'm serious," Sutter said, chortling through the words. "What I wouldn't give to track mud into Hambley's common room and listen to him prattle on about it. A race to the quarry, you and me; spying on the girls at the Harvest Bath. Now *those* were adventures," he finished, waggling his eyebrows suggestively. Then he spoke a bit more wistfully. "Or to see my father again."

But Sutter didn't linger long on sadnesses, and soon had Tahn laughing. They laughed hard and filled the room with forgetfulness for the place they were in. Sutter laughed, then moaned at the pain in his chest, but he laughed again. The odd rhythm of his jocularity and controlled winces made them laugh that much more. With it all, some feeling returned in Tahn's chest, and the relief brought a fresh dose of cackles that lasted longer than they could have hoped, and took them close to sleep.

Shivering, Tahn awoke to the sight of lesser light pooling on the floor through the window. As he pulled his blanket over his shoulders, two observations hit him with simultaneous, opposite force: he could feel his chest and legs, and the window was open. He looked to the opening and then quickly surveyed the room. In the shadows he narrowed his gaze, peering into the darkness. The fall of moonlight lent sharp contrast to their bedchamber, and left Tahn uneasy beneath his wool blankets.

"Sutter," he whispered. The sound of his own voice fell flat. No response. He could not tell if his friend's bed was occupied, or if the coverlet and sheets had been rolled back in the semblance of a body. Tahn propped himself on one elbow. "Sutter, this is no time for games."

No answer.

Tahn scooted back, aware of the weakness in his arms, but happy to have their use. He sat upright and squinted intently across the room. The bed lay empty. Then outside he heard the crunching of stones beneath boot soles. A shiver passed down his spine and prickled the hair on his legs. Vaguely, he continued to thrill at the return of sensation across his skin, but the prospect of an unseen visitor left his muscles paralyzed with fear. It might be Sutter, but something warned him that it was not.

Where is my bow?

Still watching the window, Tahn swung his legs out of bed. He started to stand, then he realized that he wore no bedclothes. His body cast a thin, ungarbed shadow against the rear wall. With no time for modesty, he forced himself up, only to collapse on weak legs at the side of his bed. He shot a glance at the window, hoping his fall had been soft, and listening for the stranger's approach.

Silence.

He looked around, searching for his weapon, and spied Sutter beneath his own bed as naked as Tahn. He was shivering, wide-eyed and searching.

Over the hard, cold wood, Tahn crawled to retrieve his cloak. Forgetting his bow, he then scuttled toward Sutter, who pushed deeper under his bed as Tahn approached.

"It's me," Tahn said. No recognition touched Sutter's eyes. He clutched at his chest, his eyes darting toward the window and back at Tahn. The grit on the floor scraped his knees and palms, but Tahn lay on his belly and crawled under the bed. Sutter drew up to the wall, his eyes darting to and fro like a ferret's. "Put this on," Tahn said, proffering the cloak. Sutter did not seem to hear.

A roll of boot heel and toe over hard soil came again. It was more distant this time, Tahn thought, but perhaps only because he was now under the bed. He finally disregarded Sutter's skittish look and forged ahead. His friend appeared to expect Tahn to produce a blade and open his throat. Tahn pulled the cloak over Sutter and scooted in close.

"What is it?"

Still Sutter could do nothing more than look about, his eyes rolling widely.

Tahn grasped his friend by the arms and shook him. "Tell me." Sutter came to himself as though he'd been asleep. He looked at Tahn, perplexed, then at the bed, then cast his eyes toward the moonlight falling in a long rectangle from the window.

"I saw it," he said. Tahn was about to question him further when the sound of boot heels came again. The air had just grown colder.

Tahn listened for several moments, looking back to his friend and wondering if Nails had seen the owner of the boots they heard. His skin prickled, the cold of the floor seeping into his bones. Having heard nothing for what seemed a long time, he took Sutter by the hand and led him out from beneath the bed. He cautiously looked around the room, then rose to his knees. Together they stood, and Tahn had started helping Sutter into bed when he again collapsed to the floor, pulling Tahn down with him.

Sutter gasped and pointed at the window. Tahn instantly looked up, but saw nothing there.

"What?" Tahn asked, the sound of it louder than he'd intended.

"Don't you see it?" Sutter cried. "By all the Skies of my life, Tahn, don't let her take me." Sutter began to crawl away, the cloak slipping from his shoulders. He stood, his bare skin covered with goose bumps, holding his hands up to ward off nothing more than the pale light of the moon that poured through the window. His mouth opened in a silent scream. Tahn jerked his attention back to the half-open window, which began to hum as though the ground shook with the flight of swift horses. A thin mist floated over the sill, into the room, and onto the floor. Tahn scrabbled back, bumping into Sutter's legs, but still he could see no one.

The freezing mist licked at Tahn's toes as it roiled across the floorboards. He tried to stand, but weak legs sent him to the floor again. In an instant, Sutter snapped out of his fear. He swung around, took up the lantern that sat upon the table, and hurled it toward the window. With a loud crash, the upper pane blew outward, a spray of shards littering the sill, the broken glass clattering on the hard ground outside. A rush of wind twisted in the fractured portal as Gehone, clad only in a nightshirt, threw open the door and stepped into the room. Across his chest he carried a large war hammer, his hands in well-worn grips along its haft. He spared a look at Tahn and Sutter before stepping over them toward the window, where shards of small glass whipped in the air like cotton-seed in a summer wind. With a flick of his wrists, he spun the hammer in a practiced movement and reared one arm with the weapon. He pointed an open palm at the window and crouched, a level eye prepared to meet an intruder. The muscles in his legs bulged, his thick waist ready to accept a blow. Gehone waited, a cat ready to strike, but the mist evaporated. The wind whistled out into the eaves and was gone.

As soon as it had left completely, Sutter lunged for his sword and clutched it to his chest. Tahn picked up his cloak and wrapped himself modestly. Gehone, advancing cautiously toward the window, studied the wreckage. When he turned, he looked blankly at Sutter. "Put on some clothes and gather your things. I'll put you both upstairs."

Tahn shuddered in the lingering cold. Gehone came close. "You need help?"

Tahn nodded. One bulky arm grabbed him around the waist. "I'll let this pass tonight, lads. But on the morrow, I'll need more answers from you. Nothing sounds so suspicious as the truth, and I'd better know the whole of it, or close to, when my commander comes to call. Hear me?"

Again Tahn only nodded. Still naked, Sutter had picked up his belongings and, with his eyes fastened on the broken glass, waited at the door to be ushered to a new room.

CHAPTER FIFTY-ONE

Revelations in Parchment

In the predawn light, Wendra lay still, listening to birdsong high in the trees and the deep melodic imitations the Ta'Opin made of them while he packed his bedroll and hitched his team. The smell of dew and koffee hung in the air, the latter a gift from Seanbea as he prepared to depart. For the time being, Jastail left Wendra alone, saddling the horses and continuing his charade of friendship with Penit. Wendra tried to ignore it all, focusing on the birds and the hopeful sounds they made.

Lingering memories of shadowy dreams troubled her, but remained vague, like memories of memories. The melodies of last night's song lingered, too, a refrain of the saddest sort.

When she could stand the inner songs no more, she rose. Seanbea sat at the fire, hunkered close to the flame, sipping a mug of koffee.

"Have a cup, Anais," he invited. "My beans are fresh from Su'Winde. I ground them myself this morning." He poured her a cup from a pot, and returned it to its rock beside the fire. "Is there a better smell when day is young?" He tilted his head back and closed his eyes. "There are advantages on the highroads."

Wendra intensely desired to plead for help. Seanbea sat just a stride away. She could whisper their trouble, ask him to intervene. Just when she thought she might do so, Jastail and Penit joined them.

"A fine day. Good fortune to our separate enterprises, Seanbea. Hardly a worry on a day such as this."

"Right you are," the Ta'Opin answered, lifting the pot of koffee to offer a second cup. Jastail amiably declined. "I'm hitched and loaded. I'll be off when my cup is empty. Is there any message I can carry for you?"

Wendra hoped the offer would raise concern in Jastail's face, betray his intentions to the Ta'Opin. The highwayman did not blink. "How good a man you are, Seanbea. Thank you, but we are fine. Is there more we can do for *you*?"

"There is."

This time Jastail's expression faltered a moment. Wendra could see her captor mentally working the positions of each of them at the fire. How the physical exchange would develop if he were forced to draw. She knew he'd cut the

Ta'Opin's throat in an instant if what the man said next jeopardized whatever business he meant to conduct with her and Penit.

Seanbea looked at Wendra, and ever so subtly she shook her head. He'd sensed it; he knew. He would ask her if she traveled with Jastail of her own free will. Ask Penit's true relationship to the highwayman. Deep inside her the thought of it terrified her, but also made her feel relieved. Perhaps Seanbea could beat Jastail in open combat. She and the Ta'Opin locked eyes; to her right, Wendra heard the soft squeak of a tightened palm over a leather hilt.

"I've something for you," Seanbea said. He reached into his coat, and Jastail began to move. Seanbea held in his hand a rolled parchment. He ignored Jastail's movement. The Ta'Opin only focused on Wendra as he passed the sheet to her with both hands. "It is your song, Anais. The one you made last night in harmony to mine." He smiled paternally. "I've rarely heard instant song so beautifully made. The lines of your music played on in my head and demanded to be written down. Keep this and remember your song. The notation is for only a single instrument, but when you can use that instrument to share the gift of this music, you gift others. Study it. And when you come to Recityv, show it to the Maesteri. They'll recognize it for what it is."

Wendra took the yellowed vellum and unfurled the music. With light, thin strokes the Ta'Opin had marked a series of vertical marks, interrupted by small circles with varying numbers of tails like a ship rudder. The circles came at longer and shorter intervals and rose or fell across a straight line, repeating several times down the parchment. She did not understand it, but the delicate work of Seanbea's hand and the intricate weave of inked symbols delighted her. She rose from her seat and put one arm around the Ta'Opin's neck, squeezing until she thought she might be suffocating the man.

Drawing back, she said, "Thank you. I never thought . . . thank you."

Penit seemed pleased with the gift. He came over to look at it as Wendra sat beside Seanbea and took his hand. Jastail's guarded look eased, and he dropped his hand from his sword. "How foolish of me," he said. "You do my fire honor. You have my gratitude as well." He bowed, but not so deeply that he lost his vantage on all three. "We should be going," he said.

"And I," Seanbea added. "Safe haven to you at your . . . uncle's, did you say?"

"Safe haven to you," Jastail responded.

Seanbea ruffled Penit's hair and squeezed Wendra's hand. He said to her, "I hope one day to hear you sing again," then mounted his wagon and drove to the road where he turned north, raising a streamer of dust until the trees obscured him from view.

Jastail's smile frayed at the edges, but only slightly. The highwayman maintained his good humor, calling Penit to take his saddle. In moments, dirt had been kicked over the fire, and Jastail led them back to the road.

For half a day they rode, Penit tirelessly asking the highwayman questions. Wendra stayed behind them, a mixture of gratitude and simmering anger contending within her. More than once the image of the Bar'dyn clutching her child erupted in her vision; each time it came when she saw Jastail put an encouraging hand on Penit as the two laughed and talked. She fought back the sounds that struggled to escape her lips, wondering what they might appear like in Seanbea's beautiful script.

Shortly after meridian, the highwayman turned them west off the road. No trail guided them, but he seemed to know his way, and never paused even when fording a shaded river running in the depths of the tall evergreens.

Night had not fully come when they emerged from a thin grove of aspen into a flat hollow at the base of three mountains. In the center of a clearing, a small log cabin sat low and virtually hidden by several holly bushes. A large moon shimmered on a narrow stream that wound through the hollow and near one side of the cabin. In the dark, the smell of wild honeysuckle and high-mountain lilac hung heavy in the air. Jastail surveyed the basin before going ahead, his sharp eyes searching the dark. Several times he turned around to watch the way behind, allowing Wendra to pass. He appeared more skittish than she'd ever seen him. The furtive look on his face pleased her. But what might make a hollow man jumpy?

Jastail left the horses saddled while he checked the cabin. No lock secured the door, and the highwayman entered so quietly that the sound of the brook concealed his entry. The fleeting thought to run teased Wendra. But she could no longer be sure Penit would follow her—the boy and the highwayman seemed good friends.

In the neutral glow of the lesser light, the boy's silhouette showed the image of the man he would become. A fuller nose, a deeper jaw, eyes set in lines earned by experience he couldn't yet dream of, broader shoulders and chest. She would fight to save the brave lad's future.

"Come," Jastail whispered.

Penit jumped down and bounded inside. Wendra climbed down with stiff legs and wrapped her reins in a nearby shrub, then did the same with Penit's. Jastail emerged from the doorway and skulked like a shadow to her side. He rolled a tobaccom leaf into a small wrapper. With a curling motion, he drew a knife across a cylinder of flint and brought an oil lamp to flame. He puffed his tobaccom alight, and stood drawing deeply of the sweet-leaf.

"We are almost done, you and I." He spoke like a merchant describing a business arrangement.

Wendra smelled the smoke on the air, and watched it, silver and dreamlike in the moonlight. She remembered Balatin striking alight his pipe, the gentle soap and tobaccom smell of his beard and sleeves as he pulled her to his chest and rocked back in the shadows of their porch. A hundred lesser cycles ago this night, this moon, and this smoke would have meant something entirely different. Tonight, they came as an insult to her memory, more bitter, cold resin than sweet, warm leaf.

She withdrew her parchment from her pocket, and followed the graceful strokes as she remembered her melody.

Without looking up from the page, she said, "I can only imagine that we will die, *highwayman*." She uttered the defamatory term with as much derision as she had. "Either in body or in spirit, but whatever trade or sale you conduct in this remote vale is meant to be kept secret. An arrangement you keep with men that are less comfortable beside the road. I come to comfort the boy, or you would have had to kill me long ago to have my obedience."

"Are you sure you've never read Toille?" She could feel his sarcastic smile in the darkness. "You speak much as he wrote, such unvarnished truth. But really you have seen an unlikely end to this." He scrubbed one side of his face. "No matter. I won't convince you. You'll know when you know. Not that you'll be any happier, but you are resilient, my dear. A good deal more so than I'd have guessed when I first found you seeking out the boy. And a good lad, too."

"You strain your hold over me, highwayman." This time Jastail bristled at the epithet.

"Meaning if you believed him lost to you that you would take to these hills alone and leave him behind?" Jastail chuckled. He drew deeply of his tobaccom, and let out the sweet-smelling smoke as he spoke. "A poor threat, my lady. I know more about you than you may realize. Learned, as a matter of fact, in just keeping your company. And what I know tells me that you will stay close to the boy until you've no more power to do so. That the child fancies me, that I've encouraged it, makes you hate me. But I really don't care."

His glib words and easy manner as he smoked and admired the waxing light of the moon rankled Wendra as nothing else had done. She wanted to tell him she'd try to kill him. She longed to clutch his throat and drive his head into the ground. The images blossomed in her head and brought with them snatches of melody that cooled her heart.

"Nothing to say," Jastail mocked. "Dear me, what can this mean?" He puffed again on his tobaccom. "I gave the boy a bed. Tomorrow will bring revelations to him for which he'll need his strength. You should sleep as well."

Wendra said nothing, and did not move. She only looked again at her parchment and followed her song in her mind.

Lost in the internal sound, she did not notice the highwayman draw nigh. Suddenly, he stood very near, hunched slightly to stare at the page she held in her fingers. A derisive smile curled his lips in the strong moonlight. "Seems we both have our favorite poets. Yours, a Ta'Opin who drives a wagon filled with useless artifacts." A quiet chuckled escaped him. "You see, even now I am not unkind. A petty scoundrel would snatch your song from your hands to deprive you of its distraction." He put one hand on his chest. "While *I* recognize the value that tinder holds for me in quieting your vengeful thoughts."

Wendra seethed at his disregard for her parchment of music. Her captor's arrogance stirred the unsettling song in her bosom.

"No poem tonight?" Wendra asked in response, her voice neutral, mocking his penchant for verse. "You would let your education slip so that you could taunt me, a piece of merchandise. Or have you just realized that your poet is a buffoon?"

Wendra knew her words seared him, for even as she spoke, the familiar callousness stole over his eyes as he turned them toward her in the lunar light. The rays of the moon in his pupils, his face very close to her own—the smell of sweet-leaf soft as a lover's kiss between them. No anger, no regret, no fear, no expectation showed in his hollowed cheeks or slash of a mouth. He stared at her, his eyes focused and unmoving. Then he recited from memory:

> *Some lift prying eyes to discover the motive hands.*
> *Some toil daylight hours to rest and dream their days a different end.*
> *Still others make brash sounds,*
> *And many tormented supplication say on bended knees.*
> *Youth scrapes and hides and practices for its own time to stare the wall.*
> *I these things observe and name them wounds,*
> *And by so doing create my inmost salve,*
> *With which to rise and watch it all again.*

Jastail held her gaze a moment more. Then he tossed his tobaccom into a bulrush and unsaddled the horses. The words leapt to spontaneous melody inside her. They felt like song that mustn't be sung. The mere thought of it chilled her heart. She rushed inside and left the highwayman to his neutral moon and dark verse. Tomorrow, she felt, would be her last chance to save the boy and herself, and to have any hope of seeing Tahn again.

She offered a silent good-bye to her brother at the lesser light, just in case . . . *I love you, Tahn.*

Light came through the window, diffused by the ungainly branches of several holly bushes growing beside the cabin. Wendra lay in a fetal position, Penit curled up against her chest. The soft intake of his breath against the blanket made her sure she'd been right to find him. Hoping that their silence would keep Jastail away, she lay watching the sun strengthen in the sky and at last heard old melodies in her head and let go the worry of imminent confrontation she'd carried since meeting the highwayman.

In another part of the cabin, she heard preparation for endfast. Penit would be hungry, but she did not want to wake him. He had not been this close to her in days. His smooth brow and downy cheeks glowed just a finger's breadth from her own, his face a portrait of unconditional trust. The memory of sleeping this way with her father, especially in the months after her mother had died, stole over her. His broad chest and strong arms had made her feel safe. Then, like now, she'd woken first, but lain still so the spell of morning calm could linger.

The way she imagined she would have done with her own child.

A soft moan, response to some fanciful childhood dream, escaped Penit's mouth. He squirmed and settled again even closer. Wendra fought the urge to hug him. He might wake if she did. In her softest voice, she began to hum, the sound delicate, so soft that Penit's breathing could be heard to keep time. She found phrases from her songbox in her mind and wove them into variations as bright and promising as the light from the window. Penit did not stir, and Wendra thought she could feel herself healing as she had in the cave, though somehow differently now.

Thinking of the cave, she remembered that she'd wanted to ask the boy what he'd seen in the mists of Je'holta when he'd broken the line and raced away. But it no longer seemed to matter, and she relaxed for the moment, lying by his side.

Then he opened his eyes and turned to look at her. "You sing well. We never had such a good voice on the wagons."

Wendra smiled. Then something she'd wanted to be alone to talk to Penit about surfaced abruptly. "Don't be fooled by Jastail, Penit. He is only playing at being your friend. He uses you to control me, because he knows I won't do—"

"I know," Penit interrupted with a secretive whisper. "I've known men like him my whole life. They're the ones that take coins out of the hat on the wagon wheel. I'm just letting him think his little pageant is working to keep his trust. I figure sooner or later it may give us an advantage—"

The bedroom door opened with a thick, heavy crack against the wall. "You'll need to eat," Jastail called and returned to the outer room. Wendra and Penit shared a conspiratorial smile. Then he leapt from the bed and pulled on his boots.

"Will we make it to Recityv today?" Penit asked, following Jastail and resuming his ruse.

"Not today, lad." Jastail put an arm around the boy and the two walked into the hall toward the kitchen.

"Maybe never," Wendra added, alone in the sunbathed room.

Fried oats covered in honey, roasted water-root, and spring water lay on the table in a bounteous endfast. Jastail sat magnanimously at the head of the table and passed dishes to Wendra and Penit. "You've both worked so hard," he said. "I wanted to treat you to a good morning meal. Have plenty."

"And where did you learn this hospitality?" she asked.

Jastail smiled thinly. "But you already know. It is my poetry that teaches me civility. And"—he looked around the cabin—"there is a certain grace amongst highwaymen, if you must know. We do not all slop from a trough."

Wendra forced herself to eat. The meal felt like an extra bale of hay, when calves and lambs were fatted for Harvest Bath. But she would need her strength when her moment arrived, and she ate a second helping of everything to ensure she did not faint when that moment came.

Penit slapped his lips with every bite, savoring the oats especially. He rushed through each helping, seeming to expect that they'd be back on the trail again after endfast. He gulped his spring water and sat looking at Jastail as the highwayman finished his water-root. Their captor ate in silence, suddenly less disposed to play to Penit's worship.

Wendra thought of Master Olear taking lambs into his shed. The animals bleated and complained, sensing the awful business intended for them, until Master Olear spoke in his soft, singsong voice to reassure them. She never saw how the lambs met their end. But she could still hear the lilting phrases of reassurance muted by the wooden walls of the shed. She heard hooves on planks coming to a halt. And she still heard a final strangled cry before the silence, and with it, the grunt of Master Olear bearing down as he plunged his implement of death into the beast. She and Penit were on the boards as surely as he'd been in Galadell. They were in the silence now, the coaxing words having brought them to the cabin. She wondered what sound Jastail would make as he made victims of them.

She put trembling hands into her lap to hold them still. The terrible uncertainty of not knowing Jastail's plan oppressed her. Wendra looked down at the fork she'd taken her meal with. *One clean movement. Take the utensil in hand and stick it into Jastail's throat.* She could smell the tobaccom smoke on him, and hated her own fear of the apathy in his eyes. Her gorge rose, sour and rank at the very look of her captor; bile burned her throat.

"We're going to stay here a day or two," Jastail said, not meeting Penit's eyes. "We could all use some rest, and I have stock here for ten days or more."

"I thought you were taking us to Recityv?" Penit asked.

"Indeed, lad, I am." Jastail instantly adopted the paternal look he'd mastered during their days together. "But the woman here needs some rest. It's not fair to push her as fast as we can go." He leaned toward Penit to make a show of solidarity.

"I am fine," Wendra responded, still clutching her hands in her lap. "I'm not at all tired."

Jastail flashed angry eyes at her, but regained his composure quickly. "Every woman will say such things, Penit, may the Will bless them for it. They'll push on until they near collapse from exhaustion. But a proper man knows to take his time, attend her needs." Jastail allowed himself a slightly lurid look. "And so we'll rest a day or two, eat well, relax. Then on to Recityv."

"And will you help us find the Sheason?" Penit asked, immediately looking at Wendra. His face said that he knew he'd just made a horrible mistake. It was the first look at the old Penit she'd had in many days, and despite the blunder, the face warmed her.

Jastail glared at Penit, then Wendra. He exuded anger like heat, catching her and Penit in its waves. "What business have you with Sheason?" Jastail inquired, his voice just barely restraining fury.

"None at all," Wendra responded, her eyes still on Penit.

"Boy," Jastail said turning toward Penit. "Tell me true. You seek one of the order. Why?" Penit looked at the highwayman and back at Wendra like a rabbit caught in a trapper's snare.

"I won't ask you again," Jastail said, his voice rising as he slowly lost control.

Wendra let the highwayman grow cross with Penit, and made no immediate move to help him. She hoped it would dispel the false countenance he'd tried to show the boy. The turn of events pleased her, and she fought her own smile even as Jastail lost his temper.

"What should I say, Wendra?" Penit finally asked, pleading for help across the table of oats and water-root.

Jastail smiled. Penit's face immediately showed regret for his mistake: He'd revealed her true name.

Wendra put a forgiving hand over Penit's own and inclined toward him. "Tell him that it might be wise of him to take us to Recityv today. Tell him that his anger or any bruises it may cause you and me will not look good to potential buyers, if we are to fetch the price he wants for us. And tell him that the poet he adores has twisted him from a fine cook of honeyed oats to a sack of grain tainted with weevils."

Penit stared back in confusion.

"Or tell him he smells bad and ought to take a bath."

The table shook. Jastail rose, his fists still trembling where he'd pounded them into the tabletop. He swallowed slowly, the rise of blood to his cheeks suffusing his entire face. Then he composed himself, the callous look that Wendra dreaded returning. "You misunderstand, *Wendra*," Jastail began, making sure she knew he'd caught her lie. He went on in his strange uninflected tone. "I only wish I might have known to raise my price on you and the child. But I've not been entirely in the dark. Why do you suppose I purchased my own lot?" He motioned at Penit without looking at him. "I saw what happened in you at the auction. I listened to you singing with the Ta'Opin. How ironic that it is my poet who has described such things to me and leaves their traces in my memory? The boy's loose tongue gives my suspicions credibility. It will help me fetch the prize I seek."

"And what is that, highwayman?" Wendra asked. "I've a poet, too, and he has defined the man you are." She studied his face. "Stuffed. And as worthless as a scarecrow. So much dried hay to fill a discarded shirt and pair of trousers. For you, no prize will stir your heart. That is what I learned from Gynedo on your gambling riverboat. It is a wonder you care at all for your own safety."

Jastail smiled then, a baleful, awful twist of his lips. "Ah, but I do." He came around the table and bent to speak at Wendra's ear. "One does not deal with Quietgiven alone."

Wendra's heart seemed to stop. She did not turn in surprise, as she thought Jastail hoped she might. But the mention of the legions from the Bourne sent chills down her back.

"They are not generally of high business principles," Jastail went on. "You may be glad of it, too, Anais. I've men coming to partner with me in this trade. Safety in numbers, you see. And your womb and the child's innocence are high market items with those out of the Bourne. Your little songs and closeness with the order are treasures I would thank the Great Fathers for, if I believed."

Wendra smiled triumphantly. "I've a gift for you then. One that may inspire belief in you for a Will of mercy."

"Indeed," Jastail mocked. "One of your pretty songs laced with insults and hatred, perhaps."

"Not at all." Wendra dug into her trousers and produced the parchment she'd found in Jastail's room at Galadell. She placed it delicately beside her plate. "A fine garnish to this meal, highwayman." She then turned and glowered at him. "There'll be no help coming. Your men will have no message."

Jastail hit Wendra full force on the side of the head, sending her sprawling to the floor. "By every death I've seen!" he howled. "I would send you to join them!"

Licking blood from her lip, Wendra said, mocking, "And what of our price, highwayman?" Penit raced around the table to kneel beside her. "Is there still value in us if my womb is cold and the boy lies dead in his purity?" She spat the blood from her mouth. "I don't know what use they have of us, you mongrel, but great is the Will that brings you to know what it is to be ruled by the hand of another. I'll pray for rough hands on your most tender skin. And to know what price a highwayman will bring on his own block should the Given take a liking to you."

Jastail swung to face her full on, savagely pointing a finger at her. "You are

small-village wise, Anais, and small-village foolish. What gain is there for Quietgiven in killing or shackling a trader in human stock? Ending a steady supply
from a consistent source?"

Wendra returned his glare. "And you are blinded by your own commerce,
and your own need to liven a hardened soul." She spat again, this time aiming
for Jastail's boots. "The Bar'dyn chased me out of my home at the very hour of my
childbirth. Do you understand? They came especially for me. They won't leave
behind any connection to me; not even the trader who brought me to them."
She got to one knee. "Your trading days are over, unless you hold a threat that
dissuades them." She picked up the scrap of parchment. "And I have taken
that advantage from you. When they come, you will join the boy and me." She
smiled, uncaring that her lips still bled. "If they don't decide to simply kill you."

Jastail stared at Wendra as she stood, shielding Penit behind her. His lip
curled, quivering behind his finely trimmed beard, when the heavy sound of
many feet announced others approaching the cabin. The emotion in Jastail's
face disappeared like smoke in the wind, and he calmly walked past Wendra
and Penit toward the door. Her hands began to shake more violently. Jastail
represented the worst of men, but her heart would not be still, for she realized
what lay for her and Penit in the clearing beyond the door.

• CHAPTER FIFTY-TWO •

Public Discipline

Tahn slept fitfully, never descending into full sleep. Sutter dreamed, muttering and calling out, but always hugging close his sword, the handle
locked into the hollow of his cheek like a child's doll.

What did he see? The mists, what were they?

In the absence of sleep, Tahn restrung his bow, grateful for a simple task to
perform. He had to blink back the images of attempting to draw an unstrung
weapon against Sevilla. After he tested the string, he put aside his bow and took
a stance to the side of the window, testing his strength. Over the rooftop of the
next building he could see the tail of the serpent stars, dipping now below the
horizon. Soon the dawn would come. But what beauty the night held for now:
Distant, shining stars with their stories and unending surety; the sleeping
world, the peace, the quiet. Perhaps the light of day would do better to remain

on the other side of the world. Would time march on if the greater light did not rise to wake men and thrust them into keening for another meal or battle for dominion?

Tahn looked away at the serpent's tail, six stars in a gentle curve that plunged into the land, hiding its head. Gone to its earth, Tahn thought. But then he imagined he could see the morn, a gentle warming of color at the farthest end of the land. "The song of the feathered," Balatin used to say. Let it come.

The thought exhausted him; recent days had been long and hard.

"You're up." Gehone's voice came softly, but startled Tahn nonetheless. "Let your friend sleep, and join me in the kitchen." Tahn looked at Sutter and smiled wanly.

Bright lamps gave the kitchen a cheerful look. A brick oven warmed in one corner, fired with ash logs that lay in a wood scuttle beside it. A black skillet rested on an iron grate, and the fragrance of cooking apples filled the air. Gehone took a seat at the table and poured a mellow-colored cider. He pushed one mug at Tahn. "Goes good with warm apples," he said, and drank.

Tahn sipped and rubbed his legs, which still tingled the way they did when he'd sat cross-legged too long.

Gehone, raising a finger the way Balatin often had, looked ready to speak. But as he opened his mouth, he seemed to think better of it, and smiled sympathetically with his eyes. He said only, "Apples first." The leagueman went to the cupboard and took down two bowls. From the skillet he scooped two large portions of sliced apples warmed in what smelled like cow cream. Gehone returned and set the dishes on the table. Before Tahn could take his first bite, Gehone spooned a brown powder over the warm, sliced fruit. Tahn ate, disappearing into the taste of cinnamon and molasses. Gehone was right; apple cider was the perfect complement. They endfasted in silence, while outside the sun blued the sky.

With his last morsel, Gehone licked his lips and studied Tahn's face. "I'm not an old man—still have use of my arms like a man twenty years younger—but I'm old enough to know striplings have no business in Stonemount. Old enough to have seen sensible boys cower at the sight of an empty window, or like to it. Now, you can keep it from me, lad, and I'm bound to respect your right to do it, but if there's trouble, I need to know. The League needs to know."

"The League," Tahn parroted before he realized he'd said it.

"Yes, is the name sour on your tongue?"

Tahn returned Gehone's careful stare. "I've no reason to trust *or* distrust you."

"I see, other than me dragging you out of a rainy ditch and giving you a warm, dry bed," Gehone said with a guileless smile.

So far. I've come so far. Maybe he can be trusted.

Tahn wanted desperately to tell Gehone everything, to unburden himself of it all. But behind his need to confess lurked his dreams of misdoubt and perhaps even of betrayal. Still, Tahn sensed he could trust Gehone, and decided to tell part. He related their run-in with Sevilla in Stonemount, withholding the part about the empty bow; of the library, but not of the sticks in his cloak; of Ariana and the great striped tents, but not of the Lul'Masi. And he told of Bar'dyn, but not Vendanj or Mira. Gehone sat, paying close attention. The smell of warm apples hung in the air. And when Tahn came to the last, Sutter appeared in the door, a weak smile on his lips.

"Smells good," he said, the question clear in his voice.

"Have a seat, lad." Gehone got up to the endfast fire. "We'll all eat. And then you will prepare to leave. It won't be good for you to be here when Commander Lethur arrives."

The clatter of hooves interrupted them. Gehone rushed to the door and poked his head out. He looked only a moment, then ducked back inside, showing Tahn a troubled brow.

"To your room, quickly!" He gathered the bowls and stuffed them back in the cupboard unwashed. "Prepare yourselves to leave, then hide in the closet. Make no sound and stay away from the window."

Gehone dashed past them and down the hall toward the front door. Sutter turned an ashen face to Tahn. Nothing needed to be said. The League of Civility had arrived, and by the sound of it, Gehone's superior had not come alone.

They dressed quietly. Sutter buckled his sword and Tahn took up his bow. Near the window, Tahn paused and eased forward, hoping to catch a glimpse of the new arrivals. Several horses stood tethered to a hitching post, their flanks steaming in the crisp morning air. A thin coat of frost still clung to the ground where the sun had not yet touched, and above it all, the sky stretched in a perfect lake of unbroken blue. Then came the sound of many boots on the porch. Tahn crept forward, hoping to catch sight of the men.

Then he saw her.

Bound at the wrists, legs tied to the saddle straps, sat a woman, holding her chin at a defiant angle. A soiled dress gathered about her waist and thighs and exposed her calves, which bore a cake of mud from her horse's hooves. Her cheeks hung slack as though from lack of sleep, but Tahn thought he knew the look: resignation. She might hold her head up, but her expression held none of the determination she affected.

A firm knock came at the front door and Tahn stepped back from the window. Sutter grabbed his arm and pulled him toward the closet. Disuse and the smell of moths clung to the tiny space. Tahn and Sutter quietly sat in the small enclosure as voices rose from below.

"We are all one," a deep, clipped voice announced.

"And therein lies our strength." Gehone's words seemed a routine reply. The exchange came muffled but understandable through the floor.

"To protect civility in every form, the surest call," the other finished on cue. A rattle of armor came next, and a series of cordial exchanges.

"You are early," Gehone said.

"First Commander Cheltan thought it best that this business come to a quick conclusion."

The other voice worried Tahn. The man spoke with eagerness, but slowly, as if he might rush toward the exacting of a long, painful punishment.

"What business is this?" Gehone answered. "I've had no reports. Is there news?"

"Indeed," the Commander said in an odd tone. It reminded Tahn of a man with a surprise to share, but one he knew would displease Gehone. His speech carried a sense of delight.

"What news then?" Gehone asked.

The gleefulness disappeared from the other's words. "A public discipline—"

"But we—"

"I have authority to exercise, Gehone. Make your complaint if you will, but even by courier bird it will arrive too late in this instance." A shuffling of feet followed, and Tahn imagined the commander walking to the door to point to the woman he'd seen. *Public discipline.* He didn't know what it meant, but it must surely have to do with the woman tied onto the horse.

"By every Sky and each man's Will, Lethur, can you mean to do this?" The desperation in Gehone's voice concerned Tahn more than the undercurrent of delight in the commander's words.

"The shadow of civil disobedience grows longer, Gehone. It spawns insurgence in every nation. The League alone appears ready to stand against it."

"By disciplining a woman in view of children? What is her crime?" Gehone's fervor grew.

"Keep your place, man!" Lethur snapped. "We have all of us unpleasant tasks to perform. But civilization is stronger when corrupting elements are removed. And so much the better if the unenlightened can be made a lesson to others. Remember your oath." Lethur's voice softened. "Petition for change if you think it will advance civil thought, but remember this"—the Commander's voice was one that would clearly brook no argument—"your right to make your own choices is not free rein; it comes with responsibility . . . and consequence. When this is understood, the choices you make will conform perfectly with His Leadership, Ascendant Staned."

Gehone did not answer. Several moments passed before Lethur spoke. "Good. I've always admired your loyalty to the League, Gehone. It is a credit to you when you follow in mind though your heart somtimes clings to the misguided traditions of uncivil men. Old Guard, maybe." Lethur laughed. "And perhaps the last of those. But you are a leader's man, to be counted on to fulfill the oath by doing your duty."

"When?" Gehone asked flatly.

"As soon as the town is fully awake," Lethur replied. "I'll expect you to be there. You will gather your four standards and meet us. Perhaps I will leave the discipline to you. It may give you sway here, cause reflection in those who do not fully understand the common interest."

Gehone's next words seemed to come through gritted teeth. "It's not really discipline at all, is it, commander?"

"What do you mean to say, Gehone? Speak up. I won't listen to mumbled words."

"Discipline ought to mean a chance to change." Gehone spoke with unfaltering passion.

"Ah, astute as ever, Gehone," Commander Lethur replied. "But you miss the point, and I am glad to make it a source of instruction to you. You see, it is not really the woman we will be disciplining at all, is it? The spectacle of her disciplines a hundred, a thousand, ten thousand. This is the value our leadership sees in such a thing. She is a willful woman, convicted of harboring known opponents to the leadership's stand against disobedience and the order. The world is changing, Gehone, the superstitions and falsehoods of our fathers no longer hold meaning for us. The Court of Judicature is beginning to see this, even though the Sheason Artixan still holds a seat there." Lethur paused, seeming to consider. "Enough. Your three brothers must be brought. Every interest must be represented. Go, and we will make our preparations." The commander paused again for a long moment. "I smell cream and apples, Gehone. What guests have you that you prepare your renowned confection?"

Tahn held his breath. Lethur seemed to know Gehone intimately. Would he detect the secret in their rescuer's eyes?

Without a moment's lapse, Gehone replied, "I take it more in solitary company these days, Lethur. I've few who warrant the effort." Tahn heard the veiled insult clearly in the leagueman's voice.

The sound of receding feet rose through the floorboards; the commander was apparently willing to leave the words uncontested. Then Lethur stopped, and spoke again. "You're a good oath man, Gehone." The footsteps resumed, and in a moment, the party of leaguemen exited, pulling shut the door behind them.

Tahn panted in the musty confines of the closet. He finally had to open the door to catch his breath. Crawling to the window, he peered over the sill. Eight men led the woman away up the street, townsfolk stopping to stare and point.

"Away from that window, you imbecile." The command was soft but direct.

"Hiding from the League makes you criminals to a mind like Lethur's. I must go to the rest of my jurshah. All four branches of the League must be present at the common for the discipline. Tahn, your horse is in the stable. And an old mare is yours for the taking," he said, nodding to Sutter. "But she's not had a rider in several months. That is the last help I can be to you."

"What are they going to do to the woman?" Tahn asked.

Gehone's eyes were fiery, but he did not speak. Tahn watched a slow burn etch red lines in the leagueman's face. Finally, he said, "It is none of your concern. Take advantage of Lethur's preoccupation and leave town. You'll have several hours if you go now. I don't know what his next orders will be, so don't travel directly upon the road. Keep a safe distance, whatever direction you go. If he spots you, you'll be questioned, and Lethur will find any petty grievance to haul you before an authority if he thinks you're hiding something from him. And you two don't look to be good liars."

"But we've done nothing," Sutter said, seething.

"Relax your sword arm, boy. I am not your enemy. It won't matter if you've done nothing. The principalities are often afraid to follow the dictates of their own laws when hearing an argument from a league commander in open court." In a soft voice, Gehone added, "Lower councils and mayors are men and women with families, easily pressed." Gehone clutched the brocade at his neck. "This wasn't the course we set," he muttered, and turned to leave.

"Wait," Tahn called. "Thank you."

Gehone stopped and turned back. Solemn eyes searched Tahn as he approached Gehone and raised a hand in gratitude. The leagueman looked down at Tahn's fingers with an odd expression, as though the gesture were foreign to him. Then, with a growing recognition in his face, Gehone took Tahn's hand in his own. Cupping his other palm under their handshake, as Balatin had taught him to do, Tahn secured his thanks. Gehone seemed surprised at the gesture.

"Go in safety, lads," the leagueman said, a peaceful look smoothing his brow. He clapped Tahn's shoulder and descended the stairs.

"Can we go now?" Sutter said with slight exasperation.

In answer, Tahn hurried to the kitchen and straight across to the rear door. Shadows still clung to the yard. Crouching low, he opened the door and scurried over to the stable. Sutter came close behind and, pushing the door inward, they crept inside.

Jole stood munching some hay. The mare Gehone mentioned had a deep sway in its back and long hair. Tahn smiled to think that the leagueman had kept the horse, which in any farming community would have been put down or released to wend its way to the end of its life. The hoary animal whickered under Tahn's hands as he brushed its flank.

"We'll get far with this one," Sutter complained. "I'll do better on foot."

"Saddle her," Tahn said, and set to doing the same with Jole. In moments they were ready. Gehone had prepared a bedroll and saddlebags filled with dried meat and flatbreads, two skins of water, and a fresh coil of rope. Tahn mounted Jole and rode to the stable door. Behind him the sound of clattering hooves drew his attention. Sutter had one foot in a stirrup, and was hopping after his ornery mount. Wide-eyed, the mare sidled away and whickered in protest.

"No good even with older women, Nails?"

Sutter was too preoccupied to retaliate. Tahn chuckled softly as his friend and the old mare kicked up hay dust in a skitter of feet and hooves. When Sutter got mad enough, he yanked the horse close and leapt atop her. The old mare half reared twice, then settled with a stamping of her feet.

"All done playing?" Tahn teased.

Sutter's glower turned to a smile of acknowledgment. "You just wait, Woodchuck. I've a long memory for insults."

"Because there's so much to love about you, no doubt," Tahn countered.

They both laughed, and Tahn led them out of the stable. From behind him, Sutter rode up and leaned close. "This is the way the League went. Shouldn't we find another way out of town?"

Tahn didn't answer.

"Oh, no. You can't be serious. What do you think you can do about it? It's you and me against a whole band of them. This is not the way to make it to Recityv, Tahn. Vendanj wouldn't approve."

Tahn looked an answer at Sutter this time.

"You're right. What do I care what the Sheason might do?"

Further on, pedestrians crowded the streets. Fine-chipped gravel had been laid down across the main avenues. Boys gathered in clumps, taking turns running and skidding through the loose rock. The sound of so many feet across the tiny stones reminded Tahn of the Huber at spring runoff, a low white roar.

Several streets up, they came to a broad avenue, nearly twice the width of the others. Instinctively, Tahn turned the corner and kept close to one side. A hundred strides on, a crowd had gathered. High in Jole's saddle, Tahn saw past them to almost three dozen leaguemen in their rich, russet cloaks preparing some kind of structure at the midpoint of the broad central concourse. Tahn could see the woman still sitting on her horse, the same resignation weighing down her pliant features.

Tahn angled Jole to a nearby hitching post and dismounted. He and Sutter tethered their horses and blended into the crowd. Tahn positioned them in the center of the pack, not close enough to be clearly seen by the League, but close enough to have a good view of the proceeding. They'd been there for only a moment when Commander Lethur came forward to address the crowd.

"We live in a glorious time, good people." Lethur looked the crowd over

from one end to the other. "Our knowledge grows every day, our wisdom re-
fines, our civility improves the quality of our lives." His voice rose stridently
over the mob, which began to stretch farther and farther back each passing
moment. "It is your birthright, each of you, to know choice and determination
and to lift yourselves up, despite the superstitions and flawed ideas of seasons
long past."

The space around Tahn became more crowded. He and Sutter found themselves pinched in as the crowd pressed forward. Firmly, he pushed back, clearing a small space for himself, to some disgruntled muttering.

"Today, we do what is right by law, having done all in accordance with the
presiding council and His Leadership, Ascendant Staned. How great a reminder is this, that you are all free to act as your conscience dictates, and not as
another would have you do."

Sutter harrumphed. "I'm a root-digger, and I can smell a cowflop when I
come across it."

The leagueman behind Lethur finished his preparations and stood back. A
tall pole stood at the center of a raised dais. Several bundles of sticks had been
placed around its base.

"Sutter . . . they mean to burn her."

Sutter looked, and muffled a string of curses in his hand.

From the left, Gehone arrived, three men in tow. Each of the others wore the
russet-hued cloak of the league, the emblem at their throats dazzling in the
morning sun. Tahn noted that each emblem had been fashioned of a slightly
different design, emphasizing the four separate disciplines of the League. Gehone climbed down from his steed and reported directly to Commander Lethur, who nodded and motioned for Gehone to stand with the rest behind him.

"A great commonwealth is Ulayla," Lethur said, puffing out his chest at the
name of the town. "A marvelous and industrious place, known for its high ethics and allegiance to the kingdom's will. It is for you that the League works; for
you we put our flesh and steel where no order"—he twisted the word into a
sneer—"would ever go. Because your concerns are our concerns. No vaunted,
meaningless philosophy or tricks of the light."

The Commander nodded to his second, who pulled the woman from her
perch and took her to the pole. Three others assisted him, though they were
unnecessary. She did not protest, and stood still as they lashed her to the log.
All returned to their positions but one, who struck flint to a torch and carried
it to Lethur.

Tahn looked desperately at Gehone, whose face showed the same awful resignation as the woman's. He would not look. He stared at the ground, his hands
clasped behind him.

A fevered excitement passed through the crowd as Lethur raised the torch, whispers and speculations and a few gasps. Tahn put a hand to his scar and canted the words of a thousand days, his mind seeking an answer.

"If there weren't so many of them," Sutter muttered.

"My friends," Lethur continued, "this is a great day. A day for casting off the past and embracing your future. For seeing the work of justice and the truest meaning of the cleansing fire. It is us, friends. Not the myths of First Ones or even the flames that burn. But each of us. In the way we support and enforce what is most right and civil among us."

Lethur strode to the platform. He stood beside the woman, who managed to look with longing toward the heavens. Tahn followed her gaze, wondering if any help existed there. Only the great blue empty sky replied, and that silently. Tahn clenched his fists, the words of the man from his dreams and the reassurance of Balatin somehow deserting him. He dropped his eyes to the woman, who continued to look up at an endless sky.

"This woman has broken the law, and persisted in spreading superstitions that hinder our civility. And so with proper authority, and a clear conscience that what I do is a step forward for each of us, I carry this sentence out in the name of the most proper civility."

With painfully slow deliberation the torch began to descend. And Tahn looked deep into the woman's eyes, his body thrumming with every pulse of his racing heart. Hot waves of protest curled his fists like a man preparing to fight, and he lunged forward. Sutter caught him, wrapping Tahn and anchoring him down. The crowd watched the platform, unaware of Tahn's reaction. He struggled against Sutter's grip, but his friend showed uncommon strength and kept him still. The sound from the crowd swelled, muting Tahn's cries. He twisted and tried to pull free, but his friend did not relent.

He turned his eyes again to the woman as the flame struck kindling into life. Wood dust laid by the practiced hands of the league ignited almost instantly, and the fire mounted around her. Lethur stood back a pace and watched the crowd, a satisfied look on his sharp features. Tahn cast a hopeful glance at Gehone. But the man's eyes never moved from the parcel of ground he watched.

"Look at her," Sutter whispered, retaining his grip on Tahn.

It pained Sutter to look upon this appalling scene.

But Tahn followed his friend's gaze back to the woman. Still, her face seemed placid. Suddenly, Tahn ceased his struggle. Words burned in his mind, the same old words he always spoke, ". . . release as the Will allows." And Tahn somehow sensed that she was not guilty, but yet meant to die. A measured calm and confusion wrestled within him.

Tahn looked on a moment more, then turned and walked through the crowd back to Jole. He and Sutter left unobserved as the smoke of flesh rose into the bright, shining sky.

CHAPTER FIFTY-THREE

Reluctantly Used

Why have you hardly aged a day since you were exiled? Was Vendanj really suggesting that Grant hadn't aged in years?

Braethen watched as Grant looked away at the fire, a sad smile rising and defining several rough lines on his face at the Sheason's question. The sodalist wondered if Vendanj had asked a literal question of age, or if his inquiry of this man meant something deeper, something about the spirit he carried. Perhaps Vendanj meant to remind Grant of the defiance and honesty that had brought him into exile in the Scar.

Grant began to nod. "My primrose, Sheason, that is your answer." He turned and gave a mournful sigh. "I rewrite the Charter, one that governs only this Delighast, this end of creation, of life, because this place, this Scar that is sterile, is the future and I am forever in it." He seemed to look through the walls at the vast, hard expanse of the Scar outside. But Braethen thought he saw some small dissemblance in the man.

"This place came into being because of the Battle of the Round, the expenditure of life and Will and promise that stole the nectar that gave the earth its vitality, that brought change in the leaves, broods in the spring. These things exist here no more, and with them, time itself has gone."

Vendanj's brow drew down in consternation. The worry in the Sheason's face sped Braethen's pulse. Braethen could not remember seeing such concern from Vendanj. Mira cast a studied look at the three in the hall.

"You do not age here," Vendanj stated. It was not a question.

"I am the same man who left the city gate those many years ago. But there is no blessing in immortality." The exile grinned feebly. "I've learned to live here. Emptiness has its own fruits, and their succor is what I'm used to now. They are the secrets of the Scar. Pray you never learn them." Grant looked at his hand, turning it over to view his palm. "I came here only because of the cradle."

Braethen heard himself ask about the cradle before he realized he'd done so. The exile again offered his sad smile.

"When the lesser cycle comes to an end, I go to the end of the Scar." Grant rose and went to the window, pulling the shutter open. "A child is left in the hollow of a great dead tree. I find a home for it, a place where it may escape the fortune of the streets, or the traveling auction blocks that do human trade with the Bourne—such fools, selling their own future for bitter coin. Most I am able to find a home. Some few—a dozen now—I could not help, and so they remain here with me." Grant looked up at the lesser light and exhaled, then turned and looked past Braethen to his foster children in the shadows of the hall. "I teach them to fight, to make choices wisely, and along the way to distrust the best intentions of others." Grant set his eyes on Vendanj.

"An unfortunate and difficult education," the Sheason said.

"Simpler than you know," Grant put in. "They share the curse of the Scar, the endless march of days. So I send them to the perimeter three weeks in four. There they watch for strangers, practice the skills I teach them, and experience the pull of age toward death."

"How have you cared for these infants? Grown food, or found water in the Scar?" Braethen asked, his natural curiosity pushing the questions ahead with naive impertinence.

Grant smiled. "I am an exile, but there are a few at the edge of the Scar," he said, his voice hushed, "who yet believe in the truths I meant to protect. They accept the risk to help me with provisions, and to watch over my wards for stretches of time while they are young."

"Some of your . . . children . . . crossed us as we came," the Far said. "Drew on us without provocation."

"Any stranger in the Scar is provocation," Grant said flatly. He did not bother to ask after their health. He went on, slightly annoyed. "Time has stopped here, Sheason. The sun still rises and scorches the land, drying our water early and killing the vegetation. But the seasons of the year are lost to us. And while I have ceased to grow, the Scar has not."

"What do you mean?" Vendanj asked in a low voice.

"Just what I said. This awful wound that I call home is expanding." Grant stepped to the table and pulled a yellowed parchment from his stack. On it, a map showed a dark line describing a shaded area scrawled with the word Scar. Around its edges, boxes of dotted lines were drawn, each one encompassing an area larger than the one inside it. "When I came," he said, pointing to the shaded area. "Each year since." He touched the dotted lines in quick succession.

"How?" Braethen asked. He walked to the table and looked more closely at the map. He suddenly became aware that Grant eyed him closely.

"You may be a sodalist yet," Grant said, seemingly impressed, though why, Braethen did not understand. Then Grant sat again, leaving the map in Braethen's hands. He resumed his vigil by the fire. The room was still cold, the night chill passing directly into the room through the open window. "I don't know how or why. Perhaps this place has become the repository for all the wounds suffered by the land. Maybe the effects of the war haven't all yet been felt. Could be they burrow deeper each day, seeking out Forza to satisfy the cost of Forda spent in that awful contest of Will. Or perhaps . . ."

Braethen got the impression that Grant did not want to finish what he'd begun to say. The man rubbed his palms together, then laid them over his knees.

"Speak, Grant, do not keep your thoughts from us," Vendanj urged.

"Perhaps," the exile continued in a softer tone, "the Quiet is among us, their draw upon Forda I'Forza increasing, the balance of light and dark shifting."

Braethen looked up from his study of the map. Grant's words disturbed him, but only because they resonated with truth. Wasn't that what forced Braethen and the others from the Hollows? Wasn't that why Bar'dyn and Maere and Velle had trespassed the groves set aside ages ago as hallowed? And now they had come through the High Plains of Sedagin, come to Widows Village . . . Braethen desperately wanted to return to an age when such things existed only in books.

"This is my ward," Grant went on, "this home in the Scar, these youths who are left by parents too selfish or afraid to serve as guardians. There are changes outside the Scar, and I want no part in them."

"Grant," Vendanj said firmly, "you made an important stand against the highest council at Recityv. No one has ever argued so eloquently against the Recityv court. It will be remembered, and we may need that kind of assistance." The Sheason took a breath and exhaled sharply. "We need not only your sword, but the moral authority possessed by a man who would rather die—and see others die—than compromise his principles."

Grant said nothing.

Vendanj frowned. "If not to address the council, then for these." He withdrew a parchment from his cloak and put it on the charter. "The names of Sheason widows and widowers left desolate with the rending of the Undying Vow. Abandoned through unnatural authority"—Vendanj's voice grew soft—"and now also by the Exigency."

Braethen realized it must be the list of names Vendanj had gotten from Ne'pheola in Widows Village. Grant took up the parchment and scanned the names written there. For the first time, Braethen thought he saw sadness touch Grant's face. Perhaps as one exiled in this place, he knew something of the desolation of the eternally severed unions of the Sheason spouses. If it was possible, Grant's sadness seemed to grow, deepen.

Grant looked at Vendanj, a deep frown upon his face. "How is this possible?"

"That is something you may help us discover. But these women are now alone, and they will go alone to the life beyond. I have seen the withering of their souls. . . ."

The room fell silent. Finally, Grant spoke again. "Then perhaps my primrose should speak for *all* the Eastlands, and I should find a voice, speak it into reality. . . ."

Vendanj cautioned with a darkly reverent whisper, "Do not utter such a thing."

Grant looked back at the Sheason. "I cannot return to that place, Sheason. That part of my life is over."

In final, humble request, Vendanj asked, "If not for the family of man, if not for its servants . . . then do it for Tahn."

Again Braethen saw a flicker of recognition in Grant's eyes, and a look of utter regret steal across his face. "I cannot," Grant said. "You may take my words with you and share them as you see fit. But this is where I've made my home. This is where I was sent to serve sentence for the crime of conscience. I know no other way anymore. I will fill your skins, give you direction, and tend your horses. But I will not reenter the world of men. Though my world here is bleak, I came to it willingly. I've no mind or patience for the politics of a council, for Vohnce or any other king or nation."

Disgust showed plainly on Vendanj's face. The Sheason could compel Grant by some other means, but instead rose, casting a look at the Charter half penned on the table. "You may be in need of your document, Grant, when the border of your Scar is much wider than your map allows. But it will not be so easy to know where the Scar ends and growth continues when Quiet and Dark attack across every border like a lengthening shadow. You know the risk. You know our hope. And you know the regent."

Grant cast a curious glance at the Sheason.

"Yes, she is still alive," Vendanj said. "Older now, slower, but her hand is still iron inside a velvet glove. And to her credit, she seeks to see past her own border. We'll leave you to your warder's task, Grant, though its purpose is likely near an end."

Vendanj went toward the door, Mira close behind. Braethen started to follow, his mind scrambled by pieces of a puzzle he didn't know how to fit together.

"East by the dog star," Grant said, his voice rough and unsteady at the edges. "Your horses are weak. Walk them if you want them to live. You've water for three days." He paused, the tension in the small home thick and smothering. "Watch closely, Far. Quietgiven have been near the last two nights. The Scar is no obstacle to them anymore. Safe passage," he said, still staring at his fire.

Vendanj went into the night. Mira paused at the door to give Braethen a summoning look. The sodalist spared another glance at the three youths in the hall, the document nailed to the back wall, and the exile poised near the small hearth. Then he rushed to join the others, the fragments of these new stories heavy in his mind.

As they found their horses, Braethen heard Vendanj curse more than once. The Sheason gave each horse a sprig, then told them to mount. The lesser light blazed in the night sky, accompanied by the brilliant glitter of countless stars. The day's heat had fled, leaving a brittle cold in the clarity of night. Braethen glanced back once to see a pale square of light cast from the exile's window, its feeble glow resting on the ground beside the house. Vendanj took his mount and rode away at a sprint. Mira checked to see that Braethen stayed close, then followed. But Braethen hesitated on Roleigh, wondering if a dozen stories, and the strong arm of this man Grant, were being left behind forever to rot in the timeless waste of the Scar. He touched the saddlebag that held Ogea's books, and promised himself he would write what he knew when time allowed, then raced after the three-ring man and the fleetfoot.

A thousand strides away, where Grant's house could no longer be seen, Vendanj rode to a stop, jumped out of his saddle, and cast a quick look to the sky, seeking, Braethen assumed, the dog star. The Sheason walked on at a fast clip, neither checking to see if he was followed nor paying any heed to his horse, which obediently trailed a few paces behind. Mira handed her reins to Braethen and disappeared into the darkness before Braethen thought to say or ask anything.

They traveled for an hour, Vendanj striding with a determined gait, Mira a blur every few minutes at the edges of Braethen's vision. Preternatural silence lay across the rocks and dry grass, broken barely by the sounds of their passage. Only the clean hint of sage and a light sweat on his upper lip left Braethen with the certainty that he was not dreaming.

Suddenly, the Sheason stopped. He turned and searched the terrain in a full circle about them. The cold came more severely, the frost of the great spaces between the stars descending upon them.

Connected.

That was the feeling. Braethen reached out experimentally and all of a sudden felt that from the farthest star above to the ground beneath him, a kind of relationship existed. That every movement was known to every other mover, like swimming in a still pool, the ripples giving away your presence. To move meant to disturb the whole, but Vendanj strode onward, a hand raised to his chest. With wary fingers, Braethen took hold of his sword, remembering the last time he'd raised it in his own defense, and grimaced a little at the touch.

They walked over a knoll, moon shadows vague and ghostly behind them. Then, in an instant, the world turned to fire. As if from nowhere, seven great hulking shapes rose from the ground. They stood against the velvety darkness of the sky, their massive silhouettes blotting out stars. Behind them stood two sleeker shapes, draped in long robes with wide cowls. *Velle!* Beside each of the Quiet renderers stood shorter figures, slumped and beaten. Each of the beings stirred, and the feeling of connection, of being close, part of everything, part of them, rippled like heated tar. Braethen drew his sword and agonized over the lethargy he felt, the way he often did in dreams when he tried to flee but his legs disobeyed.

Only Mira seemed unaffected, but Braethen believed even she had lost a step. The Far rushed in, dancing close to the Sheason, and crouched. She held one sword before her; the other cocked back over her shoulder.

One of the Velle uttered a command in a deep, rasping voice, and the Bar'dyn fanned to the sides: three moved left, three to the right, and one stayed directly before them. Mira turned to face the three on the left. Vendanj took two steps out and threw back his cloak to free his arms as he turned to face the three on the right. Braethen caught a glint of argent in the blades of the Bar'dyn facing the Sheason. The mammoth creatures out of the Bourne hesitated.

"Step in, sodalist," Mira said without looking. "Fill the gap and remember what I've showed you. Remember balance. Fight quickly, not rushed."

Braethen took three long, careful strides and held his sword out at an angle. The Bar'dyn directly ahead of him pivoted into a defensive posture, and spoke. "All this way. How fitting that you will come to an end here." His voice rasped as though damaged by the smoke of a thousand fires.

The sound of the Bar'dyn's voice flowed over Braethen like waves in that pool of connection, but beneath, his muscles tightened and suddenly the grip of the sword felt wonderfully sure and right. Braethen looked past the speaker to the two forms behind him. They stood still, implacable, the hatred in their eyes palpable, their calm disquieting.

Velle. By my father's Sky, I have lived to see Velle walk the land.

Then each of the tall, still figures reached for the closest hunched man beside him, and took vicious hold of his flesh. Weak cries came, uttered through swollen lips. In a breath, the air burned with red flames that sizzled and shot like lightning in random patterns from each free hand.

"Roll!" Mira screamed.

Braethen reacted instinctively, falling to his left and scampering. Mira leapt back, and Braethen heard the sound of the Sheason's thick cloak snapping as he dashed aside. Great shards of fire bit the ground where they had been standing. The earth boomed in protest and shook. In that moment, the Bar'dyn came on. Two rushed Mira, nearly taking her by surprise as she tried to escape the fire. A pike whirled through the air toward her head, another at her knees. The Far ducked and leapt in the same movement, landing on her feet just when the Bar'dyn were upon her. She pivoted sideways and dove between them, just escaping a second blow from a quick blade.

Braethen rolled to his knees, dust rising in his throat and forcing him to cough. He still held his sword, and got his second hand to its grip as the third

Bar'dyn dove toward him. He had no time to roll again, and tried to raise the sword to accept the charge. He was too late. The force of the massive creature bowled him back and under, a gout of saliva spraying his face with rank-smelling mucus. Pain bloomed in his chest, taking his wind. The Bar'dyn clutched his throat.

Something unbidden rose in him, then. He looked into the face of the Bar'dyn and wrapped his hand around the hilt of his sword, gripping it savagely. His chest heaved, and he roared, "I am I!"

The force of the words stopped the Bar'dyn for a moment, and in that time, Braethen brought the sword up, pulling its sharpened edge across the beast's neck. The thick, armorlike skin gave under the blade. Braethen scarcely noticed the white glow. The Bar'dyn fell back, trying to stop the blood that coursed from the wound. A frightened surprise touched its eyes as it stared at Braethen and pulled away, growing slower with each scrambling pace.

The sodalist's concern turned immediately to Vendanj. As he whirled, he saw the Sheason make a long sweeping gesture with his arm toward the closest Quietgiven. The Bar'dyn toppled forward, and struck the ground like a great piece of ironmongery.

The strangled cries of the bent and ravaged men near the Velle grew louder. Braethen suddenly realized that without Forda in the ground to draw upon in the Scar to replenish their expended Will, the Velle were using real men, stealing their Forda to fuel their fight. Anger burned hot behind Braethen's eyes and he whipped his sword in a harsh arc toward the Velle, then moved fast to join Vendanj.

Each breath he took seared his lungs. He raised his sword, which now glowed as bright as a meridian sky. Around him, a yellow mist rose, spreading quickly in every direction.

"Vendanj!" he cried, swatting at the air with his blade.

The Sheason spun at the sound of his name. In that moment, the two Bar'dyn behind him advanced. Braethen tried to yell a warning, but the yellow mist stole his voice. He pointed, and just when the Bar'dyn raised their swords at Vendanj, the Sheason lifted both arms, his fists clenched. Thunder bellowed from his mouth and struck the Bar'dyn like a battering ram, casting them back several strides. The impact drove the yellow haze from the air in an instant.

Just as quickly the soil began to bubble, then to flow like mud, and he and the Sheason began to sink. More cries screeched into the night, and Braethen saw the first men being used by the Velle pitch to the ground, spent. The sound they made as they fell was ghastly, as if even their dying breaths were stolen from them. Braethen fumed and struggled to wade from the mud in which he was now nearly knee deep. Mira leapt over the growing quagmire to meet the advancing Bar'dyn leader. The beast's great sword swept toward her. The Far feinted back and threw one of her swords at the Bar'dyn in a mighty heave. The Bar'dyn raised a quick hand to ward off the attack. Mira's sword pierced his palm through, spattering drops of blood into the Bar'dyn's face. The beast yowled and continued to sweep its steel at the Far, shaking Mira's sword from its other hand.

As Braethen fought the thickness claiming his legs, Vendanj touched his arm. Together, they began to rise from the mud, which continued to bubble and spurt. The Bar'dyn to the right had regained their feet and rushed around the mud toward Mira.

Then, several hollow pops sounded from behind them, and the whistle of fletching tore past their heads. A moment later, the Bar'dyn captain absorbed a volley of arrows with his chest and neck. Some of the shafts broke against the armorlike toughness of the Bar'dyn's skin, but many found purchase in the massive body, driving it backward in a stumbling fall.

Vendanj stood and heard the popping of another volley as the Bar'dyn tried to scramble away, arrows showering their backs and legs. Those Bar'dyn that could still move scurried off into the night. But the Velle stood firm, keeping hold of their human vessels to draw more Forda.

Braethen turned to see Grant and eight striplings standing back with bows aimed and drawn. Vendanj put his hands together and raised a bright ball of light to illuminate the entire area. The youths gasped at what they saw. Braethen turned around in the mud and saw it, too. The men the Velle held to draw upon for their Forda were a few of Grant's own wards. The first two had already fallen; the second two appeared alive enough, but firmly in the skeletal hands of the Given.

"Your brothers," Grant said evenly. Some of the striplings looked at him with horrified expressions; others nodded gravely. "See what will become of them. It is your mercy." He raised his own bow and held his aim.

The Velle were preparing some dark use of those they yet held—their last vessels of Forda.

A moment of dark regard stretched across the Scar.

As Grant began to shout, "Fire," the Quiet renderers drew the remaining life from the wards they gripped. Before anything more could happen, they vanished, like shadows when the sun dawns over a barren plain. Several arrows whistled over the Scar, sailing harmlessly high against the night. The two wards slumped when the hands of the dark emissaries disappeared.

Braethen sat tiredly in the mud, his legs weakened to exhaustion. Several of Grant's wards wandered off to mourn, some went to their fallen brothers. Others examined the bodies of dead Bar'dyn.

When Braethen regained his breath, he tromped from the mud to see for himself what Vendanj had done to the first Bar'dyn he'd faced. Just being close, Braethen felt the freezing cold emanating from the corpse. The soil around it was white with frost. Braethen imagined that the Sheason had frozen all the fluids in the beast's body with a wave of his hand. He turned to see Mira run into the dark; the Far never ceased to amaze him with her endless energy.

Vendanj had taken himself out of the slop and knelt where the Velle had been, looking over the emaciated corpses of Grant's fallen fosterlings. Grant came up beside the Sheason, Braethen came to Vendanj's other side.

They stared at the lifeless bodies.

"They were your own," Vendanj said through labored breaths. The Sheason finally succumbed to his exhaustion from the battle and sat directly on the ground.

"They were already dead," Grant answered. This man from the Scar spoke with a bluntness that chilled Braethen, even after just confronting the Velle. He then took a parchment from the saddlebag of his mount and handed it to Vendanj. "I finished reading your list of names . . . to the last. You win, Sheason," Grant said. "I'll come with you to Recityv. There are old debts to pay. But I am not the man I was when I left there. You'd do well to say as much to those who might grow hostile at the sight of me."

Vendanj nodded, still looking at the dead youths lying in front of him. The Sheason then lay back on the hardpan of the Scar to rest. He took a sprig of herb and laid it on his tongue. He looked not so different from the corpse beside him.

A thousand questions boiled in Braethen's mind. But his Sheason was in need of rest. He stood watch over him for a long time, thinking, wondering. Somewhere in that time he cleaned his sword. When Vendanj stood again, they reckoned by the light of the dog star and started on their way to Recityv.

• CHAPTER FIFTY-FOUR •

Recityv Civility

Tahn and Sutter traveled north for three days, passing towns with greater frequency. Always, as they rode closer to town, wood gave way to stone and stone to brick. And as frequent as were the towns, more frequently did they see encampments of brightly appointed wagons and carriages. Standards rose high on staffs and spears, some borne by flinty-eyed men who would not return a look. But more often the pennons appeared hand-fashioned, their dyes less brilliant and the embroidery competent but unrefined. These came lashed to lances that Tahn guessed had once been farming implements. The two of them passed unnoticed through these towns and camps. Only standard-bearers seemed to be interesting to the townsfolk and to those who bore crests of their own.

At dusk of the third day since the public execution, russet hues lit striated clouds like grand versions of the banners they saw. Dusty weeds lined the road, dirtied by the passage of hundreds of wheels and hooves. Occasionally, Tahn and Sutter passed a cluster of wagons circled in a fallow field against the evening's chill. Fires blazed in their midst, the faraway hum of conversation and vague scent of roasting meat enticing on the air. Even there, standards rose against the shadows of sundown, announcing loyalties or bloodlines. The symbols and colors stood vividly against the gathering gloom, but Tahn recognized none of them. Noble families, he assumed.

As they continued up the road, they were almost run down by a fast-moving caravan.

It was led by a lone rider carrying a horn. Behind him, eight riders clad in full dress armor and helmets galloped, one bearing a standard on a long pole. The banner showed a bright silver hammer set against a field of black. Next came a war-wagon drawn by a six-horse team. After it, four carriages, each pulled by a team of four horses, sped past, followed by another war-wagon. Behind the procession, Tahn counted no less than thirty men, most in lamellar and brigandine armor. Half of these carried bows.

The rumble of wheels and hooves filled the evening sky like thunder.

Sutter's jaw dropped, and his eyes widened. Tahn clapped him on the back in jest, but was no less impressed. The parade of standard-bearers surely meant royal delegates of some kind. Tahn did not know the crest, but one thing seemed certain. They were on the right road to Recityv. In seconds the highway was clear again, save for a lingering dust that refused to settle.

The following morning, the road widened drastically and became more pocked and rutted by the hour. Ranches of cattle, sheep, and goats sprawled over several hills alongside the winding road. Tahn noticed that many of the gates leading out to the houses bore a black iron sigil of a tree with as many roots as branches.

Then, unexpectedly, a great wall appeared in the distance, rising twice as high as any Tahn had seen before. It extended so far to the east and west that trees concealed the ends. Above it, Tahn could see even taller domes and spires and great vaulted roofs, gables pitched like the tip of a spear, each one higher than the last. From afar, he sensed the sheer size of the place, of Recityv. In the distance, the wall bore a hazy golden hue that shimmered behind heat rising up from the land.

But Tahn knew the city was no mirage.

More and more travelers joined the stream of people moving toward the gate, some walking, others riding as he and Sutter did, still others in ornately decorated carriages. Again, he felt for the sticks in his cloak. Their touch reassured him slightly, until he thought of Wendra. He only hoped that she and the others had arrived safely.

The thought of the others reawakened in him a suddenly powerful longing for Mira. He thought maybe the next time they were alone, he'd be more bold. Merely recalling her face made him flush.

"Well, Nails, this is what you came for." He gestured ahead. "That's more adventure than I think even you can handle."

A distant look passed over his friend's eyes before the familiar smile returned. "We'll find out, then, won't we, Woodchuck?"

As the road widened, it also become more congested. A league from the city wall, houses sat nestled among hosts of tents woven of bright-colored, expensive-looking canvas. More cook fires burned, the smoke settling like a low cloud over the many temporary dwellings.

Along the road, merchants had staked out space for their carts. Standing before their wares, they held samples of their goods and eagerly sought to catch the eye, pitching to anyone who looked their way. Everything he could imagine was displayed by well-manicured merchants and traders. Some hawked exotic foods, claiming origins as far west as Mal'Sent and as far south as Riven Port. Tahn noted pairs of soldiers adorned in burgundy cassocks and cloaks, a white circle prominent over the left breast bearing the sigil of the tree and its roots.

The chaos of countless merchant barkers, squealing children, stock and pets braying and barking, laughter, insults and curses, quarrels, all rushed at Tahn in a swirl of humanity.

It reminded Tahn of the road to Myrr, but much bigger, more crowded, dangerous, and somehow startlingly hopeless—these people beyond the gates. More of them here looked on with hawkish eyes and weapons on their belts; while others huddled in shadows raising dirty hands for alms.

Tahn took it all in, and thought longingly of home.

In many ways, this city outside the city differed from others he'd seen of late. But one way proved more than a little unsettling: As he and Sutter rode closer to the Recityv wall, the roadside became increasingly populated by street prophets.

Calling as enthusiastically as their trading counterparts, these men, women, and children looked at everyone with astounded eyes and seemed to see no one. Matted, dirty hair hung from tanned scalps as they gestured maniacally with their arms and turned skyward to rant.

"Every son and daughter is an abomination, a curse from the Whited One."

The man calling out a wild-eyed screed shouted through lips cracked from incessant talking and exposure to the sun. Scabs, looking like dried leeches, riddled his lips, but did not stop his raving. "The end of Forda I'Forza has long since passed, and we live in a hollow time, a dead age. A dry wind blows south from the farthest places, starting at the other end of the Bourne and passing over us like a whisper. Don't you see!" The man began to jump up and down, accentuating each word with the pounding of his heels on the soil. "We are Quiet already. We are come to our earth and haven't woken yet to taste the worms. No Exigent, no renderer, no regent or general, no one can undo what has been done. Our Song of Suffering is over, it is the echo of it from a distant cliff that we hear. And when it is gone, we'll have been dead a generation."

Tahn and Sutter swung wide of the man, tramping close to a woman seated on an elaborate rug who clicked her fingers together and spoke in words that rhymed every third phrase. She spoke of lands west of Mal'Sent, whole worlds on the other side of the oceans. She told of a place that hid beyond the Bourne like the forgotten child of orphan parents. At the end of each rhyme, she opened her eyes to see if anyone had placed a coin in the hat at the edge of her blanket. Her substantial belly hung over the waistband of her skirt, and a slender wrap that hung loosely from her shoulders more than hinted at a full bosom beneath. Straight, dark hair had been gathered in a brass ring at the crown of her head, pointing skyward like a harvest bale.

But perhaps the strangest of all was a child standing on a wooden box, who tapped answers to questions with a wooden peg leg. They paused to watch. A man standing behind the boy interpreted the responses for those who paid for knowledge. A small wooden sign leaning against the boy's box announced his ability was a gift from the First Fathers, and that he'd been rescued from the mountains fabled to house the Tabernacle of the Sky, where the fathers had sat at creation. When he raised a hand, exposing a long tear in the seam of his shirt, Tahn could see clearly the child's ribcage. *What must he do for food,* Tahn thought, as the boy tapped out another answer to some riddle.

These strange and desperate people intrigued Tahn the most. He didn't know if he felt sadness for them, or hope that one might be able to help him answer the riddles of his own life. Maybe it was both.

He and Sutter moved on.

A hundred strides from the wall, Tahn again looked up in wonder at the towering majesty of the structure. At its top, a parapet jutted up every fifty strides. From what Tahn could see, each housed two ballistae. He also saw the heads and shoulders of men walking across it at intervals, their eyes looking down to monitor the goings-on below. As he peered in each direction, it was still difficult to know exactly where the city wall ended.

Focusing on the wide gates, Tahn pressed forward through eddies of milling shoppers and travelers making their way to the city. Sutter nodded to a man in a brass helm and long crimson cloak. The soldier returned the greeting with the slightest movement imaginable. At either side, eight more men in crimson garb stood watching the flow of humanity through the city gates.

At the barrier, one line of wagons and carriages waited to be inspected; another moved more quickly where people on foot were scrutinized briefly before being allowed to enter. When he and Sutter reached a uniformed attendant who held a small copybook in one hand and a quill in the other, panic rose in his throat.

With a tired monotone, the man asked, "What brings you to Recityv?"

Before Tahn could answer, Sutter declared, "We're hungry."

A crooked smile crossed the man's lips as he surveyed them both. "You're not aspirants to any seat?"

"What?" Sutter asked.

"Move along," the soldier replied, "and keep out of trouble."

Relief washed over Tahn as he passed beneath the thick red stone wall of Recityv. He heard a distant cry in his mind—the voice of the Sheason telling them to get to this place. And now they'd arrived safely. In the shadow of the gate, he no longer felt like a child this side of the Change, regardless of the Standing. The end of the cycle might come soon, but part of him believed that when he returned to the Hollows, even if it were before then, it would somehow seem different. Smaller.

Inside the great wall, buildings towered several stories high. Just strides beyond the gate, storefronts gleamed in the daylight, the stone of their facings principally white. Some had been polished smooth, showing pale reflections of the street they faced, others were rough-hewn. On the rooftops, a variety of animal statues perched atop the stone, peering down like unmoving familiars. Windows varied in size and shape and color: Fancier inns seemed to have been crafted in straight lines and angles, fitted with rectangular panes of glass; other edifices had round, long, narrow, or polygonal windows; and many were tinted various shades of rose, azure, or gold, those on the east side of the road refracting colorful rays of light.

Some men walked the street in mail, others in cotton twill. Many wore tight leather breeches, mid-calf boots, loose-fitting coats that laced at the neck, and hooded cloaks of various lengths. Women strolled in gowns that shimmered or were oversewn with lace in intricate and delicate designs. Those that did not have such finery seemed mostly to go about in work dresses, often bearing stains deep in the fabric. Most of the women wore hats, the brims of those worn by the more stylishly dressed women long and curving subtly downward in the front and rear, while the brims of many others were short and generally flat, and often had no brim at all.

A host of richly ornate carriages lined the streets, their owners seeming to be bustling from one shop to another in pursuit of some item to purchase. A charged feeling buzzed in the air, as everywhere standards flapped in the wind.

Tahn and Sutter kept riding, hoping to see someone they recognized. Perhaps Vendanj would have someone watching for them. Deeper into the city they went, passing arbors and warehouses and multifloored taverns, past fountains and inns, and offices marked with the sigil of the tree and roots.

At the center of a broad, grassy common rose a tall, narrow building, crowned by a glass dome. Tahn could see tall cylinders within the bubble, pointing skyward. Near the foundation of the building stood a rooted pavilion with several rows of chairs facing a lectern. At the back, a tall, dark slate showed diagrams in yellow chalk.

Sutter, while agape at the marvels about him, wore an impossibly broad smile, making him look entirely conspicuous.

"Perhaps, Your Majesty, you might close the royal mouth. It makes you appear a commoner," Tahn joked.

Clearing his throat, Sutter sat straight in his saddle. "Just relishing the gems of my domain, boy. It is wise for a man to reflect upon his success and importance."

"A man, you say? And important?" Tahn laughed. "My Lord, the only thing *man* about you is your scent, which I find important indeed. You might consider washing the royal ass."

"A job for a chamber maid," Sutter said, leering. "Delicate work for a delicate girl." Dropping the conceit, Sutter added, "Where *are* we going to stay tonight?" He then resumed craning his head at nearly impossible angles to see every height and detail of the architecture around them.

"I don't know. Perhaps the others have already arrived." Tahn looked around at the sheer number of people bustling through the street. "But we'll never find them without asking someone."

"And how do you intend to do that?" Sutter chided. "Saunter up to someone and ask them if they've seen a grim-looking Sheason and a gorgeous young Far?"

Tahn considered. "We'll look for the symbol of the three rings," he said. "If we can find any member of the order, they'll be able to help us find Vendanj."

"I don't get the feeling Sheason are welcome here any more than they are anywhere else. Maybe less so. Perhaps we should find a sodalist."

Sutter started to say something more, but choked it off as they came to a densely packed crowd. The street had suddenly become a wall of humanity too congested to negotiate with a horse. Ahead, and beyond the congregants, Tahn saw a raised scaffold.

"Move over!" a gruff voice demanded.

A portly man with mottled skin over most of his face sneered at him and tried to shove Jole aside. The crowd amassed behind them. Tahn reined left and led Sutter to the edge of the street and out of the way. Then above the tumult, a loud voice echoed past the stone of the building fronts.

"It is with solemn regret, but by authority of the Court of Judicature, that we bring sentence before you today."

Tahn squinted into the distance. It looked like a gallows. He'd heard of them from stories given by Ogea at Northsun. The thin man announcing from the platform wore the color of the Recityv guard, shouting through a cone he held to his lips as he spoke. But it all remained so far away that Tahn could barely make any of it out. As the man continued to speak, two figures climbed a stair and stood behind him.

"Let it be understood that justice will not be denied. The regent will not be swayed by any threat." A protest went up from some; others cheered. "Today treason will be answered as befits the crime."

People jockeyed around for a better view. Tahn looked past the man at the front of the scaffolding at the two standing behind him. A horrible certainty dawned in his mind.

"Come on!" he whispered urgently to Sutter. Tahn jerked Jole's head about. "Out of the way!" he yelled, urging Jole to hasten back through the tightly packed crowd. Insults flew, a few swinging at Tahn's legs as, finally free of the crowd, he gained speed, racing away from the gallows.

Sutter came abreast of him as they dodged around others. "What are you doing?!"

Tahn made no answer. He focused on avoiding the various obstacles in the road. Apple cores sailed past his head and rocks struck his chest and shoulder, more than a few hitting Jole as Tahn guided him through the crowded streets. Sutter yelled at those hurling things toward them, promising to answer their hospitality. At a narrow alley, Tahn turned left. They leapt overturned barrels and broken crates, the clatter of hooves echoing off the walls. Sutter's nag struggled to keep up.

Emerging onto the next street, Tahn reined in and looked left again. Several intersections north, the crowd had just started to gather.

"There!" Tahn shouted and pulled Jole left yet again, spurring him onward.

Carriages careened to one side or the other as Tahn screamed for them to stand aside. Children clapped at the spectacle, and Tahn saw two soldiers in crimson dress look his way as he passed. He did not turn to see if they pursued him. Near to the cross street where people gathered closest to witness the sentence, he again pulled back on Jole's reins. Hooves slipped and scraped over stone as the horse fought to keep balance while skidding. The mob backed away as he came to a reckless stop near the street corner.

Sutter came in behind him, his old mare dumping him to the ground with a loud thud. Tahn quickly looked around, and found that some second-story windows had short balconies that overlooked the street. He eased to his feet to stand on Jole's saddle, and jumped. Catching a balustrade, he hoisted himself up. A few people appeared to disapprove, but also understand Tahn's desire for a clear view of the hanging. Sutter began climbing the building, using the deep grooves in the stonework as footholds.

Tahn knelt on one knee on the side of the balcony nearest the gallows. Though yet sixty strides away, it was much closer than they had been before. He could see the fear in the faces of the condemned.

". . . resolve is absolute," the guard was saying. "Be a rumor true or not, all things are subject to the rule of law and the discretion of the regent." A continued mix of approval and scoffing attended the officer's remarks.

Sutter reached the balcony and took a knee beside him. "Will and Sky, Tahn, what's gotten into you? Haven't you seen enough of this?"

"This isn't the League," Tahn said.

"No, but it's just as gruesome." Sutter tugged at his sleeve.

"Stop!" Tahn scolded. "Don't bother me now!"

"Tahn, what is this about?" Sutter's voice now held genuine concern. "There's nothing you can do for them. And even if there were, this isn't the kind of attention we need. You can't afford—"

"To what!" Tahn interjected. "To help them?"

"You don't know what's going on here," Sutter said reasonably. "Whatever it is, it doesn't involve us. Those men may deserve this."

Tahn looked his friend in the eye. "One of them does not."

Sutter stared back, confused. "How could you know that? Do you recognize one of them?"

Tahn shook his head. "Please, Sutter, just trust me." He wanted to say more, but he knew that anything he might say would sound crazy right now, and there wasn't time to explain.

"All right," Sutter said softly. "But you seem to be taking over my adventure."

The throng of watchers pressed even tighter as their numbers increased. A line of guards three deep extended in a horseshoe around the gallows, the first row pointing spears outward to keep the crowd back. The officer finished speaking and stood aside as each of the two men was fitted with a noose around his neck. A horn trumpeted the moment, calling from some high promenade above the yard where the bulk of the mob stood waiting to witness these deaths. A hush fell over the crowd as a dark-cloaked man spoke privately with each of the convicted. Tahn wondered what the man could possibly say to them at this moment. When he left them, Tahn saw the gleam of tears on one fellow's cheeks.

At one side, a second guard in Recityv crimson stood with his hand on a lever, his eyes on the front-most officer. The yard grew quiet enough to hear the birds chirrup in the eaves of a nearby building. The dart and swoop of swallows was the only movement. The sun felt suddenly heavy and too bright, exposing this scene in glaring clarity.

Tahn took his bow from his back and produced an arrow from his quiver. He moistened his fingers with his tongue and checked the fletching. He traced the scar on his hand, reminding himself not to clutch his weapon too tightly. Then he stood, holding the bow at a perfect angle to the ground. His heart raced in his chest, pounding an impossible rhythm. But he breathed easy and recited the oldest words he knew.

"I draw with the strength of my arms," he said, and exhaled.

Shouts of alarm rang up beneath him as the crowd became aware of him standing with an aimed bow. But Tahn might have been standing at the edge of some promontory, a wide, empty chasm before him and nothing else, save the scaffolding and the objects of its use. The officer looked at the guard who manned the lever-release. At that moment, the guard nodded and performed his task.

"And release as the Will allows," Tahn finished, and calmly released his arrow.

A hatch opened and the two men fell. The rope tightened with the weight of their parcels, and when the rope holding the man on the right drew taut, Tahn's arrow sailed into the sunlight of the yard and sliced the rope a fist's length from the high beam that held it. The man plummeted to the ground. A gasp of horror and shock erupted from those gathered, and several hundred heads turned to see Tahn standing with his bow still pointed toward the gallows.

Moments later, a squad of soldiers swarmed onto the balcony and put Tahn and Sutter into irons.

"I guess we won't be needing to look for a room," Sutter said. But there was no humor in his voice.

The guards led them away. With bitter irony, Tahn could only think of Wendra, her lifeless child, a moment of indecision, and how much better this moment had been.

CHAPTER FIFTY-FIVE

Darksong

Wendra stood inside the mountain cabin a pace back from the doorway, peering through the opening at Jastail and eight creatures like the one that had broken into her home and forced her child from her womb. She shivered at the sight of them, recalling the feel of coarse hands tearing her undergarments away and the incredible power in the beast's grip as she was forced to drink a pulpy fluid from a bone vial. Guttural sounds responded to the appeasing voice of the highwayman, who motioned toward her.

"Come out here," Jastail said, glancing toward her. "And bring the boy."

Wendra looked despairingly at Penit, who returned her gaze with a terrified expression. He grasped her hand and together they eased out the door. Wendra shielded her eyes against the brightness of the sun as she tentatively approached Jastail, keeping the highwayman between her and the Quietgiven. She saw cold appraisal in the heavy brows of the Bar'dyn, their attention shifting from her to Penit and back again.

"Did I tell you?" Jastail said in a confident, pleased tone. He looked back at Wendra and gestured toward her with splayed fingers, as one might do to invite inspection. "And this is why I ask my price."

The Bar'dyn did not speak at first, running another emotionless gaze over her and the boy. "Perhaps we will just take them," the foremost Given said evenly.

"Ah, Etromney, you test my patience with this needless litany each time we meet." Jastail turned his back on the Bar'dyn and paced around behind Wendra and Penit. "You come to me because I deliver goods no one else can."

"Not every time," the Bar'dyn said pointedly.

"Perhaps," Jastail admitted, unruffled. "But I have access to"—he looked at Wendra and seemed to alter his words—"circles that the pedestrian traders never will. But you know all this; I've explained to you my connections many times. So why begin with threats?"

The Bar'dyn's expression never changed, remaining as flat as Jastail's had ever been. "The times are changing." The Bar'dyn paused, raising its thick nose to the air as though it could smell what it described. Wendra remained still, feeling as much as hearing the deep resonance of the creature's voice, like a single, thick chord drawn by a heavy bow.

"More threats?" Jastail asked.

"No," Etromney answered. "Soon, there will be no need to meet here. No need of any trader or highwayman." The Bar'dyn seemed to frown, but the lines in its folded skin hardly moved. "You are an abomination, human, wretched in your Second Inheritance, and worse to betray your own kind. My gorge rises at the sight of you."

Jastail let a strange smile crawl over his face. "What do you know of humanity, of abomination, except what you see reflected in the trough you drink from."

The Bar'dyn's hoary face resumed its steady gaze. "Is the boy hers?" Etromney asked.

"No," Jastail said, "but what of that? She is still capable of breeding."

"Can you prove her womb is not barren?" the Bar'dyn went on. "And what of—"

Jastail violently ripped Wendra's dress upward, exposing her belly and hips. "See for yourself," he said with heat, pointing to the stretch marks in Wendra's skin from her recent pregnancy. "The mark of one recently with child. Now no more accusations or disbelief! She will suit your purposes well enough. And the child is pure Forda I'Forza, a suitable receptacle I'm sure. And I'll share this advice: Control the lad, and you control the girl."

Wendra knew her legs trembled as she stood exposed to the Bar'dyn. She locked her knees to keep on her feet. Jastail held up her dress for several more moments as the Bar'dyn looked on. Finally, he dropped the hem and took a wide-legged stance in front of them, facing the Quietgiven. The highwayman's zeal and confidence in the face of the Bar'dyn surprised her. The creatures out of the Bourne stood two feet taller than Jastail; the obvious strength in their massive shoulders and legs would discourage most men from such boldness.

"What of this ability you mention?" the leader of the Given asked. "You demand an unheard-of price. I must know the truth of this to grant what you ask."

"Sing him something, Wendra," Jastail said, a near hint of fatherly pride in his request.

The request caught her entirely off guard. "What?"

"A song, let's have a song." He turned, irritation creasing his brow.

She looked at the highwayman in pain and confusion. At that moment, with Jastail bartering their lives to Bar'dyn, the marks of childbirth shown openly to bear witness to her fertility, and Penit squeezing her hand so hard in fear that it ached, the idea of singing a song insulted her. Jastail wanted her to perform like a trained animal. And somehow this would raise her stock for the highwayman's purse. She gritted her teeth, seething with hatred. Then she startled herself to find the intimations of a melody in her after all. It boiled up from her belly like acid. She found it suddenly hard to breathe, and began to pant. Every lie Jastail had told Penit had here been laid bare, and Wendra held the thought of the boy's broken trust in her mind until she felt herself losing control.

"Don't make me use the boy to encourage your song," Jastail warned.

"Enough," the Bar'dyn said, shuffling mighty feet. "We did not come to trade today, highwayman. We will take what we like and leave you to hope for mercy in the seasons ahead."

Jastail snapped his head back to the Bar'dyn leader. "Hold there, Etromney." Jastail raised a finger in objection, then used it to point toward the trees. "Do not forget that I come not alone. A party of men will descend that ridge the moment you prove . . . unscrupulous."

The Bar'dyn did not bother to look. Instead, it came a step closer to Jastail, narrowing its eyes. Wendra recoiled, pulling Penit back. The little clearing tensed with the imminence of death. "I could pinch your head from your neck, grub. You are part of the abomination; I would sooner watch you die than listen to you lie."

"Have I ever come alone before?" Jastail asked with less confidence, staring up into the broad, thick musculature of the Bar'dyn's face. "My bounty ought to honor you."

The Bar'dyn stared, then finally looked toward the trees. "Done."

"Wait," Wendra cried. "He is lying. No one will come." She let go Penit's hand and stepped forward. Her legs betrayed her, and she fell to the ground. She immediately sat up on her knees amid a cloud of dust.

Jastail whirled, lashing her face with his fist. "Silence, cow! You've not been given permission to speak!"

Wendra swallowed blood, her vision swimming with tears risen suddenly from the blow. She reached into her dress and pulled free the parchment, clenching it tightly in her hand. "At Galadell he left a note for these men he says will come. But I found the note and took it, hiding it until today. You see! No party is coming. He trades alone today." She raised the note toward the Bar'dyn.

From blurry eyes she saw Jastail raise his hand again. Before he could hit her, the Bar'dyn swept its arm across the highwayman's back and drove him savagely to the ground. "You lie and then abuse our merchandise." Jastail remained on the ground, spitting dirt from his mouth as the Bar'dyn took the scrap of parchment from Wendra's hand. Revulsion rose in her throat at the touch of the rough skin. So close, she caught the scent of carrion on the creature. Etromney examined the note, then let it fall, landing in Wendra's lap.

"She creates this lie to preserve herself," Jastail quickly offered. "And regardless, I have brought you woman and child. I have brought Leiholan." Jastail crawled to Wendra and wrested from her the parchment the Ta'Opin had made for her of her song. He held it out to Etromney. "Please . . . take me with you."

The highwayman's request stunned Wendra. She'd tried to make it a threat over endfast, and now the trader wanted to go with the Bar'dyn. Perhaps the only thrill left to him was gambling with his own life.

The Bar'dyn leader snatched the parchment from Jastail's hand and returned to his band, speaking to them in a tongue Wendra did not know. He then paused to look over the rendering of Wendra's song. With each pass of his eyes over the page, Wendra thought she saw a change in the Bar'dyn's countenance. At last, Etromney lowered the written song and whispered to his companions. Immediately, two of the Bar'dyn came toward her and Penit. Wendra's eyes still stung from her tears, but she scrambled back on her hands and feet. Penit stood transfixed as the second Bar'dyn lifted him up and placed him on one great shoulder.

"Please, Etromney!" Jastail spoke stridently. "I've much to offer. There are things I know."

At that, the Bar'dyn stopped and seemed to consider. He then motioned to one of his party, who went to Jastail and helped him to his feet. The highwayman clutched his own shoulder with one hand as he strode to join the other Bar'dyn.

Before her, the Quietgiven moved more quickly, catching her and grasping her wrist with one clawed hand. With a jerk, the Bar'dyn brought her to her feet, turning to drag her back to the others. Wendra blinked the dust and tears from her eyes and saw Penit gulping air from his perch as he fought the need to cry. In that instant, Wendra recalled a conversation with a scop on songs sung from the bottom of pain and felt a hundred moments of isolation and frustration and dark melodies coalesce in her chest and rush like a flood through the gates of her teeth.

The song burst from her abruptly, unbidden—pained, tortured sounds that ascended in powerful crescendos, notes turning in and over one another in sharp dissonance. The dark song issued from her lungs in a series of screams that rasped like moving stones without the cushion of mortar.

The terrible song ripped through her, from her; yet she listened to it and watched through eyes that saw nothing but white and black, the world a stark mosaic. She saw the skin of the Bar'dyn begin to blacken, smoke rising from it. The beasts yawped with their chesty voices, a few dropping and rolling through the dirt and brush.

The strains of her song filled the entire meadow with a mighty roar. With every note she grew angrier, the contrast in her vision more severe. The black deepened, white glowed in fiery brilliance. She sang to bring it all to darkness, to divest everything of its light. Distantly, she felt her arms and legs tremble with the power rushing from her mouth. Her skin burned, but the feeling of it pleased her, and she smiled around her terrible song as it shot forth into the meadow and fell upon the Bar'dyn.

The glory of the harsh sounds enveloped her. At the sight of Penit—a white form on a dark canvas—the timbre of her awful song moderated slightly. And in an instant, she could not remember his name. She recognized the shape, the rounding of his chin, the thin chest and legs, but his name was gone to her. The sadness and frustration of forgetting the child welled up in her, cycling toward her song like a reprise, when a sweet, low counterpoint joined her. Wendra whirled toward it, seeing a shining light in the shape of a tall man. She recognized this, too, but had no idea who it might be. The harmony coming from the figure soothed her, eased her own melody, reshaped it, and she found herself naturally working to follow the progression of his simple, beautiful tune. Some phrases threatened to ride away from the new song, to take her back to the soothing certainty of singing everything black. But the gentle insistence of the countermelody assured her, guided her. Gradually, what she felt and heard became one, color coming again to the things she saw.

When their melody joined in a soft unison, she saw Seanbea walking toward her, a paternal smile on his full lips. She sang until her breath forsook her, and collapsed into the Ta'Opin's arms, her dark song at an end.

Wendra woke to the creak of axles and the jounce of hard wheels over stones in the road. A sour taste lingered in her mouth, like curdled milk and soot. Slowly, she opened her eyes to see a leafy world passing lazily by overhead. The slant of the sun said that night would soon come, and the thought displeased her, flashes of the darkness in her vision when last she had sung superimposed over the branches above. She then felt the press of a warm, small hand clinging to her own. Adjusting her head on the blanket rolled for her pillow, she saw Penit sitting in the wagon bed beside her. The boy stared into the forest beyond, a troubled look giving his young face an age beyond its years.

Wendra squeezed Penit's hand, drawing his attention.

"Hey, she's awake!" he hollered at Seanbea, climbing to his knees and scooting forward to huddle over her. "You passed out," Penit confirmed. "Are you okay now?"

Wendra smiled at the concern written on the child's brow. "I'm fine, but I could use some water."

Penit kept hold of her hand while he reached forward and lifted a waterskin from a jumble of gear stowed to each side. He uncorked it for Wendra and raised it to her lips the way she had done for Balatin with her own small hands when her father had once taken ill. The connection of the two events eased the aching in her limbs as much as anything could. The water washed the foul taste from her mouth, and she rested back on the blanket. A sudden thought plagued her and she tried to sit up, but her stomach cramped, forcing her back before Penit could do the job.

"The Bar'dyn?" she managed, coughing the word.

"Mostly dead," Penit answered. "The rest crawled beyond the trees before you stopped singing."

The memory of her song came back to her, the forceful, angry melody inviting her to give voice to it again. But her heart felt none of her former rage, and the feeling passed.

"What about Jastail?" She tried to sit again, the thought of the highwayman suddenly making her anxious.

Penit remained silent. It was Seanbea who replied. "When his deal was broken, he made his way quickly to the ridge and escaped your song."

The Ta'Opin's deep, resonant voice soothed her like honeyed tea. It lilted and trailed in easy lines, unlike the horrible evenness and clipped speech of the Bar'dyn's own deep tones. She wanted him to keep talking so she could listen, to breathe in the music of his words. But he had happened upon them and saw what she had done. The realization that he had witnessed her destuctive song made her hope he kept silent.

"He won't come after us," Penit assured her. "He's afraid of you now. And Seanbea is with us. He's taking us to Recityv so I can run in the Lesher Roon." Penit smiled, again the sunny child she loved, as if untouched by all he had endured.

But he had spoken a painful truth: Some part of her caused fear in the highwayman. She found she feared it, too. The silky invitation of the notes she'd sung had enticed her, even as she knew that they led to a state of being where she would only ever see darkness when she made the song.

Wendra also realized that Penit still clung to one of the lies Jastail had told, that Penit would take part in some kind of race once they reached Recityv. She considered correcting him, but wondered if Seanbea had offered the distraction to try and keep the boy preoccupied.

"The boy might win, too," Seanbea added. "Saw him run to you when that Bar'dyn dumped him to the ground. He's got quick feet."

"What does he win?" Wendra asked.

She heard Seanbea swivel in his seat, as though he meant to see if she asked in jest.

Wendra looked back. "You mean there really is a race that will take place in Revityv? That wasn't just something Jastail made up to trick Penit?"

"You really haven't a notion, do you?" Seanbea said.

"I'll get to meet the regent after all," Penit exclaimed.

"True enough," Seanbea began, the tone of a story about to be told filling his voice. "The Roon is an old custom, hardly anything more than a story . . . until the regent recalled the full council." The wood of Seanbea's bench creaked as he turned back to his driving. "King Sechen Baellor called the council at the height of the War of the Hand, when most of the nations had already fallen to the Quiet. He knew that many alliances had already been made with the Quiet-given, and the rest were likely to sign treaties with them in exchange for leniency in seasons to come. In his own kingdom of Vohnce, he felt an urgent need for action. But he didn't want decisions made by an unbalanced council, where nobles gathered to strut and preen. So he posted a notice that one member of the working class, any man or woman that would serve, could be raised by the people to take a seat among the rest." Seanbea paused and spoke to himself. "He was a good man." Clearing his throat, he went on, "Anyway, he also declared that a child should sit among them in the council chamber, to give voice to the thoughts and fears of the children. His own offspring were excluded from running, but it was said that he trusted the honesty and instincts of his own son and daughter more than the counsel of his scholars and the other nobles.

"Many opposed the inclusion of a youth on the council, believing that the child would only express the views of his parents. Others disliked the idea because they weren't sure how to fairly choose one representative from among the children." Seanbea chucked good-naturedly. "The king considered a number of tests, but knew these would favor noble children who could afford tutors. Combat seemed inappropriate, and the king objected to the idea of children being coached to gather votes for themselves by going about to make speeches. So, he settled on a simple footrace. Some still grumbled because the older children would have a clear advantage, so the king limited the race to those twelve years of age and younger."

Penit shook Wendra's hand to get her to look at him. "I do run fast, you know. If I win, then maybe I can tell them all about the Bar'dyn. They can send their army to save your brother."

Wendra felt a jab of memory at the mention of Tahn. She hoped he would be safe in Recityv by the time they got there.

"The palace walls still show the markers of the race course," Seanbea continued. "Children who hear the story can be seen racing one another along those walls." The Ta'Opin's voice evened to a serious tone. "The regent has called a date for a running of the Lesher Roon . . . and she's put out a call for the Convocation of Seats."

Wendra chilled at the mention of it. "Why?" she asked.

"I don't know," Seanbea replied. "I've been out visiting cities and towns, collecting instruments and looking for singers." He gave her a knowing look. "The messenger birds came into the places I've been, and word of it spread fast."

They were all quiet for a time, each seeming to think about what it could mean. The Ta'Opin started again, "But the Roon isn't just a contest, boy. It *means* something to run that race. You'd do well to remember that."

"I will," Penit said, excitement still ringing in his words.

Wendra let the discussion of the race end, and she looked about her at the instruments and parchments pushed aside to make room for her. She remembered there being a great deal more in Seanbea's wagon when she'd seen it a few nights before.

"What happened to your cargo?" she asked.

"My cargo is still in the wagon." Seanbea answered, the sound of a smile on his face as clear as laughter.

"Yes, but not all of it," Wendra persisted.

"Right you are," the Ta'Opin conceded. "I had to stow some in the hills so that you could rest. But don't you—"

"Seanbea, you can't do that. Those instruments were old, they'll—"

"—concern yourself. I'm still carrying an old instrument." The wagon bench creaked. This time she cranked her head at an angle so she could see his face. "There's nothing in this wagon as important as you, Anais. I think I knew it when you joined my song beside the fire. That's why I pretended to leave, then tracked you into those mountains where the highwayman took you." He paused, his voice then sounding far away. "I've not heard those sounds in my life. I've seen them written on parchment, different arrangements, but the same motifs, the same phrasings, the same mournful lines."

"How could you have heard—"

"Music is a response, Anais," he said reverently. "A response to what is in our heart. There have been some who put those feelings to parchment. Not exactly the way you did, but enough that I recognized the sad beauty of them . . . the danger in them."

He reined in and stopped the cart. He turned all the way around, putting his feet into the back of the wagon, and looked down at Wendra, commanding her attention. He knitted his fingers and leaned forward, bracing his arms on his knees. "You'll want to listen close, Anais. Think back and you'll probably remember a time when your songs seemed to do more than just tickle your tongue. A time when they did more, when they *caused* more. Don't bother to tell me about it, and don't try to deny it to yourself."

Seanbea looked at Penit, as if trying to decide whether to go on. He gave the boy a wink. "What you do, what you are, is more an instrument than anything Descant is expecting me to bring. Never you mind the stuff I left behind. It's covered and will keep. You, my girl, must do neither. The changes that prompt the regent to call a full council are likely the same that sent me into the land to find and haul these rusted items to Recityv. And now that I've seen Quietgiven so deep in the land, I'm almost sure of it. That they almost had you makes my blood cold." He gave her a sympathetic look. "What I saw you do to them . . . You've never done it before, have you?"

"No," she managed. Dark memories flared in her mind. She wondered if her song would have grown dark enough to steal Penit's light. "I'm not even sure what happened."

"I've never seen it," Seanbea said. "But I've heard the stories. When I trained at Descant with the Maesteri, they warned us of it. But a thousand voices could gather notes to song and offer them as painfully as you and the world would not change its form a jot. This thing in you, Anais, is a rare music indeed. And music touches eternity." The Ta'Opin reached down and placed his hand over her forehead. "But there are two eternities, Wendra; your song can inspire hope and lead men to a better tomorrow, or it can bring death and damnation. Having such power is a responsibility you must learn to shoulder. That is why we're going to Recityv," he concluded.

"What changes inspire the regent to assemble a full council or recall a convocation dead for generations . . . or cause a desire for dilapidated instruments and moldy sheets of music?" Wendra asked.

"What I know would be only half the truth, and not rightly spoken of here. Besides, there's no time to waste on unsafe roads." He pulled his legs up and spun to face forward again. "You'll have questions, I'm sure. Those at the cathedral can answer them for you better than I. You rest. I'll stop at nightfall, but just long enough to brew some koffee and rest the team. We should get to Recityv tomorrow."

Wendra looked up at the leaves and sky passing in a mosaic against the failing sun. She could smell the brass and wood of the wonderful instruments Seanbea still carried, the dusty smell of old parchment. As the wagon creaked northward, Wendra kept firm hold of Penit's small hand.

"Just wait," the boy said, his smile unfailing. "I'll take care of you."

Wendra placed her other hand over Penit's sturdy fingers.

• CHAPTER FIFTY-SIX •

A Quiet Cradle

When the greater light pushed up from the distant mountains before them, Braethen saw an end to the Scar. A thin line of green on the horizon spoke of life and growth. The promise in the color brought emotion to his throat. He had almost forgotten the simple beauty of foliage, and he found himself eager to reach it, to put the Scar behind him.

Grant had given instruction to his wards, taking them by the hand one by one before departing. For all his bitterness, he remained the common bond each of these abandoned children clung to in the waste of the Scar. In a real way, he was their father.

He was a shadow, Braethen thought, exiled by an order penned on official stationery, a man who, though he had lived here for nearly twenty years, had not aged as he traced the growth of this arid, wounded land. Yet this shadow also preserved the lives of children in a place so lonely and harsh that the only meaning in their lives seemed to be what they gave one another. Respect spread in the sodalist's bosom for Grant. What had he done to deserve this punishment?

Grant motioned to the right and angled his horse in a southeasterly direction. They followed the exile down a short slope into a featureless plain that ran outward in a pattern of grey and white earth less populated with sage and barren of trees, save one. A hundred strides from the base of the hill stood the lone tree, its branches dead to even the memory of its leaves. The trunk rose in a gentle twist of bleached wood, like bone left in the sun. Thick limbs snaked away from the trunk, ending in jagged snarls as if snapped off long ago. The bare branches offered no shade from the greater light, which rose hot in the sky even in these earliest moments of day. Braethen realized for the first time that the heat in the Scar came up from the earth as much as down from the heavens, as though the soil had no use for the sunlight, which it caught for only a moment before releasing again.

Grant stopped and slid effortlessly from his saddle. He crossed a few strides to the tree; a hollow had been carved directly into the trunk. The man paused there a moment, looking up at the tree the way Braethen might an old friend, though one he might like soon to forget. Grant then placed his head at the hole and looked inside. When he pulled away, his face was contorted by a grimace so ugly and full of pain that Braethen turned from the sight of it.

Both Mira and Vendanj dismounted and started toward the tree. Grant held up a hand to stop them. "No. The cradle is my responsibility." He waited a moment longer, his face slowly returning to the dispassion Braethen had seen the exile wear in his home. Then Grant looked back to the hollowed tree and reached inside. With a sudden jerk, he grabbed something and ripped it from the hole. His iron fist grasped a snake that writhed in his hand. A snarl twisted Grant's lip before he simply squeezed the serpent so tightly that its movement stopped. The dead snake hung limp in his hand, the exile unwilling to relinquish his death grip over the reptile.

Braethen slipped off his horse and strode to where Mira and Vendanj stood watching. Perhaps the man harbored a distaste for serpents. Grant finally dropped the lifeless creature to the dry ground; the snake fell in a heap. Blood coated the exile's fingers and hand. He inspected the blood before turning back to the tree. Realization dawned in Braethen's mind: This was Grant's cradle, the one he'd spoken of as part of his punishment, the place to which his striplings were brought and left for him to either place or raise.

Tenderly, the man's arms eased inside the hollowed tree and withdrew an infant. Even from where he stood, Braethen saw the pallor of the child's skin and the darkness around its eyes and mouth. Grant knelt on the hard earth beneath the dead tree and cradled the dead babe in his arms.

None of them moved, observing a moment of silent reflection for the passing of a life that never knew a hope. The thought of the baby wriggling its arms in ignorance as the serpent coiled nearby seared Braethen's senses. He shut his eyes to the image. A distant part of him wanted to avenge the child, but the culprit already lay dead near Grant's feet. A horrible feeling of helplessness gripped him. Whatever his own comfort in taking up the sword, he would forever be too late to change the ending that lay in the exile's arms. He thought of Wendra then, and wondered how deeply her own wound and scar must be. How she might wrestle with the loss she could not change?

Braethen took an involuntary step forward, then another. The unrealized possibilities of the babe weighed on his mind, as did the injustice and cruelty of abandoning a child this way, leaving it to the caprice of a world it could not comprehend. One hand sought his sword instinctively, as if to affirm his willingness to stand against such things, while in his mind he sought old tales given him by A'Posian, something to allay this terrible iniquity. But there was none, and he stood staring at a surrogate father mourning a child he'd never known.

Mira went to the snake and knelt to inspect it. She and Vendanj exchanged a knowing look. "Hostaugh," she said. "Not a serpent from the Scar. You won't find these south of the Pall . . . unless someone brought it here."

"What are you saying?" Braethen asked, already sure of the answer.

"The serpent was placed in the tree by Quietgiven." Mira stood and kicked the snake away with a flick of her boot.

Grant turned, catching a look of the sun low on the eastern sky. "We're not late, not by more than half a glass." His voice came questioningly but with resignation. "This is the appointed day, the appointed hour. The child is cold." He pulled the infant's blanket around its shoulders as though to warm it.

"It is the poison," Vendanj said. "The hostaugh is a sidewinder conceived in the Bourne. Its bite steals life to invigorate the beast itself."

"Why would they do this?" Braethen asked. "I thought Quietgiven sought life for its own use. Wouldn't they have taken the child?"

"The Quiet seeks Forda in any form, but in an infant it seeks something very specific," Vendanj explained, speaking directly to Grant.

Grant stared up at the Sheason, and a secret passed between them in a look.

"It is a warning," Vendanj said, coming closer to peer down at the child. "The child's parents would surely have cleansed the cradle before placing the child within. No. The serpent was put there after the child's parents had left, and the child was left to you as a sign."

"They are mistaken if they think I can be dissuaded over the death of one stripling." Grant looked away at the vastness of the Scar, a resolute expression settling over the creases in his deeply tanned face.

"It isn't your care for new wards they mean to disrupt," Vendanj said. "They will seek to destroy you if you cannot be of use to them in attaining their desire."

"And what is that?" Braethen asked, irritation edging his voice. So many private conversations and old relationships clouded the Sheason's exchange with the exile. He felt like the village yokel left out of a conversation between men and women of consequence.

Vendanj looked at him but did not answer, while Mira climbed to the top of the hill and checked their back trail. She returned quickly and shook her head—no one followed them.

Grant gave the babe a final look, his patient, steady eyes acknowledging the end of a cycle, though one closed prematurely. Braethen saw a tenderness in the man he hadn't seen before. Then the exile gently passed the child to Mira to hold and began digging a grave. Braethen watched as Vendanj knelt beside Grant and the two men dug together in silence. Beneath a dead tree, they scooped the barren earth that would be the final ground for the infant. Braethen joined them, drawing his sword to break up the packed dirt. Vendanj looked once at him as he put the sword to this new use, but the Sheason appeared to approve, and Braethen's heart gladdened in the act of honoring this tiny life in this small way.

．．．

As the three men stabbed at the earth to create a grave, Mira looked down at the child in her arms. She cradled it close, feelings both maternal and mournful touching her in quiet waves. The face of the babe was pallid but peaceful. And looking upon the infant girl, the promise of her future frozen forever in her delicate features . . . Mira fought a rising wrath that sought escape.

There would be a time for that.

Now, she honored this small life with the care and attentiveness she deserved but had never received in life. Mira thought about her own mother—her birth mother—whose face she couldn't remember, and wondered what providence had kept her from being like the child in her arms at that very moment.

The abandonment of a small life, whatever the cause, caused an ache in Mira's chest. It made the decision awaiting her beyond Recityv a heavy burden, a decision that might affect the success of the Sheason's ultimate plans.

Somehow, staring into the unrealized promise of this little girl galvanized Mira's need to act, but put her further from understanding which path to choose. Only one certainty filled her under the hard sun of the Scar and the unmoving body of this little one: If she could have given her life to save this babe, she would have.

When the child lay in its final slumber and the earth had been replaced, the four lingered a moment in the stillness. Then Grant mounted. "You have one cycle of my life, Sheason. Then I will be back at this tree. Not one more life will fall because I was not here to receive it."

Then he raced to the east, leaving the others to catch up. Mira and Braethen mounted. Vendanj lingered a moment.

The Sheason looked down at the small patch of dirt that humped slightly above the earth around it. In the barren confines of this inhospitable place they had laid to rest a life come unnaturally to its end. The hope and path that had lain in store for the child, which had been stolen by malice and cowardice, brought the Sheason's indignation surging to the surface.

To send a message, a defenseless babe . . .

Vendanj shook with the need to do something. The foul deed could not go unavenged.

But it would have to wait until next he came upon the Quiet. The helplessness of it, the vision in his mind of a baby struck unwitting by this viper and crying in pain and confusion and desperate need of the comfort it had sought and rightly deserved in coming to this world, this life . . . Vendanj fell to his knees and wept silently. The bitterness of it stole his strength and will to go on, to even stand.

What lived in the soul of those who served Quietus that they would do such a thing? He could not fathom it. In that moment Vendanj saw a glimpse into the horror that stood in store for the family of man should the veil fall. He now understood, more intimately than ever before, what the histories called the Placing: when the fathers had hidden the Whited One and his abominations from the world.

There could be no chance at greatness, at living to make this world a place worthy of its creation, if the breath of a child were to be snuffed before it could live to know that potential.

The anguish seared through him, and the Sheason raised his head and screamed all the pain in his heart into the pale blue sky. With the sound of it still echoing out on the hard, barren waste of the Scar, Vendanj thrust his hands into the grave of the babe and spoke the words of his heart, and gave unto that plot of land a portion of his spirit forevermore.

Spontaneously from the gravesite came grass and flowers, exuding their scents of life around the vale of the cradle that had been the death of the child.

When the burn of his grief subsided and his great shout had echoed its last, Vendanj drew his hands out of the now fertile soil. "Good-bye, small one," he said. "Though unknown to us, you go loved into your next life."

Then Vendanj took his knife and found the serpent. He cut off its head and put it in his pouch. He also reclaimed the fold of the child's blanket they had torn away before burying her, the portion that bore a small stain of blood.

These tokens he kept, and left the babe to its rest.

At meridian, they passed the boundary of the Scar and felt the cool whisper of breezes among the trees and undergrowth. Braethen had never considered that life was something he might actually smell, but he drew deep breaths of the scent of bark and needles and fallen leaves and moist earth. Mira scouted ahead, leaving Braethen to his two silent companions. Near a brook they stopped and ate a midday meal, speaking no words.

They moved on quickly, and stopped again at twilight, the moon rising fast and large.

Braethen cast his eyes heavenward and thought of Tahn, Sutter, and Wendra. In the Hollows, he would have come to serve as an author. His father A'Posian had taught him certain knowledge from rare texts, and with his education he would have served them.

But not protected them.

He hadn't been a sodalist then. He knew it now. Hadn't been a defender of anything except his father's library.

But now he'd been given a sodalist's sword, and by a member of the Order of Sheason that the Sodality had been created to serve. The blade upon his sigil, and the quill that danced its length, had been forever only a metaphor to him, though he had read fragments of the histories and stories authors had penned for generations. In the Hollows, the reality of what his crest really meant might never have been known to him.

Braethen dropped a hand to the steel hanging at his hip. The feel of it still caused many emotions in him: pride, willingness to stand, to defend; revulsion at the intention of a sword; despair that each time he hefted its balanced weight, the weapon became more comfortable in his hand.

Braethen stole a look at the backs of the two dark figures who had led him out of the Scar. Vendanj and Grant sat close together, confidential discussion passing between them. Lunar light carved them dully from the black landscape that stretched before them: two equally inscrutable stories sitting side by side. In their mystery, the two men felt to Braethen like a couplet of prophecy. The thought sent a chill over him, because his own story was now inextricably linked to theirs.

Finally, Braethen couldn't help but ask: "Why are you rewriting the Charter?"

Grant turned in the darkness. "Because I'm tired of fighting."

Braethen recalled the weapons racks at Grant's home. "Then why teach that skill to the children who live with you?"

"Because sooner or later, I know they'll need it. A lot of time to consider is what I have, sodalist. A lot of time to think about the ways that a man brings angry hands against you. Days and years to teach my wards and myself that personal freedom is something to safeguard, even if it involves risking physical harm." Grant put his dinner aside on a fallen log and nestled down with his back to the wood. "I *anticipate,* my friend. A thousand days I've walked through the strokes and counterstrokes of fight after fight. Different weapons, different opponents of varying sizes and ability. I've imagined different terrains over which battles might rage, compensated for wounds to myself or my enemy. All up here." He tapped his temple twice lightly. "And when I could think of no more, I considered them again, and again, seeing the results each time, varying the level of ability in my foe and anticipating his next stroke based on a hundred factors. And when I was done, I taught my striplings. And we practice. It is all there is to do in the Scar."

"Except drawing a new Charter," Vendanj put in.

"Well that, too," Grant conceded, his smile a tad more bitter in the concession.

"You still haven't answered why, though," Braethen pushed.

"You. A stripling from the Hollows carrying a glowing sword and brash enough to be ready to hold it against a stranger." He pointed at Braethen. "And an inquisitive fellow beyond that, always ready with a question, even when words ought to be left alone. The answer is: Maybe I want to believe this world has hope, could be redeemed. Or maybe it's none of your concern."

Braethen gave an embarrassed grin. He saw Grant and Vendanj share a genuine smile over the exchange, but their separate thoughts turned their countenances dark soon after, the weight of their ruminations lingering upon them until sleep relieved the tension that puckered their brows. Braethen found it difficult to sleep. He sat up watching the two men and every so often spotting Mira. *What am I doing in such company?* The question followed him down to slumber, where it played upon him in dreams of swords and books, each biting flesh and each answering a call to arms.

CHAPTER FIFTY-SEVEN

A Servant's Tale

Sutter sat in the dark, his wrists and ankles bound with chains, staring across at a troupe of scops.

If prison could descend further than its own dank breath, and if Sutter could have imagined something worse than to be caged with thieves and murderers, then being manacled in the company of players was certainly it.

There were reasons. Old reasons. But he would not let himself remember it all. The blind hate was enough. He preferred it to the despair the stone and beatings inspired.

He looked through one eye, the other swollen shut from where a boot had caught him during the first night of his stay in Recityv. He stared across through shadows at two men and two women shackled to the opposite wall. Their jailer had painted their faces in rough, garish mockery of their profession, and from time to time made them stand and dance or prattle out some folliet. Whether their performance was to his liking or not, the whip seemed to come with the same intensity. Sutter saw that whip take the eye of one of the women during a song she'd sung unaccompanied to a simple skit.

But neither did his compassion rise too high.

Old wounds.

So when Sutter discovered another cellmate, it was a welcome relief. He had not seen or heard from this other before. This new cellmate had kept himself hidden far back in the crook of the stair, but was given away finally by a moan in his sleep; no other sound came. Sutter, listening closely, realized this other's bindings were of rope rather than chain.

"Why are you here?" Sutter asked.

The man remained silent for a time, then finally said, "I was deemed unfit for my throne." A sad laugh followed. He sounded young.

Sutter liked the genuine sound of it. "You're from Recityv?"

"Not hardly. You won't have heard of my homeland: Risill Ond. We're nestled against the eastern ocean beyond the Wood of Isiliand."

"You're right. Never heard of it. And you're the king?" Sutter's skepticism rang in his words.

Again the easy laugh. "My people put away courts and high politics so many generations gone that we had to consult our oldest books to remember our own sigil."

"And what was that?" Sutter found himself grateful for the sudden conversation down in the dark.

"A scythe," the young man said.

Sutter could feel the honest surprise on his own face. "And why a scythe?"

"We're farmers."

A full silence settled between them.

"What is your name?" Sutter finally asked.

"I am Thalen Dumal. But I am no king. All our land has ever known is the peace of planting and harvest. We've lived our lives by the cycles of the crop for as long as there've been people in Risill Ond. But we did once have royalty of a kind. And when the convocation was called, a very old oath was remembered. My ancestors made those promises when we still had a palace and courtiers. I would rather be with my crops again than have come to Recityv."

At that, Sutter nodded agreement. "My name is Sutter. I'm familiar with the dirt myself."

"Then you see the senseless waste of this whole affair."

"I don't know. But if you feel that way, why come?" Sutter probed at his swollen eye.

"We were obligated. I was obligated. When the Second Promise was issued long ago and we were asked to answer, my ancestors went. But we had no army, so a vote was held, and our unmarried men who had seen the Change were called upon. They marched to Recityv, bearing the only weapons they knew, scythes. For it, the contingent out of Risill Ond were named the Reapers. They were among the few who went into the fray beside the men from Recityv. And in fulfillment of our oath, we vowed to honor Recityv's call should it ever come again.

"It came. But because we don't observe all the traditions of a ruling class in Risill Ond, there were no special vestments to wear or standards to fly. My mother stitched our emblem into an old, thin carpet." There was no shame in Thalen's voice. "And when we arrived, I was promptly taken in by some leagueman and questioned. But it was not a mere routine check, or worry over what vices we might observe. They seek to push their influence into Risill Ond. Imprisoning me leaves our lands essentially unclaimed. Which means our seat at the convocation is unclaimed. The League will claim it, and then a *civil* contingent will come to our lands—something we've been able to avoid until now."

"How have you managed that?" Sutter asked.

"I told you. There are no palaces. No royalty. We are small and remote. But then . . . the Reapers are known for the steadfastness they showed when the Second Promise failed. So we have a seat here by tradition. The League is trying to gain as many votes as it can so that when the convocation convenes, they'll be able to achieve their own ambitions. The regent . . ." Thalen's voice softened. "It will be the end of her when they do."

"We must tell someone," Sutter exclaimed.

"Who, the guards who beat us? Or the scops here who keep us company?"

Sutter looked over at the troupe, who seemed to be listening to Thalen's story from the darkness. Then he turned back to Thalen, anger evident in his voice when he spoke. "I don't understand how they can hold you here."

The fellow laughed again. "Therein lies the irony. They accused me of being a false applicant to the Seat of Risill Ond. They looked at my hand-sewn banner and meager clothes and used them as a judgment upon me."

Sutter fumed. It didn't help that this fellow accepted what had happened so temperately.

Thalen spoke again, his voice becoming sad and wistful. "I would like to be back in my fields, and smell the dew of morning on the crops and soil; till the earth, and look out upon the endless tracts of harvest under a mild sun. That is my court . . . I am no king."

The words stole some of Sutter's ire, as he thought again of his own home, his own parents. His adventure had brought him to the depths of a dark prison. And yet his first thought of the Hollows didn't remind him that he sat in chains, but of the man and woman who'd given an orphan a home. He felt suddenly homesick.

Hearing Thalen talk about his love of his work reminded Sutter of his own feelings, which he'd hardly bothered to acknowledge. His anger fell away as he sat quiet then and thought, maybe for the first time, about the things he loved.

It was, to his reckoning, the end of his second day in the bowels of Solath Mahnus. They'd separated him from Tahn, muttering something about keeping accomplices away from each other. Sutter found himself wondering if Tahn was all right as he finally fell down into sleep, and saw the dead in his prison cell.

Tahn had sat chained for two days in the dungeon chamber without food or water. The dank smell of sweating stone lay just under the stench of waste and filth and stale straw used to cover the mess. He had occasionally heard someone in the shadows squatting over a chamber hole in the corner. But down here it hardly seemed to matter. A shaft of light fell slantwise from a barred window in the door, seeming to grow weaker as it finally met the junction of wall and floor down a set of stone stairs.

The square of torchlight cast from the window fell between Tahn and the other prisoner occupying the cell, and he was grateful for it. In the night, the man moaned in his sleep. Whatever his unseen companion had dreamed about had caused the man's arms to thrash about, scraping heavy chains across the stony floor. Perhaps he moaned because of bruises caused by the unforgiving hardness of the floor which was their bed.

The manacles binding Tahn's wrists and ankles chafed until the iron stung his raw skin. He barely noticed; the guards had beaten him almost unconscious before shackling him to the wall. The ache in his ribs from hard boots and the cuts in his lips and across his cheeks throbbed with the beating of his heart. A gash in the back of his head made lying down intolerable. He slept sitting against the wall, his chin on his chest. His left eye had taken some damage. And though he didn't remember it, he thought someone had stomped on his fingers, leaving the joints too bruised to flex.

No outer window freshened the stale air. When he or his cellmate shifted or sighed, the sound of each movement reverberated loudly off the high ceiling.

They'd stripped him of his bow and belt, and ripped his cloak from his shoulders. He wished they'd left him that, at least. The cold stone chilled his flesh through his clothing. They had stripped him of Sutter, too, taking Nails to some other place. Just now he could use some of Sutter's wit, to hear how he'd respond to a dare of digging up a root in this cellar.

Tahn drifted in and out of sleep, scarcely aware of night and day save that he had awakened twice in the manner to which he was accustomed. Always able somehow to know which was east, he looked into the darkness and imagined the torchlight falling in a wan rectangle as being the greater light coming to dispel another night. The thought gave him little comfort as he looked at the prison bars cutting dark lines across the brightness there. But he felt the coming of the day in those moments, and counted the cycles as they came and fled. And when the weight of the silence threatened to crush him, he pressed the back of his left hand to his one good cheek and felt the familiar shape across his skin. The scar comforted him, if only because it was still his.

In his first imprisoned hours he had hoped that Vendanj, Mira, any of his friends might come and reclaim him from this darkness. He'd sat watching the door through his one clear eye, growing tense each time a guard paced the outer hall and passed the window. Each time that square of light dimmed with the shadow of a man's head, Tahn lost a small portion of hope. He no longer raised his head at the sound of boots beyond the door. The moments stretched on like days; hours passed like weeks. Confined by the darkness, and beaten down by the denizens of a strange city eager to witness a man hanged, Tahn felt trapped.

His own jumbled thoughts also trapped him. He tried to remember moments of freedom and happiness: hunting deep in the Hollows, swimming in the quarry with Sutter as sun glittered on the ripples of the water, and Wendra cutting apples to fill a sweet pie that she would top with grape jam and spice. But each memory clouded, shifted, became ash falling from a burning mountain on a forest slope, dragging cold water into his lungs beneath the death grip of a tracker, the Bar'dyn holding Wendra's dead babe and he unable to stop the monster . . .

All of these things Tahn eventually surrendered—at least for a time—to the serenity of the blackness, the quiet that came around him.

Except Wendra. His failure to Wendra.

They had always shared a special bond. Brother and sister yes, but more. Friends. True friends. When Tahn did for her was not simply the obligation of blood. It was honest affection and concern. That was the truth of it. And on her side of things, never had she questioned any of the small strangenesses she'd surely seen in him. Indeed, when his dreams had plagued him, it had been the soft sound of her voice singing to him in the dark hours of the night that had eased his mind and made him feel at peace once more.

Which was why these recent events hurt him so deeply. Even here, where he'd been stripped of virtually all emotion and dignity. But at last now, he had no further choices. Or so he thought.

"Two days and not a word. Where are your manners, son?" The voice penetrated the darkness, but Tahn paid them no more attention than any other dream that fevered his mind.

Again, the voice: "There's just the two of us here, so you must know I am addressing you."

Tahn raised his head in the direction of the voice. It came calmly, with patience and clarity.

"You've not spoken to me, either," Tahn said. He tried to peer beyond the shaft of light to see the man.

"That is a matter of caution," the disembodied voice replied. "The council has sent informants and spies before you to wear your shackles for a few hours, a day perhaps, believing that I might make one of them a confidant, to share my woe, and discover what they could not force from me any other way."

"Then why speak to me now?" Tahn still could not see the man.

"Because no man here by choice has ever remained as long as you." Tahn heard the man's chains rattle as though he shifted his seat. "The darkness gets to them, the light from the door mocks their little game, and they call to be let go." The man chuckled in the darkness. "My silence disturbs them. Such oaths I have heard from men to whom I never uttered a word." He heard another soft chuckle.

"So you have decided to trust me because I've been here two days?" Tahn said with incredulity.

"I did not say I trusted you," the man's voice changed, becoming flat and precise. "That I've broken my silence does not mean I've taken you to my right. But anyone beaten as you were . . . I would be pleased to know what crime causes the Recityv guard to lay into you with such enthusiasm. Even I did not suffer so much when first I came to this place." Tahn again heard chains rattle, and imagined the man raising an arm to indicate their shared cell.

Tahn considered. If he told the man what he'd done, the fellow might want to know why, and what would Tahn say? But Tahn had already learned something in the dark of a stinking cell: You heard the truth because there was nothing else to distract you from it. Tahn sensed that in this chamber where debts were paid, secrets came like confessions.

Tahn's cellmate broke the silence. "You may be ashamed of your deed," the voice said with a tone of doubt. "Or you may fret that I am the informer, here to discover your plans. Or you may even think that I simply cannot understand." The man paused; air whistled through his nostrils. "You should consider what type of man would volunteer to be chained beside a pile of his own foulness for so long just to question a prisoner. What shame could I judge *here*? And as to understanding, son, you must believe that my days in this place have instructed me in ways that scholars will never know." He again laughed gently. "Though I'd have been glad to forgo this training."

Tahn still did not speak. A thief, a murderer, whatever manner of miscreant this man was, Tahn did not believe he could unburden himself of all the suspicions and events that had occupied him since first meeting the Sheason. Vendanj would not want him sharing such things. And what might a man confined to a cell do with such information once he was free? Tahn raised his hand and again touched the pattern on his hand to the skin of his unmarked cheek.

"Still cautious," the man said with appreciation. "Then consider this, my young friend. I'll have no reprieve. No second stand before the Court of Judicature. When my turn is done here—a long turn to repudiate me—I will stand to face my death and wonder if my final earth could be any colder than this stone bed."

"At the gallows?" Tahn asked.

"Whatever they deem appropriate," the man said. "So you see, your story, whatever it is, will never reach another soul. But down in this prison it may offer us each some respite for a few moments."

An earnest undertone in the man's voice caught Tahn unaware. Patience still measured every word the man spoke, but now it sounded as if long exposure to the murk and indifferent stone edged the man's request. Yet it was more than that. Tahn could hear his honesty. The honesty that the man needed to hear a story, something to carry him beyond the walls of this cell, and the honesty that some night here would be the last he would sleep in this world before he met his end.

Still, Tahn asked simply, "Why?"

The sound of the man standing came out of the dark, and Tahn saw a shadow rise near the shaft of light that slanted in from the window up the stairs. A raised chin showed defiance. "Because the soldiers here don't brutalize simple lawbreakers whose offense is against another citizen of Recityv. And no one victimizing an immigrant is ever placed in chains; there's too much distaste for the unwashed among the footmen who keep the law." His shadowed head lowered as though he could see Tahn through the darkness. "A young man who smells of the road, whose face is new to the touch of a razor, but who excites such venom from his captors as you did, my friend, is one who has caused a wound to the guard itself, perhaps the League, and that is a story to melt away the walls of this place, if only in the telling."

Tahn swallowed against the thickness in his mouth, and suddenly felt the pains of thirst and hunger. "My mouth is dry," he said.

"You'll be fed your fourth day, and whatever you eat and drink will run through you like rain down a spout. It will likely be moldy bread and water left to sit since you came here." Tahn thought he heard a smile. "Still, it tastes good, though the rush of it into an empty stomach will give you pain."

Tahn groaned and drew himself up against the wall at his back.

"I will split my ration with you," the man said. "To keep your strength up for the words you generously share."

Momentarily, Tahn considered refusing still, when an arm emerged into the light from the window pushing a metal plate with a slice of bread and slice of cheese toward him. A moment later came a cracked decanter. The face and shoulders of the man yet remained in the shadows beyond the shaft of light. The man was silent while Tahn ate.

Never had warm water quenched his thirst so completely. He hardly noticed the sting of his shackles over his raw wrists. When he was done, the arms appeared and retrieved the plate and decanter. Tahn half expected the man to harangue him to begin. But he soon heard the long intake of a sleeper's breath, and knew the man had gone to sleep.

In the depths of his own shadows, Tahn watched the square of light, a growing feeling of abandonment gripping him. He didn't know how long he stared before he began to talk, hearing the echo of his own voice against the indifferent stone. He spoke just above a whisper, his small voice carrying in the fetid air. Almost immediately he knew the man was listening. Never did a chain stir or a scrape interrupt, but his audience heard every word, an audience of one, who lay against unyielding stone.

Somehow it did feel like confession.

He included every detail he could remember, holding back only two things:

the sticks entrusted to him by the scrivener, and drawing an empty bow at Sevilla. He told of Vendanj and his strange appearance in the Hollows on the eve of Wendra's attack. He told of the Sedagin and Sutter's dance with Wendra. He related the dark mists, and his and Sutter's separation from Mira and Penit and the others, and what had caused him to flee headlong into those roiling clouds. He spoke of the Lul'Masi and the tenendra tents, of the fire at the library of Qum'rahm'se, of Stonemount and his fight with the insubstantial creature. He retold with disgust the burning of the woman by league order. Several times he went back to fill in portions he had forgotten to include.

He finished by recounting his arrival at Recityv and discovering another public punishment about to be meted out. He described the division in the crowd that watched the hanging, and his feeling that one of the men should not be put to death.

"And here I am," Tahn said, ending his story. "It seems like a lifetime ago that I sat near a ravine and watched for a herd of elk to climb the draw." Tahn looked up. "That's where it began," he said. "With a man wearing a dark cloak that shimmered crimson when he moved. He killed the elk I spared, whipping rain into a spout that crushed the animal into the earth." Tahn shook his head. "When he was done, I watched him thrust hands into the mud and cause the wet earth to burn to glass."

Tahn wished for another draft of lukewarm water from the man's decanter. His mouth and throat were again dry. The cell was silent until his cellmate exclaimed in quiet amazement.

"In the name of Palamon, son, who are you?"

Tahn tried again to look through the shaft of light between them. The sallow glow never seemed so bright. "Tahn," he said. "Tahn Junell. My father was Balatin Junell, who took his earth just three years ago."

"And you've not seen Vendanj since the Male'Siriptus?"

"No," Tahn answered. "But I heard him call for us to gather at Recityv. I've seen nobles and gentry and others not as highborn crowding the roads and towns on their way here." Tahn tried to lean back against the wall and winced when he struck the gash on the back of his head. "There are rumors that the Shadow of the Hand is open . . ." Tahn trailed off momentarily. "They are not rumors. I've seen them. I assume that is why everyone comes in a panic. I just hope the others arrive safely."

"The Hand is a focal point, Tahn, but it is not the only passage out of the Bourne. The legions of Quiet press against their borders as far east as the forests of Saecula. But it is the land west that bleeds, Mal'Tara, Mal'Valut, Destik'Mal, even Ebon, where life so near the Bourne corrupts the soil, the air, the people. It is an inhospitable place, and the veil there that holds the darkness at bay is thin. The nations and kingdoms beyond the Divide are all but lost to us. Once they stood as a defense against the canker of the Bourne. Just an age ago, the Order of Sheason was strong there, assisting in the fight to prevent the Quiet from descending into the land the way the Lul'Masi came into our world during the War of the Hand."

Tahn listened now, the sound of the man's voice whispering over the hardened stone like a prayer.

"But the suspicions of those who followed the order in the west have grown into sanctions carried out by the League. Hysteria infects weak rulers, who are anxious to remain in good stead with His Leadership." Disgust tinged the man's words. Tahn thought he heard the gnashing of teeth before calm returned to his companion's voice. "But that is not the greater part, Tahn. The Quiet of the One grows even without the conscious assistance of men. Our fields produce less each year; our litters and folds diminish. The growing season shortens; the sharpness of winter air lingers, smothering the work of the greater light. Our land grows to resemble what we imagine of the world beyond the Pall." He quieted, conveying an import to what was to come next. "The rumor that binds us, Tahn, and moves the regent to recall her full High Council and the Convocation of Seats, is that the veil thins once more. And, in this maddened day, belief in the Tract and the Song wanes to the point of their abolition."

A chill stole over Tahn. He had heard the names, but they had the same effect on him now as they had before. Even naming these things inspired a reverence and awe that was both frightening and hopeful. The words themselves called to something deep within him, something crucial and frightful. He realized the chains that bound him were clattering on the stone paving, but he could not stop his arms from shaking.

The man did not seem to notice. "And now for *my* story, Tahn," the man said in a slightly more genial tone. "I am Rolen. And I am Sheason."

Tahn's head snapped in Rolen's direction. "Sheason," Tahn echoed. "But then you could free yourself. Why do you—"

"Easy, son. Patience."

Tahn had a hundred questions, but sat straight, wanting to know how a renderer could be held against his will in the most vile of places. A guard came to the door, looking in on them and letting out an oath before passing by, satisfied that they were sufficiently miserable. His steps retreated down the hall. Tahn listened with rapt attention, peering into the shadows where this Sheason sat. Rolen stood and began to pace slowly. The lengths of chain swayed almost musically in time with his steps. Forgotten to Tahn were the conditions surrounding him, his hunger, the cuts and bruises, even the outside world. A burning thought hampered his breathing: If a Sheason could be bound and caged, then the promise of escape, and perhaps the hope Vendanj had placed in Tahn, were foolish things. Tahn considered that he might learn more of what was true by sitting in this stinking darkness than in every dawn he had awakened to see.

"I was from Maven Wood originally," Rolen began. Though weak, his voice grew wistful. "My mother had but one book, but she read it to me every night of my life. A hundred times or more we turned the last page, only to start again at the beginning. That book was *The Will's First Son*.

"I would sit and watch my mother's lips move, forming the words on the page, and imagine that I was there, standing witness to the first battle of Palamon and Jo'ha'nel. And every night those same lips that shaped the words on the page would kiss my forehead to usher me to sleep, and I would tell mother that I would one day follow Palamon, and pledge what I am to serving others, even if it meant at the cost of my own life." A whimsical laugh escaped Rolen's lips. "I imagine now how it must have sounded to her. But she always replied, 'I know you will, Rolen,' and turned down the lamp before descending the loft.

"The day I left my melura behind and crossed the break of Change, I packed all I had and rode north over the Balens Road to this place." Wonder crept into his words. "I'd never seen such a city. I've been told Ir-Caul and Dalle are grand to behold, but I fell to my knees when the Recityv walls rose off the plain before me. It was to me almost like the Tabernacle of the Sky that had always been in my dreams.

"When I passed the gate, I wasted no time in inquiring after a Sheason with whom to train and learn. Every face, every pair of eyes scowled, oaths and taunts scorned me. 'Throwing away my youth,' they said. 'Chasing after secrets and abominations,' said others. Most called me 'fool' and turned away."

A sad laugh followed. "I couldn't understand these feelings toward the order. And more than once I tried to retell the story in my mother's one book, assuming that they did not know the tale. It earned me the taste of used bitter spewed from loose lips, and more than once I had to pick myself up off the floor. I learned that Maven Wood was smaller than I'd thought. Or perhaps my mother had been the victim of a clever but false author, crafting stories to earn money rather than to illuminate."

Rolen's breathing grew labored, and the Sheason sat again, his chains rattling, his lungs wheezing with the effort to draw breath. Tahn waited, patient but eager to hear the rest. Finally, the man caught his breath, and went on more slowly.

"For a full cycle of the lesser light I sought the order, working from one end of Recityv to the other. I searched every inn, every tavern, every store, shop, and alley. In some streets, my search was met with haughty sniffs or lancing glares down washed noses. But then one day I turned into a byway stinking of rotting cabbage and moldy wood guarded by vagrant cats. A short stair descended into a sunken bitter room with three tables and a few couches set at the back used to transact deals of the flesh, the tavernkeeper taking a price for their rental.

"I went in more from habit than any belief that my search would ever yield fruit. One man sat at one of the low tables, a wide glass filled shallowly from a burgundy bottle. One couch creaked with two occupants trading service for coin. I was grateful for weak candlelight in the place and took a seat. A man whose height kept him high in the shadows left a glass and a bottle on my table, and took himself back to a stool near a cutting board in the corner.

"I remember the smells of grit underfoot, bad candlewicks, and unmopped wine left to stain the wood. It was no place to find an honorable renderer of the Will. It was a forgotten place, a last place. It suited my mood just fine, and I poured my glass. I'd decided I would search no more.

"Silently, I drank, in no hurry to dull my senses, and waited for day to come so that I could return home and tell mother the awful truth: Her book was just a story. I watched the candle flame, and tried to block out the intermittent moans from the back of the room. It occurred to me that a coin went further than I thought." Again the sad laugh.

"When my bottle neared empty, I took it in hand to finish it when a figure appeared out of the gloom. 'Will you finish your bottle and not offer me a drink?' the man asked. I looked up into a kind face, the man's smile faint in the light of my candle. I remember thinking that his smile brightened the room, made it less woeful, less unsavory. I nodded and the man put his own glass down on the table and sat with me.

"He asked me who I was, why I had come to this little drinking room. I told him everything, expecting one of the various reactions that had followed my inquires all across Recityv. But instead he pushed his glass toward me. All that remained of my bottle was a swallow for each of us, but I poured. He then pushed his glass aside and asked me why I wanted to follow this man in my mother's book, saying that if he wasn't a fable, he was surely dead so many seasons gone that nothing remained of his noble fight.

"I looked into my own glass, my face distorted in the curved surface." Tahn heard the man's chain rattle, as though he lifted a hand toward the memory of the glass. "'If it is true, then what he began surely lives,' I said. 'But I am tired and perhaps still too young to see things for what they are.' My own nose, large in the reflection of my glass, made me feel every bit the fool. And I turned my glass over to pour out the sour wine where it would join the stains of the other fools who came to drink here.

"I then pushed my empty cup aside, and stared into the kind face of my guest. Behind us the moans came with more frequency, and my companion's eyes caught the flame between us with mild amusement. Whether for me or those on the couch in the rear shadows, I wasn't sure."

Rolen's voice fell. "The man placed his hands around his glass. I felt his concentration as he fixed me with a stare, seeming to speak with his eyes. A moment later, his brow eased, and he stretched forth a brimming glass of brandy, pouring my cup half full from his own.

"I had found the Sheason after all. His name was Artixan, and I became his pupil. For twelve years I studied and read. I walked the streets of Recityv, traveled to other towns and villages with Artixan to observe and assist. I did not acquire knowledge easily; many things I had to learn and learn again. But in the end, my desire qualified me; it pushed me to work and gain the understanding necessary to become Sheason. And the day finally did come when the power to render the Will was conferred upon me."

"Conferred?" Tahn asked. He'd always assumed the power to draw upon the Will was inborn, a natural gift.

"It surprises you." Tahn thought Rolen must be smiling. "Yes, conferred. But it isn't given without being earned; at least it wasn't in the beginning. Anyone seeking to hold the power to render was required to study no less than eight years. The trial of years was meant to prove the intention of the pupil. Very few last the course of study and training. You are either given to patience, or you learn it. Those who do not, leave the order unendowed. And the right to render the Will may only be bestowed on another by one who already possesses the authority to wield it himself."

Tahn followed the reasoning ahead. "Then what of the Velle?"

A grimace sounded from the darkness. "The Whited One has his Draethmorte that can render and have the power to bestow the ability just as a Sheason does.

"That, and"—he sighed mightily—"the Sheason order is constituted of men and women, my friend; and mankind is fallible. Among us there will always be some who cannot live the full measure of their call and responsibility. Vanity and greed bite at a Sheason as surely as the next man, and there are those who, over time, have given in to these base qualities. The promises of the One have even enticed good servants to seek a different path." His voice fell low. "And the power to render remains unaltered in them. They may even confer upon others the right to draw upon the Will as they see fit. These lost Sheason observe no trial of time, no training period. And so they often die from being prematurely given the gift. But these rogues still flock to the Whited One. And their devotion to their cause is perhaps stronger than ours because bitterness, disillusionment, and disappointment with their *original* cause sends them to the easy promises of the One's false, hollow call."

"Why are there not more of them?" Tahn asked. "Wouldn't an army of Velle easily defeat an army of swords?"

"To render the Will is still a difficult thing, Tahn. Conferring the ability does not guarantee the safety of the practitioner. And the haste of the Quietgiven to teach and qualify and confer the power to render claims most of their initiates in the first moments they attempt to direct the Will . . . as it does some Sheason."

Tahn grew impatient. "But why do you remain in chains? Even if *you* fell victim to greed, you have the power to free yourself, don't you?"

"The plate I shared with you," Rolen began, "always comes bearing small, stale portions. Moldy bread usually. And the water is barely enough to wet my tongue and make me want more." He paused, but went on when Tahn did not reply. "My rations keep me weak," he concluded. "The darkness is oppressive, and the poor food starves my flesh. My irons turn more freely around my wrists and ankles today than when I came here. My Forda I'Forza has been impoverished. If I tried to draw on the Will here, it could well mean death to me. Even if I could survive the use of Will to break my bonds, another ten barriers lay between me and freedom, and I could not survive the drain of repeated renderings.

"But this is not why I stay," Rolen added quickly, then paused.

Tahn tried to make sense of the things the Sheason said. He listened in the dark to the man panting with the exertion of relating his story. He certainly sounded weak. The rasp in his lungs reminded Tahn of the winter fever and pox he'd had several years ago. Rolen coughed with a wet tearing sound that made Tahn wince. He heard the man spit liquid onto the floor, and Tahn found himself grateful again for the darkness.

When Rolen's breathing had calmed, he chuckled again, causing a few more stifled coughs.

A troubling revelation insinuated itself into Tahn's weary mind. "You choose to stay, don't you?"

• CHAPTER FIFTY-EIGHT •

Maesteri

Wendra looked up when she heard Penit gasp. The boy's eyes were impossibly wide, staring into the distance before them. Turning, she saw what no reader's description could ever do justice to: a wall more than a thousand strides across, rising from the plain as high, it seemed, as the cliffs of Sedagin. The encampments along the road and at the base of the wall would fill the Hollows a hundred times and more. Wendra wondered what would become of these people outside the protection of the immense barrier if an army laid siege to Recityv.

"There she is," the Ta'Opin announced. "The jewel of Vohnce. Home of the regent and mendicant alike. House of song and floor of debate. Hearth to draw nigh to, and table with many seats." A wide grin split Seanbea's face—the grin of a man returning home.

"How big is it?" Penit asked with evident awe.

"Why, how big does she look, lad?" Seanbea spoke through his smile. "Mountains have fallen to quarry her stone. And forests have been harvested and replanted more times than a man can count to fuel the forges that built her." The Ta'Opin swept his gaze from far left to right. "She's a jewel," he repeated.

Seanbea drove them through the thronged highway to the expansive gate. Several dozen soldiers in deep burgundy cloaks over bright suits of ringmail checked each entrant with a critical eye. Wagons and carriages were directed to one side where they could be inspected. Merchants offered lists of the contents in their wagons, many fidgeting as their loads were examined and checked against bills of lading.

Seanbea took his place in the line behind an elaborately decorated brougham. Delicate scrollwork had been carved in dark mahogany wood. Wendra caught glimpses of a lush fabric over the seats, burnt umber in color. Brass fixtures sparkled on the regal exterior, hinges, corner fittings, and lanterns attached to the sides. From a standard atop the carriage, a white banner ruffled in the wind, bearing the image of a taloned bird in simple, elegant strokes.

At every corner of the carriage, a small platform extended, and upon each stood a man at arms in a bright white and chestnut brocade. These attendant soldiers held onto brass handles secured to the cab, and watched the Recityv inspectors with raptor eyes.

"What have you?" a voice called, drawing Seanbea's attention.

"Instruments for the cathedral," the Ta'Opin said, pulling a parchment from his coat and extending it to the same inspector who had entered the previous carriage.

The man made a cursory look over the wagon before drawing back canvas tarps to verify the list.

"And who are they?" the inspector asked.

It did not sound to Wendra like a formal question, but the man raised his eyes from the list when Seanbea did not immediately respond.

"I've never been asked that before, sir. Can it matter who they are?"

Impatience edged the inspector's tone. "There's been trouble lately with all the . . . immigrants. We like to know who's . . . visiting."

Seanbea nodded. "The boy's name is—"

"I'm Penit." The boy stood up in the back of the wagon and put a thumb to his chest. "I'm going to run in the Lesher Roon."

Seanbea smiled. "That's right. And this is Anais Wendra, who'll be a student of the Maesteri as soon as we arrive at Descant."

The soldier gave Wendra a skeptical look. "She will, will she?" he said with displeasure. "For all the good their songs have brought us, I'd tell her to do her work in a tavern. Better pay."

Seanbea maintained his smile. "There are all kinds of wages. We'll make out just fine."

The inspector handed back the bill of goods and looked past them to the next cart while waving them inside. Seanbea thanked the man and released his brake, taking them into Recityv.

Wendra thrilled at the buildings, her own surprise as vocal as Penit's. Seanbea seemed to enjoy their innocent delight at the immensity of the city around them. He pointed out certain inns, shops, and merchant exchange houses, sometimes adding a bit of history in the telling. Wendra sat in the bed of the wagon, clinging to the side and gathering in one sight after another as they rolled onward.

They passed a hundred treasures as the throng of people pressed in around them like water around an island. Then gradually, the elegance of the edifices on either side of the road diminished. Stonework seemed older, more often in disrepair and stained from seasons of rain and sun. The buildings themselves were not as tall, their mortar crumbling and leaving gaps in their facing, like missing teeth. Awnings tilted over entries to various establishments; many windows looked like sharp-toothed maws where shards of glass rimmed an opening once completely paned. Even the livestock here reflected the general dishevelment of the structures around them, horses with deep-swayed backs and ungroomed manes and tails, dogs coated with burrs and mud. People went about with heads bowed, their coats and breeches puckered from poorly mended tears, their boots creased by too many strides to remain comfortable. The streets themselves remained unpaved here. Muddy pools stood in potholes and shallow ditches at the edges of buildings where rain fell from rooftops and beat their stale troughs, which filled, too, with slops thrown from windows— the smell of human filth rose from more than a few of these.

Between buildings, pigs and goats had been penned in narrow alleys awaiting a cook's pleasure for butchering. Wendra pulled her coat up over her nose against the smell of livestock and piled table scraps untouched by the animals. Flies sought waste to lay eggs, humming at a pitch that rose and fell as Seanbea drove Wendra and Penit past the many poor inns and dilapidated trade shops. She couldn't imagine this place being a part of the same city they'd come through after entering at the gate. Hers and Penit's delighted exclamations fell to disappointed silence.

Then the Ta'Opin turned down a cross street, and Wendra suddenly forgot to hold her coat over her nose and mouth. At the end of the avenue rose a grand building in the midst of the squalid surroundings. Four times higher than the closest building, the majestic cathedral ascended in a series of spires and pitched gables that left Wendra with the impression of a castle. The roof and cupolas shone green in the afternoon light, resplendent and luminous.

"Wow!" Penit remarked.

"Descant Cathedral. I told you," Seanbea said.

Each turn of the wagon wheels brought them closer, making the cupolas seem higher and the face of the great edifice loom larger. High in its darkened stone, colored glass caught the sun and glinted violet, crimson, gold, lapis, and emerald. Nearer still, the green cupolas disappeared from view. As she looked up, the spires seemed to angle toward the sky like spears thrown toward heaven.

The wagon creaked to a stop, and brought Wendra's gaze earthward. At eye level, the windows showed none of the magnificence of those higher up. Slats of wood boarded them over, either protecting the colorful mosaics or filling gaps left behind by a vandal's work.

Yet despite the unattractive windows and the aged stone covered in patches by lichen and withered vines, the cathedral made Wendra forget the distasteful quarter around it. Descant pressed up and out like a monument of strength and nobility. It seemed to both know the future and preserve the past.

They had only been stopped a moment when a large set of double doors swept inward, and two men bustled out and down the stone steps toward them. Each wore loose breeches tied with a wide crimson sash knotted on the left hip and a simple coat with a pocket over each breast.

"We'll bring you in under time," one said cheerfully, arriving at the wagon and ignoring Penit and Wendra as he pulled off the tarpaulin and hefted some of Seanbea's load.

The second man paused on the bottom step, taking note of the extra human cargo. "What's this, Seanbea? I hope you don't expect additional pay for these." He pointed fingers toward Wendra and Penit, and smiled.

"And hello to you, Henny, Ilio." Seanbea jumped to the ground. "These are friends of mine. I intend to introduce them to Belamae." The Ta'Opin leaned against the side of his wagon and smiled as though holding a secret from the two men.

"That's nice," Henny said, and bowed awkwardly before turning to pack his armload of instruments into the cathedral. Despite his rush, he handled them with great care. "Come on, Ilio, we've work to do."

Ilio did not take his eyes off Wendra as he lifted two small boxes from the wagon. "Is she spoken for?" he asked, inclining his head toward the Ta'Opin, his stare still locked on Wendra.

"I don't think she heard you," Seanbea mocked. "Speak up and perhaps she'll answer you herself." The Ta'Opin bent over to hide his laughter.

Ilio gave Wendra an embarrassed smile. His face flushed. Holding the boxes against his chest, he rocked side to side, seeming not to know what else to do. He started suddenly, as though just hearing Seanbea's taunting laughter. His reddened face became angry.

"You'll be responsible for them," Ilio said, leaning out over his boxes. "Rooms, rations, clothing . . . manners." The man scurried up the stairs after Henny.

"I'm sure you impressed her," Seanbea called after Ilio. He turned his smile on Wendra. "Pardon me, Anais, but I simply can't resist the opportunity to see Ilio's face turn that color. If I could duplicate it, I'd make a fortune in textiles."

Wendra caught the infection of Seanbea's laughter as the Ta'Opin helped her down from the wagon. Penit giggled brightly, joining in, though he seemed hardly to understand the joke. Seanbea hoisted the boy down, and waited a moment for Henny to emerge again before climbing toward the doors.

"Will you see to my wagon and team?" Seanbea asked the man.

"Surely," Henny replied.

Seanbea patted the man's bald head, and led Wendra and Penit to the double doors, now open to admit them.

"It is a special place," Seanbea said, speaking as much to himself as to either Wendra or the boy.

At the top of the steps, the doors seemed much larger, and bore engravings Wendra could not read. The scars of time made them appear to her more like skin than doors. Past them, cool, mild air caressed her skin with the scent of cedar incense and fruit rinds, and something else . . . the faraway echo of song that came from no one direction, but seemed to emanate from the walls themselves.

"What is that?" Wendra asked, putting her hand to a pillar and looking up at the ceiling of the vestibule in which they stood.

"It is the Song," Seanbea said with a deeper reverence in his voice Wendra had never heard. The Ta'Opin moved further into the cathedral without any further explanation.

Penit trotted past her to follow Seanbea. Wendra lingered a moment, feeling the hum through the marble pillar. Under her fingers, the beautiful stone felt vibrant, imbued with life by the uttering of words and music deep within it. Pulling away proved difficult. But she sensed that the song touching her fingers—just a whisper in her ears—came from voices somewhere deeper within the cathedral. She wanted to hear it, every word, every note.

Beyond the vestibule, three hallways sprouted, each passing beneath great stone vaults and housing a few cherrywood tables bearing silver urns. Intricate scrollwork had been carved directly into the stone walls. The doors were heavy and panelled. Candles burned in long glass hurricane tubes, lending the halls an intimacy and guarding the light against the air of loud voices. Brass handles and fittings had the look of small arms and hands drawn out of the stone itself; they had grown dark with time. Their footsteps echoed flatly down the clean marble floors.

Wendra caught up to Seanbea and Penit, who had angled left and paused briefly before an oil painting—the first of many—that adorned the hallway wall. The image shone beneath the warm illumination of a candle and revealed a man holding a piece of parchment in his hands with the same type of ink notes as the sheet Seanbea had given Wendra. A thin fringe of hair circled his head just above his ears, and he peered at them with kindly patience. The gentleman sat in a modest chair, wearing a long, white robe.

One by one, Seanbea stopped at each painting, never speaking or offering insight or names. Wendra marked the same patient look in the aspect of every portrait. Some showed women dressed in the same style as the men. A few held instruments in their laps, and a few sat reposed holding a kind of baton.

As they silently proceeded down the hall, Wendra thought the music grew louder. Each step excited her. Something in this melody felt familiar, though she was sure she'd never heard it before.

As she tried to remember, three women turned into the hall ahead. The one in the middle wore a thick white cloak, the hood up, her arms wrapped about herself as though she fought the shivers. On either side of her, the other two walked attentively, supporting the one in the middle as if afraid she might fall. When they drew close, Seanbea stepped into their path.

"Sariah?"

The woman in the middle looked up. "Seanbea?" Her voice sounded weak and tired, but pleased.

"It's good to see you. I thought when we arrived that the voice of Suffering I heard might be yours. But you've just finished a turn at the Song. Our reunion can wait until you have rested."

Sariah hugged Seanbea anyway, allowing his strong arms to hold her for several moments. Wendra watched the young woman's face lay against the Ta'Opin's chest, and saw a kind of concern and frightful wisdom that didn't belong in the face of one so young. It was something she thought she recognized from her own recent past.

Then finally she drew back. "Therin sings now. He'll want to see you, too, before you go. Can you stay until his turn at the Song is complete?"

"Of course," Seanbea said. "You've a fine voice, Sariah. And I didn't even hear the transition from you to Therin. Nicely done."

The young woman smiled, and the two girls beside her helped Sariah continue toward a set of doors Wendra guessed were personal quarters. Wendra didn't understand it all, but gathered that the song she heard was sung without ceasing, one voice taking over when another was exhausted. And Seanbea had said "the voice of Suffering." Could this melody she heard now in the very air and stone of Descant Cathedral be the Song of Suffering?

Just as she opened her mouth to ask, Seanbea pointed at the last painting at this end of the hall.

Wendra gasped, covering her mouth against her outburst.

She knew this face: the paternal smile, the patient eyes.

The visage at once warmed and frightened her. It was the face of the man who had appeared to her when the fever visions had found her in the cave near Sedagin. She'd nearly forgotten the counsel he'd given her, the comfort, the instruction. Seeing him in this portrait gave the memory a reality that caused her to tremble.

She'd doubted that simply singing the song from her songbox had healed her. Even the events in the mountain meadow near Jastail's cabin had blurred in her mind. But in the presence of the eyes looking out at her from this painting, Wendra considered that perhaps her song was more than mere melody. And the burden of it burned in her. Singing had forever been an escape and source of solace. Now it seemed it might bring consequences with it, reshaping the world around her. The thought turned her mood black. After all she had lost, this one private pleasure and reminder had become something more. She looked away from the painting with a scowl.

Behind her, Wendra heard the soft rapping of knuckles at a door. As she turned around, she saw the door open, revealing the face of the man in the painting, the man from the cave. He looked out and past Seanbea, directly at her.

"You've found your way," he said.

Wendra gave him a look of surprise and wariness. The elderly man's studied gaze retained its benevolent smile, but one brow rose as though he noted her caution.

"Well, Seanbea," the man said, shifting his attention to the Ta'Opin. "Always good to see you. Am I to thank you for shepherding this young woman to us?"

"There's no fee on it, Maesteri," Seanbea said, smiling. He embraced the old man, who gathered the large Ta'Opin in his white robed arms like a mother bear cuddling her cub. The gentleman stood an apple taller than the Ta'Opin.

Releasing Seanbea, the man said, "And who's this?" He bent over to look Penit in the eye.

"I'm Penit. I'm going to win the Lesher Roon."

"Is that right?" The old man winked. "I like a confident tone. Well you've arrived just in time, then; the race is tomorrow." The Maesteri then glanced at Wendra. "And you came along with Wendra, did you?"

Penit looked back at her. "We kind of watch out for each other. The others—"

"That's enough, Penit," Wendra interrupted. "Let's not plague anyone with our problems." She stepped beside the boy and put her arm around his shoulder. "Seanbea says you might let us stay a night or two. I can work to earn our meals."

Both Seanbea and the man in the robe gave Wendra a puzzled look.

"You are both guests here," the old man said. "You will stay the night and rest for Penit's big race tomorrow. I am Belamae. I teach the art of music for the Descant." He watched Wendra closely, appearing to expect her to acknowledge him. She kept a careful ambivalence. "We've plenty of room and food, and you're invited to partake of the music given voice within these walls."

"I see they've added you to the wall," Seanbea said, indicating the portrait. "A dandy likeness, I'd say."

Belamae gave a somewhat self-conscious smile. "Not my idea," he said. "And the placement is kind of conspicuous. But I am honored to be numbered among the Maesteri. They were rather forgiving with my nose, don't you think?" He chuckled warmly.

Seanbea joined him, while Wendra made another survey of the painting. The Ta'Opin's voice drew her attention back to Belamae.

"She creates," Seanbea said, an odd tone to his words, "new song such as I've never heard." He pulled a roll of parchment from an inner pocket and unfolded it before handing it to the old man.

With a gentle smile, Belamae began inspecting the sheet. Wendra caught a glimpse of the unique musical notation and knew Seanbea had transcribed for himself a copy of the duet she had sung with him some days ago. Slight embarrassment mingled with resentment. What she had sung spontaneously from her heart was now copied and recopied and set before the old man's eyes for approval and inspection. She felt scrutinized, naked. She glared at the Ta'Opin, though he did not see.

Belamae's smile faded, the light in his eyes flickering like a candle in the wind. Wendra might have thought the man had just read a warrant or elegy. His eyes rose from the parchment and locked Wendra in a serious gaze. She returned the old man's stare, partly arrested by his inscrutable eyes, partly out of defiance. After a long moment, he stepped back inside the room and motioned her to follow.

"Take the boy to the kitchen and get him something to help him grow," Belamae directed. "Give us an hour. Then we'll join you."

In each corner of the room, stands and easels stood overflowing with large books opened to more of the musical notation like that on the parchment Sean-bea had given the Maesteri. Beside each, instruments lay carefully set on pedestals uniquely crafted to receive them. On the walls hung more paintings, smaller portraits and a few of landscape and nothing more. In the middle of the room sat a large desk with twin lamps burning brightly, one at either end. The entire study shone with a great deal more light than the hall, the several easels and pedestals casting washed-out shadows across the floor like veins under skin. Directly opposite them, another door remained closed. Wendra thought the sound of the distant song emanated more strongly from behind it. The sound still came vaguely, audible only in the silence. But it never ceased.

Belamae took a seat behind his desk and folded his hands in his lap. "Please sit down," he said.

Wendra sat and surveyed the scattering of music sheets and quills and drawing graphite. Near one lamp lay a metal instrument like a small horseshoe attached to a handle. Seeing her interest, Belamae picked it up and struck it against the edge of his desk. The tines hummed and vibrated a single musical pitch.

"Can you match the sound?" Belamae asked.

Without thinking, Wendra hummed the sustained note.

"Harmonize with it."

Wendra shifted her pitch several times to sing different harmonies on the chiming fork. She caught herself relishing the feat because the fork did not vary, and she could easily find and sing a musical dyad that rang in perfect intervals.

"Can you name the separate harmonies you've just created?" Belamae asked, deadening the instrument with a touch.

Wendra shook her head. "My father taught me how to create harmony, but I don't know their names." She looked down, embarrassed by her lack of understanding.

The teacher shook his head. "There's no shame in not knowing a thing, Wendra. Only in not attempting to learn, never asking the question."

He struck the fork again and asked her to sing a higher note. He then added his own voice in a lower register. Wendra thrilled at the sound. Sometimes in the Hollows, a few would attempt to create such sounds, but it had never come out like this. The three notes sang together in a unity she had never heard, seeming to fasten together as one, creating a triad of perfectly harmonized intervals. Her own voice faltered the wondrous unity as the awe of it pulled her lips and sank her jaw. Belamae doused the chime and ended his own note.

"You've come to study," the teacher said.

"I don't know." Wendra glanced at the music stands and their sepia parchments scrawled with notes and signatures inscribing music in a language she couldn't read.

Belamae captured her attention, his kind eyes intent. "You have a gift, Wendra. I hear it even in the single note you've just sung. It no doubt brings you great comfort, and has probably amused and delighted your friends and family. But what you possess is not meant for them alone." His eyebrows rose as though to ask whether she understood him. Wendra remained silent. "The warmth and enjoyment of a voice, a musician's hands upon his strings or fingering the notes on his flute, these are joys to be heard after evening meals are taken and tobaccom smoked to calm the day's worries. But given to some is a double portion of that ability, an excellence that requires a higher call, that *is* a higher call. For these few, the fulfillment of that gift can only be achieved by careful training. This is what I do."

"I cannot stay," Wendra blurted. "I've friends to find, my brother. There are things . . ."

"Child," Belamae began, infinite tenderness leavened with the certainty of experience. "Take stock of what you know. Look within yourself and ask if there is any priority higher than this." Wendra tried to interrupt, but the man held up his hands. "Tut, tut. Hear me. I know your mind tells you this is selfish, perhaps self-indulgent. But you may trust my ear. What I hear is more than notes. And there awaits you, child, more in the exercise of this gift than anything you've dared to imagine."

Wendra had questions, but she found she could not frame them. She looked around desperately, thoughts of Penit, her own stillborn child, and finally Tahn careening through her mind. She saw herself sweating on the floor of a cave, saw the chalked feet of women and children on the blocks, and saw the world flash in a relief of dark and bright and nothing more. She closed her eyes and heard the distant lilt and rhythm of song and grasped one question.

"What is the music that emanates from this place? Is it the Song of Suffering?" She opened her eyes and looked her question at Belamae.

The teacher let a lopsided grin light his face. "As good a place to begin as any," he answered, and stood up from his chair. "Come with me."

Belamae went directly to the rear door and opened it as a servant might, holding it for her. He ushered her through and pulled his study door closed behind them before quickly taking the lead again.

"We will educate you about a few things this very hour." All grace and flowing robes, he bustled down the hall. His white hair floated in the long bob of his stride. Wendra had to step lively to keep pace with the elderly Maesteri.

They passed more oil paintings. Many depicted what appeared to be recitals, musicians at the center of amphitheaters filled with listeners. Further on, the paintings depicted battles. In some, a single man or woman stood before a terrible onslaught, in others a chorus of men and women stood together. But in each one, Wendra saw that one side came armed as warriors, the other without weapons, though typically with mouths open in an attitude of song. In some, those without armor lay pierced beneath the instruments of war, white robes stained with the capricious design of flowing blood.

They walked through another door, and left the intimate warmth of cherrywood for the relative coolness of marble. Then they strode into a large vaulted hall, their footfalls like small things in a great cavern. Here, striations textured the smooth stone surfaces in red, blue, green, and a dozen other hues. It reminded Wendra of the play of light upon the water's surface when viewed from several strides below the surface. Ahead, on the other side of another door, the music became louder still. No more did it merely rise like a melodious hum from the stone; it fell from it like a last echo.

Up steps and across short mezzanines they went, the ceiling a full six stories above them. Statuary replaced the oils, as did great, wide, intricate tapestries four times a man's height, woven with obvious skill. Natural light fell through windows set in the ceiling high above, and through the halls wafted the smell of rosemary and water. Soon, they passed small pools set into the floor and surrounded by low benches. Within the pools, shallow steps allowed one to dip one's feet and relax them there. Warm mist curled over the water's surface.

To the left and right, arched passageways led out of sight down other halls. The glow of candles set upon simple, but elegant pieces of ironmongery gave the marble a fleshlike quality down these corridors.

At the far end of the vaulted hall, they approached two women in hooded robes who stood beside yet another door. The women bowed as Belamae approached, keeping the posture until the door closed behind Wendra. Beyond the door, a wide corridor stretched under a ceiling not much taller than Belamae himself. At the far end, there appeared to be no door, though a man stood stolidly with his back against the dead-end wall. His lips were moving, and strange incantations fell from his mouth. But it was the floor that unnerved Wendra.

At each end of the hall, two strides of the same marble provided landings. But between them, water stretched from wall to wall. The pool was recessed as those she'd just passed, and a narrow walkway proceeded through it to the landing at the far side. Here the teacher paused, considering the water and the path across it. The water was not deep, but in it Wendra sensed a warning. The vibrations that Wendra had felt in the stone seemed to ripple the water in subtle response to the music.

Belamae walked to the edge and looked back at her. "You must cross," he said. "Keep your feet and move slowly."

"Are you coming?"

"If you reach the other side I will join you."

"What do you mean, *if*?"

"The water is not precisely what it appears to be."

Wendra looked at the pool. "What is in it?"

The teacher's mouth curled into a curious expression, part frown, part smile. "Reflections," he said and nodded for her to begin.

Why was she being tested? She had not asked to come here. A distant part of her remained grateful to the man for visiting her when she'd been alone and tormented by thoughts of dying alone, of being unable to safeguard Penit once he'd left to find her help. But she chafed under these sudden expectations, the need to prove herself against standards she hadn't yet learned. A familiar discontent roiled in her bosom. But Belamae's gaze remained insistent, and Wendra realized she wanted to see the source of the music that caused the water to stir.

The length of the pathway could be no more than ten strides. Wendra sighed and started across.

Halfway to the far side, the water around her began to roil and churn fiercely. The ripples rose like small waves, the musical splash of water against stone becoming more frantic. She looked down and instantly felt light-headed. She blinked against the sensation and the image of a tree flashed through her mind in stark white relief against a blackness as deep as midnight. Her vision began to swim—things, people running in and out of focus. She rushed to reach the other side. Water splashed over the pathway as small waves crested the stone. Wendra's foot slipped on the slick surface. She felt herself falling, but slowly, like an autumn leaf drifting earthward. She fell backward toward the troubled pool. She snapped her head around in time to see the water turn black. It glistened darkly, as though fraught with anger and despair. Then the caress of cool wetness surrounded her. The water shifted and bubbled at her touch, as though it meant to escape, but could not flee its own nature. She sank deeper, her head descending beneath the surface. The wash of water over her face felt like an accusation. She refused to close her eyes, and the blackness shut her in. The music subsided, replaced by the unnatural loud silence of water. She held her breath involuntarily, but felt no urgency to leave the water's grasp. She touched the bottom of the pool; her legs strangely content to drift, still against her own rescue.

This is what it is like. The end of my song.

Then Belamae was hauling her to safety. The man in his sodden white robe supported her while she focused on his intelligent eyes. Pain in her chest forced her to breathe in quick pants, sour bile in her stomach nauseating her with every inhalation.

Before she steadied herself, Wendra thought she saw dread concern in Bela-mae's face.

But why? I don't care for his secrets!

When the dizziness had passed, Belamae led her back through the door and supported her across the expansive mezzanines and down the several short stairs, eventually finding his study again and helping her to a chair. He stepped out briefly and returned with a blanket and a cup of warm mint tea. After wrapping her and placing the cup in her hands, he took his own seat and sat quietly appraising her while she tried to forget the look and feel of dark water in her eyes.

Clumps of hair hung wet in her face. She peered up through them at the old man, whose cheek and jowls rested in the crook of his thumb and finger. She had no will to speak, wanting only to have him explain what had just happened. In answer to her questioning eyes, the teacher sat forward and picked up the parchment Seanbea had provided him.

"Our friend says you can create." Belamae looked alternately between the notation of her song from the highway campfire and at the song's composer.

"We all make our own songs in the Hollows. It is part of the cycle every—"

"He does not mean tunes, child," Belamae interjected. "He speaks of composition. Do you understand? To *create*."

She knew what he meant. The act of singing herself well, the fire and ache in her chest and throat that meant to force wailing lines of explosive song up from her bowels, the leeching of color and definition from her eyes as everything became blurs of dark and light. The folding of everything toward one or the other.

Like the dark water in her eyes.

"No," she said. "I do not know what he means. I only make simple tunes with the voice my father gave me."

Belamae frowned and fingered the tuning fork on his desk. "All knowledge, learning, and song begin with honesty, child." He chimed the fork against his desk. "Mark me, any gift may touch two eternities."

Wendra remembered the Ta'Opin saying the same thing. She said nothing in reply, only looked into her tea and saw the image of her and Tahn singing to Balatin's cithern. For the time being, she held all thoughts and desires of song safely locked away.

CHAPTER FIFTY-NINE

A Servant's Tale, Part II

I do," Rolen said with a quiet steadfastness. "I chose to stay bound here in the bowels of Solath Mahnus. But with good reason."

The Sheason cleared his throat and began again. "Eight years ago the Recityv council debated a new law. It came to the High Council from the People's Advocate. But the action fooled no one; the Exigents had rallied the support, calling it a progression in civility. Only two days did the debate rage, and when it was done, the regent's Civilization Order on all those found manipulating the Will was read into the Library of Common Understanding."

A pained silence followed.

"By my Father's name," Tahn finally muttered.

"They claimed that it made for a slothful working class, and destroyed self-reliance. They mocked us, saying ours was the work of scops, deceiving others for gain, standing, and position, manipulating them for our own ends. Some even called us spies for the Quiet.

"What followed tore at the heart of all we are, rippled into the city and carried its taint into the kingdoms bordering Vohnce." Tahn heard the anger in Rolen's words, though his voice never rose as he spoke. "The gravely sick passed to their earth ahead of their time. The protection we offered the standing guard could be no more. Small battles claimed the lives of many we were not allowed to defend. Only a handful of Sheason kept residence in Recityv. How poorly we were treated after the Civilization Order went forth! It would seem that, for most people, respect comes only by way of fear. Some thought we should abandon Recityv, move to other places. But since the new law, the three-rings are feared on every road, in every village. Mistrust and lies narrow the eyes of most men we meet. I suppose, to be fair, it was so even before the law. But since . . .

"Our call is to serve," Rolen said with halting speech. "Some of us thought we could do so without recourse to our gift.

"And in time, even our order became divided. Many sought justice for others without regard for the laws of their lands. To serve, they said, by doing what was right, even if it was not legal or ethical. For them, there could be no separation of the use of the Will and their ability to serve. The schism in the order persists, grows stronger, even as resentment grows among those the order has sought to help."

Admiration for Rolen bloomed in Tahn's chest. "You stayed in Recityv when the others left."

"As did Artixan." The Sheason swallowed, and Tahn wished he had left some water in the man's decanter. "Two months past, a young girl came to my door begging my help. Her name is Leia. She's twelve years old, and has for several months come to help me distribute supplies on beggar's row. I let her in and listened through her sobs to a plea on behalf of her sister, who she said had suddenly taken very ill.

"I remember it vividly, as it was the first time I remember seeing her hair matted and tangled; her face was drawn and soiled. I don't know why, but I marked those things that night as I agreed to go with her and offer what aid I could.

"Leia pulled me through rainy, empty roads in the small hours of the night. And at last we came to a modest house in the merchant district. One feeble lamp burned in the window, the rest of the street dark. We rushed into a one-room dwelling that had boxes and sundries cluttered near the walls and obscured in the shadows cast by the lamp.

"Her little sister, only four years of age, lay on a pile of rags and old clothes in the corner past the window. Kneeling over her were her parents, speaking softly and wiping her brow with a wet cloth. I can still recall the smell of mold and wet wood where the roof leaked in steady drips. Leia's home was one step from beggars' row itself. Theirs was a family that labored hard in the streets to get by. I guessed before even getting to the girl that it might be fever from the cold and rain, gotten inside her in that drafty hovel.

"Her father looked up as I entered. I could see concern in his face as he began to shake his head. But over his daughter's feverish body, his wife's hand came to rest on his own. He looked back at the woman, then down at his little girl. Some internal debate waged for but a few moments. I saw him let go a sigh and nod.

"I removed my cloak and came to the little girl's side, where I saw the man actually weeping silent tears. It's the kind of grief parents learn when their children are close to death . . . I've seen it too many times.

"I knelt and felt for fever, listening to the child's breath and blood. It was too late; Leia's sister was dying and there was nothing I could do for her unless I violated the law and rendered the Will to save her.

"Then I caught sight of something familiar partially tucked under the girl's head as a pillow. Pulling back one fold of the garment, I found the crest of the League emblazoned on russet wool. If there was danger in coming to the aid of any man, woman, or child by use of the Will, tenfold more would it be for aiding an Exigent, or even the family of an Exigent.

"I understood, then, the look in the man's eyes. He was a member of the

League. My presence in his home alone represented danger for him and his family. Helping his daughter by rendering . . .

"And for me, the law was clear. Using the Will meant death if I was caught.

"I cursed the law then, trying to understand how letting the girl die could be an advancement in civility. All their arguments that our order reduced the need for self-sufficiency and caused sloth in the citizenry fell like so much wax from a spent candle. They had fashioned hatred and mistrust of Sheason into a law that could bring me here to this prison." The Sheason's fist slammed against the prison stone in the darkness. "For the crime of saving a dying child."

"I turned to the girl's father, whose name I never learned, and meant to tell him of my conflict." Rolen's wheezing ceased. "I never uttered those words. I simply saw the terror in his eyes at the prospect of having to watch his little girl die. The anguish of it got inside me. I'd seen too much suffering already that might have been avoided if it weren't for this law. And perhaps helping a member of the League would somehow help change their attitude about the Sheason's call.

"So, I leaned close and put my hands on her head. I spoke the words, and called health from the Will into the child's fevered body.

"When the girl opened her eyes, her mother took her gently into her arms. Around the child, she reached and touched my hand, a strange look of gratitude and regret in her eyes.

"I understood that look," Rolen said with sympathy. "Since the woman knew that what I'd done may have forfeited my life. But there was something more. When I put my hands on the girl, I learned of the deception that had ensnared me. This child burned from a poison fabricated by Exigent hands. The truth of it passed into me as my Forda passed into her. This little one had been poisoned as a way to test both this family's loyalty to the League and my obedience to the regent's order.

"The talk of the Whited One has grown among the people, and there are some who have expressed the desire to have the Civilization Order repealed and the power of the Will again to protect them. But a rogue Sheason in open disobedience to the decision of the Court of Judicature would reaffirm the need for the Civilization Order, and focus the people elsewhere, rather than on the Quiet that creeps toward us.

"That was the ploy to which I fell victim.

"At the moment of healing I still could have withdrawn my help, and perhaps the threat out of the Bourne would have united the people, and the Civilization Order might have been repealed. But the child would have died had I done so. It is that moment of decision—a momentary willingness—that eases this grotesque place to which I have come. So I am able to better suffer my skin rubbed bare by these irons." Rolen heaved a sigh and licked his lips.

"The rest happened very quickly. The door burst open behind me and six men in russet cloaks surrounded me with raised swords. Coarse oaths were uttered, and feigned jabs from their weapons came with wild laughter as I flinched from their sharp points. I remember asking only that they close the door; the cold air was bad for the child.

"They put me in chains, then turned on the family and asked which one had sought the Sheason to heal the girl. I saw a look of surprise in the parents at the question; the child's sickness was not common knowledge—it had come on suddenly. But I knew this already. In healing the child, the poison had revealed much to me. I learned that the League had suspected this family of being sympathetic to the Sheason. Poisoning the child would either prove their suspicions, or, through bitter loss, prove their loyalty.

"The leaguemen asked again who had conspired with me to commit treason by seeking me to heal the girl. I saw Leia back into the corner, her face pale with the realization of her crime.

"Part of the Civilization Order calls for the death of not only the Sheason who renders the Will, but anyone who seeks a Sheason to do so.

"Without hesitation, her father stood. 'It was me,' he said. 'I couldn't watch my daughter suffer.'

"I could see their suspicion as he accepted the blame for the crime. A horrible silence came over the room, and the man shared a long look with his wife. They were saying good-bye.

"He gave the daughter in his wife's arms a kiss on the forehead, and then swept up Leia in a tight embrace. He whispered something in her ear, and left her weeping as the League escorted him and me from the room. As we left, I saw the woman crawl into the corner with her children, mixed tears of thanks and loss in her eyes.

"That very night I came here," Rolen said, his voice far away. "I have remained because to do otherwise would be worse than never to have helped the poisoned child. I believe they assumed I would escape. Think of what that might have meant. What better way to vilify the order of Palamon than by imprisoning a member of the order, only to have him escape, thus showing he wouldn't be bound by the laws of those he serves?" Rolen's tone became clear, proud, but his voice remained soft. "I am a servant. I have sworn to extend my hand to fashion the Will for the lives of others, to protect, console, and go to my earth in the execution of my office."

The Sheason took several breaths. "Still the snare worked doubly well: confirming the distrustful feelings of the people as to the order's commitment to lawful service, and keeping them preoccupied with small, local strife while far greater threats roll toward us."

When he finished speaking, the man wheezed again in the darkness.

"And if you escaped, you would prove the validity of the mistrust that created the law to begin with." Tahn shook his head and looked up at the door where another guard walked by, momentarily blocking the shaft of light. "But why sentence you to death? The punishment does not seem to fit the crime."

Rolen laughed quietly. "Because as the League will avow, a small act of disobedience is the sign of a dangerous man, a man who will eventually use the Will in a monstrous way to undermine the governing table, undermine the regent herself." His tone echoed with bitter amusement. "Such was the reason given. Every council seat invokes the name of the regent to buoy its argument. Helaina is respected, cherished by most in Recityv. Her rule is the only reason Artixan retains his seat at her table."

"Artixan? The man from the low tavern in your story?"

"That's right. My mentor sits on the High Council, along with the regent; General Bolermy Van Steward; the People's Advocate Hemwell Or'slaed; First Sodalist E'Sau; Commerce Advocate Tully Dwento; First Counsel to the Court of Judicature Jermond I'Meiylo; Maesteri Belamae from the Descant Cathedral; and, of course, the Ascendant himself, Roth Staned, first among the League of Civility in Vohnce. One seat sits vacant."

Tahn listened to the names. Did these people know of Vendanj? Of Tahn? Would they ever learn he'd ended up in a prison cell? Suddenly, this room of cool, sweaty stone seemed much smaller than it had the moment before.

For the first time he earnestly worried about Sutter. Perhaps Nails, too, shared his cell with someone. His friend hated to be forced to do things. Tahn imagined him putting up a fight when the guards surely beat him as they had Tahn. The thought made him smile, causing his cracked lips to sting.

"None are closer to Helaina than Artixan. He does not contend with or violate the order she signed proscribing the rendering of the Will. I suspect he is dearer to her now, having stayed beside her even after the reading of the law . . . after my imprisonment. I also suspect she signed the law under pressure from a majority vote. A regent must be a regent first, before friendship.

"For his part, Artixan is very old, a judicious use of his own Forda, I'd guess. Helaina's reliance on his wise counsel infuriates Ascendant Staned. It surprises me sometimes that they haven't succeeded in killing the old man. But then, he is keener in mind than the whole of the League taken together, so perhaps it's not surprising at all.

"I served Artixan as an assistant for a few years while he sat on the council." A fondness entered Rolen's voice. "I was allowed to stand by in the event he needed something. Each of the council members had such an attendant in waiting. The day the Civilization Order was voted into law I stood a pace behind Artixan's chair. I heard the debate. I saw the eyes that would not meet Artixan's gaze when he asked them their true feelings. Only two voted against the law. . . ."

"Who besides Artixan?" Tahn asked, his interest rising. "The regent?"

"No, it was the Sodality. The regent does not vote," Rolen explained. "Hers is the authority to accept or reject the proposals of the council. There are those who complain Helaina is nothing more than a queen. To that I say it is our good fortune. Endless councils bickering and squabbling over rights and privileges and trivial rules to regulate the people, this is what they seem to want a regent to appoint." An exhausted, irritable sigh escaped Rolen's lips. "Helaina does what she can to curtail the mindless discussion of lesser matters. All change passes through her, and she may carry out the will of the council, or elect to trust her own wisdom. Of late, when she parts with the consensus of her advisors, word of it reaches the streets. It is forbidden that it does, but some of those who serve her seek their own gain above the interests of the people, and let slip the rumors.

"Helaina sustains the council when she gives her approval, wielding the power of Van Steward's army. But most of the people follow Helaina because they love and admire her. She is not foolish with mercy; never has a fairer or more just regent occupied her office."

"Why did she approve this Civilization Order then?" Tahn asked critically.

Rolen's words boiled out of the darkness. "A regent must choose her battles. And she knew the Civilization Order's true author—the League of Civility. Even then, the rumors that the veil was weakening caused many to observe personal curfews. Word of changes in the borderlands in the far west made General Van Steward concerned enough to double the watch and offer incentives for joining the army. It was not a time to challenge the League. When the vote was taken, I saw her place a hand on Artixan's shoulder. She believed a time would come that the Order of Sheason would no longer labor under the manacles of this law." Rolen rattled his irons for emphasis. "She believes it because she believes the Quiet rumors. Believes Sheason will be called upon again to help face what descends out of the Bourne. When that day comes, it will strike a heavy blow to the League." Rolen's voice took on a strange, thoughtful tone. "Ironic that to hope the rumors of the Whited One are false is to keep Sheason in Recityv chains. Perhaps I was wrong. Perhaps I should have left this place." Anger began to harden Rolen's words. "I lose my patience with foolish men!"

Tahn recoiled at the scathing statement.

"One last seat remains to be filled," Rolen continued, the sound of his voice even again. "That of the Child's Voice." He explained before Tahn could ask. "Since the War of the First Promise, a child has been seated among the men and women who rule and lead factions of adults. The youth offers wisdom and insight for those who can hardly remember what it feels like to be melura. Some records indicate that the words of the Child's Seat have changed the course of events that might have ended badly otherwise."

Another coughing fit wracked Rolen's lungs. Tahn could almost feel the ripping in the Sheason's chest. When he'd regained control, Rolen spat again. "But it has been some time since the Child's Seat has been occupied. When Helaina could no longer ignore the rumors of Quietgiven and the thinning of the veil, she recalled every seat to the High Council, and she called for the Lesher Roon to be run. A simple affair really, where the winner of a footrace earns the right to speak for all the children."

Tahn curbed a smile, not wishing to exacerbate the cracks in his bleeding lips. But the thought of a race that gave a kid the chance to be heard among *any* group of adults delighted him. It also made a wonderful kind of sense. A child will give all to a contest of speed, and accept a loss without complaint. Tahn wished he could see this race; he would like to have run it as a boy.

"Participants must be no more than twelve years. Melura rise to the age of eighteen, but the passage of primary youth to stripling disqualifies them from the Roon." Rolen tried sit up, but collapsed back to the floor. His chest heaved from the attempt, breaking the silence as he gasped for air.

Tahn left his questions unspoken, allowing the Sheason to regain his strength. He readjusted his position, relieving the bruises imposed by the stone floor. The movement reminded him of his shackles, which jangled and pulled at his arms like boat anchors. But his discomfort was not only physical. Rolen's words had reminded him that he was close to his own Change, the days of his youth to be left behind and a mantle of choice and responsibility placed upon his shoulders. Just three days ago the lesser light had been rising toward its fullest. He'd judged that it would reach its round in four days.

It was the eve of his Standing.

He could imagine no place more bitter to pass the mark than here.

Worse than that, there would be no one to stand First Steward for him, no one to mark the moment. Hambley was a world away; the Hollows a distant memory. The rite he'd watched through windows at the Fieldstone Inn would pass him by. He would still move on in years. And the Change would come as the lesser light waned again to full dark. But the significance, the attendance of friends, would not be a part of his memory. Instead, filth, cold, indifferent rock and shadow, and lips that would sting and bleed as he announced his acceptance would be his memory. Raw skin, the unmusical sound of chains, and the unhappy story of a Sheason choosing death, these things were the appointments of his ceremony. Tahn hung his head and muttered an oath in despair about the circumstances of his own passage into manhood.

Rolen spoke with a timbre of dismay and misfortune. "Tahn, do you mean to say you are near to your own mantle?"

Tahn had never heard it expressed that way. But a third time he was glad the darkness cloaked his face and hands. He did not care to have Rolen see the sadness that gripped him. Balatin had died and would not be there to stand for him. Hambley had gladly accepted the job, and Tahn had long looked forward to his support on that day. Now *he* would not be there, either. He cursed again, and refused to answer the Sheason.

Tahn heard the renderer crawl toward him in the darkness. The scrape of flesh over the stony floor, accompanied by the dragging of iron-link tethers, freshened the emotions welling in Tahn, and threatened to push him into sobs. He bit his lip and hurriedly held his scar to his face to again feel the old familiar comfort. In his haste, he forgot which cheek remained unmarked. His wounds stung at the touch of his hand, but he did not remove it. He pushed it harder into his flesh, inviting the sting, relishing it as the sadness gave way to shards of pain shooting down his neck and around his eyes.

Then a hand came into the yellow light that fell between them. Tahn looked through the shaft of illumination and saw the blurred edges of Rolen's face, a shadow drawn with liquid smears of coal. But Tahn saw a kind face. He then glanced down at the Sheason's proffered hand. The manacle had rubbed a scar so deep that beneath it a ring of scabrous flesh showed red and raw. Rolen said nothing more. Tugging at his own chain and ignoring the burn in his shoulder, Tahn put his hand in the Sheason's amid a pale wash of light from the barred window above.

• CHAPTER SIXTY •

Sodality and the Blade of Seasons

The ramparts blazed with too many torches to count. Pennants waving in the light cast wraithlike shadows over the high stone walls. Soldiers in cloaks drawn tight around their shoulders walked at regular intervals, their eyes turned out toward the long plains around Recityv. Braethen was awed by the height and breadth of the outer fortification. In the distance, the wall blended into the night sky, but for the torches flickering in a long line in each direction. He wasn't sure if maybe his vision failed before the torches ended.

Tents and wagons and makeshift shops lined the road around them, a few drum fires burning low in the night. But those who lived or traded here now slept in anticipation of another day of work. Only a few wakeful souls sat close to the flames, not bothering to raise their eyes toward them as they passed. The smell of people living in close quarters drifted on the wind: food scraps, grease drippings, animals, waste. An emptiness touched Braethen's heart as he wended his way through the midst of the sleeping crowds.

At the gates Vendanj knocked and stood back. From above, a guard looked down, screwing up his face to say something. At the sight of the Sheason, he clutched his helmet and disappeared quickly from sight. A moment later, the hinges toiled as the left gate drew inward and the guard filled the opening.

"Sheason." He gasped for a breath. "Vendanj, you come to us late."

"Good to see you, Milon." Vendanj nodded and extended a hand.

The guard bowed his head as he clasped the Sheason's hand in a familiar greeting. "Things are astir here, my friend. It is fortunate you come at night."

"What news?"

"A writ restricts access to the city." The soldier looked over his shoulder at something behind the gate. "The regent has called the convocation again, but few nations answer so far. We're flooded with aspirants to vacant lower seats at convocation, and countrymen claiming the right to have voice in rule. Hand-sewn ribaldry set on rakes announces them." Milon offered a wry smile.

"Ribaldry?" Vendanj echoed, slight remonstration in his tone.

"My apologies, Sheason." The man bowed again. "But it hardly seems to us like heraldry here. There are maybe thirty lower seats for every king that sits at the main table at convocation. It's been so long since the Second Promise, these ladies and fellows have no idea what they should be doing. And plenty of them are pretenders, mark me. Their votes won't amount to much—if I have my guess—when the regent calls for vows at convocation. But then I may be wrong. And meantime, very few, whether true seat holders or not, would like to take command of men and lead them to chase rumors—"

Vendanj's eyes cut the man off cold.

"My Skies, they aren't rumors, are they?" The guard's face slackened visibly.

"We've urgent business, friend. You'll keep our entrance behind your teeth."

The soldier nodded and immediately signaled for the gate to be opened wider.

Riding beside Grant, Braethen came last, looking with amazement at the immense, dark shapes of buildings towering against the night sky. It was difficult to believe they had arrived. The Hollows, Bollogh, Myrr, Sedagin, and Widows Village all seemed like ages ago.

Each stop along the trail to Recityv seemed to signal an ending of some kind—of peace, of idealistic notions, even of life. He pondered whether it might always be so for the Sheason. *What must that burden feel like?* It did not show in Vendanj's face, except as a promise of action and the stolid determination to prove the rightness of his course.

Braethen's legs and back ached, and his cut hand throbbed, but all the hours of flight could not steal the wonder of beholding the grandeur of Recityv, dark though it was. A few windows glowed with faint candles; and a few, high and dark, caught the long rays of starlight like heavenly winks.

It stood in contrast to the last two days' ride. Braethen had marked farms where fields had gone to seed, and plows left in the midst of tilling a furrow in the soil. Stock pens lay empty and doors stood open as though left in a rush. Some homesteads were still occupied, but at most of these, people peered out through windows from safe distances, wariness in their eyes. Children had not ventured toward them, being held tightly to a mother's hip. Men stood with a look as though they meant to spit.

Tonight they'd arrived past dark hour, Recityv being so close. Once through the gates, Braethen's anxiety eased, his shoulders relaxed. Though he wondered what would happen to those encamped beyond the great wall should Bar'dyn follow them all the way to the city.

Mira assumed the lead and turned left, following a series of narrow alleys and rear streets where garbage lay clustered outside back doors. Cobblestone lay slick with the sour runoff of refuse, a few stinking heaps steaming warmly in the chill air. More than one beggar curled close to these sources of warmth, using the waste as pillow and blanket; they did not stir at their passing. Even the stench of offal and human filth seemed not to bother the alley people.

Soon, they passed from the merchant district to a quarter dominated by large homes and inns with stables. The Far reined in at the rear of a simple, fenced two-story house. A rear courtyard lay behind a wrought-iron barrier that stood twice the height of a man. Lesser light washed a fountain dominated by a statue of a woman bearing a vase, like a specter attending an unholy anointing.

Mira swung down from her saddle and scaled the fence. She dropped to the inner court and walked to the back door, her head turning constantly. She rapped softly, and a moment later the door opened without the accompaniment of a lamp that Braethen might have expected. Without hesitation, the fellow followed Mira to the gate, keyed the lock, and motioned them all inside. The man still wore his bedclothes, but did not seem discomfited by the intrusion. He locked the gate behind them and jogged to the small stable in one corner of the fenced yard. Again he opened the door and let them in.

When the horses had been tended, the man led them to the house, never speaking, and leaving lights off even once they sat to table in a dining area adjacent to the door. High windows admitted the neutral lunar light, paling the visage of their host—a middle-aged man with thinning brown hair and a strong face. It also hit Braethen squarely in the eye, and cast shadows of the others across the table, leaving their expressions cloaked.

"I apologize for the caution of darkness, Sheason," the man began. "But we are watched closely since the regent's order, and more yet since Rolen's arrest."

"What has happened, Malick?" Vendanj asked.

"Two months past, the Exigents laid a snare to trap him." The man shook his head in disgust. "A leagueman poisoned one of his own children, believing it could solicit Rolen's hands to heal the child. It worked. Rolen is being held in the catacombs beneath the Halls of Solath Mahnus. He will not rescue himself and waits there to be sentenced."

"The order calls for death," Mira said.

"Sentence of *how* to die, not *whether* to die," Malick added.

Braethen could not see Vendanj's face clearly, but his anger was tangible. Grant made an incredulous noise, chuffing air out his nose. Braethen looked away at the window and saw the Far's profile come into focus. She seemed poised to attempt a rescue that very moment.

"Rolen will go to his death. He will hold to his covenant." Malick shifted in his seat. "Forgive me, Sheason. You know what I mean."

"It is nothing," Vendanj said thinly. "Each man must attend the oath individually, Rolen in his way, I in mine."

"We stand with you both," Malick said, his voice serious and clear.

"I know, Malick. Thank you."

Braethen's heart leapt. *We stand with you both. Is this man a sodalist?* Searching his face and clothes, Braethen could see nothing to indicate it was so. No insignia, no weapon. Nothing in the room to show it. Yet the timbre of his voice as much as the proclamation to Vendanj told him it was true. Braethen's weariness sloughed off him like a shed garment.

"You will not be safe here long," Malick resumed. "The recall of the High Council and the Convocation of Seats has upset the league leadership. They fear a challenge to their authority. Those few of us who remain in Recityv are hounded as relics of an unfortunate age. By day men and women loiter outside, often following us upon our errands. By night they haunt shadows. I pray you weren't seen coming.

"Between us, my guess is that they are worried the council might reverse the Civilization Order. That is why, I believe, they set their snare for Rolen. Forcing his hand garnered them support among the people. It does not take much to incite suspicion of a renderer. And the example of a Sheason who is also a lawbreaker reinforces the need for that law."

"Has any appeal been made?" Grant asked.

"There can be no appeal of such a decision," Malick said ruefully. "The Court of Judicature has voted on it. Helaina could have chosen her own wisdom over that of the court, but it is unlawful to challenge the mandate once it is law. Such a thing would bring the irons to the protester's wrists."

"Perhaps not," Grant replied.

Braethen wondered how someone could defy the will of the council and later escape punishment. The exile seemed to have something in mind.

"The irony is that the leagueman was also convicted of treason and sentenced to hang." Malick smiled bitterly.

"I would have liked to have spoken with him," Vendanj said.

"You still may," Malick told him. "On the moment of his descent in the noose, an arrow severed his rope and dropped him to the ground unharmed."

Vendanj sat forward, his head inclining at an inquisitive angle. "By whose hand?"

"The League claims he is not one of theirs. But they needn't protest, not with us anyway." Malick splayed his fingers on the table before him. "We here don't believe they would try to save their man; he's to be made an example of. No, it was a stranger.

"The Convocation of Seats has brought gentry from far and wide. With them, pretenders to the same appointments come in droves. Some follow the scent of fortune and the promise of a name to be earned in gallantry, all believing that some campaign is imminent. A great many more wait beyond the wall, Vendanj." It was the first time the man had used the Sheason's name, and it raised the hair on the back of Braethen's neck. "*These* men are sent by their mothers, their wives, land folk who say that in the great stretches between Recityv and Con Laven Flu they hear the coming of the Quiet. Men and boys sent here to prepare for war because they want to protect their homes and families.

"Leather jerkins, hay forks, crooked staffs, sharpened hoes, old plow horses, and cabbage boots, Vendanj. They sit in open fields, held at bay by a necessary writ that keeps them beyond the city wall. While inside, the streets teem with charlatans, profiteers, conscripted leagueman eager for a little authority, and the soft scions of noble houses expecting a commission from Van Steward in a battle they claim is nonsense behind the backs of their hands. I've not seen such things in all my skies.

"The rescuer is one of these fellows, no doubt," Malick continued. "Seeking to earn a name for himself by cutting free a leagueman sentenced to hang to death." Malick shook his head again.

"You believe the leagueman is innocent?" Vendanj asked incisively.

Malick drew his head back sharply at the question. "As innocent as any Exigent. Fah. But the man had a family. There's a sadness in that."

"Where is this man now who cut him loose?" Grant demanded.

"According to those sympathetic to us, the archer is confined to the same cell given Rolen—an Exigent's idea of insult and justice. They'll attempt to try it as a high crime. Claim it repudiates the wishes of the regent—"

"Did this archer act alone?" Mira cut him off.

"He came with another. Both are imprisoned. None know his name, but he is cursed in the streets as the Archer."

"This other who came with the archer," Mira pressed, "did he wear a glove?"

"The glove of the Sedagin," Malick said. "Do you know this man?"

Braethen's head whirled. Tahn and Sutter had made it to Recityv safe.

"We do," Braethen broke in. "They are friends of mine from the Hollows." For the first time Malick gave Braethen a long look. "I am Braethen," he said, introducing himself and extending a hand toward Malick in the cold light of the moon.

Malick met the greeting. As they clasped hands, Braethen instinctively folded his first finger back into Malick's palm. At the token, Malick's jaw dropped visibly. He likewise folded his first finger back, and squeezed Braethen's hand in an iron grip. "And we are one," he said.

Braethen could think of only one response. "I am I," he intoned softly. In the neutral light, Braethen watched as amazed eyes whipped to Vendanj, seeming to seek confirmation.

The Sheason nodded gravely. "He wears the Blade of Seasons, Malick. I have entrusted it to his hands. His stripling years are not long behind him, but he has studied the books. And at Will's door he accepted the metal, though its edge was and is yet a stranger to him."

"Pardon my doubt, Sheason, but how can this be so? A boy to wield the blade. And how will he learn his duties to it, to us . . . to you?"

"He knows some. I give you leave to teach him as you can," Vendanj said. "For but an hour. Tomorrow's work will require sleep."

"An hour?" He shook his head. Then focused again. "What's to be done about the rest?" Malick dropped his hand from Braethen's grip and looked back at Vendanj.

"We will speak with the regent. The man they call Archer must be set free, both he and his friend. The Whited One pursues them, even into the Hollows, even to the forests beyond the Nesbitt Hills." Vendanj looked away as though seeing the western hills they'd traversed to reach Recityv. "Helaina was right to call the convocation. Pray it has not come too late."

"Late or no, the Wynstout Dominion, the Principality of Aiyrs, and several other thrones ignore the call." Malick spoke bitterly. "It is enough for them that Quietgiven have not yet assailed their vales and hamlets. It is the curse of the Second Promise. This age of rumor makes cautious men silly."

"But an audience at the regent's High Office will be difficult." Malick bent his attention to the table to think. "Artixan might be petitioned to use his influence with Helaina, but if news of it got out, he would be in a hot kettle." Malick looked up. "The Sodality's seat at the High Table is tenuous at best. Reforms suggested by the League would remove our presence there. If we bring up the desire of a Sheason to free a traitor, days would not pass before we would join the order in being as openly scorned and denied the practices that define us. Some even fear exile."

"Speak carefully when you speak of exile," Grant said coolly.

Malick went on. "They might be snatched from the prison. We have friends among the soldiery. Van Steward's son studies our ways. The general's men are taught respect for the Sodality. It gnashes at the gums of the League, but Van Steward's men are fiercely loyal to him, and have less love for Exigents because of it. With proper preparation, the Archer and his friend could be plucked from their chains."

"No," Grant said, seething.

The air seemed cold with his words.

"This is why you've brought me, Vendanj." Grant turned to Malick. "Take a message to the Halls at Solath Mahnus at first light. Announce that justice demands a hearing on the conduct of this Archer. That there is evidence this leagueman is not guilty and was rightly saved from execution. Claim the law of Preserved Will against the protestations of any who try to deny the hearing."

None spoke. The room looked very like the garden beyond the door—pale statues in the pallid light.

"Can this argument prevail?" Malick asked, uncertainty thinning his voice.

"If it does not," Vendanj said, "there is yet more the regent might consider on behalf of this criminal."

Grant turned a heavy brow on the Sheason and nodded once. The Sheason then looked to Mira. "Go to the convicted leagueman's family. Bring them here so that we may speak with them."

Without hesitation the Far went out the door; she could not be heard racing away into the Recityv night. Braethen saw a wan look steal over Grant's features. The exile appeared to feel the weight of time in his face, as he had not in the Scar. Or perhaps it was memories written there that Braethen saw.

"You will take the message yourself, Malick," Vendanj said, breaking the silence. "Trust no one else with the things we have spoken, even your brothers." The Sheason said this with a note of finality.

Malick nodded. "There are rooms upstairs, if you are ready to rest." He turned to Braethen. "I will stay behind to talk if you would like."

The sodalist from the Hollows licked his lips with a dry tongue. "I would, yes."

Vendanj and Grant followed a hall deeper into the home and could be heard ascending the stairs. Braethen did not speak, nor did Malick as the sounds of trod floorboards came to a halt. Braethen had longed for the day when he might speak with one who shared his ideals, the hopes that had grown in him under the tutelage of A'Posian.

"What do you carry in the satchel?" Malick asked as a beginning.

Braethen looked down at Ogea's books, having forgotten them. "The books and scrolls of a reader. He came late to Northsun Festival, attacked by Quietgiven on the roads. He went to his earth after breaking the seal on a parchment and telling his last story. He entrusted them to me."

Malick eyed Braethen with reservation, but said no more.

Braethen then remembered something this sodalist had said. "Earlier you told Vendanj that you stand behind both him and this other Sheason, Rolen. Vendanj spoke of an oath regarded differently. What does that mean?"

Malick arched one eyebrow. Braethen wondered if the man was impressed or dubious. "The order was conceived too many seasons ago to count, and it was conceived as a way to serve. But as the world moves on, *how* to serve is not always a matter of agreement. The veil of the Bourne grows thin, treachery inviting Quietus like never before. Men undo themselves in their own self-interest: as the League does in forbidding the drawing of the Will here in Recityv; as nations do by adding their silence to the quiet voice of the Whited One.

"Against these changes some Sheason continue patiently to serve in the way Rolen did, accepting what need the people have of them, even if it comes as a law that prohibits their use of the gift. I admire Rolen, Braethen." Malick's face rose as he turned to look into the moonlight. "There is courage in his steadfastness. He chose to see his covenant as one tied in harmony with the laws of the people he served."

Braethen looked at the ceiling, beyond which Vendanj took his rest. "And what of Vendanj?" he asked. "Is he not true to his covenant?"

"Those aren't words that you should ever speak," Malick said in reproach. The stern look in his face faltered quickly. "Some serve as Rolen, but others believe their oath is to ensure what is best for this world, for today and all the skies to come. This they do regardless of the laws and disfavor of those they serve. It is said of them that they give 'What is needed, not what one *thinks* is needed.'"

"But who decides what is needed?" Braethen asked, speaking almost to himself as he considered the question.

"Indeed. That is the division we fear." Malick returned his gaze to Braethen, fixing him tightly. "But we stand beside a Sheason, Braethen, no matter how he chooses to serve. That is our calling. To step into the breach that allows a Sheason the time necessary to make his own sacrifice."

Braethen shook his head. "What if their intentions are not proven by their actions? Or what should happen if two Sheason come against one another?"

"It has never happened. Nor will it. What one man of Will does is easily recognized by another man of Will as an act of hope. If it were otherwise, he should cease to be Sheason, and would be called something darker." Malick considered. "Perhaps simpler than that even. If it were an act of greed or pride, he would not take the company of other Sheason in the first place. It would not suit his spirit."

"Then Vendanj is Sheason of the second kind?"

"And a powerful one. I've heard other Sheason say they marvel at his gift. The authority to render is conferred upon those deemed worthy, but it does not come in equal measures. Vendanj understands the potent blend of Forda I'Forza as naturally as you or I breathe. I trust him implicitly, but his path is one that men do wisely to avoid. When he looks upon you, he sees beyond the flesh, beyond the spirit. He looks upon the soul—the marriage of Forda I'Forza."

Braethen recalled a hundred looks he'd had from the Sheason, and wondered what Vendanj knew of him from them. He remembered his feelings when Vendanj prepared to draw on the Will in their defense, and the words that had boiled unbidden to his own lips when danger and need pressed in about them: *I am I.* The thought of those words sent chills racing through him. Declaration. Defiance. Certainty. Braethen's heart stirred and he understood the tone Malick had taken when regarding Vendanj in the company of Mira and Grant. There was singleness of purpose, unclouded. All of it invested in the simple phrase that he'd come to on his own.

One question remained.

Braethen rested his hands on the table to steady them and looked around the room in order to mark this moment before putting his query to Malick. So much had changed since he'd left home. He felt like a single blade of grass on an ashen plain. Alone, fragile, needing nourishment. At last, his thirst to understand consumed him most. But he also sensed that some knowledge brought further expectation, and this moment (this next question) had weight enough to crush him under.

Braethen stared straight at Malick. "And what of this?" He put his palm to the sword on his hip. Malick did not follow the movement. It was not necessary. The man's face looked back at Braethen, impassive, unreadable. The muscles in his back and chest tensed.

Malick let a quirky half grin move his lips. "That, my friend, is more than I could tell you . . . more than I know, myself. Vendanj gave you its name. I dare not repeat it. The blade itself is a threat I do not understand. Guard it, Braethen. Raise it if and when you must, but learn by it as surely as you have by your books." Malick's eyes seemed to see something through Braethen, past him. "My final Sky . . . you are only a boy."

CHAPTER SIXTY-ONE

Dreadful Majesty

The morning of his Standing, Tahn opened his eyes to blackness so complete he could not be sure he had opened them at all. The familiar pallor of the lamps beyond his cell door was gone. Beneath his cheek, a twist of chain served as an unfortunate pillow, and reminded him where he slept. The chill of the stone urged him to sit up, and he slowly obeyed, his muscles quarreling with him over the movement. His hips and shoulders ached from bearing his weight against the hard rock surface.

Tahn turned his head, hoping to catch any glint of light. He blinked, and studied, and saw emptiness. Yet it felt like those same hours each morning when he considered another day. He peered into the impenetrable gloom about him and remembered sunrise from the top of Windy Peak. For the briefest of moments he was there, and saw the eruption of light into a pale blue sky over the Selia Hills. But the moment passed, replace by the sable depths that surrounded him. It seemed not even memory lived long here, the darkness absorbing light even in thought. Tahn sat and listened to himself breathe, and knew by that sound that he still lived.

If his reckoning was correct, the lesser light had come full last evening, a full cycle since his day of birth. In the Hollows, preparations would have been made for a ceremony at the Fieldstone Inn. The town elders would have gathered in the private room. Tahn had imagined his nervousness about passing out of melura to the mantle that awaited him beyond. He'd thought about what it would mean to the girls, how they might glance differently at him. And he wondered what new wisdom might dawn inside him once the ceremony was complete.

Afterward, there would have been food, music, men gathering around him to speak sage advice in quiet, serious tones. The womenfolk would have appraised him anew, especially those with daughters. Younger boys, anxious to have the secrets of the Change, would have crowded in and asked endless questions, just as he had done to boys who had Stood before him. And deep inside, Tahn had hoped that the memories of an insistent voice, the one belonging to the man in his dreams, would disappear forever, or that he'd finally understand what those cryptic words meant.

Today his sunrise came as guards passed in the hall and lit an oil lamp back out of sight. Today there would be no ceremony. The smell of ovens preparing goose and lamb and vegetable pies, and fruits baked with honey and cinnamon, were not here; in their stead here were the smell of old stone, human waste, and his own sweat coating his skin and clothes. No crowds attended here—friends, townsfolk—only another prisoner, a man capable of escape, but unwilling to use his power to free himself.

What choices have I made that brought me here? On this day of my life, I have none of the things I hoped to have.

Tahn began to consider the possibility that he could die here before Vendanj or the others found him. Nearby lay Rolen, a Sheason of the order, a strong man whose arms, Tahn could tell even without seeing them, were too weary to be held up for more than a moment. If the Sheason went so quickly to death's door, then Tahn might join Rolen in the earth in a week's time.

In his solitude of darkness and cold and pain, the thought was a comfort. It sated him as a cold drink after a day's labor. Yet, in his weariness, even death seemed too much to wish for. Tahn rested his head against the wall and waited, resigned. He abandoned expectations without deliberate thought; behind so many barriers, they seemed now inconsequential.

The sound of a key in their cell door throwing back tumblers echoed down to him. Tahn looked up and saw a prison guard through the window. The door swept inward and a larger wash of light spilled into the cell. The brightness hurt his eyes, and he shaded them from the intrusion. The first man through carried a tray of bread and a carafe. A second guard followed bearing a short spear. The man who had opened the door replaced the keys on his belt and drew a short sword, following the others down toward Tahn and Rolen.

Their booted feet stamped loudly to the bottom of the stairs. The first man approached Tahn cautiously, stooping to place the tray on the floor just beyond a line chalked across the stone to mark the limit of the chain's tethering distance. Tahn stared at the bread and small decanter, then raised his eyes to those of the guard still hunkered down before him. A maniacal grin touched the man's lips. With a playful slowness, he began to tip the carafe over. Tahn realized there would be no more for perhaps several days, and his heart jumped in his chest. The guard tipped the container nearer a spill, his eyes regarding Tahn with wicked delight. The two men behind him began to laugh openly.

Tahn lurched from the wall and fell to his chest. His cheek cracked against the stone floor, bringing an intense explosion of laughter from his jailers. The man's fingers still tipped the carafe ever closer to a fall. Tahn struggled to crawl forward. His muscles strained, cramped from the cold and still bruised from his beating.

"Come save this bit of water, Archer," the man taunted. "How nimble are you? Can you reach it in time to preserve what it holds?"

Tahn worked his legs and arms, his knees difficult to bend. He dragged himself toward the man, the rasp of his chains a merry accompaniment to the unmusical sound of the guards' continued tittering. The shackles tore at his wrists anew, but Tahn ignored the wounds and concentrated on the water. It must have been a game they played all the time, but if he did not reach the carafe, Tahn did not know if he'd be alive to play a second time. Deep behind his eyes, waves of emotion beat at him. Perhaps he did care to live, after all. Else why crawl in this sadistic game? Anger roiled through him more violently still. He used it to propel him onward.

"Ah, this time you won't save the day." The guard gave the carafe a final push.

The decanter fell, beginning to spill its precious liquid out over the prison floor.

Tahn crawled harder. One of the guards slapped a knee and doubled over in laughter. Another cocked his head back to emit his harsh bray. The third man, standing before Tahn, remained squatting, watching with interest and dark amusement as Tahn inched toward the water.

He reached it and pulled one arm around to right the container. But a finger's length from it, his chain snapped tight and prevented him. Another round of mocking laughter filled the cell like a chorus. Tahn collapsed to the floor, again smacking his cheek, but too tired to move again. Prostrate on the stone, he looked into the shadows and saw Rolen's eyes, sad and disappointed.

Then Tahn heard the carafe raised from the floor. The tray was scooted closer, and his tormentor returned to stand with his friends at the bottom of the stairs.

"A fitting guest for our cherished Sheason." The spear-bearing guard grunted.

"Saviors both, and see them wallow in their own filth." This from the guard with the sword.

"Saviors to what?" The tray bearer said acidly. "A leagueman, a witless child. And what does it earn them? The Exigent will likely go free, while these two are sure to find a traitor's death at the end of their own rope. And that if they're lucky."

Tahn gasped for more breath, unable still to lift his head. Beyond the darkness, Rolen sat unmoving, his own chains silent.

"Did I ever tell you of the novice I met?" the first guard asked, a licentious lilt to his voice.

"You've been holding back," another replied, and sat himself on the bottom stair, resting his sword across his knees.

"A fitting time for the story," the man continued. "It was my first year in the guard. I found me a bitter hall one night and set to dulling the pain of numbness in my fingers and toes. 'Twas a harsh, cold winter.

"A young woman comes in. Had the look of a stripling, but she was full where a woman ought to be full."

The others chuckled knowingly.

"I made a comment about the cold and the company of a woman. Well, I expected a grunt or curse or something. But she comes over and takes my hand like I'd paid her the highest compliment. Made no difference to me. She had the prettiest face I ever saw so close. Then she reaches into her robe and takes out a small vial. I kept working my glass with my free hand, glad of the attention, but still thirsty, mark me. She didn't look to be for hire, but I wasn't closing my options."

Again the three men chuckled lasciviously.

"Anyway, she puts this oil on my hands. Says I've got winterbite and could lose the use of them if I don't take care to protect them." He jabbed an elbow into his friend's ribs. "Wouldn't want that. What good's a woman then, I ask you?" The guards shook their heads at one another in exaggerated motions, then broke down laughing again. "Well, the oil put fire into my skin, and I started to feel much better. Of course, the bitter was lighting fires of its own." He chuckled at his own innuendo.

"So I offered to escort the lady home. Along the way she tells me about how she's studying with some Sheason so that she can join the order. Oh, she said a lot of things, but all I really remember was the generous wealth of her bosom beneath her winter cloak. I suspect even without her oils my hands would have been itching with fire to get under her garments."

Tahn slunk back to the wall as the men went on. Their laughter and insults fell over the cell in abrasive tones.

"Well we get to where she's going, and I ask to come inside and pay my respects to her mentor, her Adwilor. And bless my luck, the man's not at home. The sweet young flower tells me it is not proper for me to come in while he's away, and gives me a gentle embrace in parting. But that's not the end of it, lads. Not by a thousand suns."

The man shifted his weight to his other leg to set himself for the meat of his tale. He gathered his companions' eyes and proceeded. "When she turned to go in, I checked the street and slipped in after her before she could utter a sound. My, what a look she gave me. Nothing so stokes the coals like innocence coming to knowledge. Mark me. She tried to remain stern, but it melted from her fast enough.

"I ripped her cloak and bodice off with little trouble. Let me tell you, she was clean and smooth. And I fancied her cries as inclination for more. Took her right there in her master's home. The thought of it gave me a pinch of thrill, there's no lie in that. Had me a fine time. And when I was done with my business, I thanked her for everything"—again he jabbed his friend's ribs—"and off I went. Never had so blessed a time since."

"So blessed a time . . . you're too much," the man sitting on the stair cackled.

"It's a lie," the other said. "You don't have the stomach to rape a novice and invite the anger of a Sheason."

The storyteller gave them both a feigned look of hurtfulness. "You doubt me, friends? Take a gander at this then." He stretched his collar down and lifted his chin. "This is the reminder she left me. Looks more painful than it came," he added.

Tahn could see the pale thin scar etched from the man's collarbone to the middle of his chest. The fellow turned to give each of his companions a clear view of his badge. The guards nodded appreciatively.

"And you say she was as pure as a virgin's honeypot." The seated guard sounded envious and enthralled.

"The best fit I've ever had," the rapist proclaimed.

As the men fell into another round of lecherous laughter, Tahn pressed himself against the wall. His gorge rose at the ease with which they amused themselves over the defilement of a woman. He thought of Wendra, bearing a child in the youth of her womanhood, the victim of one such as these.

"Hear my contribution," the man who'd carried the tray said next. "In the meager quarter of the city, the noble Sheason erected an orphanage to house the bastards produced by the loins of careless men and unfit women. The look of it is a shambles, a desecration that it exists at all, however poor its surroundings. These rotten bastards come to us and haven't a place to go. I know what I'd do with them."

The other men agreed, their voices now solemn. Tahn tucked his head between his knees to try and shut out the words. But the hard stone echoed the tale as though directly into his mind.

"Helaina has a giving heart, a credit to her. But some business must be transacted by men whose hearts aren't so afflicted." The man paced around in front of his friends as though prancing upon a stage. "The order was given leave to build their palace of neglected children by reasoning that these orphans would grow to serve Recityv, and that they should be safeguarded due to the trade value for children on the highways. Always spreading their propaganda about the Quiet's lust for the children of men, they warned against poor mothers who might choose to sell their babies." He turned with sudden viciousness. "Now I warrant you, were you not told such horrible tales in your own stripling years to get you to behave?"

The men readily agreed, held rapt by the speech of the third man.

"Worse still, these filthy orphans did not grow to serve their city." The man sneered as he paced back and forth before the other guards. "Many grew to devise schemes and swindles to rob and scavenge the streets and people of the city that housed and protected them. And those were the better of the lot. Fah." He growled at his listeners, and raised his voice as if to be sure Rolen took note. "The secret desire in the establishment of this bleak house was to raise up a new generation of Sheason. The insects were schooled and groomed and indoctrinated to become the disease that preserved them." He wheeled about and peered into the shadows toward Rolen, pointing a finger. Slowly, he dropped his arm and grinned, a hidden triumph in the gleam of his eye.

"But I was not fooled by their plans." He turned casually back to his cohorts. "Some of the creatures did follow in the footsteps of their benefactors." He twisted the last word into a sneer. "Perhaps, Bryon, your triumph was one of these." He pointed to his friend and chuckled as he performed a grinding motion with his hips. They all three barked a laugh. "But most of them did nothing but soil the city. And I would not have it."

The malevolence in the man's voice chilled Tahn to the bone. His heart pounded in his chest, anticipating what this city guard had done in his displeasure over the practices of the Sheason. He wanted to stand and rebuke him for speaking ill of babes. But his limbs hung heavy and numb.

"A friend of mine prepares the wretches their slop," the man said. "The year before the Civilization Order was ratified to exterminate the Sheason, I made an extermination of my own. I delivered their oats personally one morning and dropped a flask of a rather sweet, potent tincture in the morning kettle."

"The Tainted Repast," the rapist said. "That was you?"

"None other." The man bowed munificently.

"One hundred sixty and eight went to their earth that day," the seated man remembered. "I was called to remove the bodies to the city graves."

"One hundred sixty eight fewer criminals," the speaker declared. "One hundred sixty eight fewer renderers and their unholy power to call lightning, move earth, influence *us*." He beat a fist against his chest. "They are no different than the Velle. Worse perhaps, cloaking their deeds in the raiment of service. If you ask me, they are closer in nature and purpose to the Whited One than any legend of the Bourne." He started to pace back and forth in an agitated manner. "Stories, all of them. And we are left to bear the burden of their philosophies and grand plans." He gestured broadly. "No sirs, not I. I put the poison to their strange brood and ended an experiment that should have never been allowed.

"And I sent no lye to the pits either. Let their bodies grow rank in their own liquid decay."

Will and War, can he be saying these things about children?

Tahn shoved his fists into his ears. The clank of his chains traveled up his hands and arms and into his head.

"Well those are fine enough pearls," the man seated on the stairs said dismissively. "But they lack ingenuity. Effective to be sure, and I hail your best efforts. But let me tell you of my humble deceptions. Yield, will you, Jep?"

The man on the stair stood and shooed Jep back to his place beside Bryon. They both clapped their hands indifferently at his assumption of the stage. He mugged a close-lipped smile before hunching over in a conspiratorial manner. Tahn stole another glance into Rolen's shadows. The Sheason had not moved.

The insults may not have penetrated his private darkness. Tahn wished the things he'd heard had forever remained unknown to him.

"I've been the turnkey for quite some time now," he began. "Came the year Van Steward named his predecessor, Ulian, a minion of the Quiet. Why, Bolermy was no more than an infantry leader at the time. But the regent gave him command of her army, and put the laurels on his sleeve.

"General himself appointed me here. No favor in that. The smell of oil and wax and stone down here, not to mention the prisoners and all their loveliness." He pinched his nose. "It all gets ripe and tiresome. But," he said confidentially, "those condemned to the irons are crafty with how they hide up bribes to get a little attention once the cell becomes their home."

"Bribes?" the two guards said almost in unison.

"Aye, and you can forget sharing a part in them, 'less you intend to ask for permanent reassignment here, and come to help me clean and serve our fine guests." He fanned his nose in comment on his odious task.

"And what bribes do searched criminals have with them?" the rapist asked, skeptical.

"How about rings, necklace charms, gold sometimes." The turnkey fairly giggled through his list of illicit booty.

"And how do they manage these things past the guards who search them?" Jep asked, a hint of understanding in his voice.

"Resourceful people will use every cavity available to them, friends, including those between their legs," he said, smiling as though vindicated.

"Not an attractive way to make a living," Bryon critiqued.

"What does that matter?" he said, shrugging his shoulders. "I wash the items and sell them the same day. It comes out all right by me." He sniggered at his own joke.

The other men shared a disgusted look and chortled.

"But this is not all," the turnkey went on. "Some cause themselves to spew small gems or bits of platinum once they are safely shackled. Then they pick the finer bits from the mess and offer them to me to buy favors."

"Favors?" Jep said. "From bribes to favors. Come, what is it they ask for?"

"A flask of bitter, sometimes, to salute the birth of a child. Or a whore for such time as it takes to satisfy a manly urge. Most often, they want a spot of meat, roasted vegetables, sweet bread." The turnkey looked about like a thief. "And always they think to purchase freedom, my friends. They kneel there and hold up small offerings—their last, most valuable items still reeking of their own ass or slick with the offal of their own guts—and grovel to be let out of their chains.

"The biggest fools confide in me their absolute innocence, and the shrewder ones their guilt, but each hopes to tender a deal that appeals to my softer side."

He patted his rump and made an indelicate sound as though it were choreographed. "They speak of ailing families, pining lovers, motherless children. They weep for sunlight, companionship, the warmth of a soft bed. And for these things they are willing to trade their last valuable in return for my mercy."

"And which one do you give them, Beattie, mercy or greed?" Bryon asked, sarcasm thick in the query.

A snorted laugh came from Beattie the turnkey, and Tahn looked up in time to witness the man's sordid response.

The man drew himself up and puckered his lips as a woman preparing to kiss. Then spoke with a high, coquettish tone. "Why, no one ever bought a thing with mercy."

The three belted laughter. The raucous clamor of it echoed around the room.

"How do you do it, then?" Jep asked, stifling his own giggles.

"Oh, lads, that is the best part." He hunkered over again as though sharing important secrets, his head swiveling like a ferret before he began. "I accept these bribes with a glad heart and promise all the inquirer seeks, sometimes more. These pitiful fools cry and thank me, blessing me for my tender mercy, promising me more than they'll ever have for my willingness to make such an exchange. I smile at them, and tell them how I can see how good a person they are, and wrongly accused, and how I will do all I can to send my good word of them upstairs to the halls where leniency or clemency might be granted. And then they fuss more over me and weep some more, kissing my boots and praising my name.

"And I drop the booty into a pail of soap and water and leave them to their happiness." A malignant grin spread over his damaged teeth. "On appointed days I return to deliver their meager meals, sometimes throwing a bucket of water over them and dropping a shake of soap and a wet rag. And they ask about our arrangement. And that is when I squat before them and wait for them to be still. Then while their eyes are steadfast and hopeful on mine, I say to them, 'What arrangement?'"

Bryon and Jep dropped their jaws, then hooted and clapped each other in amusement.

"You should see their faces," Beattie went on. "Oh, nectar, pure nectar. That look of hopelessness, betrayal, from a criminal yet, is the wages of my post, lads. Robbing these convicts of their last petty desire, a bit of hope. It makes the stench almost bearable."

Tahn cringed and wanted to sink into the stone, cover himself over, and take himself from the company of these men. Their vile oaths and curses, obscene jests, and despicable acts rankled. Was this the city of light Vendanj had meant to bring them to?

Then Rolen rose to his feet.

The sound of his chains was like a harbinger in the echoing chamber, slicing the laughter to silence.

He stepped into the shaft of light thrown by the door, emaciated and filthy, but with a terrible countenance. He opened his mouth and spoke with a thunderous voice.

"Enough! I will bear your devilish tongues no more! By the Will that forms and sustains us, I command you to be silent! Or I will rain down your deaths upon you without mercy!"

His words echoed about them as he stood in dreadful majesty. Bound with irons, he stared at his jailers, still and solemn.

The men cowered, their blades falling from their hands, their arms and legs quivering violently. They bent low to where the floor and wall met and pleaded Rolen's forgiveness.

Tahn watched in silent reverence and awe. He recalled all the stories he had ever heard about the Court of Judicature; he thought of the first Convocation of Seats called to answer the threat of the Whited One; he remembered readers' tales of nations and kings and dominions assembled to act on the word of the First Promise; but grace and nobility Tahn would forever associate with this moment, as he stood fettered at dark hour in the vaults below the Halls of Solath Mahnus.

Tahn felt it then. The call of the Will: small, silent. He bore witness to the dignity of this imprisoned Sheason, long suffering and dutiful even in this vile pit, and rested easier in his own chains, if only for the moment. And in that instant, he thought he knew something of where to draw the line and where to stand.

They stared at Sutter, unspeaking, wide-eyed as though amazed that they could be seen at all. Or perhaps the glossy whites of those eyes were simply the hundred-league stare of the untabernacled.

The mists licked at him, creeping across the stone floor, swirling around the feet of the ethereal creatures who stood with yearning expressions that suggested the need to speak with Sutter, but could not.

The cold had awakened him, as it had the night he'd spent in the home of the leagueman Gehone. This time, he could do nothing more than cower into his corner as far as his chains would permit, and hope these beings were not like the creature that called itself Sevilla.

Sutter's heart raced; panic seized him. He wanted to cry out, but his voice failed. This time, neither Tahn nor the powerful arms of a leagueman would rescue him. And these two creatures—maybe more of them lost in the mists that churned around him—stood in full view, their wide eyes caught in that eternal look of surprise and need.

Perhaps they were a nightmare. Perhaps a fever dream.

If he did grow sick and vomit it would shock him. He'd scarcely eaten, and what he had had been rotten fruit and fetid water.

All this gave Sutter the feeling that he lay already interred, bound up in the great room of a tomb with other waking dead. The trembling in his arms and legs grew so violent that his chains began to rattle. The sound of it rose into the deathly scene, and he feared he would never see his own fields again, nor offer the gratitude to his papa that he now so badly wished to give.

It was the chill of the grave to be sure, and he pressed himself into the floor, waiting to die, and heard distantly in his ears his own weak moan.

"Sutter." An intruding voice. "Sutter!" It came again.

He stared up into the face of Thalen at the end of his tether, calling his name. And in that instant, something changed. Sutter looked around at the cell. The mists were gone. The figures were gone. In a great gasp he took a long, painful breath, exhaling in a cry that resounded in the prison cell.

"He's having the tremors." It was one of the scops against the other wall. "Give him some water."

Thalen took up a bowl and wetted Sutter's lips.

"He'll be all right. Have him keep drinking, even the filth they're providing. It will help." The man spoke with the assurance of a father who's had sick children.

Moments passed, and Sutter soon began to feel normal again. "Thank you," he managed.

"No thanks necessary, my boy," the scop said. "Precious little to be done here." His chain rattled as he waved a hand at the room. "I figure what I can do, I must."

Sutter pushed himself up. "Why are you here?"

"We await trial on grounds of sedition."

Another scop piped in. "We played the cycle of the First Promise in the square south of Solath Mahnus. The League did not take kindly to the subtle suggestion that its formation was not only unnecessary, but unfortunate."

A weak laugh came out of the dark from yet another of the beaten players.

On their left the door opened, spilling harsh light down on them. Sutter blinked back tears at the intrusion, then shaded his eyes so that he could catch a better look at the scops across from him. One of the women had buried her head in her knees, whether shielding her eyes from the light or in abjectness Sutter could not tell. But the faces he could see still held the sloppy, exaggerated application of face paint done by their jailers to make the scops up like jesters or fools.

It was the jailers' way to mock what these people did to make their way.

"Quiet down there," a voice barked. "You'll get yer chance to entertain us later. You'd best save yer strength for yer performance."

The door shut with a bang, echoing down on them and blessing Sutter with darkness once again.

"I am Niselius. Why are *you* here?" the first man asked Sutter in a whisper.

"A friend of mine saved a leagueman from his rope. I guess heroism is no longer honored." Sutter smiled, but his swollen face twinged and he let it go.

"That may be our fate, as well," a woman said. "Some believe an example will be made to scare all troupes from their wagons. I am Mapalliel. Nice to share the darkness with you."

The woman uttered a mild laugh—something he could appreciate in the bowels of this dungeon.

"I am Sutter. If it's really so dangerous, why do you do it?" Sutter thought of Penit standing up to a leagueman in Myrr.

Mapalliel answered. "For me, there aren't many choices. For most women, come to that. If you've no husband and no dowry, there are precious few things a man with coin will pay you to do." She thought a moment. "And the wagons have a kind of honor of their own. It may be true enough that some of the folliets carry double meaning meant to teach people of the past and the lessons they may have from it. But execution for playing a pageant? The regent has lost the fist inside her glove if it comes to this."

"Isn't it the League?" Sutter slid to his right, his chains scraping the stone floor.

"Yes," Niselius said. "But law requiring such severe punishment would have had to be ratified by the High Council. She oversees its affairs. Something is amiss that the regent is not able to reject such a law."

"Maybe she doesn't know," Sutter offered.

"Maybe." This was a new voice, softer, yet still male, and still too deep in the dark to see clearly. But it came as through the swollen lips of one beaten badly in the face. "This then is civility," the unnamed man added, "that the League suppresses the stories they believe threaten their own liberty. But what of the liberty to tell a story in the first place? Much stands to perish in this. Not just some few of us."

Sutter understood most of what the man said, coming though it did through ruined lips.

The darkness resumed its silent pall upon them. Sutter did not know what else to say. These were their own choices. And the old wounds revisited him, making sympathy a hard thing to summon.

Though something about the maniacal, painted grins on the beaten faces of these simple pageant players left him uneasy and with a small portion of pity.

"Come, enough of this brooding. Let us employ our talents and make a folliet even here. This one for ourselves." Niselius stood, extending a hand to Mapalliel to help her to her feet.

Sutter watched as the the other two scops dragged themselves up. They all then stood in a line.

Niselius bowed. "What will it be, my friends? What story would you have of us?"

Sutter could think of nothing, but didn't have to. From his nook behind him, Thalen said evenly, "The Last Harvest of the Reapers."

The troupe stood in silent reverence for a few moments. Then, with a grave nod from their leader, they began. They told an amazing tale of heroism at the farthest reaches of the north and west, of the time that gave name to the Valley of Sorrow. When the Quiet stood in awful might against a small Recityv army and a band of Sheason.

> *The Velle rained down fire and wind upon the surviving few of the Second Promise, and the advancing line of Quietgiven came as a dark wave that would roll them under in minutes. Near upon their utter defeat, with the trained, armored soldiers of Recityv all but destroyed, the small battalion out of Risill Ond arrived after a three-day forced march with no sleep.*
>
> *But the farmers, come with pole-length scythes and many short upon a handle, did not pause. They marched past the Sheason, who needed enough time and relief to join their hands for a final rending of earth and heaven to bring an end to their war. Directly into harm's path they went, creating a mighty line of men with little else but their trust in their sickles.*
>
> *Their muscles hardened by long summers and autumns of work held the Quiet at bay, cutting down the enemy in a hard wave. They gave the Sheason the time they desperately needed. And when the great calling of the Will went up, every last man from Risill Ond lay dead upon the ground, most with their tools still gripped tight in their fists.*
>
> *It would always be said of them that they thrust their implements of harvest with strength and faith after crossing the world to buy a moment's time with their very lives.*

When the troupe finished, they stood in respect of the story they'd just played to a dark dungeon cell and two farmers from the hidden places of the east.

A quiet pride filled Sutter's chest, the kind that made you want to stand and die with the valor of those memorialized in the telling. And the root-digger from the Hollows heard a sniff from behind him, making him think of a hand-sewn emblem on an old rug and the honor to fulfill an oath made generations past.

Then an abrupt intrusion of light and the slam of an opened door stabbed the darkness again. Their turnkey bustled in and unfastened two of the scops without a word, herding them up the stairs toward the outer door. One of these was the woman who'd spent most of her time with her head laid upon her own knees. As she began to shuffle her bare feet over the cold stone, she looked down at Niselius and said with all the earnestness of her soul, "Tell my children I love them."

Tears coursed down her face, which bore an awful cast of uncertainty.

At the door she and her fellow scop looked back at their friends, and that's when Sutter knew their faces. Captured differently in the light at the door, the bruises and blood and garish paint faded in his eyes to the true faces beneath.

They were the faces in his waking nightmare.

The faces of the dead.

It hit Sutter with a horrible certain prescience, just as he now realized that he'd seen the spirit of the woman burned at Ulayla in his window the night before her execution.

The door closed, leaving them to their troubled hush and obscurity.

Sutter wept silent tears, knowing that the woman would never see her little ones again.

Nor would those small ones see their mother one last time. And that, too, touched upon his old wounds, and Sutter cried for each of them.

• CHAPTER SIXTY-TWO •

The Lesher Roon

Wendra stepped into the street that fronted the Descant Cathedral. Seanbea accompanied her on her right, Penit holding her hand on the left. The boy involuntarily squeezed her fingers as he took in the festive decorations of a city virtually transformed overnight. Even the streets in the mercantile district celebrated the Lesher Roon, streamers dipping in low arcs between shops, lintels and sills adorned in makeshift garlands fashioned from corn husks and dried vines. Men and women walked about with small sprigs of various green herbs fastened to a lapel or hanging from a breast pocket, showing their awareness and support for the race.

Penit started ahead, pulling Wendra along. She hadn't expected that the boy would actually run the race, but it gave her a good reason to leave behind the ruminations brought on by Belamae's words and lose herself in the gaiety of the event.

The teacher wanted her to remain with him for several months at the cathedral to study, imparting a warning to her should she choose to do otherwise. Twice more—once last evening and once this morning—they had spoken since her arrival. Belamae had shown her the wonders of music, hinted at the methods and techniques she could learn to master her craft. The ways to compose and organize music astounded her. And she'd sensed that the things Belamae shared with her were merely those tools he taught to each student he mentored. Beneath these things, beyond them, his eyes seemed to tell her that her true training would consist of greater methods, things not spoken of among the other pupils. But she continued to maintain that she could not create as Seanbea had suggested. Each time she denied the ability, Belamae's eyes darkened with disappointment and concern.

But there was no time for this. For her own reasons, she'd agreed to enter Penit in the race: She wanted to find the others, if they'd made it at all; and with the streets as full as they were, she felt safe from hidden or surprise dangers.

Past the end of the street, the crowds thickened. Barkers called out foods and souvenirs of the Lesher Roon for sale. Street performers sang songs that Wendra soon realized must attend race day as traditionally as the songs of Northsun— old folk tunes, by now, that most everyone knew. A general buzz of excitement hummed in the streets, bystanders speaking excitedly to one another but, she noted with relief, happy noise, not the kind of dangerous crowd she'd recently heard in Galapell. Very like Northsun, Wendra thought, a fraternal air prevailing in every face and word and song.

Carriages and wagons plied the streets, bridles and wheels woven with yet more garlands. The sweet fumes of spicy drinks filled Wendra's nose, and here and there a child near Penit's age received advice from parents or other adults as they streamed toward the Halls of Solath Mahnus.

Beyond the merchant quarter, the avenues and lanes thrummed with life, the people moving with more purpose but no less enthusiasm. Men dressed in fine cloth coats with two rows of buttons down the front and glossy boots carried tall, thin glasses of what looked like a rum punch that Wendra fancied to taste. Other men moved about in full armor polished to a bright shine, one hand swinging in time with their strut, the other settled comfortably on a ceremonial weapon. Women carried bouquets in the crooks of their arms, slender white and green grasses interspersed with deep red flowers and yellow roses. Here, the children sat politely, their shoes less worn, their shirts bright with vertical stripes that often matched the clothes of their parents.

Girls and boys alike seemed appareled for the race, though always near to the age of twelve, with longer legs and more visible coordination than the younger runners. Some of the potential entrants to the run had begun the growth of their stripling years and stood much taller than the rest—more than one boy had the beginnings of facial hair and a thickening in the chest. Wendra didn't see how the younger runners could compete. But that was just as well. She did not want Penit to win; she was, in fact, glad to see competitors who so clearly overmatched him.

Through the thronged streets they wove, keeping an eye on the upper spires and domes of the Halls of Solath Mahnus on its low hill, towering above the surrounding city. As the time of the race drew near, movement became difficult, people jamming the thoroughfares and halting all progress except by foot. Soldiers in Recityv colors could be seen everywhere, their cloaks and helmets a constant reminder of the purpose of the race.

The Ta'Opin moved effortlessly through the masses, his powerful shoulders twisting to slip through narrow openings, sometimes creating more room for Wendra and Penit. Seanbea seemed to share the bubbling excitement, a constant smile exposing his teeth.

They moved past men and women with entourages—standards raised on poles staked an area of the street for a family of station or a member of the gentry. People crowded around acrobats, but peered away often in expectation of the race. Penit occasionally jumped to gain a view of what lay ahead, his small hand slick and sweaty with anticipation.

Seanbea led them down two less-crowded alleys and brought them out onto a wide concourse that crossed to the wall that separated Solath Mahnus from the rest of the city. "This is part of the course," he said. "The children follow the line engraved into the street. It takes them around the Wall of Remembrance and through a few of the old streets of Recityv where the first regents lived. The race passes beneath their verandas. Then back here, ending at the gate to the courtyard of Solath Mahnus. Those with runners are allowed to stand against the wall to cheer them on. The rest line the outer half of the streets; the General's men keep them well in hand, but it is largely unnecessary. Since, though it's been a long time since the Roon was run, few would interfere with the race— the tradition and stories of it are often and fondly recounted."

Wendra listened distractedly. She searched the crowds for signs of Tahn, Sutter, and the others. People milled around and were gone so quickly she soon realized the folly in hoping to chance upon them in such a vast city. But she still looked, even as Seanbea began leading them toward a table set near the inner city gate.

While they stood in a line of parents giving last-minute instructions to their children, others called cheers and encouragement to the kids. A few slurred voices offered less fitting support, but most hailed them and wished them well.

"A regent's right lad," one yelled.

"The truest voice at the High Table, you'll be," another called. "Don't let them intimidate you."

"Hey, Simba's jaybird is small enough," one fellow bellowed. "Don't that qualify him to race?" Those around him bellowed with laughter.

Wendra couldn't help but smile, naturally assuming the meaning of "jaybird." In no time, they stood at the table, where two men sat with pleasant, intelligent faces.

"Are you running today, boy?" one asked.

"Yes, please," Penit enthused.

"Very well. Is this your mother?" The man looked up at Wendra with thoughtful eyes.

Wendra froze. She stared back at the man blankly.

"That's right," Seanbea interjected. "She's a little overwhelmed here. Their first time in Recityv."

"Ah, well, don't let it frighten you, Anais. We're a little crowded these days, but Recityv goes on because its people are decent. Isn't it so?" The man turned to his partner at the table.

"It is," the other said. "May we have your names?"

Wendra gave hers and Penit's names to the recorder, who wrote them in a ledger. After their names lay scrawled upon the page, the man gave Penit a blue pin to place on his shirt. He then leveled a serious gaze at the boy.

"Run hard but run fair, son. The only loser is the one who doesn't give the Roon all he has. But the cheater disgraces the Roon, and earns himself a month in the regent's stables as a helpmate to Gasher." He turned to his partner. "Would you ever want to work for old Gasher?"

"Oh, my, no!" his friend said. "He's an awful crank. Every minute would be drudgery. Wouldn't want that."

"I won't cheat," Penit put in. "And I'll win. You'll see."

"A champion's attitude," the recorder said. He winked at Seanbea and Wendra and motioned for them to move to the left.

The children lined up behind a broad ribbon stretched from the gate to a building across the concourse. A line of guards held the crowd back on the far side. More of the soldiers were beginning to clear a number of streets branching from the main thoroughfare where the Roon tailed away from the wall and took the racers through several city blocks. A man holding a baton came forward and offered to escort Wendra and Seanbea to a place along the wall from which to observe the race. She looked down at Penit, the boy's eyes brimming with confidence.

"Just have fun," she said, and kissed him on the cheek.

Penit nodded and suddenly cried out, "Dwayne!" He rushed to a boy amid a host of other children. He talked excitedly with the other boy, the two jabbering over each other about things Wendra could not quite discern. Then the man with the guiding baton led her and the Ta'Opin to a place along the wall right near the gate to the courtyard.

For nearly an hour, more contestants gave their names and were herded to the ribbon. The mass of children stood a hundred across and perhaps ten deep. Some of those waiting there stood no more than six years old, eager parents enrolling them in the Roon with vain hope. The largest boys bulled their way to the front. Girls made up nearly half the runners, some taller even than the largest of the boys.

The racers fidgeted and looked over their shoulders toward parents who continued to shout instructions to them over the din. Youthful faces wore unsure expressions but nevertheless nodded understanding; other children shook their heads side to side in confusion. Penit stood in the middle of the pack with Dwayne, the two still avidly talking. Neither met the largest boys in height, but neither was short. He wouldn't finish last, Wendra thought gratefully. *I can make him proud of his placement.*

The hum of the crowd rose suddenly to a roar as trumpets blared into the sunny air over the wall. The men at the table closed their books and drew their instruments back from the street into the courtyard. A stiff-looking man with a thin mustache appeared from the inner gate door and began to speak. His first words were lost beneath the tumult, but the gathering quickly quieted.

"... this running of the Lesher Roon for the Child's Seat at the High Table, to sit at council with those who speak for their constituents. So then, do we, by tradition and law, draw our Child's Voice from this worthy field of contestants."

Another roar rose from the throng. The man went on, but his words ended before the people quieted again. The gentleman walked in stately fashion to the head of the ribbon and solemnly cast his gaze upon the runners. Over the frenzied speculation and last-second admonitions of parents, Wendra could just make out the same exhortation that the recorder had made of Penit: "Run hard but run fair."

Then, from above them, confetti rained in the air, streamers fell from the windows and rooftops. The trumpets blazed, calling a triumphant fanfare, and the children hunched, ready to run.

The man strode to the wall and lifted his baton, taking the ribbon in hand. At the far side of the concourse, another did likewise. Amid colored confetti and shouts and horns, the two men dropped their batons simultaneously, letting go of the ribbon. In a spurt, a thousand children dashed ahead to claim the coveted prize of the Lesher Roon.

Several fell as legs locked and intertwined, but each quickly jumped up and joined the lurching mob. Without realizing it, Wendra was caught up in the thrill of the race as she watched the children find their pace. She could still see Penit, his head bobbing with quick steps. He ran firmly ensconced in the pack. The same excitement and anticipation that always attended the Kottel Rhine now swept through her, and she forgot her reservations and raised a cheer for Penit. The shouts and exultation of the masses overpowered Wendra's own, but she waved toward Penit's back as the first children rounded a corner in the wall.

When all the runners had disappeared, Wendra looked up at Seanbea, who gave her a quirky smile. "Gets in you, doesn't it?"

Only slightly abashed, Wendra nodded and turned in the opposite direction, where they would next see the children. The crowd simmered, their jubilation falling to murmurs and bubbling expectation. Men and women continued to fill the air with confetti and streamers as the crowd awaited the return of the children from around the outer wall of Solath Mahnus. In the distance, the roar of spectators rose in a moving wave as the runners passed them in their course. The sound of it grew more faint as the race approached the far side of the hill.

"What will you do if the boy wins?" Seanbea asked, interrupting her auditory tracking of the race.

She started as the question penetrated her concentration. "He won't win," she answered, disappointed in herself for the sentiment. "He's fast, but the older boys will have the day."

"The Roon goes to the runner with the largest heart," Seanbea countered. "There are tales of a girl three years younger than the tallest, strongest boy finding speed in her legs that even she hadn't believed existed." His eyebrows lifted to mark his point. "The Roon chooses who bears the seat, Wendra, not the child. It is a race, yes, but after all the child can do, something more aids the winner in crossing the ribbon."

"It sounds like a legend, like that of the White Stag or the Pauper's Drum." She stood on her tiptoes and looked in the direction the children would come.

"Legends come to us for reasons, Anais," Seanbea said. "Like the legends of songs that do more than entertain."

Wendra shot him a hot glance, but the Ta'Opin stood firm under her glare.

Far away, the cheering from the crowd began to cycle back toward them. As the roar of the crowd drew closer, those around Wendra and Seanbea began to fidget and call, the excitement of the race coming before it like leaves stirred by a wind presaging the storm.

Moments later, a pack of children rounded a corner and broke into a sprint down the long concourse. Twelve youngsters ran, their arms pumping, their hair whipping in the wind of their own speed. Across the cobbled street they flew, feet pounding in an impossible rhythm. Hands and arms rose in support as the runners raced past. Twenty strides behind them, a second group of children came around the corner and caused another surge in volume from the onlookers. Behind this cluster of contestants, more children came in staggered formations, each individual racer working feet and knees and arms in ardent strain.

The first grouping came into clear view. Wendra rose up again on her toes and scanned their faces. At the back of the pack, Penit and Dwayne labored to keep pace with those at the front. Sweat streaked their cheeks and temples, matting hair to heads. Two boys ran at the head of the lead group, effortlessly sprinting and seeming untaxed in their exertion. A handful of girls made up the middle of the pack, ponytails flipping to and fro with each long stride. A few more boys flanked the girls, eyeing their counterparts as they drove their legs forward. Penit and Dwayne ran with the third at the back of the group, their strides shorter and quicker then the long, graceful strokes of the others.

Wendra yelled Penit's name, but she could scarcely hear her own voice. In the midst of the deafening noise, she suddenly wondered if an unheard song held any power. But the thought fled her mind in the exuberance of cheering Penit on. The colored bits of confetti showered like a blizzard in the street, swirling around the bodies of the children as they passed. Some small bits sticking to the sweat on their faces and forearms. Whistles pierced the din, noisemakers popped and rattled, and a few celebrants blew horns of their own.

Then the first pack turned and followed the course down a narrow side street. The crowds lined the route there, too, jostling one another for a view of the children as the first runners dashed past them. Now innumerable voices rose all around Wendra, racers passing constantly in a long procession, the throng lifting its roar down the streets where the Roon snaked into the city. The sound reverberated off stone buildings, and Wendra fancied it the voice of Recityv, a multitude of pitches and words commingled to one great, giant voice.

The last runners passed them and followed the course down the street to Wendra's left just as the return route began to thrum with the excitement of the lead pack. Wendra clutched her bodice, trying to will her heart to slow, but to no avail. The thrill resonated through her, in her. Every beat in her chest fell like the blow of a hammer.

The intensity of the crowd might have been nothing to what it now became. Every onlooker howled and cheered with the fullness of his own lungs. Taken together, it felt like the air must surely rend. Or else the density of the noise might have weight and substance enough of its own to be touched. The force of the volume pressed at Wendra's eyes and raised every hair on her body. She felt simultaneously like one dropped into a winter river and one roasting on an oven spit, but none of it was painful. Instead, she felt buoyed, as if she might raise her arms and float upward.

Then Penit appeared on the return avenue.

His shoulders were bent, his arms driving with sheer determination. He emerged from the byway ten strides ahead of Dwayne. He'd found his own sure stride, his legs churning like a champion horse in long, powerful rhythms. His feet glided across the cobblestone, his heels never touching the ground. Tears of pride welled in Wendra's eyes as she added her voice to the incredible chorus of exultant celebrants.

Through the wide concourse Penit sprinted, seeming to gain speed with every stride. The crowd knew their winner, and reveled in anticipation of the ribbon, now again raised by the men bearing the batons.

Through the riverbanks of proclaiming attendants Penit ran. Their own frenetic energy contrasting the smooth, elegant pace Penit kept as he dashed down the open concourse toward the finish line. He came closer, and Wendra could see the calm but determined set of the boy's features—the same one she'd seen when he'd gone out to find her help from the cave. She gloried in his impending triumph and all that had transpired to bring him safe to Recityv. Forgotten were her fears of what winning could mean. She held her breath and embraced the joy that raced her heart.

Suddenly, a strange look passed over Penit's features, a kind of thoughtful concern. He looked back over his shoulder at Dwayne, now twenty strides behind him, and the rest of the lead pack just emerging from the far avenue. His legs carried him forward, but Wendra thought she saw in his eyes a realization not yet communicated to his feet.

Fifteen paces from the ribbon, Penit stopped.

• CHAPTER SIXTY-THREE •

Winners and Wisdom

Penit came to a skidding halt, his breathing labored, his eyes regarding the ribbon so close ahead.

The crowd erupted with frustrated expectation. Some jeered, others roared in confusion. Wendra noted the pitch shift to something deeper, less appreciative. Violent gestures exhorted Penit to finish the race, continue on. A few heads shook in annoyance. Wendra was sure this had never happened in all the history of the Lesher Roon.

Penit could have jogged the remaining distance and still won the contest.

Instead, he turned and watched as Dwayne came racing on. His friend gave him a curious look. Penit nodded, lending a contented, reassuring expression to Dwayne, who passed him with a brief glance.

A moment later, Dwayne broke the ribbon. A roar of victory followed, and the boy was snatched up and extolled by those gathered in the streets as the next Child's Voice to the High Table. Other children buzzed past Penit to finish for honor's sake. Some slowed and stopped, moving off to rejoin parents.

The crowd filled the street, many seeming to forget Penit as they rushed to congratulate Dwayne. A few sauntered close and gave him bewildered stares. Wendra fought through the wall of people to Penit, and heard harsh, critical comments aimed at the child before she gathered him close and silenced the critics with a scathing glare. Seanbea forged a path for them back to the wall near the gate, where she knelt and embraced Penit for several moments before realizing he was not crying or otherwise upset.

She drew back and gave him a guarded look. "Penit, why did you stop?"

He peered over her shoulder, presumably at Dwayne, his face a study in satisfaction that burgeoned into a smile.

Wendra turned to follow Penit's eyes and found the race coordinator marching toward her, baton in hand. Behind him a number of attendants vested in city colors surrounded Dwayne and escorted him watchfully. She thought the man intended to pass them with his brusque, sensible stride. But he came to an abrupt halt next to them.

"You will come with me, all three of you," he said, pointing at Wendra and Seanbea while keeping his eyes fixed on Penit. "I'll have no discussion about my race. The regent and her table will hear an account of it from both you and Master Dwayne, and let her say out upon it."

He paused long enough to indicate which ones they were to his staff with a wave of his baton, then stepped smartly away, heading for the gate. The men in bright Recityv crimson enfolded them in the circle they formed for Dwayne and a shifty-looking man Wendra thought she recognized but couldn't place. Together, the five of them passed through the inner gate and onto the smooth surface of the Solath Mahnus courtyard. The stone clacked beneath their heels. Long slate slabs had been meticulously fitted together, rendering the yard virtually seamless. Dark marble benches edged the perimeter, here and there occupied by men in full armor and women in neatly pressed dresses. Planters stood on both sides of each stone bench, where manicured trees offered little shade, but prim decoration.

On the far side of the yard, an archway large enough to permit two carriages abreast tunneled into the hill. Above it rose the sprawling courts and halls of Solath Mahnus. Each roof showed crenellated abutments more decorative than useful. The stone of the outer walls had been carved with various crests denoting houses and families. The crests formed pyramids, each successive level holding fewer as if showing the genealogy of the seats housed within.

Their steward ushered Wendra, Seanbea, and Penit into a tunnel lit brightly with oil lamps. Several intersecting passages ran at perfect angles to the one they traversed before finally they came to a wide stair guarded by four men bearing halberds. The fastidious baton wielder did not even bother to acknowledge the guards, fussing past them and up the stairs at a sturdy clip. Gates hung from the ceiling above them. A short stroke would bring them swinging down to block their ascent. Wendra saw strange clips bolted to the outer edges of the stair, where it looked as though the gate locked home once it fell.

Wendra's legs had started to burn by the time they stepped into a wide, vaulted chamber, appointed with suits of armor and weapons resting on oiled wood stands, and pedestals bearing glass cases where sepia parchments sat atop easels, many of them singed around the edges or burned through in places as if with a hot stick. Murals hung painted on canvases several strides to a side, and long drapes in solid, dignified colors descended from brass rods fastened in the heights of the room's great ceiling. All around, charcoal-colored marble set in feathered patterns announced the dignity of court, and the refinement of artistry.

Seemingly inured to his surroundings, their guide led them through the hall into a second chamber bordered by doors and dominated by a narrow stair that began in the middle of the room and ascended past the second and third floors, issuing them directly to the fourth story. Marble balustrades ran along the edges of each level, though Wendra had no idea how people found their way to those floors.

At the top, several soldiers stepped into their path in a practiced manner, and waited until the race coordinator said something to them before they would withdraw. They pushed through a large set of double doors and saw a number of maps and long scrolls on tables where men and women sat, harried looks upon their faces, some gesticulating, others with heads cradled in their hands. There were deliberations going on.

Soldiers numbered half the room's occupants, most in unsullied uniforms and looking ill at ease to be so clean and tailored. Sun streamed through long, high windows, bathing the room in light; looking through those windows, Wendra could see the breadth of Recityv even from the doorway. It made her woozy; she reaffixed her attention onto following the bustling little gentleman.

Some of the room's occupants looked up as they passed, a few appearing to understand who they were and forgetting whatever concern currently occupied them. Behind them, men with pitchers of water stood at the ready to refill glasses on the table. Wendra found her mouth dry and wanted to ask for something to drink. The hush that followed them into the room dissuaded her from making any requests.

At the back of this room stood another set of double doors guarded by eight men. The race coordinator impatiently waved them away as he approached. The soldiers gave way and the doors were drawn back to admit them. Through the doors stretched another hall, more doors at long intervals on either side and engraved with words from a tongue Wendra did not know. Past these, a final set of stairs led to doors that stood unattended. To these, their trenchant guide took them. Wendra's stomach churned. She took Penit's hand and as an afterthought, took Seanbea's hand as well, just as they came to the end of the hall.

Their guide stopped at the door and turned to face them.

"I've sent ahead for an audience." He looked them over one by one, pointing at each person with a crooked finger as though taking count. "This is an interruption the regent will permit because it bears on the completion of her High Table, but it is not an invitation to speak. If you are asked something, you may answer. 'My Lady' is quite appropriate when addressing the regent. Otherwise, keep quiet."

The fellow did not wait on questions or protests, and with a small grunt pushed open the heavy doors to the regent's High Office.

Every surface shone in alabaster marble. Only the slightest variant of color showed it to be anything but pure white. Arched windows running from floor to ceiling in broad stripes let light into the chamber. Wendra did not remember seeing any windows from the courtyard. Each corner housed a hearth attended by a cluster of high-back chairs and flat benches. A table set before the each fireplace held books, some open as though left while being used. At the back of the High Chamber, a brass tableau had been set into the wall. It showed a king in full regalia removing his crown. Upon it, inscriptions gleamed in the light. Beneath it, on a raised stone dais, sat an elegant elderly woman in a large, upholstered chair—the regent, Wendra guessed.

At the sight of her, Wendra felt the sudden urge to kneel. The woman had a commanding gaze, and gave Wendra the feeling that she stood in the presence of real power. She would never have thought she'd be in the same room with such a woman. Her heart beat stronger as though in a kind of sisterhood.

At the center of the High Office stood a great circular table. Across from Wendra, the table showed a gap where one might enter the area inside the ring it created. Around the outer edge sat men and women at odd intervals, separated by empty chairs. As the doors closed behind them, Wendra's attention fell on a gaunt gentleman adorned all in black and pacing the area inside the ring of the table. He walked casually in a smaller circle, alternately facing those seated around him as he spoke in relaxed, confident tones.

"Our regent's call for the Lesher Roon is a worthy one, even if the rumors that shift opinion in the streets are the fancy of empty bellies eager for a scapegoat to sacrifice to their malcontent." He opened his hands, palms up, to emphasize the image he described. "There, neither she nor the people are to blame, my fellows. It is proper to find consensus as the reunification of the High Council could. And when men and women move listlessly in their markets and homes, leadership is what is needed.

"But as to the naming of Quiet in the land"—he shrugged his shoulders and threw up his hands—"have any of you seen it? What evidence of these things do we have? Our respected friend Artixan champions this belief," the man said, pointing to a white-bearded gentleman who sat in stately fashion though his age drew his shoulders forward in the slump of his advanced age. "But his people take it upon themselves to violate the law."

Artixan half rose. "To save one of your own men's children, Ascendant Staned. Let us not forget who benefited by such generosity."

Wendra looked at this man, Artixan. He was Sheason, she could feel it.

"It is no matter who was saved, my fellow. None at all. It might have been the regent herself, and still the law was broken. I held out for no favor in the League's defense when one of my own was brought under condemnation. And I will address it now as I have before: the Archer is no member of the League. He may be sympathetic to that which elevates our cause, but he acted independently. I'll swear on it."

"Your words are vile enough, Roth, without such oaths," Artixan said, drawing polite laughter from the others seated at the table.

Brief indignation crossed the Ascendant's face before diplomacy resettled his features. "It is no wonder the regent keeps you on, Artixan; a better scop no regent could ever hope to have."

"And you are my rightful heir, Your Leadership . . . your prattle is an endless joke," Artixan riposted. The Sheason's smile fell. "And yet I'll have an end to our dispute. Rumor or none, many despair over their condition, and in their dismay is a fiend. Let us pluck it out, whatever the cause."

"Truly said," Roth replied. "And have courage should that thorn be called Sheason."

"Or Exigent," Artixan finished.

Ascendant Staned sat with a forced smile, holding his composure with some difficulty.

When all were seated, the race coordinator cleared his throat and stepped forward. "My Lady, I present you the winner of the Lesher Roon and his father."

The woman seated in the chair on the raised step now stood. Her mantle fell to the floor in flowing folds. She, too, stood hunched from age. Deep creases told of a life of fret and laughter. Brown spots on her brow and neck and hands came in the same color of her close earth. Yet her eyes sparkled with fire and clarity. She seemed not to miss anything in its detail, reserving speech until she'd looked and considered those she addressed. She spared a glance at the table, and at an unspoken command, each of those seated there stood as well, and turned to face Wendra and her companions.

"I'm told the winner of the Child's Seat isn't as evident as you suggest." The regent indicated both boys.

"The boy who crossed the ribbon first isn't in dispute, my Lady," the race coordinator replied. "But the winner may be."

"Don't draw it out, Jonel," she urged. "Bring us to your purpose."

"This child," he began, motioning Dwayne to stand beside him, "crossed the ribbon ahead of the rest." He looked at Penit and brought him forward with a glance. "But this child led the race to within a house-length of the finish before stopping and letting the ribbon-taker pass him by."

The regent held up a hand. "Is this true?" she said, looking directly at Penit.

He nodded. The race coordinator gently pressed a knuckle in his back. "Yes, Anais, I mean, my Lady."

Penit immediately looked up to see what danger he had caused for himself in referring to the regent in such a way. Helaina surprised them all by smiling graciously.

"A long time since anyone honored me so," she said, sharing a look with the Sheason. "Wouldn't you agree, Artixan?"

"I would," the old man stated.

"We are concerned that the children may have conspired to thwart the natural delegation of the Lesher Roon, my Lady," the coordinator said. "And I put the matter before you to decide whether another race must be run, or the results of this Roon should stand. I'll have the records reflect my diligence in selecting the appropriate Child's Voice."

The regent nodded once. "So noted, and wisely so, Jonel. Thank you." She then descended her single stair and walked around the table, making her way with a slow, deliberate step, aided by a pearl white cane formed of two intertwined pieces of wood. No one moved or spoke while she came to Penit. The sound of her shuffling steps and the tick of her cane upon the marble floor filled the silent chamber.

At last she stood before them. "Come to me," she said, propping her cane against her hip and proffering her hands to Penit and Dwayne.

With a gentle shove from Jonel on each boy's back, they did as they were asked, stepping up and each taking one of the regent's hands.

"Your names?" she asked.

Each boy gave it.

, She looked down at Dwayne, her eyes gripping him in a solemn stare. "Did you conspire with Penit to win the Roon?"

Dwayne shook his head. "No, my Lady. I ran my hardest. I didn't expect Penit to stop, but when he did I just ran past him."

The regent gave a nod of satisfaction before turning to Penit with her iron stare. "And you, son, if you were sure to take the race, why did you stop?"

Penit looked back at Wendra. His eyes pleaded, but she could do nothing but nod for him to answer. The gesture seemed to reassure him, and he turned back to the regent.

"Dwayne is much smarter than me, my Lady, much smarter." He tried to look at his feet, but the regent took his chin and lifted it again.

"And what has this to do with deliberately losing the Roon?"

Penit shrugged. "I wanted to win. Wendra and I have come all the way from Myrr, and I thought if I won I could get us out of trouble with the Quietgiven and Vendanj and everybody." Wendra caught a start in the regent, who tightened her gaze on Penit. "But after we got close to the ribbon, something kind of hit me. Whoever wins the race gets to make important decisions for the whole city. Dwayne will do a better job of it than I could. He knows more; he figures things out better than I do. If the children are going to have one to speak for them, it should be Dwayne before me."

The regent gave Dwayne another look. He stood dumbfounded.

"How do you know this of Dwayne if you are from Myrr? I was informed that our new Child's Voice is a resident here of Recityv."

"I don't know about that," Penit shook his head. "We met at Galadell, that's where—"

"Hold," the regent stopped him.

Wendra watched as Dwayne's father began to look backward toward the door, perspiration gathering at his temples.

"We will adjourn," the regent called. "At first hour the table will reconvene." The tone of command in her voice belied her age, and those sitting at the round table silently filed past them and through the only doors to the High Office. The league leader hesitated near them to make a close observation of each boy. Then the Sheason came, his step slower and less steady. "Attend me, Artixan," the regent said. "I could use your counsel, I think."

"As you say," Artixan answered.

When the hall was cleared, the regent gestured for them each to take a seat at the table. She slowly retook her own, resting her aged body in the cushioned seat and gathering a breath before speaking.

"Go on now, Penit. And mind you speak the truth. We've no leniency for lies." The regent rested her cane against an armrest and settled her keen eyes on the boy again.

"Wendra and I got taken by a highwayman to Galadell. First he took me because Wendra got sick and I went out looking for help." Penit rushed ahead with his story. "Wendra came and rescued me, but before she got there, I met Dwayne. He was being held for sale, too. They made us run a lot, the faster kids separated from the slower ones. Dwayne and I got put together, and food was better after that.

"Dwayne is very smart. He doesn't know as many of the stories as I do, because I had to learn them for the wagon-plays. But he had a whole plan for escape, and I saw how he helped the younger kids when they got scared. He even helped the men and ladies, teaching them how to deal with the traders. I'm just glad he finally got out." Penit shot a look at Dwayne's father.

The regent held a finger to her lips as she listened. Her sharp gaze did not vary as she assessed Penit's words. "But you must know the Roon selects its own. It is not for you to decide who takes the Child's Seat." Helaina spoke with a dignified calm, but certain sternness.

"Yes, my Lady," Penit said. "But maybe the Roon is what made me stop. That's what I think." Penit ran his arms across the gloss of the table. "The race doesn't have a brain, it can't think. I decided that what the Roon meant was a race where all the children run and do their best to select one to sit at this table. I might be the fastest, my Lady, but the best thing I can do is be sure you get the smartest one to help you do your ruling. That's Dwayne, no doubt."

The regent smiled around her finger.

"And anyway, now maybe I don't have to worry about the Bar'dyn and Vendanj and the rest. *You* can help them."

Helaina's smile faded from her aged lips. "You've seen the Bar'dyn, boy? And Vendanj, you've spoken with him?"

"Yes. Vendanj helped us get away from the Bar'dyn. So did Seanbea." Penit turned and smiled at the Ta'Opin. "But we got separated from Tahn and Sutter and Braethen and Mira. And we haven't seen them since."

"We will speak of these things later," the regent declared in an authoritative voice. "For now, I am left with an unprecedented event in the Lesher Roon, and the trouble of who shall claim a seat at my table." She scrutinized each boy's face. "The rightful winner should have been Penit, who shows more wisdom and humility yet in forfeiting the race as he believes it is in the highest interest of the council.

"Still, the people have witnessed the ribbon falling to Dwayne, and will claim him as the rightful voice." She sat back into her chair, straightening her hunched shoulders. Wendra thought that she glimpsed a moment of the regent's former beauty and majesty as Helaina raised her voice from a head held royally aloft. "More than this," the regent spoke forcibly, "young Penit reminds us of the spirit of the Roon, the spirit of the table. We dishonor ourselves to question his sacrifice." She looked at Penit. "Besides, son, though I would be glad to have you take a permanent seat here, I trust your judgment of the young Dwayne. I hope to benefit from the wisdom you ascribe to him."

The regent then looked at Artixan, who'd remained quiet the entire time. The Sheason nodded with a look of satisfaction. Just then, the door opened and a page bowed deeply in apology.

"Excuse me, regent," the page said. "But the Court of Judicature has been convened on a moment's notice to hear the defense of the Archer."

"What is this?" the regent said, standing and taking up her cane. Fire burned in her eyes. "We cannot open this to law, there'll be riots."

"Pardon, my Lady," the page went on. "Against the protest of our magistrate, the right to Preserved Will has been claimed, and the law still holds in the annals. I've been asked to convey you there to hear the entreaty and pronounce upon it. Lord Hiliard of the Court of Judicature does not wish to rule on the dissent without your endorsement."

The regent looked around, the ire clear and bright in her face. On her wrinkled cheeks color rose. She did not speak, her mouth a thin, tight line. Finally, she tapped her cane once and descended the stair to the chamber floor.

"Follow me, Artixan," she said. "The rest of you, too. I won't ascend these steps again today. We'll talk over the rest of your revelations at our day's last meal."

She bustled past them, her cane metering out time as it tapped against the marble floor. Wendra went to Penit and gave him a gentle squeeze as they all followed the regent through the door and down the many steps toward the Court of Judicature.

• CHAPTER SIXTY-FOUR •

Preserved Will

Wendra could hear the court chamber before they came anywhere near it. The voices of speculation and discontent rose like the buzzing of a hive. Attendants fluttered in and out of view, hastily performing errands and delivering messages. Guards stood stoically beside the entry, many more milling about in the open halls, some clustered in small groups, whispering and shaking their heads. As the regent passed, these men stood at attention. She ignored them completely.

The court chamber doors opened at her arrival, sending a wave of chatter and noise over everyone. Helaina paused a moment and drew herself up. Then the door guard led her in, raising standards once she'd passed out from beneath the covered entryway and entered the room proper, whereupon the entire assembly rose to its feet and bowed. The regent acknowledged the crowd with a wave of her hand, and went forward into a great ringed amphitheater. All around them rose circular rows of seats, each bounded by a low balustrade. Not a seat was vacant. Even the aisles teemed with gawkers hunkered down or seated on the stairs. Men and women, old and young, pressed cloth and rumpled shirttails, sat beside one another. The smell of expectation and the heat of cramped bodies filled the chamber.

On one side of the floor, a number of men sat behind a long, burnished hardwood table coated with a deep chestnut lacquer. These gentlemen wore high-collared coats woven in black tightcloth and trimmed with white epaulets. Before them on their table rested dozens of books and mottled scrolls in hasty disarray. Four of them sat in utter silence, their faces gaunt and unsmiling. Wendra thought that beneath the austere visages the look of a trapped animal wrestled their near impeccable control.

On the other side of the round chamber rested a second table identical to the first. In its lacquered surface were reflected the grim stares of Vendanj and a second man Wendra did not recognize. Behind them, against the short wall that raised to the first row of the theater, sat Mira and Braethen—the Far a statue, Braethen with wide, amazed eyes.

They made it!

Wendra was stunned. She realized that part of her hadn't expected to see them again.

When the shock wore off, she could barely restrain herself from rushing to Braethen and embracing him. But now was not the time. Vendanj had noted them with a nod, as had Mira. Braethen mouthed something before Mira put a hand on his arm to end it. Wendra understood. Braethen was asking about Tahn and Sutter. Wendra shook her head.

The regent crossed between the two sides and mounted a low set of stairs to a modest platform and an old wooden chair lined with a horsehair fabric. The chair was chipped and marred, but its stout legs did not grumble or budge as Helaina eased her weight into it. She took a moment to gather her breath before propping her cane and settling her gaze upon the men wearing the formal counsel gowns across from Vendanj.

Still no one spoke. With the inclination of her chin and the intensity of her eyes, the regent set the mood for the entire room. The gossiping and accusations and excitement of a life hanging in the balance of the deliberations of free men all ebbed, replaced by the power of the regent's presence. Even as elderly as she was, she commanded attention merely by the way she looked and comported herself. Wendra wondered if the woman became regent because of this quality, or if being regent had imbued her with it; having heard her speak before, she believed the former.

The guard closed the doors to the Court of Judicature; the boom of it reverberated in the hall. Wendra and Penit and the others quickly sat upon the floor in the covered entryway.

"This is a matter already put to bed, written upon the ledger." The regent directed her comments to the first counselor, who wore a white braided rope slung over his shoulders, its ends knotted above a series of thin fringes. "Why are we convened again upon it, First Counsel?"

The man stood and cleared his throat. He came around his table and assumed a posture of oration. "My Law," he said, addressing Helaina, "indeed this matter was heard and ruled upon. The offender sits this day in chains he has rightly earned. I, for one, have no desire to put the argument to the Court of Judicature again. And you may make an end of it here and now—"

"I know my authority, First Counsel," the regent said curtly.

"Your pardon, my Law." He bowed.

"To the point," the regent said with rising impatience.

Again he cleared his throat, his thin, aged cheeks puffing as he did so. "Our ruling has found a challenge. An old one to be sure." He looked back at the dusty scrolls upon his table. "But we've not found sufficient cause to disregard it. We may circumvent this, my Law, if you will delay the hearing until we may read upon it."

"The dissent?" the regent asked.

"Preserved Will, my Law."

A sudden flurry of whispers and gasps rose like the soughing of wind.

The regent raised her eyes to the many circular rows and brought the crowd to silence. Wendra watched Helaina, and could not tell how the regent herself felt about the challenge. Not until she looked down at the table of the challenger, which she'd carefully avoided to that moment. Then her face showed all its age, and the stern, ruling set of her brow and cheeks slackened. Her face bore a mask of terrible remembrance and guilt. The look quickly passed, though, and the regent regained her composure.

"Can you prove this?" the regent asked, locking on Vendanj with a strict gaze. Wendra noted Artixan seated beside her, nodding his own answer.

But it was not Vendanj who rose. Instead, the other man with him stood, coming around his table and taking a wide stance in the center of the Court of Judicature chamber. He looked from his far right to his far left, seeming to want to meet every set of eyes. Finally, he leveled his grim regard on the regent.

"We can, my Lady. We will show you today how honest men suffer in the prisons you create for them."

The regent looked on with quiet intensity. "You will hoist yourself up on your own rope, Counsel, if you intend to disgrace this Chamber."

"I intend no disgrace to the *Chamber*," he said, unduly emphasizing his final word.

The insult was plain, but as Wendra watched, the regent let it pass. Wendra had the immediate sense that this challenger, who shared Vendanj's table, had known the regent before today. She likewise sensed that, history or not, Helaina would not suffer another subtle slight. To do it would undermine her authority in the minds of all those present. The challenger appeared to know this as well, and retook his seat.

"Your books," the regent said, returning her attention to the first counsel, who had maintained his orator's pose. "What do they say on this? We've not had it spoken of here in a very long time."

"This is the issue, my Law," the man replied, his thin cheeks uninvolved in the formation of his words. He spoke in a dour, pessimistic tone. "The use of it is well beyond the memory of most of those gathered here. Tradition holds that laws so long out of use are not always of particular relevance to our ruling body, my Law." He bowed again.

The challenger rose from his seat again. "Tradition also holds that laws granted in the Charter supercede the wiles of crafty counselors or the reformations of government."

The regent would not be distracted and continued to hold the first counselor's eyes. "Have you established the rightness of this dissent, then, Pleades?"

The counselor seemed caught off guard by the use of his name. But he nodded. "Indeed, my Law, if you've no mind to controvert it, we have no place to deny the audience of a hearing to examine their argument." The man sounded defeated as he made his report. "But you may give us leave to review it more closely, my Law, and some things . . . pass away, as time permits."

Wendra heard an ominous note in the way the man finished. She realized that whoever was being held would likely be dead before the Court of Judicature reconvened to discuss him if the first counselor succeeded in persuading the regent to grant this review.

"No," Helaina said. She turned to Vendanj. "And you sit attendant to this challenge, Sheason?"

Vendanj nodded.

"You are aware of the strictures placed upon your order within the walls of Recityv and throughout the nation of Vohnce."

"I am," Vendanj said.

"We will accept as evidence all that our esteemed first counsel has brought to light through his good efforts and the light of Will in the first argument on this offender." She refocused her penetrating gaze upon the challenger. "What can you add to dissuade us from the proper course we've taken? And watch that you do not trifle with our time or patience. We do not abide liars or miscreants here."

"I've no time for either, my Lady, today any more than in years past."

The regent nodded primly, and signaled the entry of six men and six women through doors Wendra had not seen, on either side of the regent's chair. The new entrants stepped formally down the stairs, men to the left, women to the right. From their shoulders flowed long robes in the colors of Recityv, a white emblem of the tree and roots over each breast. Wendra could see pant cuffs beneath the robes, shirt sleeves and collars, as though these people had donned their outer ceremonial garments hastily. They filed to separate rows of chairs similar to the regent's that were set on the first ring from the hall floor, and sat with hands cupped and resting in their laps.

When they had settled themselves, the regent lifted her cane and struck the marble with a loud crack, signaling the first counselor to begin. She then sat back into her chair. Wendra followed Pleades's long gait as he clasped his hands behind his back and paced before the men seated at his own table. Several moments passed, and low chatter began to rise in the high seats of the circular chamber. The first counselor's face held a scowl, the thick skin of his forehead bunched over his thin white brows. Abruptly he stopped and folded his arms. He squared himself to face the challenger.

"The ledger needs your name," Pleades said. There seemed a hidden ridicule in the simple request that Wendra could not discern.

The challenger stared unblinking, his skin dry and lustrous dark from long exposure to the sun. Then a smile appeared on his lips and he nodded appreciatively. "A fine gambit, First Counsel, worthy of every book of logic you've studied to earn your post. Adding my name hurts our credibility, given my history in this court, is that it?" He shook a finger at him in a playful mockery of scolding. "What say you to putting the name of the three-ring, Vendanj, on your ledger? I shall merely be the voice to this challenge."

Pleades began to protest.

"Ah-ah." The challenger cut him off. "The records don't require that they be the same, so let us dispense with clever ploys to discredit me before we begin, and instead redress this abuse of power."

The first counselor threw up his hands, exasperated, it seemed, with his adversary's disrespect for the Court of Judicature.

"Very well," the challenger said. "Now, log his name as you find time. I don't want to bicker with you while innocent men languish in your dungeon. You have arrested and imprisoned two melura for thwarting your effort to execute a leagueman accused of conspiracy to violate the regent's law. While tradition holds that melura are not accountable in spirit for their errors, they may be punished for them in body." The challenger pointed a savage finger at the first counselor. "You mean to put to death this Archer and his friend for interfering with your rite of justice, and likewise hang the leagueman he saved because you believe the leagueman sought the assistance of a Sheason to heal his dying daughter. Have I my facts straight?"

"Facts, yes. Deportment, no," Pleades said tersely.

From the gallery, a murmured laughter ensued.

The challenger stepped into the center of the great round and turned a slow circle, as though casting a momentary glance into every set of eyes in the amphitheater. "Our challenge is this: that the actions of this Archer are not punishable, because the leagueman is innocent."

A rustling hum flared in the audience: gasps, sighs, denial, speculation.

"In the rush to assign blame, the counselors overlooked the most obvious evidence available to them: a witness." The challenger shook his head and began walking in a slow, tight circle, still addressing the assembly of citizens, as though deliberately refusing to acknowledge those seated in counsel robes against the walls beside the regent.

The challenger then raised his hands and closed his eyes. He mumbled something to himself, and Wendra thought she saw the word "Charter" on his lips. Eyes still closed, he went on. "Let's start simply. You have, in the city of Recityv and the nation of Vohnce, a law known as the Civilization Order, which holds that any Sheason who renders the Will, or any citizen who *seeks* a Sheason to render the Will, are guilty of a crime. This crime is punishable in many ways, including death."

Assent came with the nodding of heads.

"So," the challenger submitted, "if the leagueman did not ask or conspire with this Sheason to render the Will, then he is not guilty and does not deserve death. And if he was spared the punishment of a false charge by this Archer and his friend, then these melura you've condemned did what any men of conscience should."

"Your logic is sound," the first counselor admitted with a tone of reservation. "But someone should have informed you—and spared us all a lot of time—that the accused confessed to this crime. He chose to not even speak in his own defense." The counselor then paced away, deliberately turning his back toward the challenger in a show of contempt. "Something you'd have done well to choose in your own trial many years ago."

Wendra recoiled at the dark look that gripped the challenger's features. Just then, she feared for the first counselor's life. Mira actually sat forward in her chair, as though preparing for a physical outburst. But the challenger did not move. All the chamber fell silent. Penit reached over and took Wendra's hand.

The challenger stared blankly at the counselor's back, then turned to face the council in their crimson robes. "Mark me," he began, and Wendra fought a chill spreading down her back. "You hold three men accountable for crimes they did not commit. You've sentenced them to death, or will see them die as you deliberate their fates. I will answer for my own transgressions . . . will you?"

No one spoke for several moments. The first counselor finally retook his seat and attempted to look busy reviewing parchments lying on the table. His hands shook as he did so. Finally, the challenger turned and nodded at Mira, who stood and went to another door near her own chair. The Far went through the door, and promptly returned with a young girl adorned in sooty rags, her hair pulled back in a frayed band to keep matted strands from falling in her eyes. At the urging of the Far, she hesitantly came forward. The challenger went to her; Mira passed the girl's hand to him, and gently the challenger led her to the center of the circle. He whispered into her ear. The girl cowered, then stared at the floor as she gave witness, the challenger standing behind her with a supportive hand on her shoulder.

"My name is Leia," she began. "It wasn't my father who went to get the Sheason . . . it was me."

The gallery erupted in shock and shouts. For a full minute the regent could not restore order. Finally, the pounding of her cane against the marble floor brought silence to the court. "Go on, child," the regent said.

"I know Rolen," Leia continued, "because I help him give out food to the poor on beggar's row. I've done it for months because it makes me feel fortunate for what *my* family has. And Rolen always gives me a loaf of bread for my help. When my little sister, Illia, got sick, and Mother couldn't help her and we had no money for a healer . . ."

"Go on," the challenger urged.

"I thought of Rolen, because I know Sheason can use the Will to make people better. I knew mother and father would never go to Rolen because of the law. Or, at least, I didn't think so. But I couldn't just let Illia die. And Rolen is so good to me—"

Before the girl or the challenger could say more, another of the counselors at the other table stood. This one wore the emblem of the League below his epaulets. He steepled his fingers under his chin and showed the girl a fatherly smile. "Are we to reverse the dignified resolution of this council on the words of a child? It is notable that she would lie to preserve her father, but hardly admissible."

"And why not admissible?" the challenger demanded. "Why are you so eager to execute a member of your own fraternity when I am here to tell you he is innocent? That he did what any father would, accepting the blame for a sin to save his child?"

The league counselor fumed a moment before a retort occurred to him. "Let me answer with a question: Why are you so eager to substitute the fatherly valor you speak of with the life of the girl here to answer for this crime?"

Again the gallery murmured with the turn of logic. And Wendra found herself in agreement. This challenger sitting with Vendanj seemed to be arguing that the lawbreaker who should hang was a young girl, maybe twelve years old. She looked down at Penit, realizing again how fragile safety really was.

The man with the deep brown skin standing behind the girl put his other hand on her empty shoulder. He stood as a father might, in full support of what the girl was about to say. "You have not heard the end of it," he announced, and waited patiently for Leia to resume.

The girl trembled; she could look only at the floor, terrified of what must come next.

With a voice cracking with emotion, she spoke. "Mother has tended us many times when we've gotten sick. She's not a healer or a sodalist, but she knows about sickness. She asked us if any of our friends had been ill, or if any of the beggars on beggars' row had looked sick when I went to help Rolen pass out bread. She says you can get sick by being around them. But Illia and I told her no. It wasn't until after they took Rolen away that I remembered Mother telling us that eating too many sweets and fruits could give us stomach pain . . . that, and the gifts Illia and I had gotten that morning."

The challenger turned, then, to look at the league counselor, who'd gotten to his feet yet again. Wendra thought the man appeared a shade paler. He addressed the regent, "Your Law, the child is emotional and should never have been forced to come here. And, despite her love for her father, this is a waste of the Court of Judicature's time. We should—"

"Sit down," the challenger interrupted. "The girl will say what she has come to say." He did not ask the regent for leave to say it, nor did he look to her for assent. He merely gave the girl a reassuring pat on the shoulder to continue.

"Illia and I were behind our home, playing. Some of Father's fellow leaguemen came into the yard. It didn't really startle me, since they often came by for supper or just to gather Father on their way to a watch. But that morning, they brought Illia and me each a gift. They gave me a sheaf of flowers and told me I was growing into a fine woman. And to Illia they gave a box of sugared sweets . . ."

The challenger gave Leia another paternal pat on the shoulder, this time whispering something to her so low that it could not be heard. Then he raised his head to the robed council. "The trial record of the Sheason Rolen states that he testified of a poison in the body of child Illia—"

"Don't you dare suggest it!" The league counsel shot to his feet a third time. It was his turn to point a savage finger, thrusting his hand at the challenger.

The challenger turned to look directly at the man as he said, "I submit that the conspiracy in this affair is not the imprisoned leagueman's, nor this child's solicitation of the Sheason to heal her sister. The conspiracy belongs to the league itself, who poisoned a child to force the family of one its members to make an impossible choice: the death of a four-year-old girl, or loyalty to its immoral law."

A torrent of speculation, rumor, shock, and jeering cascaded down on the floor of the council from the gallery. Even the jury showed concern on their customarily impassive faces. The regent appeared to have need to speak, but could find no words.

It was the league counsel who finally found words. Composed again, he stared back at the challenger. "With all due respect, we still have only the word of a young girl, one who's emotionally distraught with the imprisonment of her father. A girl, I might add, who appears to have been *prepared* for her testimony by our esteemed challenger. A man, as we know, who has no respect for this council, and who seeks the freedom of those who tried to save the girl's father." He smiled. "It doesn't take much reasoning to determine what is really going on here. And I can assure that you any league confection is not only harmless, but actually quite tasty."

Mellow laughter rippled in the hall.

To this, the challenger whispered again in Leia's ear. The girl reached into the pocket of her ragged smock and pulled out a small wrapped morsel. "Illia gave me one of her sweets before she ate them all. I was saving it for a special occasion." She extended it in an open palm before the Court of Judicature.

The challenger took the sweet from her hand and walked to Pleades's table. He held it up to the league counselor. "Do you recognize the emblem on this wrapper? Unless things have changed in the last few decades, I'm going to guess that only members of the league can procure this confection."

The league counselor's eyes never went to the sweet. "And anyone could have tampered with it in the weeks since the crime," he observed.

The challenger reset his feet. "The seal is unbroken. Let's make this even simpler. Eat this. Eat it and prove that a simple gift to a child was not the instrument of conspiracy and death."

Whispers rushed like seeping winds. The league counselor again opened his mouth to rebut, but words failed him. The challenger had woven a trap, and his opponent had ensnared himself. Several times he started to speak, giving him the appearance of a brook trout pulling water through its mouth and past its gills. Finally, he managed to say something.

"This is an author's tale. A child's fancy. Aside from which, where Sheason are involved, anything with this sweet is possible." The league counselor looked over at Vendanj.

Vendanj rose for the first time. He looked across the aisle at the leagueman. His countenance shone with a terrible frown. Wendra saw genuine concern in the faces of even the regent and Artixan. The air felt charged with an imminent threat.

The force of the words resonated in the very stone, though spoken softly. "You will not make this intimation again. The court will not consider it in its deliberation. And I will not suffer false accusations upon my character, regardless of your laws. Am I understood?"

The league counselor could only nod.

"Eat this," the challenger repeated.

The counselor picked up the sweet and turned it over in the air before his eyes. "I will not," he concluded. "This is all so much speculation. I think we have heard enough of this dissent for the jury to render a decision on its merits."

"I'll have that back," the challenger said of the morsel. With some hesitance, the man returned it. Immediately, the challenger turned to the regent. "Your Law, what is your confidence in your league counselor? Would you risk partaking of this confection? Prove that the court's trust in this man is justified?"

Silence crept over the entire hall.

The regent stared back at the challenger with royal disdain. "We are done here," she announced, and tapped her cane. "Make your final argument or let this matter lie."

The challenger motioned the girl back to Mira, and turned to look first at the regent, then at the league counselor. Into the thick stillness he said, "You have benefited by the imprisonment of the Sheason Rolen. The opinions of the people turned to your favor in the wake of his purported crime and conviction. To such as yourselves, the life of one man means less than the directives of your leadership. And with all this distraction, you have caused men to forget the threat out of the Bourne that rushes toward us."

The league counselor ground his teeth at the challenger's rhetoric, his jaw flexing muscles near his temples. "There is no threat—"

"Do not interrupt." The challenger turned back to the council. "The League was worried that this family was sympathetic to the Sheason, perhaps because it knew or had heard that Leia had spent time helping Rolen distribute bread, or perhaps for other reasons. So, they devised a way to test where this family's loyalties lay.

"Either that," the challenger said, "or this man's family served as pawns in a larger scheme. One to reassert the Civilization Order or to divert the people's attention from rumors of Quiet in the land. And the reasons the League would seek such a diversion should make us all worry.

"But I am not here to expose plots. I am here because two more are now touched by this shameless ploy, two boys who freed a man innocent of the crime that nearly condemned him. It is provident that they came along. They must be set free. They may have interfered with the execution of our regent's order. But in doing so they answered the higher law of the Charter, and for that they must be held blameless this day. Or have we forgotten the foundation that stretches back through all ages?"

"This is careful logic," the league counselor exclaimed. "We still have only the word of a child against the conclusion of the Court of Judicature. We have a man defying the law—"

"We have," the challenger broke back in with renewed vehemence, "one of your very own, preserved, and you stand ready to see him hanged before you'll let me prove his innocence. What logic in this offends you?"

"No one is more pained than I at the prospect of one of my civil brothers going to his ground before he could do all that he might have done," the league counselor said, affecting a visage taut with dismay. "But among all else we do, we stand behind the rules that give us order and peace. We do not exempt ourselves from these things, even when they affect us heavily and personally."

"That is good to hear," the challenger said, his voice betraying his true feelings. "Nevertheless, we have a witness, the young girl Leia, who testifies that the man you prepare to hang is not guilty of seeking the Sheason's help. And we have leaguemen arriving at his home where the poisoned girl had just been healed by the Sheason, as though they were anticipating his arrival and prepared to pounce upon him. The timing is interesting—"

"The circumstance of the timing suggests nothing of conspiracy in this matter," the league counselor said forcefully. He folded his arms.

"The question before the Court of Judicature," the challenger continued, "is this: A Sheason saving the life of a poisoned child, an innocent man accused of seeking that Sheason's help, and two boys preserving the Will and life of the accused are all caged in the wet stone of your catacombs.

"You may argue that the Sheason still violated the law, to which I would ask you to consider how he came to do so. Because if he is to die, then you must make an inquiry into the leaguemen who gave tainted candy to the girl he chose to save." The challenger's voice lowered to a whisper. "And the only other lawbreaker here is Leia, a sister who sought help to save her sibling. The law condemns her for seeking the Sheason's help. But I put it to you now: Is she truly guilty? She would not have had need to seek help were it not for the fatal sweets given her sister. Or perhaps in a simpler way, do you hold her guilty for preserving the Will of a loved one, regardless the circumstance?" A long pause stretched throughout the assembly. Then the challenger finished. "Surely you will set them free."

The challenger sat again beside Vendanj, whose face betrayed no emotion, though Wendra thought the Sheason seemed satisfied. The challenger's words seemed to ring in the round chamber. For long moments afterward, no one spoke or appeared to move. The counselors across from Vendanj's table stared blankly at them. Slowly, low voices muttered to one another. No one attempted to quiet them.

Wendra watched the robed council, their faces unreadable. Seanbea leaned back and spoke into her ear. "The council will not rise until they are prepared to render a decision. They have been known to sit for three days in deliberation."

"They do not discuss the new evidence?" Wendra asked, looking past the Ta'Opin to the colorful robes of the council.

"Each member decides alone and makes a ruling. The largest number of votes prevails." Seanbea followed Wendra's gaze. "The regent may overturn their decision, but it is so rare that I cannot recall it happening. Though stories tell of trials in seasons gone by when the regent defied the court."

Wendra nodded and settled back to await the decision. Braethen looked on intently; Mira stood next to her chair, which she'd given to the witness. The challenger and Vendanj, subtle contempt visible on their features, looked out across the intervening floor at the line of court counselors.

The whispering continued, often interrupted by a self-remonstrating attendant shushing the congregants. By turns, the air thickened, growing dense with heat and a mix of human smells. Wendra caught a glimpse of Artixan seated against the wall just behind her. The Sheason eyed Vendanj closely. He blinked slowly as if unconcerned with the trial, some inner question claiming his attention.

Abruptly, one of the council members stood. Her robe fell in long deep folds. Then other members stood, one by one. The deliberations concluded, the regent nodded and the council member on the far left raised an arm in the direction of the counselor's table. The man next to her did likewise. In turn, each lifted an arm, the wide sleeve hanging in a low arc beneath his or her wrist. Each arm pointed toward the first counselor and his companions. The chatter of those assembled grew with each vote, gasps of surprise and delight and uncertainty escaping hundreds of mouths at once, followed by a renewed furor of speculation.

The accounting continued, council votes pointing toward the distinguished men in their fine black attire. Looks of self-assurance replaced the austere severity in their hollowed cheeks. Every hand confirmed the merits of their prior judgment. All save the last, whose arm lifted calmly toward the challenger. Uproar ensued, which quickly quieted before the regent could quell it. But the shock stirred the chamber, all eyes falling on the final voter. This last council member looked directly at the man with deeply tanned skin, then at Vendanj and Braethen and Mira and the girl. She did not seem to seek approval for casting her vote in their direction, but Wendra thought the woman sought to have them know of her resolve apart from the extension of her robed arm.

The challenger nodded appreciation, though the look of disgust and defeat contorted his lips and brow. A small man raced forward and produced a ledger into which he began to make an inscription.

"Your pardon," Vendanj called with his resonant voice.

The Court of Judicature became instantly silent, and the diminutive recorder lifted his pencil from his book.

Vendanj pushed back his chair and came round the table. He disregarded the counselors opposite him; he disregarded those still holding their arms to designate their votes. All the assembly seemed outside his consideration. He approached the regent as a sole individual with a stride of sure defiance. He came to the foot of the marble stair and placed one boot upon the first step. He stood staring at the regent, who returned his fixed gaze for many moments. The two appeared locked in a contest of wills.

As Vendanj began to speak, Wendra heard restless shifting behind her from Artixan. The old renderer muttered under his breath. Wendra could not make it out, but the tone was one of approval.

"Regent Storalaith, I invite you to look past the dictate of this Court of Judicature and appeal to your privilege as regent." Vendanj lowered his voice a note. "Set these men free. There could be no greater injustice than to uphold this ruling."

"Sheason," the regent said, "I still do honor what your emblem represents. I have championed the seat of your order at my table. But this council is just. I will not allow it to be subverted in the performance of its calling."

"My Lady," Vendanj persisted. "Is it not possible that after all the words are spoken we have not yet arrived at the truth? Or that what is lawful is yet not the proper course?"

"I'll not argue philosophy with you, Sheason." The regent spared a look at the table of counselors and the challenger over Vendanj's shoulders. "But if you ask me to rule according to my conscience and ignore the mandate of this Chamber, you'd not like my conclusion. I am unconvinced. I would spare you the humiliation of requesting my privilege only to have me send you away twice denied."

Vendanj did not immediately reply, seeming to consider alternatives. He half turned and looked at Wendra and Penit, then Braethen. The flinty look in his eyes and press of his lips unsettled Wendra, the brief hesitation. Why? Then he turned to the regent and spoke in an even tone.

"Will you follow us to his cell," Vendanj pointed toward the challenger. "Look upon the accused once before closing the ledger on this matter?"

The regent lowered her chin. She held Vendanj's eyes, seeming to search for his motivation in such a desire. Abruptly, she raised her chin again.

"No." She summoned the recorder, who rushed to her side with his tome and his graphite. As the book was placed in her lap, she pointed her cane at the counselor's table. "You are dismissed." She then looked up at the ascending circular rows of the assembly. "You have seen the work of justice and reason. Now go into your homes and keep yourselves clean of any offense that might bring you here." Her voice rang like iron from a clear throat, though the skin of her neck hung loose.

The hall began to empty. Vendanj did not move. The council folded robed arms and passed back through the doors by which they'd entered. Wendra and the others stood and flattened themselves against the entrance walls to allow the attendees to exit. In moments, the great round chamber had been vacated. Wendra rushed to Braethen and, of a sudden, found tears in her eyes. Penit stuck out a hand and greeted the sodalist in formal fashion. Braethen smiled and shook the boy's outstretched hand.

"You are well," Mira commented, surveying first Wendra and then Penit.

"Fine," Wendra said.

"Very fine," Penit added.

Braethen held onto Wendra's hands. "There is so much to tell you."

"We've stories of our own," Wendra said, rolling her eyes in exhaustion.

"Enough time for that later," Mira cut in, turning as Vendanj and the regent crossed toward them.

Seanbea then hugged Wendra and promised to see her later before taking his leave. Wendra returned the embrace, wondering if it would be so.

Helaina called the door guard to her. "Escort the girl home," she said, indicating the witness. "See that she is not troubled for her testimony here today." The witness bowed and followed two soldiers out of the chamber. Then Helaina turned to the challenger. "I can't believe it is you, Denolan. You've not aged."

"I am Grant, Regent," the challenger said coldly. "And you've not changed any more than I." He looked upon the empty council chamber to emphasize his meaning. Wendra suddenly had the thought that the two had met together in this place before.

"Belay your insults," the regent said icily. "I have adjourned the council because it will not do to meet the demands of strangers in our highest assembly of law. But I will accompany you to look upon this archer in deference to the order that serves me still." She glanced at Artixan, who stood a few paces off, then back at Grant. "Vendanj requests that you accompany me into the prisoner's cell. I will allow it. But do not think that your years of exile have earned you a place in my ears for bitter accusations and angry words. I won't hear it." She did not raise her voice, but no room remained for disagreement. "Follow close," she said to the recorder, who held his book across his chest as though it might fly away. "Artixan," the regent said, motioning the old Sheason close, "Dwayne will take the Child's Voice at my table. Watch over him until I can speak with him privately."

Artixan gave a smile and returned to Dwayne and his father, ushering them from the room.

"Now . . . Grant," the regent said, "take my arm and assist me to this stranger you care so much about. And if fortune favors you, I will not remind my council that your return here warrants execution."

Reluctantly, the challenger extended his arm. The regent linked her arm over his elbow and together they started out. Wendra took Penit's hand as they followed Vendanj. A joyful anxiety grew inside her. It had to be Tahn they were going to see. He was alive!

Mira led the witness back to her mother before she joined the others. The girl's small hand in Mira's own was cold and trembling. Through a narrow hallway they went to a dimly lit room beneath the raised court gallery. The weight of expectation hung heavy on the air as they entered.

The woman stood, and her daughter ran to her. The two fell into a close embrace as Mira stood just inside the door.

Then the woman looked at Mira, a question in her eyes. Mira looked down at Leia, expecting her to relate the judgment. The girl had been so frightened that it seemed she either hadn't heard or hadn't understood the regent's ruling. Her eyes, too, looked up at Mira, waiting, hoping.

The silence enveloped them.

Then Mira steeled herself. "I'm sorry. The regent would not overturn the ruling. The dissent failed."

"Papa," the child cried. "Papa." And she buried herself in her mother's side.

The woman tried to hold strength in her face and deny her tears. But the suffering and finality of it all overwhelmed her and her tears came. She fell to her knees, unable to support herself against her grief, and took her little girl in her arms. Together they wept anew for the loss of Leia's father, wept for the failure of the girl's honesty and bravery to convince the court that this was a mistake.

They wept and held each other, now left without a husband and father.

As Mira watched them grieve, she thought about what future this family might have without the support of this innocent leagueman. If they had no other family or means, women in a city had few options to make their way. And what they had to sell would be taken roughly by men with liquor on their breath.

The accumulated loss and sorrow of it swirled in Mira's head as she stood witness to this private scene of heartache and hopelessness.

Not this time.

Mira crossed the floor and dropped to one knee in front of the mother and daughter. She again took up the girl's hand and drew her attention. "Leia, listen to me, and mark what I say. You take heart and give your mother the strength you showed today in the Court of Judicature. Can you do that?"

With just a small bit of hesitation, the girl nodded. "Yes, I can." She looked at her mother. "I will help you, Mama." Then she looked back at Mira. "What are you going to do?"

Determination filled Mira as she looked down at the child. "I am going to free your father."

The girl stared at Mira with large tears still upon her cheeks. "Can you really do it? Can you save Papa?"

From the distant past, Mira heard her own questions about the loss of her parents. And she thought about what she was preparing to do now to keep her promise to this young girl. There were high costs. But the right costs. And Mira would not let doubt enter in.

Mira gave the girl's mother a confident look, then took the girl's wet face in her hands. "I believe I can, Leia. You hope, and I'll hurry." And with that, Mira gave mother and daughter's hands a squeeze and left to catch the others, thinking through precisely what must be given to keep her word—both to the Sheason and the Hollows folk, and to this girl so that she might not lose her father.

• CHAPTER SIXTY-FIVE •

Standing

Blackness held Tahn in its grip, the light from the cell door window paler and more diffuse than usual. It might still have been night beyond the walls of Tahn's prison for all the darkness that pervaded the space. But instinctively, he knew another day had come, and this day he knew more than any other—the day of his Standing.

He ached with hunger, the pain of deprivation grumbling inside and leaving his mouth sour and pasty. His bruises and cuts had oozed and swollen further in the hours since the guards had finally left him and Rolen alone. Merely breathing hurt his ribs. His muscles burned from rigid immobility. When Tahn attempted to reposition himself upon the hard stone, the use of his hands and legs brought exquisite pain every time the iron shackles scraped over raw scabs. Tahn felt momentarily grateful that no flies penetrated the darkness. He cringed at the prospect of having to constantly shoo them away or else let them lay their eggs in his wounds. He decided that somehow this low cellar was too fetid for even carrion eaters.

Will they bring me food today?

Tahn tested his wrist lightly against his manacle before yielding to the sting. Lying still, he smiled into the dark at the image of Rolen standing tall against the foulness in the mouths of their jailers. That one triumphant moment kept him warm when thoughts of Sutter or Wendra or Braethen came to him. Or when the old words he repeated in his dreams offered him no solace.

He cast his eyes toward Rolen's corner. He could see nothing, but the Sheason surely occupied the shadows there. And in that thought Tahn found another small comfort.

Then, from the curtain of darkness he heard, "It is your time, Tahn. Fit or not, you traverse a boundary today as sure as night yields to day." Rolen sat up, his chains rattling in the stillness. "I will stand First Steward for you if you wish it."

The offer stunned him. He had resigned himself to the passage of this day without the rite or ceremony meant to mark it. Three years ago Balatin had gone, and days ago the hope of Hambley at his side had fled him. In the endless darkness since he'd come here, the Change had come to mean much less to him. Whatever lay on the other side of this day could look no better from where he currently stood, bound and hungry. Some moments he preferred his chances against the Bar'dyn to the winnowing death he felt seeping into this bones from filth, cold, hunger, and impenetrable stone.

"No," Tahn answered. "Not here. It doesn't make sense to celebrate in this place. I'm not sure it matters now."

"It always matters, perhaps here more than anywhere else," Rolen said, his voice mildly remonstrative. "Do not let your circumstances rob you of what you cherish, Tahn. Even chained, you possess the most important of gifts. That is what the Change should teach." The Sheason sighed in the darkness. "It is the unfortunate case that when one is basking in warmth and celebrations of food and song, the truth of this day sometimes goes unrealized."

"What do you mean, unrealized?" Tahn asked.

Rolen did not immediately speak. But moments later, his voice rose in the stillness. "Every child becomes accountable, Tahn, each of us comes of age. But not all of us Stand. Standing requires a steward, and during those moments of change, the steward is able to impart a portion of his spirit to the one passing into adulthood. It is a special gift, Tahn. Something many melura are robbed of because they have no one to stand with them, or because their stewards have forgotten there's a gift to bestow."

Tahn groaned to sit up. He winced against the scrape of iron on his tender skin and slowly stretched his arms and legs from their cramped positions. "Tell me about this gift?" Tahn asked.

"Stand, Tahn," Rolen said, his chains rattling again. "Perhaps you may be counted lucky among the rest that the trappings of your Standing are stone and iron and your first meal the froth of a hungry mouth."

Tahn could hear the Sheason rise to his feet and begin to shuffle toward him. He knew he would not sleep again, anyway. And soon, the insistent image of dawn would rouse him anyway. Reluctantly, he got to his feet, biting back the oaths his ravaged body tried to coax from his lips. He faced the weak fall of light from the window at the top of the stone stair, and watched as a ghost of a man stepped into the shaft.

White, smudged skin drawn tight against the bone displayed sharp features. Wavy brown hair hung in matted clumps, some spots on his head thin or bare as if his scalp had lost the will to support those locks. Tahn wondered if this dungeon cell and poor diet had caused the patches. A wiry beard filled Rolen's face, covering his mouth. His robe hung from his shoulders like a sheet upon a drying line. Whatever meat there had been to him before he came here was now gone. Dark half circles under his eyes spoke of many sleepless hours.

Tahn thought he saw a vague smile on the man's lips. But the look in his eyes captured him most. Against the gross backdrop of darkness, hunger, and indignity, Rolen looked at him with gentle hope. He looked not at all like a man in chains or nearer his earth with every breath. He might have been standing at the head of a Northsun repast, his children at his feet, his wine cup full, and nary a friend with a harsh thought of him.

The Sheason beckoned him with a gesture, and Tahn scuttled forward. "Do you know which way is east?" Rolen asked.

Tahn nodded.

"Look that way, then."

Tahn turned and stared into the darkness as Rolen shuffled two steps and took position on his left and half a pace back. The Sheason put his right hand on Tahn's left shoulder and looked east with him into the darkness where no sun would ever rise. Into the cool, stale air he spoke with a voice soft and clear.

"From the cradle you come, son, through the march of a hundred days, a thousand, and more. Legs that first crawled then walked then ran. Hands that clutched a mother's finger then carried stones then learned to write. But in innocence all, in sport, jest, and growth, sometimes seeing the end of your actions, but never owning them."

Rolen's warm tones deepened in his chest. "Remember to run for the sake of working your legs; remember to write, that those after us may know your mind. Your days walk out before you now as a string of pearls, priceless and yet formed in imperfection. These imperfect moments are the choices that you must wear, be they good and true, or selfish and false. And you may know of this only in the ripples created by the choices you make. But whether you claim them or let them be, they belong to you now as they have not as melura."

Rolen paused. Warmth spread suddenly in Tahn's chest, arms, and legs. Heat flushed his cheeks, and the chill of his prison receded for the moment.

"I pledge to be your marker, Tahn." At this, chills swept Tahn's newly warmed skin. "To show you the ends you create. But only when you invite me to do so. I can reside in you as memory, a companion, even to incite you. But you may prove or condemn yourself on the merits of the paths you alone choose. I stand with you in the place of this promise, Tahn. But that promise moves as you move, for the promise is the fertile soil for your soul, which will be a refuge for you."

Tahn raised his hand and covered Rolen's fingers. He hardly heard the rattle of his chains. He stared into the blackness of the room and forgot the rasp of irons at his ankles, the emptiness in his gut. All the hell of his condition remained, but seemed of no consequence as he stood with this cellmate firmly at his back and looked past this day to what life lay ahead.

"You join the great fraternity now, Tahn." The cadence changed, now more reverent. "Take care how you comport yourself. The inclinations of youth are not gone. This passage you take does not leave behind all that you have been." Rolen turned Tahn around, clasping his shoulders with both hands, chains dangling and rattling impertinently in the stillness. "Your course is a deep river, Tahn, filled with currents that pull and rush. They will often seem separate from you, but know that they are yours. Each contending emotion proves that you live and breathe and are. Do not let go that self-assurance. No matter the personal cost, Tahn, do not question your own breath. It is as sure a thing as the sun that divides night and day."

Rolen's voice now quavered, his words coming in snatches, as though he reported images flashing before his eyes. "Beware though, Tahn. The line that separates light from dark is an easy place to lose your conviction. It is the dark backward, the light upside down. It invites but confounds. It is a stupor of thought that eases you toward the Whited One. And the foulness beneath his facade will corrupt the soul you wish to preserve: your own."

Tahn frowned at the words. They made no sense to him. But Rolen only smiled at his bewilderment, patting one shoulder and causing his chain to clink unmusically. "I might have hoped still for a roast goose to endfast with you." He gave a crooked smile.

"Is this the Change?' Tahn asked. "Is this all?"

"What more would you have it be?" Rolen looked at him with penetrating purpose and faith.

"Sutter and I have waited on this time for so long," Tahn lamented. "Girls . . ." He let an embarrassed grin flicker at the corners of his mouth. "We always just thought that . . ."

But secretly, Tahn had always hoped the Change would restore the childhood he could not remember, disclose the secrets of the words he was compelled to speak whenever he drew his bow, reveal the face of the man in his dreams, and—though it frightened him—the voice that answered him at times when he rose to envision another sunrise, a voice that spoke with a paternal tone. The Change had been the one true, last hope Tahn harbored for those answers. A heavy despondence crept into his heart.

"I know," Rolen said, mildness in his voice. He squeezed Tahn's shoulders to force his attention. "But it is no less important than your expectations led you to believe, Tahn. I have given you a gift of myself, one your own father surely meant to give. It is fire for your heart if you so choose."

Tahn stared blankly.

Rolen looked back with understanding. "It is not something you feel right now, I know. But trust me in this." He dropped one arm, grimacing with pain as he did so.

Tahn remembered the moment of warmth that had come over him as Rolen recited his words, and wondered if that was the gift of which the Sheason spoke. Beneath the years of anticipation, Tahn had hoped for a grand, new ability or understanding. Instead, he felt only a new burden upon him.

Rolen seemed to read his thoughts in the expression of his face. "Don't despair, my friend. Look within yourself and see if you don't already possess a ready calm. No sure revelation is the Change, no granting of immeasurable wisdom or strength. It is the freedom to stand or sit in your chains, Tahn, to bear the bite of steel on flesh, to subdue your hunger, and feel no threat of death."

The same placid look filled the Sheason's bedraggled features as he'd seen when first Rolen had stepped into the dirty shaft of light, but Tahn still did not understand. And yet, he did feel changed. Looking at Rolen, half his face aglow in sallow light, the other half veiled in shadow, Tahn saw suffering nobly borne. He saw the face of age, too. Tahn wondered if he'd ever again run through the Hollows' groves in autumn and kick at the fallen leaves simply because they heaped into drifts on the forest floor.

What consequence did that choice bring? Just running and kicking leaves?

He felt very much in the country of Rolen's dark backward and light upside down.

Rolen disappeared again into the darkness of his corner, dragging his chains after him. Tahn had no will to sit or even move. He did not know how long he stood there, thinking and yet trying not to think. Finally, he turned and cast his eyes upward into the vaults of the darkened cell and pictured the creep of heaven's greater light into an ashen sky cloaked by bruised clouds and imminent showers. The image held for the time it took Tahn to gather the courage to sit back upon the indifferent stone. Once there, he curled into a ball and gathered his chains into a pile to rest his head upon. With his face to the wall, carefully shielded from even the sallow light of the high window, he chased old memories down toward sleep. The last he thing he recalled was the image of Sutter ruffling the dresses of girls as they wandered too close to his and Tahn's concealed seats beneath the rear steps of Hambley's inn. He hoped Sutter was all right.

The day of Sutter's Change arrived.

He knew it because he'd been counting the days for many cycles now. Always before, he'd imagined it would be the day he would set out from his root farm and do something more with his life. But that day had come a bit sooner, and its path had brought him here.

It was still deep into the dark hours of night. He'd awoken as if in anticipation of seeing again the eyes of the dead.

Instead, only the stillness and darkness greeted him.

The others here still slept.

Sutter sat up off the rough stone, his bones and muscles aching with every movement. He looked at the wall opposite him; the two scops had not returned. He hadn't seen their forms yet this night. Sutter tried not to think of what that could mean. Perhaps these nightmares really were just fever dreams, or maybe, if they were the spirits of the dead before they met their end, he saw them only when they were near. Or perhaps the scops had been freed.

Sutter turned his mind to his Standing. Today of all days he missed Filmoere; his father would not be there to stand for him. No one would. He guessed he would still leave his melura years behind him, but they would go with a whimper, nothing to commemorate the occasion except the dank, cloying smell of filth and a few humble cellmates.

He spent a moment peering into the dark at Thalen. He could barely make out his form. Perhaps he could stand as First Steward, but would he know what to say or do? Sutter had always heard the same words, or near to them, when someone spoke the Change. A Reaper from Risill Ond would not be a bad choice, though, he thought. Not after the tale the scops had told.

He surveyed his cell companions from the pageant-wagons. Perhaps they would know the right words, and add something ceremonial besides. But the dark irony of it stole up on him—more of his old wounds. Even should they agree, Sutter wasn't sure he could ever stand with a wagon trouper.

But he still would not let his mind spiral down into his past.

And he lamented, for a long time in those small hours of night, his flight from the Hollows. Not in homesickness for the place, but in unspoken gratitude to the simple people who had given him a home and enough hope to think he deserved to ever leave the Hollows behind for something bigger, better. Leave, and cause them to suffer costs both practical and emotional.

Again he wished he'd had the chance to say a few things to his mother and father before this journey had begun. And just now he wondered if they'd be proud of him. He realized suddenly he wanted that. On the day of his Change, he wanted that most of all.

Then, as always, his thoughts turned to Tahn.

Now that fellow had some secrets.

A few he'd shared with Sutter just days ago on the banks of a deep river. But Sutter sensed more. And yet, none of that mattered. His friend had ever treated him well, something many in the Hollows found difficult due to his own unending jokes.

He hoped Tahn had survived his own beatings here in the Recityv dungeon. If he had, what would his friend do for his own Change? What would either of them do if they never escaped or were freed? Would the others find them? Why did a Sheason and Far come to the Hollows in the first place?

Sutter knew his solemn musings grew from his own beatings, lack of sleep, and the dreariness of this place.

He certainly was weary.

And not, he knew, simply from their flight since the Hollows. The costs were older, deeper.

So he lay back down on the stone, seeking escape in sleep for a few hours yet. And sleep took him quickly, easing the many pains.

Until another face rose up with the mists.

Until another waking dream.

Though this time, Sutter did not start or shiver quite so much. Perhaps because he grew more accustomed, or perhaps because the sadness of it tempered the fear.

He stared back for a long time into the vacant eyes of this one who soon would die.

CHAPTER SIXTY-SIX

Choices and Revelations

The echo of many feet brought Tahn half awake. The hallway beyond their cell door stirred with an unusually large number of guards. Then the sound of a key turning the lock caused Tahn to come full awake. Always before, the sound had brought to him a degree of hope. Today he did not turn to greet the guards. Instead, he kept vigil on the stone and waited for them to either leave his food or set to beating him again.

A harsh wash of light came suddenly into the cell. Tahn squinted against the intrusion, even with his back to the door. Murmuring voices interrupted the solitude as sharply as the light upon the stone stair, and soft shoes carried their owners down toward Tahn and Rolen's world. The guards moved about in hard soles, leaving Tahn to wonder what visitors these might be. He raised his head, the effort shooting a stabbing pain down his neck. The bright light blinded him, causing his eyes to water. From the corner of his vision he could see several people descending the stairs, dark shapes like the figures in his dreams.

"There," he heard one say.

A collection of feet, all shuffling gracefully down the steps. Slowly, Tahn's eyes adjusted. He blinked away the water and attempted to focus. Faces swam in and out, seeming familiar before blurring again.

One of the forms began to approach him, when a man beside her clasped her arm. "Patience, Anais. There will be time for reunion and mending. There is a dispute to be settled first."

Tahn knew this voice, but a haze remained over his mind. He struggled to sit up, managing only to roll onto his back. He panted shallowly from the effort. Though lying flat against the stone, he no longer had to support his head. He squinted against the light now directly in his eyes, and peered toward the gathering, anger growing in him that they stood and gawked as he lay bruised and winded on the first day of his alchera.

"What are you staring at?" he said, unable to invest it with the recrimination he'd intended, sputtering the words unevenly through his gasps.

No one replied. Tahn suddenly felt as though he were in a dream: vaguely familiar faces and voices, soft shoes, the quality of light thin yet penetrating.

Perhaps it had all been a dream: Rolen standing with him; the trembling of the guards at the Sheason's command; the taunts, the beatings. Perhaps he would yet wake to find that he slept in his Hollows bed and Wendra would have apples and cream on the iron for breakfast when he woke.

Then in his dream, one of the forms assembled at the foot of the stair detached itself and came toward him. The figure did not pause at the chalked line drawn upon the stone floor to indicate a prisoner's reach. The man stepped across it, fixed his eyes on Tahn, and fell to one knee beside him. The figure's head blocked the light from the door, becoming a misshapen silhouette in which Tahn could distinguish no face. He blinked, trying to clear his vision, and still saw nothing. The man took Tahn's hand, lifting it into the light from the door and seeming to study the mark there. Gently, the stranger placed it back on the floor, and turned to the rest.

"You must see this for yourself," the man said. And again Tahn thought he knew the voice, though it came with more rasp than he thought he remembered, as though too much wind and heat had traveled through it.

A second figure then came fully into the light. Tahn thought she looked old, though not fragile. She walked with a cane, her slow steps accented by the tapping of her stick upon his hard bed.

"Be sure he behaves," the woman said.

"He's in no condition to threaten you," the man above Tahn replied. He stood and stepped aside, making room for her. "This archer you've chained, Helaina, is the boy Tahn."

The woman tapped her way closer and bent over him. A look of understanding bloomed in her eyes. She dropped her cane and fell to her knees, taking Tahn's face in her wrinkled hands. Tears welled over her lower eyelids, falling directly onto Tahn's chin. All in a moment, Tahn witnessed joy, relief, concern, and shame. The old woman thrust her face into Tahn's neck and cried in silent heaves. Hot tears rolled down his skin into his collar. He was confused, but grateful for the warmth of both the woman's tears and embrace.

The woman repeated something over and over, but Tahn could not make it out, her cheek muffling his ear. When the tears ceased, she drew back, looking through eyes already clouded with age. An expression of grief stood on her brow as she put her forehead to Tahn's and whispered, "Good Will."

The woman let go of Tahn's face, wiped her eyes and cheeks, and extended a hand for help in standing. The first man came to her aid.

"Release him," she said, at which a sentry rushed forward and set upon Tahn's manacles. The rattle of the irons stabbed at his tender skin, but he had no energy to complain. "Take him to the levate healers immediately. We will join you shortly. Do not leave him until I come to you." She pivoted. "Recorder." The man with the ledger scurried to her side. "Write that Recityv honors the season of the Charter. The ordinance of Preserved Will is just in this matter and prevails upon the High Council. The prisoners are free." She tapped his ledger. "See that the Court of Judicature is made aware. I will come to you later to be sure that it is done. Go."

Tahn watched as people leapt at her bidding, this strange woman who a moment ago had wept upon his neck. She pointed to a second guard, this one the man who'd poured his water upon the stone floor. The guard strode swiftly to her and went to one knee. "You will release the other. Is he in need of a levate's hand?"

"I regret to say that he is, my Lady."

"Take him likewise to the healer," she said, her tone indicting. "See that no incident causes either of these boys another whit of harm."

The first guard finished removing Tahn's shackles and hoisted him as easily as a father might a child. Tahn's muscles sang painfully at the sudden jostling, but he bit back his cries. The guard began to carry him off. A sudden bright bolt of clarity and action filled him.

"Wait," Tahn said. The guard did not stop. "Wait!" Tahn yelled, filling the chamber with a violent threat. This time the guard halted, sending a look of inquiry to the woman for instruction.

Tahn ignored them both and turned toward the shadow where Rolen remained cloaked and forgotten.

"You must free him, too," Tahn said. He clenched his teeth against pain drumming in every cut and sore. "If I am innocent, if the man I cut free is—"

"Tahn." It was Rolen. His voice came like a calm out of the shadow-veiled corner, interrupting his plea. A moment after, the Sheason stepped slowly into the light. "Do not worry for me. Remember, I chose this."

"But Rolen," Tahn protested. "They see it was a trap. They are letting me go because the man I cut free was innocent. You should not have to—"

"Tahn." Again a voice of serenity and assurance. "Whether a trap or not, I have violated the law. I knew what I was doing. And I have new strength in my confinement after what I have seen here today."

"What do you mean?" Tahn asked. "This isn't fair. It isn't right." He wrestled to free himself from the guard's arms, but his body held little fight.

"I will not accept a pardon from the regent that would bring criticism of her." He turned to look at the woman.

Realization spread through Tahn, and he ceased his struggle.

In the same moment, he saw clearly for the first time the faces of those standing near the wall: Vendanj, Wendra, Braethen, Penit, and Mira. Even in the dark, even weakened, he could see her grey eyes, and even now they lit fire in his loins. A crash of emotions descended upon him. His heart swelled to see his sister safe, to see his old friend. Even the sight of Vendanj was comforting. Emotion tightened his throat and he could not speak. Soon Sutter would join them, too. And as he reeled from intense gratitude and the alarming words of the woman Rolen had called regent, Vendanj approached him.

"You are weak, but you are well," Vendanj said.

"Vendanj," Tahn began. His mouth betrayed him, his tongue clucking dryly and robbing him of words. He licked his lips and swallowed. "Vendanj, don't let them do this, please. You have to know about Rolen. He is one of your order. He was only trying to help a dying child, and for that he is condemned. Please."

Vendanj gave Tahn a watchful look, then stepped past him toward Rolen.

"Is this how you intend to serve, fraterna?" Vendanj asked.

"It is," Rolen answered. "If I seek to avoid punishment for my crime, the strife between the people and the councils will grow." He smiled weakly. "I do not believe in this law, but I am bound to it as others are bound to the rules that govern them. What servant am I if *I* choose which laws are just?"

"We will not agree on that," Vendanj said. "And I make no such covenant. If you ask it, I will accept the risk for you, and remove you from this place."

"No," Rolen said. "This is how it must be. I've no regret." He looked past Vendanj to Tahn. "I've found meaning in it beyond merely maintaining my oath." He returned his eyes to Vendanj. "Yours is a great stewardship, my brother. Give to it well."

Vendanj inclined his head. Rolen did likewise.

The guard started away, bearing Tahn with him. As they mounted the stair, eyes followed them up—all save the woman's and Rolen's.

At the door Tahn reached out and grasped the wall, stopping them again. He looked down at the prison cell, and saw the regent in her resplendent dress facing the filthy Sheason, who yet stood nobly before her. "I will not forget your gift, Rolen. Thank you."

The Sheason turned and looked up at him. "My friend, it was the most honored moment of my life."

The guard bore him away.

Tahn lay still while attendants worked swiftly but methodically through their ministrations. One woman wearing a scarf tight around her face applied a cool salve to his wrists and ankles. The cream smelled of peppermint and nut oils and burned icily, soothingly. Afterward, she wrapped the areas with clean, white strips of fabric. A second woman soaked a rag in a pungent liquid and rubbed it over the purple bruises that covered Tahn's body. Another forced him to sip water from a glass, and washed his head and face with a damp towel.

When they finished, another woman came and dismissed them. She walked around the bed, eyeing Tahn's naked body with observant detachment. Tahn wished to cover his nakedness; he'd never been exposed in such a way in front of a woman except in the baths of Myrr. She made a small grunt and came forward, leaning over his bed and looking at each of his eyes by turns. She took her hands from the folds of her heavy robe and placed her thumbs beside Tahn's nose, her fingers cradling the sides of his head. A look of confusion rose in her.

Just then Vendanj came in. "Thank you for your help. I will see to what is left."

The woman did not acknowledge the Sheason.

"Do as I say," Vendanj said. The command in his voice caused the woman to remove her hands from Tahn's face. Her head bobbed up and a faltering expression passed over her.

"This one, he is not whole. He—"

"He is weak, Anais," the Sheason said, more gently. "Thank you. I will tend to him." Vendanj motioned toward the door.

The woman tucked her hands into her robe and scuttled from the room. The pallor in her face left Tahn disquieted. Or perhaps it was the way her lip quivered. But then, Vendanj had that affect on a lot of people.

As the woman exited, a set of guards brought in Sutter, his arms holding onto their shoulders for support. One eye was swollen shut, and dried blood was caked upon his collar. His friend did not use his left foot.

"What happened to you?" Tahn asked.

"I complained about my food," Sutter said as the guards hefted him into a second bed. "I see you've had it pretty light." With his one good eye, Sutter looked around at the spacious room.

"Yeah, they just don't care much for root-diggers here." Tahn chuckled, the laughter descending into his chest in a fit of wracking coughs.

"Save your talk for later," Vendanj admonished.

The Sheason came to Tahn's side as the first three women reentered and began dressing Sutter's wounds. "You've undergone your Change," Vendanj said. It was not a question.

"This morning," Tahn answered. "I knew the turn of the cycle."

"Rolen stood for you." Again the Sheason spoke with certainty.

"Yes. Though I'm not sure why we get so excited over this day. I think I might prefer to live my life as melura . . ."

Tahn thought Vendanj's lip curled ever so slightly into an honest grin. The Sheason drew his thin wooden case from inside his cloak and produced a sprig. Rather than hand it to Tahn, Vendanj placed it on Tahn's tongue. The bit of greenery dissolved quickly, leaving a hint of something nearly peppermint, though not quite. Almost immediately, Tahn began to feel a relaxation of the stiffness in his flesh.

The Sheason moved to Sutter's side and placed a hand on his eye. Vendanj gave to Sutter a sprig as he had to Tahn, and shared a long stare with Nails as the three women finished their dressings and made a silent exit. Tahn had the impression the Sheason was looking past Sutter's eyes. Unbidden, the image of his friend cowering naked beneath a leagueman's bed flashed in his mind. *Could Vendanj see such things?*

"You've had your Change as well," Vendanj said, still looking at Sutter.

Nails nodded.

"Let's have your story," Tahn insisted. "I've just got to know what low one stood steward for you."

Sutter laughed without humor. Then he focused on the Sheason. "The League has arrested a seat holder under false pretense, Vendanj. They mean to assume the seat of Risill Ond in his place."

"The Reapers," Vendanj said softly.

"I fear worse than mere imprisonment for him. Is there anything you can do?" Sutter's words grew more anxious.

"Be still, Sutter. I will speak to the regent about it." Vendanj put a reassuring hand on Sutter's chest. "Now rest, both of you."

Just as the levate women left, Wendra burst into the room and rushed to Tahn's side. "Thank the Will and Sky." She gave him as firm a hug as she dared, and kissed him on the cheek. "What a mess you got yourself into." Her mouth tugged into a smile to belie her scolding. "What happened?"

Tahn gave Vendanj a look. "Later," he said, lifting his hand to gently take hers. "I'm kind of tired right now."

"Of course, I'm sorry." She kissed him again, and turned as Penit came in and stood beside her. "We're all safe," she added, putting her arm around Penit's shoulders.

Tahn noted the look Wendra gave the boy. In a glance, it reminded him of the motherhood she'd lost, but also something else. Something had changed. It seemed more like a mask than like the desperately powerful protectiveness she'd shown him before. He shook the feeling away; he'd been through his own share of troubles. Everything he saw was bound to seem somehow different. Perhaps the Change brought this perspective.

Mira stepped into the room. The Far came to Tahn's side, freezing him with a look. "A lot of grit to cut a man loose from the gallows, even if he was a leagueman." And she gave him her small smile. "A day in irons is worth a hundred in battle. A man once held captive fights with more purpose. Do not forget those days."

The sight of her helped his spirits as much as the healing levate hands.

"I'm glad you are well." And she returned finally the impetuous kiss he'd given her some days before, pressing soft lips briefly to his cheek.

He barely had time to think how slow the kiss seemed in counterpoint to the precise speed of most of her life when Braethen came in carrying Tahn's weapons and pack and cloak. At the sight of it all, Tahn sat up. "Bring them here," he ordered.

"Easy, Tahn," Braethen said. "You should be resting. Your things are safe."

"Now. Bring them here now!" Tahn insisted.

"All right," Braethen said. "Nice to see you, too."

Tahn shook his head. "It's important."

As Tahn tore his cloak from Braethen's hands, behind them, four guards strode into the room. Two took position against the wall left of the door, two to the right. Then came the woman they had called regent. She walked carefully, placing her cane in a steady rhythm. Behind her strode the man who'd first knelt at Tahn's side in the cell. Everyone in the room bowed, except the man behind the regent, whose weathered face held little emotion.

The last to enter was an old man who wore at his throat the same symbol as Vendanj. A snowy white beard fell upon his chest, and wavy white hair hung to his shoulders. Spectacles adorned his bulbous nose, and the man moved with the deliberateness of the regent, his steps careful. Once he'd entered, he closed the door, and nodded at Vendanj before turing his attention on the regent.

"No doubt," the old woman began, "this has much to do with the rumors that skulk the council walls of Solath Mahnus." She spoke with a voice not to be crossed. "You know my heart in this, Sheason. I have called for the Convocation of Seats. Detractors accuse me of politics, but I'm too old to be concerned with my own legacy. I sent the birds and criers because there are reports of Bar'dyn in the south, because every day the gate is flooded with those who've abandoned their homes for the protection of Recityv's walls. I suspect it is much the same in cities across the nations of the south.

"Though I can't abide the opportunists"—she scowled—"men and women putting on colors, others adopting a sigil, all in order to compete for commissions or sit in seats on councils dead since the Second Promise. A hundred generations or more and now they swagger in all pomp and posture. It is a disgrace, and it's become the single reason I am glad so many of the Promise Seats remain empty.

"No matter," she finished. "What is it that coaxes Grant from his Scar?"

Grant made no response; he simply looked at the regent's back.

When Vendanj answered, he looked at Tahn. "The same urgency that compels you to fully recall your High Council and Convocation of Seats, my Lady: the threat of the Quiet. He bears us company to the Heights of Restoration to test the fate of one against the design of the Will."

"You don't mean that Grant intends to stand at Restoration." The old woman's voice held a hint of amusement.

Vendanj then turned and came to Tahn's bedside.

"You will rest today," Vendanj said, looking down at him. "We cannot wait any longer than that. Before a week's time, we must come to Restoration. If we do not, then whatever else we do may be without meaning."

Tahn started to ask a hundred questions burning in his mind. The Sheason held up a hand before he could utter a word. "Save your strength, Tahn. There are things to discuss, I know. And I'll want to know what has happened to you since Sedagin, who you've met, every detail. But it must wait. There are preparations that I must make."

Tahn struggled up to his elbows. "No!" he shouted. The effort weakened him, and his head dropped back to the pillow. "I will not follow you another step without knowing about these Heights of Restoration."

Vendanj stared down at him, a thoughtful expression on his face. Then softly, though loud enough all could hear, he began to speak. "The Heights of Restoration lay in the far north and east, beyond the Soliel Stretches and deep within the Saeculorum Mountains. The Heights are a series of great cliffs known to some as Creation's End, to others as Endland, and in some histories as the Well of Worlds."

The Sheason looked over at Braethen, whose rapt attention yet conveyed a sense that he knew these things. "Beyond those cliffs lay the mists of the abyss. A primordial power lives within those mists, a power that exists nowhere else . . . a power to test the spirit."

Vendanj looked back at Tahn, fixing him with a firm but reassuring stare. "That has been our final destination from the beginning, Tahn, since fleeing the Hollows."

The words chilled him. Tahn wrestled with what suddenly felt like a certainty: This Restoration had everything to do with him.

"The Quiet have entered the Hollows?" the regent asked, clearly disconcerted.

The Sheason nodded. "We were chased from there by Velle and other creatures from the Bourne. On the north face of the Sedagin we were separated. It is good Will and a favored Sky that all of us came here alive."

"Tahn is one of these from the Hollows?" The regent stared at Tahn, but seemed to be seeing something more distant.

"He is, Helaina." Vendanj turned to face the regent. "It was hidden from you because of the eavesdropping ears of Solath Mahnus. The Scar is safe, but it is the safety of men. The Hollows offered the consecration of the First Ones, and good men besides."

"But the Quiet have entered there?" She shut her eyes.

"They have," Vendanj said. His words came like an epitaph. "Changes corrupt the old ways, all the things we thought we knew." Vendanj looked at Grant. "Denolan looks much like the man you exiled so long ago because time has little meaning in the Scar. The cycles do not turn in its earth or sky as rapidly as they do beyond its borders. The curse of the Velle still seeps into its soil and spreads like contagion. The protections we have enjoyed tear apart. I have seen the monstrous rank and file of the wastes beyond the Pall tread upon the fertility of our choicest groves while governments bicker over station and influence, while secret alliances are sealed in the antechambers of base taverns and grand palaces alike. Men and women, who know nothing of the dark covenants they make, enter rash and bloody contracts as the veil breaks and the Shadow of the Hand comes to fulfill its bargain."

Tahn felt instantly cold. Penit curled into Wendra's hip, Tahn's sister clutching her chest defensively. Everyone looked on agape. Only Mira's stoic face and the unmoving expression of this new man, Grant, seemed indifferent to the chilling words.

"What of the Mal and Northwatch?" the regent asked.

"There is no word from the Mal Nations." Vendanj lifted a hand, palm up, and then turned it over. "Many would no sooner journey there than to the Bourne itself." Vendanj lowered his hand. "Northwatch has likely fallen. I doubt we can expect any warning or defense from them."

The regent blinked and leaned heavily on her cane. "We'll need to know if the Hand is fully open," she said. She lowered her voice, seeming to speak to herself, "And we a divided front."

"The Whited One stirs against the old bonds," Vendanj said, "hoping to call an end to creation and lead us to the day when the air itself is as final as grave soil . . . Delighast." At this, Mira gave Vendanj a wary glance. "His darkness spreads one soul at a time, as some are robbed of life and others offer themselves up to the One in exchange for empty promises. From both is extracted what is needed of Forda I'Forza to meet his purposes.

"And those that have always followed him, those races sealed behind the veil, will come. A long time in the Bourne are they. Their hatred and envy are powerful."

Tahn suddenly remembered the strange words he'd heard from the Bar'dyn as he and Sutter had fled the black winds from the north face: *You run only from lies . . . your lies and the lies of your fathers will we show you.* He wanted to ask the Sheason what it meant, but he felt weak, and still struggled with the feeling that Restoration had to do with him, and that even now it hid more secrets from him.

"And against this you take a child to Restoration," the regent said, a hint of confusion in her words.

"Precisely because of his youth, my lady. But no longer a child," Vendanj replied. "He has passed his Change. We race time now to reach the Heights."

"And what of the others?" The regent lifted her cane and swept it around the room. "What justifies their risk?"

Vendanj's head turned a bit aside, his eyebrows rising. "Their choice," Vendanj said finally, as though he could not help but believe the regent knew the answer. His face again became placid. "And more, my Lady, but none of the rest matters."

The answer seemed to satisfy her, but she did not look pleased. Tahn thought this elderly woman's stately eyes yet flashed talons and teeth.

The regent turned to steal a look at Artixan, who lowered his head in a half nod. Somehow, this put her more at ease. When she looked back, a resolved expression showed upon her face. "Very well, Sheason. What help are we to you?"

"An envoy must be sent immediately to the library at Qum'rahm'se. Quiet-given will seek it out to own or destroy. It is known, even to them, to be the greatest repository of knowledge we have on the covenant language. It will become among their primary goals to restore to themselves a conversant tongue with the lost language, since it has the power to make or unmake inherent in its use. Send General Van Steward's best hundred men. Armored wagons. And bring the entire library here where it can be kept safe."

Tahn suddenly remembered his cloak. Quickly, he thrust his hands inside, and sighed with relief at the shape of the sticks still concealed within. He'd not had an opportunity to locate Dolun'pel, and decided that he would have to trust the Sheason with the contents of the parchments hidden within his garment. He pulled them out and held them up. "Sutter and I were forced from the road out of Squim. We traveled east to the river, then north, where we smelled fire."

Vendanj took the sticks from Tahn's trembling fingers. The Sheason seemed to know the end of the tale from the beginning.

Tahn told of Edholm the scrivener and the melted rock of Qum'rahm'se Library. He explained how they had gone inside and how the scrivener had made them each write an account of what had happened, and how he told them to carry the parchments in these sticks to Recityv.

Vendanj broke the seals and withdrew the testimonies. He read Sutter's, then Tahn's. Next he rolled open Edholm's parchment and looked it over. As his eyes scanned the lines, a still, calm anger touched his features. When he finished, he lowered the scroll, his fury emanating from him in palpable waves. Finally, he held up the fourth, larger stick but did not open it.

"The library is burned. Nothing remains." Vendanj replaced the scrolls into their respective sticks. "There is no copy now of the Tract of Desolation. Translation would be impossible without the generations of research and scholarship it inspired. What we might have hoped to gain for ourselves of the covenant language is lost." Vendanj turned to the regent. "Send word to Descant. They no longer have the protection of redundancy. If something should happen to the Tract, we have the memory of its singers alone by which to recall it."

Tahn's mind raced. A dozen stories told at Northsun descended upon him in a rush, things he hadn't thought of in years, tales he'd read to himself in the waning hours of day. Everyone held their silence in the wake of the revelation. Tahn noted a kind of serenity in Mira's face that either welcomed death or was not concerned over the loss at Qum'rahm'se. He lay captivated—maybe more now that he'd passed the Change—by the Far's steadfast calm. And her soft, luminous eyes.

Vendanj continued. "Regent, the hundred that you might have sent to Qum'rahm'se send instead to keep watch over the cathedral. Dress them in common clothes. Metal and color would invite speculation. But chance not to leave it unprotected. The Tract of Desolation, though a fable to this season of men, is a keystone we cannot afford to lose. Without it, we would be unmade."

Penit tapped Wendra, who had pulled him so tightly against herself that when she released him, he drew a ragged breath. She smiled an apology, and he amiably took her hand. Behind a grave expression, she, too, seemed to harbor secrets. Tahn hated the look of it. Wendra had always, even at work, whether forking out the barn or washing the cook pots, worn a smile.

The regent cleared her throat, a small sound. "It will take a vote of the High Council, but it will be done. We will put to the test our new Child's Voice." The regent looked down at Penit. "You should know the boy has shown the highest honor and wisdom, Sheason, refusing to take the ribbon at the Lesher Roon so that another better suited might sit at my table. His personal sacrifice for the common good emboldens me. For that, I nearly gave him the seat. But it would seem now that he has other works to perform."

Vendanj gave Penit a knowing look, eyed Tahn briefly, and then turned again to the boy. "Indeed he has."

Tahn did not like the way Vendanj said it. It was the ominous, multiple-layered speech of the Sheason. And the look in Vendanj's eye felt like nothing so much as a farmer looking over his spring stock. It reminded Tahn of the indifference he'd previously witnessed in the Sheason. He must not forget it. And when he looked over at Sutter, Tahn saw his friend's obvious concern for the lad. Clearly, Sutter, too, had heard some second meaning in the Sheason's words.

"What needs to be done?" Grant interjected. "The boys will sleep until dark. I don't intend to spend one unnecessary moment in the marble arrogance of Solath Mahnus."

The regent stiffened. She rounded slowly on the man to face him. "If it weren't more cruel to leave you in exile, I'd have you strung up this hour. What a waste of a man you are. I'll allow you to accompany the Sheason for his sake. But curb your tongue until you find yourself outside with the animals, or you'll wear stripes as easily as your boots. I may be old, but I am *not* too old to exercise the powers of my office."

A terrible authority filled the regent's voice as she spoke, something Tahn did not believe could be learned simply by filling a role. The guards beside the door straightened at the sound of it.

Grant stood still beneath her threat. Without any trepidation, he spoke in a soft voice. "Does all this not show you that I was right even then?" He returned the regent's stare a moment more, then opened the door and departed, closing it softly.

"Go with him," Vendanj said to Mira. "Make all things ready."

In the silence that followed Mira's departure, Braethen walked a bundle of clothes to Sutter, laying his sword at the foot of his bed. "Sweet of them not to pawn my belongings," Sutter quipped.

Braethen smiled without conviction. The others ignored him.

Wendra said, "Penit should not come with us. He is a boy. Whatever needs to be done at the Heights of Restoration can't possibly involve him." She paused, looking into unsympathetic faces. "I won't allow it."

Instead of responding to her, Vendanj walked around Tahn's bed and knelt in front of Penit. He peered into the boy's eyes. "Child, it is a dangerous thing we do. If you come, you may be asked to pay a very high price. An ultimate price. Do you understand?"

Penit seemed to consider it.

"It is your choice," Vendanj went on. "No one will choose for you."

"He is a boy," Wendra repeated. "Ten years old. How can you expect him to decide this?"

Vendanj turned impatient eyes on Wendra. "I would rather this wait, Anais. But it cannot. No one stopped you joining us in the Hollows when you were asked to come. Penit may choose this for himself. He is aware of the risk."

Wendra began to argue, but Vendanj pinned her with a stare. "Wendra, your concern is noble, but you are not his mother."

Words hung in Wendra's open mouth. The Sheason's statement had opened a wound as surely as if he had cut her. In her cheeks, Tahn saw the look of winter bark—cold, inflexible, but also perhaps strong, resilient.

The Sheason returned his attention to Penit. "Choose."

Penit recoiled under his stern gaze. "I will go," he said, turning into Wendra and hugging her belly.

Vendanj stood. Tahn thought he would look satisfied, but the Sheason merely turned to the regent. "Will you require a moment alone here?"

"No," she said, shaking her head. "I have much to do to prepare for the convocation." She then moved with her cane to Tahn's bedside. Though her back stooped slightly, she remained regal. Her clouded blue eyes peered down at him; Tahn thought he saw a concern behind them. But at last she put a soft hand on his arm and said, "Watch safe." Then she turned and brushed past Vendanj. The guards led her out. And the man with the white hair and beard, bearing the order symbol at his throat, extended toward Vendanj a cupped palm facing the floor. Vendanj did the same, and Tahn saw an admiration in the token. Then the older man followed the regent from the room.

"How can we come quickly to the Heights of Restoration?" Braethen asked as the door closed. "The legend of Restoration puts it in the Saeculorum Mountains, by my sky. That is weeks . . . months of travel by the fastest horse."

"There are ways," the Sheason said. He folded his arms and gave Wendra a knowing look. "Have you been to the cathedral?" he asked her.

Wendra had taken to running her hands through Penit's hair, her eyes far away. She looked up, startled. When she saw who asked, her eyes drooped as if reminded again of what the Sheason had said. She nodded and quickly looked away, focusing again on Penit, who continued to hold her close.

"When evening meals are done, and most the city is to bed, we'll leave Solath Mahnus and find your cathedral, Anais. The talents there will make our journey short." Vendanj drew a long breath. "Sodalist, it is time to look closely at Ogea's books. Learn from them what you can of Restoration."

"You haven't been there?" Braethen asked.

The thought that Vendanj might be leading them somewhere he didn't know, and then expected Braethen to assist him, filled Tahn with sudden anxiety.

"I have," Vendanj answered. "You have not." The response made Tahn feel no less concerned. The last time he'd heard Ogea speak, the reader had shouted unreal things from Hambley's roof.

What might Braethen learn if he begins looking through those books?

Tahn wasn't sure he wanted to find out.

Vendanj took the scroll of Edholm the scrivener and tucked it into the lining of his cloak. "I will return after evening meal. Eat well. Penit, walk with me. We have things to discuss."

The Sheason and the boy left without a further word, leaving the four from the Hollows alone in the room. Tahn rested back onto his pillow, and sighed.

"I want him at my next birthday," Sutter jested.

The rest stifled a bout of giggles that lifted the pall they all felt. Soon they spoke hurriedly of all that had happened to them, sharing freely and laughing in amazement over wondrous events. Tahn kept back a few things, unwilling to worry his friends, and unable to shake the Sheason's words to Penit: *an ultimate price.*

CHAPTER SIXTY-SEVEN

Tokens

Vendanj strode the marbled halls of Solath Mahnus. He had an appointment to keep. Or rather, the regent and his old friend Artixan had to receive him. There were matters to discuss, and he would no longer be patient or silent. So he did not notice the grandeur of the halls, the history engraved in the marble, the sculpture and art depicting kings and war and the beautiful promise of the land that filled the high vaulted ceilings of the seat of the regent and her council.

This night, Helaina and Artixan would take his counsel.

Mira accompanied him. Vedanj had told her he meant to visit the regent and the venerable Sheason by himself. But she'd insisted, which was unusual for her. So he acceded to her request.

He knew where they would be: The regent's High Office, the singular room at the top of Solath Mahnus, the eight sides of which each showed a unique view of Recityv. After the events of the day, there would be strategy to create; she always started with Artixan, as well she should.

At the final stair, two of her elite Emerit guard stepped in front of Vendanj and Mira. Other watches on their ascent through Solath Mahnus had deferred to the three-ring sigil at Vendanj's neck. These did not.

"I am not Sheason Rolen," Vendanj said coolly. "If I'd wanted to harm the regent, she would already be dead. You know I have been in her company today already."

The two shared a wary look, then stepped back. Vendanj climbed the long marble stair, this one windowless and dark, and at the top did not knock, but threw back the double doors and went in. Mira slipped in silently and stood like a shadow just inside the door against the wall.

"Do join us," the regent said.

"I told you he would come," Artixan said to the regent with a smile.

"Yes, but you did not say he would show such disrespect." She gave Vendanj a measured look.

"I do not have time for etiquette or the show of deference. You know of my esteem, my Lady, but we are running out of time." Vendanj shut the doors behind him.

"It is worse than you know." Artixan stepped in front of the great window that faced the south. "The leader of the League, Ascendent Staned, has called for a meeting of the High Council to review the regent's special clemency in releasing the two boys."

"That is the regent's privilege. It has been a part of Recityv law for ages." Vendanj looked at the old woman. "Do not allow him to convene such a hearing. It will undermine you utterly. And we will need the strength of your office when the Convocation of Seats begins."

The regent shared a wan smile. "It is too late. I knew that releasing Tahn and the others would invite Roth to this action. Long has he wished to limit the power of this office—if he cannot have it for himself. He likewise is lobbying for shared control of the Recityv army. Van Steward is well loved and a mighty general, so that's a political front on which the Ascendant is currently losing. But," she said, "if he prevails in this attack on my right to overturn the decisions at court, it won't be long before the office of regent will be merely ceremonial." She looked around the grand High Office.

Vendanj spared a look at the greatroom, a sanctuary built atop the several halls and palaces that comprised a man-made mountain in the heart of Recityv. Here she kept her precious books, strategic war maps, and other secrets a regent must have. It spoke, too, of her refinement, the white marble bedecked sparingly, but elegantly.

"What of your journey to Restoration?" Artixan still looked south at the window.

"When the boys are rested, we will go. They are still weak."

The regent took a seat at her long desk. "You'll need to leave quickly, tonight, under the cover of dark. And know that even then, I may be compelled to add my guard to pursue you. Roth does not remain idle."

Vendanj nodded understanding.

"Restoration, Vendanj. Do you believe in the boy?" Artixan asked.

"He has many questions. And they are worthy questions. But they cloud his mind." Vendanj crossed the room and looked from the northwest window. "Nothing is certain but that the Quiet descends upon us. No amount of rhetoric in these halls can make that untrue. The League's denial is either naive or bears a more insidious meaning. Either way, they are dividing the people's attention and leaving us all unprepared."

"The people's attention is not all that is divided, Vendanj." Artixan came into the middle of the High Office. "You know this. The Order of Sheason itself is fractured. If you fail at Restoration, support for the way you would have the order meet this threat will also fail. Your only recourse will be to become an outlaw." He sighed. "You are a mere half step from that now."

Vendanj turned on them. "There is more. The League has arrested the seat holder from Risill Ond. After all this time, and their peaceful seclusion, they answered the call of the regent's convocation only to be treated to the hospitality of your dungeons. The League will take that vote in your convocation if you do not free the man and set it straight."

At this news, the regent's brow furrowed.

"And if that seat, how many others have been compromised?" Artixan's question came low and sad and ominous.

"I leave you to deal with the League leadership. But as for the rest . . ." Vendanj walked to the long table that served as the regent's desk. He looked across its polished surface at her weary face, feeling some pity but also indignation. He recalled a list of names and an infant's grave and fire again touched his heart. With steady fingers he drew open his pouch and tossed a snake's head and a swatch of a child's blanket onto the desk before her.

The regent recoiled not in fear but surprise, then studied the artifacts. Artixan came close.

"The ignominy you foisted upon Denolan may have been warranted, but the sentence was not. This cradle at the edge of the Scar is finished."

"You do not have the authority—"

"I *claim* the authority!" Vendanj railed. "I bear no hate for you, Helaina. But with the power of the Will that I bear I will strike down even you if you do not put an end to this vile chain that keeps Denolan there."

"You forget yourself!" The regent stood.

Artixan came to stand at her right shoulder. "Vendanj, your passion makes you unwise."

"No," he said. "I see more clearly than you both because I walk in the places where the suffering is dire and the cries of the afflicted go unanswered and unremembered." He took up the swatch of blanket, his heart aching at its very touch. The token brought quiet reverence to what he said next. "Not three days since did I come upon your cradle in the Scar with your exile, and found a babe dead, bitten by a viper brought down out of the Bourne. A sign, a message."

The regent and her Sheason counselor looked at the snake's head, understanding in their eyes.

"The Quiet knows how you fetter your former Emerit, Helaina, and they persecute him by stealing the life of one too young to even know it needed defense." Vendanj stared them down. "It ends. Now."

They stared back, beginning, he thought, to bear some grief over the loss. They said nothing, he hoped, because their throats were tight with the awful image of what had happened.

"Grant will stay in the Scar if you ask him to, if that's what you deem fit for his treason. But he goes with me to Restoration—though he would rather not leave his barren home, and though he no longer feels at ease in the company of men—and he goes to help these children out of the Hollows try to answer a need that is larger than they realize. I don't know how long we will be gone. But the one thing I would spare him, the one thing you should wish to spare us all, is the concern that a babe may die if he is not there to receive it.

"And mark me: I will not bury another babe. The day I do, I will forsake these vestments and make a mortal enemy of any who put such children at risk."

The regent heard the threat but did not falter under Vendanj's hard glare; neither did she rebuke him.

"Do this," Vendanj finished, "or when we return from the end of all things, kill Denolan. Execute him as you do any traitor. You know him, Helaina. He would stand up for that."

The regent looked back thoughtfully. "Yes," she said, "he would."

Vendanj's wrath receded. He looked at these old friends. "I ask this," he said, "because it is right. If you search your hearts, you will know it, too."

The regent reached out, and Vendanj put the portion of the child's blanket in her hand. As she looked down, tears came to her eyes. For that instant, the regent was replaced by the mother who had lost her child. Without looking up, she nodded. "No more children will I send to the cradle," she said softly. "Please tell Denolan."

Vendanj reached out and placed his hand over the regent's as she smoothed the child's blanket. "Thank you, Anais."

He looked up at Artixan, whose wrinkled face held a glint of pride despite the roughness he'd seen in Vendanj. *Each servant has his way,* the look said. And for his part, Vendanj had meant every word he'd uttered. In some things, you went all the way, or not at all.

"I meant to ask you," Artixan said. "What was in the fourth scrivener stick? What did it hold?"

Vendanj looked past the regent and the aging Sheason to the window that showed a sweeping vista of the west. "I have not opened it yet. My heart restrains me. But I know its purpose, and I dread the day that breaking that seal becomes necessary. I pray it never does."

He then remembered a promise he had made, and added, "Our friend Ogea has gone to his earth. It was the Quiet that brought him to it." Vendanj paused, reflecting on the reader. "He wanted you to know that it was something you taught him which helped him evade the Bar'dyn long enough to reach the Hollows before his wounds overcame him."

Vendanj had turned to leave, his business done, when Mira stepped into the room's center and took the regent's attention.

"And what would you say to us, Mira Far? I would hope to be better used by your words than I have been by your friend's." The regent offered a slight smile.

Mira stared silently for a moment at the woman, sparing a last thought for what she was about to do. The regent looked back, still mighty in spirit and with the command and loyalty of an army, not to mention the favor of many nations, though not all. "I have a trade to make. One you can ill afford to ignore."

The regent shared a look with Artixan and even Vendanj, whose eyes still registered some surprise that Mira had chosen to speak at all, and with a bargain no less. "Go on," the regent said.

"Your Convocation of Seats will not be full this third time, any more than it was the second or first ages ago." Mira held the regent's steady stare. "And this time, my Lady, with all due respect, anything short of *full* participation dooms your efforts before they are begun. Do you disagree?"

The regent paused to consider before responding. In her eyes, Mira saw the weight of a lifetime of experience. "No, I don't disagree. But then, what does full participation mean? We have never had the Mal Nations join us, nor the lands across the seas. And those few principalities that haven't lent us their swords don't add much to our political or military strength anyway—"

"The Far have never answered your call," Mira cut in. "Both prior requests that the Far king attend the convocation to represent his quiet, distant nation went unanswered."

The regent sat forward in her chair, anticipation of what was coming clear on her brow. "No, they have not. And yet, the Convocation of Seats has prevailed anyway."

There was challenge in the regent's words. But Mira knew it was hollow.

Artixan came up close, staring over the regent's head. "Be wary of what you say, Mira Far. In the seclusion of the High Office the regent is more herself, but always she is the reigning voice in Recityv and all of Vohnce. So mind your words and promises."

Mira had already weighed what came next. She leveled her gaze. "Regent of Vohnce, my sister is the Far queen, or was until several days ago, when she passed from this life."

"I am sorry to hear it," the old woman said.

"Thank you, my Lady." Mira paused a moment, for what she was about to commit was not only unprecedented, but had many ramifications. "I will guarantee that King Elan, or whoever the rightful successor may now be, will return here promptly to take the Far seat. And may the convocation be blessed by our presence."

The regent stared, unbelieving. Mira knew that other races and kingdoms long ago had ceased to depend on the Far, so much so that most no longer believed—if they ever had—that her people existed. "And what would you have in trade?" the regent asked.

Without hesitation, Mira replied, "The freedom of the leagueman framed in our dissent today."

The regent began to shake her head. "No, that would undermine my power—"

"On the contrary, your decision in this would show to your people that you are not afraid to make decisions that defy the League. And it would have the added benefit of letting your people know that you are not afraid to have the Sheason in the streets to do their duty." Mira then waited while the regent and her counselor thought.

"How can you guarantee the actions of the Far king?"

Mira nodded in appreciation of the question. "You'll have to trust me. But if you need a witness to my honor, Vendanj can speak it well enough."

The regent finally stood again, and came around her long table to stand in front of Mira. She stared at one eye, then the other, and seemed to wait for some internal question to solidify. "Why?" she asked. "What is it to you if he dies?"

It was a cold question, Mira thought. But not unexpected from a woman who had sent armies to war, where lives were lost. Mira wondered if the regent still would have asked the question if she'd seen the mother and daughter grieving in the small room beneath the gallery. "Eventually you'll have to decide if Recityv will continue to follow the growing ignorance that would ultimately enslave it, or recognize the war that no longer waits, but comes against you even now. I have seen the smallest hints of the war that is about to come upon you." Mira's sharp gaze did not relent, and she made sure the regent noted every word that came next. "Your Convocation of Seats will be a magnificent failure in your hour of need, unless the Far join with men to repel the Quiet, now and for good."

"But what is it about the leagueman?" the regent repeated.

"It is simple really." Mira spoke with soft tones. "He is innocent. He is a father. This injustice is affecting more than the man you wrap with chains."

The regent nodded understanding. "Very well. I will release him to his family. But I will hold you to your vow, Mira Far."

As though she hadn't heard, Mira pressed on. "I need your word on more than simple release. You must have a court guard assigned to him and his family, to keep them safe. If anything unnatural happens to him, those responsible will be accountable . . . to me. I will see to that accounting, and it will be bitter."

"You and the Sheason practice a unique brand of diplomacy." The regent's words elicited a soft laugh from Artixan. "Very well, the leagueman shall be freed this very day and given a new life, far enough from here that no one will remember them from this unseemly event, so that they can live in peace."

Mira nodded. Warm satisfaction flooded her.

She caught a look from Vendanj that suggested he'd never heard her say so much at one time. She thought she saw approval, and a new level of respect.

Now she had only to convince King Elan to attend this convocation. This gathering of standards and crowns would be the last, she felt, before the idea of the convocation was lost or replaced or dismantled forever. If the Far nation were ever going to rejoin the world of mankind, it was now, especially if Tahn failed at the Heights of Restoration. Because if the Hollows boy failed, then the defenses of nations would be all that stood between the races south of the Pall, and the Quiet.

She may have just commited the Far to war to save a man and his family. But her people could no longer remain aloof to the concerns of mankind, nor could they remain alone in their covenant and commission to protect the covenant tongue. Perhaps the covenant, from the beginning, had meant more than simply preserving a language anyway. If the Quiet came, the stillness of the Bourne came in equal measure to *all* the races in the eastlands. And mankind surely needed the Far.

It was time to fight or die.

But King Elan had his own thoughts on the matter. And he would be exceedingly angry.

Mira had a plan to deal with that, too.

• CHAPTER SIXTY-EIGHT •

Garlen's Telling

Beyond the window of the levate healing room, darkness had fallen, interrupted only by the glow of lights from distant windows in the Recityv night. Braethen stared out, new knowledge weighing upon him. The others had returned, dressed for the cold in thick cloaks and high-collared coats. Vendanj and Grant spoke softly near the door. Mira had not yet returned.

An uneasy feeling tugged at Braethen's gut.

He'd spent hours reading all he could find on Restoration. It was an end place: at the other side of the Eternal Grove.

Much of what he had found had been written in other tongues, writings he struggled to decipher. But the most he could discern was the idea of atonement.

And no story Braethen knew that took this idea as a theme ever ended well.

The sodalist watched as his newly freed friends took turns rushing to a basin set in the healing room to disgorge the food they'd eaten. Their tender stomachs, so long without food, could not bear the feast. They'd simply eaten too much, too fast. When their stomachs were again empty, they leaned against the wall to catch their breath.

"Ready," Sutter said, pulling on the leather bracelet with the strange loop over his middle finger. "To the Heights." Still holding a crust of bread, he took a bite.

Tahn smiled. "Glutton."

The door opened and Mira stepped in. She conversed with Vendanj and Grant in a low tone. She then opened the door, looked into the hall, and nodded to Vendanj.

"Come," Vendanj said. "It is time. Keep silent. The halls of Solath Mahnus are alive with argument over the regent's decision to exercise her right to free Tahn and Sutter. The league has called her action into question. Soon she will be forced to add her guard to the search for us, while they convene a formal council."

Grant laughed. "Doesn't that defeat the purpose of her sovereign right to grant amnesty?"

Vendanj nodded. "Nevertheless, it is true. It is the time we live in. They search for Tahn and Sutter even now. We are safer if we go unheard and unseen. Quickly."

Mira led them down the hall and across a mezzanine. As they went, Braethen realized suddenly—for the first time—that he was actually in the great halls of Recityv. Walls of rich marble flowed into ceilings with intricate carved designs. The floor shone in the light of a hundred lanterns. Here and there islands of wide, deep chairs sat grouped in circles on burgundy carpets cut in great squares. In their midst, small tables held bottles of mulled wine and boards of bread and honey butter.

They descended a stairway into a second hallway. Recessed alcoves on either side of them harbored statues, empty suits of mail, and occasionally a door into another room.

At the hall's end, another stair spiraled down. Mira still led them, and in short order they arrived at a workroom. Large tables stood laden with mallets, steel rings, sharp shafts, and rolls of leather. Along the walls, pegs were hung with unfinished suits of armor, saddles, tack, and harness rigs, lengths of hide still curing. To the right blazed a forge with water troughs beneath it to cool heated metal. The entire room was redolent with the smell of armor oil and rawhide. A dense, humid heat thickened the air, as well as the smell of a man's labor.

At this hour, the room was empty save for three men. One held something in the blistering fire of the forge. As Mira started toward a broad open entrance opposite them, the man put a piece of red-hot iron into the water, a gout of steam and a loud hiss rising from the trough.

The other men beat at folds of doubled leather, driving studs into them at even intervals. They worked without their shirts, thick stomachs glistening with sweat beneath corded chests and shoulders. Each swing fell precisely where they intended it.

One of the men working at his leather looked up as they passed two tables away. He continued to hammer, uninterrupted, grunting at a casual nod from Vendanj.

The far end of the armory was open to ventilate the fires and keep the men cool. The wind was blowing hard, sending strong gusts into the armory. Ten paces from that open yard, Mira abruptly stopped, drawing her swords in an impossibly quick, dual motion. Braethen heard Grant pull his own weapon. In the blink of an eye, four leaguemen walked into sight, blocking their passage into the stable yard.

"His leadership was right. Look what we have found." One of the leaguemen laughed as they all drew their swords.

"We've no quarrel with you," Vendanj said. "But we have urgent business, and will not be delayed."

"Will not," the leagueman mocked. "Sheason, you are going to the pit for this. And if you raise your hands to draw the Will, you will be put to death. Do you understand your choices?"

Mira leaped forward, blades slicing the air. Sparks rose from the furnace in the wind, streaking the air like light-flies around her as she moved. Before the leagueman could defend himself, she had her blade at his throat.

"I will cut your throat if you utter another insult," Mira said. To the remaining leaguemen, she said, "We are leaving. If you try to stop us, your friend will die."

"Hurry," Vendanj called.

Braethen ran with the others into the stable yard, where they found their horses ready.

They had all mounted when the leagueman gambled on Mira's threat and began to shout an alarm. His cries rose on the still night air. Down distant alleys, running steps echoed toward them from every direction.

Braethen waited for the Far to dispatch the man, his stomach roiling at the thought. Instead, she severed the tendons above the ankles on both his feet—he would not be following them. Then she jumped onto her own horse. Vendanj clucked twice, sending Suensin into a gallop toward the stable-yard gates. The clop of hooves rose like applause across the stone mall.

They rode hard and fast, the cobblestone underfoot too slick for iron-shod hooves to stop. A horse-length from the barred doors, Vendanj shoved a flattened palm toward the gates, casting them open as though straw in a summer storm. Into the street they poured, turning south along the outer wall of Solath Mahnus. Warning cries rose behind them, but they soon were lost to distance and the rush of blood in Braethen's ears.

Around a sharp turn, the cobbled road ended, passing to soil. Braethen chuffed a sigh of relief as their horses' hooves quieted in the dirt.

They raced under a full moon that lit their way. Around them, the city had begun to fall to sleep: fewer lights shone in the windows, fewer dogs barked at their passage.

After just a few minutes, Vendanj pulled up abruptly, jumping from his saddle and taking two running strides to a door with a faint yellow glow at its edges. He rapped lightly at the lintel as Braethen and the others came to a stop and looked down in confusion. This was no cathedral. Mira gestured them off their horses, gathering the reins and pulling the mounts into a covered alcove beside the house. Grant assisted her, his eyes searching the night with the same intense awareness as the Far.

The door squeaked, drawing Braethen's attention. He saw a sliver of an old face between the door and its jamb, sallow cheeks beneath a shock of snow white hair. An expression of unhappy surprise was clearly evident on the portion of face Braethen could see. But the man opened the door to admit the Sheason. Vendanj half turned and silently gestured them to follow.

All responded save Mira and Grant, who looked a perfect pair, aware of one another but their focus outward into the Recityv night.

Braethen had just cleared the door when Vendanj shut it fast and directed the sodalist to watch the street through the window. The Sheason then stepped into the direct glow of a lantern hanging from a rafter. He eyed their host carefully. The old, tired-looking man stared back with arched brows.

"I need a telling, Garlen, and I need it with the pass of one quill's dip into your ink." Vendanj spoke fast but clear.

"What else," the man replied. "I should know the sound of Suensin's hooves by now. Each time they clatter to my stoop, you expect some words. And in a hurry." A recalcitrant tone entered the old man's voice. "As things go, just talking to you could earn me some stripes. And on from that, those bumble-fools at council may decide the author's craft is like to yours and put an end to the meager coin I can still earn from tight-fisted merchants."

Braethen stared. An author. He'd been so focused on his task he'd completely missed the house full of books and parchments. Within this cluttered home tucked away in a squalid quarter of Recityv, tables overflowed with scraps of parchment and books in various sizes, some bound in animal hide, some in cloth, others wrapped in twine; crowded shelves bowed from the weight of their volumes, sitting like a series of thin smiles; trunks sat open on the floor where the contents overflowed their lids; and amidst it Garlen seemed to bring a perfect order to it all. Braethen thought that he might be looking at the mind of the author, a vault of accumulated knowledge, the thoughts and impressions of a thousand historians, stories preserved throughout the ages, stories wrought by Garlen's own pen, and everything a knot, a riddle, a mess to Braethen, yet all of it an extension of the mind of this ornery old writer.

"Please, Garlen," Vendanj said. "I haven't time to debate the decay of a society that doesn't esteem your skill. And I've always made generous payment for your work."

"You're the only one," Garlen shot back, wheezing as he climbed a short stair and perched atop a high stool set beside a lectern that rose two full strides from the ground.

"We must go north and east," Vendanj went on. "The words must tell of a place at the edge of what is known in common history. Or else to your memory."

"Now we come to it." Garlen smiled and winked. "To me you come when my age suits your purpose, but younger pens dally at your scryer's beck when other concerns press you."

"Nonsense," Vendanj shouted. "There's not another pen in Recityv I trust or use. None sharper, none quicker. And haste is the nut inside, my friend. Those same bumble-fools at court trail us this instant, surely due to lies from the mouths of leaguemen."

"Don't end there, Vendanj," Garlen sputtered through a laugh. "Say it all. We've Quiet in the land. Patient shadow-stuff that bring with them a taint, a taint not just of foulness but of secrets mankind has ignored for far too long. I've put it on parchment a thousand times, my friend. A thousand times this cycle alone. Fellows and anais alike clap slavishly, but fail to place a copper in my hand for my clever tales and elaborated histories. They all hold to the texts that bear the regent's sigil, you know. The lies about our safety."

"I know, Garlen. But enough! Can you write it?" Vendanj may as well have thrust his fist into the lectern. The force of his cry rattled in the fibers of the wood.

Garlen raised his chin and one eye squinted. Upon his writing perch at the impossibly tall lectern, his white hair glowed in the light of the lamp hanging close by. His spectacles caught a glimmer of the flame inside. The author peered for a dreadful moment at Vendanj, testing the Sheason's patience. Then he pointed a quill at him.

"You're going to Restoration." He paused, twisting the quill in his fingers. "It is a dangerous place, my friend. Not a place to go gallivanting off to with such a tribe as this." The quill swept across the room to indicate all those from the Hollows and Penit.

Vendanj opened his mouth to speak.

Garlen stopped him before he could utter a word. "Yes, I can write it. Or near to it. I've seen the Soliel. Wandered like a lost pup in the places most men won't write about." The author became quiet, his gaze reflective. "But I've not written of such things, ever. What lays claim to that region of the Far is better left alone." Then, as though waking, Garlen spoke up. "But yes, I can write it! I'll take double on what you usually pay. And I'd have you make mention to your cathedral hootenanny that we tone-deaf louts find plenty of song in the spoken word alone."

Vendanj said nothing to that. Finally, he added, "We need to get to Naltus."

A look of concern touched the author's face. "I've not been there. I'm not sure I can write that telling accurately. But I can put you on the Soliel. From there—"

"Do you have Hargrove's *Collected Works*?" Braethen interjected.

A'Garlen looked down from his perch, squinting into the dimness near the window where Braethen stood watch. "Who's that? What do you care about my book collection?"

"Do you have it?" Braethen demanded.

"No author considers himself—"

"Where?"

The author began to point, and Braethen dashed to a bookcase to the man's left on the far wall. He scanned the books and found it quickly. There were eight volumes. He fingered the bindings in a blur, and pulled down the second book. With an audible crack, he opened the tome and flipped by memory a third of the way through the pages. He scanned, his mind and heart racing with remembrance and urgency.

"Here!" Braethen passed the open book up to A'Garlen. "Halfway down the left page."

The author took the book with a look of skepticism, but read the printed page. His face took on a conspiratorial smile. And before he did anything more, he reached down. Braethen took the author's grip, one he knew well.

"I thought so," the old man said. "Thank you, lad. Of course, this is pedestrian language, and won't do for a telling." He harrumphed. "But it gets me what I need." He shook his head, and cast a gleefully wicked eye over Braethen and the rest. Then the diminutive man stretched his arm up to draw back his sleeve, and made a grandiose movement of dipping his quill in an inkwell. His gaze flitted over the top of his glasses toward Vendanj as he withdrew the instrument, seeming to ask if the Sheason really meant to use what the author was about to produce. Vendanj nodded gravely.

As Braethen returned to the window to watch the street, the Sheason caught his arm and gave him a brief grateful nod. For Braethen, it was a world distant from the feelings of disappointment he'd once felt over his choices and aptitude. He settled one level deeper into the skin of a sodalist.

Garlen looked down at his lectern, put his quill to parchment, and began to write. The scratch of the quill against the parchment came loud. But Garlen never looked up once. His hand moved with practiced ease to the inkwell, but so quickly that it scarcely seemed anything more than another stroke in his current word. No pause came, no waiting on something more to write. The scribbling was feverish but not panicked. Braethen watched the author's eyes look beyond the page under the quill to whatever he created. In those moments, Garlen's gaunt cheeks seemed robust and his elderly eyes clear. Braethen's skin prickled at the sheer thought of what the man might be creating inside his mind and committing to parchment.

No one spoke or moved. None wanted to break the spell of silence. In the quiet, the only sound was the solitary quill roughing its way with black ink over a patch of vellum. That sound seemed to Braethen immeasurably lonely, and in the same instant impossibly important. It reminded him of his father's work, and somehow, so far from home, his esteem for A'Posian grew manyfold.

The sodalist stood near the door, one hand idly draped over the sword at his hip. Penit smiled as he stood next to Wendra. The boy appeared to revel in the idea of words, of story being written out. Braethen had almost forgotten that Penit had until quite recently earned his way by using the words of authors and acting the parts of characters in an author's scenario. Wendra herself had an odd expression on her face. Braethen thought he'd seen it come upon her when Garlen mentioned the cathedral.

But he watched the man with quiet reverence. Vendanj waited on the author with perfect attentiveness, the Sheason's face upcast into the soft glow of the old man's lamp.

Braethen did not know how long they'd stood waiting, watching Garlen create his telling. However long it may have been, it seemed an instant. The author was creating words that Braethen—from his years of study—knew could be sung in order to bridge great distances. The legends of tellings were like legends of the Far.

Suddenly the door burst open. Mira swept past Braethen to Vendanj, who did not look away from Garlen.

"A mob searches the next street," she said in a quiet, urgent voice. "They come here next. If we don't leave now, we will be overmatched."

Vendanj appeared not to hear her. And Garlen could not be disturbed. The author was alone with his words in a room full of strangers.

"Shall I run a decoy south? Grant and I could lead them false long enough for you to reach the cathedral." Mira looked up at Garlen. "Is he near to finished?"

Vendanj raised a hand to silence her. That same moment, fighting broke out in front of the house. Mira bolted from Vendanj's side and into the street as clashes of metal and heaving grunts told of swordplay beyond the door. Shouts of alarm rose up.

"Over here," one man called in a fierce bellow.

Rearing horses whinnied loudly, and frantic hooves echoed in increasing volume toward them. Scuttling boots pounded the soil of the road; the clink of armor and blade jangled Braethen's nerves. The shouts and calls became furious. Oaths accompanied the sounds of sword blows. Protestations echoed down the hard-packed dirt of the street.

The Sheason looked up at Garlen again. The author's quill still leapt across the page, undisturbed by the combat outside his door, unperturbed by the intrusion of voices and the threat of weapons in his own house. The fight seemed to rage closer to the stoop, impacts slamming the walls from without. Panes of glass rattled in their frames and wall hangings bumped occasionally, displaced momentarily by the force of a blow. A shrill cry rose—the sound of a mortal wound. The rumble of a mob, the shriek of dissonant voices, and the tumult of blind aggression advanced toward them. Still Garlen wrote; still Vendanj watched him write. Neither could be disturbed.

Someone came to the door, hollering an oath of death. The words gurgled in his throat, Mira's blade cutting short the imprecation. A hollow thud followed as the man fell across the entry.

Tahn looked up and saw a maniacal look in Garlen's eyes. His lips worked over his yellowed teeth. The hair upon his head and in his ears seemed to stand on end. It was as though he experienced a chill, yet he did not stop. His quill worked now at such a pace that it sounded as one long stroke, the individual letters and words indistinguishable from the whole.

"Here!"

Garlen dropped his quill into the inkwell and dusted the parchment with sand to dry it. Then he rolled the parchment with stubby fingers. The author lashed it with a braid of horsehair and tossed it at the Sheason.

Vendanj caught the scroll with a deft hand, and swept it into the folds of his cloak in the same motion.

The lantern rocked slightly over Garlen's head. The author leaned out over the lectern he used to write upon. "Never forget that you asked this telling of me, Vendanj. I am glad I don't know the names of your company."

Vendanj pulled a small bag from his cloak and placed it on a nearby table. "For a great many skies to come, my friend. Watch yourself well. I regret what finds your street tonight." With that, Vendanj whirled and strode to the door.

The others followed. Braethen lingered a moment to note the strange look on Garlen's face. It was as though he'd just returned from another place, and found the world he'd come back to a relief. The author turned toward him. Garlen did not speak, but he smiled thanks again to Braethen and nodded.

Then the sodalist moved fast to the door. He stepped across the body lying there and onto the stoop. Eight men stood near Mira and Grant, wearing the color of the League. The two had successfully kept them at bay.

Vendanj rushed into the center of the street and pushed his cloak off his shoulders. With one fist drawn to his right hip, he pointed splayed fingers toward the sky.

The wind began to stir.

Vendanj dropped his arm toward the men. A faint yellow luster engulfed them, and in that same moment, the wind descended in punishing waves. Small pieces of wood from houses down the street tore loose from their nails, rocks and cast-off bits of iron rose from the ground. Panes of glass shattered; shutters, barrels, everything light ripped into splinters, streaking through the air toward the glow around the men. A rain of detritus struck them like a swarm. A few fled; some fell to the ground under the assault, their bodies writhing beneath hundreds of pointed pricks and the bludgeoning of stone and metal.

In a moment Braethen and his companions all clambered aboard their horses and bolted as the wind howled past them, tearing at their cloaks and whipping dust into their eyes.

• CHAPTER SIXTY-NINE •

Leaving Peace Behind

More shouts followed them. Searchers, spotting them as they raced through the streets, called alarms and pointed accusing fingers, spurring their mounts to move faster. Shadows blurred past, smears of grey beneath a bright moon. Wendra had the impression of long, sleek arms snaking toward her as they passed beneath the more profound dark of tall, narrow alleys.

Then they turned onto a broad street that ended at the steps of Descant Cathedral. The sight relieved her. Beneath the lesser light, it rose like a monolith against the starry sky. Great domes marked dark half circles against the night. From there, upper windows showed the dim light of candles.

They headed for the cathedral, looking behind them to see if they were still being followed. Wendra glanced back, too, noting the strain on the faces of Grant and Braethen, who brought up the rear. Sutter rode beside her, chin lowered, giving his steed his head as he kicked the horse's flanks. Wendra held Penit against herself with one arm, coaxing her mount on with her reins.

More lights flickered in windows on both sides of the street, a few men coming to doorways as they notched sword belts over nightshirts.

"You there," a man called.

"Hey, slow or be stopped!" another demanded.

Ahead, the street began to line with more denizens of this dusty quarter of Recityv. Mira pushed harder, pointing her sword at one man who stepped into the street with violent intentions. Her warning stopped him in his tracks.

Suddenly, behind them a roar erupted. Wendra looked over his shoulder and saw many horses burst onto the street, a block behind them. A chorus of battle cries came after them, raised from men in league chestnut and Recityv crimson all muted in the neutral tones of the large moon. Their pursuers bore down on them, the sound of bloodlust in their cries.

Looking ahead again, Wendra's heart fell as three horsemen emerged from the end of the street and took position in front of the cathedral steps to block them. If they should somehow evade these new challengers, those behind would surely be upon them before they found safety beyond the cathedral doors.

Bur Mira did not slow. She pulled both swords and rode with an easy grace and rhythm on Solus's back, eyeing the obstacle. As they fast approached the end of the street, Grant rode past Wendra and took up position beside the Far, barreling down upon the three horsemen.

Nearer to the cathedral, Wendra saw that the men sat in old saddles on horses as shaggy as meadow mares. They wore armor pieced together from whatever they had at hand, and bore sigils that looked as though they had sewn them themselves. They meant to earn a reputation and esteem at Solath Mahnus in this time of convocation. But they seemed little more than highwaymen or opportunists. All save one, who wore a plain suit of black leather and carried a pike forged of a metal equally black. Though he wore no cloak, a hood shielded his face. This, most of all, struck fear in Wendra's heart.

And still Mira did not slow.

A cacophony of angry shouts rose from those who stood in the way. Wendra lowered her own chin and followed the others into the melee.

The man in the hood reared his horse and pointed his mace at Mira. The Far hurtled forward undaunted, driving her mount directly toward him. Grant angled right for the rider on the end. Vendanj leaned forward, urging his mount on.

Of a sudden, Braethen passed Tahn on the left, whipping his steed forward and drawing his own blade as he raced to the front and arrowed toward the horseman at the far left.

On the sides of the street, torches flared into life, the growing crowd eager to see as well as hear the contest about to take place. Men howled loudly with glee, asking for blood and declaring their own ability. But the words rose and fell, waves of violent sound, joining the white noise of the blood roaring in her ears.

She turned to see their pursuers. The mob now filled the street, a wall of men and horseflesh. The glint of fire on dull metal winked at her, and she realized she and Sutter now held the rear position. If the three horsemen stopped them long enough, the swarm would find them first, and she and Sutter would be pulled under like capsized boats in an angry sea.

Ahead, the man in the dark hood lifted his black mace and began swinging it at a dizzying speed, creating a wide, whirling barrier of himself and his weapon. In the air, an ominous, painful moan began to grow, like the deathbed sighs of an entire generation—this was no ordinary warrior. The sound stole Wendra's breath, and she began to choke. She clutched at her throat and looked over at Sutter, who was doing the same.

A squeal pierced the air, and Wendra turned toward the sound in time to see Mira rein in hard on Solus, using the forward momentum to vault herself from her saddle toward the man in black armor. For a long moment, she seemed suspended in air, sailing toward the whirling mace. Then her arm flashed and caught the weapon in its arc, stopping it in the same instant as her second blade sliced toward the hooded face. The rider leaned back to escape the blow and rolled from his horse to the ground, keeping hold of his weapon.

Grant forced his mount into a collision with the rider on the right, who made a weak attempt to thrust a sword into Grant's chest. The man out of the Scar twisted his fist into the other's hair and wrenched him from his saddle. A jarring crunch of mismatched armor accompanied a snap of bone, and the man scuttled away on his knees, dragging one arm uselessly.

To the left, Braethen raised his blade, which began glowing a bright white in the night. He took a path that would carry him to the side of the rider, holding his sword ready for a strike. As the sodalist closed in, Wendra caught a flash of shadow well to his left. At the corner of the last building, two men huddled with crossbows aimed at him, their heads lowering to the stillness Wendra knew came just before firing.

Tahn pulled his bow from his back, nocked an arrow, and loosed it at the first man.

The arrow hit the very corner of the stone building, striking sparks into the shadows. But it was enough to disrupt the crossbowman's concentration.

The bolt sailed high and disappeared into the blackness across the street. A wicked eye turned on Tahn—the man who had not yet shot his bolt. His crossbow turned on Tahn, the point aimed at him.

At full ride, Tahn could not nock another arrow as quickly as he could on his feet. He would be too late. Sutter could not help. Wendra looked at the man and loosed a burst of angry song. The sound filled the end of the street before the great face of Descant Cathedral, the force of it pounding the crossbowman like the impact of a great gavel. In but a moment, he lay motionless on top of his own weapon. The echoes of her short song rose with the din of the mob.

A scream broke the sound of her dying note.

Wendra followed the wretched sound and saw the left-hand rider pulling a barbed sword from Braethen's leg. She knew what had happened. Her harsh melody had also struck Braethen, and ruined his stability. The sodalist had tried to swing in the direction of his attacker with his bright blade, but his stroke, off balance, had been weak and unthreatening. Braethen had managed to keep hold of his sword, but he was exposed to attack and unable to defend himself. The rider flashed a triumphant grin, batting his gauntlet twice against his breastplate in self-acknowledgment. Then he raised his blade to finish Braethen.

His sword never fell. His mouth opened in surprise, his eyes closed in mortal pain. Wendra saw Mira shove the man from his saddle while pulling both blades from his back.

Vendanj now rode past the fray and up the cathedral steps. To her relief, Maesteri Belamae drew back the wide double doors. Wendra and Penit followed him up, Tahn and Sutter close behind.

Hooves clatterd noisily on stone. Roars of displeasure and foulness echoed from the tall face of the cathedral. The wall of pursuers bore down upon Braethen, Mira, Grant, and the man with the black hood.

Again the moan of human wailing rose up. The man in black armor, who stood behind Mira, had begun to swing his mace in crushing arcs toward her. The Far danced back a step and brought her swords up in defense.

Less than twenty strides separated the charging mob and Mira. She could easily have escaped them all and mounted the stair, but she stood between the dark rider and Braethen like a mountain cat before her litter.

Vendanj ordered Wendra and the others inside, where a handful of men waited, eyes wide.

"Quickly!" Vendanj shouted. "Theirs is not your fate!" The Sheason followed, looking toward the bottom of the steps.

Maesteri Belamae drew Wendra and Penit inside. Sutter jumped from his horse and started down the stair, both hands on his blade.

"No!" Vendanj commanded. "Your one blade means nothing against so many."

Sutter scowled at Vendanj, but stopped and looked again toward Braethen.

The din of shouts and howls and hooves and clattering armor rang around them.

Then, as if from nowhere, Grant appeared. He lunged quickly and purposefully at the back of the hooded man, ducked low at the last moment, and drove a knife into the fellow's calf.

The mace ceased, the moan slowed. But a screech of anger and betrayal echoed like a malefic prayer. The shadow inside the cowl turned on Grant, who pulled back to wait for a counterattack.

Mira did not hesitate. She took Braethen's reins and her own and began racing up the steps. Grant took his own and followed, as the hooded rider disappeared into the darkness of a nearby alley. A rain of arrows began striking the steps about them, chips of rock flying, sparks leaping where metal met stone. But none found its mark, the arrows slipping from their trajectory by fractions, as if parting around their quarry.

It was then that Wendra realized she heard a melody like a battle song, but low, directed. She turned to make way for Mira and Grant and their steeds and saw Belamae's gaze fixed upon her friends and singing just under his breath.

The leaguemen and city guard had reached the cathedral steps. They brought their horses to a skidding halt. Several voices shouted commands and warnings. But they faded as Braethen at last was pulled inside and Vendanj ushered the last of them through the doors, which the gentleman with white hair pulled closed with less haste than Wendra expected.

As soon as the door was closed, two men and two women pulled crossbars through great iron rings to hold them shut. Belamae gave some quiet instruction to these men and women, who then quickly led the horses away.

Then Belamae turned his clear, patient gaze on Vendanj, looking a question at him.

"A telling," Vendanj said. "And quickly. It must be sung with precision, nothing erring." Vendanj paused, pulling the scroll from his cloak and handing it to the man. "And my apologies for bringing this on you, Maesteri. This will not be easy for you, even if the regent shows you favor."

Belamae smiled as he received the parchment from Vendanj. "You are right in that, Sheason." His voice rang deep and clean. "But though our gables and spires are tarnished, our purpose is not. It was easier to open our doors because you bear this one company." He looked at Wendra. "You've kept her safe. In this you've won an ally of me. She must now remain here, though. Wherever your author has written you, it is certainly not a haven if this mob is any indication."

Vendanj turned to Wendra, his impatience to be about his business momentarily forgotten. The Maesteri and Vendanj then drew Wendra from the others.

The Sheason gave her a solemn look, but spoke softly. "Wendra, when I came to the Hollows, I came not only for Tahn . . . I also came for you. I knew your parents." He paused briefly, seeming to consider what to say. "Before you knew it yourself, I knew the gift you possess. It is a mighty endowment, and one desperately needed here." The Sheason glanced up, indicating the Descant.

Wendra felt like the wind had been knocked out of her. Vendanj had known? Had her father also known, her mother? She felt manipulated, deceived. She'd nearly been sold to the Bar'dyn through all of this. Then she realized it was also her voice that had saved her from that fate. And, of course, she would never have met Penit. She turned to look at the boy. Her heart relaxed briefly just seeing him safe.

Then she looked back at Vendanj and Belamae. "Why?" she asked. "Is it for what lay beyond your pools of reflection, Belamae?"

The Maesteri explained to her that the Song of Suffering was the singing of the Tract of Desolation, that it must be constantly sung to keep in place the veil that held the Quiet within the Bourne. He told her that the Lieholan were few . . . and tired.

When he had finished, Vendanj again spoke. "You are the reason we came to Recityv, Wendra. There is still much to be done, and that is work we go now to do. But your place is here."

Again she found it hard to breathe. The revelations had come hard and fast. "What about Penit?"

Vendanj did not turn away when he said, "He is coming with us. You'll have to let him go."

In some ways, this scared Wendra more than everything else she'd heard. Desperation filled her chest. She could feel the weight of her decision bearing down on her, and felt trapped.

Often, in her panic, she would sing or hum, or even play in her mind a tune to calm herself. But now the thought of doing so only reminded her of the choice before her. It was impossible. . . . Then she looked at the boy again, and thought of her lost baby, and all she had done to reclaim Penit after she had lost him, too.

Calmness returned to her. She looked back at Vendanj, returning his stare. The Sheason's penetrating gaze took in her brow and cheeks and chin before he looked at the Maesteri.

"She has chosen," Vendanj said. "She will accompany us. But my oath to you, Belamae, that I will protect her."

The man's demeanor shifted noticeably; Wendra thought it less one of anger than concern. The Maesteri nodded and stepped away, leading them down a dark hall.

No one spoke, and Vendanj went directly after Belamae, followed closely by

Wendra and Penit, then Tahn and Sutter. Mira and Grant came last, supporting Braethen between them. Distantly, Wendra heard the same melodic humming she'd heard before: the Song of Suffering, being sung deep within the cathedral.

Beyond the walls, shouts could still be heard, lending haste to their steps.

If they rush the cathedral, will the doors hold?

Belamae led them through several halls where small candles burned on shallow shelves to dimly illuminate their steps. They went past closed doors, catching phrases of song, and musical passages played on citherns, flutes, and violins—sometimes together, sometimes solo. The snatches of song sounded mournful to Wendra's ear.

The Maesteri strode to a closed door. He produced a key, turned back the tumbler, and admitted them before he himself entered and locked the door behind them.

"What voice?" Vendanj asked.

"I would trust none other than myself, Sheason," Belamae replied.

Without further words, the man went around the room and lit several lamps. Gradually the shadows receded, revealing to Wendra's eyes an oval chamber with a ceiling fifty strides high. Murals had been painted there, the details of which faded from the eye at such a distance. A great oval rug of blue and white interlocking patterns stretched to the walls but left bare a smaller concentric oval of stone at the room's center. The stone there was seamless, and shone like a black mirror.

Chairs were placed at even intervals around the perimeter of the inner oval, appearing as though set at the edge of a dark, placid pool. At the back of the chamber stood a lectern like Garlen's, wrought from the same sleek stone as the floor.

The Maesteri went to Wendra and stood quietly before her. He gently took her hand, cupping it between his own. He let out a sigh and smiled wanly. "You'll never know how difficult it is for me to see you go," said Belamae. His voice caught with emotion. He swallowed and patted her hand. "Go safely, young one," he said. "Remember that when you open your mouth to make song, there is responsibility in it. Rough, strained tones have their place, child, but are always forgotten and never create. There's a special endowment in you, Wendra. And you are the only one who can look after it once you pass from this place. Please, come back to me. So much depends—" The Maesteri cut himself off, though wanting, it appeared, to say more.

Wendra realized as the words died that they did so after a slowly fading roll of echoes. The chamber resounded with the cast of Belamae's voice, making each word larger than itself, a quality of depth and dimension Wendra had not quite heard before.

"Your horses will be with you shortly," the Maesteri said to Vendanj without turning away from Wendra, who still held Penit's hand.

She smiled appreciatively at the old man, but in her heart she held reservations. It had been a long time since she'd felt anything she could use that word to describe—*endowment*. The Maesteri might not use the word if a child had been ripped from his womb, or another sold on the blocks, or had himself been the wager in a game of chance.

The Maesteri left her and walked around the black oval to the lectern. He climbed a stair behind it, and soon stood overlooking the room from several strides above them. Carefully, he untied the scroll and unrolled it on the lectern. His eyes read the words. He looked up. "This is A'Garlen, I can tell." He smiled. "Please be seated," he said.

Vendanj pointed to the seats. Each of them took a chair, Wendra yet keeping her hold of Penit's hand.

Sitting last, the Sheason spoke to the Maesteri. "Belamae, speak strongly for Helaina when you are given the opportunity to do so. With laggard seat holders, pretenders, the League, and the Quiet . . . Help her where you can with this convocation. We go to attempt an important task, but our success may mean nothing if the convocation fails."

The old man smiled devilishly, as if he relished the debates in store for him with the likes of Roth Staned. He laid a finger aside his nose in what looked like a salute. The Sheason gave a grateful nod.

When they settled, the Maesteri began to hum in a rich, deep voice, the sound of it resonating in the chamber until the entire space seemed filled with it. The sound came at Wendra from every direction, washing over her like her most vivid dream. The music thrummed with life of its own, so that she could not be sure the Maesteri sang it at all.

Then the man began to sing the words on Garlen's vellum. The telling unfolded in glorious detail, the words fitting together as naturally and rhythmically as any lyric Wendra had ever heard. The dance and play of each phrase gave life to the words and what they described, and from the lips of the Maesteri, the music soared as though it might stretch outward and upward without end.

In moments, the words ran together with the song and became something more. It touched Wendra deeply, striking a chord at once in flesh and spirit. Wendra felt the chamber about her begin to recede, becoming insubstantial, visible more as elements of something much more vast.

Above the brilliant oval, the air began to draw itself into threads like the weave of a loom. Tendrils of space with the color of what lay beyond it reflected in thin, wavy lines. Hundreds, then thousands of these strands shimmered together and grew until they filled the space between the chairs.

Through it, Tahn saw the faces of Grant and Mira undulating as though through rippling water, but in slow vertical lines, and thin, like strands of hair.

As the song unwound itself, Wendra glimpsed the gift that lived inside her. She thought she might have been afraid, but in the embrace of Belamae's song, she felt safe.

The Maesteri sang a crescendo that wove itself in a shifting, scintillating pattern above them. Garlen's words given voice began to create a picture. The threads moved, changing color, weaving in new patterns. Wendra felt a pull as though the world, the physical space of the chamber, was realigning itself. The strands danced to the song, the words gave direction, and thousands of hair-line rents in the air obeyed, moving and reshaping what she saw.

The weave coalesced, pulling tight and firming. The strands began to disappear from view, creating a new order in place of the old. On the Maesteri sang, until the breeze became a wind, and Wendra smelled the plains she looked upon, and heard the sound of thunder in a dark sky.

"Step through," Vendanj said, his voice low so that he would not disturb the song.

Though she could not see past this new curtain draped in the air before her, Wendra saw Mira and Grant suddenly appear on the soil of the scene rising up from the black oval mirror. Then Vendanj, and Braethen. To her left stood Sutter, who gave an enthusiastic salute to Tahn, and stepped through himself. Then Tahn. And Penit.

Wendra looked back at the Maesteri, who continued to sing, but gave her a reassuring nod. With a rush of sound entreating her mind and poetic language quelling all disbelief, Wendra stepped into the tapestry. With a sudden sadness and doubt, she left the Descant behind.

• CHAPTER SEVENTY •

Children of Soliel

Tahn crunched fine shale underfoot as he emerged into the vast dark plain. A damp wind gently lifted his hair as he quickly took visual count of his friends. All had arrived safely. He looked back at the fabric and saw a scene torn from open space showing the chamber and its chairs, where the Maesteri was bringing his song to a close in softer tones. The woven strands began to unravel, pulling back to a previous form and distorting the picture behind it. In moments, the lighted chamber was gone, replaced by unbroken terrain that met dark clouds at the horizon.

Vendanj went to Braethen and laid the sodalist on the ground, rolling his cloak for a pillow to cushion his head.

"Breathe easy," the Sheason said mildly.

Then Vendanj put one hand over the wound in Braethen's leg, holding his other palm over his navel. He said something that Tahn lost in the wind's flapping of his cloak. Moments later, Braethen's face relaxed. Vendanj applied an ointment and carefully wrapped the wound.

A shearing sound drew Tahn's attention. Looking up, he witnessed a display of ever-changing, dazzling light mere paces away. Mira approached the coruscating brilliance, and shortly their mounts walked through another window of shimmering strands. The Far gathered the horses and left the breach before it could close, soon handing reins to the appropriate owners.

A distant flash of light blazed near a range of jagged mountains, followed by a muted roll of thunder. The charcoal darkness of the shale blended gradually with the darkness of the mountains and storm clouds that closed them in.

"The Soliel Stretches," Mira said evenly. "Garlen is full of surprises." She jumped astride Solus, and looked around in a full circle. "Naltus is close. We should take shelter from the storm."

Another flash lit the night. Soon the grumble of thunder cracked and boomed around them; faraway coyotes or wolves raised howls of protest to the sound.

As they traveled, Tahn now and again caught glimpses of the silhouette of the man with tan skin looking at him. Perhaps Grant only *appeared* to be watching him, but in a dim streak of lightning, his eyes rested solely on Tahn, menacing with hidden purpose.

They passed tangles of bleached bone in the shale; small prongs of calcified skeletons jutted up from the earth, the size of the creatures' bones confounding any guess Tahn had about what they'd been in life. More than once, Tahn thought he saw rows of shale piled in mounds like graves, where the hardness of the earth permitted only a covering and no final rest in the bowels of the land.

Then in front of them, as if appearing from no where, rose a city.

Massive walls had been mortared together from the same shale around them, making the city hard to discern, especially in the shadows of twilight. Watching close, Tahn realized something more. He could see no watch or movement; could, in fact, see no gate in the seamless outer wall, no congregants or merchants without the walls to harangue them on their way into the city.

What traveler would come here? Everything here feels isolated . . . abandoned . . .

As they approached, Mira spoke to them. "Strangers are seldom admitted past the gate." She sounded unapologetic. "Be respectful."

Sutter whispered, "I guess if you're not a Far, you're an outsider." He smiled.

"We haven't even seen anyone, let alone been stopped. How safe will we be?" Wendra asked.

"There are no secrets on the Soliel," Vendanj explained, having heard their whispering. "Not to the Far. They have known of us since we came through the telling. News of our presence has surely been announced. A decision to admit us likely awaits our arrival at the city wall."

"And what if they will not let us in?"

"The errand we bear will prevail over any protest, I'm sure. But you are more than guests here." The Sheason looked over them intently. "Every man and woman who comes into the Soliel is an unwitting model of life as it persists in the lands south and west: sometimes merchants, sometimes vagabonds, sometimes vain men given to adventure. The intentions of such men cast our kind in an unfavorable light. Beyond here is the Bourne to the north and the Saeculorum to the northeast. And beyond the Saeculorum the land comes to an end.

"But you pass this way with a different purpose than these others I name." Vendanj leveled a threatening gaze over them all. "Do not sully that purpose with tricks or your own private contentions."

The walls of Naltus Far were much taller and broader than they had appeared from farther away. Tracking the parapets proved difficult in the dark, but their tops were clearly visible each time the sky erupted in flashes of lightning.

Drawing closer, Tahn saw that the walls rose in smooth, sheer planes. No joints or extruded rock offered a foothold, and there was no gate. Mira led them to the base of the great wall. With sure movements, she traced a design on the smooth surface with her fingertips. Then she again made the pattern. And a third time.

When she'd completed her last pass, a whisper of escaping air came from the wall and a large door began to swing inward. Tahn strained to see what the Far had done, but saw no marking on the door, nor a traditional latch. The entry moved in a slow, deliberate arc but made no sound, no grinding of rock or squeak of hinges. Shortly, an entry large enough to admit a horse had opened in the wall. Mira rode through.

When they had all passed, Tahn found Mira standing silently before a male Far. Mira lifted her right hand and placed her middle three fingers on the other's lips with a tenderness Tahn envied. While her hand still rested there, the male Far returned the gesture. Neither spoke a word. Mira withdrew her hand and motioned them to follow.

The city rose in sleek lines of shale. In places a dark wood augmented the architecture in the way of support posts or window dressing. But the impenetrable dimness of black slate prevailed in almost every structure.

"It's not very attractive," Tahn muttered.

"I don't know," Braethen said from behind him. "There's a stark beauty in it, I think, a kind of simplicity, if nothing else. Besides, I don't believe the slate is used because it is all they had."

"What do you mean?" Nails turned in his saddle to look at the sodalist, who was avidly taking in their surroundings.

"I mean that I think the Far chose the Soliel Stretches *because* they are dominated by shale." Braethen looked back at Tahn. "Or that the Noble Ones *sent* them here because of the shale."

"Why? Has it got something to do with their personalities?" Sutter asked, quickly checking to be sure he hadn't been overheard.

Braethen smiled as he explained. "Shale is noted in the histories as an element without Forda. Or at least, so little that it possesses no value to—"

"Quietgiven." Grant silenced them with his intrusion. He looked straight ahead, but seemed to be seeing neither the stone nor Tahn and his companions. Tahn had a feeling that what the man saw was still in the Scar, that the man himself might forever inwardly tarry there. "The land may, with time, replenish itself. If left alone . . . if it is Will that it be so.

"This place, though. It is already at final rest." Grant focused on Mira at the lead. "How they thrive here as they have done since the first turn . . . it is a wonder. There must be a reason to exile an entire people."

The Far who had greeted them led on through only a few turns. Hooves beat at cobbled shale bordered by countless homes and shops and storehouses, but Tahn saw not one Far step into the street to watch them pass. Nor were any casually sauntering by, and he saw no faces peering from windows. He did not hear the usual strains of music from a tavern or the raucous laughter and shouts of men and women drinking toward inebriation. Everything was still as though slumbering, though many windows burned with light, even at this late hour.

An entire city like Mira. Are they all as beautiful?

They stopped before a large rectangular building with round, fluted pillars supporting a roof that covered an outer walk. Well within the pillars stood a hall three stories high. Long terraced steps rose in groups of two from the street to the first story. Mira dismounted and handed her reins to the man who had conveyed them there.

"Thank you, Secretary Bridgoe," Mira said softly, her words barely carrying to Tahn's ears.

"They convened when we learned of your return to Soliel. You are expected," the secretary replied.

Tahn and the others stepped down from their mounts, and the male Far took their reins as well, escorting the horses away while Mira led Vendanj and the rest toward the large building, her gait slow but certain. Near the stone wall she went to one knee, bowing her head in the direction of the inner hall and holding her unguarded pose for what seemed a long time.

The sound of their passage came like the rustling of cloaks, and Tahn thought that they all walked on the balls of their feet to diminish the click of boot heels. The small hours of the night held sway in the quiet and depthless shadows.

Several paces on, they mounted a stair that led to a mezzanine. The light of large lamps gave Tahn a view of bookcases set in long rows. The tall shelves cast large, square shadows upon the vaulted ceilings above. Ahead of them were several closed doors. Upon each portal hung a different weapon as if an indication of what one might find within.

Immediately to Tahn's right, a large wall was covered by an enormous map that stretched from floor to ceiling. Across it, names had been written in a tight, fine hand. Upon it he saw notation for cities he'd never heard of, and cities nearer to the Hollows than Myrr, and beside them all he found dates. Mostly, though, Tahn saw the names of battles, wars, and leaders, some of whose legacies lived in the stories they told at Northsun and late at night when mortal thoughts crept in upon even young boys.

Calem Heelstone at the Rise of Shalin during the War of the First Promise; Vancet Jonasilith I'Nesbitt, Lord of Nallan, who held Sever Ens while his people fled south to safety; Olan Forant's name written beneath the Stand at Mal Point South. And more, so many that the map was crowded with its ink. Names Tahn had not heard, and handfuls of them in the northeast near Naltus, the writing smaller to keep each name discrete. One among them was penned in red: Kieronit Dalo, whose name dominated the rim of the mountains that lay beyond Naltus and the Soliel. The surname showed a tailing serif on the last stroke denoting gender—female, which Tahn surmised by finding Helaina's name near Recityv. This Kieronit had earned a place of prominence for whatever she had done, and her name was nearly the last to be seen before the markings of the Saeculorum Mountains.

There was one last name: Elan. This one looked recent, and ran into the markings of the Saeculorum to the far north. It seemed clear some battle had taken place, and that this Far, Elan, had led his people to victory—his name was actually written in several places near the top of the map.

Tahn scanned past the sharp scores and jagged scrawls to a final legible writing, expecting to find the Heights of Restoration. But the word written there was not one Tahn knew. He peered through the dim light, straining to see. There, scrawled at the farthest corner of the map were the words *Rudierd Tillinghast.*

Simply reading the words filled Tahn with hot chills. At times, musicians traveling into the Hollows had played their songs, calling upon the noblest qualities Tahn could imagine to describe the value of surrendering life for liberty. More than once, A'Posian had sat for them at Festival and read aloud the fruits of his pen, his words carrying over the fire and evoking images in Tahn's head that raised the hair on the nape of his neck. And when first Tahn had seen the Bar'dyn, rough hands cradling what fruit it could wrest from his sister's womb, this, too, had caused severe feelings in his bosom.

The internal feeling wrought by these words at the edge of the Far map exceeded the sum of all these, was somehow both a threat and promise, condemnation and freedom, in the same breath. He shaped the words with his mouth, unwilling to give them voice. The act of merely reading them had stolen his ability to speak.

What might saying them aloud actually do?

Before he continued, Tahn knew in his heart that this notation on the map was the place they sought, the place Vendanj had set course for from the hearth at Hambley's inn. With every step between, the Sheason had surely known more of what awaited Tahn than he ever shared. That corner of the map remained a mystery to him, a distant place more myth than reality. But those words, *Rudierd Tillinghast,* etched themselves on his mind and heart as though they had always been there. And of a sudden he believed he had likewise always feared them.

Would I have come if I'd known? Perhaps Vendanj had been right to be secretive.

The Far had gone to the left. They followed her down another stair that descended in long steps to the level below. Coming to the edge of the mezzanine, Tahn looked down on a small assembly of Far sitting in rows divided by a center aisle. Before them stood a young man who held a short crook in his hands, which he stroked thoughtfully.

Light-bearers stood stoically around the group, lanterns hanging from poles only slightly taller than their owners. The lamps glowed small in the vastness of the hall. Their presence felt merely symbolic to Tahn, rather than to actually provide light. He recalled Mira keeping vigil in the night with her bright grey eyes, taking in all that the darkness deigned to hide, not seeming to need light to peer into the night. If it were so, then he imagined the Far here possessed the same ability. Perhaps, then, the lanterns were for Mira's friends—a welcome.

None of the Far looked up at them as they descended the stairs. Flat

footsteps echoed in the hall, announcing their arrival. Still not a s
turned to greet them. At the base of the stairs, Mira held up her ha
them before she crossed to the man heading the congregants.

A pace from him, she stopped and bowed her head. She did not raise it again
until the man had softly touched her shoulder with his crook. Something
seemed odd to Tahn about the gathering. Perhaps it was the meekness of the
gestures they used to communicate with one another, nothing like he'd seen of
the Far in her dealings since coming to the Hollows. But that wasn't quite it.
Something else.

Mira spoke to the man, her words inaudible to Tahn. Then she stepped back,
and Vendanj strode forward, his tall frame commanding even in the depths of
the great hall. He humbly bowed his head to the man, who quickly touched the
crook to Vendanj's shoulder, the speed of the gesture seeming to indicate respect. Vendanj looked up for only an instant before turning to rest the rest of
the assembly. He did not immediately speak, his gaze passing over each Far.

He realized what had seemed strange to him. As Tahn followed the Sheason's gaze, not one of the Far could be any older than either Sutter or himself.
Looking closer, he saw that some appeared several years younger. Many wore
experience outwardly, giving their faces a cast of years beyond what their bodies might indicate. Not one showed the innocence of a melura, though each
also sat with a placid brow as though forever untroubled. And each in his or her
own way was as beautiful as Mira, perhaps, he thought, because of their youth,
or perhaps because they all seemed to have a sure sense of themselves.

The renderer finished assessing his audience, his bright eyes ablaze, reflecting
the light of the light-bearers' lamps. He took the vertical hems of his cloak and
drew them back over his shoulders, exposing the three-ring pendant that hung
from the short chain around his neck. A rustle of movement swept through the
Far. No words came, no exclamations, but the stirring of feet and straightening
of backs to take full view of the Sheason bespoke the same surprise.

"Children of Soliel," Vendanj said. "Thank you for sheltering us against the
storm and the shadows walking upright in the land. I ask your patience for
one night, then we leave you to your duties here."

Vendanj stopped, and Tahn thought the Sheason might be considering the
duties of which he spoke. The renderer nodded, as if he had just come to some
decision.

"Your stewardship becomes more dear today with the news I bring. No record ever speaks of a time when you have not honored and kept your First Inheritance: a life lived only until your Standing, your spirits thereafter going to
what lies beyond death. As reward for keeping your commission to safeguard
the Language of the Covenant, you've been given the blessing of another life
after leaving this world, where you may gather your family around you. And

you have carried this trust well." Vendanj's brow darkened. "But the Whited One grows restless after countless ages in his tomb. His misshapen creatures slip through the veil at the Shadow of the Hand, crossing from the Bourne in the west. They would rob you, rob all of us, of the hope you guard."

Sutter whispered to Tahn. "What's he talking about?"

Tahn shrugged.

"Keep still and you may have a sense of it," Grant said quietly over their shoulders. "Nothing so alerts another of melura as the opening of its mouth." Tahn thought it the closest thing to a joke the man from the Scar had uttered, but he held back a grin.

"I've seen the dolmen across your shale, and others yet toppled to the ground. It is a desecration unique to the Quiet who've come against you. Even in this shale valley you are not safe. You know this. It is inevitable that the spill from the Bourne will widen, and its hazards seek you out specifically."

Vendanj stepped closer, capturing them with a serious gaze. "But they have already struck deep into the land. This fortnight the Library at Qum'rahm'se was burnt to cinders, destroying generations of scholarship on the covenant language. Other repositories exist, but the library was protected by more than its mountain, with Sheason wards round about it." Vendanj paused. "And it contained the only other copy of the Tract of Desolation beyond that held at Descant Cathedral. The knowledge of the covenant tongue is now gone from the hands of men. Your stewardship here over the Language of the Covenant is more crucial than ever, more endangered." Vendanj looked past them, his eyes growing distant. "If Quietgiven made so easy a task of it at Qum'rahm'se, I fear for the coming of Delighast . . . the end of things." He paused. All the Far listened, attentive.

"Whatever action men take to answer this threat, you mustn't fail here to keep your commission: The Language of the Covenant must never be destroyed or stolen. No shrouded night amidst the shale is as black as what awaits us if it is." He paused again. "I fear the threat will come to Naltus again . . . stronger this time . . ."

It was the only time Tahn could remember Vendanj not finishing a thought.

The Sheason stepped back beside Mira. The young man with the crook placed the small staff upon the table behind him. The Far assembly rose as though formally dismissed and quietly took their leave. The light-bearers placed their staffs in holes in the floor before likewise exiting the room. Moments later, the hall stood empty save for Tahn's companions and the one Far who'd borne the crook.

He sat on the edge of the table. "It is good to see you, Vendanj. You are a worthy reminder of men to us. You are always welcome here." Tahn thought he heard a request more than an invitation.

"Thank you, King Elan," Vendanj said, nodding his head in gratitude and respect. "But there is more to say, and I would that we held this conversation without your captains."

"I suspected as much," the king replied, a wry half smile quirking his lips. "Shall I have water drawn?"

"They need it," Mira answered, nodding to indicate Tahn and the others.

Elan turned to look at an attendant standing post at the rear wall and half raised an arm. The attendant went straight out, returned quickly with two carafes of water and a tray of small glasses, placed them on the table, and withdrew immediately.

Elan poured the water, inviting them all to take a glass. As Tahn drank, he stared at Elan, realizing he was seeing not just the living king of the Far, but one who had taken his army to battle more than once and had returned victorious every time. When all had drunk, Vendanj paced to the center aisle of the chairs and pivoted sharply on his heel to look back at Elan and the rest of them.

"There are a dozen other places of study between Naltus and Qum'rahm'se, and the Quiet will likely visit them all. But should they ever take possession of the Tract of Desolation . . ."

Elan drank again, his forehead smooth, unconcerned. "Recityv will hold."

"It is not so easy as that," Vendanj continued. "Already the Given have come near the city, one coming . . ." The Sheason stopped, his eyes alighting on Tahn. "They have walked without regard into the Hollows, those hallowed groves consecrated during the Age of the Tabernacle. The land grows barren." Vendanj shared a look with Grant. "The balance of Forda I'Forza is upset. It is not a battle with a front this time, Elan. Yours is a crucial role, but we are as strands laid across a loom, and one miswoven thread flaws the whole." Vendanj grew quiet for a moment, his eyes downcast in his own thoughts.

"Did you come all this way to bring this news, and with a child no less?" Elan looked at Penit, a disconcerted look clear upon his features, as though he recognized something in the boy that Tahn could not see.

Vendanj looked up from beneath a lowering brow. "We pass this way into the Saeculorum . . . to Rudierd Tillinghast."

Elan shot Vendanj a look of horrified surprise. The Far turned to stare in the direction of the mountains where the storm raged. Still looking away, he said, "This is unfortunate news, Sheason. Quiet so deep in the land, attacks on the vaults of wisdom, these are alarming . . ." Elan turned back toward Vendanj. "But men returning to Restoration . . . that you will test the mountains is the darkest jest known to the Far; that you believe you must go to Tillinghast disheartens me. What can be gained by this?" He awaited an answer.

Vendanj blinked slowly. "The Far keep their First Inheritance, Elan, living without the shackles of consequence because you return to your earth before your Standing. Restoration may return to you nothing, for nothing can be restored to one for good or ill who hasn't felt his own Change. But for man it has ever been so only in his youth, and even there he is not protected as you are by your covenant. And beyond the day he Stands, the Heights become something altogether different. The abyss that presses in at Tillinghast is the substance of things unseen, the formulation of Forda I'Forza. And it will ask of those who alight there the most profound question . . ."

What question? More unfinished thoughts. Tahn was yet more alarmed.

He tried to ferret out the answer. The Sheason was taking Tahn to this place, the mere mention of which had the power to disturb the stoic countenance of Elan. *What is the most profound question?*

Interrupting his thoughts, Vendanj said, "We must know the answers to understand how we will face the servants of the Whited One and every hoof or foot that steps forth out of the Bourne."

Elan sipped at his water, his eyes again distant as though remembering something. "The Heights are too pure, too supernal for the flesh of men. The great cloudwood trees grow there only because they are as hard as iron and can withstand the mists. They are older than recorded history, and their roots reach to great depths to secure their trunks against the winds."

"Nay, more," Vendanj added, with deep reverence. "Their roots at the Heights of Restoration grow into the mists themselves, forming new soil. It is a marvel. There is special providence in the cloudwood. No mere tree is it."

"And how unlike this tree is a man," Elan said. "Your hopes may wither with the very decaying of human flesh when it comes in contact with the mists of Tillinghast that churn beyond the Heights. The pure potential that exists there will tear out the heart of a man who is less than the full promise inherent within him."

Vendanj nodded agreement. "These are necessary risks. What awaits us in the seasons ahead must be met by those whose very life is a gift of Will. We cannot know this about anyone who has not stood at Tillinghast. And anyone who actually walks away from the Heights has perhaps earned nothing more than a fated death if the Whited One escapes his sepulchre."

Elan raised a sober eye. "Yet you ask these here to have restored to them the memory and consequence of all their own choices, so that you can be satisfied of their worthiness?"

The Sheason frowned at the Far king. Elan did not retreat, but a look of uneasiness filled his face. Vendanj stared back with grim resolve.

Tahn felt a flicker of betrayal at the revelations that continued to unfold about his part in the journey to the Heights of Restoration. He'd always hated to be deceived, even when it came in the form of surprise gifts. But the fire in Vendanj's eyes was unrelenting, showing no mercy for whatever sacrifice must be made.

A peal of thunder reverberated around the great hall.

"Your pardon, Sheason," Elan finally said. "I do not question your intentions. But our own history shows more than a few who have perished in the mountains that rise from the Soliel. Their beauty is savage and deceptive. What thrives there is not edible by man, and the life that feeds upon it has crept from crags and pits where the work of creation is imperfect."

"How can that be?" Wendra cut in. Tahn started at the intrusion of a new voice, and turned to find concern in his sister's eyes. "The cycles of life are as steady and certain as the turn of the greater light. The mountain cat is a fierce predator, but part of the balance even when it kills."

Elan faced Wendra. "Imperfect, Anais, only because the change and growth wrought in the mountains near Tillinghast is not meet for your survival. New life there is born out of the mists and the potential they bear. It is the irony of Tillinghast that it be used to discern balance, and yet is surrounded by a terrain that threatens the harmony of man." Elan looked again toward the wall that faced the mountains to the north. "Tillinghast," he whispered. "Its purpose is not wholly known; its secrets are well preserved. Even authors who claim to have been there do not agree. Restoration it grants, that is sure, but—"

"Enough," Vendanj said, softly putting an end to Elan's words. "Fear of Restoration has crippled the efforts of otherwise good men. Generations ages past have labored to know how the Whited One could ever slip his bonds, and their search led them round to their tails while the rancor and legions beyond the Bourne grew. The Shadow of the Hand lengthens, and today's rumors hint toward the commencement of Delighast. Enough!" Vendanj's voice boomed in the large hall. "The blood of many stains my hands, as it does the hands of those who bear me company. Even their families were asked to follow painful paths. These sacrifices will not be mocked or go unremembered." His voice turned cool and even. "But it is part of our weakness that most in this current age are no longer willing to sacrifice to answer the threat of the Bourne. Our great 'civility' breeds indignation at the thought, or worse, disbelief and complacency." Vendanj stopped, and cast his eyes upward. Tahn heard the Sheason take a long inward breath. When Vendanj lowered his head again, an indomitable expression lit his face. "It will not be so this time."

Goose bumps rose almost painfully across Tahn's skin. He had the feeling that the Sheason was implying that Tahn and the others might be called upon to sacrifice something more before this was over.

Mira looked at Tahn, a kind of empathy in her eyes he had not seen before. It both comforted and frightened him.

The Sheason pulled his cloak about his shoulders and weighed the looks of those around him. Only Grant seemed to have no expression at all. The exile out of the Scar sniffed and waited. Any other time, the callousness in Grant's eyes might have bothered Tahn. But the stillness that followed the Sheason's words fell like a pall over everything.

"You'll have rooms at my home," Elan finally said, shattering the silence. "Sheason, I must insist that you take attendants into each room."

"To sleep with us?" Sutter blurted.

The Far king smiled. "Not to sleep. It is custom that visitors to Naltus be watched over continually, even at rest. It is rare that human boots tread Far shale, but the custom has always been observed, and I'll not diverge from it."

"Wisely said," Vendanj interjected. "My regret is that in harboring us you put yourselves at greater risk."

"We accept the responsibility of our stewardship." He looked up at Vendanj. "It would not be the first time that Quiet has come against us. And if they do, we will be ready."

Vendanj turned to Mira. "You will sit with Tahn. The others will be attended by members of Elan's guard."

The Far king nodded, took up his crook, and strode away. Vendanj followed. In a dozen paces, his long, powerful strides brought him abreast with Elan. The two conferred as Mira motioned for the rest to come after her. Sutter said nothing. He just shook his head with a wry smile.

Tahn looked back over his shoulder at the great hall, seeing the light standards, the rows of chairs, and the mezzanine where he'd first seen the map showing Rudierd Tillinghast. He thought about the things Vendanj had said to Elan's captains. Somewhere in those words, he felt there were answers for him, at last; yet at the same time, he thought maybe he no longer wanted to know.

At the door, Grant put a reassuring hand on his shoulder as he urged him through.

• CHAPTER SEVENTY-ONE •

One Bed, the Same Dream

Mira stepped past Tahn and surveyed the chamber: bed and chest of drawers to one side, and a table and chair set beside the window on the other. Tahn never got past the bed—there was only one. A thrill raced through him, followed quickly by anxiety. Slowly, he shut the door. When he turned, Mira had already seated herself in the chair beside the window and had taken out her oilcloth to clean her blades. As she set to wiping down one of her swords, Tahn unshouldered his bow and threw off his cloak, tossing it over the foot of the bed.

Beyond the window, lightning still flashed against the darkness to the north. Gouts of wind buffeted the eaves, whistling like thin reeds. A single lamp burned on the table, its wick so low that the oil threatened to extinguish the flame.

Tahn turned up the wick, brightening the room, and put his hands near the glass as though to warm them. He then sat beside his cloak, and shifted to look at the Far. Mira seemed to take no notice of him, running her cloth evenly over the edge of her weapon, which caught reflections of the flame.

Questions spun in his head, things he wanted to ask but did not dare: *How much of all this did she know from the beginning? Did she think it was possible that a boy from the Hollows and a Far girl . . .*

Tahn regarded her in the lamplight. No delicate square-cut blouse overlaid her bosom as the women of the Hollows wore when spring came full. Mira's cloak remained clasped at her neck, the grey folds cascading around the chair to the floor. No tincture colored her lips or eyes. But the glow of the flame gently touched her skin, giving it warmth even over her determined features. In contrast, white flashes burst from the sky, starkly lighting half her face for brief moments.

"Something on your mind?" she said, turning over her blade to inspect both edges.

Tahn groped for words. "I don't know. Yes."

"You should say it, then, so that you won't waste sleep wondering if I might answer."

"All right. I left the Hollows because I thought being there put the town in danger. I know now that Bar'dyn and Velle hunt me. But I don't know why." He leaned toward her, emboldened by his words. "And the only time I learn much about this Heights of Restoration is when I hear Vendanj telling someone else about it. He could kill me with a wave of his hand, but I'm tired of being the last to know just what, by my father's name, this is all about."

Mira sheathed one sword and withdrew the other. Without a look, she said, "You don't really need me to answer that, do you?"

Tahn's momentum ebbed. He eased back to an upright position. Thoughtfully, he touched the mark on the back of his hand. "Why me?" he finally said.

"Will that make it easier for you?" Mira said, folding over her oilcloth.

Tahn's fist tightened into a ball. "Wouldn't it make it easier for you?"

Mira continued to work. "No."

"Well that's just fine for you," Tahn steamed. "You're a Far. Sure! Fast!"

"Keep your voice down," Mira said calmly. "Others are trying to sleep."

"Is it that you don't know?" Tahn said with some ire. "Are you a puppet, too?"

Mira went on with her careful cleaning of the weapon. "We are all puppets, Tahn," she said. Tahn felt Mira's words might have personal implications for herself, as well. "Yet," she continued, "the end is not always known from the beginning. Especially for a puppet. Be glad your life will give you time to know that your road is your own."

"That's another thing," Tahn retorted. "I'm tired of riddles. Tell me why you say that. Tell me why I am here. If I am going to stand at Tillinghast, I have the right to know why it is me and not someone else." Emotion caught in his throat.

Mira stopped cleaning her blades, and showed him compassionate eyes. "I don't have all the answers you seek, Tahn. And even if I did, I don't believe hearing them from me would ease your heart. But what I can do is tell you about me. And maybe that will help you live with the uncertainty for now.

"You have recently had your Standing. A day to mark the putting away of childhood things, and the embracing of life that comes after it. In the light of ten thousand more skies you will toil and laugh and suffer. But what you call your day of Change is a Far's last sky. It is a day of ceremony for man, but for the Far, it is an epitaph. It is part of our stewardship that we do not live beyond the Change. It gives us the liberty to speak and do what is necessary to guard the covenant language left behind by the Framers of the Charter, and in so doing never be accountable for those things we must to do keep it safe. Never endanger our own souls. But we do not mourn . . .

"My sister's passing leaves me the sole remnant of my family line. She was Elan's wife. And before I go he will ask me to stay. To take up her crown. And to bear an heir. It will be an honor to be asked. And our people need this very badly." She paused and looked closely at him. "But I do not want to be the queen. And I do not wish to have a child that I will never hear use my name."

Tahn forgot to breathe. Through her speech, Mira never showed any anguish over any of it. Tahn marveled at her strength.

"It's strange. You don't remember your parents because they went to their earth while you were too young to remember. While I can see my father's face in my mind even now, still hear his voice and see his face, yet I cannot remember my childhood."

He'd said it. He'd shared one of the great burdens he carried. And it felt good to do so with Mira.

The Far looked back thoughtfully. He could see in her face that she understood the gravity of what he'd just said. "Why does the memory of your childhood matter so much to you, Tahn? Who you are is defined by the choices you make now. And for you this is truer than most."

Tahn considered her words. "Perhaps you're right." And then added, "And the same would hold true for any child of yours."

They sat looking at one another, and he wished he could wrap his arms about her, but didn't know how not to do it clumsily. The hiss of the lamp was suddenly very loud.

Tahn thought about how his life seemed almost a reverse of the Far's. Tahn could not remember most of his melura years, but had the possibility before him of a long life. Mira's life was nearly over. But in one way they were the same: Most of their childhood was fatherless, whether through death or the absence of memory. He wondered if that had shaped who both of them had become. For Mira, that question didn't seem to matter; for Tahn, it still did. The things that most defined him stemmed from a past unknown to him.

Maybe there was a lesson for him in her commitment to this journey to Restoration, where she would give so much of her life that would end so soon.

Considering it, Tahn felt selfish.

But so many things were still unknown. The Bar'dyn had come into the Hollows, and now a Sheason and a Far led Tahn and the others to the Heights of Restoration. He harbored feelings that compelled him to make choices he didn't understand. There was the mark on the back of his hand. What did these things mean?

And under it all was the vague memory of a man whose face he couldn't remember, but whose advice resonated deep within in his mind.

The faceless man in his dreams, and the voice out of his nightmares.

He tried to recall Rolen and the wisdom he spoke to Tahn in the bowels of Solath Mahnus. He thought he did feel some easing in his heart when he recalled the Sheason, a reminder to look beyond himself.

Then from habit, before unstringing his bow, he pulled it deep several times, limbering the wood and stretching the string. In his mind he heard the words: *I draw with my arms, but release as the Will allows.* Their familiarity also comforted Tahn, and he repeated them twice out loud, interrupting the stillness. The words fell from his lips like a prayer.

He had forgotten Mira was there.

When he looked up, she was looking intently at him. Neither of them spoke until he asked her what had been on his mind ever since he had met her in the Hollows. "Has a Far ever married a man?"

Mira smiled her glorious lopsided grin, but did not answer. He somehow knew she meant to tease him by withholding a reply. He had one more question, but she answered it before he could ask.

"I will sit vigil. You will have the bed to yourself."

· · ·

Fog and mist roiled over the precipice, licking at the stone. The darkness felt like wet leaves sticking to his skin. Only the faintest trace of light illuminated the emptiness beyond the ledge, as though the shroud that separated the solid from the ethereal held its own dark energy. . . .

As stones grated beneath his heel, the mists absorbed the sound, leaving Tillinghast as quiet as a tomb.

Tahn clenched his fist around his bow. The leather creaking beneath his grip was the only sound. To his right on the precipice stood an immense tree that rose into the shroud of fog and darkness. The bark of the tree was as black as the night around it. It was a forgotten sentinel at the edge of nowhere.

A shrill hissing rose up like wind over jagged rocks. Swirls of fog eddied and faded. And in the darkness, several strides from the land's end, the mists of Rudierd Tillinghast began to coalesce. A shadow formed in the shape of eyes and a mouth, streamers blowing through it and momentarily shaping the image before passing away. The lines of the face never varied, the mists only giving more detail as they passed.

Then, as Tahn watched, the eyes narrowed, glaring.

There is no morning here, Tahn. No greater light risen from the ashes of yesterday.

The words came into his head with the force of a thousand bells. Tahn pressed his hands to his ears, but could not stop the tumult in his mind.

Restoration, Quillescent, is the handmaiden that will undo the injustice of every age that has passed since the council parted. You will suffer the torment of countless lifetimes as the pawn of those too weak to answer for the crime committed against me.

The voice's final word tolled like a death knell and shook the very earth of Tillinghast. The mighty branches of the tree beside him swayed through the thick banks of mist.

I will not remain forever silent for doing that which I was asked to do, that which has been done as many times as stars shine from the sky. It is their failure, Quillescent, their crime that condemns you. Do you think you can balance a land, a people . . . a world? You are not even sure yourself what light means. *Tahn caught a glimpse of a malevolent smile in the twist of the fogs across the visage.* And how beautiful that the instrument that will lay all low to the dust is the very thing so revered by those nobles who first abandoned this place to the devices of men. Do you know it, dead man? Has the insult of your birth spoken it to you?

Tahn recoiled from the words, raising his arm to shield his face, the very sounds reverberating in his head, stinging his eyes. Rumbling in the earth caused large rocks to shift and pitch. The cracking of limbs at the top of the tree boomed like a peal of thunder. Tahn frantically looked around for help, but no one stood upon the path that led to the ledge. In that moment, the world grew darker, leaving the contorted face etched into the mists a shade paler.

An awful certainty stole through Tahn, causing the face to lighten yet another shade. The face grew whiter against the stark blackness of the Abyss, and laughter began to ring through Tahn's head, deep, resonant vibrations like the tearing of the land and the sound of falling sky.

Tahn fell to his knees, still holding his ears. He shook his head. Then the face brightened a last time, threads of mist whipping across its features. Wretchedness drew itself deep into the lines of its jaw and malefic eyes. In a hoarse whisper it spoke again.

It is nothing less than your choice, husk. It will also condemn your past and foreclose your future. And all will become eternal night. Just as it has been on every world without end. That is your birthright, Quillescent. That is your Tillinghast.

Deafening laughter erupted around Tahn. He pitched forward onto the hard stone of the cliff and tried to block it out. Mists lapped and caressed his face like dirt falling down through a crack in a coffin.

Tahn sat up in his bed, slick with sweat and breathing heavily. For a moment he did not know where he was. He frantically looked about. Mira was watching him.

She said nothing, but came to his bedside and took his hand in her own. He'd hoped for that touch ever since he met the Far. But tonight, it barely pushed back the dread growing in his heart.

The world beyond the window was still dark. But not for long. Slowly, he lay back down and turned his head east, his hand still held in Mira's. He managed to imagine a sunrise over the top of Balatin's stock barn before even that image mattered too little to remain in his mind's eye. He focused on his breathing and soon regulated the rhythm enough to calm his heart and leave the waking world again, if only for a short while.

CHAPTER SEVENTY-TWO

Leave-takings

Mira knelt at her sister's tomb in the Hall of Valediction. The shale shone brilliantly dark here in the glow of large braziers, which lit the names and dates inscribed deep in the dark stone.

It pained her to say good-bye.

Saying good-bye to a Far was not supposed to be a sad thing. Their passage beyond came vouchsafed by a covenant as old as the world itself. And Lyra had lived a joyful life, ruling so well and so thoughtfully that she'd earned a rare esteem.

But she had not produced an heir.

The Far shared their stewardship of the covenant language, but to only a few bloodlines were the gifts of that tongue given. And such was needed to maintain their commission, otherwise . . .

With Mira's sister gone to her earth, her line was at an end.

And childbearing years for a Far were understandably short.

That was not the source of her grief. She held no ill will for her sister having thrust this responsiblity upon her. It was not a law that she take her sister's place. But if she was honest, it *was* a fair expectation. More than that, it might prove to be an absolute need. The line should not be allowed to end; only a few Far possessed the special ability to both protect *and* understand the covenant tongue.

This was the angst in her heart.

And for the first time she could remember, that angst had called her away from a watch—just this hour, over Tahn. He would be safe in Naltus, and in the king's manse no less, but it was not customary for her.

She had needed this moment to think, to pray. Her path seemed so unclear to her.

However, there was another need in the world of men, one to which she'd joined herself with the Sheason many months ago. Meeting the melura from the Hollows had been a pleasant surprise. He was courageous, if willful in his ignorance. And she felt comfortable around him.

And yet it was a dream. She had but a few years to live. She should not be thinking beyond the promise of her call: to safeguard the Language of the Convenant.

But over the tomb of her loving sister, she argued with herself that her course had been to do precisely that—forsake her own covenant. Only her path took her beyond the black shale gates of Naltus. She hated to think how like the exile Grant that might make her. The man's leathery face would show a bright smile at that were she to share it.

Lyra, what shall I do?

As if in response, footsteps sounded on the hard floor. She needn't turn to know their owner.

"Can I not have but an hour to pray for my sister?"

"Prayers are not needed, Mira. You know this. And I would not interrupt the respects you pay her. She was my wife, and I loved her. But your companions are readying for their ascent into the Saeculorum, and I would have your answer."

"Mankind would not find your proposal to be tender." Mira ran her hands over the inscribed name of her sister.

The Far king's voice softened. "We are not mankind. Ours is a different destiny."

"Better?" Her voice rang with accusation.

True to his nature, Elan replied, "No, Mira. But it is a high calling to which we are bound. And I myself am not long for this world. I seek only the best interest of our commission here at the far end of the world. You must know that."

Silence settled in the Hall of Valediction. Elan neither pressed nor departed. Mira continued to kneel, searching.

"Tell me what to do," she whispered over her dead sister's body.

She stood and turned to Elan. He was a good king, strong and a better strategist than any single person she'd met in all her travels. He approached gently. He touched her face, and his eyes showed genuine compassion for her equivocation over this choice.

"It is not so easy," she said.

"Even with a people like the Far, the mantle of leadership is not easy to wear." He smiled, a wan look touching his face—something she had never before seen. Perhaps to sit at his side, to produce an heir, would be a happy last chapter to her short life.

"I am honest and kind," he said. "That is as true as the need to perpetuate the traditions and leadership we have put in place, for which there must be a child."

Mira looked back at the Far king and gave her own wan smile. "Subtle," she said.

A confused expression rose on his face, but fell quickly as he began walking her to the stable yard. There in the bright sun of Naltus, as her companions began to file out of the king's manor, she kissed his cheek. "I must see this through to the end first." She looked away toward the Saeculorum. "But I have a request of my king."

King Elan raised an eyebrow, waiting.

"You say the destiny of men is not ours. But if the veil comes down, our fates are inextricably tied with theirs." Mira came to her request softly but resolutely. "We must take our place at the Convocation of Seats. The world of men needs our strength and wisdom. Most no longer believe in who we are. And the regent faces sedition in her own courts. The Sheason are hunted. Elan"—Mira touched his arm gently—"you must go and sit at convocation, and remind them of what they have forgotten and the hope they may yet have in the stewardship we bear."

Moments passed before the king answered. "Mira, you're asking me this extraordinary thing even as you delay answering my own request. Our people need a queen, they need a continuing line. What you ask is more impractical if you do not take your place at my side, because I would then rule alone. What should happen if I died without a successor? It is an impossible thing you ask."

"Can you not see that this convocation will fail if you do not go? In times past they succeeded without our help, but narrowly, and the cost was dire for that. And because of it the Quiet better learned the weaknesses of man. It is different in this season, Elan. I have seen it." Mira thought of her sister's tomb. "Our covenant must be to more than those First Ones who gave us this trust. We are part of this world; our fates are joined." Then Mira touched her stomach and thought about mothers and daughters. "And there are promises to keep," she whispered.

King Elan's brow drew down. He was fair, but he would not be manipulated. "You are not thinking clearly, Mira. This simply cannot be. I will hear no more about it."

She then looked back at him with a calm defiance. "Elan, if you will not go, then I will take my place as queen and go myself."

Mira could see that her audacity struck him like a fist.

Mira did not wish to undermine him. But neither would she let this pass. "Think on it, Elan. But don't think long. They already assemble at Recityv. Two, maybe three, weeks, and all who will have heard the call and chosen to answer will have arrived at Solath Mahnus. From Naltus, it should be you who goes. The threat that comes needs the finest minds and stoutest hearts. I don't say that idly."

Her king smiled softly. "I know, Mira. It seems we each have something to consider."

"I am proud that you are my king, and were my sister's husband," Mira said. "And I will keep only good thoughts of you."

"Thank you, Mira. I loved Lyra. I still do. And I shall keep only good thoughts of you, as well." He then held up Mira's hand and passed her a note, her sister's last message for her, on a small roll of parchment. "Read it when your journeys are at an end."

They followed Vendanj into a grand stable yard. Soft loam gave generously beneath their feet. They emerged into the light of day, a thin steam rising from the soil warming in the sun. Around them, the rich smell of tilled ground hung sweet in the air. A series of outbuildings arranged in a perfect row bordered the far side of the yard. In front of the centermost structure, their horses stood tethered to a hitch post. Beside Solus, Mira spoke with Elan, both of them framed against the dark stone of the stable behind them.

As they approached, Tahn saw Elan take Mira's arm by the wrist and hold her hand flat. With his other hand, Elan placed something into Mira's opened palm. He squeezed her fingers over the item and she hid it within her cloak.

When she turned, Tahn thought he saw genuine gladness to see him. Mira came to his side, out of earshot of the others.

As she helped him check his saddle and tack, she said, "You speak in your sleep. It is a dangerous flaw."

He could not read the look on her face. It seemed an odd thing to find fault with, especially since he was sure she hadn't meant to sleep anyway.

"And just why is that?" he asked.

"Because you tend also to answer when someone speaks to you."

They stared a long moment at each other before Mira smiled. Tahn forgot to breathe, and grinned as he fought an expression of shock.

"What did I say?" Tahn finally managed.

Her smile held a moment more, then fell. "Never mind, Archer," she said. She was about to go, then leaned back in and whispered, "Oh, and it's not wise to sleep naked. You never know when you're going to have to get up in a hurry."

She ducked away before Tahn could laugh or blush.

"My scouts returned this morning and reported no sign of Quietgiven in the valley," King Elan was saying to Vendanj. "But the Soliel is not an easy place to hide. I'd rest little until you reach the Saeculorum. Even the Quiet may think twice before following you; such are the dreadful secrets that lay hidden there.

"Your packs are full, and your skins refreshed." Elan cast his careful gaze over their mounts. "We've seen to your horses. They'll be in need of little besides water until you pass beyond the Stretches." His brows lifted a question. "Tillinghast?"

Vendanj only nodded.

"We are come to the fabric of the Charter and the Tract, then. I pray what is restored to you there is the necessary sum of your First Inheritance, my friends."

them with a glance much as he had their horses. He seemed to lin-
ent on Tahn. "Be watchful. Resolve weakens when one nears a goal's
on. The Saeculorum will likely see to that. And if it does not, Tilling-
h. ."

Tahn looked down at the Far king. A wave of doubt stole through him.

"Thank you, Elan," Vendanj said, and took his saddle.

The others stepped into their stirrups in a riot of creaking leather. It reminded Tahn of the moment in the Kottel Rhine when men took to their plow
horses to partake in the ritual hunt. A thrill raced through him. Sutter's face
was a perfect mirror to the emotion; Nails had never looked so enthused. Tahn
thought his friend sat taller in his saddle at the prospect of what they were
about to do. Braethen sat his horse, reading, one fist filled with reins, the other
holding a book.

The Far had prepared a horse for Penit. Wendra drew even with him, put a
hand on his arm, and gave it a squeeze.

Grant rode up to Tahn and fixed him with a steady gaze. Tahn thought the
exile looked wistful, an expression that couldn't possibly seem any more incon-
gruous on the man's face. Then Grant held a daypack out to Tahn. Tahn took
the pack.

"You were late coming down to endfast, so I put some things aside for you,"
Grant explained.

"Thank you," Tahn said, confused.

"It is time," Vendanj said, looking straight at Tahn. He kicked his mount
into motion.

"Woodchuck, I don't know what you did to earn that man's adoration, but I
think I'd prefer a nest of angry hornets down the front of my pants to the
strange bond he seems to have with you."

A single chuckle escaped Grant. When Sutter and Tahn turned quizzical
stares on him, the exile only pointed toward the yard gates, prompting them to
get moving. Mira heeled Solus without looking back and led them from the
stable yard.

In the light of the sun, shale sparkled. They rode for eight straight hours,
taking only brief breaks to rest their horses.

Late in the day, shale gave way to russet earth broken by an occasional oasis
of long green grass around pools of water. Thorny flowers grew across the
earth, crawling over the ground in a huge network of interconnected creepers.
Stout trees with long thin leaves dotted the land, their shade giving rise to
bloodred ferns and yellowed bushes with leaves that rustled together like dim
rattles.

Ahead, the mountains loomed closer, reaching up with suddenness from the
basin as though thrust into the sky in a violent quaking of the land. The nearer

they drew, the less friendly the crags and sheer ravines appeared. Still Vendanj never slowed. It was as though he fled something yet unseen, though he never looked back.

Behind them, the sun began to set, aureate hues fading to russet and finally to the muted blues of twilight. With the passing of the light, they finally stopped to rest. Mira strung a tether line near another pool and tied Solus to it. The others did likewise, unlashing bedrolls from their saddles.

Sutter sat gingerly, grimacing against the pain in his thighs and buttocks. Once down, he promptly pulled a hunk of salted meat from his daypack and took a large bite. Around it he said, "No need to stop just yet. I still have feeling in my ass."

Tahn sat beside him and drank deeply from his water skin. When he was done, he said, "It's a lie, you've never felt a thing below your neck."

Braethen and Wendra laughed weakly, and found patches of ground on which to lay out their bedrolls. Braethen managed the fire. Vendanj strode to the center of their makeshift circle. "Eat and get to sleep quickly. We will move before it is light. Are any of you in undue pain?"

Even Sutter was silent.

But then he slapped Tahn's leg to call him from his thoughts. "Let's have a story," he said. "Penit, come over and give us one of your fancies. I'm paying." Sutter tossed a rock in the semblance of a coin into the center of the circle they'd formed. "And spare not the wit."

Tahn had noticed Sutter seemed to feel a kind of fatherly affection for Penit that surprised him.

Penit came as bidden, and smiled in embarrassment. Grant perched on a rock, his back to them, watching the southern horizon where stars flickered into view against the spread of dark.

"What story do you wish?" Penit asked.

"Anything," Wendra said. "Something stirring. Something familiar, perhaps. Oh, you choose."

Penit eyed the back of the exile and cleared his throat. Braethen had just finished readying wood for a fire, and struck it alight as Penit began.

Grant shifted a quarter turn, though not far enough to watch the boy spin his tale.

Penit raised his chin as Tahn had seen him do atop his stage-wagon in Myrr, and the words began to take a familiar form, scripted by a gifted author no doubt.

"Years ago, the great court of Recityv convened to rule on the life of a man condemned, the people said, because he held no regard for life." Penit paced once toward the growing fire, adopting an orator's pose.

Sutter chuckled enthusiastically. Tahn smiled at the words so eloquently fashioned as they came from the boy's youthful lips. The fire licked higher, casting shadows around them. At the far edge of their circle, Vendanj came, peering on with little interest.

"Go on," Wendra enthused.

With another tilt of his head, Penit resumed, this time raising an open hand to dramatize the tale. "Our man in this tale stood beneath the weight of his accusation while the gentry, the ruling seats, and the merchant classes all looked on." Penit lowered his voice to a whisper. "And the words he spoke are said to reverberate still in the great court of Recityv.

"And so it goes," Penit said, as if ready to tell one of the greatest rhea-fols he knew.

CHAPTER SEVENTY-THREE

Rhea-fol: The Dissent

And so it goes," Penit said again, and turned a circle where he stood. When he'd made one full round he wore a grave expression and tightly folded arms, his eyes stern and turned earthward toward the fire. The flicker of the flames lent much to the look of condemnation the boy wore.

"You are accused here of high treason, Denolan SeFeery," Penit said with a surprisingly authoritative voice.

Braethen had looked wistful. Now his face fell into a doleful frown.

Penit went on. "You are aware of the crimes that bring you here?"

He turned a circle—a character change—and stared upward into the starry night, defiance clear in the set of his chin. "I know why you have brought me here, my Lady," Penit said with firm resolve and a second adopted voice, this one calm but implacable. "But it is your arrogance and ignorance that call my actions crimes. Stop these proceedings before you condemn yourselves in your haste to place blame. I am not a traitor."

Penit whirled, again with arms folded. "Enough!" The vehemence of the command caught Tahn off guard. "You will answer as you are asked, and nothing more." Penit pointed an accusatory finger toward the fire, disgust curling his upper lip.

"There is ample evidence that I might wish to forgo these . . . pleasantries . . . but I will obey the law of the land before all else."

Penit sneered. "Blessed be Will and Sky that we are *civilized* here, or you'd be well acquainted with your earth by now. I've no ear to listen to what defense you intend to make, SeFeery. Still, we will proceed as with every dissent brought to the Halls at Solath Mahnus. And you will uphold the standard of citizenship throughout. Counselor, lead on."

Penit turned again, swirling plumes of dust at his feet drawn into the stream of heat now rising from the fire. He spun to a new stance two paces from where he'd been, a calm, calculating expression in his features—the Counselor. "Two nights ago our good and noble regent brought forth her child from the womb. Trumpets heralded the arrival, and songs came in chorus. Celebrations began at the announcement . . . though a secret remained strictly held by the regent's closest servants." Penit paused, his eyes narrowing farther. "The child arrived without breath."

Penit spun in one long turn back to the place of the accused. With an up-turned face and the poise of one beyond his years, he said, "These words weave a deception that hopes to demonize me, my Lady. No such jubilation existed in the city. The regent's child is not heir to her seat, and many suspect the timing of the child's birth—"

Penit shuffled in a tight spin to his first position. "Silence!" Clear hatred shot from Penit's eyes toward the fire. "You have been warned about violating the dignity of our procedure here. Now, go on, Counselor."

Again Penit turned, the cool, intelligent gaze returning. "Yes," he began, confident. "The child had no birthright to rule. That is not our way. But it is not the threat of losing a monarch that brings you to us today." Penit grinned with malice, and shook his head. "Rather, you must answer why you felt it your place to stop the restitution of that child's life by the benevolent abilities of the Order of Sheason. I might add, trying to stop the Sheason from saving the child is not so different from murder. For to take life and to prevent its reclamation are close cousins, are they not?" A snide look passed over Penit's face.

In the darkness, Vendanj appeared to scowl, his own arms crossed in front of him as he looked on at Penit's dramatic telling of the tale.

Penit again performed his circular dance, and landed in the guise of the accused. "Though framed as a question, sir, I take it you did not mean it so. I'll leave the question to its own destruction through every man's wisdom."

Once more the boy twisted around to the place of prosecutor, a thin haze of dust floating in the circle around his feet near the fire. "Very well. A semantic discussion for another time." Penit paced back and forth a few steps before cocking his head and staring inquisitively into the fire. "How is it that you knew where the ceremony would take place?"

Penit turned, this time more slowly, his form casting shadows. As a defendant he spoke toward the sky. "I was taken into the regent's trust as a special aid and protector. First to teach and inform as a benefit of my years in tutelage to Julian A'sa. Second to vouchsafe for her in special circumstances when the regent's guard were too conspicuous. I am Emerit."

Penit turned. "I see." His eyes shone as a child's who had captured something with which to play. "Then by her confidence, you knew when and where the stewards of the Will would minister to the child to give it a chance at life. And with this knowledge you undertook not only to deny that chance, but to contravene the wishes of the regent. Is that," Penit said, raising a dubious brow, "also a weave of deception? Or have I fairly described the circumstance and your intentions in its regard?"

Penit stepped much more deliberately in his slow arcing circle. Tahn watched the change in expression take place as the boy came to the position of the accused. A calm shaped his mouth, as again he seemed to speak toward the spray of stars. "It is . . . incomplete. It is true that there is little I did not know about the affairs of the regent. And with time, she came to trust my judgment."

Penit shifted his focus, as if turning from his inquisitor to view the unseen judge presiding over the dissent. "I became perhaps the only one able . . . or willing," Penit said in a sudden burst of anger, as he looked back to where his questioner might be standing, "to tell her she was wrong."

Wendra and Sutter let out a gasp, so thoroughly engrossed in the tale that they felt the shock of the seditious words in the Court of Judicature. Tahn found himself unwittingly looking in the direction Penit did when addressing the judge, attempting to see the object of Penit's fancy. Braethen nodded knowingly.

For a long moment Penit let the words hang over the fire and his rapt listeners. When Tahn spied Vendanj again, the Sheason had not moved, shadow playing across his darkened features as the fire spat and surged, glinting dully over his three-ringed pendant. He undoubtedly knew the story; the recognition of it was clear in his eyes. But something more rested there, something inexorable like floodwater in a spring of heavy rains.

The boy then stepped twice, gracefully completing his turn to change his guise back to the counselor. A thin smile spread on Penit's lips. "'Tell her she was wrong,' you say. With an adversary like you, SeFeery, I hardly need to present evidence here. Your arrogance about my Lady's trust in you is hardly the indemnification you might hope it to be." Penit let his grin fall. "And in any case, wide is the gulf between the liberty to provide strong counsel and taking measures to inhibit the actions or choice of the regent. In the instance of the latter, we have witnesses who attest to your treason. Do you wish to hear their testimony, or will you concede their words as truth?"

Penit twisted back and raised his eyes in calm compliance. "I've read their written testimonies. They are true accounts of what they saw." One eyebrow rose as Penit said, "But I admonish the Court of Judicature on this point. Each of the documents varies in detail; each is given with a level of dislike or affinity for me. They are of no use in determining whether my actions were *right*."

With a short step and a quick turn, Penit returned to his first position, a harsh glare on his face. "Quiet!" The shrill cry caused Grant to turn in full profile to the fire. Heavy creases in his tawny skin held the shadow of night. "We do not assemble to determine if *you* believe in the correctness of your own actions. What zealous insanity could be produced as defense here if we ignored the law in exchange for a criminal's earnest belief that he was justified in his crime?" Penit approached the fire and bent close. He glared down with disdain. "You, fellow, would likely be a handful of coins in an assassin's purse if I offered pardon for the vengeance that killed you, feeling justified in my *actions*."

"It was *her* child," Wendra whispered in realization. "The judge is the regent herself, and it is her child the man tried to kill." She looked over at Tahn, all slack jaw and wide eyes.

"The particulars are irrelevant," Penit continued. "By your own words you admit to speaking in open defiance to our Lady. You are well known to be privy to the most delicate information in the realm. You accept as truth the testimony of witnesses that describe your actions as contrary to our Lady's wishes. And you arrive today prepared to place your ethics above the law of this Court of Judicature and the tradition of Recityv since the Craven Season." Penit waved a hand as though to erase the insufferable image of the defendant, and stood up slowly from his slight crouch. "We could well be done now. Your head aches for the rope. Do you deny any of this?"

Penit rounded deliberately, his face slackening to near tranquility. "Yes."

Again Wendra and Sutter gasped. Braethen looked up at Penit, his attention newly won.

"This chamber has not been house to safe, peaceful traditions since the dark seasons which followed the Tabernacle of the Sky. Solath Mahnus is a monument to possibilities, but today the chairs of many sit vacant in the council rooms, where they remain abandoned since the Second Promise. Bloodlines of families as far back as the War of the First Promise today run diluted with the cowardice of *civility*. We are now only several nations loosely acquainted across a wide land, but our vaunted speech might make it seem that we are greater than we are." Penit widened his stance and looked heavenward, even more defiant. "We are men, women, and children. We are hopeful and able. We are grown in our understanding of much and have enjoyed peace for generations." Penit stopped. His eyes seemed to gather the light of stars. His voice softened, deepened. "But we are *not gods*."

A chill ran down Tahn's spine. Penit stood resolute, maintaining his fiction, eyes peering up at a judge no one could see.

A scowl rose on the Sheason's face.

Penit then whirled violently, his feet throwing rocks and dirt in a shower as he forced himself to a stop. "Such impudence! Such disrespect! How dare you say such things to she who is the sovereign authority, the great leader of our land! You are a mule. You desecrate the very nobility this chamber was built to honor. Such an accusation! You are not here to cast petty judgment on our regent. I will have you bound—"

Penit leapt, forgoing the turn. "Interesting that you believe my words speak only to our regent. Either you are clever to focus them so and try to provoke your Lady's wrath, or you yourself are uncomfortable with your part in claiming the rights and powers rightly reserved for none other than the First Ones. Such arrogance has consequences!"

Sutter shook his head, then nodded, then shook it again. Wendra looked every bit the mother she would have been with her own child: proud, attentive, happy.

Penit slid to the spot of his fiction's regent. "We return to pride so often, it seems." Consternation slipped from his brow, replaced by pity. "But to us was given the power and use of the Will through the Order of Sheason. That gift is administered as they see fit. I may make requests of them, but I cannot compel one to give of his own Forda for my sake. It is both immoral and unlawful. So in your reasoning, have you considered that trying to subvert the renewal of a life, as you did, is precisely the aggrandizement of power over life and death of which you accuse us? You," Penit reproached vehemently, shoving a regent's finger toward the fire, "are the one guilty of claiming godhood. You are a traitor. More, you are a hypocrite."

A brief turn, and Penit raised his head. "I do not believe the Sheason acquiesced so. What coercion bought their complicity? What promises were made? Their calling is sanctified; they would not be a willing party to this, since revivification is a known heresy. Only Velle draw the Will for gain. A true holder of the Will would suffer every indignity before being brought to this." Penit clenched his fist and raised it to his mouth, his voice trembling. "Or else resist you with all the power that is his."

Again Penit paused. Wood crackled and popped in the flames, sparks rose in orange flares against the night and winked out. The boy's words froze them all, the severity of the recriminations casting a pall throughout the camp, though it was nothing more than a rhea-fol.

Penit did not turn this time, completing a wide circle as he resumed the role of accuser. "Let us put an end to this," he said with a note of finality, and motioned with his right hand, bidding someone to come. Then he stepped to the far side of the fire and peered levelly over the flames. "We will hear from Artixan.

The Sheason in counsel to the regent, and the renderer who began to revive her child before SeFeery came to prevent him."

Penit gravely walked to the opposite side of the fire, where he took his place and looked back across the top of the flames. In a pained whisper, "Artixan, no. Please, don't do this."

Round again the boy went, his gait slow. Penit's eyes became glassy with tears as he adopted an expression of anguish and spoke for Artixan. "A perfect child, a handsome child, came through her womb. But the babe did not awake in this world. Her Grace was grieved, and prepared to begin the arrangements to bury a stillborn infant. Such courage I've rarely seen. Helaina is long known to possess a barren womb, yet this miracle began, and swelled her stomach to her own delight." A tear tracked across Penit's cheek. "What pain then to await the miracle, and at its very accomplishment know such tragedy.

"It is not given to us by custom to call upon the Will to redeem all a child's skies. But there was sufficient purpose in it to disregard the custom. And I agreed to it willingly." Penit looked across the fire imploringly. "It was necessary, Denolan. Can't you see that? You of all people? Must I say it aloud in this court? Rethink your position, please, before it is too late—"

Penit stepped quickly to his left; his countenance changed to a look of reproof. "That is all, Sheason, thank you."

"Too late" for what, Tahn wondered. Something lingered there unspoken, cut short by the clever questioner.

In the voice of the accuser Penit turned toward the accused, who Tahn felt he could almost see. "You now have the witness of the very man who you tried to thwart. He has vowed before the council that he freely and of his own desire sought to help the child. And"—Penit raised a finger as he kept track of each issue—"he is an honored member in good standing with the order, lest you think to sully his reputation here by naming him Quietgiven." Penit lowered his hand, looking up and around where the court gallery might have been sitting in the great round chamber. "It is your good fortune, I should think, that you are not left to the opinions of the people." Penit folded his arms as though concluding his argument in the role of questioner.

The boy gracefully took the place where he spoke in the voice of the regent. He performed a turn and frowned toward the fire with a melancholy aspect. "You may make a rebuttal if you so choose. But be warned that lies here are likely to invite a sharper punishment." Penit let out a long breath through his nose before continuing. "One thing more. I call on you to use discretion in the defense you make. But you mustn't feel restricted from conveying any information you believe has merit or bearing in this dissent. No matter the costs to others." Penit raised his brows, deeply furrowing his forehead, and said, "You are free to speak of any and all things to exonerate yourself of these allegations. Do you understand?" Penit looked into the fire expectantly.

Then, another proud turn, and his head inclined toward the stars low on the southern horizon. He nodded, and in that moment Tahn watched the boy adopt the most steadfast, honorable demeanor he could imagine. "I tremble at what is about to take place here," Penit said in low, resigned tones. "At the foot of Julian A'sa I sat when all the floors were swept and all the animals tended, and I listened. The stories of a hundred other authors I know in every detail, and the meanings behind their words.

"Hour after hour, for years I studied the art and tactics of combat, becoming a student of the body, its movement, its capabilities, its purpose. My preparations made me of value to the men and women who occupy seats in the councils. Soon I stood in attendance to these people when they convened their ruling sessions. I saw and heard how the life of a single man could be so blithely dismissed. Later, in higher, grander rooms, it was the lives of scores of men. And not soldiers alone, but innocent people of the city and of the great tracts of this nation, whose livelihoods precariously turn on the decisions a few make around a banquet table." Penit swallowed, his throat thick with emotion. "All this I witnessed, but I retained my hope in the simple, elegant balance of life, having an assurance that we yet choose our paths, and that the only real measure of our lives is our response to it."

Sutter was nodding. Tahn saw that Wendra and Braethen, too, nodded in agreement with Penit's words. Several strides away, still seated on his rock, Grant sat in profile to the fire, its light illuminating his tough, sun-baked skin. He had not yet acknowledged Penit's tale, but his eyes showed clearly his attention to the words.

Vendanj lurked a farther distance behind Penit. The Sheason eyed the boy as though he wanted Penit to get the words right.

Then something happened in Tahn. He had the strong impression that what he was hearing was, indeed, true. But that wasn't quite right. Not the story itself, though it might be exact in every detail, for all Tahn knew. But an overwhelming feeling of surety suffused him, as though the essence of what Penit's characters said was right. A familiar feeling of comfort and support washed over him, dispelling his momentary fears and all that had happened since the Hollows. In an instant, he recognized the sensation as the same he'd felt when Rolen had Stood for him in their shared prison cell.

"What I have done I do not deny," Penit continued with firm resolve. "It was mine to choose, and I'd choose it again. I've no guilt or shame of it." Penit raised his arms slightly, palms up. "We meet together, build cities and communities, and draw boundaries across land to establish wealth or create the feeling of security. But our attempts to define law are paltry things. They grow out of the misconception that one group of people knows better than another. And we err when we choose a course that abuses the power of Forda I'Forza, when we assume more authority than is ours to wield. It is inconvenient, this life. But to rob it of its sting is to divest it of the very reason to live." Penit took a deep breath and looked about, capturing the eyes of each of his audience in turn, ending with Tahn.

Looking back to where the regent might be, he said, "I do not recognize the authority of this Court of Judicature to pass judgment on me for my actions. It is a body of men and women too steeped in their own traditions to acknowledge a higher law. I hereby grant myself amnesty from the ruling of this court. Its deliberations shall have no bearing on my life. You will do as you will. But for my part, I say again that I reaffirm and grant myself freedom and liberty independent of this mockery."

From across the fire, Braethen sighed in sympathy for this man Penit played. The sodalist hung his head and clutched the book in his hand. Beside him, Wendra stared on, seeming equally pleased by what Penit said as the fact that he had said it. Tahn thought she might in an instant sweep the boy up and hug him close. Sutter only stared, weighing, Tahn thought, the things said. Whoever the man was who Penit spoke for, he was much like Nails in his fierce independence. But Tahn felt neither pity nor pride, only the assurance that the fabric of the tale was right.

Vendanj stroked his beard with thumb and forefinger and turned away toward the night. And while the scene Penit had played stood static as each considered what they had heard, Grant finally looked at the boy, his face catching the firelight and reflecting its warm glow. It might have been the heat from the flame, or simply the brightness of the fire, but the man's eyes seemed to glisten with emotion, the stoic face momentarily discountenanced, if only by a sheen of moisture. The exile shared a long look with Penit, silently appreciating the tale before turning back to the darkness and his vigil.

Penit turned a final time, retaking the first position of his narration. A resolute look stole over him, a look different from those of the other characters he'd portrayed. Looking at the fire, the boy began to speak in the voice of the regent. "I will excuse your blasphemy because I know you face a great challenge in reconciling justice with your own actions." With a malicious glance Penit said, "You are no different than the host of men and women brought here who endeavor to cover up their crimes or justify them because they fear the harshness of their sentence." In an angrier tone yet, he continued. "I only regret that I took you into my confidences. I wonder if you'd feel so beneficent had you never risen to the station of Emerit to the regent. Perhaps you have become the very sanctimonious nobility you despise."

Penit waved a dismissive hand. "I will abide no removal of the council for deliberation. By a raising of hands I want a vote now on the dissenter's guilt." Penit cast his glance around. The boy's haunted expression as he looked around the fire circle chilled Tahn to the bone. Without seeing a single juror, he knew the vote. With disquieting pleasure Penit announced, "The record will indicate unanimous conviction. Set the rest down as I now say." Penit raised his chin so that he might look down his nose at the flames, at the convicted. "For the crime of treason it is hereby declared that Denolan SeFeery is unfit for citizenship in the free city of Recityv. It is further known and witnessed to in this writ that Emerit SeFeery has willfully committed treason against the stewardship entrusted to him and against the right order of progress as held by the Higher Court of Judicature and the Exigents.

"Denolan SeFeery is thus remanded to permanent exile, and in the interest of justice will be given a sentence in the emptiness known as the Scar. With the exception of the First Seat at the regent's Table, he will remain the only one to know of the trust this judgment represents.

"Anyone known to abet Denolan SeFeery will be adjudged a traitor like unto him and punished accordingly.

"From this day forward, Denolan SeFeery will no longer be referred to with the Emerit honors of his former office. And return to the free walls of Recityv shall be construed as an act of aggression and punished by immediate execution.

"And so it is," Penit ended, his final word at once the crack of a gavel and the sound of a closing book. All that was spoken hung in the air, seeming to dare contradiction. It came as an epitaph, like words one reads in the stone or journal of a dead man. The Soliel swallowed the feeling, absorbed it. Deafening silence remained, broken only by the hiss of wood.

Then with a touch of familiarity Penit leaned forward. He spoke in a sweet, conversational tone. "Death is too good for you, Denolan. In exile you will feel the weight of your crimes, and the barrenness of the Scar will remind you of the barrenness of my womb, whose only fruit has now been taken from me. There you will live, your sinews growing hard and eventually inflexible. And what will keep you there, you are wondering? Your honor? A guard? An army?" Penit laughed caustically. "Hardly any of these. No, it will be the establishment of an orphanage for foundlings, castaways, the children of unfit parents. The very thing you hoped to prevent will be the tie that holds you to your heated rock. Derelict guardians will be forced to surrender their offspring to the council, which will decide where the babes are to be reared. And to you will be sent a share. A tree will be hollowed as a waypoint and cradle at the edge of your domain. On an appointed day a child will be placed there, given into your care." Penit sneered with severe reproof. "And if you do not arrive to retrieve the babe, it will die. And thus every cycle of the lesser light will you check the cradle. Some days you will return with only what you bring. Others you will nestle

life to your breast and ride more slowly to your home." Standin
a satisfied smile tug at his lips. "Either accept the sentence, or be
derer you conspired two days ago to be. My officers will be wat
other than you attempting to retrieve the children will be killed
still resides in you may fetter the sentence to you. If not"—Penit's ....e faded,
his eyes blank in the firelight—"then the deaths of countless innocents will
follow your every sky and cry against you when your life is at its end.

"Grant yourself amnesty? Grant yourself freedom and liberty from this
mockery? The mockery is yours, Denolan SeFeery. Mockery of life itself. I am
done with you." Penit ceased, staring into the fire.

Glassy eyed, the boy did nothing more than raise his head heavenward, a
last character change. "And I with you. My name in your mouth and the gossip
of your court is like the sting of vipers. I will no more answer to it. I am not
yours to hold accountable when your law is corrupt. When you violate the basic
Charter of man, my obligation to you is annulled. I am free. I am clean . . . I am
Grant."

Wendra and Sutter turned at the same time Tahn did to look at the broad
shoulders of their traveling companion who sat upon a nearby rock. Shock and
respect showed in Sutter's face as he mouthed something Tahn could not understand. Braethen alone did not look. Had he known? Why had he said nothing?

Suddenly, the sound of rushing air rolled toward them. Grant jumped to his
feet and took a step into the night, his sword a flash in his hand. In an instant,
Mira sprinted out of the darkness toward them. Over her head streaked flaming arrows, humming past her and flashing through the air above their circle.

"On your feet!" the Far yelled, drawing to a quick stop beside the exile to
prepare for unseen pursuers.

Tahn jumped up, nocking an arrow and pulling a deep draw in one fluid
motion. But he pointed the tip aimlessly toward the darkness beyond the fire,
unsure of a target.

Out of the night more flaming arrows brightened against the night, soaring
swiftly toward them, the shafts flying in an arc, seeking their target. Streaks of
light angled down first toward Mira and Grant, parting the night in rapid,
bright lines. As Tahn looked on, the Far and the exile danced away from of the
arrows, and just as often turned them harmlessly away with a quick flick of
their swords.

Sutter and Braethen took positions a few strides behind Mira, and Wendra
placed herself between the arrows and Penit.

In the distance, Tahn heard the deep, resonant beat of a drum. Hearing the
ominous droning beat, the hackles on his neck stiffened. Somewhere out there,
cloaked by the night, Bar'dyn advanced toward them. How many would be

hard to say, but before anyone could think to test the horses' endurance and flee north, an echoing call of drums answered the first from behind them. They were surrounded. Tahn pulled his draw around, but still saw nothing. Wendra shuffled her feet, trying to decide which direction to shield the boy from.

"Terror tactics." Grant spoke with a loud but calm voice, never looking away from the south. "They won't have moved this quickly after us with an entire collough. But the Bar'dyn did not find us without help."

The drums grew louder, closer. Where was Vendanj? Tahn searched the darkness for the Sheason, but saw nothing. Beyond the close veil of night, Tahn heard the approach of feet—labored, heavy steps, but not clumsy or careless. The sounds bore down on them from the dark.

Then in the distance, a glint of light reflected from two orbs bobbing in the darkness. A second set of eyes appeared, catching the light. Behind these came yet two more. Then all four Bar'dyn emerged from the night at a full run, their stout legs carrying their considerable forms at impossible speeds. No crazed look of ambush or bloodlust characterized their faces as maces and swords were raised to meet Grant and Mira.

Flaming arrows continued to light the sky above them, but these flew straight and seemed more an attempt at confusion than any real attack.

Still there was no sign of Vendanj.

The sound of drums drew closer still. Chaotic rhythms pounded. And just as the Bar'dyn came within three strides from Mira, the sound of footfalls fairly shook the ground behind them. Tahn whirled to see two Bar'dyn barreling in from the north. Wendra shot Tahn a dark look. His sister pivoted to meet the flank attack, and Tahn aimed at the first Bar'dyn coming in from behind.

He whispered his old phrase, now a thought more than anything else, and let fly his arrow.

Tahn's arrow struck the lead creature in the arm. Without slowing, the Bar'dyn plucked it away as if it was a mere splinter and let it fall beneath his feet. As Tahn drew again he heard weapons and bodies clash behind him. He thought he heard Sutter cry out, but had no time to check on Nails. He released again, aiming for the Bar'dyn's head. The arrow caught the creature just below the eye. A maddened shriek tore from its throat. The second Bar'dyn raced past his wounded brother and surged into their camp, closing on Wendra and Penit.

As Tahn raised a third draw on the Given closest to his sister, Wendra sang a string of syllables in a sharply dissonant melody. The air began to shimmer, looking like a horizon baking in heat. As Wendra's voice grew louder and more angered, the camp swirled. Blood began to flow from the first Bar'dyn's eyes, nose, and ears. But it pushed on as though fighting a river current, moving with deadly intent toward Wendra. A moment later it thrust a massive fist toward Wendra's neck and grasped her around the throat.

She ceased to sing. The shimmer in the air stopped, and the Bar'dyn's sluggishness ended. Wendra struggled against the beast's grip and was thrown to the ground on top of Penit. Tahn tried to retreat a few steps, but the two Bar'dyn slipped behind him and began to drive him away from the firelight. Tahn began to fire his arrows in a blur, as fast as all his speed and skill would let him. Some deflected off the Bar'dyns' tough skin. Others found home, sticking in the creatures, who wailed as they were struck. Yet Tahn had the feeling that the Bar'dyn did not swing their weapons to kill. And still they came on, pushing him farther from the fire. Tahn realized they were isolating him from the others.

And he was out of arrows.

He looked over at Wendra. He couldn't tell if she was breathing. Penit struggled to free himself from beneath her. Behind the Quietgiven herding Tahn, Mira and Grant descended on a Bar'dyn simultaneously, swords flashing in the weak light; the Given dropped in a heap. At their side, Sutter brandished his longsword in a huge, sweeping figure eight. His arms worked with fluid intensity as he drove one Bar'dyn back several paces. Another Bar'dyn tried to sideswipe Nails, but before it could land a blow, Braethen was there. A radiant white flash of blade arced in the darkness, followed by a hopeless cry where the Bar'dyn fell.

Mira and Grant parted and drew the advance of two more Given. The whistle of steel wielded by mighty arms sliced toward the Far. One arm went up, deflecting the blow, the other came directly after, catching the Bar'dyn in the neck. A gout of blood splashed Mira across the face.

A second, more cautious creature waited on Grant's attack. It held a menacing ax, ready to swing. The exile outlasted the Bar'dyn's patience, his sword held dangling at his side. The Given swung, its great ax descending like a judgment. Grant anticipated the move and leapt close to the Bar'dyn's wide chest. In a furious thrust, the exile swung his sword up through the underside of the creature's chin. The creature's movement ceased immediately.

Tahn looked back at the Bar'dyn pushing him far from his friends. They appeared unconcerned about the deaths of their comrades. The drums continued to pound, filling the night with sound.

Tahn looked around. *Where is Vendanj?*

"I am I!" Out of nowhere, Braethen flashed into Tahn's view. His battle cry erased the sound of the drums, and caused Tahn's skin to tingle. With fury, the sodalist came at the Bar'dyn that were pushing Tahn farther away from camp. Sutter rushed to Braethen's side. But before they could be of any help, arrows hit them in the legs and they both went down in a tumble.

Tahn stood alone.

Then something occurred to him.

He drew his empty bow, rehearsed the oldest words he knew, and aimed.

A look of recognition caught in the Bar'dyn eyes. "We did not choose this, Quillescent. Beware your own destruction if you first seek ours." It spoke with a soothing intelligence that caught Tahn off guard.

In the next moment the camp grew still. Quiet.

The drums ceased.

All light dwindled; the fire guttered. Tahn's own wakefulness seemed to ebb. An apparition cloaked in white, parting the two Given that separated Tahn from the others, floated in the air. Even the stars flickered, their immutable light straining in the shadow that surrounded the figure. Icy fear immobilized Tahn, and he dropped his bow. A willowy hand, draped in deep sleeves, rose. It came to point at Tahn. Tahn looked away. He thought he heard the whispers of a generation all rushing into his ears in an instant. With sudden, total weakness in his legs, he fell facefirst into the ground.

But almost immediately, an explosion of flame ripped the apparition apart, and there stood Vendanj, his arms extended toward Tahn. The Sheason swept his hands up toward the sky, and a wave of soil swallowed the last two Bar'dyn. The creatures fell, snatched down into the earth amid the grinding of rocks and twisted roots. They shrieked into the Soliel, their throaty voices calling wildly as they went until their mouths filled with dirt and sand that seemed to flow there intentionally to strangle their cries.

But in the sudden calm, before their mouths were no longer of use to them, one of the Bar'dyn looked up at Tahn with blank, scrutinizing eyes. "You still don't understand, do you?" the Bar'dyn said, turning a brief look toward the ground where his dead comrades had been swallowed up. "You cannot win a war against an enemy who hasn't anything to lose."

Then its mouth was full and its eyes lost their life.

Vendanj rushed to Wendra's side. The Sheason took his wooden case from the inner lining of his cloak. He produced a single sprig, opened Wendra's mouth, and placed it on her tongue. Then he took her hand and placed it splay-fingered on his own chest, placing his fingertips against Wendra's throat. A throaty hum rose from the Sheason's lips.

Penit sat close, watching Vendanj with fascination and concern. As Vendanj worked, the others were still, watching and hoping.

A few moments later, Wendra convulsed, then took a long, ragged breath. Her eyes shot open, immediately searching for Penit. Seeing him, she settled beneath Vendanj's hands, and began to breathe normally.

The Sheason then quickly tended to Braethen and Sutter, whose wounds were not severe. Sutter limped back into camp, his sword held loosely in his hands. Sweat ringed his armpits and collar. Between heavy gasps he muttered, "Had . . . them . . . worried."

Still shaking from his encounter with the apparition, Tahn crawled his way back to camp and asked Vendanj what they all must have been thinking. "Where were you?" His face felt raw and dirty, but he didn't bother to brush the dirt away. He propped himself up on his hands and stared through the fire at the Sheason. "We could have used you in this fight. My sister almost died!" Tahn began to cough.

Vendanj's countenance remained impassive as he looked at Tahn. "I had to know what they know, Tahn. I need to understand their intentions. So I exposed you to this threat. I was always close. But it was safer here than it will be in the Saeculorum."

The Sheason looked out into the dark. "They came to test us. It was just a band of advance scouts." Then Vendanj sat back on the ground, the expenditure of personal Forda claiming him, his face gaunt and pale. In the firelight, sweat shone on his brow like tiny pearls.

"They have reached the hills ahead of us. They know there's only one reason for us to travel north." He shook his head. "It doesn't matter. We must go. They know what we bring with us." Vendanj looked at Wendra. "They know your gift. That is why they sought first to silence you. And you." The Sheason settled a heavy gaze on Tahn. "Mark this: They have learned of you. Not as they knew you when first they came to the Hollows. Since you showed them an empty bow, they will now believe you know yourself." This time Vendanj shared a look with Grant before turning back to Tahn. "It is better you die than live in their service. Remember this when you have to make choices."

Tahn looked back at Vendanj. Hearing the Sheason talk of choices, much as others had done over the last few weeks, Tahn began to understand that whatever awaited him in these mountains would require him to make a difficult decision.

"Rest a while. We will ride north when you've collected your strength." Vendanj closed his eyes and breathed deeply, taking a sprig from his wooden case for his own tongue.

Tahn caught his breath, wondering what it meant that he'd raised an empty bow. He wasn't even sure he understood why he did it. Then the Sheason's words rang again in his ears: . . . *better you die* . . .

Tahn gathered his arrows. Sometime later they mounted again, and rode toward the Saeculorum.

CHAPTER SEVENTY-FOUR

Lineage

It was dark hour when Vendanj woke him.

They had ridden several hours to put distance between themselves and the Quiet, then found some shallow caves high on a defensible ridge. Tahn had barely fallen asleep.

"Tahn, please come with me. There are things we must discuss."

It was the heart of night. Tahn crept from his cold bed and joined the Sheason far from the others under starlight and a hard moon. Vendanj waited as another dark figure joined them in the shadows. For several long moments, they kept a silent company before the Sheason began in a low voice.

"Very soon, Tahn, I will tell you your purpose here in the Saeculorum, at Restoration. I will tell you all. But some things that have been kept hidden must be revealed first. Because you must know of them beforehand; they must not surprise or frighten you when you come to Tillinghast." Vendanj reached out and gave Tahn's arm a reassuring squeeze.

"These are hard things to hear, Tahn. And you will know, in time, that my secrecy to this point has been to allow you to focus on this one goal. Do you understand?"

Tahn did understand, much as he hated the secrets. "But why tell me now? Is there something at Restoration that threatens me?" He looked at the dark shape just deep enough in the shadows that he could not recognize who it was.

Vendanj was quiet a moment. "Tillinghast threatens us all, but you more than the rest. And more will I say when we have drawn nearer the Heights. But right now, I want to give you a gift. It is a restoration of a sort, and will answer many of your questions." He drew very close, and whispered. "Have courage, Tahn, and remember your Standing. You are now accountable."

The Sheason put his hands on Tahn's head and began to speak in a tongue Tahn had never heard. The touch of Vendanj's hands warmed his head, relaxed him, made him feel safe and comfortable. He could not understand the Sheason's words, but somehow understood them by the feeling in his heart. Then slowly, what Tahn could only call a veil slipped from his mind. As it did, memories returned to him, memories from his youth, before the Hollows.

Tahn fell to the hard rock.

In his mind, he fell still, down a long tunnel of forgotten things that made sense of thoughts and feelings that for years had made him feel odd, or sometimes even sick. Memories cascaded down on him like rushing waters.

He shut his eyes against the images. He knew without seeing that the shadow behind him was the man Grant.

And he knew that the man was his father.

The faceless man from his dreams and nightmares; the man who had taught him how to stand on a cliff and draw, and that what mattered was the *intention* of his pull, since there would be no target; the man on the barren plain—the Scar—the man with the wind-tortured voice; the man who taught him how to recognize his latent gift to hear the whispering of the Will and bring it into harmony with his weapon by reciting those words with every string drawn throughout his life: *I draw with the strength of my arms and release as the Will allows*—words that had defined him in ways which had often made him feel quite mad.

These words had stayed his hand when he should have defended his sister from the Bar'dyn. . . .

Tahn's eyes shot open, and he looked at the shape in the shadow. "You *fiend*! Wendra! Is she my sister?!"

Grant rushed to Tahn, but Tahn put his boot in the man's chest. "Answer me!"

The wind soughed around the cliff's edge under the brittle moon. "No," Grant said. "She is not."

Tahn stared out at the long, dark plain of the Soliel far below. "Balatin! Why didn't you tell me?!"

He saw in his mind a hundred memories of singing, dancing, hunting, playing, eating, celebrating Northsun, and feeling the warm love of the man . . . and it was all *false*! The life he had clung to, even while he could not recall the long past, had been nothing more than a hoax, a scheme, conceived by the people who claimed to love him.

And now, underneath it, he could see and feel his years of dry, lonely hopelessness spent in the Scar with Grant. He understood he had learned to fight and examine and live, all in anticipation of the day he would come into this place of last things and prove a sacrifice for a Sheason and his martyr's quest to be right. Murder rose in Tahn's mind.

The Sheason must have sensed it, because his hands took hold of Tahn again, imbuing a measure of peace to his troubled heart. Again Tahn felt warmth.

But it was not sufficient to quell the anger seething inside him. When Vendanj removed his hands, Tahn knelt under the harsh glare of the moon and swore an oath. "I will see you both plucked on the plains of death's decay and expunged from every book that bears your name for good. And if there is some quality in me that qualifies me to stand at Tillinghast then you. Have. Failed!" he screamed into the vaulted heavens. "Because I will not go! For your lies and deception, and for stealing everything that was simple and honest and true from me, I would rather the Quiet come and the sun die in the east than help you fulfill that plan that made me its sacrifice." He drew in a great breath. *"No!!"*

He collapsed again and wept bitter tears.

He understood so much now, so many of the questions he had asked tentatively all his life, because probing too deep touched on possibilities he did not care to learn. But in awful revelation under the hands of this Sheason, he understood. He was Grant's son, trained for ten years in the barrenness of the Scar, prepared for a time none of them hoped would come, but then sent away to the Hollows, where they held safe their secret. Where Grant had sent his best friend and his wife, whom he had known and loved from his life at Recityv before his exile, to care for Tahn as their own son.

"Balatin," Tahn cried. "Why?" The tears on his cheeks streaked hot and painful.

As he lay beneath those same stars that had once been the far points of dreams, he realized that the man who should have loved him first and best, his real father, was the one who had sent him away.

And slipping farther into the abyss—successive shadows of his own eternal nightmare—Tahn realized that though he now knew the awful truth about his birth father, he still could not recall the face of the woman who had given birth to him. Even now, there remained secrets.

Tahn again cried out, anger and frustration and sadness competing in his heart. He had been an instrument. That was all his life had ever been about. The days since his forgotten youth, the days of the Hollows, had been his to live and remember. But they were a disguise to hide the purpose Vendanj and Grant thought might one day come, and for which he had been removed from the company of those who should have loved him.

But his heart also wept for the loss of the memories of the life and family he'd believed were his own. For Balatin, Voncencia, and Wendra. His heart broke the most because of her. He'd not even been able to defend her because of these things they'd put in his head about the Will. The guilt and torment belonged more appropriately to these awful stewards bending over him in this far place. Would that he could transfer *that* cost to them, as the Velle did with their villainous art! He knew now that the Sheason had placed a veil over his memory, causing him to forget everything before he came to the Hollows; likewise, he knew the Sheason had done something to Wendra's memory, since she believed Tahn was her brother.

Into the dark, unyielding stone of the Saeculorum he cried, "Who am I? Who am I!"

He wondered if those strange men and the unknown crests he'd seen at Balatin's funeral had belonged to these conspirators. Had his real father been there and not come to make himself known?

As he wept bitter tears into the crags of the mountains, Tahn's anger turned to hatred, and he decided that he did not care. He hoped that Grant remained forever in the Scar, where the endless sun and lifelessness could beat on him until time passed him by.

Only for the little ones at the cradle . . . which he recalled with painful clarity. Even now he heard the cries of babes he'd held as he and Grant had sought homes for them.

Then the Sheason spoke. "There were many reasons for Grant to accompany us, Tahn. But this is first among them: He's your father. Hear what he has to say."

Tahn glared up at the exile.

Grant looked back, his eyes hard to read. "Tahn, you remember now that you lived with me in the Scar. For ten years you trained before I sent you away. I could tell you it was to give you a better life, and that wouldn't be a lie. But neither is it the real reason, because I would have sent you there regardless."

The exile looked up at Vendanj, then resumed. "Early in your life, Tahn, it became clear that you possess a special gift, a certain bond between you and the Will, so that sometimes you can sense things about it that virtually nobody else can perceive. Not all the time. And not for all things. At least not when you were a child. But with time, the ability grew. I knew I could not hide this, even in the Scar, from those who would seek to abuse your gift or even take your life . . . as the Quiet now tries to do. That is why I sent you to the Hollows. It was once set apart—hallowed—by the First Ones, as a safe haven from the Quiet. I thought you would be safe there, especially in the care of my closest friend . . . Balatin Junell."

A fresh wave of anguish thickened in Tahn's chest and throat, and he bit back more tears. Grant tried to touch him, to console him, but Tahn jerked away. The man withdrew his hand.

"But even before sending you to the Hollows, Tahn, we suspected your gift might one day be needed in the way it now is. That is why I taught you to draw with the strength of your arms, but release as the Will allows."

Hearing the words that had plagued him all his life, had often driven him mad, and that had stayed his hand when he wanted to aid his sister—not his sister, Wendra—the words spoken here, by this man who had abandoned him . . . it was almost more than Tahn could bear. He shut his eyes and waited for this nightmare to end.

"You see, Tahn. When you go to Restoration, all your choices will return to you. Even for melura, such is a grave risk. But you . . . your choices have been guided by your unique sensitivity and bond to the Will. You possess less guile, Tahn. It will still be painful, but your gift may make you the one person who can stand at the Heights of Restoration, feel the caress of the abyss, and survive having to confront all at once a lifetime of any doubts, misdeeds, arrogance, and bitterness."

Tahn opened his eyes again, and stared with hatred at the exile. "Why? What happens if I survive Restoration?"

Neither the Sheason nor Grant immediately replied. Finally, Vendanj said, "Soon, Tahn, we will prepare you for it. But you have learned enough tonight. Too much, perhaps. Nevertheless, you must make your peace with what we have shown you. Not this instant, but soon. Very soon. You have had your Standing, Tahn. More, now, is required of you."

Tahn took a deep, bracing breath, trying to gather his composure. But it would be no use, not tonight, anyway. To endure these things, he could only harden his heart. These many long years he'd suffered with doubt of the deepest kind; his own sense of identity and worth had been taken from him. Looking back now, he thought he could see the questioning glances of those in his own home, Balatin, Voncencia—had they ever really worried about Tahn, the instrument of schemes plotted by exiles?

Distantly, he realized the Sheason and the exile (whose name he did not wish even to utter) were trying to talk to him. But Tahn no longer heard them.

He crawled over the rough stone back to the shallow cave and lay down, wondering if the dreams that came would at last be truly his own. And if they might, after tonight, be darker than all the secrets and lies and doubts that had plagued him these many years.

As he fell down toward nightmare, he shivered not from the cold of the Saeculorum, but from wounds of the soul he didn't know how to heal.

The guilt descended on Grant in a rush.

He sat at the edge of the cliff as his son crawled away, and let the self-recriminations scourge him. The gentle but firm hand of the Sheason on his shoulder did little to reassure him before the three-ring left to tend to his own needs. In the dark solitude, his own remembrance grew full and bitter.

He knew and still believed that sending Tahn away into the Hollows had been the right thing. The boy had received from him that which would serve him all his life, but the Scar and being in Grant's company were not healthy for the lad. More important, he'd be safer in the the Hollows.

Still, he'd sent away his own son, and the thought of it had never been far from him. If his exile held any real punishment, it had been that.

He'd not stood beside his son through it all.

He'd done the next best thing, convincing his closest friend, Balatin, to leave his life in Recityv and take his young bride into the Hollows to rear Grant's son. Balatin had been a good father, and Voncencia a good mother. The boy had had a good, simple, safe life. Still, though, remorse and shame touched his heart.

Abandonment. Something Grant knew about, and hated in himself.

As he stared into the distance, he knew that the long years of placing the children from the forgotten cradle in the homes of those who might better care for them had been a kind of personal atonement. Not because Helaina had sentenced him to it. But because he sought to correct, by that service, his own act of desertion.

And if he was honest, he even resented his old friend, Balatin, despite the immense favor the man had done him. For he imagined the moments his friend had shared with Tahn that Grant would never know.

But those many years of rearing wards in the Scar, of protecting those he'd placed into homes here and there, gave him confidence that he knew what was best for a child, for a young man. He would have to find some comfort in that knowledge. He might even have to use it to guide Tahn yet later in the Saeculorum.

Or afterward, if Tahn was not destroyed at Restoration.

And though the Scar had not gotten into Tahn as it had gotten into him, he nevertheless saw much of himself in his son: honesty and doggedness in service of what was right. It pleased him in the same way it would any father, but those traits had also caused Grant a lifetime of sorrow. He could only hope it would not be the same for Tahn.

In the end, though, the guilt was unavoidable. His heart ached with it. He could not undo what had gone before. He might hope it had prepared his son for what lay ahead, but he was not deceived that even should Tahn survive, he would never truly be the boy's father.

He had given away that honor.

And so on this rocky ledge, the Sheason's restoration had been dual. Grant's own lifetime whirled back on him, and left him as immeasurably and completely in the Scar as if he had never left its barren confines.

Grant needed the stoniness of his heart to creep back in, to relieve the pains of memory and choice.

If there was any blessing to his life in the Scar, it was the emptiness it inspired. And there were times the exile could call upon it to soothe him.

Here at his own Tillighast, he hoped it would come to him.

CHAPTER SEVENTY-FIVE

Waking Dreams and Forgiveness

Tahn woke to the crush of dirt and scree under Sutter's boots. His friend was uncustomarily up before the sun, and walking away into the night alone. A moment later, Tahn followed.

Frigid winds swept down the face of the mountain, tamed by the heat that rose off the Soliel. On the face of the short, sheer bluff, Tahn hunkered down next to Sutter, who'd found a crag to sit in. Out of the wind, everything became suddenly quiet, and he stared with his friend into the predawn dark out over the Stretches, away to the far south and west, and out of sight.

They shared a companionable silence.

In an hour maybe, all would waken to the birth of a new day. Tahn tried to remember the excitement morning used to hold for him, when the smell of sweet-root and eggs filled the air as they sizzled over a griddle on the hearth. Strong warm tea brewed in Balatin's pot, and from the yard came the sounds of wood being split to fuel the endfast fire and feed being thrown down for the animals. Then he would race through chores before he took to the trees and discovered a new way through the woods to Sutter's house, where hopefully his friend would be stooped over his furrows, and Tahn could send a dirt clod into his ass without being heard.

As he peered deep into the darkness from the Saeculorum arête, Tahn beheld in his mind a greater-light that shone weakly and indifferent over the crests of these far mountains. The promise he'd always felt when imagining the sun was somehow gone.

Why does anyone believe in their next day? Why do they want it?

Tahn shut his eyes and rested his head against the rock, grateful in the world for only one thing: his friend, Sutter, who did not try to fill the air with word or jest at this predawn hour. Nails was the only person in all the world he could talk to about the horror of his last few hours. And Sutter, perhaps better than anyone, would understand.

His friend had himself been abandoned.

Finally Tahn broke the silence.

"You've been a good friend, Sutter," he began. "Despite the strange things you've seen of me all these years, questions I'm sure you've had . . . you never asked. And it never affected our friendship."

Sutter, still staring into the darkened plain, gave a wan smile. "You were my friend, too."

"Then can I ask you something? Something about your parents . . . *all* of them?"

Sutter turned, and nodded.

Tahn didn't need to debate if he would tell Sutter the whole truth. "Last night the Sheason somehow restored my memory of my childhood. And among all the memories and secrets, Sutter, I learned that I am not Balatin's son. The dreams and loss of memory, all the things that have plagued me, they're all because of my real father . . . Grant."

In the dark, Sutter's eyes widened. But he did not speak, allowing Tahn to go on uninterrupted.

"I spent many years with him, but eventually he sent me away to live in the Hollows with Balatin and Voncencia, who knew but said nothing. A Sheason clouded my mind so that I would not remember my true father or mother, or even who I really was." Tahn choked the words out. "Why didn't he want me, Sutter? Why do parents not want their children?"

Silently, Sutter wept with his friend and took his hand in a firm Hollows grip. He spoke through the tears. "Tahn, Grant is not your father. Your father is Balatin; your mother is Voncencia. I don't know all the reasons why they made the mistake of not telling you the truth, but they loved you, Tahn. Do not doubt it. I was in your home, I knew your father. Hold to that."

"How do you do it? How do you put a parent's abandonment aside?" Tahn waited, hoping for some truth that would help him. If anyone would have it now, it would be Sutter.

His friend looked back, his eyes distant. "Maybe you never do." A calm touched his face. "I think you have to find a way to live past it. For me . . . I consider myself an orphan. Not because the parents who bore me were already dead. They weren't." Sutter looked out on the vista before them. "They just didn't want me."

He wept more silent tears and spoke of the pain he'd held secret from Tahn all their lives.

"I thought for a long time that I wanted them to die. I remember wishing I could watch it happen. I hated them. They were performers on a pageant wagon much like Penit, and didn't want to be burdened in their vagabond lives. My true father, Filmoere, saw them in a field one day when they'd come to the Hollows with their wagons to play the rhea-fols."

Sutter's eyes stared into the past. "They were alone in the high grass, hidden, but my father walks the field every day to survey his farm, and came upon them.

They had just given birth, Tahn. There in a field under the sky, they'd brought their child into the world between sketches on the wagon they trod for coin."

Then Sutter looked back at Tahn, his eyes streaming their sorrow as he said, "The man who sired me was about to put me in a bucket of water to silence my cries and end my life before it had begun."

The revelation stole Tahn's breath. How long had his friend lived with this knowledge? Tahn ached just hearing it, and the image rose up like a specter that even Tahn knew he would never be able to forget.

Sutter held Tahn's gaze, and went on in a low voice. "He rescued me, Tahn. Filmoere, my father, took me in as his own. Raised me. Gave me a life. And he told me the truth of it because he said truth was the only way." Then Sutter wept again, but silently. "He told me the better truth was that he was proud of me, and that none of that business in the field meant a thing. Told me he loved me."

Sutter looked back at Tahn, quiet again. "So your father is still Balatin. He made mistakes, and he should have told you the truth, but he did not abandon you. And I am a witness to that."

They sat together for a time in the dark of the crag staring out over the Soliel. Tahn's spirits rose a little. And he imagined the dawn but briefly.

Until Sutter spoke again.

"Tahn, have you ever dreamed with your eyes open?" Sutter asked. He let the inquiry hang. "Ever stood at a window, seeing unearthly things that you did not want to believe were real?"

A gust of wind howled around the bluff above them, and with its passing, the breezes vanished altogether. In the distance, the earliest trace of the new day touched the sky in shades of deep violet.

At last, Tahn shook his head.

"I've seen some things," Sutter continued. "Like dreams in the moments I first rise, and the last moments before I fall to sleep. I don't know what to think, fatigue maybe. No harvest ever worked me so hard as this." He pointed back toward the horses and the others. "But I think it's more than just dreams. I see them when I know I am awake, and try as I do, they don't leave when I tell them to go. It's hard to sleep. I need to tell someone about them, Tahn. I need to tell you."

Tahn nodded. "What have you seen?"

Sutter looked away at the horizon. Traces of light streaked the sky. "Last night, sleeping under the eyes of the Far, it was the strongest. But I've seen it each night since the prison at Recityv . . ."

"What is it?" Tahn shifted, uncomfortable with the import of his friend's words.

"I see faces, Tahn. All the time, and not like you do when you just think of them and remember. It's not like that." Sutter's voice began to tremble.

"Sometimes I think they're looking at me, trying to tell me something. But their eyes are empty; it's like they're looking through me, or that they're not really here at all in this world, and I can just glimpse them in whatever world *they* inhabit."

"Who?" Tahn prodded. "Who do you see?"

Sutter's head swiveled with ominous deliberation. He settled Tahn a fixed gaze. "Will you believe me if I say it? Will you forgive me if it's true?"

"What?" Tahn asked. But inside he wasn't sure he wanted to know.

"Have you ever thought the stories we told around the fire were more than just an evening's entertainment? Have you ever"—Sutter swallowed—"seen the soul of a man, Tahn? Because I think I see them. I think I see death before it comes." With a quiet tone he finished, "And I think it walks with us to Tillinghast."

Sutter looked away from his friend again.

Tahn patted Sutter's leg. "Maybe you just need some sleep, Nails. I know I could use some."

"Maybe," Sutter agreed, unconvinced. He tugged at the leather loop around his finger that the Sedagin had given him. Tahn thought it must remind Sutter of a different strength and truth he knew he could possess. He clenched his fist and sat straighter. "The night we stayed at the leagueman's home," Sutter said slowly. "Do you remember?"

"Of course. You spent half the night under your bed with fever dreams."

Sutter corrected him. "Not fever dreams. I don't know what it was, Tahn. I was falling asleep but still awake when I began to feel cold. I got up to close the window a little. When I got to the sill, a face rose up out of the dark beyond the glass."

"You were pretty sick," Tahn offered. "Could you have seen your reflection?"

"That's what I thought at first. I even remember laughing at myself for spooking at my own mirrored image . . . until I moved, and the image didn't."

"But this all sounds like a fever dream, Nails," Tahn reasoned. "You could well have imagined it, and ended up falling out of bed and rolling beneath the mattress."

Sutter stared at him; even now he dreaded saying it out loud. "The face I saw that night beyond the window belonged to the woman they burned the next day."

His friend's face went slack, and Tahn's own heart pounded. His mind swam.

"Will and Sky, Nails, are you sure?"

"As if she was my own mother," Sutter replied.

"Do you suppose she got away from Lethur? Got away long enough to find our window and throw a scare into us?" Tahn wasn't convinced of his own explanation.

"I might have convinced myself of that, until I saw the spirits of two scops in my cell at Solath Mahnus. Two faces, Tahn . . . that were hanged after I'd spent a night under their unearthly stares." He looked Tahn in the eye. "I'm seeing the dead before they go to their final earth. And it scares me, Tahn. It scares me."

Silence settled over them. Sutter turned and stared thoughtfully into the cold of dawn.

Tahn took Sutter's hand again in the Hollows clasp, stirring in him a look of gratitude so overwhelming that he nearly wept. Sutter surely knew that whatever caused him to see the things he did, Tahn would believe him.

Death walked with them to Tillinghast.

"That's not all of it, Tahn." Sutter pulled his legs in against his chest, and wrapped his arms around his knees. The greater light offered no warmth of body or mind. A soft sussuration of leaves stirred by a cold breeze whispered a warning, as Sutter prepared to tell Tahn the rest.

It must be such a burden. The anguish and loss and confusion and regret in the faces of those panaebra, unhoused from their bodies in anticipation of their death. And drawn to Sutter. Was this thing in him permanent? How would he live with this? How would he ever find love and have a family, knowing that he would one day see their souls before they died, and then have to spend that last day with them knowing what would come?

And what of his parents, Filmoere and Kaylla, who had given him a life and home? Already Sutter must dread the day he would see harbingers of their deaths and grieve for them while they yet lived.

It was too much.

I'd like to return to my roots. Just till the earth and leave Restoration and everything else behind. No waking nightmares anymore. No shadows of death coming to me. Not my friends. Not my parents. . . .

But he gripped Tahn's hand hard and looked him in the eye, as though somewhere inside him he wanted to believe that the things he saw could be changed. "The face I see now, every night since Solath Mahnus . . . is Mira."

Tahn sat in silence. Forgotten were the mark that scarred his hand—a brand he knew now belonged to the children of the Scar—and his misgivings about secrets and Vendanj and Tillinghast. His eyes ached from sleepless nights and the endless stream of days that had preceded them. In his mind he saw the image of a terrible water funnel beating a helpless elk into the mud, and remembered the animal wasn't meant to die. What did he feel about Mira's death? Was *she* meant to die?

Tahn shook away the thought when Sutter spoke once more. "Do you think it will be like this forever? Will I now see those soon to die all my life, until I join them?"

"I don't know, Sutter. But I will tell you what I do know. For as long as you need me, I will help you however I can against these visions."

Tahn could see his words helped his friend. Sutter's jaw set with determination. "I don't know what's at the end of these mountains, Tahn. I don't know what waits for us at Restoration. But whatever it is, I will give everything I have to help you. And if we falter, the faces we'll remember, the faces we go to the end for, are our fathers, the ones who stood by us when others would not."

Tahn's throat tightened and his eyes started to water. He gave his friend a strong embrace and stood, his head still filled with the ache of revelations, but now also of warning and doubt and a nameless desire. He left Sutter sitting low against the rock, and returned to Jole to check his saddle, his provisions, to busy himself with any task normal and mundane.

As he fidgeted with the saddle belts, Wendra drew up beside him.

"How are you?" she asked, her voice husky.

Tahn realized it was the first time he and his sister had spoken since she had been attacked by the Bar'dyn, and a prick of guilt brought a weak, blushing smile to his lips. "I've had better days. How are you?" He pointed to her throat.

Wendra gingerly touched her neck. "Still hurts," she managed. "Feels like the bruise goes down my throat. Just talking is a strain." She coughed lightly.

"Then don't," Tahn said. "We can talk later. But I'm glad you're on your feet. I guess I've one reason to thank Vendanj." Tahn looked up the hill, where several strides away the Sheason cast his hawkish gaze back over the same vista he'd left Sutter appreciating. "You ever feel like it might have been better if we'd just stayed in the Hollows?"

Wendra followed Tahn's gaze, then pointed toward Penit, who methodically rubbed his mount's legs and sang soft snippets of a song Tahn had often heard Wendra singing. She whispered, "Sometimes. But mostly I'm grateful to have come along. I'd never have met Penit otherwise, and in spite of the danger, it's been a kind of blessing for me to watch after him." She turned back to Tahn. "And Balatin would have wanted me with you. He spoke to me often of our duty to each other." She took his hand. "I love you. You're my only family now."

Strong emotions rose in Tahn. Looking at Wendra, he still loved her as a sister. But new knowledge darkened his tenderness. She was not his true sister, though she didn't know it. Tahn shot a look at the Sheason, wondering if he should tell her. What consequence might that have? He decided to leave it be for now. She'd been through too much already.

"Besides, when this loveliness is over, we'll go back, and Hambley will keep our plates hot and full for the stories we'll have to tell his patrons." Wendra playfully rolled her eyes. "It might even fetch me some attention from eligible men besides Sutter." She coughed again, quickly stifling the noise with her palm.

Tahn marveled at his sister's resilience, and was grateful for this moment, so like the days before her pregnancy, before the night he'd watched the foulness out of the Bourne hover over her birth bed when he'd been unable to defend her. But then, how much could he have helped? The words he spoke when he drew his bow, the need for him to feel in harmony with the Will . . . were they really him? Perhaps the secrets of the Sheason and Grant—his father—were responsible for his inaction. Suddenly, he wanted badly to tell Wendra everything, so that she could understand what had happened when her child had been stolen away into the night.

So he did. He unburdened himself to her one of his oldest secrets, the need to seek the correctness of his every draw, the words he recited. And he explained how he'd uttered those words when he'd aimed at the Bar'dyn who'd come into their home to take her child.

"I had the feeling that I should not shoot," he said. "I can't explain it, Wendra. It doesn't make any sense. But I'm so sorry. If there was ever a time in my life when I wish I had not heeded those feelings . . ."

She smiled wanly.

"I want that shot back," he said. "Even if I couldn't have saved the baby, I want the chance again to make that shot."

In his heart of hearts, though, he didn't know if he could do it differently if he was given the chance.

Wendra shook her head. "Don't say such things. If these feelings in you are true, you must listen to them."

Tahn looked over at the Sheason, who stood preparing to continue upward into the Saeculorum. "They tell me that this ability is the reason they came for me in the Hollows." He looked at her, hoping to find the sisterly compassion he'd always found there. "They want me to use it at Restoration. They think it may be enough to preserve me . . ."

"Preserve you? From what?" Wendra quickly asked. She then looked toward Vendanj herself.

"I don't know," Tahn replied. "But it feels like a long time since we left the Hollows. So much has happened. I don't feel like myself anymore." He stopped, and refocused. "I'm sorry, Wendra. I'm so sorry."

When he finished, he wondered what she would think of it, after all.

Wendra placed her hands on his cheeks and turned his face fully to her own. She looked at him tenderly, and Tahn saw there the might of his father, Balatin, a strength surpassing all he'd seen: a willingness to forgive.

With an intent gaze, Wendra whispered, "Let it go. I do not blame you."

Of a sudden, he thought he might just go to Tillinghast and succeed. This woman had forgiven him when he had been unable to forgive himself. He wished for a bit of her strength. He pulled Wendra close and folded her tightly into his arms. "Thank you," he said, and looked up to see Vendanj watching them.

Tahn spared a look at Penit, whose attention had likewise been drawn by his and Wendra's embrace. A look of gladness played across his smooth features.

Then Wendra drew his attention. "Revelations have been part of this whole journey." She gave him a steady look, her words carrying a double meaning.

"How do you mean?" Tahn asked.

"I've learned a little about myself, too, Tahn. Apparently, gifts run in the family." She smiled at him, and explained about the power of her song. She told him about Jastail, and the slave blocks, and the terrible song she'd sung down on the Bar'dyn. She told of Seanbea and the Descant Cathedral and the Maesteri.

"I learned why Vendanj brought me out of the Hollows," she said. "He meant for me to study music at the Descant, and join the Leiholan in singing the Song of Suffering." A look of regret crossed her face. "Belamae needed my help, but I couldn't stay, Tahn. I have to be sure Penit remains safe. Still, the look of disappointment on his face . . . I hope I haven't made my own worst choice. The Sheason drove us all to Recityv because of me. And I didn't stay. . . ."

The realization sank in: Wendra was the other half of whatever Tahn was being marched to Restoration to do. Vendanj had meant for her to help keep the Veil strong through her gift of song; and the Sheason meant to have Tahn's spirit tested at the place where the world touched the abyss, to relive every moment he would hope never to recall. Why? It had to have something to do with Wendra and the Veil. He believed the answer must be treacherously simple, and yet it eluded him, and filled his heart with dread.

Until Wendra took him by the shoulders and drew back to arm's length.

"Now, to more important matters." She looked around, taking inventory, it seemed, of all the company she kept, then whispered, "How true are these rumors of your feelings for the Far?" A playful smile spread on her lips.

Tahn shook his head. "You've been talking to Sutter."

"No, I've overheard Sutter. You'd think a root-digger so used to his own company might have learned a softer voice. But he seems to have only one volume, and I couldn't help but hear more than one reference to your fondness for her."

Tahn put his hands on Wendra's shoulders. "Sister, if I ever choose to do anything with regard to Mira, you'll be the first to know."

"Good enough, brother," Wendra answered. "It's clear you're drawn to her, but I wonder if you've thought what could come of it."

The question caught Tahn off guard. "Don't worry about me," he said. "I've just ended my days as a hopeless melura." He smiled wanly. "I suppose it's natural for me to make some mistakes in matters of love. You just take care of that voice. I miss your songs."

She kissed his cheek and went to Penit, the two of them returning to her horse with arms intertwined.

"She's a strong woman."

The voice startled him. He turned to find Grant at his side.

"Wendra, your sister." Grant nodded toward Wendra. "She will be your greatest ally, if you keep faith with her."

Bile rose at the back of Tahn's throat. His anger thrummed in him so that he could not even get out the words to revile the man.

"Tahn, I want—"

His words found him. "I don't care what you want, exile. You forfeited your right to give me advice a long time ago. You are an insult to any who know you."

The stoic look in Grant's eyes flickered. Another man might have risen to the bait. This man stared back with the patience of long isolation. "Whatever you decide to think is your choice. But you'd better search your newfound memory. You have a task at the end of these mountains and you need to be straight in your heart and mind to do it.

"I did not want to send you away. It was the best, safest thing for you. And I prevailed on my best friend and his wife to go into the Hollows to raise you and their young daughter because I wanted you to have the best possible life." Grant's voice came without apology.

Not the voice of reconciliation. Not the voice of a father.

And Tahn hated him the more for it. "Yet I understand you are father to children in your Scar. How did you decide that *they* were worthy of your care and protection, but your own son was not?" Tahn raised his hand. "No. I don't want an answer. You could have none but lies, and I won't listen to them anymore. Balatin may have been too weak to tell me the truth, but he loved me. He was good to me. *He* was my father. You are only a tired, used husk that keeps vigil in a dying place. Even death is too good for you."

"It wasn't easy . . ." Grant started, and failed.

Tahn held no sympathy. "You stole my childhood from me twice: Once when you used it to prepare me for your own purpose, and again when you wiped it from my mind and sent me away. If I go to Tillinghast it will be because of the decency of another man, not the secrets and lies of an exile."

Grant stood a moment, as if he might try to say something more, but finally only walked away.

CHAPTER SEVENTY-SIX

Stain

Winds drove the clouds from the Saeculorum, leaving Tahn and the others in brittle cold under clear skies. For two days they trekked into the mountains, attended by a groaning that was as much a vibration under their feet as a warning to their ears. The mountains themselves seemed to resist them, denying whatever purpose Vendanj had brought them here to achieve.

For most of that time, Tahn kept his own company in silence. He had not turned back, but neither had he decided he would go to Restoration. And he would take no counsel on it from anyone.

On the morning of the third day, beneath the shimmering sun, glittering points of refracted sunlight sparkled like gems on a blanket of snow. The clean, bright vista relieved, if only slightly, the sullenness that had afflicted them all since they'd entered the Saeculorum. Somehow, this brightness spoke of another season in which dormant seeds nourished on melting ice would flourish and set in motion another cycle.

For the first time since her kiss, Tahn sought out Mira. "We're close, aren't we?"

Her eyes continued to search the tree line. "Yes. And how are you?"

A bitter smile rose on Tahn's chapped lips. "I'm still headed to Tillinghast."

"I heard your cries on the bluff above the Soliel. And I inquired of the Shea-son. It does you honor that you have stayed on this path."

Tahn hurried to clarify. "I haven't turned back. But I also don't know if I can go to the Heights, Mira. I'm trying to understand . . ."

"That is all anyone can ask, Tahn. But I have faith that you will find your way. There is much more in you than the hunter who left the Hollows. I have seen it." She smiled. "And not just under a Far blanket."

Tahn laughed for the first time in longer than he could remember.

He looked down then at the ground. "Won't the snow make it easy for Quiet-given to track or hear us?" Tahn had often taken immediately to the Hollow Wood after a good winter fall of snow had made hunting simpler.

"Yes but there is no mystery about where we're headed. The Bar'dyn know it. The Velle assuredly have counseled their scouts to find an opportune place to make their stand." She looked out over the delicate green and white blanket of pine and snow spread below them. "And you, Tahn, have sacrificed yourself in showing the Bar'dyn scouts which of us is the prize."

"What do you mean?" Tahn's breath billowed in the air.

"When last the Quiet came upon us, you showed them your awareness of something within you, when you drew your bow with no arrow. They won't hesitate to kill us all." She paused, seeming to judge whether to say anything more. "But I think they will want you captive, to employ your gifts in the interest of those who lay within the Bourne . . . the interest of Quietus himself."

The unanswered questions from their night together at Naltus came again to him with renewed anger. "I'm weary of the threat of secrets. If the Quiet wants me, tell me why. Why do a Sheason and a Far come into the Hollows to find a hunter? It must be more than my connection to the Will. And what is it that awaits us at Tillinghast? Haven't I a right to know?"

Tahn's last words echoed over the tops of the trees below them, startling several ravens from their perch. As the flutter of wings answered Tahn's fury and filled the morning air, Mira turned to him. "Let me speak to you plainly, hunter." The replacement of his name with the common term felt like a slap across the face. "I respect your willingness to be here, to place your faith in a renderer and his designs. But do not put us at greater risk with your foolishness, your insecurities. Why do you think Vendanj has kept his tongue about so many things? Perhaps it is because a child, barely become a man, hasn't the fortitude to hear the fullness of truth. Perhaps if you knew all, you might have shrunk from a task clearly greater than you, greater than any of us.

Tahn felt the bite in her words and wished to retreat. But there was no place to go, and he became aware that all ears heard this exchange.

"We may well reach Tillinghast safely. I suggest you make peace with your decision to come, and lend us whatever skills you possess to reach our destination. Do you understand? What a waste of words to have to say all this to you. You may have alerted our pursuers with your declaration of your *rights*. Turn back if you cannot stand it another moment, if insecurity causes your heart to falter. Because that will surely cause you to fail at Tillinghast."

She stopped; the silence that followed was deafening. Tahn could bear her gaze no more and looked out over the peaceful scene he'd shared happily with her a mere moment before. When at last Vendanj proceeded down into the trees, the others following, Mira shocked Tahn by placing a hand over his own as it rested on his saddle horn. "Sometimes we must speak sharply to those we care about. But fear not, Tahn, I have faith in you."

With that she kicked Solus ahead, passing everyone and disappearing deep within the pines.

Tahn thought of what Sutter had said, about the horror of his true parents and what almost happened to him. He thought of what his friend had said about their fathers, the ones who hadn't abandoned them. He thought of Wendra's forgiveness.

And then he thought of the cutting truth in the words Mira had just spoken to him.

The indecision he had felt since the painful revelations had threatened to undo him was gone. These many small wonders of words and actions had stiffened Tahn's resolve. He would stand at Tillinghast, whatever it meant to do so.

And stronger still than this, though still a small thing, was a love for the Far that he could neither explain nor deny. Yet even that concerned him, when he considered Sutter's vision.

They moved with caution over the undisturbed blanket of snow. Towering pines rose around them, many with an ivory bark Tahn had not seen before. Patches of sunlight fell through the trees, producing crystalline shards of reflected light. With the scent of pine needles and snow, the air smelled clean, free of the mold of last year's leaves. The crunch of hooves broke the silence, much louder than usual in the stillness, but even Grant seemed at relative ease until the boom of a beaten drum shattered the morning air.

The deep sound spooked the horses. Several of them reared up, as though they recognized the portent the drums bore. Their shrill whinnying filled the morning with chaos as another drum answered the first, and a third called back to both, from ahead, downslope, and upslope. . . . They were trapped.

When the horses quieted, Tahn quickly surveyed every direction. He pulled his bow and nocked an arrow. Braethen already had his sword in hand, touching the blade in a thoughtful fashion. Then distantly, the sound of feet breaking through the snow rose from every quarter like a mother shushing her child, rushing in upon them.

Mira dismounted and pulled Tahn from Jole. They ran into a clearing, just up the hill from the path they'd been taking. Vendanj and Grant already stood at the northern edge, the Sheason preparing his hands, the exile kicking snow back and clearing a wide circle in which to stand. Wendra sheltered Penit behind Sutter and Braethen as she strode into the small clearing and shot worried glances at Tahn. Only Sutter seemed both prepared and anxious. He made several figures in the air with his Sedagin blade, his muscles now more used to its employ.

Again the drums sounded, closer and deeper, resonating in the thick ivory trunks of the evergreens around them. The very ground shivered with the beat, snow sifting and crusts of ice cracking. Birds took to the air, calling as they dispersed, leaving the band utterly alone.

The pounding of heavy footfalls came closer, the gentle shushing increasing until it sounded like a stampede of hooves. The splintering of wood came with them, and Tahn imagined small trees being snapped like kindling beneath the girth of towering Bar'dyn. Movement caught Tahn's eye, and he looked up in time to see a treetop thirty strides north disappear. The Quiet were crashing down upon them; the air was taut with the expectation of violence and death.

Then, into the clearing just to the left of Vendanj and Grant, came six Bar'dyn. The exile waited patiently in the small area he'd cleared. The Sheason smote his hands together, calling a whirlwind from the ground that twisted ice and snow and the hard, cold rocks and earth beneath it into a maelstrom. He then thrust both hands at the coming Quietgiven. The whirlwind leapt at the Bar'dyn. Three were drawn into the tangle of snow, stone, and ice, and lifted from their feet, tumbling over as they were battered and slashed.

Two Given turned on Grant, the remaining one fixing his eye on Tahn and heading for the center of the clearing. As it did, six more Bar'dyn emerged at a full run from the east. But these were different; they wore charcoal tunics with a grey insignia in the center of their chest: a single tree whose roots spread and grew downward to become several smaller, withered trees. These six each carried a heavy pike in one hand and a spiked shield in the other.

Sutter turned on the six as Tahn loosed his first arrow at the leftmost Given. With his shield, the Bar'dyn batted Tahn's arrow away as though it were a fly.

Braethen began to dash to Vendanj's side, but the Sheason shouted at him to stand with Sutter against their flank.

The three Bar'dyn caught in Vendanj's swirl had crashed down in a dead heap. The two spoiling for Grant came within the exile's circle. They fanned out quickly to opposite sides of the man, but before they could calculate a strike, Grant drew a small hidden knife from his belt and threw it not at the first Bar'dyn's face, but at its ankle. Its howl thundered terrible and low. Tahn seemed to feel it in his gut. The second Bar'dyn, taking advantage of Grant's first attack choice, simply threw itself at the exile, and went tumbling with him to the ground.

Vendanj turned his attention to the dark-clad six, and began gesturing at them with first one hand, then the other. Bits of bark dislodged from tree trunks and hurtled toward Bar'dyn eyes, as sharp and menacing as tiny daggers. Two lost their sight immediately. The others pushed against the onslaught, covering their faces as they came.

The single Bar'dyn heading for Tahn slowed as it came near Mira. It drew a second sword, and swung each in tight, quick, looping figures, its arms working together so that a wall of whistling blades began to advance on the Far.

Mira did something Tahn had never seen her do before. She simply lifted one sword to eye level, and dropped it. Surprise brought the Bar'dyn's impressive display to a pause. The Far sprang, dropped low, and thrust her sword with savage intent. The sound of shattered bone cracked in the bright morning air as Mira's blade found the Bar'dyn's knee. It staggered backward, its guttural scream erupting in the air, until Mira leapt and buried her blade in its open maw.

A mighty flail hit Sutter. The spiked ball lifted him into the air and sent him heavily to the ground. The attacking Bar'dyn lifted its weapon to deal a death blow. In an instant, Tahn let fly an arrow at full draw. The missile caught the Bar'dyn in the neck. Nearly before the first arrow had found its home, he'd released a second, and then a third. All three hit the Bar'dyn in the same place, driving it backward.

A second Bar'dyn leapt at Sutter, who lay in the snow. Before it could strike, a cry filled the air. *"I am I!"*

The call, utterly primal and inarguable, raised the hair on Tahn's neck. Braethen surged into the space between Sutter and the Given, whipping a blow at the creature in a vicious, tight arc. His sword hummed in the air, glowing faintly in the morning light. Then the steel found home, and burned the flesh of the beast as it tore a deep gash in its chest.

Grant escaped the Bar'dyn that had wrestled him to the ground, and as he did, Vendanj raised his hands in a grand motion, sending the creature skyward thirty strides. Then the Sheason fell to the ground, breathing heavily in the snow.

The two remaining Given ran past Braethen and headed for Wendra. Their dark tunics marked a dread contrast to the white powder snow they kicked up ahead of them. Nothing lay between them and Tahn's sister, and Tahn knew he would not reach her in time.

He nocked another arrow. From his bowstring to the Bar'dyn was but a moment, but when his arrow struck its side it hardly slowed the beast.

Wendra pulled Penit behind her and stared savagely at the Given as they bore down upon her. She then opened her mouth, as though to speak or sing. But alarm lit in her face as she rasped out something completely devoid of vocal timbre. She tried again, but also began to back away, pushing Penit along.

Tahn fired again, this time missing completely. A horrible rasping sound rose from his sister's throat as she pushed harder to vocalize something. Nothing could be heard but the pounding of feet.

In a final effort, Wendra turned to Penit, trying to force him to flee. The child shook his head. Wendra slapped him hard, and pushed him in a safe direction. Penit rubbed his face twice, and began to sprint away. Wendra wheeled about and headed in another direction, hoping to draw the Bar'dyn's attention from the boy, to preserve him with the lure of her own life. But as she dashed aside, the two Given rushed past her in pursuit of Penit. Tahn could not understand why, but the race was on. Only Mira could catch up to them. Tahn shouted to the Far, who instantly saw the dilemma and gave chase. In eight strides she had matched the Bar'dyn's distance, and looked like she would rescue Penit.

Wendra stood helpless, watching Mira streak toward the boy. One of the Bar'dyn pursuing Penit turned suddenly to meet the Far. Caught unaware, Mira nearly ran into the beast. A menacing grin spread on the thick, rough features of the Given as it knocked Mira down and planted a foot on her arm, kicking the sword from her other hand.

In unison, Tahn and Wendra lifted their cries: "No!" He for Mira, she for the child.

Vendanj lay spent in the bright snow several paces away.

Grant, Sutter, and Braethen started to plow through the snow toward them. But they were too far away.

Only Tahn . . .

He raised his bow and nocked an arrow.

He drew down on the Bar'dyn pursing Penit, then shifted his aim to the Given hovering over the woman he loved. The moment lengthened, and the world grew dreadfully still. Plumes of labored breath hung in the air, billowing with unnatural lethargy.

Tahn looked at the exhausted Sheason, his face gaunt and as pale as the snow, then to his sister, who'd taken the boy as her own. Wendra gave Tahn a pleading look, and his mind filled with the memory of his own suspended action when another child had been taken from her.

The memory seared him still, despite her forgiveness.

Not the son of Balatin. Not Tahn.

He had not truly stood passive in her moment of need, had he?

But Tahn also thought of the face in Sutter's visions, Mira's face. Nails had seen the haunted, anguished visage of a woman burned by the League the night before her death; at least, he thought he had. Sutter believed it, and so Tahn believed it.

He spoke his words in his mind as cries and yells sounded all around him. He recalled Rolen Standing for him in a dank prison cell, and was instantly reminded that he was now accountable for his choices.

Then Tahn narrowed his aim, and between the towering pines and over the fallen snow, he released his shot.

The arrow sailed true, slicing the brittle morning air, and whistling toward its target. As it struck down the Bar'dyn, Wendra raised a cry to end all the Skies known to her. The Given pinning Mira fell back, releasing the Far. A moment later, Penit was caught and whisked away into the forest.

Tahn dropped to his knees, tears burning his eyes, though he could hear none of the scream coming from his own throat. All sound and light dissolved as well, leaving him alone with his thoughts. He pitched forward into the snow, but caught the tortured look on his sister's countenance shortly before the comforting cold of the ice soothed his face, as he buried in the snow both his head and his own cries of anguish.

The quiet sound of sobs came to him sometime later. His eyes fluttered open, revealing the close, impassive face of the Sheason, and over his shoulder, Mira. The Far wore a mixed look of gratitude and disappointment. Vendanj helped Tahn sit up, where he could see the stoic expressions on the faces of the others. Only Sutter's eyes held no indictment. Tahn wiped the snow from his cheeks and unhanded the bow he'd been clenching with distaste.

"You made your choice, Tahn." The Sheason fixed Tahn with an unrelenting gaze. "You must own it. Do not disclaim it by relinquishing your weapon."

Tahn looked away at his friends. Braethen stood with one arm heavily bandaged and blood on his neck. The sodalist looked too weary to stand, swaying as he attempted to steady himself with his sword. Sutter winced every few moments and finally sat on a large rock to roll up his pant leg, which revealed a purpled bruise that ran from his calf to his knee. Nails then placed tentative fingers on the crown of his head, and pulled them away bloody. He shook his head but gave a sardonic smile before wincing again. The exile seemed to have no injuries and kept his distance.

Then Tahn looked at Wendra, collapsed at the far side of the clearing. She wept bitterly, but softly, hiding her face deep in her garments. The sound rasped from her bruised throat. The pitiful scene surrounding Tahn found its emblem in the covered face of a crying woman. He'd chosen to save Mira over the life a child, the child Wendra had virtually claimed as her own. The sheen of sunlight off the snow and the newness and delight it represented only made Tahn's abjectness darker, more bitter.

Putting words to it, Vendanj said low and even, "It was a selfish draw."

Tahn snapped his head in the direction of the Sheason. Anger flared in him, and he was momentarily grateful for it as it replaced the ache growing in him for Wendra and the lost boy, the ache for having failed her twice. What did those words mean, *I draw with the strength* . . . if when he should most adhere to them, he chose instead to serve himself.

And yet, looking at Mira, he was not sorry. The ache within ebbed further still as he briefly imagined the possibility that they could one day be together, that he could escape the pull of waking dawns, and she the vigil she seemed forever to keep. The thought calmed him even in his deepest grief.

"Sutter, Braethen, gather the horses," Vendanj ordered. "Be quick and quiet. If they've wandered too far, leave them to their instincts." Then the Sheason turned sharp eyes back to Tahn. "I will accept part of the blame," he began, "for not telling you something that might have prevented your mistaken arrow."

"Mistaken arrow!" Tahn repeated, incredulous. He focused on his anger, preferring it to the shame he felt when he heard Wendra's cries. "I know the child was young, but he was of little use to us in reaching Tillinghast. Mira is Far, a skilled fighter; her contribution outweighs his loss." The words rang out in the cold stillness, and brought Wendra's face from the depths of her cowl.

"You bastard," she said coldly. "Will you weigh the life of a child against anything? What man lifts his arms in the defense of a boy or his family and fails even to act? No son of Balatin, I tell you!" Her tears streaked over cheeks etched hard with hatred and indignation. "I've no dislike for Mira, but what choice was it to let an innocent be taken by the hands of Quietgiven. You are a coward!" she screamed with her damaged voice. "You disgrace me; you disgrace your father!" Her words plumed into the cold mountain air. "If I had voice for it, I'd sing the curse of a lifetime down upon you!"

Then Wendra began to weep more openly, her hand outstretched toward Tahn as if conveying apology, her own wearied spirit and confusion and loss.

Tahn turned back to Vendanj, who exhaled slowly, then began to explain. "Tahn, what I kept back was the importance of the child as a contingency against your own misstep. I feared we would not reach the Heights of Restoration before you stood to pass your melura years and take upon you your own will. By fortunate coincidence, the child came along with us, deeply protected by his youth against the consequences of his choices. His innocence, Tahn, was his value, besides the value of any life."

Tahn shook his head, failing to understand.

"He was to be a sacrifice, Tahn, to answer for a poor choice on your part, should you do so before reaching Tillinghast. Not a blood sacrifice. But to Penit we could have transferred the stain of that choice. His purity meant he could accept—and thus cleanse you of—whatever mistake you made that might have led you down a false path."

Understanding dawned in Tahn's mind. "Like shooting to preserve my own desire rather than releasing as the Will allows."

Vendanj nodded. "But in this choice, Tahn, you not only brought the stain of selfishness upon you, you also let slip the vessel to which we would have transferred that stain to reclaim you from a state of blemish." Vendanj drew back and looked about him, appraising the situation. When at last his eyes rested again on Tahn, he reiterated in a soft, defeated voice, "It was a selfish draw."

The Sheason crawled a few strides away and rested his back against a rock, appearing to fall deep into thought and weariness himself, leaving Tahn staring at Mira. The Far returned his gaze for several long moments, her grey eyes sympathetic but also sorrowful. She took a small step and touched Vendanj's shoulder lightly. They shared a look that seemed to communicate much in but a moment, ending with a mutual nod. Mira then drew near to Tahn, and knelt in the snow beside him. She searched one eye, then the other. Without a sound, she mouthed the words, "Thank you."

It was all the reward Tahn needed.

Then she began to speak. "Melura is a word from the covenant tongue, the language of the Charter, meaning *First Inheritance*. It is the providence of the Far to abide in this condition all their short life." She gave Tahn a reassuring look.

And in that moment, the realization of what she was about to suggest came upon him.

"As one who stands spotless in her First Inheritance, I offer to accept the stain you brought upon yourself by seeking to preserve my life."

The creak of snow could be heard as Grant wheeled about and finally showed his face to the scene behind him, his impassive, sun-worn visage drawn taut with concern and amazement. He partially raised one hand, but to no apparent purpose, before dropping it again to his sword. Tahn didn't know how to respond, and shot Vendanj a look. The Sheason gave no indication of approval or disagreement. He appeared to wait on Tahn's reply. Tahn stole a look at Wendra, whose face showed a bitter judgment.

Looking back into Mira's smooth face and clean eyes, he searched for direction from within. "What would this mean for you?"

"It is not yours to count the cost, Tahn. It is only yours to accept or deny my gift." Her voice fell to a whisper. "But there is no alternative. If you will not allow the transfer of this transgression to me, then all we've done thus far will have been in vain. You cannot go to Restoration burdened . . ."

Her words trailed off without an end, leaving Tahn doubting that even Mira could be completely honest with him. It pained him that his love for her had brought her to such a choice. Sutter and Braethen were nowhere to be seen, on an errand Tahn thought the Sheason had put them to precisely to take them away from here. Vendanj, his eyes unblinking, offered no council. He wished Balatin were here; he'd surely speak wisdom to Tahn. But for the first time in his memory, he felt utterly alone.

Unable to decide, he simply said, "I don't know what to do."

"Then do as I ask, Tahn, and let me do this for you, for all of us."

"Isn't it selfish of me to be delivered from my own mistake?"

"You have not sought this of me," Mira said, "I offer it freely." She leaned closer, and noted his reluctance with a kind smile. The sight of it eased Tahn's concern, if only slightly. But perceiving his need to know more, she explained, "In accepting this stain, I forfeit my First Inheritance."

Tahn's eyes grew wide. "I can't let you give back the blessing bestowed on you by the Noble Ones so that you can bear the mark for something I have done."

She smiled again her slight, nearly imperceptible smile. "People often do such things for those they care about."

The revelation spread through Tahn and made him certain he could not ask this of her. As he began to protest, she interrupted.

"There isn't time to deliberate or act feebly. You feel that you are in the dark, but I ask you to have courage and trust me. I know that this is right."

Tahn thought of his compulsion to await sunrise, of his restored memory, and of the things he and Sutter had shared on their way to Recityv.

"Trust me," Mira repeated, "and believe that this must be done."

Again Tahn began to argue. This time Mira put her finger to his mouth.

"Tahn, even if you were a stranger traveling to Tillinghast to answer the threat of the Quiet, I would insist."

He stared into her grey eyes a long time.

"It is so much easier that you are not," she finished.

Tahn felt like he was again unable to defend someone he loved, as he had in his Hollows home at the start of all this madness. But the truth was, he did trust Mira. Slowly, he acquiesced with but a simple nod.

Vendanj stood and came to them. He placed Tahn's hands on Mira's and bound them with a silken cord he produced from his mantle. Clasping their shared grip in his hands, the Sheason began to chant cryptic phrases. Warmth spread up Tahn's arm, and light radiated around the intersection of their four hands even brighter than the sun shining off the snow below it. In a flash, Tahn saw his moment of choice. He saw it from high above the clearing where he now sat, his bow drawn toward the Bar'dyn. He watched in terrible clarity the release of his arrow. The moment came like a knot in his throat, suffocating him. He felt keenly his deliberate betrayal of trust in the appropriate shot. And while Mira had been spared, he realized something more: The new repercussions in the life of the child, Penit, were also his.

Soon to be Mira's.

In that instant, a wave of horror overcame Tahn as he understood that what had been born of his error would touch the lives of many. For he saw a rain of burning pages, and a rending of the very air as though the world had been undone. And in the midst, an ashen figure with upraised arms showed an open mouth to the sky, but whether of triumph or travail Tahn could not discern.

Then Tahn felt lighter, new. He opened his eyes and saw Vendanj staring intently, not at him but at Mira. Her eyes still shone with razor awareness, but her brow furrowed now with a concern he'd never before seen in her.

And Tahn knew it was done.

Mira crept away on her hands and knees. Over the snow she went, assuring the others she was fine, but wanting to be alone.

Where she could feel the stinging tears of relief and regret.

Carrying Tahn's stain, she could no longer sire an heir for Elan, for her people. Her long fear of nurturing a child for the few short months before she moved beyond this life was over. And that eased her heart in a way that surprised her, since now her covenant could not be fulfilled. But blemished, she would not inherit the promise of the Far. Whatever awaited her beyond this life, it fell to a lesser place, which meant she would not rejoin any of those whose faces she had known and learned to love.

Then an awful realization hit her and she put her face into the snow and cried bitterly. The end of her line was now sure. And with it might come the end of the Far as a people. And in turn, the end of the covenant to safeguard the language, the promise of which held the hope of men.

Had she, however well-intentioned in her sacrifice for this quest, for Vendanj, for Tahn, just delivered them all into ruin?

The magnitude of it struck her. Nothing was sure. But there existed the possibility that she was right. And if it was true, then no sacrifice could exist large enough to transfer the scale of this stain.

Mira shuddered and could only hope that this boy out of the Hollows would fulfill all the needs for which they were depending on him.

Vendanj slumped back onto the snow and lay down, staring up into the deep blue. His body and spirit were weary. And not just from the use of the Will. This flight from the Hollows had reminded him of a past he'd tried to forget. As they came closer to Tillinghast and their losses mounted, that past came into sharper relief in his mind.

His heavy breathing plumed in the frigid air above him as he thought of the boy, Penit, now gone, just like his wife and child. He shut his eyes and gave himself up to a more recent memory. In the Halls of Solath Mahnus he and Penit had walked together, and Vendanj had learned what a remarkable lad he was. Vendanj had suspected so, in seeing the boy play the stories of the past with such meaning. Then he'd told Penit of the purpose that qualified him to go with the others to Restoration—becoming the possible receptacle of a stain, should that occur.

Even asking the boy had been a burden of guilt for Vendanj. But the Will had provided a failsafe against Tahn's possible lapse, and Vendanj recognized that he must ask. It was for the boy to choose. Vendanj would like to *not* have asked, except that there were shadows in the future he could not discern, and there needed to be recourse. The advent of the boy's company seemed more than happenstance.

The consequences of all these choices bore down on him. Vendanj twisted fists of snow in his hands, inviting the bite of the ice into his skin. As much as the rendering, these thoughts caused his labored breathing in the frosted air.

For he also knew the Quiet had marked them. Their pursuers knew the minds and fates of his companions. They surely knew that the boy was the key to controlling Wendra, whose lieholan talents had begun to bloom. Vendanj thought by now they might also know that Mira stood on the brink of succession to the Far bloodline and her people's great commission. The Bar'dyn attack had almost certainly had multiple targets beyond Tahn. And at least one of the Quiet's purposes in it may have been to try to take the boy, whom they would have known could accept the stains of mistaken choices, which would leave—if they couldn't kill her—only one other who could, Mira. And if the Far took any stain upon her, then the threat to the Language of the Covenant would become far too real.

And Quietus's plans of descent into the world of men would come more speedily still.

The boy might yet be alive. Vendanj felt it was so, and when his strength returned, he would tell his companions, especially Wendra. Still, they couldn't look for Penit right now.

Restoration awaited them.

For Vendanj, each moment of this long journey had already restored something to him. He was in the dark, and would not be free of it for a very long time.

Wendra sat in the snow as Tahn crawled toward her. She made no effort to move, or to acknowledge him. The snow ceased to creak as her brother came to a stop a mere stride away.

"Wendra . . . I'm so sorry," he said.

She did not bother to look at him.

"I don't expect you to forgive me. I can only imagine how you must feel . . ." Tahn faltered, searching for words. "I had a simple decision to make, Wendra. I couldn't save them both. I know how much you cared for Penit."

"He's not dead," she said flatly.

Tahn waited a moment, then went on. "It was the wrong draw, Wendra, if I account it by the Will only . . . but in that moment, even when I knew I must shoot to save Penit, I realized I loved Mira. And I had to try and save her. Please understand. It's the only time I have ever disregarded the whispering in my head. I don't kow how this all works out, Wendra. But after what happened back home, I decided that I would never be on the wrong side of that kind of draw again. Never fail to release where love was concerned."

Tahn stopped speaking again for a long time. She imagined that he was feeling the horrible irony of a lesson he had learned at her expense the first time, returning to grieve her again. She hoped it caused him pain, since she could not.

Finally, he finished, saying simply, "I had to do it, Wendra . . . I love her."

Wendra remained indifferent to his pleas and apologies, and sat without looking at him. Eventually, her brother crawled away, leaving her once again blessedly alone.

Then she fell deep into her own pain, but could not give it voice.

She'd rasped her recriminations and hatred at her brother in the first moments after his shot. She no longer felt bound to honor Balatin's admonishment to hold to Tahn above all else. Twice now, he had abandoned her and the young lives she'd sworn to love and protect despite the rough circumstances that brought those children to her. In her heart of hearts she knew it wasn't malice on his part, but neither was it the observance of their father's counsel for them to watch out for each other.

Misery filled her.

Visions of helpless children in the hands of tormentors plagued her. For Wendra, it was one thing for men and women to suffer the effects of their own bad judgment or even the imposition of another's will upon their own. But it was something else entirely for children, who looked to their elders for safety, to have their cries unanswered.

That song throbbed inside her, and she ached to give it voice, though even she could not be sure she wanted to hear and feel its effects. Its darkness blurred her sight, so that color seemed to have fled the waking world.

She thought of her own baby, taken, leaving her with a mother's arms that would never know the feel of holding their own child. Remembered the still moments when she'd lain and felt the movements of it inside her womb, loving it before it ever came into this world. She thought of a boy put up for sale to bidders who surely had a host of hideous intentions; remembered the courage he'd shown as he left their cave and set out alone to find her help when she was wounded. She thought of her own inability, ultimately, to protect either child. She felt like nothing so much as a vessel, used for the pleasure of others, to do their bidding. The torment of her thoughts wracked her with uncontrollable sobs. She knew only the sound of her own grief now, and it came, she thought, as though she wailed at the death of herself.

Her few choices lay before her. Either see this whole thing through to Restoration, or follow Penit. She had little mind for the first, but no ability for the second. She drew handfuls of snow and washed her face, its icy sting bracing her. She would continue to Tillinghast for now. But the time would come when she would carry her hope and dreadful songs after the boy, for rescue, retribution, or ruin.

Until then, the weight of her own scorn filled her heart, easing the pain of loss, and weaving sounds she knew would one day find a voice, once she'd healed and come upon her opportunity. And at that time, she would trust no one.

No one.

CHAPTER SEVENTY-SEVEN

A Blade of Grass

As Braethen helped Vendanj into his saddle, Grant ended the suffering of the crippled horse.

"Do not tarry," Mira ordered, her voice again an even tone that brooked no argument.

They all mounted up, Wendra wincing a bit as Sutter climbed on Penit's mount. Braethen surveyed the line of travelers. They were all unsteady in their saddles as they fought the pain of their wounds. Wendra searched the trees as though believing she might find the young Penit, and occasionally shot Tahn a withering glance. Vendanj slouched in his saddle, looking more drawn than ever. He'd lain in the snow for a long time, unmoving, Braethen doing what he could to help him. Mira remained resolute and watchful, but looked like a woman staring back over an unusable bridge. Grant held a twist of regret and displeasure in his sun-weathered face; perhaps, Braethen thought, for having had to end a horse's life, but maybe, too, for the loss of the boy, Penit.

Turning again toward a narrow pass to the northeast, they trudged on toward Tillinghast. Braethen measured the cost his companions paid, and considered what price lay ahead for him.

As they rose higher into the Saeculorum, he fought harder for breath. He could no longer completely fill his lungs, but found if he breathed slowly, he could abate his panic a little. But regardless of what he did, the dread remained; and it grew, not only from reflection on what had just happened, but from the simple knowledge that they neared Tillinghast.

It was a place mentioned in authors' tales, but actual historical accounts couldn't be found. It wasn't a place men were meant to visit. The high places of the Saeculorum, the passes that took them to Restoration, might have been myth, except that Braethen stared at it all around him. The dark stone of the mountains struck him with its stark beauty. Cliffs rose hundreds of feet, defying anyone to pass. Small clouds floated near and were pulled into the coursing updrafts, drawing them into wisps that soon became nothing. The sweat on their horses' flanks had begun to freeze. By the time they cleared the trees and became exposed to the wind, ice crystals hung from their mounts' hair.

By mid-afternoon, the sky itself began to reveal deeper truths. Looking up, even through the light of midday, Braethen could faintly see the stars beyond. At times all appeared blue, then by some trick of light he thought the sky the deepest violet, and he believed he glimpsed the very vault of heaven.

As they crossed into the shade and shelter of a towering cliff, the Far brought them to a pause.

"The horses will die if we push them farther. We'll leave them here and go the rest of the way on foot. Take a moment to gather your breath and drink deeply before we proceed." She then sat with her back to the cliff and took her oilcloth to her blades.

Wendra wandered to the edge of safety, and sat looking back the way they had come. Braethen watched Tahn twice start to go to Wendra to speak with her, both times returning to his horse without doing so. Vendanj and Grant sat conferring, then arguing. The blare of their voices rose up the cliff's face, becoming lost in the howl of wind around sharp outcroppings. Braethen no longer cared what they had to say.

Favoring one arm, he huddled over his book, passing one finger of his good hand under each successive line he read. Tahn finally took a seat next to him.

"Long way from the Hollows," he offered.

Braethen paused, then went on reading.

Tahn had maneuvered himself to read along with him, when Braethen stopped again. He stared ahead at the page, lost in memory. "I used to sit on my porch and watch the rain. My father taught me that a story could be born of every drop that came to earth, and that the chorus of their landing on a Hollows roof or lawn was a lifetime of revealed truth."

He turned to look at Tahn. "He used to say such things when I grew impatient for Ogea to come and share the old stories, or when my insistence to learn made me insolent. And once," the sodalist said, shutting his eyes as if doing so might shield him from his own words, "when I sought the understanding of the blade, he sat with me to watch a wild rose near our well as it opened to the rays of day. While night still held firm he woke me, and we went by lantern out and sat in wet grass before the wild bush.

"I remember the call of birds to announce the morn, the coming of smoke from chimneys newly lit with endfast fires. I shivered until the sun rose high enough to light the area around our well. But even then, the rose remained closed. Not until late morning did its petals unfurl to greet the sun." Braethen opened his eyes.

"I don't know if I have learned what A'Posian meant to teach me by such lessons, Tahn. Because all I can think is that our time is dreadfully short. There is knowledge here." He hefted his book and replaced it again in his lap. "But I don't seem to glean what is necessary. And each time I lift my sword, I fear being consumed. It opens . . ."

Tahn put a hand on Braethen's arm. "Later, you'll better understand what I'm about to say, but for now take comfort in the decency of the life of your father. I know he wanted you to be an author, and I know your dream to become a sodalist sometimes caused strain between you, but those moments with those flowers, Braethen . . . you are fortunate to have had that man at your back from the cradle. I think . . . I know it makes being here, this far from the Hollows, easier."

Braethen said, "Indeed, my friend. But I have neither Sutter's desire for battle, nor the patience you seem to possess."

"Patience?"

"I've watched you pull your bowstring, Tahn, as though something hinged on the result of your draw. It seems a considered—"

Tahn held up his hand. "There is more indecision than consideration in my actions, Braethen. Look what it has earned me." He pointed toward Wendra. "And things in my own life are turned upside down . . ."

The sodalist looked away at Tahn's sister. Then he offered, "Family is yet stronger than her pain."

At that, Tahn showed him expressionless eyes that yet carried something deeper behind them. Moments later, an anguished frown came upon his friend's face that for some reason reminded Braethen of when he had broken his father's goblet.

Tahn finally blinked and focused a look on Braethen, focused on someone else's burden—the quality Braethen had always liked best about him. He looked down at the book in Braethen's lap. "Perhaps you're not reading the right stories," he suggested. "What exactly are you hoping to find?"

The sodalist lifted his finger from the book. "I'm not sure. I'm trying to learn about Restoration, but most if it is cloaked in riddles, or written in ancient tongues I can't decipher. The Sheason gives me little instruction."

Tahn chuckled. "It is his gift of evasion."

Then Braethen remembered the day Ogea finally arrived at the Hollows, and the reader's slow climb up the ladder of Hambley's inn. The old man had broken the seal on a scroll, and spoken from memory the words all had assumed were written on the parchment. Speaking mostly to himself, he said, "What of the story Ogea spoke at Northsun last?"

"What does it say?" Tahn asked.

Braethen put his hand over the satchel at his side. "I've opened it three times . . ."

"Only opened it?" Tahn asked, confused.

Braethen turned calm eyes on Tahn. "It's blank."

They shared a long, troubled look.

"What have you discovered?" The voice startled them.

Both Tahn and Braethen looked up to find Vendanj standing over them. The

Sheason wore his hood up, shading his hollowed cheeks. He spoke quietly, as though conserving energy.

Braethen spared a glance at the empty scroll. "Nothing, Sheason." Braethen's voice came equally low, failure evident in his tone.

"Nonsense," Vendanj replied, though the lack of inflection left the words unconvincing. "Put your book aside a moment, sodalist, and tell me this: Have you a sigil of your own?"

"I wear the crest of the Sodality. It is—"

"A worthy emblem," Vendanj finished. "But it is yours only as the sky is yours, or the earth. We are all of us adopted into larger families, grafted onto longer vines. This is necessary and important. But it is not individual. Do you understand?"

Braethen nodded. "I have no family mark. It never seemed necessary in the Hollows. Everyone knew me by name—"

"That is not the purpose of a personal insignia, sodalist." Vendanj paused to consider, his eyes never leaving Braethen. "Perhaps you have discovered precisely what you say." Nothing. While the Sheason spoke with little inflection, his words conveyed clear disappointment.

After all he had done and hoped and given, the disappointment burned.

Still, the Sheason did not move, seeming to scrutinize Braethen, perhaps to compel him to some realization by the imposition of his presence.

Then Braethen softly touched the blank scroll and muttered again, "Everyone knew me by *name*. . . ."

With unhurried hands he withdrew from his pack a green-colored vial and a quill. Removing the stopper from the vial, he dipped the quill and set the ink aside. Then, placing Ogea's empty parchment on the book in his lap, he drew a single blade of grass at the topmost center. He rendered it expertly, as though he saw in his head precisely what he meant to draw.

Braethen did not look up at the Sheason, but stared down at the image as the ink dried. After several moments he whispered, "Ja'Nene."

Vendanj looked satisfied. He nodded and said, "Your own story, sodalist. An important one," and walked away.

Braethen rolled the scroll and carefully replaced it in his pack. When he withdrew his hands, he held a needle and several strands of thread. Taking up his cloak, he set to the wool, fashioning over the left breast the symbol he'd drawn on the parchment.

"You're planning on telling me why you've chosen this as your sigil, right?" Tahn smiled, nudging Braethen.

"We'll share a sack full of secrets sometime soon," Braethen answered, and went on with his stitching. He allowed a thin, dubious smile as he met Tahn's questioning gaze.

"I look forward to it," Tahn said, nudging his friend again.

Moments later, Mira called, "Gather your things."

Braethen closed his book and put his belongings away. He shouldered Ogea's satchel and sheathed his sword. "Well, let's go see Tillinghast."

Once through the pass, the air suddenly warmed, as though the seasons of men held no sway beyond it. A shallow valley stretched before them, the mountains rising again at its far side.

Across the valley floor, trees had fallen heavily to the earth, their trunks half buried in the soil. Once-elaborate root systems stood exposed in twisted knots. It struck Tahn like a garden of stone statuary tumbled by a quake. Simply seeing the length of these trees suggested to Tahn the majesty that had belonged to them when they had stood and reached heavenward.

The inscrutable visage of the Sheason fell to a kind of despair Tahn couldn't remember seeing.

In a careful whisper, the sodalist explained. "The mountains at the end of the Saeculorum are described as being filled with the beauty and grandeur of the Cloudwood, trees reaching up more than a hundred strides, their branches and trunks denser than steel folded a dozen times. It is known as the Eternal Grove or Undying Forest, because its wood was said to be impervious to the axes of men, its bark resistant to disease. It is written that during each century, the cloudwood grows by but one growth ring, and each ring comes so near its neighbor they can scarcely be distinguished."

As the Sheason followed Mira onward, Braethen spoke, his voice hushed in reverence to a woodland now vanished, the land somehow denuded, and left dotted with scrub oak, low cedars, and grasses brown as from an early autumn.

"History records that the First Ones created the grove at the end of the world to be a source of renewal and growth. In its strong roots, the weave of the earth could continue should men prove to be poor stewards. Though the Fathers abandoned this world once the Artificer tainted its potential with his ruthless ambition, it is believed that they hoped the land and its people might survive through the strength of the iron roots weaving a new loam in which men might plant, and through the reemergence one day of the covenant language." Braethen paused a moment, considering his own words.

"Much of the balance of Forda I'Forza is the special rendering of the Cloudwood as it claims form from the abyss into which its roots crawl."

Tahn turned back to him. "That is where we'll find Tillinghast, isn't it?"

Braethen looked from one eye to the other. "Yes." The sodalist paused briefly before resuming. "But the Cloudwood is . . ." he trailed off.

The party had descended into the midst of the fallen sentinels, the girth of the half-sunken trees twice and three times the height of Vendanj. Mira led them between two parallel trees, the trunks forming a roofless conduit along the basin. Braethen walked near one tree, placing a hand on the gnarled bark. "This is why the Scar expands. The balance is undone."

From several strides ahead, Vendanj's voice boomed, "That is not the whole of it!" The Sheason whirled about, halting them all in mid-stride. "The loss of these stewards and emblems"—he gestured around him at the dead wood without looking—"is an indictment of us all. A blemish we wear as a race, every man and woman on the comfortable side of the Bourne. But it is also the vile product of Quietgiven, prideful, lustful, scornful creatures who would take for themselves and leave the penalties of their avarice for us all to pay in the body of a wounded land.

"We have but one thing that is truly our own, truly ours to give. Everything else belongs not to us, but is ours to watch over, or ours to squander." Vendanj looked around, seeking each pair of eyes in reproachful instruction.

"There is no great mystery in it, and yet it is priceless beyond all you might own." Then his voice softened. "Still, some give it away as cheap and sullied as a harlot's bed linen." His eyes came to rest on Tahn. "It is our will. Nothing else is forever ours, nothing else so keenly sought by those who hope to Quiet our world, and nothing else much less regarded by the noble, reasoning beasts we have become." Again his eyes sought each companion, silently naming them.

"Beyond this valley lies the last earth and stone risen from the roots of these fallen sentinels." He pointed to the peaks of another range just visible over the top of the dead cloudwoods. "And where that earth comes to an end is Tillinghast, the Heights of Restoration, beyond which there is only emptiness, the mists of Restoration that bristle with the permutations of countless lives and choices. It is a cauldron of breath, of Forda, a mirror to help us see behind our own mask." Vendanj lifted his arms skyward, clenching his fists as though he might take something in hand.

Tahn felt for the lines of the scar on the back of his hand, so like a mallet.

"We come with our petty differences, our disinclinations. And when we taste the mists on our tongues, they will be a scourge that threatens to unmake us. Or when Tillinghast shows us our true selves, we will *wish* to be unmade."

Vendanj stood motionless for long moments. Then he softly stepped close to Tahn and whispered in his ear, "Prove me wrong. Stand fast at Tillinghast."

Deep inside, Tahn felt a seed of hope. He wanted badly to do just that.

He turned to Sutter. His friend was white, as though he'd seen a ghost, the very penaebra of lost life.

What has he seen?

They continued on, and as they neared a narrow canyon at the far end of the valley, the sun slid behind the mountains behind them, casting everything in blue shadow. With it came a preternatural stillness, absent the whir of crickets or the call of larks taking to their nests, making every footfall large in the quiet. Sutter started a fire to ward off the chill.

But before Tahn could make his way there, Grant cornered him near a fallen cloudwood. "I know you don't want to listen to me, but this once, if never again, please."

It was the only time Tahn had heard the exile use that word. The plea inside it softened Tahn enough to nod.

"I didn't come to Recityv or with the Sheason to entreat a reunion with you, Tahn. I'll be honest with you; I don't know if anything we can do will turn back the tide of what has begun in our world. I sit in the midst of it every day, and sometimes I believe the Quiet has already come, and we are just hearing the echo of our own death throes. It is said by dark poets that we are nothing more than walking earth, upright dust, consuming breath in ignorance."

Tahn instantly remembered hearing these last words from the creature in the wilds of Stonemount. He'd thought then that they were familiar. He knew now, with his restored memory, where he'd first heard them.

"There are days," Grant continued, "when I half believe that. But . . ."

He paused, searching for the right words.

"But whatever you end up thinking or feeling about me, I want you to understand, especially as you go to the Heights, that your mother and I are proud of you. She loves you, Tahn. Her ache when we conceived the plan to hide you away from scrutinizing eyes almost killed her. And for my part, I might have accepted a death sentence rather than go into exile in the Scarred Lands. But we wanted you to have a chance at a good life. And if it came to it, I wanted you to have the strength of body and character to stand at Restoration."

He put a hand on Tahn's shoulder.

"I know now that you have become all that we ever could have hoped. What comes after may be black and may destroy you or even yet the land of men, I don't know. But up to this moment, here, now, nothing more could have been asked of you.

"And come Quiet or chorus, Tahn, I stand behind you with anything that is mine to give . . . anything."

With that, he removed his hand and left Tahn without another word or look.

Tahn did not know how to feel. But he did see something he'd not seen before, since the man for once did not wear his battle gloves: a scar on the back of his left hand in the shape of a hammer or mallet. The image suggested to Tahn's beleaguered mind yet more similarities between him and the exile. But he put them out of mind. Right now, this near Restoration, he could bear no more.

The exile took to the fire for some warmth.

Vendanj stared at Tahn, flame flickering in his steely eyes. He stroked his beard and began to speak. "Tomorrow we will come to Tillinghast. You must be prepared."

Tahn believed the Sheason was talking to everyone but more specifically to him.

"Tomorrow, at dawn, you will come to the place where Forda and Forza meet, Ars and Arsa. It is a place of absolute power, absolute potential . . . for now, at least. There can be no prevarication at Tillinghast, Tahn. While it represents the finest and most potent gift given to men in life, it is indifferent to your hopes, indifferent to you. Take care to comport yourself with utter honesty."

Then the Sheason looked deep into Tahn's eyes, again making him think that the renderer could know his private thoughts. While holding his gaze, he began in a softer voice, "You will have restored to you all that you have done, all that you are. You have the shield of melura to answer for most of your years, but we have not come quickly enough to make that the fullness of your protection, nor would it be enough in any case. Even though you are not accountable before you Stand, these things must be restored to you—every misgiving, every ill thought. That will be painful enough.

"The ripple effect of your every malice and mischief is something you can't deny, and will be yours to see and feel again, yours to admit to."

Tahn realized then why the Sheason had restored his memory: if he hadn't, Tillinghast would have. The shock of it there might have undone them all.

"But Restoration is more than remembrance," Vendanj explained. "More than a scale to measure worth or value. Restoration will put a name to who you have become, who you are capable of being."

"This is our purpose," the Sheason explained. "This is the purpose of every night you've spent away from your Hollows skies. It is the meaning in your sunrise."

Tahn puzzled at this, knowing the Sheason was aware of Tahn's morning vigil, but sensing that Vendanj did not fully know any more than he did why he was compelled to witness the birth of every dawn.

"We have seen the destruction of that which we once thought timeless. In coming here, we have learned the threat is present from the simplest blade of grass"—Vendanj spared a look at Braethen—"to the greatest of our nations. The Whited One is restless; his influence widens, and does so at our own bidding. Against legions without number and his mastery in rendering the Will, we are of no consequence.

"And yet he has sought to put our purpose at an end. Why? Because he fears anyone he cannot enslave." Narrowing his gaze, Vendanj lent fervor to his words. "You will draw your bow tomorrow at Restoration, Tahn, to know if you are chosen to continue to resist Quietus, and . . . Will and Sky . . . stand against Quietus himself if the time comes."

The Sheason said even more softly, "This is the final answer to your question of what we set out to do."

The revelation descended on Tahn and stole his breath. *Dear Fathers, they mean for me to stand against the Whited One!* He tried to speak, and could not. He looked at Sutter and saw a stark, dumbfounded expression on his face. Tahn then looked at each of his companions, seeking he knew not what, but feeling as though he needed to grasp onto something, someone.

Then from the crevasse, a deep wind rose up, shrilling into the night air. "When will you tell the boy the truth, Sheason? He is Quillescent."

The word chilled Tahn to the marrow. Though pronounced in the awful voice of this dark intruder, it somehow held the ring of truth. Tahn didn't know what it meant, but as he whipped about to look into the crevasse, he saw an ominous figure float up unaided from its depths, and knew that whatever its meaning, it would bring him harm.

Vendanj threw back his cloak, and rose in a single, graceful motion. Grant and Braethen jumped to his side, brandishing their blades as the Sheason crossed his arms across his chest and stared over them at the deep cowl of the floating form.

The figure rose three strides above the edge of the crevasse, and peered down at them. "This is the hope to which men cling?" A bitter laugh chafed the very air, and shook the stone beneath and around them. "Quillescent or no, the measure of your Will is feeble." The cowl shifted noticeably, facing Tahn. "A mistake that I might rectify with but a word."

"You've no dominion here!" Vendanj shouted above the howl of wind still emanating from the crevasse. "And no heart among us will yield!"

"No dominion? I am Zephora," the creature declared. "My authority is as old as the first Draethmorte called after the injustices of Juliad, the closing of the Bourne, and the imprisonment of Quietus and all the works of his hand." Zephora's voice grew harsher still. "I am more lord here than all your councils; I am more enduring than all your restored choices." He threw his head back and laughed with the voice of the damned.

Tahn hadn't needed a name to feel the difference of this creature from the Quietgiven that had pursued them since the Hollows. His concealed countenance emanated abjection, the hint of a visage within the cowl frowning at them with pity and anger. Beneath its glare, Tahn's skin prickled with goose bumps and his fingers tingled with an itch he could not sufficiently rub away. Somehow it reminded Tahn of the taste and feel he'd had of the sweating prison stone in his cell beneath Solath Mahnus. Only the light and will of Rolen had mitigated the debasement that place had forced on Tahn's beleaguered mind. And yet that memory approached the despair and malevolence of this new being only as near as an aspen stripling might a cloudwood. His very voice reminded Tahn of the soughing of winter winds through dead trees, and the anguish of a mourner too overcome to articulate the words of his grief. That, and the patience and stillness of an ossuary. He invaded Tahn's mind like a secret plaguing his conscience, and moved as one with the soil beneath his feet, as one presiding over interment.

Mira backed away from the creature, her swords held defensively before her.

Tahn raised his bow, nocking an arrow as Sutter drew alongside him, his sword gripped firmly in both hands. Speaking mostly to himself, Nails said in a whisper, "He said the first Draethmorte."

Braethen's sword began to thrum with a single, pure note as it started to glow, the light pulsing. The sodalist stepped protectively in front of Vendanj, but was recalled to his place with a soft spoken command.

Zephora descended to the edge of the crevasse, landing softly, always facing Tahn. On the ground, he stood as tall as Vendanj, though thinner and frailer looking. "Concede," the Given said. "Do not martyr yourselves against the ages of my desire and power to wield more perfectly the Will that binds you." He pointed toward Vendanj. "You labor under the misjudgments of generations that did not correctly interpret the meanings inherent in a Charter whose authors held no authority to write it. Your handling of these precious gifts dishonors you as you seek to keep locked a prison without knowledge of its prisoners."

Anger flared, and Zephora's next words came pushed on breath heated as by a furnace. "And we grow tired! The prattling of these generations fuels our passion for Quiet. No more will we accept the tethers placed on us for something—" The creature's words degenerated into an anguished roar. "Prepare yourselves!"

As the folds of Zephora's cloak began to unfurl, his arms stretching preparatory to some invocation, Vendanj lowered his wrists and cupped his palms. Light sparked in the Sheason's hands and grew rapidly in intensity. The mountain pass lit as though from two suns, when suddenly Vendanj brought his hands together, and closed them into fists. Light streaked from between his fingers and sought Zephora, shooting from the renderer's hands like brilliant shafts of sunlight through a darkened cloud.

The attack swept Zephora back, but only briefly. The rays of light began bending around him, unable or unwilling to touch him any longer. From within the depths of Zephora's cowl, Tahn thought he saw a dark smile.

Vendanj grabbed Mira's shoulder and roughly pulled her close, focusing his eyes upon hers, but saying nothing. The Far nodded, as if hearing something unvoiced. She broke past Vendanj and Grant and grabbed hold of Tahn. "Come!" she commanded.

Tahn did not hesitate to follow as Mira dashed to the far side of the pass. He stretched his strides to keep from slowing her. Reaching the far side, Tahn turned back to see the others position themselves between him and Zephora. As he watched, the member of the dark Draethmorte did not make any great or hasty countermove, no flames or shifting of earth. Instead, the fugitive from the Bourne slowly and with a darkly beguiling smile, opened his arms as though to receive them all unto his bosom. And with that graceful gesture, a cold silence settled across the pass, stealing sound and replacing it with an ineffable sadness, a mortal grief that chilled Tahn more completely than any rain or ice ever had. It stopped him in his tracks. It bore down upon everything, seeming to press in upon the stone and sand, weighing heavy in the air, touching their hearts with the gall of bitterness. The malevolent and destructive moment was rendered almost lovingly by Zephora, reminiscent of a mother looking into the face of her sleeping child, as though this was the creature's purest, most powerful emotion and need.

A death of silence . . .

The moment lengthened, threatening to consume them utterly, when shattering the silence came a triumphant cry: "I am I!" The resounding blare leapt from Braethen's lips, erupting into the pall like the dawn, and sending shivers of hope down Tahn's back. The spell broken, Mira yanked him forward, and up they raced. He realized, with a sudden sense of dread, that she was taking him toward Tillinghast.

As they sped over star shadows and stone, Tahn looked back over his shoulder at the scene unfolding at the rim of the pass. Wendra's head bobbed as she retreated and tried to force audible tones from her injured throat. He wondered if this would be the last time he would ever see her, and wished he had tried to speak to her again. Grant and Braethen danced in close to Zephora, attempting to use their dual attack to confuse and cripple the Quietgiven. With a casual pass of his hand, Zephora sent them both skidding across the rough ground like scarecrows ravaged in an autumn gale.

Vendanj spared a look up the mountain at Tahn before calmly lowering one palm earthward and splaying his other fingers over his breast. In the next moment, the rock itself seemed to come to life and lick at Zephora with shard tongues and clutch toward him with indifferent fists. One lashed the Given's chest before Zephora went to one knee and drove a bony hand into the hard soil. With frightening speed, the earth took on a deathly pallor that began to spread around them.

Tahn and Mira swept over the rise and found level ground as behind them the world lit in an explosion of darkness as searing and painful as live coals. The concussion thrust them forward, driving Tahn to the ground. The blast echoed past them in long, diminishing waves, leaving in its wake an emptiness that he thought might have claimed the shrieks and suffering of friends. Tahn heard only his own labored breathing, and the sound of his boots grinding against Saeculorum gravel as he followed the Far toward Restoration.

The sky above shone darkly, revealing every star Tahn had ever looked at long enough to fix in his memory. He'd hoped to have time to consider Vendanj's words, consider everything that led him to this moment. All his thoughts clouded in his mind, and were finally pierced by the sound of footsteps, far down the mountain, climbing in pursuit with a steady, purposeful rhythm. Perhaps Vendanj . . . perhaps not. Tahn fought to climb faster, pushing the Far to quicken the pace.

• CHAPTER SEVENTY-EIGHT •

Rudierd Tillinghast

Sweat drenched Tahn, stinging his eyes. The higher they crept, the tighter his chest felt, the pressure causing him to gasp. Deep breaths sent piercing pains through his body.

But up they climbed.

Twice Tahn looked back and saw nothing. But, holding his breath for a moment, he could hear the continued steps down the rocky way.

With renewed determination, he attacked the path, sliding in behind Mira as they forged through dense mountain brambles. At times, the steep pitch of the mountain made it seem like they ran up walls; the Far's sure steps showed Tahn where to place his feet. The sound of his own heart pulsed in his head, behind his eyes, and in his wrists. He did not ever remember being so aware of the flow of his own life's blood, and yet feeling so close to his own final earth.

Rushing after Mira up a steep leftward jag, he thought of his Hollows friends, Sutter, Braethen, and Wendra, and felt a pang of mourning. Surely the dark explosion had seared them utterly, claiming the lives of them all. In that instant, his concentration lapsed and he missed a step, crashing down and slipping toward the edge on loosened dirt and flat stones. He clutched at dry grass and sharp, buried rocks that ripped at his hands, tearing rough wounds in them.

His legs and chest slid over the edge of the path, dangling in the emptiness that cut away a hundred feet to a spray of jagged rock. Hanging by his hands, he stared up past the mountain at the sky, flooded with bright stars that blurred in his vision. He hadn't the breath even to scream, and could feel his hands weakening.

He smiled, finding irony in failing this way after coming so far, after all the expectations he was supposed to meet at Tillinghast. He slipped closer to disaster. Mustering the reserves of his strength, he fought the momentum and tried to pull himself back up. He'd almost gotten his legs up over the edge when he dropped back again, hanging again by his hands ... and he was losing his strength. Then one hand slipped. A weak moan escaped his lips.

Where is the tragedy in this? he thought, turning his gaze downward toward his imminent fall. *My family is gone, as are my friends. And I cannot endure another day. I am not who they hope I am. Could I not simply have lived out my life in the Hollows? I would have been content.*

As he began to slip farther, he was not sure that his fall was entirely due to weak hands.

From above, a hand flashed down and took hold of his arm before his fingers could give out. His head lolling back, he saw the furrowed brow of the Far. Her hair hung down around her face, but Tahn thought he saw something new in her eyes. She took Tahn's wrist with her other hand and hauled him up in one powerful effort. He sat a moment, the wind stirring his hair, and tried to gather enough breath to thank her. Before he could say anything, she put his bow in his hand and helped him to his feet. As she nodded and resumed their climb, the resolve in her features rivaled the Sheason's.

He cast a look backward over several tight switchbacks, and caught a flash of a dark figure gaining ground. His mind shouted a warning and he raced after Mira.

As the slope began to level off, the air began to thicken with mist, streaming as though with the onset of a storm. Moving forward through it, Tahn suddenly became aware of his skin. As he and Mira ran, the mists parted, coursing smoothly over his forehead, cheeks, and the backs of his hands. Unsure how, Tahn thought it felt as though these clouds were sentient. His skin came alive at their touch, communing with the ethereal element independent of his own thoughts. The mists thickened, reducing visibility and slowing their pace.

Mira paused, appearing to get her bearings. Standing together in the dense mist with the rasp of leaves stirring around them, Mira grabbed Tahn's shoulder and thrust him forward, falling in a half-stride behind.

Then, out of the mists, a low ridge appeared. They headed directly toward it, angling for a break to their right. They passed through the rim of black rock which let out abruptly on a few strides of soft loam before a sheer cliff fell away to nothingness.

Mira stopped. "Tillinghast."

The mist roiled in slow patterns, turning back on itself and folding endlessly together. Looking skyward, Tahn could see more of the same, though thinner. Beyond the ledge, the mist thickened to obscurity. He took a tentative step, and his foot sank into the rich-smelling soil. He looked at his sunken boot, then peered right along the cliff to where he could see the vague silhouette of one cloudwood rising at the edge of the land. Its roots grew partially into the abyss, twisting down into the clouds like bony, scrabbling fingers. The tree disappeared up into the mist, its top lost completely to view. At its base, a single branch lay fallen as though broken away in a storm.

He looked once at Mira, whose eyes shone with confidence.

Then Tahn crept toward the ledge, desiring to look down, his boots tracking deep in the loam. Halfway to the edge, he heard Mira draw her swords, and turned to see Zephora ease from the rim of rock. The mists parted around his black cloak as though in aversion.

The Quiet disregarded Mira, looking past her to Tahn. "Quillescent."

Mira did not wait. With blinding speed, she set upon the Draethmorte, her blades slicing through the fog so quickly that it did not stir at their passing. Several blows appeared to land directly on the creature, but Zephora did not flinch, the insult of a blade apparently of no consequence to his flesh. Mira sprang back, landing in a defensive posture.

Tahn could not see clearly, but whatever rents or marks Mira's attack had made seemed to have healed themselves.

"Your destiny is larger than the race of men allows, Quillescent." The Draethmorte's words rang darkly. "You are more than they know. Their arrogance and greed have opened a way to put right the abominations of the First Ones. You can be the deliverer, and erase ages of neglect and cruelty."

"His words are all lies, Tahn," Mira shouted. "Absurdities meant to confuse you. Give no heed to words that make darkness light and light dark. The trick of the Artificer is to lead you gently first, before tightening shackles that unmind you forever."

With a slight gesture, Zephora shoved a burst of dark light that took Mira full in the chest and hurled her to the very edge of Tillinghast.

"She can be yours, too, Tahn," Zephora said in a silken tone. "In the protective hollow of the Quiet's hand, you'll have restored to you only what you wish, and you'll be endowed in all the ways you could desire: memory, power, security. You may, Quillescent, even undo things you have done. Does there remain any act you wish you could take back? This is true power, the offering I make to you. It is not villainy, Tahn."

Zephora's use of his name unnerved him.

He relaxed his grip on his bow. "Why does the order fear you, then? What have they to lose?" he asked the Draethmorte.

Mira groaned, struggling to get up, but Tahn focused on the cloaked form.

"Their own power, their own control." Zephora took a casual step toward Tahn. "It has always been so. Your histories are incomplete, and they tell a flawed version of accounts which demonize all those trapped within the Bourne."

"Bar'dyn have sought my life, forced me to leave my home . . . they claimed the life of my sister's child! And you speak as though *you* are the casualties! Mira is right, you merely seek to deceive me!"

With more ire Zephora explained, "We have not sought your life, Quilles-cent. Though it were better that you die than have you give your gifts to those who would use them to confirm and sustain our abandonment."

Better that you die . . . They were words Tahn had heard now from both sides of this hateful conflict.

"In ignorance, you are filled with hatred and fear. Do not let it be so. I can supply you with answers, and open all the world to you." Zephora's voice deep-ened, resounding in the very loam beneath Tahn's feet. He drew back his cowl to reveal a skeletal face. The skin might have parted with a smile. "Or I can end at Tillinghast forever the life that never belonged to you."

Uncontrollable shivers wracked Tahn. Through them he struggled to ask, "Why do you call me Quillescent?"

The Draethmorte laughed. "It is who you really are, Tahn. The secret the Sheason isn't ready to share with you. You were—"

Just then, a loud clanging interrupted the creature. Tahn looked to see Mira holding one broken sword over a rock. In her other hand she held the stone with which she had just snapped her blade in two. Fury raged in her eyes as she stood and pointed the broken sword toward Zephora. "In the name of the Far, I rebuke you. By the covenant of those given special age, I call you out."

Tahn had no idea what Mira had just said or done, but Zephora's face regis-tered a brief glimmer of concern. Just as quickly, the expression passed, and he turned to face the Far, lifting his robed arms in preparation.

"Oathbreaker," the creature hissed at Mira, a kind of awful delight sounding in its voice as it spoke the word.

Then a shriek arose from him, emanating from his mantle, his pores, his eyes. It touched the air with a sourness that coalesced into a palpable form that Tahn believed would tear skin from muscle. It flew at Mira, streaking through the mists. The Far leapt to the right out of the way, the shriek sailing like a great spear into the mists and abruptly losing its potency to silence. Mira danced to her feet, and trod lightly nearer Zephora with the jagged stump of her sword.

"You waste my time!" Zephora roared.

Before Tahn knew what he was doing, he had again drawn his weapon. He saw blood from his wounded hands seeping between fingers tightly clenched on his bow, but he aimed and drew back the string.

This time, with certainty, he used no arrow.

The bow was always just a way, when the time came, to focus. He knew, from years ago, standing with Grant in the Scar, that it was only the *intention* of his draw that mattered. And along his path from the Hollows, he'd learned some-thing new about himself, some deeper ability when he drew an empty string.

In his mind he began to speak deliberately the words.

I draw with the strength . . .

"Don't be a fool, Quillescent! You've no understanding of what you do!"

Mira circled closer to the Draethmorte.

A low hum began in Tahn's head.

. . . of my arms . . .

"Do not cause me to destroy you! Choose now, or I will make the fall of the Cloudwood seem a rose's death compared to the anguish your Ars and Arsa will forever know!"

Tahn drew deeper yet, his body still quivering, his flesh weak and cold. He remained uncertain even now, questions and grief plaguing him as the hum in his mind grew loud like the faster and faster turning of a potter's wheel. Mira raised her truncated sword and began to say something in a low whisper. Tahn thought her body looked less substantial, perhaps a trick of the mist.

. . . And release as . . .

"Will you serve injustice, Quillescent? Will you honor and harbor those who hid from the face of the sun creations equal to themselves in glory and potential?" Zephora took a defiant step forward. With it, Tahn's body shook, his mind filled with shapeless fears and doubts. "I defy you! I name you unforgiven! A doleful little archer come to Tillinghast without his own childhood. You raise your aim, and I mark you for all the brothers out of the Bourne as a deliverer become betrayer. The ravages of time I invoke upon you! Across ages the darkness speeds to find you, Quillescent. With the power of hatred and despair tempered in the farthest reaches of the Bourne they will fall upon you and yours! Now, enough of this! I will have my reward!"

Zephora loosed a wave of awful darkness from his outstretched hands. Tahn was knocked savagely to the loam at the ledge; his body felt as though he had fallen into the rough stones of a winter river. The silent pulse throbbed in his flesh. He could hear nothing, but images of all his dreams and visions raced through his mind: burning pages falling like cinders from the air; rivers of blood coursing from the Tabernacle of the Sky; men and women stumbling with their throats ripped from their necks as the last notes of the Song of Suffering ended; the veil falling and a great white mountain at the bitter end of all that is light quaking and thrumming with the hatred of ages.

As these terrible scenes flowed before his mind's eye, his soul quailed, and he hoped for solace. But instead he saw himself seated in the dark of predawn awaiting the miracle that never came.

That was something he knew he could not bear.

He thought then of Sutter's ramblings in the wilds: *The spirit is not whole, Tahn. It's not whole. It can be divided. Given out. Taken. Small portions separated from the whole . . .*

And of the feeling in those moments when he'd drawn with no arrow, and what he intended to release.

Tahn again drew his bow, pulling hard and fast and releasing at the vileness escaped from the Bourne. An unseen arrow flew from his string and struck Zephora in the chest. The fiend wailed, a cry like a chorus of mourners both old and young at the deaths of their dear ones.

Tahn marveled at what had happened, but knew that he had used his bow, an instrument of this world, to fire his heart upon his adversary—a small portion of his spirit, unacquainted with the stains that might diminish him. The stains that in their fullness became the foulness that stood before him.

But Zephora was not done.

The enemy had a heart of its own, and in a moment of defiance to Tahn's small act of bravery, it rent its garment and exposed its awful flesh. From the earth and abyss and heavens all at once came a thunderous boom that Tahn knew was only ever heard in his mind.

There came to him a taste of the Quiet.

Malice and hatred and the energy that might give them life coalesced into the splendor of the Whited One and filled Tahn's mind. It stole his own voice and any power to fight or defend against the coming of the end of the world, stole any power yet left to choose, to hope.

Tahn fell, his body numb. He was still aware. He lay there unmoving after a horrible rain of dark applause, in a deafening silence. His will to act bled from him, as he felt the burden of unending grief and despair.

In that moment, he lost his name and all the history for good or ill that had been his own.

Accountability no longer even mattered.

And suddenly he watched himself fade into a canopy of white so immense and stark that he couldn't be sure he wasn't blind. The universe was as empty as new parchment, on which he was an indistinguishable speck.

At the far side of his defeat, when meaninglessness had all but taken him, came the ringing of another blade being broken in the air of Restoration.

Then came the soft words of a familiar voice uttered low in an ancient tongue. Perhaps a covenant tongue.

It somehow gave him enough mind to cry out for help to the one who'd helped him in the pit at Solath Mahnus: *Rolen!*

The scream filled up his mind, echoing out to silence, where he heard simply: *Be still, Tahn. Be still. Remember standing in the dark, and in the glorious gentle light of a thousand sunrises.*

These things at the last Tahn did hear. He opened his eyes to see Mira standing between him and Zephora, invoking some ancient promise and holding one of Quietus's great ones at bay, if only for another moment.

His body and mind were spent. There was nothing left but what his will could muster. Tahn put his ravaged hand out and clutched his bow with fingers dirtied by the loam of Tillinghast. The movement brought to mind Sutter and a flood of memories: Wendra, her lost child, fathers left behind. In the barrage of so many sacrifices, Tahn remembered Rolen and his Standing, and heard the man's small, soft voice. Rolen, a servant unto his own demise.

Tahn pushed himself to his feet behind the prayerful and broken-sword defense of the Far. As Zephora shrieked out madness, Tahn finished his own prayer:

. . . the Will allows . . .

And released an empty string.

Not at Zephora.

But into the Abyss.

With it, he was swept away, carried into the roiling mists, the arrow of his own shot.

A great roar erupted behind him, making Tahn think of the dying of nations. Then it was gone, shut out by Tillinghast.

He disappeared into the clouds, seeing not himself, but only the rush of forms accreting and dissipating all around him in the empty mist. He sensed that he had left his body behind, becoming something more pure, more vulnerable. A feeling of motion captured him, but not physical movement, movement through time, through possibility.

Faces appeared before him, as though sculpted from the mist. Some of the faces were smiling, some frowning, others talking, though Tahn could hear no words. Then suddenly, a flood of images descended upon him. So strange were they, that though he thought they were familiar, he could not name them. But more than that. He had the feeling some things were being hidden from him.

The will of the Will.

His mind raced on, streaming through the abyss, light and dark swirling in close and flitting away again. Each time, he saw a choice, a word, a deed, a way of responding that directed him to other choices. He marveled at the winding of his own path through this matrix of interconnected moments.

Some of these brought him shame, causing him to turn away, though he could never escape the scenes playing before him. More painful yet were scenes from his past where he did nothing, choosing inaction that resulted in hardship for others. These brought further images showing the lives of many cascading in dark consequences resulting from Tahn's indecision. He knew immediately the raw feelings of people as they struggled with sadness or loneliness, because of his inattention in a crucial moment. Opportunities to make a difference cascaded in wild succession before him, opportunities he'd passed up, too selfish to render aid.

Other images made him laugh, especially those with Balatin and Sutter. The feelings of love and togetherness felt as strong as when they had first occurred.

Tahn's longing to speak again with his father caused him to cry out to the memories. Though he thought he spoke, he heard nothing. Nonetheless, he gloried in the recollections, so many lost to him, and reveled in the carefree smile Wendra so often used to wear. He watched Balatin smoke his pipe and sing and tell stories. He watched Hambley put another contender down in a game of shoulder-wrestling and then help the man up to buy him a cup of bitter. He saw light falling through the aspen trees on the Naghen Ridge during a hunt years ago. He'd waited on dawn there as he always did, taking a small pleasure in the birth of a new day, feeling somehow a necessary witness to the event.

Then the mist shifted, and Tahn watched his journey out of the Hollows that had brought him to Tillinghast. He felt his own suspicion and resentment. He was reacquainted with his first stirrings at the sight of Mira. He felt again the manacles and the bite of steel on an open wound while imprisoned where he believed himself forgotten. He recalled an empty city and the unexpected defense he made for Sutter with an empty bowstring.

Most of all, he remembered his failures to save Wendra. The first time because he hadn't believed he should release on the Bar'dyn. The second time because he believed he was in love. The latter was his most painful single memory in Tillinghast. But the choice did not sting as it had before, and Tahn knew it was because of Mira's sacrifice.

A great rushing began, mist flowing in toward him, gathering speed as it came. He watched in utter astonishment as a thousand varying paths from a thousand different choices sped through his mind. Against the increased awareness of who he had become, he was suddenly being shown countless versions of himself that he would never be. By turns, he felt gratitude for small victories, and guilt for missed opportunities. With it all came a sense of the meaningless measurements of time and space. He likened it to standing atop a grand mountain where he had a view of every trail and its intricacies as each one led upward to the summit. Or perhaps he was standing atop a thousand mountains all at once.

Like a storm, the mists produced flashes of light and wellings of darkness. Frightening images emerged, interwoven with peaceful moments. The interplay of conflicting images became somehow less difficult to experience, and Tahn relaxed at the center of the maelstrom. Everything began to gather toward him—his memories, his choices—touching his mind with possibilities, some things sure and inevitable, others unlikely but understandable.

The mist licked at him, through him, invaded his senses, and lulled him to acceptance. It all became deafening, filling him until he was no longer capable of conscious thought. He floated in the abyss and simply was, and that was enough.

Then it ended, and the silence shocked him. His eyes already open, he suddenly could see again, and found himself where he'd stood to shoot toward Tillinghast, his feet still rooted in the loam.

He felt . . . peace. Then he collapsed and fell unconscious.

• CHAPTER SEVENTY-NINE •

A Solitary Branch

The smell of rich soil awakened him, as fresh as a pot of brewed cloves. For a moment, he imagined Sutter holding a handful of his roots beneath Tahn's nose in jest. The thought of his friend brought a smile to his face, and he held it there, sensing that if he were to open his eyes, the fancy would shatter. He breathed deeply, and felt the cool density of the air as it rushed into his lungs: mist.

The abyss.

Tahn opened his eyes and saw, but a few strides away, the place where the Heights of Restoration became nothingness, obscured by the graceful billows of the clouds. He did not immediately move, suddenly aware that he had not rested in quite some time. As he stared vacantly outward, ripples in the mist threatened to coalesce into familiar shapes, as though drawing upon his thoughts. But the mist swirled onward.

Then, like a pail of winter river water poured over him, he remembered the coming of Zephora, and Mira. He pushed himself up, a wave of nausea and unsteadiness sweeping up from his belly to his head. When his vision cleared, he looked frantically for the Far, remembering her last stance as she created a barrier between him and the Draethmorte.

Will and Sky, I left her here alone to contend with him.

He struggled to his knees and forced himself to crawl to where he'd last seen her standing. As Tahn crept ahead, a form came into view. He could not be certain, but the prostrate figure lay utterly motionless. He hastened, pushing himself beyond his strength, and went facefirst into the dirt. The soft earth cushioned his fall, and he took a mouthful of soil.

He spat it away. "Mira!" The cry rasped from his throat, which felt as bruised as Wendra's had last sounded.

At the thought of Wendra, his heart stopped.

The last he'd seen, an explosion of dark and bright had ripped out of the summit pass, and the only one to follow Tahn to Tillinghast had been Zephora. He pounded his fists weakly into the loam as salty tears streamed down his nose and into his mouth. "No," he whispered. "No. Not you, too, Wendra!"

Tahn again rose to his knees. With resignation, he moved toward the body. In his grief, he paid no mind to caution, and coming upon the lifeless shape, tugged the creature's shoulder to turn it faceup.

The gaping maw and bony ridges of Zephora's face smiled its death back at him. Tahn recoiled, scrambling back. Instantly, his hands began to burn. He thrust them into the loam, scrubbing them as with soap. Slowly, the pain subsided, and he was left in the company of the ancient being. Mira was nowhere in sight.

He tried to stand, but his legs wobbled, and he collapsed back to his knees. His mind raced with panic, mostly in response to his growing belief that he was now truly alone. The Draethmorte must have somehow consigned Mira to the mists before dying. All his loved ones were now surely gone. Kneeling just strides from the end of the world, Tahn turned a hateful eye toward Tillinghast.

The sacrifices that had brought him here, most of them by others, raced in his head. Of what use or purpose was this place to him, to anyone, when it could restore nothing save what had already come and gone? It seemed to Tahn an instrument of pain, and he shuddered with loathing for it. He looked into the roiling mist.

Something more had taken place here. Had Tillinghast gotten inside him?

The ability to understand it was beyond him, and he was left able to do nothing more than stare emptily at the abyss as it moved before him.

After a moment's reflection, Tahn tore several long twigs from nearby brush. He wove them into a shallow, makeshift basket. When he finished, he rose shakily to his feet and, using his bow for support, took the basket to the base of the cloudwood. There, he eased himself to his knees again and placed the basket near the trunk between two large roots. Then Tahn rummaged around for a small stone. Finding one, he dropped it into the basket. "And one for every visit I pay Tillinghast, my friend." Somehow he thought he'd be back.

Tahn picked up the fallen cloudwood limb resting near his basket, and with some effort stripped it of its dead leaves. Using it for balance, he rose, and began shuffling toward the edge. He felt ashamed and angry that so much had been lost on his behalf. One way or another, he did not mean to let those offerings go unrewarded.

As he came near to Zephora, he paused. With sudden fury, he began to roll the dead body toward the ledge with his makeshift cane. Though tall, the Draethmorte weighed very little. When he rolled the body over, a silver necklace bearing a pendant fell onto Zephora's pale, thin neck. Each turn caused it to swing about, until Tahn stopped to inspect the token.

Using his knife, Tahn moved it around, trying to make sense of the design. A single hoop of silver hung from the necklace, and at its center lay a small disk, creating a sort of bull's-eye. But nothing connected the inner piece to the outer ring. Tahn thrust his dagger through the emptiness around the center disk—it passed through unimpeded. Tapping the centerpiece itself, it did not budge from its place.

Tahn pulled the necklace free of the dead Draethmorte. Standing, he heaved the Given into the abyss. It fell soundlessly, dropping away from the ledge and out of sight in the space of a breath. The mist enshrouded it as completely as its every other secret.

Tahn pivoted and began to ease away from Tillinghast. Just past the ridge, the sound of leaves being trodden underfoot came to him as from a great distance. He paused, unsure whether he merely heard the stirring of the Cloudwood remnants on a subtle breeze. The crunching became louder.

Hope leapt in his breast, and Tahn began to hurry back the way he and Mira had come. "Wendra, Sutter . . . Mira?" he hollered as he raced, stumbling often, his legs threatening to betray him. From the other side of the field, voices were raised in response. He could not understand the words, but the meaning was clear enough. At least some of them had survived!

He raced on, ignoring the burn in his chest as he fought for breath. Tahn came around a tangle of roots from a fallen cloudwood and saw his friends running at full stride. He collapsed, exhausted, but with joy swelling in his breast. They came, each of them, Mira leading them all. Their boots kicked up the hard leaves, cracking others underfoot. Momentarily, Mira reached him. She took him in a strong, tight embrace, and held him for long moments. She then dashed past him toward Tillinghast. He assumed she went to check on Zephora, but Tahn hadn't time to tell her he'd disposed of the Draethmorte, nor to ask her how she'd defeated him.

Then his friends were upon him. Sutter fell into a slide, shoving a pile of the leaves between them and into Tahn's lap. "Woodchuck, my skies, I never thought I'd be so glad to see you." Sutter planted a big kiss on Tahn's cheek, and flung some leaves in the air as if showering him with festival streamers. The heavy leaves fell down on Tahn's head like small pebbles.

Tahn grinned. "And I've never been so glad to bear the company of a man who plays in the dirt."

Sutter laughed, but then his face drew taut. "When I saw you disappear from the pass, I wasn't sure I'd see you again." His friend took Tahn's hand in the familiar Hollows grip, clasping him tight. "Not that I doubted you, Tahn. But no one knew what Tillinghast held in store, and I wish I could have come. . . ."

"You'd love it," Tahn said. "The loam there is six inches deep, and rich with the smell of expected growth." Then Tahn gave Nails a mischievous grin before wrapping him in an embrace.

Braethen came up as the two broke their hug. "It is good to see you, Tahn." The sodalist hunkered down on Tahn's other side. "It would seem that you've proven yourself at Restoration." Then he whispered, "Thank you."

Tahn took the sodalist's hand in the same Hollows shake.

Wendra came next, slowing to a stop a few strides away. She held his gaze long enough to say, "I am glad you are alive, Tahn . . . though others do not share your fortune."

Even with her words hanging between them, Tahn's throat closed with emotion at the sight of her. He wanted to stand and take her in his arms, apologize for his misdeeds, promise that all would be different. He wanted to feel her heart thaw, to regain the closeness they'd always shared.

Wendra then moved aside as Vendanj came up next, Grant trailing him close behind.

The Sheason looked deathly ill. He sweated as they all did, but his flesh hung from his face, dark circles ringing his eyes. His hood was back, revealing dark hair slick with perspiration that clung to pallid skin. His shoulders hunched deep as though the weight of his own cloak was too much for him to bear.

He stopped, and made no quick attempt to speak. Looking at Tahn, he leveled his eyes, which never seemed to dim, even now. Again, Tahn had the feeling he was being measured, weighed, by the penetrating gaze of the Sheason.

Then Vendanj asked Grant's assistance in helping him to sit. The exile eased the Sheason to the ground, and propped a large fallen branch behind him so he could recline.

Standing straight again, Grant gave Tahn a look both proud and relieved. But he said nothing.

When Vendanj had fully recovered his breath, he folded his hands in his lap. His first question caught Tahn off guard. "What stick is this that you carry?"

Tahn looked into his hand, finding that he had not let go of the cloudwood branch.

"A walking cane," Tahn answered, confused.

"It is cloudwood," Vendanj stated. "But not greyed yet as these fallen sentinels." Without lifting his stare, he pointed at the tree behind Tahn.

"I've seen only one live tree. It grows at the edge of Tillinghast."

A look of relief showed on the Sheason's face. "One tree." His look grew distant. "A forest, a world, can be sired from one tree." Then his scrutiny blazed. "Tell me, did Zephora speak to you of Quillescent?"

Beside Tahn, Braethen flinched.

Tahn had been called this name, he realized, many times. He had no idea what it meant. The Sheason's interest disquieted him, nearly as much as the name itself. But Zephora had used it to darkly ingratiate himself to Tahn, hoping to inspire Tahn's allegiance or alliance.

"No, he said nothing of it," Tahn answered. He watched carefully for another sign of relief in the Sheason's face. Vendanj gave no indication of either relief or concern.

A small silence stretched out between them all, broken thankfully by Mira returning from the ledge.

"Tahn rolled the body into the abyss," she said, as if answering a question Tahn hadn't heard.

"It is just as well," Vendanj replied. "The One has ways of reclaiming his own. In the abyss, Zephora is forever lost."

Shifting, Tahn looked up at Mira. "Why did you break your own sword? It drew Zephora's attention and gave me time. . . . What did he call you? Oathbreaker?"

"It's not important right now," Mira said, then shared a strange look with Vendanj.

Clearly it *was* important, but Tahn hadn't the energy to pursue any more mysteries. But he did have one question. "How did you kill him?"

The Far stared back with her bright grey eyes. "It was not I, Tahn. When you turned and fired into the abyss, things began rapidly to change around us. The mist pulsed with reflections of light like lightning streaking inside a cloud. At the ledge, each pulse changed the landscape, the position of rocks and trees. The very air was one moment fragrant and new, the next burnt and sharp. The ghosts of proud cloudwoods flickered around the edge as though showing the possible gardens that might have grown there. At times, the ledge itself extended, leaving Zephora and me standing in a dense wood. In other moments, our feet hung over the abyss, the cliff strides behind us as the mist caressed our bodies and lit our minds with flashes of opportunity."

Mira looked back in the direction of Tillinghast. "And in other moments, Tahn, Zephora wasn't there at all. In still others, he lay dead upon the loam."

She stopped, turning her gaze directly at him. "In the flash of some moments . . . I was not there, either. And at times . . . I was conscious of my own lifeless body fallen deep into the soil."

Mira went on. "You alone remained unchanged in your pose and permanence, Tahn, staring into the clouds as though you looked upon realities I could not see.

"Then the mist began to whip, the fluctuations of light nearly blinding me. Streaks of the mist began to lash over the ledge, stabbing toward Zephora. I jumped away just as the fury of the clouds shot in a thick streamer and wrapped Zephora in its fierce embrace. I watched the mist penetrate his cloak, his skin.

It wove in and out of his mouth and nose, streaming from his ears and seeping from his eyes. The mist seemed to invade his every pore, passing through him as though he was insubstantial.

"The creature shrieked, his howls shattering the stone around him and causing my flesh to ache. Even in the grasp of Tillinghast, Zephora reached out to transfer his own pain, and its touch tugged at my skin. Shafts of light began to shoot from his nails, and his eyes, and soon he was so bright that I could no longer look at him. He blazed a moment in a state of sheer brilliance. Then the light abruptly faded, and Zephora fell to the ground. The mists receded, but you did not move.

"As the ground began to shake so that I considered pulling you back from the edge . . . it stopped. The mist became at once still, the wind gone, the ground quiet. No further flashes of light or dark, only the soft light of the mists.

"And you collapsed. I could not revive you, and so went to get Vendanj."

"What happened in the pass? The last I saw, a great blast rose out of the mountain. It pushed me to the ground."

Sutter chimed in, his eyes alight with a tale to tell. "Zephora shoved his hand into the soil. A circle began to spread, stripping color from the dirt. His eyes blackened and then a great burst threw us back. It felt like what I imagine the Bourne might be like. I suddenly felt all my desires drain away. I could feel myself being lifted and hurled by the force of the blast, and knew I would soon strike stone, but in that moment, I didn't care."

Sutter swallowed hard. "It was like that time when Haley Reloita, Shiled's son, got trapped in the well just before the rains came. Do you remember?"

Tahn nodded. No one had been able to get Haley out. The well was too narrow for men, too dangerous for a child. Haley's fall had brought loose wellstones down upon him, half burying him in the stagnant, shallow water at the well's bottom. Hours later, it began to rain, swelling the river, and from an underground tributary, the water in the well, too. They watched as the water rose, and Haley cried. Frantic men lowered ropes that Haley could not hold firm enough to pull him from the stones. Eventually, the water covered him completely. . . .

"That was the way I felt in the darkness," Sutter said. "I've never had anything hit my chest harder than the force of that blast, but I'd take twenty such blows to not feel the anguish that crawled inside my mind as the blackness surrounded me . . ." Then Nails smiled weakly. "Just give me my roots back."

"The veil weakens," Vendanj said in an ominous voice. "The First Ones created the Tract of Desolation to form a veil which might hold the malefic ones at bay. It is safeguarded and sung by Leiholan at the Descant Cathedral. Its design is to restrain all those sworn to Quietus, but especially those capable of calling upon the Will. That is why we've known only Bar'dyn in the Land for some time. Zephora's emergence into the light of men represents a threat we cannot imagine. It means other Draethmorte may soon pass through the Hand."

"It means more than that," Grant added, his voice gruff. He looked at Vendanj, then at Wendra. "It means the Tract has been compromised somehow. Or the Leiholan fail."

Tahn's sister turned an icy look on the exile, seeming to take his words as an indictment.

Vendanj did not respond to Grant's grim theory. Instead he focused again on Tahn. "And you, are you resolved to stand evermore as you did at Tillinghast?"

What real option did he have? He clenched his teeth at the thought. But sitting in the company of Sutter and Braethen, and to a lesser degree, Wendra, he realized he would do what he had always done. He would speak the words and he would rise in the earliest moments of dawn, while the world remained dark, and imagine a sunrise to light the sky. And though he had no reason for it, he took the smallest comfort from these patterns of his life.

Returning Vendanj's severe gaze, Tahn mustered his confidence and said, "I will give my best."

"Then give me your cane," Vendanj replied.

He handed the branch of cloudwood to the Sheason, who took it and hefted it twice in his upturned palms. He then clasped his fingers around it and closed his eyes. The wood began to reshape itself, coming alive in the renderer's hands. Slowly, it turned, moving as though alive, but drawing itself into a definable shape. Within moments, the branch had become a sleek bow, fashioned of the ebony cloudwood.

"Newly fallen from a live tree, the branch still courses with the nourishment of Restoration." He handed the bow to Tahn. "I have sealed the mist inside, giving the branch eternal vigor. It will serve you when you draw fittingly."

Tahn admired his new bow for a moment. Then his mind returned to where they had been interrupted by Mira returning from the ledge. "What is Quillescent?"

Vendanj gave him a penetrating look. "Let us speak of that another time, Tahn. Be glad in the knowledge that you have survived Tillinghast. Whatever comes will not come uncontested. This is mighty, and will surely anger Quietus. For now, let us rest." With that, the Sheason eased himself onto his side and closed his eyes.

Still keeping secrets. Well, I've now secrets of my own. Tahn patted his tunic where he'd pocketed the necklace he'd lifted from Zephora's dead body. That, and the results of choices he'd witnessed at Tillinghast which lingered in his mind—the ends of choices yet to make.

CHAPTER EIGHTY

A Refrain from Quiet

The stars still held sway when Tahn stirred awake. Gentle dew coated his face with freshness he took a moment to enjoy. Around him, the hulking shapes of fallen trees rose up. Tahn folded back his blanket and crept past his companions to the end of a nearby cloudwood. There, he used the snakelike roots to climb atop the tree, where he stood and surveyed the world around him. In that broad valley, he became the highest point, and quietly mourned for the forest now blanketing the ground. Looking up, the sky shone with stars Tahn did not remember ever seeing. For a moment, he felt as though he stood between the earth and sky, the strength of soil and the hope of the untouchable.

And there, he imagined the coming of the sun, a slow, beautiful dawn that turned the skies a hundred shades of blue.

He shut his eyes and took deep, deliberate breaths, not allowing the intrusion of other thoughts, and briefly recaptured a portion of the peace the ritual had long ago given him.

"There's a kind of glory in it, isn't there?"

Tahn's eyes snapped open, and he whirled around to see the Sheason standing a few strides behind, watching him.

"In what?" Tahn asked, discountenanced by the intrusion.

"In the coming of another day, the awakening of the world from its slumber."

Tahn turned back to his view of the valley. "A small comfort, yes."

"And why small?" Vendanj asked, his tone calm, almost fatherly.

Taking a moment to survey the devastation around him again, Tahn said, "Morning sun used to thrill me, the very look of it on a farmer's neatly planted field, the hazy way it fell through the leaves, dancing in patterns on the frosted ground below. I liked the idea that things were made visible again, that the light held a promise of reuniting friends, shared meals, and that one's dreams might find their form in the light of a new day."

He waited, feeling suddenly ungrateful. "But the covenant we make with the sun is not what I once thought . . . I still seek its return to the sky, but now only for warmth and a sure place to put my feet."

"And where is the smallness in that?" Vendanj persisted.

Tahn exhaled a deep breath, watching it cloud the bracing air. "There are days that the warmth of my blanket is enough for me, days when I fear the path the sun lights for us." Tahn turned to face the Sheason. "I don't know why it matters to me to witness the birth of each day. It does not feel to me that we are a world watched over."

Vendanj seemed to weigh the things Tahn said. He regarded him for a long time without moving. Finally, he spoke, his voice firm but low. "The Council of Creation is said to have ended with the First Ones abandoning their work on behalf of men, because they thought the work was lost. Once Quietus had been sealed up and whited, the land was given into the stewardship of those who would have it; our lives are our own. But the work of the Artificer had already tainted that stewardship, and has pressed in upon us since recorded time.

"In all the ages past, we have warred with each other, warred with the Quiet, and so perhaps you wonder if we deserve another day, if the Quiet that would blight our world is not inevitable."

Tahn nodded. "And what difference can the bow of a simple hunter from the Hollows make when added to the nations, the armies, that stand against the darkness that comes at us from the Bourne?"

Tahn saw something in Vendanj's eyes: knowledge, perhaps comfort. The Sheason spoke of neither. "There is more to you than your bow, Tahn. You know this about yourself. However desperately you wish to be only a woodsman from the Hollows, it is folly to cling to such obvious self-deception. Your moment at Tillinghast should have taught you as much."

Tahn remained mute. In response, the Sheason's brows rose perceptibly in surprise. Seeing that look, Tahn realized that even at Restoration, the Will had controlled the moment, obscuring revelations Vendanj had apparently expected Tahn to have. Still, the renderer said nothing of it.

As if in response, Vendanj narrowed his gaze as a father might to reprove a willful child. "It is the opportunity of free men to choose their own path, to direct their will as they deem fit. But freedom is not license to waste the gifts bestowed on you."

"And what might those be?"

Vendanj settled back as a father does when he sets out to explain. "Shall I name all those who have raised their arms and placed their lives in the breach in order to safeguard the land that houses your narrow tract in the Hollows? Men and women who knew not the politics, nothing of the old war or the ancients, who put themselves in harm's way and went to their final earth because they were called to it by nothing save their desire to be free, to preserve their children's morrow?"

Vendanj showed Tahn compassionate eyes. "I am well pleased in your triumph at Restoration. But now you have been qualified, selected to act as the Will would have you. Don't ever make demands or assert your own needs, or you will have undone what we came here to do."

After a moment, Tahn offered meekly, "Is my life not my own?"

Vendanj's features softened to a paternal smile. "Every answer to that is true, Tahn. Make peace with them all."

Vendanj stood in Tahn's company for some time, then began to take his leave. As he strode away he spoke. "Keep safe the token you hide in your tunic. It may serve you well someday."

The evening of their second day, they spotted the Soliel Stretches beyond the lower peaks of the last range of mountains. Their rations gone, Sutter dug some roots he recognized, and they drank from a nearby stream. Tahn sought an opportunity to talk with Wendra, but his sister still kept her distance, speaking only occasionally to Braethen. Like Wendra, Sutter was changed, too, but Nails seemed to fight that change, turning their minds toward home.

"Can you imagine the welcome we're going to get from Hambley?" Sutter licked his lips. "I can taste his roast duck already. Hey, Woodchuck, maybe you can hunt us up something good for him to roast in those magic Fieldstone ovens. This time, we'll be the ones people buy spiced bitter for. I think I'll take a glass of warmed cinnamon and some plum brandy to wash it down with." As he spoke, Sutter casually rolled his own sword in his hands, its use seeming to have become increasingly familiar to him.

"Well, so long as you put some fine roots beside that duck, root-digger, I'll spare not the carafe."

Distantly, Tahn could hear Wendra using her voice, drawing more water from the stream, and choosing songs both high and low to test her vocal limits and strength. If nothing else, it gladdened his heart to hear her sing again.

Braethen wore a quizzical half smile, his books for once put away, and only his sword in sight, lying near to hand. "Hollows men," the sodalist added, "you will place another plate at that table, and a handful of cups for me alone."

Sutter gave Braethen a look of pleasant surprise. "And when Hambley sets the glasses down, will our resident scop favor us with an emotional retelling of the events since Northsun?" Having baited him, Sutter waited expectantly to see how the sodalist would respond.

Braethen cleared his throat, preparing to orate something, but with his first word broke down and laughed. His laughter was contagious, and soon they all were laughing as they had not since Tahn could remember.

"That's all right, sodalist, after all," Sutter said, standing and drawing a deep breath as though he meant to issue a battle cry, "you are you!"

That got them all laughing again. Tahn rolled off his rock, holding his stomach, while Sutter struck a noble pose.

The Far king shifted around abruptly, and gave the Sheason a despairing look. "Then the floodgates are nearly open." Elan glanced over them all in his central hall, quickly searching their faces. Lighting on Tahn, the king asked, "You made it to Tillinghast?"

Vendanj answered. "He did. And is come again into the land."

"Then we have an instrument to be grateful for." Elan smiled crookedly at Tahn, though Tahn did not like being described in such a way. "Still," the king added grimly, "I fear there is not time to sire a larger generation of Far before . . ."

Tahn saw Mira's discomfort at the turn of the conversation. "Whatever else you decide, you should know Mira's actions made my stand at Tillinghast possible."

No one responded, though understanding came to Elan's face. He nodded at Mira, a silent acknowledgment passing between them.

"They will seek the covenant language, and Naltus is now its sole repository. But they will not make their ambition dependent on that alone." Vendanj leveled a serious look at the king of the Far. "It will be necessary for you to place a select few of the Far in areas that will prove critical should the Shadow of the Hand be laid fully open, or should the Veil fail utterly. First though, the convocation. It is necessary for you to occupy your seat at Recityv. Tahn has survived Restoration, but that is only our first step. The time is short now before convocation begins, if it has not already. We need your leadership, Elan. The politics of kings, the subterfuge of the League . . . the coming of the Quiet. You must not stand idle."

Attending closely the Sheason's words, the king nodded in such a way that Tahn knew he would consider all Vendanj asked. But concern stayed in the Far king's aspect, causing Tahn to wonder if Elan's burdens amounted to more than even a Far could manage. In that instant, Tahn felt empathy for King Elan, a kinship he decided they shared as creatures given a role that left them few choices for themselves.

That night, after all the details had been shared, they were treated to hot baths, assigned beds, and allowed to sleep, this time, without the company of standing guards—an exception the king made in order to give the weary companions some privacy. Braethen went with Vendanj, a fealty having grown in the sodalist for the Sheason. Grant went with Mira to the training yards, where immediate work would begin to instruct the Far in battle techniques unfamiliar to them. Wendra took her own room, saying a soft good night to them all before taking a loaf of bread and some freshly warmed milk to bed. Tahn and Sutter bunked together, opening their window to let the night air touch their chests as they had always done on hunting trips into the Hollows.

"What's next?" Sutter asked, staring over the foot of his bed at a bright moon through the opened window.

"I'm sure they'll tell us," Tahn remarked, lending both contempt and humor to his words.

Sutter raised his hand that bore the unique glove of the Sedagin. "Do you suppose I'd be welcome back into the High Plains again?"

"Sure. You make a wonderful impression wherever you go." Tahn chuckled and turned likewise to view the risen moon.

Sutter laughed.

It felt good to banter with his friend again, even if the familiarity of that banter did not put him completely at ease. Looking at the moon, Tahn recalled the last room he shared with Sutter, and the disturbance at their window that had caused Nails to take refuge under his bed. The memory of the leagueman's charity and his friend's vision sent a chill down Tahn's back, and he drew his covers up over his chest.

"Do you think Wendra will ever forgive me?"

Sutter exhaled into the cool, comfortable air. "I've never seen her this way," Sutter said thoughtfully. "But I have faith in her. And why not; I intend to marry her one day."

Tahn gave his friend a playfully quizzical look. "Do you suppose she'll return to Recityv?"

"I think Vendanj would like that," Sutter replied. "But I've a feeling Wendra will make up her own mind. What I want to know is if Braethen intends to tag along with the Sheason now forever."

"Not me," Tahn shot back. "That's a secret I'll gladly let them keep."

"The real question," Sutter said, a smile audible in his voice, "is what you intend to do about Mira. I mean, a Hollows boy finding romance with the elusive Far. I'm starting to think you're keeping things from me."

"I don't have any secrets from you," Tahn said. *But that's not true anymore, is it?*

"Well don't delay, that's my advice. A ripe root goes soft if left in the ground too long." Sutter belly laughed.

Tahn joined him, unable to resist Sutter's infectious laughter. When they'd finished, Sutter wiped his eyes free of mirthful tears, and asked, "What do you think happened to Penit?"

The mention of the boy's name caught Tahn off guard. "I hope he gets away," he said. "If there's a lad in the world who could do it, it's Penit."

They both nodded at that.

"And what have you decided about Grant?" Sutter asked, treading lightly.

Tahn did not immediately reply. "There's a lot to think about."

Sutter nodded at that, too. "I don't know. He's just so full of fun and love. You know, if the exile career doesn't work out, maybe we could put in a word for him at the tenendra. I hear they have a few empty cages to fill."

They went back and forth for some time, their jests and laughter resounding in the room, and pealing through their open window toward the moon.

When they had calmed down, and Tahn was starting to feel sleepy, he turned his head on his pillow. "Thanks for not letting me come alone, Nails."

Sutter shifted in his bed and returned Tahn's grateful look. "And thanks to you, Woodchuck. You got me out of the fields. . . ."

"Well, you may thank me the day we dine on that duck and plum brandy. Until then, simply call me . . . master."

Sutter sat up and bowed his head in jest. "Especially now that you've passed your Standing, right?"

"Of course, boy," Tahn said in a kingly tone.

"Woodchuck, that might have worked out fine, but it is common knowledge that a master's generosity springs from his loins. And when we shared a room tonight for our baths, I noticed that despite what you might have hoped, in that regard the Change hasn't been terribly kind to you, has it?"

Again their laughter rose, even louder this time, so that they almost feared a knock on the door to calm them as they'd often heard during their childhood when sharing a night together at home. Forgotten were Sutter's greatsword and Tahn's new bow.

Down the hall, Vendanj sat up, quietly placing a sprig of herb on his tongue. With the sodalist fast asleep, the Sheason reflected on the brightness of the moon and listened to the laughter echoing from a few doors away. His first thought was to quiet them, afraid their noise would draw undue attention from the sober-minded Far, and perhaps any Quiet that took to the air. But easing into his pillows, he let them alone. If they could find even small joys here and now, then perhaps there remained hope for them all. Perhaps it was that one quality that most suited them to this endeavor, perhaps the very thing that gave Tahn success at Tillinghast, restoring to him a greater measure of light than of darkness. With that thought, Vendanj nodded silently to himself. "You are the one, Tahn. Given life out of death, so may you do for the family of man."

With their laughter in his ears, Vendanj drifted to sleep with belief ever more alive in his heart.

For more information about THE VAULT OF HEAVEN—
stories, glossary, maps, interviews, art, video, and more—
visit www.orullian.com.

ABOUT THE AUTHOR •

• ABOUT THE AUTHOR •

Peter Orullian has worked in marketing at Xbox for nearly a decade, most recently leading the music and entertainment marketing strategy for Xbox LIVE, and has toured internationally as a featured vocalist at major music festivals. He has published several short stories. *The Unremembered* is his first novel. He lives in Seattle. Visit him at www.orullian.com.